Uncollected Stories
of William Faulkner

Uncollected Stories
of
William Faulkner

Edited by
Joseph Blotner

Vintage Books
A Division of Random House New York

Published in the United States by Random House, Inc., New York, and
simultaneously in Canada by Random House of Canada Limited, Toronto.
Originally published by Random House, Inc., New York, in November 1979.

Library of Congress Cataloging in Publication Data
Faulkner, William, 1897-1962.
Uncollected stories of William Faulkner.
Bibliography: p.
I. Blotner, Joseph Leo, 1923-   . II. Title.
PS3511.A86A6 1981   813'.52   80-6120
ISBN 0-394-74656-2

Manufactured in the United States of America

To Albert Erskine,
his editor—
and mine

Acknowledgments

I want first to thank Jill Summers for her help over the years. I am particularly grateful also to Professor James W. Webb of the University of Mississippi for the extraordinary kindnesses and scholarly assistance I have received from him, to the staff of the University of Mississippi Library, to Joan St.C. Crane, Edmund Berkeley, Jr., and their colleagues at the University of Virginia Library, and to Mrs. Lola L. Szladits of the Berg Collection of the New York Public Library. I shall always be grateful to the University of Mississippi for the gracious hospitality extended to me during the semester I taught there and to Marilyn Majors Monroe for her accurate, cheerful, and untiring labors as a research assistant which aided me so much in my work. My special thanks go to my daughter, Nancy Wright Blotner, and my wife, Yvonne Wright Blotner, for their careful and patient labor during many hours spent sitting with me and taking turns reading aloud manuscripts and typescripts of William Faulkner's stories against magazine versions and then for reading the setting copy against the proofs. Once again it gives me particular pleasure to express my gratitude to the Horace H. Rackham School of Graduate Studies of the University of Michigan for the research grant which helped me to complete this book.

Introduction

This book consists of three kinds of stories: those which William Faulkner published but never reprinted in any of his short-story collections, those which he later revised to become parts of later books, and those which have remained until now unpublished.* Some of the third group are clearly apprentice work, but some of all three groups display qualities to be found in his best fiction. A number in each group were refused, some more than once, by various magazines, but so were a number of his most brilliant stories, and these rejections were usually a reflection upon the nature of the literary marketplace or editorial taste rather than the artistry of the author. Taken together, these stories present a view of Faulkner's developing art over a span of more than thirty years. They embody a wide variety of styles and subject matter. His attitude toward them quite naturally varied too. Some he wrote because he was a craftsman who depended exclusively on his pen for his livelihood and very often had to write what he thought would sell rather than what he wanted to write. Some he wrote for personal pleasure. Others he wrote because they engaged his deepest interests as an artist and led in at least one instance to some of his greatest work.

Because of William Faulkner's stature and the importance of his

---

*The stories designated as unpublished had not been published at the time this book went into production. Two among the uncollected stories are called by the same title: "Once Aboard the Lugger." The second of these has not heretofore been published, but it is printed among the uncollected stories because of its organic connection with its predecessor of the same name.

contribution to literature, it is fitting that all of his completed work should be made available in convenient and easily accessible printed form. Some of these stories will be of particular interest to scholars and critics, who hitherto have been able to consult them only by traveling long distances to the libraries which house them. Most of them, it seems to me, will appeal to readers who love fiction. All of them, I think, will be of interest to admirers of his work.

Excluded here are stories previously collected in *Collected Stories of William Faulkner* and *Knight's Gambit,* incomplete stories such as "Love" and "And Now What's to Do?," and excerpts from novels printed in magazines without change, such as "The Waifs" and "Hell Creek Crossing." Also excluded are *The Wishing Tree* and *Mayday,* which, like the one-act play *The Marionettes,* Faulkner produced and bound himself as presentations and which are readily available in separate editions.

Where two treatments of the same short-story material exist, as in "Rose of Lebanon" and "A Return," the one that seemed the better of the two has been used.

The texts of the unpublished stories have been taken from scripts typed by Faulkner. Editorial alterations of these texts have been kept to a minimum. Idiosyncratic punctuation and certain inconsistencies have been retained but typographical errors and misspellings have been corrected. Problematical material has been printed in brackets.

The texts of the published stories have been taken from the magazines or monographs in which they appeared, with errors and omissions corrected. Typescripts of these stories which still exist have been collated with the published versions. Manuscript stages of the works are discussed where they throw light on Faulkner's intentions. When variants between typescripts and published versions go beyond changes in capitalization, indentation, paragraphing, punctuation, and non-substantive changes in words or phrases, the nature of these variants has been described in the Notes. In almost every instance the published story is not only fuller than the typescript version but also more effective, so that though Faulkner may have acceded, sometimes no doubt unwillingly, to mechanical changes required by magazine house style, changes which went beyond these considerations seem to have been dictated mainly by his own characteristic meticulousness in revision. In the cases of stories which were further revised to become parts of books, I have tried to outline the process of growth from inception to completion. The stories are printed here in the order in which they appeared in the magazines, not the order in which they were written or the order in which Faulkner rearranged them in the books. Although some of these stories in their magazine versions are virtually identical with the versions of them in books, others are very different in the two forms, reflecting the quite different aesthetic demands of the short story and the novel.

Joseph Blotner

Contents

II. UNCOLLECTED STORIES

III. UNPUBLISHED STORIES

NOTES AND BIBLIOGRAPHY

I

STORIES REVISED FOR LATER BOOKS

Ambuscade

Behind the smokehouse we had a kind of map. Vicksburg was a handful of chips from the woodpile and the river was a trench we had scraped in the packed ground with a hoe, that drank water almost faster than we could fetch it from the well. This afternoon it looked like we would never get it filled, because it hadn't rained in three weeks. But at last it was damp-colored enough at least, and we were just about to begin, when all of a sudden Loosh was standing there watching us. And then I saw Philadelphy over at the woodpile, watching Loosh.

"What's that?" Loosh said.

"Vicksburg," I said.

Then Loosh laughed. He stood there laughing, not loud, not looking at me.

"Come on here, Loosh," Philadelphy said. There was something queer about her voice too. "If you wants any supper, you better tote me some wood." But Loosh just stood there laughing, looking down at Vicksburg. Then he stooped, and with his hand he swept the chips flat.

"There's your Vicksburg," he said.

"Loosh!" Philadelphy said. But Loosh squatted there, looking at me with that look on his face. I was twelve then; I didn't know triumph; I didn't even know the word.

"And I tell you nuther un you ain't know," Loosh said. "Corinth."

"Corinth?" I said. Philadelphy had dropped the wood which she held and she was coming fast toward us. "That's in Mississippi too. That's not far."

"Far don't matter," Loosh said. He sounded like he was singing. "Case it's on the way!"

"On the way? On the way to what?"

"Ask your paw," Loosh said. "Ask Marse John."

"He's at Tennessee. I can't ask him."

"You think he at Tennessee?" Loosh said. "Ain't no need for him at Tennessee." Then Philadelphy grabbed him by the arm.

"Hush your mouth, nigger!" she said. "Come on here and get me some wood."

Then they were gone, and Ringo and I standing there looking at each other. "What?" Ringo said. "What he mean?"

"Nothing," I said. I set Vicksburg up again. "There it is."

"Loosh laughed," Ringo said. "He say Corinth too. He laughed at Corinth too. What you reckon he know?"

"Nothing!" I said. "Do you reckon Loosh knows anything that father don't know?"

"Marse John at Tennessee," Ringo said. "Maybe he ain't know either."

"Do you reckon he'd be away off at Tennessee if there were Yankees at Corinth? Do you reckon that if there were Yankees at Corinth, father and General Pemberton both wouldn't be here?" I stooped and caught up the dust. But Ringo didn't move; he just looked at me.

I threw the dust at him. "I'm General Pemberton!" I said. "Yaaay! Yaaay!" Then we both began and so we didn't see Louvinia at all. We were throwing the dust fast then and yelling, "Kill the bastuds! Kill them! Kill them!" when all of a sudden she was yelling louder than we were:

"You, Bayard! You, Ringo!" We stopped. The dust went away and she was standing there with her mouth still open to shout, and I noticed that she did not have on the old hat of father's that she wore on top of her head rag even when she just stepped out of the kitchen for wood. "What was that word?" she said. "What did I hear you say?" Only she didn't wait to be answered, and then I saw that she had been running too. "Look who coming up the big road!" she said.

It was Ringo and I who ran then, on around the house, and Granny standing at the top of the front steps and Jupiter just turning into the gate from the road. And then we stopped. Last spring when father came home we ran down the drive to meet him and I came back standing in one stirrup and Ringo holding to the other one and running. But this time we didn't, and then I went up the steps and stood by Granny while father came up and stopped, and Jupiter stood with his head down and his chest and belly mud caked where he had crossed at the ford and the dust had dried on it, and Loosh coming around the house to take the bridle.

"Curry him," father said. "Give him a good feed. But don't turn him into the pasture. Let him stay in the lot. . . . Well, Miss Rosa," he said.

"Well, John," Granny said. "I've been expecting you."

"You have?" father said. He got down stiffly. Loosh led Jupiter away.

"You rode hard from Tennessee, father," I said.

Father looked at me. He put his hand on my shoulder, looking at me. Ringo was standing on the ground.

"Tennessee sho gaunted you," he said. "What does they eat up there, Marse John? Does they eat what folks eats?"

Then I said it, looking at father even while he looked at me: "Loosh says you haven't been at Tennessee."

"Loosh?" father said.

Then Granny said, "Come in. Louvinia is putting your dinner on the table. You will just have time to wash."

That afternoon father and Joby and Loosh and Ringo and I built a pen down in the creek bottom, and just after dark Joby and Loosh and Ringo and I drove the mules and the cow and calf and the sow down there. So it was late when we got back to the house, and when Ringo and I came into the kitchen Louvinia was closing one of the trunks that stay in the attic. And when we sat down to supper, the table was set with the kitchen knives and forks and the sideboard looked bare as a pasture.

It didn't take us long to eat, because father had already eaten in the afternoon, and that's what Ringo and I had been waiting for —for after supper. Back in the spring when father was home before, he sat in his chair in front of the fire and Ringo and I lying on our stomachs on the floor. Then we listened. We heard: The names—Chickamauga and Lookout Mountain—the words, names like Gap and Run that we didn't have in this country; but mostly the cannon and the flags and the charges and the yelling. Ringo was waiting for me in the hall; we waited until father was settled. Then I said, "How can you fight in mountains, father?"

He looked at me. "You can't. You just have to. Now you boys run on to bed."

We went up the stairs. But we did not go to our room. We stopped and sat on the top step, back out of the light from the hall lamp. That was the first night I could remember that Louvinia had not followed us upstairs, to stand in the door and vow threats at us while we got into bed; after a while she crossed the hall without even looking up the stairs, and went on into the room where father and Granny were.

"Is the trunk ready?" father said.

"Yes, sir. Hit ready," Louvinia said.

"Then tell Joby to get the lantern and the shovels, and wait in the kitchen for me."

"Yes, sir," Louvinia said. She crossed the hall again without even looking at the stairs.

"I seed in that trunk," Ringo whispered. "Hit's the silver. What you reckon—"

"Sh-h-h-h," I said. We could hear father's voice. After a while Louvinia came back. We sat on the top step, in the shadow, listening.

"Vicksburg?" Ringo whispered. I couldn't see anything but his eyes. "Fell? Do he mean hit fell off into the river?"

"Sh-h-h-h," I said. We sat close together in the dark, listening to them talking. Maybe it was because of the dark, the quiet, because suddenly Louvinia was standing over us, shaking us awake. She stood in the door, but she did not light the lamp and she did not even make us undress. Maybe she forgot about it; maybe she was listening to them carrying the trunk out of the kitchen, as we were. And I thought for a minute that I saw the lantern in the orchard, and then it was morning and father was gone.

He must have ridden off in the rain, because it was still raining at breakfast, and at dinner, too, until at last Granny put the sewing away and said, "Very well. Marengo, get the cookbook." Ringo got the book and we lay on the floor beside the hearth, with the loaded musket on the pegs above the mantel. "What shall we read about today?" she said.

"Read about cake," I said.

"Very well. What kind of cake?" Only she didn't have to ask that, because Ringo said, almost before she finished speaking, like he did every time:

"Cokynut cake, Granny."

"I reckon a little more won't hurt us," Granny said.

The rain stopped in the middle of the afternoon. We went out the back. I went on past the smokehouse. "Where we going?" Ringo said. Before we reached the barn, Joby and Loosh came into sight across the pasture, bringing in the mules from the new pen. "What we ghy do now?" Ringo said.

I didn't look at him. "We've got to watch him."

"Watch who?"

"Loosh." Then I looked at Ringo. His eyes were white and quiet, like last night.

"Loosh? Why Loosh? Who tole you to watch him?"

"Nobody told me. I just know it."

"Bayard, did you dream hit?"

"Yes. Last night. It was father and Louvinia. Father said, 'Watch Loosh because he knows.' He will know before we know. He said Louvinia must watch him too. He said Loosh is Louvinia's son, but she will have to be white a little while longer. And Louvinia said for father not to worry about Granny and us."

Ringo looked at me. Then he breathed deep, once. "Then hit's so," he said. "If somebody tole you, hit could be a lie. But if you dremp hit, hit can't be a lie case ain't nobody there to tole hit to ou. So we got to watch him."

We followed them when they put the mules to the wagon and went down beyond the pasture to where they had been cutting wood. We watched them for two days, hidden. We realized then what a close watch Louvinia had kept on us all the time. Sometimes while we were hidden watching Loosh and Joby load the wagon, we would hear her yelling at us, and we would have to sneak away and then run to let Louvinia find us coming from the other direction. Sometimes she would even meet us before we had time to circle, and Ringo hiding behind me then while she scolded at us: "What devilment yawl into now? Yawl up to something. What is it?" But we didn't tell her, and we would follow her back to the kitchen while she scolded at us over her shoulder, and when she was inside the house we would move quietly until we were out of sight again, and then run back to hide and watch Loosh.

So we were outside of his and Philadelphy's cabin that night when he came out. We followed him down to the new pen and heard him catch the mule and ride away. We ran, but when we reached the road, too, we could only hear the mule loping, dying away. But we had come a good piece, because even Louvinia calling us sounded faint and small. We looked up the road in the starlight, after the mule. "That's where Corinth is," I said.

He didn't get back until after dark the next day. We stayed close to the house and watched the road by turns, to get Louvinia calmed down in case it would be late before he got back. It was late; she had followed us up to bed and we had slipped out again, and we were passing Joby's cabin when suddenly Loosh kind of surged out of the darkness and into the door. When we climbed up to the window, he was standing in front of the fire, with his clothes muddy from where he had been hiding in swamps and bottoms from the patter rollers, and with that look on his face again, like he had not slept in a long time and he didn't want to sleep, and Joby and Philadelphy leaning into the firelight and looking at him, with Philadelphy's mouth open and the look on her face too. And then I saw Louvinia standing in the door. We had not heard her pass us, but there she was, with her hand on the jamb, looking at Loosh, and again she didn't have on father's old hat.

"You mean they gwinter free us all?" Philadelphy said.

"Yes," Loosh said, loud, with his head flung back; he didn't even look at Joby when Joby said, "Hush up, Loosh!" "Yes!" Loosh said. "Gin'ral Sherman gonter sweep the earth and the race gonter all be free!"

Then Louvinia crossed the floor in two steps and hit Loosh across the head hard with her flat hand. "You black fool!" she said. "Do you think there's enough Yankees in the whole world to whip the white folks?"

We ran to the house, we didn't wait for Louvinia; again we didn't know that she was behind us. We ran into the room where Granny was sitting beside the lamp with the Bible open on her lap and her neck arched to look at us across her spectacles. "They're coming here!" I said. "They're coming to set us free!"

"What?" she said.

"Loosh saw them! They're just down the road. It's General Sherman and he's going to make us all free!" And we watching her, waiting to see who she would send for to take down the musket—whether it would be Joby, because he was the oldest, or Loosh, because he had seen them and would know what to shoot at. Then she shouted, too, and her voice was strong and loud as Louvinia's:

"You Bayard Sartoris! Ain't you in bed yet? . . . Louvinia!" she shouted. Louvinia came in. "Take these children up to bed, and if you hear another sound out of them tonight, you have my permission and my insistence, too, to whip them both."

It didn't take us long to get to bed. But we couldn't talk, because Louvinia was going to bed on the cot in the hall. And Ringo was afraid to come up in the bed with me, so I got down on the pallet with him. "We'll have to watch the road," I said. Ringo whimpered.

"Look like hit haf to be us," he said.

"Are you scared?"

"I ain't very," he said. "I just wish Marse John was here."

"Well, he's not," I said. "It'll have to be us."

We watched the road for two days, lying in the cedar copse. Now and then Louvinia hollered at us, but we told her where we were and that we were making another map, and besides, she could see the cedar copse from the kitchen. It was cool and shady there, and quiet, and Ringo slept most of the time, and I slept some too. I was dreaming—it was like I was looking at our place and suddenly the house and stable and cabins and trees and all were gone and I was looking at a place flat and empty as the sideboard, and it was growing darker and darker, and then all of a sudden I wasn't looking at it; I was there—a sort of frightened drove of little tiny figures moving on it; they were father and Granny and Joby and Louvinia and Loosh and Philadelphy and Ringo and me [and we were wandering around on it lost and it getting darker and darker and we forever more without any home to go to because we were forever free; that's what it was]—and then Ringo made a choked sound and I was looking at the road, and there in the middle of it, sitting on a bright bay horse and looking at the house through a field glass, was a Yankee.

For a long time we just lay there looking at him. I don't know what we had expected to see, but we knew what he was at once;

I remember thinking, "He looks just like a man," and then Ringo and I were glaring at each other, and then we were crawling backward down the hill without remembering when we started to crawl, and then we were running across the pasture toward the house without remembering when we got to our feet. We seemed to run forever, with our heads back and our fists clenched, before we reached the fence and fell over it and ran on into the house. Granny's chair was empty beside the table where her sewing lay.

"Quick!" I said. "Shove it up here!" But Ringo didn't move; his eyes looked like door knobs while I dragged the chair up and climbed onto it and began to lift down the musket. It weighed about fifteen pounds, though it was not the weight so much as the length; when it came free, it and the chair and all went down with a tremendous clatter. We heard Granny sit up in her bed upstairs, and then we heard her voice: "Who is it?"

"Quick!" I said. "Hurry!"

"I'm scared," Ringo said.

"You, Bayard!" Granny said. . . . "Louvinia!"

We held the musket between us like a log of wood. "Do you want to be free?" I said. "Do you want to be free?"

We carried it that way, like a log, one at each end, running. We ran through the grove toward the road and ducked down behind the honeysuckle just as the horse came around the curve. We didn't hear anything else, maybe because of our own breathing or maybe because we were not expecting to hear anything else. We didn't look again either; we were too busy cocking the musket. We had practiced before, once or twice when Granny was not there and Joby would come in to examine it and change the cap on the nipple. Ringo held it up and I took the barrel in both hands, high, and drew myself up and shut my legs about it and slid down over the hammer until it clicked. That's what we were doing, we were too busy to look; the musket was already riding up across Ringo's back as he stooped, his hands on his knees and panting, "Shoot the bastud! Shoot him!" and then the sights came level, and as I shut my eyes I saw the man and the bright horse vanish in smoke. It sounded like thunder and it made as much smoke as a brush fire, and I heard the horse scream, but I didn't see anything else; it was Ringo wailing, "Great God, Bayard! Hit's the whole army!"

The house didn't seem to get any nearer; it just hung there in front of us, floating and increasing slowly in size, like something in a dream, and I could hear Ringo moaning behind me, and farther back still the shouts and the hoofs. But we reached the house at last; Louvinia was just inside the door, with father's old hat on her head rag and her mouth open, but we didn't stop. We ran on into the room where Granny was standing beside the righted chair, her hand at her chest.

"We shot him, Granny!" I cried. "We shot the bastud!"

"What?" She looked at me, her face the same color as her hair almost, her spectacles shining against her hair above her forehead. "Bayard Sartoris, what did you say?"

"We killed him, Granny! At the gate! Only there was the whole army, too, and we never saw them, and now they are coming."

She sat down; she dropped into the chair, hard, her hand at her breast. But her voice was strong as ever:

"What's this? You, Marengo! What have you done?"

"We shot the bastud, Granny!" Ringo said. "We kilt him!"

Then Louvinia was there, too, with her mouth still open, too, and her face like somebody had thrown ashes at her. Only it didn't need her face; we heard the hoofs jerking and sliding in the dirt, and one of them hollering, "Get around to the back there, some of you!" and we looked up and saw them ride past the window— the blue coats and the guns. Then we heard the boots and spurs on the porch.

"Granny!" I said. "Granny!" But it seemed like none of us could move at all; we just had to stand there looking at Granny with her hand at her breast and her face looking like she had died and her voice like she had died too:

"Louvinia! What is this? What are they trying to tell me?" That's how it happened—like when once the musket decided to go off, all that was to occur afterward tried to rush into the sound of it all at once. I could still hear it, my ears were still ringing, so that Granny and Ringo and I all seemed to be talking far away. Then she said, "Quick! Here!" and then Ringo and I were squatting with our knees under our chins, on either side of her against her legs, with the hard points of the chair rockers jammed into our backs and her skirts spread over us like a tent, and the heavy feet coming in and—Louvinia told us afterward—the Yankee sergeant shaking the musket at Granny and saying:

"Come on, grandma! Where are they? We saw them run in here!"

We couldn't see; we just squatted in a kind of faint gray light and that smell of Granny that her clothes and bed and room all had, and Ringo's eyes looking like two plates of chocolate pudding and maybe both of us thinking how Granny had never whipped us for anything in our lives except lying, and that even when it wasn't even a told lie, but just keeping quiet, how she would whip us first and then make us kneel down and kneel down with us herself to ask the Lord to forgive us.

"You are mistaken," she said. "There are no children in this house nor on this place. There is no one here at all except my servant and myself and the people in the quarters."

"You mean you deny ever having seen this gun before?"

"I do." It was that quiet; she didn't move at all, sitting bolt upright and right on the edge of the chair, to keep her skirts spread over us. "If you doubt me, you may search the house."

"Don't you worry about that; I'm going to. . . . Send some of the boys upstairs," he said. "If you find any locked doors, you know what to do. And tell them fellows out back to comb the barn and the cabins too."

"You won't find any locked doors," Granny said. "At least, let me ask you—"

"Don't you ask anything, grandma. You set still. Better for you if you had done a little asking before you sent them little devils out with this gun."

"Was there—" We could hear her voice die away and then speak again, like she was behind it with a switch, making it talk. "Is he —it—the one who—"

"Dead? Hell, yes! Broke his back and we had to shoot him!"

"Had to—you had—shoot—" I didn't know horrified astonishment either, but Ringo and Granny and I were all three it.

"Yes, by God! Had to shoot him! The best horse in the whole army! The whole regiment betting on him for next Sunday—" He said some more, but we were not listening. We were not breathing either, glaring at each other in the gray gloom, and I was almost shouting, too, until Granny said it:

"Didn't—they didn't— Oh, thank God! Thank God!"

"We didn't—" Ringo said.

"Hush!" I said. Because we didn't have to say it, it was like we had had to hold our breaths for a long time without knowing it, and that now we could let go and breathe again. Maybe that was why we never heard the other man, when he came in, at all; it was Louvinia that saw that, too—a colonel, with a bright short beard and hard bright gray eyes, who looked at Granny sitting in the chair with her hand at her breast, and took off his hat. Only he was talking to the sergeant.

"What's this?" he said. "What's going on here, Harrison?"

"This is where they run to," the sergeant said. "I'm searching the house."

"Ah," the colonel said. He didn't sound mad at all. He just sounded cold and short and pleasant. "By whose authority?"

"Well, somebody here fired on United States troops. I guess this is authority enough." We could just hear the sound; it was Louvinia that told us how he shook the musket and banged the butt on the floor.

"And killed one horse," the colonel said.

"It was a United States horse. I heard the general say myself that if he had enough horses, he wouldn't always care whether there was anybody to ride them or not. And so here we are, riding peaceful along the road, not bothering nobody yet, and these two little devils— The best horse in the army; the whole regiment betting—"

"Ah," the colonel said. "I see. Well? Have you found them?"

"We ain't yet. But these rebels are like rats when it comes to hiding. She says that there ain't even any children here."

"Ah," said the colonel. And Louvinia said how he looked at Granny now for the first time. She said how she could see his eyes going from Granny's face down to where her skirt was spread, and looking at her skirt for a whole minute and then going back to her face. And that Granny gave him look for look while she lied. "Do I understand, madam, that there are no children in or about this house?"

"There are none, sir," Granny said.

Louvinia said he looked back at the sergeant. "There are no children here, sergeant. Evidently the shot came from somewhere else. You may call the men in and mount them."

"But, colonel, we saw them two kids run in here! All of us saw them!"

"Didn't you just hear this lady say there are no children here? Where are your ears, sergeant? Or do you really want the artillery to overtake us, with a creek bottom not five miles away to be got over?"

"Well, sir, you're colonel. But if it was me was colonel—"

"Then, doubtless, I should be Sergeant Harrison. In which case, I think I should be more concerned about getting another horse to protect my wager next Sunday than over a grandchildless old lady" —Louvinia said his eyes just kind of touched Granny now and flicked away—"alone in a house which, in all probability—and for her pleasure and satisfaction, I am ashamed to say, I hope—I shall never see again. Mount your men and get along."

We squatted there, not breathing, and heard them leave the house; we heard the sergeant calling the men up from the barn and we heard them ride away. But we did not move yet, because Granny's body had not relaxed at all, and so we knew that the colonel was still there, even before he spoke—the voice short, brisk, hard, with that something of laughing behind it: "So you have no grandchildren. What a pity in a place like this which two boys would enjoy—sports, fishing, game to shoot at, perhaps the most exciting game of all, and none the less so for being, possibly, a little rare this near the house. And with a gun—a very dependable weapon, I see." Louvinia said how the sergeant had set the musket in the corner and how the colonel looked at it now, and now we didn't breathe. "Though I understand that this weapon does not belong to you. Which is just as well. Because if it were your weapon —which it is not—and you had two grandsons, or say a grandson and a Negro playfellow—which you have not—and if this were the first time—which it is not—someone next time might be seriously hurt. But what am I doing? Trying your patience by keeping you in that uncomfortable chair while I waste my time delivering a homily suitable only for a lady with grandchildren—or one grandchild and a Negro companion." Now he was about to go, too; we could tell it even beneath the skirt; this time it was Granny herself:

"There is little of refreshment I can offer you, sir. But if a glass of cool milk after your ride—"

Only, for a long time he didn't answer at all; Louvinia said how he just looked at Granny with his hard bright eyes and that hard bright silence full of laughing. "No, no," he said. "I thank you. You are taxing yourself beyond mere politeness and into sheer bravado."

"Louvinia," Granny said, "conduct the gentleman to the dining room and serve him with what we have."

He was out of the room now, because Granny began to tremble now, trembling and trembling, but not relaxing yet; we could hear her panting now. And we breathed, too, now, looking at each other. "We never killed him!" I whispered. "We haven't killed anybody at all!" So it was Granny's body that told us again; only this time I could almost feel him looking at Granny's spread skirt where we crouched while he thanked her for the milk and told her his name and regiment.

"Perhaps it is just as well that you have no grandchildren," he said. "Since, doubtless, you wish to live in peace. I have three boys myself, you see. And I have not even had time to become a grandparent." And now there wasn't any laughing behind his voice, and Louvinia said he was standing there in the door, with the brass bright on his dark blue and his hat in his hand and his bright beard and hair, looking at Granny without the laughing now: "I won't apologize; fools cry out at wind or fire. But permit me to say and hope that you will never have anything worse than this to remember us by." Then he was gone. We heard his spurs in the hall and on the porch, then the horse, dying away, ceasing, and then Granny let go. She went back into the chair with her hand at her breast and her eyes closed and the sweat on her face in big drops; all of a sudden I began to holler, "Louvinia! Louvinia!" But she opened her eyes then and looked at me; they were looking at me when they opened. Then she looked at Ringo for a moment, but she looked back at me, panting.

"Bayard," she said, "what was that word you used?"

"Word?" I said. "When, Granny?" Then I remembered; I didn't look at her, and she lying back in the chair, looking at me and panting.

"Don't repeat it. You cursed. You used obscene language, Bayard."

I didn't look at her. I could see Ringo's feet too. "Ringo did too,"

I said. She didn't answer, but I could feel her looking at me; I said suddenly: "And you told a lie. You said we were not here."

"I know it," she said. She moved. "Help me up." She got out of the chair, holding to us. We didn't know what she was trying to do. We just stood there while she held to us and to the chair and let herself down to her knees beside it. It was Ringo that knelt first. Then I knelt, too, while she asked the Lord to forgive her for telling the lie. Then she rose; we didn't have time to help her. "Go to the kitchen and get a pan of water and the soap," she said. "Get the new soap."

It was late, like time had slipped up on us while we were still caught in the noise of the musket and were too busy to notice; the sun shone almost level into our faces when we stood on the edge of the back porch, and when we spit, we spit straight into it. At first, just by breathing we could blow soap bubbles, but soon it was just the taste of the spitting. Then even that began to go away, though the impulse to spit didn't, and then away to the north we saw the cloud bank, faint and blue and far-away at the base and touched with copper sun on the top. When father came home back in the spring, we tried to understand about mountains. At last he pointed out the cloud bank and said how it looked like mountains, and so, ever since then, Ringo believed that that was Tennessee, where father was, just like now.

"There they," he said, spitting. "There hit. Tennessee, where your pappy use to fight um at. Looking mighty far too."

"Too far to go just to fight Yankees," I said, spitting too. But it was gone now, even the taste of it.

Retreat

By suppertime we had everything loaded into the wagon but the bedclothes we would sleep under that night. Then Granny went upstairs, and when she came back down she had on her Sunday dress and her hat, and there was color in her face now and her eyes were bright.

"Is we gonter leave tonight?" Ringo said. "I thought we wasn't going to start until tomorrow."

"No," Granny said. "But it's been three years now since I have started anywhere; I reckon the Lord will forgive me for getting ready one day ahead of time." She turned to Louvinia. "Tell Joby and Loosh to be ready with the lantern and the shovels right after supper."

Louvinia had put the corn bread on the table and was going out. But she stopped and looked at Granny. "You mean you gonter take that heavy trunk all the way to Memphis with you?"

"Yes," Granny said. She was eating; she didn't even look at Louvinia. Louvinia stood there looking at the back of Granny's head.

"Whyn't you leave hit here where hit hid good and I can take care of hit? Who gonter find hit, even if they was to come here again? Hit's Marse John they done called the reward on; hit ain't no trunk full of—"

"I have my reasons," Granny said. "You do what I told you."

"All right. But how come you wanter dig hit up tonight when you ain't leaving until tomor—"

"You do what I said," Granny said.

"Yessum," Louvinia said. She went out. I looked at Granny eating, with her hat sitting on the exact top of her head, and Ringo looking at me across the back of Granny's chair with his eyes rolling a little.

"Why not leave it hid?" I said. "It'll be just that much more load on the wagon. Joby says that trunk will weigh a thousand pounds."

"A thousand fiddlesticks!" Granny said. "I don't care if it weighed ten thousand—" Louvinia came in.

"They be ready," she said. "I wish you'd tell me why you got to dig hit up tonight."

Granny looked at her. "I had a dream about it last night."

"Oh," Louvinia said. She and Ringo looked exactly alike, except that Louvinia's eyes were not rolling so much as his.

"I dreamed I was looking out my window, and a man walked into the orchard and went to where it is and stood there pointing at it," Granny said. She looked at Louvinia. "A black man."

"A nigger?" Louvinia said.

"Yes."

For a while Louvinia didn't say anything. Then she said, "Did you know him?"

"Yes," Granny said.

"Is you going to tell who hit was?"

"No," Granny said.

Louvinia turned to Ringo. "Gawn tell your pappy and Loosh to get the lantern and the shovels and come on up here."

Joby and Loosh were in the kitchen. Joby was sitting behind the stove with a plate on his knees, eating. Loosh was sitting on the wood box, still, with the two shovels between his knees, but I didn't see him at first because of Ringo's shadow. The lamp was on the table, and I could see the shadow of Ringo's head bent over and his arm working back and forth, and Louvinia standing between us and the lamp, her hands on her hips and her elbows spread and her shadow filling the room. "Clean that chimney good," she said.

Joby carried the lantern, with Granny behind him, and then Loosh; I could see her bonnet and Loosh's head and the two shovel blades over his shoulder. Ringo was breathing behind me. "Which un you reckon she dremp about?" he said.

"Why don't you ask her?" I said. We were in the orchard now.

"Hoo," Ringo said. "Me ask her? I bet if she stayed here

wouldn't no Yankee nor nothing else bother that trunk, nor Marse John neither, if he knowed hit." Joby set the lantern down and he and Loosh dug up the trunk where we buried it last summer. Granny carried the lantern, and it took Ringo and me both to help carry the trunk back to the house, but I don't believe it weighed a thousand pounds. Joby began to bear away toward the wagon.

"Take it into the house," Granny said.

"We better load hit now and save having to handle hit again tomorrow," Joby said.

"Take it into the house," Granny said. So, after a while, Joby moved on toward the house. We could hear him breathing now, saying "Hah!" every few steps. Inside the kitchen he let his end down, hard.

"Hah!" he said. "That's done, thank God."

"Take it upstairs," Granny said.

Joby turned and looked at her. He hadn't straightened up yet; he turned, half stooping, and looked at her. "Which?" he said.

"Take it upstairs," Granny said. "I want it in my room."

"You mean you gonter tote this thing all the way upstairs and then tote it back down tomorrow?"

"Somebody is," Granny said. "Are you going to help or are me and Bayard going to do it alone?"

Then Louvinia came in. She had already undressed. She looked tall as a ghost; she came and shoved Joby away and took hold of the trunk. "Git away, nigger," she said. Joby groaned, then he shoved Louvinia away.

"Git away, woman," he said. He lifted his end of the trunk, then he looked back at Loosh, who had never let his end down. "If you gonter ride on hit, pick up your feet," he said. We carried the trunk up to Granny's room, and Joby was setting it down again, until Granny made him and Loosh pull the bed out from the wall and slide the trunk in behind it; Ringo and I helped again. I don't believe it lacked much of weighing a thousand pounds.

"Now I want everybody to go right to bed, so we can get an early start tomorrow," Granny said.

"That's you," Joby said. "Git everybody up at crack of day and it be noon 'fore we get started."

"Nummine about that," Louvinia said. "You do like Miss Rosa tell you." We went out. And then Ringo and I looked at each other, because we heard the key turn in Granny's lock.

"I didn't even know she had a key, let alone hit would turn," Ringo said.

"And that's some more of yawl's and Joby's business," Louvinia said. She was already in her cot; when we looked at her she was already covering her head up with the quilt. "Yawl get on to bed."

We went to our room and undressed. "Which un you reckon she dremp about?" Ringo said.

We ate breakfast by lamplight; Ringo and I had on our Sunday clothes. When Granny came out to the wagon, she was carrying the musket. "Here," she said to Joby. Joby looked at the musket.

"We won't need hit," he said.

"Put it in the wagon," Granny said.

"Nome, we won't need nothing like that," Joby said. "We be in Memphis so quick won't even nobody have time to hear we on the road. I speck Marse John got the Yankees pretty well cleant out twixt here and Memphis anyway."

This time Granny didn't say anything at all. She just held the musket out, and Joby put it into the wagon and we drove away, with Louvinia standing on the porch with father's old hat on top of her head rag. Granny sat on the seat by Joby, with her hat on the top of her head and her umbrella already raised before the dew began to fall. Then I didn't look back, but I could feel Ringo turning every few feet, even after we were outside the gates and in the road to town. Then we began to go around the curve. "Hit gone now," Ringo said. "Good-by, Sartoris; Memphis, how-de-do!"

The sun was just coming up when we came in sight of Jefferson; we passed a company of troops bivouacked in a pasture on the edge of town, eating breakfast. Their uniforms were not gray any more now; they were almost the color of dead leaves and some of them didn't even have uniforms, and one man waved a skillet at us and he had on a pair of Yankee pants. "Hey, Miss-'ippi!" he hollered. "Hooraw for Arkansas!" We left Granny at the Compsons' to tell them good-by and to ask Mrs. Compson to see about her flowers now and then, and Ringo and I drove the wagon to the store, and we were just coming out with the salt when Uncle Buck McCaslin came hobbling across the square, waving his stick and hollering, and behind him the captain of the company we had passed eating breakfast.

"By Godfrey, there he is!" Uncle Buck hollered, shaking his stick at me. "There's John Sartoris' boy!"

The captain looked at me. "I've heard about your father," he said.

"Heard of him?" Uncle Buck hollered; by now they had begun to stop along the walk to listen to Uncle Buck, like they always did. "Who ain't heard about him in this country? Git the Yankees to tell you about him sometime. By Godfrey, he raised the first damn regiment in Mississippi out of his own pocket, and took 'em to Ferginny and whipped Yankees right and left with 'em before he found out that what he had bought and paid for wasn't a regiment of soldiers but a congress of politicians and fools. Fools, I say!" he hollered, still shaking the stick at me and glaring at everybody, and the captain looking at him funny, because he hadn't listened to Uncle Buck before yet, and I kept on thinking about Louvinia standing there on the porch with father's old hat on, and wishing that Uncle Buck would get through or hush, so we could go on.

"Fools, I say!" he hollered. "I don't care if some of you folks here do still claim kin with men that elected him colonel and followed him and Stonewall Jackson right up in spitting distance of Washington without hardly losing a man, and then next year turned around and voted him down to major and elected in his stead a damn whippersnapper that never even knowed which end of a gun done the shooting until John Sartoris showed him." He quit hollering just as easy as he started, but the hollering was right there, waiting to start again as soon as he found something else to holler about. "I won't say God take care of you and your grandma on the road, boy, because, by Godfrey, you don't need God's nor nobody else's help; all you got to say is 'I'm John Sartoris' boy; rabbits, hunt the canebrake,' and then watch the blue-bellied sons fly."

"Are they leaving, going away?" the captain said.

Then Uncle Buck began to holler again: "Leaving? Hell's skillet, who's going to take care of them around here? John Sartoris is a damn fool; they voted him out of his own regiment in kindness, so he could come home and take care of his family, knowing that if he didn't, wouldn't nobody around here be likely to. But that don't suit John Sartoris, because John Sartoris is a damned, confounded, selfish coward, askeered to stay at home where the Yankees might get him. Yes, sir. So skeered that he has to raise him up another batch of men to protect him every time he gets up within a hundred feet of a Yankee regiment. Scouring all up and down the country, finding Yankee brigades to dodge; only, if it had been me, I would have took back to Ferginny and I'd have showed that new colonel what fighting looked like. But not John Sartoris. He's a coward and a fool. The best he can do is dodge and run away from Yankees until they have to put a price on his head, and now he's got to send his family out of the country; to Memphis, where maybe the Union Army will take care of them, since it don't look like his own government and fellow citizens are going to." He ran out of breath then, or out of words, anyway, standing there with his beard trembling and the tobacco running onto it out of his mouth, and shaking his stick at me. So I lifted the reins; only the captain spoke; he was still watching me.

"How many men has your father got in his regiment?" he said.

"It's not a regiment, sir," I said. "He's got about fifty, I reckon."

"Fifty?" the captain said. "Fifty? We had a prisoner last week who said he had more than a thousand. He said that Colonel Sartoris didn't fight; he just stole horses."

Uncle Buck had enough wind to laugh though. He sounded just like a hen, slapping his leg and holding to the wagon wheel like he was about to fall.

"That's it! That's John Sartoris! He gets the horses; any fool can step out and get a Yankee. These two damn boys here did that last summer—stepped down to the gate and brought back a whole regiment, and them just— How old are you, boy?"

"Fourteen," I said.

"We ain't fourteen yit," Ringo said. "But we will be in September, if we live and nothing happens. . . . I reckon Granny waiting on us, Bayard."

Uncle Buck quit laughing. He stepped back. "Git on," he said. "You got a long road." I turned the wagon. "You take care of your grandma, boy, or John Sartoris will skin you alive. And if he don't, I will!" When the wagon straightened out, he began to hobble along beside it. "And when you see him, tell him I said to leave the horses go for a while and kill the bluebellied sons. Kill them!"

"Yes, sir," I said. We went on.

"Good thing for his mouth Granny ain't here," Ringo said. She and Joby were waiting for us at the Compsons' gate. Joby had another basket with a napkin over it and a bottle neck sticking out and some rose cuttings. Then Ringo and I sat behind again, and Ringo turning to look back every few feet and saying, "Good-by, Jefferson. Memphis, how-de-do!" And then we came to the top of the first hill and he looked back, quiet this time, and said, "Suppose they don't never get done fighting."

"All right," I said. "Suppose it." I didn't look back.

At noon we stopped by a spring and Granny opened the basket, and she took out the rose cuttings and handed them to Ringo.

"Dip the roots into the spring after you drink," she said. They had earth still on the roots, in a cloth; when Ringo stooped down to the water, I watched him pinch off a little of the dirt and start to put it into his pocket. Then he looked up and saw me watching him, and he made like he was going to throw it away. But he didn't.

"I reckon I can save dirt if I want to," he said.

"It's not Sartoris dirt though," I said.

"I know hit," he said. "Hit's closer than Memphis dirt though. Closer than what you got."

"What'll you bet?" I said. He looked at me. "What'll you swap?" I said. He looked at me.

"What you swap?" he said.

"You know," I said. He reached in his pocket and brought out the buckle we shot off the Yankee saddle when we shot the horse last summer. "Gimmit here," he said.

I took out the box and gave him half of the dirt. "I know hit," he said. "Hit come from 'hind the smokehouse. You brung a lot of hit."

"Yes," I said. "I brought enough to last."

We soaked the cuttings every time we opened the basket, and there was some of the food left on the fourth day, because at least once a day we stopped at houses on the road and ate with them, and on the second night we had supper and breakfast both at the same house. But even then Granny would not come inside to sleep. She made her bed down in the wagon by the chest, and Joby slept under the wagon with the gun by him like when we camped on the road. Only it would not be exactly on the road, but back in the woods a way; on the third night Granny was in the wagon and Joby and Ringo and me were under the wagon, and some cavalry rode up, and Granny said, "Joby! Get the gun!" and somebody got down and took the gun away from Joby, and they lit a pine knot and we saw the gray.

"Memphis?" the officer said. "You can't get to Memphis. There was a fight at Cockrum yesterday and the roads ahead are full of Yankee patrols. How in hell— Excuse me, ma'am [Behind me, Ringo said, "Git the soap."]—you ever got this far I don't see. If I were you, I wouldn't even try to go back, I'd stop at the first house I came to and stay there."

"I reckon we'll go on," Granny said, "like John—Colonel Sartoris told us to. My sister lives in Memphis; we are going there."

"Colonel Sartoris?" the officer said. "Colonel Sartoris told you?"

"I'm his mother-in-law," Granny said. "This is his son."

"Good Lord, ma'am! You can't go a step farther. Don't you know that if they captured you and this boy, they could almost force him to come in and surrender?"

Granny looked at him; she was sitting up in the wagon and her hat was on. "My experience with Yankees has evidently been different from yours. I have no reason to believe that their officers —I suppose they still have officers among them—will bother a woman and two children. I thank you, but my son has directed us to go to Memphis. If there is any information about the roads which my driver should know, I will be obliged if you will instruct him."

"Then let me give you an escort. Or better still, there is a house about a mile back; return there and wait. Colonel Sartoris was at Cockrum yesterday; by tomorrow night I believe I can find him and bring him to you."

"Thank you," Granny said. "Wherever Colonel Sartoris is, he is doubtless busy with his own affairs. I think we will continue to Memphis as he instructed us."

So they rode away and Joby came back under the wagon and put the musket between us; only, every time I turned over I rolled on it, so I made him move it and he tried to put it in the wagon with Granny, and she wouldn't let him, so he leaned it against a tree and we slept and ate breakfast and went on, with Ringo and Joby looking behind every tree we passed. "You ain't going to find them behind a tree we have already passed." I said. We didn't. We had passed where a house had burned, and then we were passing another house with an old white horse looking at us out of the stable door behind it, and then I saw six men running in the next field, and then we saw a dust cloud coming fast out of a lane that crossed the road.

Joby said, "Them folks look like they trying to make the Yankees take they stock, running hit up and down the big road in broad daylight like that."

They rode right out of the dust cloud without seeing us at all, crossing the road, and the first ten or twelve had already jumped the ditch with pistols in their hands, like when you run with a stick of stove wood balanced on your palm; and the last ones came out of the dust with five men running and holding to stirrups, and us sitting there in the wagon with Joby holding the mules like they were sitting down on the whiffletrees and his mouth hanging open and his eyes like two eggs, and I had forgotten what the blue coats looked like.

It was fast—like that—all sweating horses with wild eyes, and men with wild faces full of yelling, and then Granny standing up in the wagon and beating the five men about their heads and shoulders with the umbrella while they unfastened the traces and cut the harness off the mules with pocket knives. They didn't say a word; they didn't even look at Granny while she was hitting them; they just took the mules out of the wagon, and then the two mules and the five men disappeared together in another cloud of dust, and the mules came out of the dust, soaring like hawks, with two men on them and two more just falling backward over the mules' tails and the fifth man already running, too, and the two that were on their backs in the road getting up with little scraps of cut leather sticking to them like a kind of black shavings in a sawmill. The three of them went off across the field after the mules, and then we heard the pistols away off like striking a handful of matches at one time, and Joby still sitting on the seat with his mouth still open and the ends of the cut reins in his hands, and Granny still standing in the wagon with the bent umbrella lifted and hollering at Ringo and me while we jumped out of the wagon and ran across the road.

"The stable," I said. "The stable!" While we were running up the hill toward the house, we could see our mules still galloping in the field, and we could see the three men running too. When we ran around the house, we could see the wagon, too, in the road, with

Joby on the seat above the wagon tongue sticking straight out ahead, and Granny standing up and shaking the umbrella toward us, and I expect she was still hollering. Our mules had run into the woods, but the three men were still in the field and the old white horse was watching them, too, in the barn door; he never saw us until he snorted and jerked back and kicked over something behind him. It was a homemade shoeing box, and he was tied by a rope halter to the ladder to the loft, and there was even a pipe still burning on the ground.

We climbed onto the ladder and got on him, and when we came out of the barn we could still see the three men; but we had to stop while Ringo got down and opened the lot gate and got back on again, and so they were gone, too, by then. When we reached the woods, there was no sign of them and we couldn't hear anything, either, but the old horse's insides. We went on slower then, because the old horse wouldn't go fast again, anyway, and so we tried to listen, and so it was almost sunset when we came out into a road.

"Here where they went," Ringo said. They were mule tracks. "Tinney and Old Hundred's tracks bofe," Ringo said. "I know um anywhere. They done throwed them Yankees and heading back home."

"Are you sure?" I said.

"Is I sure? You reckon I ain't followed them mules all my life and can't tell they tracks when I see um? . . . Git up there, horse!"

We went on, but the old horse still wouldn't go very fast. After a while the moon came up, but Ringo said he could still see the tracks of our mules. We went on; once Ringo almost fell off and then I almost fell off, and we came to a bridge and we hitched the old horse and got under the bridge and slept.

It was something like thunder; I was dreaming I heard thunder, and it was so loud it waked me up, and then I knew I was awake, and I could still hear the thunder too; and then I knew it was the plank bridge, and Ringo and I sitting up and looking at each other, and the hoofs banging on the bridge right on top of us. Maybe it was because we were still half asleep, because we hadn't had time to think at all, about Yankees or anything; we were just running all of a sudden before we knew we had started. I looked back one time, and it looked like the whole rim of the world was full of horses running along the sky. Then it all kind of ran together again like yesterday; Ringo and me diving into the briers and lying on our faces, and men hollering and horses crashing all around us, and then hands dragging us, clawing and kicking and fighting, and then there was a circle of men and horses, and I saw Jupiter, and then father was shaking me and hollering, "Where's your grand-mother?" and Ringo saying, "We forgot Granny!"

"Forgot her?" father said. "You mean you ran away and left her sitting there in the wagon in the road?"

"Joby is with her," I said.

"Lord, Marse John," Ringo said. "You know hit ain't no Yan kee gonter bother her if he know hit."

Father swore. "How far back did you leave her?"

"It was about three o'clock yesterday," I said. "We rode some last night."

Father turned to the others. "Two of you boys take them up behind you; we'll lead that horse." Then he stopped and turned back to us. "Have you-all had anything to eat?"

"Eat?" Ringo said. "My stomach think my throat been cut."

Father took a pone of bread from his saddle bag and broke it and gave it to us. "Where did you get that horse?" he said.

After a while I said, "We borrowed it."

"Who from?" father said.

After a while Ringo said, "We ain't know. The man wasn't there." One of the men laughed. Father looked at him quick, and he hushed. But just for a minute, because all of a sudden they all began to whoop and holler, and father looking around at them and his face getting redder and redder.

"Don't you say a word, colonel," one of them said. "Hooraw for Sartoris!"

We galloped back; it was not far; we came to the field where the men had run, and the house with the barn, and in the road we could still see the scraps of harness where they had cut it. But the wagon was gone. Father led the old horse up to the house himself and knocked on the porch floor with his pistol, and the door of the house was still open, but nobody came. We put the old horse back into the barn; the pipe was still on the ground by the overturned shoeing box. We came back to the road and father sat Jupiter in the middle of the litter of harness scraps.

"You damn boys," he said. "You damn boys."

When we went on now, we went slower; there were three men riding on ahead out of sight. In the afternoon, one of them came galloping back, and father left Ringo and me [with] three others, and he and the rest rode on; it was almost sunset when they came back with their horses sweated a little and leading two new horses with blue blankets under the saddles and U.S. burned on the horses' hips.

"I tole you they wasn't no Yankees gonter stop Granny," Ringo said. "I bet she in Memphis right now."

"I hope for your sake she is," father said. He jerked his hand at the new horses. "You and Bayard get on them." Ringo went to one of the new horses. "Wait," father said; "the other one is yours."

"You mean hit belong to me?" Ringo said.

"No," father said. "You borrowed it."

Then we all stopped and watched Ringo trying to get on his horse. The horse would stand perfectly still until he would feel Ringo's weight on the stirrup; then he would whirl completely around until his off side faced Ringo; the first time Ringo wound up lying on his back in the road.

"Get on him from that side," father said, laughing.

Ringo looked at the horse and then at father. "Git up from the wrong side?" Ringo said. "I knowed Yankees wasn't folks, but I never knowed before they horses ain't horses."

"Get on up," father said. "He's blind in his near eye."

It got dark while we were still riding, and after a while I waked up with somebody holding me in the saddle, and we were stopped in some trees and there was a fire, but Ringo and I didn't even stay awake to eat, and then it was morning again and all of them were gone but father and eleven more, but we didn't start off even then; we stayed there in the trees all day. "What are we going to do now?" I said.

"I'm going to take you damn boys home, and then I've got to go to Memphis and find your grandmother," father said.

Just before dark we started; we watched Ringo trying to get on his horse from the nigh side for a while and then we went on. We rode until dawn and stopped again. This time we didn't build a fire; we didn't even unsaddle right away; we lay hidden in the woods, and then father was waking me with his hand. It was after sunup and we lay there and listened to a column of Yankee infantry pass in the road, and then I slept again. It was noon when I waked. There was a fire now and a shote cooking over it, and we ate. "We'll be home by midnight," father said.

Jupiter was rested. He didn't want the bridle for a while and then he didn't want father to get on him, and even after we were started he still wanted to go; father had to hold him back between Ringo and me. Ringo was on his right. "You and Bayard better swap sides," father told Ringo, "so your horse can see what's beside him."

"He going all right," Ringo said. "He like hit this way. Maybe because he can smell Jupiter another horse, and know Jupiter ain't fixing to git on him and ride."

"All right," father said. "Watch him though." We went on. Mine and Ringo's horses could go pretty well, too; when I looked back, the others were a good piece behind, out of our dust. It wasn't far to sundown.

"I wish I knew your grandmother was all right," father said.

"Lord, Marse John," Ringo said, "is you still worrying about Granny? I been knowed her all my life; I ain't worried about her."

Jupiter was fine to watch, with his head up and watching my horse and Ringo's, and boring a little and just beginning to drive a little. "I'm going to let him go a little," father said. "You and Ringo watch yourselves." I thought Jupiter was gone then. He went out like a rocket, flattening a little. But I should have known that father still held him, because I should have seen that he was still boring, but there was a snake fence along the road, and all of a sudden it began to blur, and then I realized that father and Jupiter had not moved up at all, that it was all three of us flattening out up toward the crest of the hill where the road dipped like three swallows, and I was thinking, "We're holding Jupiter. We're holding Jupiter," when father looked back, and I saw his eyes and his teeth in his beard, and I knew he still had Jupiter on the bit.

He said, "Watch out, now," and then Jupiter shot out from between us; he went out exactly like I have seen a hawk come out of a sage field and rise over a fence.

When they reached the crest of the hill, I could see sky under them and the tops of the trees beyond the hill like they were flying, sailing out into the air to drop down beyond the hill like the hawk; only they didn't. It was like father stopped Jupiter in mid-air on

top of the hill; I could see him standing in the stirrups and his arm
up with his hat in it, and then Ringo and I were on them before
we could even begin to think to pull, and Jupiter reined back onto
his haunches, and then father hit Ringo's horse across his blind eye
with the hat and I saw Ringo's horse swerve and jump clean over
the snake fence, and I heard Ringo hollering as I went on over the
crest of the hill, with father just behind me shooting his pistol and
hollering, "Surround them, boys! Don't let a man escape!"

I didn't know how many there were; it was the fire I saw first
in the dusk, and then I sort of saw it all at once: The creek running
along quiet under the bridge and the muskets all stacked careful
and neat, and nobody within fifty feet of them, and the men, the
faces, squatting about the fire with cups in their hands and watching the crest of the hill with exactly the same expression, like dolls,
and father and me coming down the hill and father jerking my
bridle up, and off to the right in the trees Ringo's horse crashing
and blundering and Ringo yelling. Father's hat was flung onto his
head and his teeth were showing and his eyes were bright as a cat's.

"Lieutenant," he said, loud, "ride back up the hill and close in
with your troop on the left! Git!" he said, jerking my horse around
and slapping him across the rump with his hand. "Make a fuss,
holler! See if you can keep up with Ringo! . . . Boys," he said, and
they looking up at him; they hadn't even put down the cups. "Boys,
I'm John Sartoris and I've got you."

Ringo was the one that was hard to capture. The others came
piling over the hill, reining back, and I reckon for a minute their
faces looked about like the Yankees' faces did, and now and then
I would quit thrashing the bushes and I could hear Ringo on his
side hollering and moaning and hollering again, "Marse John! You,
Marse John! You come here quick!" and hollering for me, calling
Bayard and Colonel and Marse John and Granny until it did sound
like a company at least, and then hollering at his horse again, and
it running back and forth. I reckon he had forgotten again and was
trying to get up on the nigh side again, until at last father said, "All
right, boys. You can come on in."

It was almost dark then. They had built up the fire, and the
Yankees still sitting around it and father and the others standing
over them with their pistols while two of them were taking the
Yankees' pants and boots off. Ringo was still hollering off in the

trees. "I reckon you better go and extricate Lieutenant Marengo," father said. Only about that time Ringo's horse came bursting out with his blind eye looking big as a plate and still trotting in a circle with his knees up to his chin, and then Ringo came out. He looked wilder than the horse; he was already talking, he was saying, "I'm gonter tell Granny on you, making my horse run—" when he saw the Yankees. His mouth was already open, and he kind of squatted for a second, looking at them. Then he hollered, "Look out! Ketch um! Ketch um, Marse John! They stole Old Hundred and Tinney!"

We all ate supper together—father and us and the Yankees in their underclothes.

The officer talked to father. He said, "Colonel, I believe you have fooled us. I don't believe there's another man of you but what I see."

"You might try to depart, and prove your point," father said.

"Depart? Like this? And have every darky and old woman between here and Memphis shooting at us for ghosts? . . . I suppose we can have our blankets to sleep in, can't we?"

"Certainly, captain," father said. "And with your permission, I shall now retire and leave you to set about that business."

We went back into the darkness. We could see them about the fire, spreading their blankets on the ground. "What in the tarnation do you want with sixty prisoners, John?" one of father's men said.

"I don't," father said. He looked at me and Ringo. "You boys captured them. What do you want to do with them?"

"Shoot 'em," Ringo said. "This ain't the first time me and Bayard ever shot Yankees."

"No," father said. "I have a better plan than that. One that Joe Johnston will thank us for." He turned to the others behind him. "Have you got the muskets and ammunition?"

"Yes, colonel," somebody said.

"Grub, boots, clothes?"

"Everything but the blankets, colonel."

"We'll pick them up in the morning," father said. "Now wait."

We sat there in the dark. The Yankees were going to bed. One of them went to the fire and picked up a stick. Then he stopped. He didn't turn his head and we didn't hear anything or see anybody move. Then he put the stick down again and came back to his blanket. "Wait," father whispered. After a while the fire had died down. "Now listen," father whispered. So we sat there in the dark and listened to the Yankees sneaking off into the bushes in their underclothes. Once we heard a splash and somebody cursing, and then a sound like somebody had shut his hand over his mouth. Father didn't laugh out loud; he just sat there shaking.

"Look out for moccasins," one of the others whispered behind us.

It must have taken them two hours to get done sneaking off into the bushes. Then father said, "Everybody get a blanket and let's go to bed."

The sun was high when he waked us. "Home for dinner," he said. And so, after a while, we came to the creek; we passed the hole where Ringo and I learned to swim and we began to pass the fields, too, and we came to where Ringo and I hid last summer and saw the first Yankee we ever saw, and then we could see the house, too, and Ringo said, "Sartoris, here we is; let them that want Memphis take hit and keep hit bofe." Because we were looking at the house, it was like that day when we ran across the pasture and the house would not seem to get any nearer at all. We never saw the wagon at all; it was father that saw it; it was coming up the road from Jefferson, with Granny sitting thin and straight on the seat with Mrs. Compson's rose cuttings wrapped in a new piece of paper in her hand, and Joby yelling and lashing the strange horses, and father stopping us at the gate with his hat raised while the wagon went in first. Granny didn't say a word. She just looked at Ringo and me, and went on, with us coming behind, and she didn't stop at the house. The wagon went on into the orchard and stopped by the hole where we had dug the trunk up, and still Granny didn't say a word; it was father that got down and got into the wagon and took up one end of the trunk and said over his shoulder, "Jump up here, boys."

We buried the trunk again, and we walked behind the wagon to the house. We went into the back parlor, and father put the musket back onto the pegs over the mantel, and Granny put down Mrs. Compson's rose cuttings and took off her hat and looked at Ringo and me.

"Get the soap," she said.

"We haven't cussed any," I said. "Ask father."

"They behaved all right, Miss Rosa," father said.

Granny looked at us. Then she came and put her hand on me and then on Ringo. "Go upstairs—" she said.

"How did you and Joby manage to get those horses?" father said.

Granny was looking at us. "I borrowed them," she said. . . . "Upstairs and take off your—"

"Who from?" father said.

Granny looked at father for a second, then back at us. "I don't know. There was nobody there. . . . Take off your Sunday clothes," she said.

It was hot the next day, so we only worked on the new pen until dinner and quit. It was even too hot for Ringo and me to ride our horses. Even at six o'clock it was still hot; the rosin was still cooking out of the front steps at six o'clock. Father was sitting in his shirt sleeves and his stockings, with his feet on the porch railing, and Ringo and I were sitting on the steps waiting for it to get cool enough to ride, when we saw them coming into the gate—about fifty of them, coming fast, and I remember how hot the blue coats looked. "Father," I said. "Father!"

"Don't run," father said. . . . "Ringo, you go around the house and catch Jupiter. . . . Bayard, you go through the house and tell Louvinia to have my boots and pistols at the back door; then you go and help Ringo. Don't run, now; walk."

Louvinia was shelling peas in the kitchen. When she stood up, the bowl broke on the floor. "Oh Lord," she said. "Oh Lord. Again?"

I ran then. Ringo was just coming around the corner of the house; we both ran. Jupiter was in his stall, eating; he slashed out at us, his feet banged against the wall right by my head twice, like pistols, before Ringo jumped down from the hayrack onto his head. We got the bridle on him, but he wouldn't take the saddle. "Get your horse and shove his blind side up!" I was hollering at Ringo when father came in, running, with his boots in his hand, and we looked up the hill toward the house and saw one of them riding around the corner with a short carbine, carrying it in one hand like a lamp.

"Get away," father said. He went up onto Jupiter's bare back like a bird, holding him for a moment and looking down at us. He didn't speak loud at all; he didn't even sound in a hurry.

"Take care of Granny," he said. . . . "All right, Jupe. Let's go."

Jupiter's head was pointing down the hallway toward the lattice half doors at the back; he went out again, out from between me and Ringo like he did yesterday, with father already lifting him and I thinking, "He can't jump through that little hole." Jupiter took the doors on his chest, only they seemed to burst before he even touched them, and I saw him and father again like they were flying in the air, with broken planks whirling and spinning around them when they went out of sight. And then the Yankee rode into the barn and saw us, and threw down with the carbine and shot at us pointblank with one hand, like it was a pistol, and said, "Where'd he go, the rebel son?"

Louvinia kept on trying to tell us about it while we were running and looking back at the smoke beginning to come out of the downstairs windows: "Marse John setting on the porch and them Yankees riding through the flower beds and say, 'Brother, we wanter know where the rebel John Sartoris live,' and Marse John say, 'Hey?' with his hand to his ear and his face look like he born loony like Unc Few Mitchell, and Yankee say, 'Sartoris. John Sartoris,' and Marse John say, 'Which? Say which?' until he know Yankee stood about all he going to, and Marse John say, 'Oh, John Sartoris. Whyn't you say so in the first place?' and Yankee cussing him for idiot fool, and Marse John say, 'Hey? How's that?' and Yankee say, 'Nothing! Nothing! Show me where John Sartoris is 'fore I put rope round your neck too!' and Marse John say, 'Lemme git my shoes and I show you,' and come into house limping, and then run down the hall at me and say, 'Boots and pistols, Louvinia. Take care of Miss Rosa and the chillen,' and I go to the door, but I just a nigger. Yankee say, 'That woman's lying. I believe that man was Sartoris himself. Go look in the barn quick and see if that claybank stallion there' "—until Granny stopped and began to shake her.

"Hush!" Granny said. "Hush! Can't you understand that Loosh has shown them where the silver is buried? Call Joby. Hurry!" She turned Louvinia toward the cabins and hit her exactly like father turned my horse and hit him when we rode down the hill and into the Yankees, and then Granny turned to run back toward the house; only now it was Louvinia holding her and Granny trying to get away.

"Don't you go back there, Miss Rosa!" Louvinia said. . . .

"Bayard, hold her; help me, Bayard! They'll kill her!"

"Let me go!" Granny said. "Call Joby! Loosh has shown them where the silver is buried!" But we held her; she was strong and thin and light as a cat, but we held her. The smoke was boiling up now, and we could hear it or them—something—maybe all of them making one sound—the Yankees and the fire. And then I saw Loosh. He was coming up from his cabin with a bundle on his shoulder tied up in a bandanna and Philadelphy behind him, and his face looked like it had that night last summer when Ringo and I looked into the window and saw him after he came back from seeing the Yankees. Granny stopped fighting. She said, "Loosh."

He stopped and looked at her; he looked like he was asleep, like he didn't even see us or was seeing something we couldn't. But Philadelphy saw us; she cringed back behind him, looking at Granny. "I tried to stop him, Miss Rosa," she said. "'Fore God I tried."

"Loosh," Granny said, "are you going too?"

"Yes," Loosh said, "I going. I done been freed; God's own angel proclamated me free and gonter general me to Jordan. I don't belong to John Sartoris now; I belongs to me and God."

"But the silver belongs to John Sartoris," Granny said. "Who are you to give it away?"

"You ax me that?" Loosh said. "Where John Sartoris? Whyn't he come and ax me that? Let God ax John Sartoris who the man name that give me to him. Let the man that buried me in the black dark ax that of the man what dug me free." He wasn't looking at us; I don't think he could even see us. He went on.

"'Fore God, Miss Rosa," Philadelphy said, "I tried to stop him. I done tried."

"Don't go, Philadelphy," Granny said. "Don't you know he's leading you into misery and starvation?"

Philadelphy began to cry. "I knows hit. I knows whut they tole him can't be true. But he my husband. I reckon I got to go with him."

They went on. Louvinia had come back; she and Ringo were behind us. The smoke boiled up, yellow and slow, and turning copper-colored in the sunset like dust; it was like dust from a road above the feet that made it, and then went on, boiling up slow and hanging and waiting to die away.

"The bastuds, Granny!" I said. "The bastuds!"

Then we were all three saying it—Granny and me and Ringo, saying it together.

["The bastuds!" we cried.

"The bastuds! The bastuds!"]

Raid

Granny wrote the note with pokeberry juice. "Take it straight to Mrs. Compson and come straight back," she said. "Don't you-all stop anywhere."

"You mean we got to walk?" Ringo said. "You gonter make us walk all them four miles to Jefferson and back, with them two horses standing in the lot doing nothing?"

"They are borrowed horses," Granny said. "I'm going to take care of them until I can return them."

"I reckon you calls starting out to be gone you don't know where and you don't know how long taking care of—" Ringo said.

"Do you want me to whup you?" Louvinia said.

"Nome," Ringo said.

We walked to Jefferson and gave Mrs. Compson the note, and got the hat and the parasol and the hand mirror, and walked back home. That afternoon we greased the wagon, and that night after supper Granny got the pokeberry juice again and wrote on a scrap of paper, "Colonel Nathaniel G. Dick,—th Ohio Cavalry," and folded it and pinned it inside her dress. "Now I won't forget it," she said.

"If you was to, I reckon these hellion boys can remind you," Louvinia said. "I reckon they ain't forgot him. Walking in that door just in time to keep them others from snatching them out from under your dress and nailing them to the barn door like two coon hides."

"Yes," Granny said. "Now we'll go to bed."

We lived in Joby's cabin then, with a red quilt nailed by one edge to a rafter and hanging down to make two rooms. Joby was waiting with the wagon when Granny came out with Mrs. Compson's hat on, and got into the wagon and told Ringo to open the parasol and took up the reins. Then we all stopped and watched Joby stick something into the wagon beneath the quilts; it was the barrel and the iron parts of the musket that Ringo and I found in the ashes of the house.

"What's that?" Granny said. Joby didn't look at her.

"Maybe if they just seed the end of hit they mought think hit was the whole gun," he said.

"Then what?" Granny said. Joby didn't look at anybody now.

"I was just doing what I could to help git the silver and the mules back," he said.

Louvinia didn't say anything either. She and Granny just looked at Joby. After a while he took the musket barrel out of the wagon. Granny gathered up the reins.

"Take him with you," Louvinia said. "Leastways he can tend the horses."

"No," Granny said. "Don't you see I have got about all I can look after now?"

"Then you stay here and lemme go," Louvinia said. "I'll git um back."

"No," Granny said. "I'll be all right. I shall inquire until I find Colonel Dick, and then we will load the chest in the wagon and Loosh can lead the mules and we will come back home."

Then Louvinia began to act just like Uncle Buck McCaslin did the morning we started to Memphis. She stood there holding to the wagon wheel and looked at Granny from under father's old hat, and began to holler. "Don't you waste no time on colonels or nothing!" she hollered. "You tell them niggers to send Loosh to you, and you tell him to get that chest and them mules, and then you whup him!" The wagon was moving now; she had turned loose the wheel, and she walked along beside it, hollering at Granny: "Take that pairsawl and wear hit out on him!"

"All right," Granny said. The wagon went on; we passed the ash pile and the chimneys standing up out of it; Ringo and I found the insides of the big clock too. The sun was just coming up, shining back on the chimneys; I could still see Louvinia between them, standing in front of the cabin, shading her eyes with her hand to watch us. Joby was still standing behind her, holding the musket barrel. They had broken the gates clean off; and then we were in the road.

"Don't you want me to drive?" I said.

"I'll drive," Granny said. "These are borrowed horses."

"Case even Yankee could look at um and tell they couldn't keep up with even a walking army," Ringo said. "And I like to know how anybody can hurt this team lessen he ain't got strength enough to keep um from laying down in the road and getting run over with they own wagon."

We drove until dark, and camped. By sunup we were on the road again. "You better let me drive a while," I said.

"I'll drive," Granny said. "I was the one who borrowed them."

"You can tote this pairsawl a while, if you want something to do," Ringo said. "And give my arm a rest." I took the parasol and he laid down in the wagon and put his hat over his eyes. "Call me when we gitting nigh to Hawkhurst," he said, "so I can commence to look out for that railroad you tells about."

We went on; we didn't go fast. Or maybe it seemed slow because we had got into a country where nobody seemed to live at all; all that day we didn't even see a house. I didn't ask and Granny didn't say; she just sat there under the parasol with Mrs. Compson's hat on and the horses walking and even our own dust moving ahead of us; after a while even Ringo sat up and looked around.

"We on the wrong road," he said. "Ain't even nobody live here, let alone pass here."

But after a while the hills stopped, the road ran out flat and straight; and all of a sudden Ringo hollered, "Look out! Here they come again to git these uns!" We saw it, too, then—a cloud of dust away to the west, moving slow—too slow for men riding—and then the road we were on ran square into a big broad one running straight on into the east, as the railroad at Hawkhurst did when Granny and I were there that summer before the war; all of a sudden I remembered it.

"This is the road to Hawkhurst," I said. But Ringo was not listening; he was looking at the dust, and the wagon stopped now with the horses' heads hanging and our dust overtaking us again and the big dust cloud coming slow up in the west.

"Can't you see um coming?" Ringo hollered. "Git on away from here!"

"They ain't Yankees," Granny said. "The Yankees have already been here." Then we saw it, too—a burned house like ours, three chimneys standing above a mound of ashes, and then we saw a white woman and a child looking at us from a cabin behind them. Granny looked at the dust cloud, then she looked at the empty broad road going on into the east. "This is the way," she said.

We went on. It seemed like we went slower than ever now, with the dust cloud behind us and the burned houses and gins and thrown-down fences on either side, and the white women and children—we never saw a nigger at all—watching us from the nigger cabins where they lived now like we lived at home; we didn't stop. "Poor folks," Granny said. "I wish we had enough to share with them."

At sunset we drew off the road and camped; Ringo was looking back. "Whatever hit is, we done went off and left hit," he said. "I don't see no dust." We slept in the wagon this time, all three of us. I don't know what time it was, only that all of a sudden I was awake. Granny was already sitting up in the wagon. I could see her head against the branches and the stars. All of a sudden all three of us were sitting up in the wagon, listening. They were coming up the road. It sounded like about fifty of them; we could hear the feet hurrying, and a kind of panting murmur. It was not singing exactly; it was not that loud. It was just a sound, a breathing, a kind of gasping, murmuring chant and the feet whispering fast in the deep dust. I could hear women, too, and then all of a sudden I began to smell them.

"Niggers," I whispered. "Sh-h-h-h," I whispered.

We couldn't see them and they did not see us; maybe they didn't even look, just walking fast in the dark with that panting, hurrying murmuring, going on. And then the sun rose and we went on, too, along that big broad empty road between the burned houses and gins and fences. Before, it had been like passing through a country where nobody had ever lived; now it was like passing through one where everybody had died at the same moment. That night we waked up three times and sat up in the wagon in the dark and heard niggers pass in the road. The last time it was after dawn and we had already fed the horses. It was a big crowd of them this time, and they sounded like they were running, like they had to run to keep ahead of daylight. Then they were gone. Ringo and I had taken up the harness again; when Granny said, "Wait. Hush." It was just one, we could hear her panting and sobbing, and then we heard another sound. Granny began to get down from the wagon. "She fell," she said. "You-all hitch up and come on."

When we turned into the road, the woman was kind of crouched beside it, holding something in her arms, and Granny standing beside her. It was a baby, a few months old; she held it like she thought maybe Granny was going to take it away from her. "I been sick and I couldn't keep up," she said. "They went off and left me."

"Is your husband with them?" Granny said.

"Yessum," the woman said. "They's all there."

"Who do you belong to?" Granny said. Then she didn't answer. She squatted there in the dust, crouched over the baby. "If I give you something to eat, will you turn around and go back home?" Granny said. Still she didn't answer. She just squatted there. "You see you can't keep up with them and that they ain't going to wait for you," Granny said. "Do you want to die here in the road for buzzards to eat?" But she didn't even look at Granny; she just squatted there.

"Hit's Jordan we coming to," she said. "Jesus gonter see me that far."

"Get in the wagon," Granny said. She got in; she squatted again just like she had in the road, holding the baby and not looking at anything—just hunkered down and swaying on her hams as the wagon rocked and jolted. The sun was up; we went down a long hill and began to cross a creek bottom.

"I'll get out here," she said. Granny stopped the wagon and she got out. There was nothing at all but the thick gum and cypress and thick underbrush still full of shadow.

"You go back home, girl," Granny said. She just stood there. "Hand me the basket," Granny said. I handed it to her and she opened it and gave the woman a piece of bread and meat. We went on.

When I looked back, the woman was still standing there by the road. We went on up the other hill, but when I looked back this time the road was empty again.

"Were the others there in that bottom?" Granny asked Ringo.

"Yessum," Ringo said. "She done found um. Reckon she gonter lose um again tonight though."

That was early on the fourth day. Late that afternoon we began to go around a hill and I saw the graveyard and Uncle Denny's grave. "Hawkhurst," I said.

"Hawkhurst?" Ringo said. "Where's that railroad?"

The sun was going down. We came out where the sun shone level across where I remembered the house; we didn't stop; we just looked across at the mound of ashes and the four chimneys standing in the sun like the chimneys at home. We came to the gate. Cousin Denny was running down the drive toward us. He was ten; he ran up to the wagon with his eyes round and his mouth already open for hollering.

"Denny," Granny said, "do you know us?"

"Yessum," Cousin Denny said. He looked at me, hollering, "Come see—"

"Where's your mother?" Granny said.

"In Jingus' cabin," Cousin Denny said; he didn't even look at Granny. "They burnt the house!" he hollered. "Come see what they done to the railroad!"

We ran, all three of us. Granny hollered something and I turned and put the parasol back into the wagon and hollered "Yessum!" back at her, and ran on and caught up with Cousin Denny and Ringo in the road, and we ran on over the hill, and then it came in sight. When Granny and I were here before, Cousin Denny showed me the railroad, but he was so little then that Jingus had to carry him. It was the straightest thing I ever saw, running straight and empty and quiet through a long empty gash cut through the trees, and the ground, too, and full of sunlight like water in a river, only straighter than any river, with the crossties cut off even and smooth and neat, and the light shining on the rails like on two spider threads, running straight on to where you couldn't even see that far. It looked clean and neat, like the yard behind Louvinia's cabin after she had swept it on Saturday morning, with those two little threads that didn't look strong enough for anything to run on running straight and fast and light, like they were getting up speed to jump clean off the world.

Jingus knew when the train would come; he held my hand and carried Cousin Denny, and we stood between the rails and he showed us where it would come from, and then he showed us where the shadow of a dead pine would come to a stob he had driven in the ground, and then you would hear the whistle. And we got back and watched the shadow, and then we heard it; it whistled and then it got louder and louder fast, and Jingus went to the track and took his hat off and held it out with his face turned back toward us and his mouth hollering, "Watch now! Watch!" even after we couldn't hear him for the train; and then it passed. It came roaring up and went past; the river they had cut through the trees was all full of smoke and noise and sparks and jumping brass, and then empty again, and just Jingus' old hat bouncing and jumping along the empty track behind it like the hat was alive.

But this time what I saw was something that looked like piles of black straws heaped up every few yards, and we ran into the cut and we could see where they had dug the ties up and piled them and set them on fire. But Cousin Denny was still hollering, "Come see what they done to the rails!" he said.

They were back in the trees; it looked like four or five men had taken each rail and tied it around a tree like you knot a green cornstalk around a wagon stake, and Ringo was hollering, too, now.

"What's them?" he hollered. "What's them?"

"That's what it runs on!" Cousin Denny hollered.

"You mean hit have to come in here and run up and down around these here trees like a squirrel?" Ringo hollered. Then we all heard the horse at once; we just had time to look when Bobolink came up the road out of the trees and went across the railroad and into the trees again like a bird, with Cousin Drusilla riding astride like a man and sitting straight and light as a willow branch in the wind. They said she was the best woman rider in the country.

"There's Dru!" Cousin Denny hollered. "Come on! She's been up to the river to see them niggers! Come on!" He and Ringo ran again. When I passed the chimneys, they were just running into the stable. Cousin Drusilla had already unsaddled Bobolink, and she was rubbing him down with a croker sack when I came in. Cousin Denny was still hollering, "What did you see? What are they doing?"

"I'll tell about it at the house," Cousin Drusilla said. Then she saw me. She was not tall; it was the way she stood and walked. She had on pants, like a man. She was the best woman rider in the country. When Granny and I were here that summer before the war and Gavin Breckbridge had just given Bobolink to her, they looked fine together; it didn't need Jingus to say that they were the finest-looking couple in Alabama or Mississippi either. But Gavin was killed at Shiloh and so they didn't marry. She came and put her hand on my shoulder.

"Hello," she said. "Hello, John Sartoris." She looked at Ringo. "Is this Ringo?" she said.

"That's what they tells me," Ringo said.

"How are you?" Cousin Drusilla said.

"I manages to stand hit," Ringo said.

"I'll finish Bobolink for you," I said.

"Will you?" she said. She went to Bobolink's head. "Will you stand for Cousin Bayard, lad?" she said. "I'll see you-all at the house, then," she said. She went out.

"Yawl sho must 'a' had this horse hid good when the Yankees come," Ringo said.

"This horse?" Cousin Denny said. "Ain't no damn Yankee going to fool with Dru's horse no more." He didn't holler now, but pretty soon he began again: "When they come to burn the house, Dru grabbed the pistol and run out here—she had on her Sunday dress—and them right behind her. She run in here and she jumped on Bobolink bareback, without even waiting for the bridle, and one of them right there in the door hollering, 'Stop,' and Dru said, 'Get away, or I'll ride you down,' and him hollering, 'Stop! Stop!' with his pistol out too"—Cousin Denny was hollering good now—"and Dru leaned down to Bobolink's ear and said, 'Kill him, Bob,' and the Yankee jumped back just in time. The lot was full of them, too, and Dru stopped Bobolink and jumped down in her Sunday dress and put the pistol to Bobolink's ear and said, 'I can't shoot you all, because I haven't enough bullets, and it wouldn't do any good anyway; but I won't need but one shot for the horse, and which shall it be?' So they burned the house and went away!" He was hollering good now, with Ringo staring at him so you could have raked Ringo's eyes off his face with a stick. "Come on!" Cousin Denny hollered. "Le's go hear about them niggers at the river!"

Cousin Drusilla was already talking, telling Granny mostly. Her hair was cut short; it looked like father's would when he would tell

Granny about him and the men cutting each other's hair with a bayonet. She was sunburned and her hands were hard and scratched like a man's that works. She was telling Granny mostly: "They began to pass in the road yonder while the house was still burning. We couldn't count them; men and women carrying children who couldn't walk and carrying old men and women who should have been at home waiting to die. They were singing, walking along the road singing, not even looking to either side. The dust didn't even settle for two days, because all that night they still passed; we sat up listening to them, and the next morning every few yards along the road would be the old ones who couldn't keep up any more, sitting or lying down and even crawling along, calling to the others to help them; and the others—the young strong ones —not stopping, not even looking at them. I don't think they even heard or saw them. 'Going to Jordan,' they told me. 'Going to cross Jordan.' "

"That was what Loosh said," Granny said. "That General Sherman was leading them all to Jordan."

"Yes," Cousin Drusilla said. "The river. They have stopped there; it's like a river itself, dammed up. The Yankees have thrown out a brigade of cavalry to hold them back while they build the bridge to cross the infantry and artillery; they are all right until they get up there and see or smell the water. That's when they go mad. Not fighting; it's like they can't even see the horses shoving them back and the scabbards beating them; it's like they can't see anything but the water and the other bank. They aren't angry, aren't fighting; just men, women and children singing and chanting and trying to get to that unfinished bridge or even down into the water itself, and the cavalry beating them back with sword scabbards. I don't know when they have eaten; nobody knows just how far some of them have come. They just pass here without food or anything, exactly as they rose up from whatever they were doing when the spirit or the voice or whatever it was told them to go. They stop during the day and rest in the woods; then, at night, they move again. We will hear them later—I'll wake you—marching on up the road until the cavalry stops them. There was an officer, a major, who finally took time to see I wasn't one of his men; he said, 'Can't you do anything with them? Promise them anything to go back home?' But it was like they couldn't see me or hear me speaking; it was only that water and that bank on the other side. But you will see for yourself tomorrow, when we go back."

"Drusilla," Aunt Louise said, "you're not going back tomorrow or any other time."

"They are going to mine the bridge and blow it up when the army has crossed," Cousin Drusilla said. "Nobody knows what they will do then."

"But we cannot be responsible," Aunt Louise said. "The Yankees brought it on themselves; let them pay the price."

"Those Negroes are not Yankees, mother," Cousin Drusilla said. "At least there will be one person there who is not a Yankee either." She looked at Granny. "Four, counting Bayard and Ringo."

Aunt Louise looked at Granny. "Rosa, you shan't go. I forbid it. Brother John will thank me to do so."

"I reckon I will," Granny said. "I've got to get the silver anyway."

"And the mules," Ringo said; "don't forget them. And don't yawl worry about Granny. She 'cide what she want and then she kneel down about ten seconds and tell God what she aim to do, and then she git up and do hit. And them that don't like hit can git outen the way or git trompled."

"And now I reckon we'd better go to bed," Granny said.

We went to bed. And this time I don't know how late it was either, except that it was late. It was Cousin Denny shaking me. "Dru says to come on out if you want to hear them passing," he whispered.

She was outside the cabin; she hadn't undressed even. I could see her in the starlight—her short jagged hair and the man's shirt and pants. "Hear them?" she said. We could hear it again, like we had in the wagon—the hurrying feet, the sound like they were singing in panting whispers, hurrying on past the gate and dying away up the road. "That's the third tonight," Cousin Drusilla said. "Two passed while I was down at the gate. You were tired, and so I didn't wake you before."

"I thought it was late," I said. "You haven't been to bed even. Have you?"

"No," she said. "I've quit sleeping."

"Quit sleeping?" I said. "Why?"

She looked at me. I was as tall as she was; we couldn't see each other's faces; it was just her head with the short jagged hair like she had cut it herself without bothering about a mirror, and her neck that had got thin and hard like her hands since Granny and I were here before. "I'm keeping a dog quiet," she said.

"A dog?" I said. "I haven't seen any dog."

"No. It's quiet now," she said. "It doesn't bother anybody any more now. I just have to show it the stick now and then." She was looking at me. "Why not stay awake now? Who wants to sleep now, with so much happening, so much to see? Living used to be dull, you see. Stupid. You lived in the same house your father was born in, and your father's sons and daughters had the sons and daughters of the same Negro slaves to nurse and coddle; and then you grew up and you fell in love with your acceptable young man, and in time you would marry him, in your mother's wedding gown, perhaps, and with the same silver for presents she had received; and then you settled down forevermore while you got children to feed and bathe and dress until they grew up, too; and then you and your husband died quietly and were buried together maybe on a summer afternoon just before suppertime. Stupid, you see. But now you can see for yourself how it is; it's fine now; you don't have to worry now about the house and the silver, because they get burned up and carried away; and you don't have to worry about the Negroes, because they tramp the roads all night waiting for a chance to drown in homemade Jordan; and you don't have to worry about getting children to bathe and feed and change, because the young men can ride away and get killed in the fine battles; and you don't even have to sleep alone, you don't even have to sleep at all; and so, all you have to do is show the stick to the dog now and then and say, 'Thank God for nothing.' You see? . . . There. They've gone now. And you'd better get back to bed, so we can get an early start in the morning. It will take a long time to get through them."

"You're not coming in now?" I said.

"Not yet," she said. But we didn't move. And then she put her hand on my shoulder. "Listen," she said. "When you go back home and see Uncle John, ask him to let me come there and ride with his troop. Tell him I can ride, and maybe I can learn to shoot. Will you?"

"Yes," I said. "I'll tell him you are not afraid too."

"Aren't I?" she said. "I hadn't thought about it. It doesn't matter anyway. Just tell him I can ride and that I don't get tired." Her hand was on my shoulder; it felt thin and hard. "Will you do that for me? Ask him to let me come, Bayard."

"All right," I said. Then I said, "I hope he will let you."

"So do I," she said. "Now you go back to bed. Good night." I went back to bed. After a while I was asleep.

And by sunup we were on the road again, with Cousin Drusilla on Bobolink beside the wagon.

It took us all that day to get through them, like Cousin Drusilla said. We began to see the dust almost at once, and then I began to smell them, and then we were in the middle of them—men carrying babies, and women dragging children by the hand, and women carrying babies, and old ones kind of pulling themselves along with sticks or sitting beside the road and holding up their hands and even calling to us when we passed, and one old woman even running along holding to the wagon and hollering at Granny to at least let her see the water before she died.

But mostly they didn't even look at us. We didn't try to ask them to let us through; it was like we could look at their faces and know that they couldn't have heard us. They were not singing yet; they were just hurrying, with our horses pushing slow through them, and their blank eyes not looking at anything out of faces caked with dust and sweat, and our horses and Bobolink shoving slow through them like trying to ride up a creek full of floating logs, and the dust everywhere, and Ringo holding the parasol over Granny and his eyes getting whiter and whiter, and Granny with Mrs. Compson's hat on, and the smell of them, and Granny looking sicker and sicker. Then it was afternoon. I had forgot about time. All of a sudden we began to hear them where the cavalry was holding them back from the bridge.

It was just a sound at first, like wind, like it might be in the dust itself, and Cousin Drusilla hollering, "Look out, Aunt Rosa! Oh, look out!"

It was like we all heard it at the same time—us in the wagon and on the horse—and the faces all around us under the sweat-caked dust. They made a kind of long wailing sound, and then I could feel the whole wagon rise up and begin to run forward. I saw our old rib-gaunted horses standing on their hind feet one minute and then turned sideways in the traces the next, and Cousin Drusilla leaning forward a little and holding Bobolink, and I saw men and women and children going down under the horses, and we could feel the wagon going over them and we could hear them screaming. And we couldn't stop any more than if the earth had tilted up and was sliding us all down toward the river.

It went fast, like that, like it did every time; it was like the Yankees were a kind of gully, and every time Granny and Ringo and I got close to them, we would go rushing down into the gully like three rocks. Because all of a sudden it was sunset; there was a high, bright, rosy glow quiet behind the trees and shining on the river, and we saw the bridge full of Yankee soldiers running across to the other bank. I remember watching horses' and mules' heads mixed up with the bayonets, and then the barrels of cannon tilted up and kind of rushing slow across the high air, like split-cane clothespins being jerked along the clothesline, and the singing everywhere up and down the river bank, with the voices of the women coming out of it high, and then hollering "Glory!" and "Jesus!"

They were fighting now. There was a cleared space between the end of the bridge and the backs of the cavalry. I was watching the horses rearing and shoving against them, and the men beating at them with their scabbards, and the last of the infantry running onto the bridge, and all of a sudden there was an officer holding his scabbarded sword by the little end like a stick and hanging onto the wagon and hollering at us. I could see his little white face with a stubble of beard on it and a long streak of blood, and bareheaded, and with his mouth open.

"Get back!" he hollered. "Get back! We're going to blow the bridge!" and Granny hollering back at him, with Mrs. Compson's hat knocked to one side of her head, and hers and the Yankee's faces not a yard apart:

"I want my silver! I'm John Sartoris' mother-in-law! Send Colonel Dick to me!" Then the Yankee officer was gone, right in the middle of hollering and still beating at the nigger heads with his saber, and with his little hollering face and all. I don't know what became of him; he just vanished holding onto the wagon and flailing about him with the sword, and then Cousin Drusilla was there, on Bobolink; she had our nigh horse by the bridle and she was trying to turn the wagon sideways. I started to jump down. "Stay in the wagon," she said. She didn't holler; she just said it. "Take the lines and turn them." When we got the wagon turned sideways, we stopped. And then for a minute I thought we were going backward, until I saw that it was the niggers. Then I saw that the cavalry had broken; I saw the whole mob of it—horses and men and sabers and niggers—kind of rolling toward the end of the bridge, like when a dam breaks, for about ten clear seconds behind the last of the infantry. And then the bridge vanished. I was looking right at it; I could see the clear gap between the infantry and the wave of niggers and cavalry, with the little empty thread of bridge joining them together in the air above the water, and then there was a bright glare, and then I felt my insides suck, and then a clap of wind hit me on the back of the head. I didn't hear anything at all. I just sat there in the wagon with a funny buzzing in my ears and a funny taste in my mouth, and watched little toy men and horses and pieces of plank floating along over the water. But I couldn't hear anything at all; I couldn't even hear Cousin Drusilla. She was right beside the wagon now, leaning toward us, hollering something.

"What?" I hollered.

"Stay in the wagon!" she hollered.

"I can't hear you!" I hollered. That's what I said; that's what I was thinking; I didn't realize even that the wagon was moving again. But then I did; it was like the whole side of the river had turned and risen up and was rushing down toward the water, and us sitting in the wagon and rushing down toward the water on another river of faces that couldn't see or hear either. Cousin Drusilla had the nigh horse by the bridle again, and I dragged at them, too, and Granny was standing up in the wagon and beating at the faces with Mrs. Compson's parasol, and then the whole rotten bridle came off in Cousin Drusilla's hand.

"Get away!" I hollered. "The wagon will float!"

"Yes," she said, "it will float. Just stay in it. Watch Aunt Rosa and Ringo."

"Yes," I hollered. Then she was gone. We passed her; turned, and holding Bobolink like a rock again and leaning down talking to him and patting his cheek, she was gone. Then maybe the bank did cave. I don't know. I didn't even know we were in the river. It was just like the earth had fallen out from under the wagon and the faces and all, and we all rushed down slow, with the faces looking up and their eyes blind and their mouths open and their arms held up. High up in the air across the river I saw a cliff and a big fire on it running fast sideways; and then all of a sudden the wagon was moving fast sideways, and then a dead horse came shining up from out of the yelling faces and went down slow again, exactly like a fish feeding, with, hanging over his rump by one stirrup, a man in a black uniform, and then I realized that the uniform was blue, only it was wet. They were screaming then, and now I could feel the wagon bed tilt and slide as they caught at it. Granny was kneeling beside me now, hitting at the screaming faces with Mrs. Compson's parasol. Behind us they were still marching down the bank and into the river, singing.

A Yankee patrol helped Ringo and me cut the drowned horses out of the harness and drag the wagon ashore. We sprinkled water on Granny until she came to, and they rigged harness with ropes and hitched up two of their horses. There was a road on top of the bluff, and then we could see the fires along the bank. They were still singing on the other side of the river, but it was quieter now. But there were patrols still riding up and down the cliff on this side, and squads of infantry down at the water where the fires were. Then we began to pass between rows of tents, with Granny lying against me, and I could see her face then; it was white and still, and her eyes were shut. She looked old and tired; I hadn't realized how old and little she was. Then we began to pass big fires, with niggers in wet clothes crouching around them and soldiers going among them passing out food; then we came to a broad street, and stopped before a tent with a sentry at the door and a light inside. The soldiers looked at Granny.

"We better take her to the hospital," one of them said.

Granny opened her eyes; she tried to sit up. "No," she said. "Just take me to Colonel Dick. I will be all right then."

They carried her into the tent and put her in a chair. She hadn't moved; she was sitting there with her eyes closed and a strand of wet hair sticking to her face when Colonel Dick came in. I had never seen him before—only heard his voice while Ringo and I were squatting under Granny's skirt and holding our breath—but I knew him at once, with his bright beard and his hard bright eyes, stooping over Granny and saying, "Damn this war. Damn it. Damn it."

"They took the silver and the darkies and the mules," Granny said. "I have come to get them."

"Have them you shall," he said, "if they are anywhere in this corps. I'll see the general myself." He was looking at Ringo and me now. "Ha!" he said. "I believe we have met before also." Then he was gone again.

It was hot in the tent, and quiet, with three bugs swirling around the lantern, and outside the sound of the army like wind far away. Ringo was already asleep, sitting on the ground with his head on his knees, and I wasn't much better, because all of a sudden Colonel Dick was back and there was an orderly writing at the table, and Granny sitting again with her eyes closed in her white face.

"Maybe you can describe them," Colonel Dick said to me.

"I will do it," Granny said. She didn't open her eyes. "The chest of silver tied with hemp rope. The rope was new. Two darkies, Loosh and Philadelphy. The mules, Old Hundred and Tinney."

Colonel Dick turned and watched the orderly writing. "Have you got that?" he said.

The orderly looked at what he had written. "I guess the general will be glad to give them twice the silver and mules just for taking that many niggers," he said.

"Now I'll go see the general," Colonel Dick said.

Then we were moving again. I don't know how long it had been, because they had to wake me and Ringo both; we were in the wagon again, with two Army horses pulling it on down the long broad street, and there was another officer with us and Colonel Dick was gone. We came to a pile of chests and boxes that looked higher than a mountain. There was a rope pen behind it full of mules and then, standing to one side and waiting there, was what looked like a thousand niggers, men, women and children, with their wet clothes dried on them. And now it began to go fast again; there was Granny in the wagon with her eyes wide open now and the lieutenant reading from the paper and the soldiers jerking chests and trunks out of the pile. "Ten chests tied with hemp rope," the lieutenant read. "Got them? . . . A hundred and ten mules. It says from Philadelphia—that's in Mississippi. Get these Mississippi mules. They are to have rope and halters."

"We ain't got a hundred and ten Mississippi mules," the sergeant said.

"Get what we have got. Hurry." He turned to Granny. "And there are your niggers, madam."

Granny was looking at him with her eyes wide as Ringo's. She was drawn back a little, with her hand at her chest. "But they're not—they ain't—" she said.

"They ain't all yours?" the lieutenant said. "I know it. The general said to give you another hundred with his compliments."

"But that ain't— We didn't—" Granny said.

"She wants the house back, too," the sergeant said. "We ain't got any houses, grandma," he said. "You'll just have to make out with trunks and niggers and mules. You wouldn't have room for it on the wagon, anyway."

We sat there while they loaded the ten trunks into the wagon. It just did hold them all. They got another set of trees and harness, and hitched four mules to it. "One of you darkies that can handle two span come here," the lieutenant said. One of the niggers came and got on the seat with Granny; none of us had ever seen him before. Behind us they were leading the mules out of the pen.

"You want to let some of the women ride?" the lieutenant said.

"Yes," Granny whispered.

"Come on," the lieutenant said. "Just one to a mule, now." Then he handed me the paper. "Here you are. There's a ford about twenty miles up the river; you can cross there. You better get on away from here before any more of these niggers decide to go with you."

We rode until daylight, with the ten chests in the wagon and the mules and our army of niggers behind. Granny had not moved, sitting there beside the strange nigger with Mrs. Compson's hat on and the parasol in her hand. But she was not asleep, because when it got light enough to see, she said, "Stop the wagon." The wagon stopped. She turned and looked at me. "Let me see that paper," she said.

We opened the paper and looked at it, at the neat writing:

Field Headquarters,
—th Army Corps,
Department of Tennessee,
August 14, 1864.

To all Brigade, Regimental and Other Commanders: You will
see that bearer is repossessed in full of the following property,
to wit: Ten (10) chests tied with hemp rope and containing silver.
One hundred ten (110) mules captured loose near Philadelphia in
Mississippi. One nundred ten (110) Negroes of both sexes belonging to and having strayed from the same locality.

You will further see that bearer is supplied with necessary
food and forage to expedite his passage to his destination.

By order of the General Commanding.

We looked at one another in the gray light. "I reckon you gonter
take um back now," Ringo said.

Granny looked at me. "We can get food and fodder too," I said.

"Yes," Granny said. "I tried to tell them better. You and Ringo
heard me. It's the hand of God."

We stopped and slept until noon. That afternoon we came to the
ford. We had already started down the bluff when we saw the troop
of cavalry camped there. It was too late to stop.

"They done found hit out and headed us off," Ringo said. It was
too late; already an officer and two men were riding toward us.

"I will tell them the truth," Granny said. "We have done nothing." She sat there, drawn back a little again, with her hand already
raised and holding the paper out in the other when they rode up.
The officer was a heavy-built man with a red face; he looked at us
and took the paper and read it and began to swear. He sat there
on his horse swearing while we watched him.

"How many do you lack?" he said.

"How many do I what?" Granny said.

"Mules!" the officer hollered. "Mules! Mules! Do I look like I
had any chests of silver or niggers tied with hemp rope?"

"Do we—" Granny said, with her hand to her chest, looking at
him; I reckon it was Ringo that knew first what he meant.

"We like fifty," Ringo said.

"Fifty, hey?" the officer said. He cursed again; he turned to one of the men behind him and cursed him now. "Count 'em!" he hollered. "Do you think I'm going to take their word for it?"

The man counted the mules; we didn't move; I don't think we even breathed hardly. "Sixty-three," the man said.

The officer looked at us. "Sixty-three from a hundred and ten leaves forty-seven," he said. He cursed. "Get forty-seven mules!" he hollered. "Hurry!" He looked at us again. "Think you can beat me out of three mules, hey?" he hollered.

"Forty-seven will do," Ringo said. "Only I reckon maybe we better eat something, like the paper mention."

We crossed the ford. We didn't stop; we went on as soon as they brought up the other mules, and some more of the women got on them. We went on. It was after sundown then, but we didn't stop.

"Hah!" Ringo said. "Whose hand was that?"

We went on until midnight before we stopped. This time it was Ringo that Granny was looking at. "Ringo," she said.

"I never said nothing the paper never said," Ringo said. "Hit was the one that said it; hit wasn't me. All I done was to told him how much the hundred and ten liked; I never said we liked that many. 'Cides, hit ain't no use in praying about hit now; ain't no telling what we gonter run into 'fore we gits home. The main thing now is, whut we gonter do with all these niggers."

"Yes," Granny said. We cooked and ate the food the cavalry officer gave us; then Granny told all the niggers that lived in Alabama to come forward. It was about half of them. "I suppose you all want to cross some more rivers and run after the Yankee Army, don't you?" Granny said. They stood there, moving their feet in the dust. "What? Don't any of you want to?" They just stood there. "Then who are you going to mind from now on?"

After a while, one of them said, "You, missy."

"All right," Granny said. "Now listen to me. Go home. And if I ever hear of any of you straggling off like this again, I'll see to it. Now line up and come up here one at a time while we divide the food."

It took a long time until the last one was gone; when we started again, we had almost enough mules for everybody to ride, but not quite, and Ringo drove now. He didn't ask; he just got in and took the reins, with Granny on the seat by him; it was just once that she told him not to go so fast. So I rode in the back then, on one of the chests, and that afternoon I was asleep; it was the wagon stopping that woke me. We had just come down a hill onto a flat, and then I saw them beyond a field, about a dozen of them, cavalry in blue coats. They hadn't seen us yet, trotting along, and then I saw Granny and Ringo watching them.

"They ain't hardly worth fooling with," Ringo said. "Still, they's horses."

"We've already got a hundred and ten," Granny said. "That's all the paper calls for."

"All right," Ringo said. "You wanter go on?" Granny didn't answer, sitting there drawn back a little, with her hand at her breast again. "Well, what you wanter do?" Ringo said. "You got to 'cide quick, or they be gone." He looked at her; she didn't move. Ringo leaned out of the wagon. "Hey!" he hollered. They looked back quick and saw us and whirled about. "Granny say come here!" Ringo hollered.

"You, Ringo," Granny whispered.

"All right," Ringo said. "You want me to tell um to never mind?" She didn't answer; she was looking past Ringo at the two Yankees who were riding toward us across the field, with that kind of drawn-back look on her face and her hand holding the front of her dress. It was a lieutenant and a sergeant; the lieutenant didn't look much older than Ringo and me. He saw Granny and took off his hat, and Granny sitting there. And then all of a sudden she took her hand away from her chest; it had the paper in it; she held it out to the lieutenant without saying a word. The lieutenant opened it, the sergeant looking over his shoulder. Then the sergeant looked at us.

"This says mules, not horses," he said.

"Just the first hundred was mules," Ringo said. "The extra twelve is horses."

"Damn it!" the lieutenant said. He sounded like a girl swearing. "I told Captain Bowen not to mount us with captured stock!"

"You mean you're going to give them the horses?" the sergeant said.

"What else can I do?" the lieutenant said. He looked like he was fixing to cry. "It's the general's own signature!"

So then we had enough stock for all of them to ride except about fifteen or twenty. We went on. The soldiers stood under a tree by the road, with their saddles and bridles on the ground beside them —all but the lieutenant. When we started again, he ran along by the wagon; he looked like he was going to cry, trotting along by the wagon with his hat in his hand, looking at Granny.

"You'll meet some troops somewhere," he said. "I know you will. Will you tell them where we are and to send for us? You won't forget?"

"They's some of yawl about twenty or thirty miles back that claim to have three extry mules," Ringo said. "But when we sees any more of um, we'll tell um about yawl."

We went on. We came in sight of a town, but we went around it; Ringo didn't even want to stop and send the message in, but Granny made him stop and we sent the message in by one of the niggers.

"That's one more mouth to feed we got shed of," Ringo said.

We went on. We went fast now, changing the mules every few miles; a woman told us we were in Mississippi again, and then, in the afternoon, we came over the hill, and there our chimneys were, standing up into the sunlight, and the cabin behind them and Louvinia bending over a washtub and the clothes on the line, flapping bright and peaceful.

"Stop the wagon," Granny said.

We stopped—the wagon, the hundred and twenty-two mules and horses, and the niggers we never had had time to count.

Granny got out slow and turned to Ringo. "Get out," she said; then she looked at me. "You too," she said. "Because you said nothing at all." We got out of the wagon. She looked at us. "We have lied," she said.

"Hit was the paper that lied; hit wasn't us," Ringo said.

"The paper said a hundred and ten. We have a hundred and twenty-two," Granny said. "Kneel down."

"But they stole them 'fore we did," Ringo said.

"But we lied," Granny said. "Kneel down." She knelt first. Then we all three knelt by the road while she prayed. The washing blew soft and peaceful and bright on the clothesline. And then Louvinia saw us; she was already running across the pasture while Granny was praying.

Skirmish at Sartoris

I

When I think of that day, of Father's old troop on their horses drawn up facing the house, and Father and Drusilla standing on the ground with that Carpet Bagger voting box in front of them, and opposite them the ladies on the porch and the two sets of them, the men and the ladies, facing one another like they were both waiting for the sound to charge, I think I know the reason. I think it was because Father's troop (like all the other Southern soldiers too), even though they had surrendered and said that they were whipped, were still soldiers. Maybe from the old habit of doing everything as one man; maybe when you have lived for four years in a world ordered completely by men's doings, even when it is danger and fighting, you don't want to quit that world: maybe the danger and the fighting are the reasons, because men have been pacifists for every reason under the sun except to avoid danger and fighting. And so now Father's troop and all the other men in Jefferson, and Aunt Louisa and Mrs. Habersham and all the ladies in Jefferson were actually enemies for the reason that the men had given in and admitted that they belonged to the United States but the ladies had never surrendered.

I remember the night we got the letter and found out at last where Drusilla was. It was just before Christmas in 1864, after the Yankees had burned Jefferson and gone away, and we didn't even know for sure if the war was still going on or not. All we knew was that for three years the country had been full of Yankees, and then all of a sudden they were gone and there were no men there at all any more. We hadn't even heard from Father since July, from Carolina, so that now we lived in a world of burned towns and houses and ruined plantations and fields inhabited only by women. Ringo and I were fifteen; we felt almost exactly like we had to eat and sleep and change our clothes in a hotel built only for ladies and children.

The envelope was worn and dirty and it had been opened once and then glued back, but Ringo and I could still make out *Hawkhurst, Gihon County, Alabama,* on it even though we didn't recognize Aunt Louisa's hand at first. It was addressed to Granny, and that showed how long ago it had been written because Aunt Louisa didn't even know that Granny was dead now. It was six pages cut with scissors from wallpaper and written on both sides with poke berry juice, and I thought about the time two years ago when Granny and Ringo and I went to Hawkhurst on the way to catch the Yankee army that stole our silver and we found how the Yankees had come and burned Hawkhurst too after Uncle Dennison and Gavin Breckbridge were killed at Shiloh, and Aunt Louisa and Drusilla and Denny were living in a Negro cabin just like we did at Sartoris in Mississippi. And Drusilla had cut her hair off short like mine almost and she wore a shirt and jeans pants just like Ringo and me and her hands were rough from working too, and Aunt Louisa began to cry and tell us how Drusilla had cut her hair and put on man's clothes the day the news came that Gavin Breckbridge was dead too. But Drusilla didn't cry; it was just that night we were there; the Negroes were still passing in the road all night long, and she waked me and we went down to the road and listened to them passing in the darkness, singing, trying to catch the Yankee army and get free. Then they were gone and Drusilla told me to go on back to bed and I asked her if she wasn't going to bed too and she said she didn't sleep any more, that she had to stay up and keep a dog quiet; it wasn't a bad dog only she just had to get up now and then and show it the stick and then it would be quiet, and I said, "What dog? I haven't seen any dog." And then she turned and put her hand on my shoulder (I was already taller than she was) and said:

"Listen. When you see Cousin Johnny again, ask him to let me ride in his troop with him. Tell him I can ride and maybe I can learn to shoot and that I won't be afraid. Will you tell him?" But I didn't tell Father. Maybe I forgot it. Then the Yankees went away, and Father and his troop went away too. Then, six months later, we had a letter from him about how they were fighting in Carolina, and a month after that we had one from Aunt Louisa that Drusilla was gone too, a short letter on the wallpaper that you could see where Aunt Louisa had cried in the pokeberry juice about how she did not know where Drusilla was but that she had expected the worst ever since Drusilla had deliberately tried to unsex herself by refusing to feel any natural grief at the death not only of her affianced husband but of her own father and that she took it for granted that Drusilla was with us and though she did not expect Drusilla to take any steps herself to relieve a mother's anxiety, she hoped that Granny would. But we didn't know where Drusilla was either. She had just vanished. It was like the Yankees in just passing through the South had not only taken along with them all living men blue and gray and white and black, but even one young girl who had happened to try to look and act like a man after her sweetheart was killed.

So then the next letter came. Only Granny wasn't there to read it, and so for a while Ringo and I couldn't make out what Aunt Louisa was trying to tell us. This one was on the same wallpaper too, six pages this time, only Aunt Louisa hadn't cried in the pokeberry juice this time: Ringo said because she must have been writing too fast:

DEAR SISTER:

I think this will be news to you as it was to me though I both hope and pray it will not be the heart-rending shock to you it was to me as naturally it cannot since you are only an aunt while I am the mother. But it is not myself I am thinking of since I am a woman, a mother, a Southern woman, and it has been our lot during the last four years to learn to bear anything. But when I think of my husband who laid down his life to protect a heritage of courageous men and spotless women looking down from heaven upon a daughter who had deliberately cast away that for which he died, and when I think of my half-orphan son who will one day ask of me why his martyred father's sacrifice was not enough to preserve his sister's good name. . . .

That's how it sounded. Ringo was holding a pineknot for me to read by, but after a while he had to light another pineknot and all the far we had got was how when Gavin Breckbridge was killed at Shiloh before he and Drusilla had had time to marry, there had been reserved for Drusilla the highest destiny of a Southern woman —to be the bride-widow of a lost cause—and how Drusilla had not only thrown that away, she had not only become a lost woman and a shame to her father's memory but she was now living in a word that Aunt Louisa would not even repeat but that Granny knew what it was, though at least thank God that Father and Drusilla were not actually any blood kin, it being Father's wife who was Drusilla's cousin by blood and not Father himself. So then Ringo lit the other pineknot and then we put the sheets of wallpaper down on the floor and then we found out what it was: how Drusilla had been gone for six months and no word from her except she was alive, and then one night she walked into the cabin where Aunt Louisa and Denny were (and now it had a line drawn under it, like this:) in the <u>garments not alone of a man but of a common private soldier</u> and told them how she had been a member of Father's troop for six months, bivouacking at night surrounded by sleeping men and not even bothering to put up the tent for her and Father except when the weather was bad, and how Drusilla not only showed neither shame nor remorse but actually pretended she did not even know what Aunt Louisa was talking about; how when Aunt Louisa told her that she and Father must marry at once, Drusilla said, "Can't you understand that I am tired of burying husbands in this war? That I am riding in Cousin John's troop not to find a man but to hurt Yankees?" and how Aunt Louisa said:

"At least don't call him *Cousin* John where strangers can hear you."

The third letter did not come to us at all. It came to Mrs. Compson. Drusilla and Father were home then. It was in the spring and the war was over now, and we were busy getting the cypress and oak out of the bottom to build the house and Drusilla working with Joby and Ringo and Father and me like another man, with her hair shorter than it had been at Hawkhurst and her face sunburned from riding in the weather and her body thin from living like soldiers lived. After Granny died Ringo and Louvinia and I all slept in the cabin, but after Father came Ringo and Louvinia moved back to the other cabin with Joby and now Father and I slept on Ringo's and my pallet and Drusilla slept in the bed behind the quilt curtain where Granny used to sleep. And so one night I remembered Aunt Louisa's letter and I showed it to Drusilla and Father, and Father found out that Drusilla had not written to tell Aunt Louisa where she was and Father said she must, and so one day Mrs. Compson came out with the third letter. Drusilla and Ringo and Louvinia too were down in the bottom at the sawmill and I saw that one too, on the wallpaper with the pokeberry juice and the juice not cried on this time either, and this the first time Mrs. Compson had come out since Granny died and not even getting out of her surrey but sitting there holding to her parasol with one hand and her shawl with the other and looking around like when Drusilla would come out of the house or from around the corner it would not be just a thin sunburned girl in a man's shirt and pants but maybe something like a tame panther or bear. This one sounded just like the others: about how Aunt Louisa was addressing a stranger to herself but not a stranger to Granny and that there were times when the good name of one family was the good name of all and that she naturally did not expect Mrs. Compson to move out and live with Father and Drusilla because even that would be too late now to preserve the appearance of that which had never existed anyway. But that Mrs. Compson was a woman too, Aunt Louisa believed, a Southern woman too, and had suffered too, Aunt Louisa didn't doubt, only she did hope and pray that Mrs. Compson had been spared the sight of her own daughter if Mrs. Compson had one flouting and outraging all Southern principles of purity and womanhood that our husbands had died for, though Aunt Louisa hoped again that Mrs. Compson's husband (Mrs. Compson was older than Granny and the only husband she had ever had had been locked up for crazy a long time ago because in the slack part of the afternoons he would gather up eight or ten little niggers from the quarters and line them up across the creek from him with sweet potatoes on their heads and he would shoot the potatoes off with a rifle; he would tell them he might miss a potato but he wasn't going to miss a nigger, and so they would stand mighty still) had not made one of the number. So I couldn't

make any sense out of that one too and I still didn't know what
Aunt Louisa was talking about and I didn't believe that Mrs.
Compson knew either.

Because it was not her: it was Mrs. Habersham, that never had
been out here before and that Granny never had been to see that
I knew of. Because Mrs. Compson didn't stay, she didn't even get
out of the surrey, sitting there kind of drawn up under the shawl
and looking at me and then at the cabin like she didn't know just
what might come out of it or out from behind it. Then she begun
to tap the nigger driver on his head with the parasol and they went
away, the two old horses going pretty fast back down the drive and
back down the road to town. And the next afternoon when I came
out of the bottom to go to the spring with the water bucket there
were five surreys and buggies in front of the cabin and inside the
cabin there were fourteen of them that had come the four miles out
from Jefferson, in the Sunday clothes that the Yankees and the war
had left them, that had husbands dead in the war or alive back in
Jefferson helping Father with what he was doing, because they
were strange times then. Only like I said, maybe times are never
strange to women: that it is just one continuous monotonous thing
full of the repeated follies of their menfolks. Mrs. Compson was
sitting in Granny's chair, still holding the parasol and drawn up
under her shawl and looking like she had finally seen whatever it
was she had expected to see, and it had been the panther. It was
Mrs. Habersham who was holding back the quilt for the others to
go in and look at the bed where Drusilla slept and then showing
them the pallet where Father and I slept. Then she saw me and
said, "And who is this?"

"That's Bayard," Mrs. Compson said.

"You poor child," Mrs. Habersham said. So I didn't stop. But
I couldn't help but hear them. It sounded like a ladies' club meeting
with Mrs. Habersham running it, because every now and then Mrs.
Habersham would forget to whisper: "—Mother should come, be
sent for at once. But lacking her presence . . . we, the ladies of the
community, mothers ourselves . . . child probably taken advantage
of by gallant romantic . . . before realizing the price she must—"
and Mrs. Compson said, "Hush! Hush!" and then somebody else
said, "Do you really suppose—" and then Mrs. Habersham forgot
to whisper good: "What else? What other reason can you name

why she should choose to conceal herself down there in the woods all day long, lifting heavy weights like logs and—"

Then I went away. I filled the bucket at the spring and went back to the log-yard where Drusilla and Ringo and Joby were feeding the bandsaw and the blindfolded mule going round and round in the sawdust. And then Joby kind of made a sound and we all stopped and looked and there was Mrs. Habersham, with three of the others kind of peeping out from behind her with their eyes round and bright, looking at Drusilla standing there in the sawdust and shavings, in her dirty sweated overalls and shirt and brogans, with her face sweat-streaked with sawdust and her short hair yellow with it. "I am Martha Habersham," Mrs. Habersham said. "I am a neighbor and I hope to be a friend." And then she said, "You poor child."

We just looked at her; when Drusilla finally spoke, she sounded like Ringo and I would when Father would say something to us in Latin for a joke. "Ma'am?" Drusilla said. Because I was just fifteen; I still didn't know what it was all about; I just stood there and listened without even thinking much, like when they had been talking in the cabin. "My condition?" Drusilla said. "My—"

"Yes," Mrs. Habersham said. "No mother, no woman to . . . forced to these straits—" kind of waving her hand at the mules that hadn't stopped and at Joby and Ringo goggling at her and the three others still peeping around her at Drusilla. "—to offer you not only our help, but our sympathy."

"My condition," Drusilla said. "My con . . . Help and sym—" Then she began to say, "Oh. Oh. Oh." standing there, and then she was running. She began to run like a deer, that starts to run and then decides where it wants to go; she turned right in the air and came toward me, running light over the logs and planks, with her mouth open, saying "John, John" not loud; for a minute it was like she thought I was Father until she waked up and found I was not; she stopped without even ceasing to run, like a bird stops in the air, motionless yet still furious with movement. "Is that what you think too?" she said. Then she was gone. Every now and then I could see her footprints, spaced and fast, just inside the woods, but when I came out of the bottom, I couldn't see her. But the surreys and buggies were still in front of the cabin and I could see Mrs. Compson and the other ladies on the porch, looking out across the pasture toward the bottom, so I did not go there. But before I came to the other cabin, where Louvinia and Joby and Ringo lived, I saw Louvinia come up the hill from the spring, carrying her cedar water bucket and singing. Then she went into the cabin and the singing stopped short off and so I knew where Drusilla was. But I didn't hide. I went to the window and looked in and saw Drusilla just turning from where she had been leaning her head in her arms on the mantel when Louvinia came in with the water bucket and a gum twig in her mouth and Father's old hat on top of her headrag. Drusilla was crying. "That's what it is, then," she said. "Coming down there to the mill and telling me that in my condition—sympathy and help— Strangers; I never saw any of them before and I don't care a damn what they— But you and Bayard. Is that what you believe? that John and I—that we—" Then Louvinia moved. Her hand came out quicker than Drusilla could jerk back and lay flat on the belly of Drusilla's overalls, then Louvinia was holding Drusilla in her arms like she used to hold me and Drusilla was crying hard. "That John and I—that we— And Gavin dead at Shiloh and John's home burned and his plantation ruined, that he and I— We went to the war to hurt Yankees, not hunting women!"

"I knows you ain't," Louvinia said. "Hush now. Hush."

And that's about all. It didn't take them long. I don't know whether Mrs. Habersham made Mrs. Compson send for Aunt Louisa or whether Aunt Louisa just gave them a deadline and then came herself. Because we were busy, Drusilla and Joby and Ringo and me at the mill, and Father in town; we wouldn't see him from the time he would ride away in the morning until when he would get back, sometimes late, at night. Because they were strange times then. For four years we had lived for just one thing, even the women and children who could not fight: to get Yankee troops out of the country; we thought that when that happened, it would be all over. And now that had happened, and then before the summer began I heard Father say to Drusilla, "We were promised Federal troops; Lincoln himself promised to send us troops. Then things will be all right." That, from a man who had commanded a regiment for four years with the avowed purpose of driving Federal troops from the country. Now it was as though we had not surrendered at all, we had joined forces with the men who had been our enemies against a new foe whose aim we could not always fathom but whose means we could always dread. So he was busy in town all day long. They were building Jefferson back, the courthouse and the stores, but it was more than that which Father and the other men were doing; it was something which he would not let Drusilla or me or Ringo go into town to see. Then one day Ringo slipped off and went to town and came back and he looked at me with his eyes rolling a little.

"Do you know what I ain't?" he said.

"What?" I said.

"I ain't a nigger any more. I done been abolished." Then I asked him what he was, if he wasn't a nigger any more and he showed me what he had in his hand. It was a new scrip dollar; it was drawn on the United States Resident Treasurer, Yoknapatawpha County, Mississippi, and signed "Cassius Q. Benbow, Acting Marshal" in a neat clerk's hand, with a big sprawling X under it.

"Cassius Q. Benbow?" I said.

"Co-rect," Ringo said. "Uncle Cash that druv the Benbow carriage twell he run off with the Yankees two years ago. He back now and he gonter be elected Marshal of Jefferson. That's what Marse John and the other white folks is so busy about."

"A nigger?" I said. "A nigger?"

"No," Ringo said. "They ain't no more niggers, in Jefferson nor nowhere else." Then he told me about the two Burdens from Missouri, with a patent from Washington to organize the niggers into Republicans, and how Father and the other men were trying to prevent it. "Naw, suh," he said. "This war ain't over. Hit just started good. Used to be when you seed a Yankee you knowed him because he never had nothing but a gun or a mule halter or a handful of hen feathers. Now you don't even know him and stid of the gun he got a clutch of this stuff in one hand and a clutch of nigger voting tickets in the yuther." So we were busy; we just saw Father at night and sometimes then Ringo and I and even Drusilla would take one look at him and we wouldn't ask him any questions. So it didn't take them long, because Drusilla was already beaten; she was just marking time without knowing it from that afternoon when the fourteen ladies got into the surreys and buggies and went back to town until one afternoon about two months later when we heard Denny hollering even before the wagon came in the gates, and Aunt Louisa sitting on one of the trunks (that's what beat Drusilla: the trunks. They had her dresses in them that she hadn't worn in three years, and Ringo and I never had seen her in a dress until Aunt Louisa came) in mourning even to the crepe bow on her umbrella handle, that hadn't worn mourning when we were at Hawkhurst two years ago though Uncle Dennison was just as dead then as he was now. She came to the cabin and got out of the wagon, already crying and talking just like the letters sounded, like even when you listened to her you had to skip around fast to make any sense:

"I have come to appeal to them once more with a mother's tears though I don't think it will do any good though I had prayed until the very last that this boy's innocence might be spared and preserved but what must be must be and at least we can all three bear our burden together"; sitting in Granny's chair in the middle of the room, without even laying down the umbrella or taking her bonnet off, looking at the pallet where Father and I slept and then at the quilt nailed to the rafter to make a room for Drusilla, dabbing at her mouth with a handkerchief that made the whole cabin smell like dead roses. And then Drusilla came in from the mill, in the muddy brogans and the sweaty shirt and overalls and her hair sunburned and full of sawdust, and Aunt Louisa looked at her once and begun to cry again, saying, "Lost, lost. Thank God in His mercy that Dennison Hawk was taken before he lived to see what I see."

She was already beaten. Aunt Louisa made her put on a dress that night; we watched her run out of the cabin in it and run down the hill toward the spring while we were waiting for Father. And he came and walked into the cabin where Aunt Louisa was still sitting in Granny's chair with the handkerchief before her mouth. "This is a pleasant surprise, Miss Louisa," Father said.

"It is not pleasant to me, Colonel Sartoris," Aunt Louisa said. "And after a year, I suppose I cannot call it surprise. But it is still a shock." So Father came out too and we went down to the spring and found Drusilla hiding behind the big beech, crouched down like she was trying to hide the skirt from Father even while he raised her up. "What's a dress?" he said. "It don't matter. Come. Get up, soldier."

But she was beaten, like as soon as she let them put the dress on her she was whipped; like in the dress she could neither fight back nor run away. And so she didn't come down to the log-yard any more, and now that Father and I slept in the cabin with Joby and Ringo, I didn't even see Drusilla except at mealtime. And we were busy getting the timber out, and now everybody was talking about the election and how Father had told the two Burdens before all the men in town that the election would never be held with Cash Benbow or any other nigger in it and how the Burdens had dared him to stop it. And besides, the other cabin would be full of Jefferson ladies all day; you would have thought that Drusilla was Mrs. Habersham's daughter and not Aunt Louisa's. They would begin to arrive right after breakfast and stay all day, so that at supper Aunt Louisa would sit in her black mourning except for the bonnet and umbrella, with a wad of some kind of black knitting she carried around with her and that never got finished and the folded handkerchief handy in her belt (only she ate fine; she ate more than Father even because the election was just a week off and I reckon he was thinking about the Burdens) and refusing to speak to anybody except Denny; and Drusilla trying to eat, with her face strained and thin and her eyes like somebody's that had been whipped a long time now and is going just on nerve.

Then Drusilla broke; they beat her. Because she was strong; she wasn't much older than I was, but she had let Aunt Louisa and Mrs. Habersham choose the game and she had beat them both until that night when Aunt Louisa went behind her back and chose a game she couldn't beat. I was coming up to supper; I heard them inside the cabin before I could stop: "Can't you believe me?" Drusilla said. "Can't you understand that in the troop I was just another man and not much of one at that, and since we came home here I am just another mouth for John to feed, just a cousin of John's wife and not much older than his own son?" And I could almost see Aunt Louisa sitting there with that knitting that never progressed:

"You wish to tell me that you, a young woman, associated with him, a still young man, day and night for a year, running about the country with no guard nor check of any sort upon— Do you take me for a complete fool?" So that night Aunt Louisa beat her; we had just sat down to supper when Aunt Louisa looked at me like she had been waiting for the noise of the bench to stop: "Bayard,

I do not ask your forgiveness for this because it is your burden too; you are an innocent victim as well as Dennison and I—" Then she looked at Father, thrust back in Granny's chair (the only chair we had) in her black dress, the black wad of knitting beside her plate. "Colonel Sartoris," she said, "I am a woman; I must request what the husband whom I have lost and the man son which I have not would demand, perhaps at the point of a pistol.—Will you marry my daughter?"

I got out. I moved fast; I heard the light sharp sound when Drusilla's head went down between her flungout arms on the table, and the sound the bench made when Father got up too; I passed him standing beside Drusilla with his hand on her head. "They have beat you, Drusilla," he said.

II

Mrs. Habersham got there before we had finished breakfast the next morning. I don't know how Aunt Louisa got word in to her so quick. But there she was, and she and Aunt Louisa set the wedding for the day after tomorrow. I don't reckon they even knew that that was the day Father had told the Burdens Cash Benbow would never be elected marshal in Jefferson. I don't reckon they paid any more attention to it than if all the men had decided that day after tomorrow all the clocks in Jefferson were to be set back or up an hour. Maybe they didn't even know there was to be an election, that all the men in the county would be riding toward Jefferson tomorrow with pistols in their pockets, and that the Burdens already had their nigger voters camped in a cotton gin on the edge of town under guard. I don't reckon they even cared. Because like Father said, women cannot believe that anything can be right or wrong or even be very important that can be decided by a lot of little scraps of scribbled paper dropped into a box.

It was to be a big wedding; all Jefferson was to be invited and Mrs. Habersham planning to bring the three bottles of Madeira she had been saving for five years now when Aunt Louisa began to cry again. But they caught on quick now; now all of them were patting Aunt Louisa's hands and giving her vinegar to smell and Mrs. Habersham saying, "Of course. You poor thing. A public wedding now, after a year, would be a public notice of the . . ." So they decided it would be a reception, because Mrs. Habersham said how a reception could be held for a bridal couple at any time, even ten years later. So Drusilla was to ride into town, meet Father and be married as quick and quiet as possible, with just me and one other for witnesses to make it legal; none of the ladies themselves would even be present. Then they would come back home and we would have the reception.

So they began to arrive early the next morning, with baskets of food and tablecloths and silver like for a church supper. Mrs. Habersham brought a veil and a wreath and they all helped Drusilla to dress, only Aunt Louisa made Drusilla put on Father's big riding cloak over the veil and wreath too, and Ringo brought the horses up, all curried and brushed, and I helped Drusilla on with Aunt Louisa and the others all watching from the porch. But I didn't know that Ringo was missing when we started, not even when I heard Aunt Louisa hollering for Denny while we rode down the drive. It was Louvinia that told about it, about how after we left the ladies set and decorated the table and spread the wedding breakfast and how they were all watching the gate and Aunt Louisa still hollering for Denny now and then when they saw Ringo and Denny come up the drive riding double on one of the mules at a gallop, with Denny's eyes round as doorknobs and already hollering, "They kilt um! They kilt um!"

"Who?" Aunt Louisa hollered. "Where have you been?"

"To town!" Denny hollered. "Them two Burdens! They kilt um!"

"Who killed them?" Aunt Louisa hollered.

"Drusilla and Cousin John!" Denny hollered. Then Louvinia said how Aunt Louisa hollered sure enough.

"Do you mean to tell me that Drusilla and that man are not married yet?"

Because we didn't have time. Maybe Drusilla and Father would have, but when we came into the square we saw the crowd of niggers kind of huddled beyond the hotel door with six or eight strange white men herding them, and then all of a sudden I saw the Jefferson men, the men that I knew, that Father knew, running across the square toward the hotel with each one holding his hip pocket like a man runs with a pistol in his pocket. And then I saw the men who were Father's troop lined up before the hotel door, blocking it off. And then I was sliding off my horse too and watching Drusilla struggling with George Wyatt. But he didn't have hold of her, he just had hold of the cloak, and then she was through the line of them and running toward the hotel with her wreath on one side of her head and the veil streaming behind. But George held me. He threw the cloak down and held me. "Let go," I said. "Father."

"Steady, now," George said, holding me. "John's just gone in to vote."

"But there are two of them!" I said. "Let me go!"

"John's got two shots in the derringer," George said. "Steady, now."

But they held me. And then we heard the three shots and we all turned and looked at the door. I don't know how long it was. "The last two was that derringer," George said. I don't know how long it was. The old nigger that was Mrs. Holston's porter, that was too old even to be free, stuck his head out once and said "Gret Gawd" and ducked back. Then Drusilla came out, carrying the ballot box, the wreath on one side of her head and the veil twisted about her arm, and then Father came out behind her, brushing his new beaver hat on his sleeve. And then it was loud; I could hear them when they drew in their breath like when the Yankees used to hear it begin:

"Yaaaaa—" But Father raised his hand and they stopped. Then you couldn't hear anything.

"We heard a pistol too," George said. "Did they touch you?"

"No," Father said. "I let them fire first. You all heard. You boys can swear to my derringer."

"Yes," George said. "We all heard." Now Father looked at all of them, at all the faces in sight, slow.

"Does any man here want a word with me about this?" he said. But you could not hear anything, not even moving. The herd of niggers stood like they had when I first saw them, with the Northern white men herding them together. Father put his hat on and took the ballot box from Drusilla and helped her back onto her horse and handed the ballot box up to her. Then he looked around again, at all of them. "This election will be held out at my home," he said. "I hereby appoint Drusilla Hawk voting commissioner until the votes are cast and counted. Does any man here object?"

But he stopped them again with his hand before it had begun good. "Not now, boys," he said. He turned to Drusilla. "Go home. I will go to the sheriff, and then I will follow you."

"Like hell you will," George Wyatt said. "Some of the boys will ride out with Drusilla. The rest of us will come with you."

But Father would not let them. "Don't you see we are working for peace through law and order?" he said. "I will make bond and then follow you. You do as I say." So we went on; we turned in the gates with Drusilla in front, the ballot box on her pommel— us and Father's men and about a hundred more, and rode on up to the cabin where the buggies and surreys were standing, and Drusilla passed the ballot box to me and got down and took the box again and was walking toward the cabin when she stopped dead still. I reckon she and I both remembered at the same time and I reckon that even the others, the men, knew all of a sudden that something was wrong. Because like Father said, I reckon women don't ever surrender: not only victory, but not even defeat. Because that's how we were stopped when Aunt Louisa and the other ladies came out on the porch, and then Father shoved past me and jumped down beside Drusilla. But Aunt Louisa never even looked at him.

"So you are not married," she said.

"I forgot," Drusilla said.

"You forgot? You *forgot?*"

"I . . ." Drusilla said. "We . . ."

Now Aunt Louisa looked at us; she looked along the line of us sitting there in our saddles; she looked at me too just like she did at the others, like she had never seen me before. "And who are these, pray? Your wedding train of forgetters? Your groomsmen of murder and robbery?"

"They came to vote," Drusilla said.

"To vote," Aunt Louisa said. "Ah. To vote. Since you have forced your mother and brother to live under a roof of license and adultery you think you can also force them to live in a polling booth refuge from violence and bloodshed, do you? Bring me that box." But Drusilla didn't move, standing there in her torn dress and the ruined veil and the twisted wreath hanging from her hair by a few pins. Aunt Louisa came down the steps; we didn't know what she was going to do: we just sat there and watched her snatch the polling box from Drusilla and fling it across the yard. "Come into the house," she said.

"No," Drusilla said.

"Come into the house. I will send for a minister myself."

"No," Drusilla said. "This is an election. Don't you understand? I am voting commissioner."

"So you refuse?"

"I have to. I must." She sounded like a little girl that has been caught playing in the mud. "John said that I—"

Then Aunt Louisa began to cry. She stood there in the black dress, without the knitting and for the first time that I ever saw it, without even the handkerchief, crying, until Mrs. Habersham came and led her back into the house. Then they voted. That didn't take long either. They set the box on the sawchunk where Louvinia washed, and Ringo got the pokeberry juice and an old piece of window shade, and they cut it into ballots. "Let all who want the Honorable Cassius Q. Benbow to be Marshal of Jefferson write Yes on his ballot; opposed, No," Father said.

"And I'll do the writing and save some more time," George Wyatt said. So he made a pack of the ballots and wrote them against his saddle and fast as he would write them the men would take them and drop them into the box and Drusilla would call their names out. We could hear Aunt Louisa still crying inside the cabin and we could see the other ladies watching us through the window. It didn't take long. "You needn't bother to count them," George said. "They all voted No."

And that's all. They rode back to town then, carrying the box, with Father and Drusilla in the torn wedding dress and the crooked wreath and veil standing beside the sawchunk, watching them. Only this time even Father could not have stopped them. It came back high and thin and ragged and fierce, like when the Yankees used to hear it out of the smoke and the galloping:

"Yaaaaay, Drusilla!" they hollered. "Yaaaaaay, John Sartoris! Yaaaaaaay!"

The Unvanquished

When Ab Snopes left for Memphis with a batch of mules, Ringo and Joby and I worked on a new fence. Then Ringo went off on his mule and there was just Joby and me. Once Granny came down and looked at the new section of rails; the pen would be almost two acres larger now. That was the second day after Ringo left. That night, while Granny and I were sitting before the fire, Ab Snopes came back. He said that he had got only four hundred and fifty dollars for the nine mules. That is, he took some money out of his pocket and gave it to Granny, and she counted it and said:

"That's only fifty dollars apiece."

"All right," Ab said. "If you can do any better, you are welcome to take the next batch in yourself. I done already admitted I can't hold a candle to you when it comes to getting mules; maybe I can't even compete with you when it comes to selling them." He chewed something—tobacco when he could get it, willow bark when he couldn't—all the time, and he never wore a collar, and nobody ever admitted they ever saw him in a uniform, though when father was away, he would talk a lot now and then about when he was in father's troop and about what he and father used to do. But when I asked father about it once, father said, "Who? Ab Snopes?" and then laughed. But it was father that told Ab to kind of look out for Granny while he was away; only he told me and Ringo to look out for Ab, too, that Ab was all right in his way, but he was like a mule: While you had him in the traces, you better watch him. But Ab and Granny got along all right though each time Ab took a batch of mules to Memphis and came back with the money, it would be like this: "Yes, ma'am," Ab said. "It's easy to talk about hit, setting here without no risk. But I'm the one that has to dodge them durn critters nigh a hundred miles into Memphis, with Forrest and Smith fighting on ever side of me and me never knowing when I will run into a Confed'rit or Yankee patrol and have ever last one of them confiscated off of me right down to the durn halters. And then I got to take them into the very heart of the Yankee Army in Memphis and try to sell them to a e-quipment officer that's liable at any minute to recognize them as the same mules he bought from me not two weeks ago. Yes. Hit's easy enough for them to talk that sets here getting rich and takes no risk."

"I suppose you consider getting them back for you to sell taking no risk," Granny said.

"The risk of running out of them printed letterheads, sho," Ab said. "If you ain't satisfied with making just five or six hundred dollars at a time, why don't you requisition for more mules at a time? Why don't you write out a letter and have General Smith turn over his commissary train to you, with about four wagonloads of new shoes in hit? Or, better than that, pick out the day when the pay officer is coming around and draw for the whole pay wagon; then we wouldn't even have to bother about finding somebody to buy hit."

The money was in new bills. Granny folded them carefully and put them into the can, but she didn't put the can back inside her dress right away. She sat there looking at the fire, with the can in her hands and the string looping down from around her neck. She didn't look any thinner or any older. She didn't look sick either. She just looked like somebody that has quit sleeping at night.

"We have more mules," she said, "if you would just sell them. There are more than a hundred of them that you refuse—"

"Refuse is right," Ab said; he began to holler now: "Yes, sir! I reckon I ain't got much sense, or I wouldn't be doing this a-tall. But I got better sense than to take them mules to a Yankee officer and tell him that them hip patches where you and that durn nigger burned out the U. S. brand are trace galls. By Godfrey, I—"

"That will do," Granny said. "Have you had some supper?"

"I—" Ab said. Then he quit hollering. He chewed again. "Yessum," he said. "I done et."

"Then you had better go home and get some rest," Granny said. "There is a new relief regiment at Mottstown. Ringo went down two days ago to see about it. So we may need that new fence soon."

Ab stopped chewing. "Is, huh?" he said. "Out of Memphis, likely. Likely got them nine mules in it we just got shet of."

Granny looked at him. "So you sold them further back than three days ago, then," Granny said. Ab started to say something, but Granny didn't give him time. "You go on home and rest up," she said. "Ringo will probably be back tomorrow, and then you'll have a chance to see if they are the same mules. I may even have a chance to find out what they say they paid you for them."

Ab stood in the door and looked at Granny. "You're a good un," he said. "Yessum. You got my respect. John Sartoris, himself, can't tech you. He hells all over the country day and night with a hundred armed men, and it's all he can do to keep them in crowbait to ride on. And you set here in this cabin, without nothing but a handful of durn printed letterheads, and you got to build a bigger pen to hold the stock you ain't got no market yet to sell. How many head of mules have you sold back to the Yankees?"

"A hundred and five," Granny said.

"A hundred and five," Ab said. "For how much active cash money, in round numbers?" Only he didn't wait for her to answer; he told her himself: "For six thou-sand and seven hun-dred and twen-ty-two dollars and six-ty-five cents, lessen the dollar and thirty-five cents I spent for whisky that time the snake bit one of the mules." It sounded round when he said it, like big sawn-oak wheels running in wet sand. "You started out a year ago with two. You got forty-odd in the pen and twice that many out on receipt. And I reckon you have sold about fifty-odd more back to the Yankees a hundred and five times, for a grand total of six thousand, seven hundred and twenty-two dollars and sixty-five cents, and in a day or so you are aiming to requisition a few of them back again, I understand."

He looked at me. "Boy," he said, "when you grow up and start out for yourself, don't you waste your time learning to be a lawyer or nothing. You just save your money and buy you a handful of printed letterheads—it don't matter much what's on them, I reckon—and you hand them to your grandmaw here and just ask her to give you the job of counting the money when hit comes in."

He looked at Granny again. "When Kernel Sartoris left here, he told me to look out for you against General Grant and them. What I wonder is, if somebody hadn't better tell Abe Lincoln to look out for General Grant against Miz Rosa Millard. I bid you one and all good night."

He went out. Granny looked at the fire, the tin can in her hand. But it didn't have any six thousand dollars in it. It didn't have a thousand dollars in it. Ab Snopes knew that, only I don't suppose that it was possible for him to believe it. Then she got up; she looked at me, quiet. She didn't look sick; that wasn't it. "I reckon it's bedtime," she said. She went beyond the quilt; it came back and hung straight down from the rafter, and I heard the loose board when she put the can away under the floor, and then I heard the sound the bed made when she would hold to the post to kneel down. It would make another sound when she got up, but when it made that sound, I was already undressed and in my pallet. The quilts were cold, but when the sound came I had been there long enough for them to begin to get warm.

Ab Snopes came and helped me and Joby with the new fence the next day, so we finished it early in the afternoon and I went back to the cabin. I was almost there when I saw Ringo on the mule turning in at the gates. Granny had seen him, too, because when I went inside the quilt, she was kneeling in the corner, taking the window shade from under the loose floor board. While she was unrolling the shade on the bed we heard Ringo getting off the mule, hollering at it while he hitched it to Louvinia's clothesline.

Then Granny stood up and looked at the quilt until Ringo pushed it aside and came in. And then they sounded like two people playing a guessing game in code.

"—th Illinois Infantry," Ringo said. He came on toward the map on the bed. "Col. G. W. Newberry. Eight days out of Memphis."

Granny watched him while he came toward the bed. "How many?" she said.

"Nineteen head," Ringo said. "Four wid; fifteen widout." Granny just watched him; she didn't have to speak at all for the next one. "Twelve," Ringo said. "Out of that Oxford batch."

Granny turned to the map; they both looked at it. "July the twenty-second," Granny said.

"Yessum," Ringo said. Granny sat down on the saw chunk before the map. It was the only window shade Louvinia had; Ringo had drawn it, with Granny showing him where to draw in the towns. But it was Granny that had done the writing, in her neat spidery hand like she wrote in the cookbook, written on the map by each town: "Colonel, or Major, or Captain So-and-So, Such-and-Such Regiment or Troop." Then, under that: "12 or 9 or 21 mules." And around four of them, town and writing and all, in purple pokeberry juice instead of ink, a circle with a date in it, and in big neat letters, "Complete."

They looked at the map, Granny's head white and still where the light came through the window on it, and Ringo leaning over her. He had got taller during the summer; he was taller than me now; maybe from the exercise of riding around the country, listening out for fresh regiments with mules, and he had got to treating me like Granny did—like him and Granny were the same age instead of him and me.

"We just sold that twelve in July," Granny said. "That leaves only seven. And you say that four of them are branded."

"That was back in July," Ringo said. "It's October now. They done forgot about hit. 'Sides, look here"—he puts his finger on the map now—"we captived these here fourteen at Madison on the twelfth of April, sont um to Memphis and sold um, and had all fourteen of them back, and three more besides, here at Caledonia on the third day of May."

"But that was four counties apart," Granny said. "Oxford and Mottstown are only a few miles."

"Phut," Ringo said. "These folks is too busy keeping us conquered to recognize no little ten or twelve head of stock. 'Sides, if they does recognize um in Memphis, that's Ab Snopes' trouble, not ourn."

"Mister Snopes," Granny said.

"All right," Ringo said. He looked at the map. "Nineteen head, and not two days away."

Granny looked at the map. "I don't think we ought to risk it. We have been successful so far."

"Nineteen head," Ringo said. "Four to keep and fifteen to sell back to um. That will make a even two hundred and forty-eight head of Confed'rit mules we done recovered and collected interest on, let alone the money."

"I don't know what to do," Granny said. "I want to think about it."

"All right," Ringo said. Granny sat still beside the map. Ringo didn't seem patient or impatient either; he just stood there, thin and taller than me against the light from the window, scratching himself. Then he began to dig with his right-hand little fingernail between his front teeth; he looked at his fingernail and spat something, and then he said, "Must been five minutes now." He turned his head a little toward me without moving. "Get the pen and ink," he said.

They kept the paper under the same floor board with the map and the tin can. I don't know how or where Ringo got it. He just came back one night with about a hundred sheets of it, stamped with the official letterhead: UNITED STATES FORCES. DEPARTMENT OF TENNESSEE. He had got the pen and the ink at the same time, too; he took them from me, and now it was Ringo sitting on the saw chunk and Granny leaning over him. Granny still had the first letter—the order that Colonel Dick had given us in Alabama last year—she kept it in the can, too, and by now Ringo had learned to copy it so that I don't believe that Colonel Dick himself could have told the difference. All they had to do was to put in the right regiment and whatever number of mules Ringo had examined and approved, and sign the right general's name to it. At first Ringo had wanted to sign Grant's name every time, and when Granny said that would not do any more, Lincoln's. At last Granny found out that Ringo objected to having the Yankees think that father's folks would have any dealings with anybody under the General-in-Chief. But at last he realized that Granny was right, that they would have to be careful about what general's name was on the letter, as well as what mules they requisitioned. They were using General Smith now; he and Forrest were fighting every day up and down the road to Memphis, and Ringo always remembered to put in rope.

He wrote the date and the town, the headquarters; he wrote in Colonel Newberry's name and the first line. Then he stopped; he didn't lift the pen.

"What name you want this time?" he said.

"I'm worried about this," Granny said. "We ought not to risk it."

"We was on 'F' last time," Ringo said. "It's 'H' now. Think of a name in 'H.' "

"Mrs. Mary Harris," Granny said.

"We done used Mary before," Ringo said. "How about Plurella Harris?"

"I'm worried about this time," Granny said.

"Miz Plurella Harris," Ringo said, writing. "Now we done used up 'P' too. 'Member that, now. I reckon when we run out of letters, maybe we can start in on numbers. We will have nine hundred and ninety-nine before we have to worry, then." He finished the order and signed "General Smith" to it; it looked exactly like the man who had signed the one Colonel Dick gave us was named General Smith, except for the number of mules. Then Granny turned and looked at me.

"Tell Mr. Snopes to be ready at sunup," she said.

We went in the wagon, with Ab Snopes and his two men following on two of the mules. We went just fast enough so that we would reach the bivouac at suppertime, because Granny and Ringo had found out that that was the best time—that the stock would all be handy, and the men would be too hungry or sleepy or something to think very quick in case they happened to think, and we would just have time to get the mules and get out of sight before dark came. Then, if they should decide to chase us, by the time they found us in the dark, there wouldn't be anything but the wagon with me and Granny in it to capture.

So we did; only this time it was a good thing we did. We left Ab Snopes and his men in the woods beyond the bivouac, and Granny and Ringo and I drove up to Colonel Newberry's tent at exactly the right time, and Granny passed the sentry and went into the tent, walking thin and straight, with the shawl over her shoulders and Mrs. Compson's hat on her head and the parasol in one hand and hers and Ringo's General Smith order in the other, and Ringo and I sat in the wagon and looked at the cook fires about the grove and smelled the coffee and the meat. It was always the same, Granny would disappear into the tent or the house, and then, in about a minute, somebody would holler inside the tent or the house, and then the sentry at the door would holler, and then a sergeant, or even sometimes an officer, only it would be a lieutenant, would hurry into the tent or the house, and then Ringo and I would hear somebody cursing, and then they would all come out, Granny walking straight and stiff and not looking much bigger than Cousin Denny at Hawkhurst, and three or four mad Yankee officers behind her, and getting madder all the time. Then they would bring up the mules, tied together. Granny and Ringo could guess to the second now; it would be just enough light left to tell that they were mules, and Granny would get into the wagon and Ringo would hang his legs over the tail gate, holding the lead rope, and we would go on, not fast, so that when we came back to where Ab Snopes and his men waited in the woods you could not even tell that they were mules. Then Ringo would get onto the lead mule and they would turn off into the woods and Granny and I would go on home.

That's what we did this time; only this time it happened. We couldn't even see our own team when we heard them coming, the galloping hoofs. They came up fast and mad; Granny jerked up quick and straight, holding Mrs. Compson's parasol.

"Damn that Ringo!" she said. "I had my doubts about this time all the while."

Then they were all around us, like the dark itself had fallen down on us, full of horses and mad men hollering "Halt! Halt! If they try to escape, shoot the team!" with me and Granny sitting in the wagon and men jerking the team back and the team jerking and clashing in the traces, and some of them hollering "Where are the mules? The mules are gone!" and the officer cursing and hollering "Of course they are gone!" and cursing Granny and the darkness and the men and mules. Then somebody struck a light and we saw the officer sitting his horse beside the wagon while one of the soldiers lit one light-wood splinter from another.

"Where are the mules?" the officer hollered.

"What mules?" Granny said.

"Don't lie to me!" the officer hollered. "The mules you just left camp with on that forged order! We have got you this time! We knew you'd turn up again. Orders went out to the whole department to watch for you a month ago! That damn Newberry had his copy in his pocket while you were talking to him." He cursed

Colonel Newberry now. "They ought to let you go free and court-martial him! Where's the nigger boy and the mules, Mrs. Plurella Harris?"

"I don't know what you are talking about," Granny said. "I have no mules except this team I am driving. And my name is Rosa Millard. I am on my way home beyond Jefferson."

The officer began to laugh; he sat on the horse, laughing. "So that's your real name, hey? Well, well, well. So you have begun to tell the truth at last. Come now, tell me where those mules are, and tell me where the others you have stolen from us are hid."

Then Ringo hollered. He and Ab Snopes and the mules had turned off into the woods on the right side of the road, but when he hollered now he was on the left side. "Heyo the road!" he hollered. "One busted loose! Head um off the road!"

And that was all of that. The soldier dropped the light-wood splinter and the officer whirled his horse, already spurring him, hollering, "Two men stay here." Maybe they all thought he meant two others, because there was just a big noise of bushes and trees like a cyclone was going through them, and then Granny and I were sitting in the wagon like before we had even heard the hoofs.

"Come on," Granny said. She was already getting out of the wagon.

"Are we going to leave the team and wagon?" I said.

"Yes," Granny said. "I misdoubted this all the time."

We could not see at all in the woods; we felt our way, and me helping Granny along and her arm didn't feel any bigger than a pencil almost, but it wasn't trembling. "This is far enough," she said. I found a log and we sat down. Beyond the road we could hear them, thrashing around, hollering and shouting and cursing. It sounded far away now. "And the team too," Granny said.

"But we have nineteen new ones," I said. "That makes two hundred and forty-eight." It seemed like a long time, sitting there on the log in the dark. After a while they came back, we could hear the officer cursing and the horses crashing and thumping back into the road. And then he found the wagon was empty and he cursed sure enough—Granny and me, and the two men he had told to stay there. He was still cursing while they turned the wagon around. Then they went away. After a while we couldn't hear them. Granny got up and we felt our way back to the road, and we went

THE UNVANQUISHED · 83

on, too, toward home. After a while I persuaded her to stop and rest, and while we were sitting beside the road we heard the buggy coming. We stood up, and Ringo saw us and stopped the buggy.

"Did I holler loud enough?" he said.

"Yes," Granny said. Then she said, "Well?"

"All right," Ringo said. "I told Ab Snopes to hide out with them in Hickahala bottom until tomorrow night. All 'cep' these two."

"Mister Snopes," Granny said.

"All right," Ringo said. "Get in and le's go home."

Granny didn't move; I knew why, even before she spoke. "Where did you get this buggy?"

"I borrowed hit," Ringo said. " 'Twarn't no Yankees handy, so I never needed no paper."

We got in. The buggy went on. It seemed to me like it had already been all night, but it wasn't midnight yet—I could tell by the stars—we would be home by midnight almost. We went on. "I reckon you went and told um who we is now," Ringo said.

"Yes," Granny said.

"Well, I reckon that completes that," Ringo said. "Anyway, we handled two hundred and forty-eight head while the business lasted."

"Two hundred and forty-six," Granny said. "We have lost the team."

It was after midnight when we got home; it was already Sunday. Ab Snopes would not get back with the new mules until tomorrow morning. But they had already heard about it. Then I remembered that it would be Ab Snopes' Memphis trip that they had heard about, because when we came to the church there was the biggest crowd waiting there had been yet. We were late, because Granny made Ringo get up at sunup and take the buggy back where he got it; so when we came to the church they were already inside, waiting. Brother Fortinbride met us at the door, and they all turned in the pews and looked at Granny—the old men and the women and the children and the maybe a dozen niggers that didn't have any white people now—they looked at her exactly like father's fox hounds would look at him when he would go into the dog run, while we went up the aisle to our pew. Ringo had the book; he went up to the gallery; I looked back and saw him leaning his arms on the book on the balustrade.

We sat down in our pew, like before there was a war, only for father—Granny still and straight in her Sunday calico dress and the shawl and the hat Mrs. Compson had loaned her a year ago; straight and quiet, with her hands holding her prayer book in her lap like always, though there hadn't been an Episcopal service in the church in almost three years now. Brother Fortinbride was a Methodist, and I don't know what the people were. Last summer when we got back with the first batch of mules from Alabama, Granny sent for them, sent out word back into the hills where they lived in dirt-floored cabins, on the little poor farms without slaves. It took three or four times to get them to come in, but at last they all came—men and women and children and the dozen niggers that had got free by accident and didn't know what to do about it. I reckon this was the first church with a slave gallery some of them had ever seen, with Ringo and the other twelve sitting up there in the high shadows where there was room enough for two hundred; and I could remember back when father would be in the pew with us and the grove outside would be full of carriages from the other plantations, and Doctor Worsham in his stole beneath the altar, and for each white person in the auditorium there would be ten niggers in the gallery. And I reckon that on that first Sunday when Granny knelt down in public, it was the first time they had ever seen anyone kneel in a church.

Brother Fortinbride wasn't a minister either. He was a private in father's regiment, and he got hurt bad in the first battle the regiment was in; they thought that he was dead, but he said that Jesus came to him and told him to rise up and live, and father sent him back home to die, only he didn't die. But they said that he didn't have any stomach left at all, and everybody thought that the food we had to eat in 1862 and '63 would finish killing him, even if he had eaten it with women to cook it instead of gathering weeds from ditch banks and cooking them himself. But it didn't kill him, and so maybe it was Jesus, after all, like he said. And so, when we came back with the first batch of mules and the silver and the food, and Granny sent word out for all that needed, it was like Brother Fortinbride sprang right up out of the ground with the names and histories of all the hill folks at his tongue's end, like maybe what he claimed was true—that the Lord had both him and Granny in mind when He created the other. So he would stand there where

Doctor Worsham used to stand, and talk quiet for a little while about God, with his hair showing where he cut it himself and the bones looking like they were coming right out through his face, in a frock coat that had turned green a long time ago and with patches on it that he had sewed on himself—one of them was green horsehide and the other was a piece of tent canvas with the U.S.A. stencil still showing a little on it. He never talked long; there wasn't much anybody could say about Confederate armies now. I reckon there is a time when even preachers quit believing that God is going to change His plan and give victory where there is nothing left to hang victory on. He just said how victory without God is mockery and delusion, but that defeat with God is not defeat. Then he quit talking, and he stood there with the old men and the women and children and the eleven or twelve niggers lost in freedom, in clothes made out of cotton bagging and flour sacks, still watching Granny —only now it was not like the hounds used to look at father, but like they would watch the food in Loosh's hands when he would go in to feed them—and then he said:

"Brethren and sisters, Sister Millard wishes to bear public witness."

Granny stood up. She would not go to the altar; she just stood there in our pew with her face straight ahead, in the shawl and Mrs. Compson's hat and the dress that Louvinia washed and ironed every Saturday, holding the prayer book. It used to have her name on it in gold letters, but now the only way you could read them was to run your finger over them; she said quiet, too—quiet as Brother Fortinbride—"I have sinned. I want you all to pray for me."

She knelt down in the pew; she looked littler than Cousin Denny; it was only Mrs. Compson's hat above the pew back they had to look at now. I don't know if she prayed herself or not. And Brother Fortinbride didn't pray either—not aloud anyway. Ringo and I were just past fifteen then, but I could imagine what Doctor Worsham would have thought up to say—about all soldiers did not carry arms, and about they also serve, and how one child saved from hunger and cold is better in heaven's sight than a thousand slain enemies. But Brother Fortinbride didn't say it. I reckon he thought of that; he always had plenty of words when he wanted to. It was like he said to himself, "Words are fine in peacetime, when everybody is comfortable and easy. But now I think that we can be excused." He just stood there where Doctor Worsham used to stand and where the bishop would stand, too, with his ring looking big as a pistol target. Then Granny rose up; I didn't have time to help her; she stood up, and then the long sound went through the church, a sound kind of like a sigh that Ringo said was the sound of the cotton bagging and the flour sacking when they breathed again, and Granny turned and looked back toward the gallery; only Ringo was already moving.

"Bring the book," she said.

It was a big blank account book; it weighed almost fifteen pounds. They opened it on the reading desk, Granny and Ringo side by side, while Granny drew the tin can out of her dress and spread the money on the book. But nobody moved until she began to call out the names. Then they came up one at a time, while Ringo read the names off the book, and the date, and the amount they had received before. Each time Granny would make them tell what they intended to do with the money, and now she would make them tell her how they had spent it, and she would look at the book to see whether they had lied or not. And the ones that she had loaned the brand-blotted mules that Ab Snopes was afraid to try to sell would have to tell her how the mule was getting along and how much work it had done, and now and then she would take the mule away from one man or woman and give it to another, tearing up the old receipt and making the man or the woman sign the new one, telling them on what day to go and get the mule.

So it was afternoon when Ringo closed the book and got the new receipts together, and Granny stopped putting the rest of the money back into the can and she and Brother Fortinbride did what they did each time. "I'm making out fine with the mule," he said. "I don't need any money."

"Fiddlesticks," Granny said. "You'll never grow enough food out of the ground to feed a bird the longest day you live. You take this money."

"No," Brother Fortinbride said. "I'm making out fine."

We walked back home, Ringo carrying the book. "You done receipted out four mules you ain't hardly laid eyes on yet," he said. "What you gonter do about that?"

"They will be here tomorrow morning, I reckon," Granny said. They were; Ab Snopes came in while we were eating breakfast; he leaned in the door with his eyes a little red from lack of sleep and looked at Granny.

"Yes, ma'am," he said, "I don't never want to be rich; I just want to be lucky. Do you know what you done?" Only nobody asked him what, so he told us anyway: "Hit was taking place all day yestiddy; I reckon by now there ain't a Yankee regiment left in Mississippi. You might say that this here war has turned around at last and went back North. Yes, sir. That regiment you requisitioned on Sattidy never even stayed long enough to warm the ground. You managed to requisition the last batch of Yankee livestock at the last possible moment hit could have been done by living man. You made just one mistake: You drawed them last nineteen mules just too late to have anybody to sell them back to."

It was a bright warm day; we saw the guns and the bits shining a long way down the road. But this time Ringo didn't even move. He just quit drawing and looked up from the paper and said, "So Ab Snopes was lying. Gre't God, ain't we gonter never get shet of them?"

It was just a lieutenant; by this time Ringo and I could tell the different officers' ranks better than we could tell Confederate ranks, because one day we counted up and the only Confederate officers we had ever seen were father and the captain that talked to us with Uncle Buck McCaslin that day in Jefferson before Grant burned it. And this was to be the last time we would see any uniforms at all except as the walking symbols of defeated men's pride and indomitable unregret, but we didn't know that now.

So it was just a lieutenant. He looked about forty, and kind of mad and gleeful, both at the same time. Ringo didn't recognize him because he had not been in the wagon with us, but I did—from the way he sat the horse, or maybe from the way he looked mad and happy both, like he had been mad for several days, thinking about how much he was going to enjoy being mad when the right time came. And he recognized me, too; he looked at me once and said "Hah!" with his teeth showing, and pushed his horse up and looked at Ringo's picture. There were maybe a dozen cavalry behind him; we never noticed especially. "Hah!" he said again, then he said, "What's that?"

"A house," Ringo said. Ringo had never even looked at him

good yet; he had seen even more of them than I had. "Look at it."

The lieutenant looked at me and said "Hah!" again behind his teeth; every now and then while he was talking to Ringo he would do that. He looked at Ringo's picture. Then he looked up the grove to where the chimneys rose out of the pile of rubble and ashes. Grass and weeds had come up out of the ashes now, and unless you knew better, all you saw was the four chimneys. Some of the goldenrod was still in bloom. "Oh," the officer said. "I see. You're drawing it like it used to be."

"Co-rect," Ringo said. "What I wanter draw hit like hit is now? I can walk down here ten times a day and look at hit like hit is now. I can even ride in that gate on a horse and do that."

The lieutenant didn't say "Hah!" this time. He didn't do anything yet; I reckon he was still enjoying waiting a little longer to get good and mad. He just kind of grunted. "When you get done here, you can move into town and keep busy all winter, can't you?" he said. Then he sat back in the saddle. He didn't say "Hah!" now either; it was his eyes that said it, looking at me. They were a kind of thin milk color, like the chine knucklebone in a ham. "All right," he said. "Who lives up there now? What's her name today, hey?"

Ringo was watching him now, though I don't think he suspected yet who he was. "Don't nobody," he said. "The roof leaks." One of the men made a kind of sound; maybe it was laughing. The lieutenant started to whirl around, and then he started not to; then he sat there glaring down at Ringo with his mouth beginning to open. "Oh," Ringo said, "you mean way back yonder in the quarters. I thought you was still worrying about them chimneys."

This time the soldier did laugh, and this time the lieutenant did whirl around, cursing at the soldier; I would have known him now even if I hadn't before. He cursed at them all now, sitting there with his face swelling up. "Blank-blank-blank!" he hollered. "Get to hell on out of here! He said that pen is down there in the creek bottom beyond the pasture. If you meet man, woman or child and they so much as speak to you, shoot them! Get!" The soldiers went on, galloping up the drive; we watched them scatter out across the pasture. The lieutenant looked at me and Ringo; he said "Hah!" again, glaring at us. "You boys come with me. Jump!"

He didn't wait for us; he galloped, too, up the drive. He ran;

Ringo looked at me. " 'He' said the pen was in the creek bottom," Ringo said. "Who you reckon 'he' is?"

"I don't know," I said.

"Well, I reckon I know," Ringo said. But we didn't talk any more. We ran on up the drive. The lieutenant had reached the cabin now, and Granny came out the door. I reckon she had seen him, too, because she already had her sunbonnet on. They looked at us once, then Granny went on, too, walking straight, not fast, down the path toward the lot, with the lieutenant behind her on the horse. We could see his shoulders and his head, and now and then his hand and arm, but we couldn't hear what he was saying. "I reckon this does complete hit," Ringo said.

But we could hear him before we reached the new fence. Then we could see them standing at the fence that Joby and I had just finished—Granny straight and still, with her sunbonnet on and the shawl drawn tight over her shoulders where she had her arms folded in it so that she looked littler than anybody I could remember, like during the four years she hadn't got any older or weaker, but just littler and littler and straighter and straighter and more and more indomitable; and the lieutenant beside her with one hand on his hip and waving a whole handful of letters at Granny's face with the other.

"Look like he got all we ever wrote there," Ringo said. The soldiers' horses were all tied along the fence; they were inside the pen now, and they and Joby and Ab Snopes had the forty-odd old mules and the nineteen new ones hemmed into the corner. The mules were still trying to break out, only it didn't look like that. It looked like every one of them was trying to keep the big burned smear where Granny and Ringo had blotted the U.S. brand turned so that the lieutenant would have to look at it.

"And I guess you will call those scars left-handed trace galls!" the lieutenant was hollering. "You have been using cast-off band-saw bands for traces, hey? I'd rather engage Forrest's whole brigade every morning for six months than spend that same length of time trying to protect United States property from defenseless Southern women and niggers and children. Defenseless!" he hollered. "Defenseless! God help the North if Davis and Lee had ever thought of the idea of forming a brigade of grandmothers and nigger orphans, and invading us with it!" He hollered, shaking the letters at Granny.

In the pen the mules huddled and surged, with Ab Snopes waving his arms at them now and then. Then the lieutenant quit hollering; he even quit shaking the letters at Granny.

"Listen," he said. "We are on evacuation orders now. Likely I am the last Federal soldier you will have to look at. And I'm not going to harm you—orders to that effect too. All I'm going to do is take back this stolen property. And now I want you to tell me, as enemy to enemy, or even man to man, if you like. I know from these forged orders how many head of stock you have taken from us, and I know from the records how many times you have sold a few of them back to us; I even know what we paid you. But how many of them did you actually sell back to us more than one time?"

"I don't know," Granny said.

"You don't know," the lieutenant said. He started to holler, then he didn't. He looked at Granny; he talked now with a kind of furious patience, like Granny was an Indian: "Listen. I know you don't have to tell me, and you know I can't make you. I ask it only out of pure respect. Respect? Envy. Won't you tell me?"

"I don't know," Granny said.

"You don't know," the lieutenant said. "You mean, you—" He talked quiet now. "I see. You really don't know. You were too busy running the reaper to count the—" We didn't move. Granny wasn't even looking at him; it was Ringo and me that watched him fold the letters that Granny and Ringo had written and put them carefully into his pocket. He still talked quiet, like he was tired: "All right, boys. Rope them together and haze them out of there."

"The gate is a quarter of a mile from here," a soldier said.

"Throw down some fence," the lieutenant said. They began to throw down the fence that Joby and I had worked two months on. The lieutenant took a pad from his pocket, and he went to the fence and laid the pad on the rail and took out a pencil. Then he looked back at Granny; he still talked quiet: "I believe you said the name now is Rosa Millard?"

"Yes," Granny said.

The lieutenant wrote on the pad and tore the sheet out and came back to Granny. He still talked quiet, like when somebody is sick in a room. "We are under orders to pay for all property damaged in the process of evacuation," he said. "This is a voucher on the

quartermaster at Memphis for ten dollars. For the fence." He
didn't give the paper to her at once; he just stood there, looking
at her. "Confound it, I don't mean promise. If I just knew what
you believed in, held—" He cursed again, not loud and not at
anybody or anything. "Listen. I don't say promise; I never mentioned the word. But I have a family; I am a poor man; I have no
grandmother. And if in about four months the auditor should find
a warrant in the records for a thousand dollars to Mrs. Rosa
Millard, I would have to make it good. Do you see?"

"Yes," Granny said. "You need not worry."

Then they were gone. Granny and Ringo and Joby and I stood
there and watched them drive the mules up across the pasture and
out of sight. We had forgot about Ab Snopes until he said, "Well,
hit looks like that's all they are to hit. But you still got that ere
hundred-odd that are out on receipt, provided them hill folks don't
take a example from them Yankees. I reckon you can still be
grateful for that much anyway. So I'll bid you, one and all, good
day and get on home and rest a spell. If I can help you again, just
send for me." He went on too.

After a while Granny said:

"Joby, put those rails back up." I reckon Ringo and I were both
waiting for her to tell us to help Joby, but she didn't. She just said
"Come," and turned and went on, not toward the cabin but across
the pasture toward the road. We didn't know where we were going
until we reached the church. She went straight up the aisle to the
chancel and stood there until we came up. "Kneel down," she said.

We knelt in the empty church. She was small between us, little;
she talked quiet, not loud, not fast and not slow; her voice sounded
quiet and still, but strong and clear: "I have sinned. I have stolen,
and I have borne false witness against my neighbor, though that
neighbor was an enemy of my country. And more than that, I have
caused these children to sin. I hereby take their sins upon my
conscience." It was one of those bright soft days. It was cool in the
church; the floor was cold to my knees. There was a hickory branch
just outside the window, turning yellow; when the sun touched it,
the leaves looked like gold. "But I did not sin for gain or for greed,"
Granny said. "I did not sin for revenge. I defy You or anyone to
say I did. I sinned first for justice. And after that first time, I sinned
for more than justice; I sinned for the sake of food and clothes for

Your own creatures who could not help themselves—for children who had given their fathers, for wives who had given their husbands, for old people who had given their sons to a holy cause, even though You have seen fit to make it a lost cause. What I gained, I shared with them. It is true that I kept some of it back, but I am the best judge of that because I, too, have dependents who may be orphans, too, at this moment, for all I know. And if this be sin in Your sight, I take this on my conscience too. Amen."

She rose up. She got up easy, like she had no weight to herself. It was warm outside; it was the finest October that I could remember. Or maybe it was because you are not conscious of weather until you are fifteen. We walked slow back home, though Granny said she wasn't tired. "I just wish I knew how they found out about that pen," she said.

"Don't you know?" Ringo said. Granny looked at him. "Ab Snopes told them."

This time she didn't even say, "Mister Snopes." She just stopped dead still and looked at Ringo. "Ab Snopes?"

"Do you reckon he was going to be satisfied until he had sold them last nineteen mules to somebody?" Ringo said.

"Ab Snopes," Granny said. "Well." Then she walked on; we walked on. "Ab Snopes," she said. "I reckon he beat me, after all. But it can't be helped now. And anyway, we did pretty well, taken by and large."

"We done damn well," Ringo said. He caught himself, but it was already too late. Granny didn't even stop.

"Go on home and get the soap," she said.

He went on. We could watch him cross the pasture and go into the cabin, and then come out and go down the hill toward the spring. We were close now; when I left Granny and went down to the spring, he was just rinsing his mouth, the can of soap in one hand and the gourd dipper in the other. He spit and rinsed his mouth and spit again; there was a long smear of suds up his cheek; a light froth of colored bubbles flicking away while I watched them, without any sound at all. "I still says we done damn well," he said.

We tried to keep her from doing it—we both tried. Ringo had told her about Ab Snopes, and after that we both knew it. It was like all three of us should have known it all the time. Only I don't believe now that he meant to happen what did happen. But I believe that if he had known what was going to happen, he would still have egged her on to do it. And Ringo and I tried—we tried —but Granny just sat there before the fire—it was cold in the cabin now—with her arms folded in the shawl and with that look on her face when she had quit either arguing or listening to you at all, saying just this one time more and that even a rogue will be honest for enough pay. It was Christmas; we had just heard from Aunt Louisa at Hawkhurst and found out where Drusilla was; she had been missing from home for almost a year now, and at last Aunt Louisa found out that she was with father away in Carolina, like she had told me, riding with the troop like she was a man.

Ringo and I had just got back from Jefferson with the letter, and Ab Snopes was in the cabin, telling Granny about it, and Granny listening and believing him because she still believed that what side of a war a man fought on made him what he is. And she knew better with her own ears; she must have known; everybody knew about them and were either mad if they were men or terrified if they were women. There was one Negro in the county that everybody knew that they had murdered and burned him up in his cabin. They called themselves Grumby's Independents—about fifty or sixty of them that wore no uniform and came from nobody knew where as soon as the last Yankee regiment was out of the country, raiding smokehouses and stables, and houses where they were sure there were no men, tearing up beds and floors and walls, frightening white women and torturing Negroes to find where money or silver was hidden.

They were caught once, and the one that said he was Grumby produced a tattered raiding commission actually signed by General Forrest; though you couldn't tell if the original name was Grumby or not. But it got them off, because it was just some old men that captured them; and now women who had lived alone for three years surrounded by invading armies were afraid to stay in the houses at night, and the Negroes who had lost their white people lived hidden in caves back in the hills like animals.

That's who Ab Snopes was talking about, with his hat on the floor and his hands flapping and his hair bent up across the back of his head where he had slept on it. The band had a thoroughbred stallion and three mares—how Ab Snopes knew it he didn't say—

that they had stolen; and how he knew they were stolen, he didn't say. But all Granny had to do was to write out one of the orders and sign Forrest's name to it; he, Ab, would guarantee to get two thousand dollars for the horses. He swore to that, and Granny, sitting there with her arms rolled into the shawl and that expression on her face, and Ab Snopes' shadow leaping and jerking up the wall while he waved his arms and talked about that was all she had to do; to look at what she had made out of the Yankees, enemies, and that these were Southern men and, therefore, there would not even be any risk to this, because Southern men would not harm a woman, even if the letter failed to work.

Oh, he did it well. I can see now that Ringo and I had no chance against him—about how the business with the Yankees had stopped without warning, before she had made what she had counted on, and how she had given most of that away under the belief that she would be able to replace that and more, but as it was now, she had fixed up most everyone in the county save herself; that soon father would return home to a ruined plantation and some of his slaves gone; and how it would be if, when he came home and looked about at his desolate future, she could take fifteen hundred dollars in cash out of her pocket and say, "Here. Start over with this"—fifteen hundred dollars more than she had hoped to have. He would take one of the mares for his commission and he would guarantee her fifteen hundred dollars for the other three.

Oh, we had no chance against him. We begged her to let us ask advice from Uncle Buck McCaslin, anyone, any man. But she just sat there with that expression on her face, saying that the horses did not belong to him, that they had been stolen, and that all she had to do was to frighten them with the order, and even Ringo and I knowing at fifteen that Grumby, or whoever he was, was a coward and that you might frighten a brave man, but that nobody dared frighten a coward; and Granny, sitting there without moving at all and saying, "But the horses do not belong to them because they are stolen property," and we said, "Then no more will they belong to us," and Granny said, "But they do not belong to them."

But we didn't quit trying; all that day—Ab Snopes had located them; it was an abandoned cotton compress on Tallahatchie River, sixty miles away—while we rode in the rain in the wagon Ab Snopes got for us to use, we tried. But Granny just sat there on the

seat between us, with the order signed by Ringo for General Forrest in the tin can under her dress and her feet on some hot bricks
in a crokersack that we would stop every ten miles and build a fire
in the rain and heat again, until we came to the crossroads, where
Ab Snopes told us to leave the wagon and walk. And then she
would not let me and Ringo go with her. "You and Ringo look like
men," she said. "They won't hurt a woman." It had rained all day;
it had fallen gray and steady and slow and cold on us all day long,
and now it was like twilight had thickened it without being able
to make it any grayer or colder. The crossroad was not a road any
more; it was no more than a faint gash turning off at right angles
into the bottom, so that it looked like a cave. We could see the hoof
marks in it.

"Then you shan't go," I said. "I'm stronger than you are; I'll
hold you." I held her; her arm felt little and light and dry as a stick.
But it wasn't that; her size had no more to do with it than it had
with the Yankees; she just turned and looked at me, and then I
began to cry. I would be sixteen years old before another year was
out, yet I sat there in the wagon, crying. I didn't even know when
she freed her arm. And then she was out of the wagon, standing
there looking at me in the gray rain and the gray darkening light.

"It's for all of us," she said. "For John and you and Ringo and
Joby and Louvinia. So we will have something when John comes
back home. You never cried when you knew he was going into a
battle, did you? And now I am taking no risk; I am a woman. Even
Yankees do not harm old women. You and Ringo stay here until
I call you."

We tried. I keep on saying that because I know now that I didn't.
I could have held her, turned the wagon, driven away, holding her
in it. I was just fifteen, and for most of my life her face had been
the first thing I saw in the morning and the last thing I saw at night,
but I could have stopped her, and I didn't. I sat there in the wagon
in the cold rain and let her walk on into the wet twilight and never
come out of it again. How many of them there were in the old
compress, I don't know, and when and why they took fright and
left, I don't know.

We just sat there in the wagon in that cold dissolving December
twilight until at last I couldn't bear it any longer. Then Ringo and
I were both running, trying to run, in the ankle-deep mud of that

old road pocked with the prints of ingoing hoofs, but of no wheel, knowing that we had waited too long either to help her or to share in her defeat. Because there was no sound nor sign of life at all; just the huge rotting building with the gray afternoon dying wetly upon it, and then at the end of the hall a faint crack of light beneath a door.

I don't remember touching the door at all, because the room was a floor raised about two feet from the earth, so that I ran into the step and fell forward into and then through the door, onto my hands and knees in the room, looking at Granny. There was a tallow dip still burning on a wooden box, but it was the powder I smelled, stronger even than the tallow. I couldn't seem to breathe for the smell of the powder, looking at Granny. She had looked little alive, but now she looked like she had collapsed, like she had been made out of a lot of little thin dry light sticks notched together and braced with cord, and now the cord had broken and all the little sticks had collapsed in a quiet heap on the floor, and somebody had spread a clean and faded calico dress over them.

Vendée

They all came in again when we buried Granny; Brother Fortinbride and all of them—the old men and the women and the children and the niggers—the twelve that used to come when Ab
Snopes would get back from Memphis, and I reckon a hundred
more besides, coming in from the hills in the rain. Only there were
no Yankees in Jefferson now, and so they didn't have to walk in;
I could look across the grave and beyond the other headstones and
monuments, and see the dripping cedar grove full of mules with the
long black smears on their hips where Granny and Ringo had
burned out the U.S. brand.

Most of the Jefferson people were there, too, and there was
another preacher—a big preacher refugeeing from Memphis or
somewhere—and I found out how Mrs. Compson and some of
them had arranged for him to preach the funeral. But Brother
Fortinbride didn't let him. He didn't tell him not to; he didn't say
anything to him at all; he just acted like a grown person coming
in where the children are getting ready to play a game and telling
the children that the game is all right, but that the grown folks need
the room and the furniture for a minute. He came walking fast up
from the grove, where he had hitched his mule with the others,
with his gaunted face and his frock coat with the horse-hide and
the Yankee-tent patches, and into where the town people were
standing around under umbrellas with Granny in the middle, and
the big refugeeing preacher with his book already open, and a town
nigger holding an umbrella over him, and the rain splashing slow
and cold and gray on the umbrella and splashing slow on the

yellow boards where Granny was, and into the dark-red dirt beside
the red grave without splashing at all. Brother Fortinbride just
walked in and looked at the umbrellas and then at the hill people
in cotton bagging and flour-sack clothes that didn't have umbrellas, and went to Granny and said, "Come, you men."

The town men would have moved. Some of them did. Uncle
Buck McCaslin was the first man there of all of them, town and
hill. By Christmas his rheumatism would be so bad that he couldn't
hardly move his hand, but he was there with his peeled-hickory
walking stick, shoving up through the hill men with crokersacks
tied over their heads and town men with umbrellas getting out of
his way; and then Ringo and I stood there and watched Granny
going down into the earth with the quiet rain splashing on the
yellow boards until they quit looking like boards and began to look
like water with thin sunlight reflected in it, sinking away into the
ground. Then the wet red dirt began to flow into the grave, with
the shovels darting and flicking slow and steady and the hill men
waiting to take turns with the shovels because Uncle Buck would
not let anyone spell him with his.

It didn't take long, and I reckon the refugeeing preacher would
have tried again even then, but Brother Fortinbride didn't give him
a chance. Brother Fortinbride didn't even put down his shovel; he
stood there leaning on it like he was in the field, and he sounded
just like he used to in the church when Ab Snopes would be home
from Memphis again—strong and quiet and not loud:

"I don't reckon that Rosa Millard or anybody that ever knew
her has to be told where she has gone. And I don't reckon that
anybody that ever knew her would want to insult her by telling her
to rest anywhere in peace. And I reckon that God has already seen
to it that there are men, women and children, black, white, yellow
or red, waiting for her to tend and worry over. And so you folks
go home. Some of you ain't come far, and you came that distance
in carriages with tops. But most of you didn't, and it's by the grace
of Rosa Millard that you didn't come on foot. I'm talking to you.
You have wood to cut and split, at least. And what do you reckon
Rosa Millard would say about you all standing around here, keeping old folks and children out here in the rain?"

Mrs. Compson asked me and Ringo to come home and live with
her until father came back, and some others did—I don't remem-

ber who—and then, when I thought they had all gone, I looked around, and there was Uncle Buck. He came up to us with one elbow jammed into his side and his beard drawn over to one side like it was another arm, and his eyes red and mad like he hadn't slept much, and holding his stick like he was fixing to hit somebody with it and he didn't much care who.

"What you boys going to do now?" he said.

The earth was loose and soft now, dark and red with rain, so that the rain didn't splash on Granny at all; it just dissolved slow and gray into the dark-red mound, so that after a while the mound began to dissolve, too, without changing shape, like the soft yellow color of the boards had dissolved and stained up through the earth, and mound and boards and rain were all melting into one vague quiet reddish gray.

"I want to borrow a pistol," I said.

He begun to holler then, but quiet. Because he was older than us; it was like it had been at the old compress that night with Granny. "Need me or not," he hollered, "by Godfrey, I'm going! You can't stop me! You mean to tell me you don't want me to go with you?"

"I don't care," I said. "I just want a pistol. Or a gun. Ours got burned up with the house."

"All right!" he hollered. "Me and the pistol, or you and this nigger horse thief and a fence rail. You ain't even got a poker at home, have you?"

"We got the bar'l of the musket yet," Ringo said. "I reckon that's all we'll need for Ab Snopes."

"Ab Snopes?" Uncle Buck hollered. "Do you think it's Ab Snopes this boy is thinking about? . . . Hey?" he hollered, hollering at me now. "Hey, boy?" It was changing all the time, with the slow gray rain lancing slow and gray and cold into the red earth, yet it did not change. It would be some time yet; it would be days and weeks and then months before it would be smooth and quiet and level with the other earth. Now Uncle Buck was talking at Ringo, and not hollering now. "Catch my mule," he said. "I got the pistol in my britches."

Ab Snopes lived back in the hills too. Uncle Buck knew where; it was midafternoon by then and we were riding up a long red hill between pines when Uncle Buck stopped. He and Ringo had crokersacks tied over their heads. Uncle Buck's hand-worn stick stuck out from under his sack with the rain shining on it like a long wax candle.

"Wait," he said. "I got a idea." We turned from the road and came to a creek bottom; there was a faint path. It was dark under the trees and the rain didn't fall on us now; it was like the bare trees themselves were dissolving slow and steady and cold into the end of the December day. We rode in single file, in our wet clothes and in the wet ammonia steam of the mules.

The pen was just like the one Ringo and Yance and I had built at home, only smaller and better hidden; I reckon he had got the idea from ours. We stopped at the wet rails; they were still new enough for the split sides to be still yellow with sap, and on the far side of the pen there was something that looked like a yellow cloud in the twilight, until it moved. And then we saw that it was a claybank stallion and three mares.

"I thought so," Uncle Buck said.

Because I was mixed up. Maybe it was because Ringo and I were tired and we hadn't slept much lately. Because the days were mixed up with the nights, all the while we had been riding I would keep on thinking how Ringo and I would catch it from Granny when we got back home, for going off in the rain without telling her. Because for a minute I sat there and looked at the horses and I thought that Ab Snopes was Grumby. But Uncle Buck begun to holler again.

"Him, Grumby?" he hollered. "Ab Snopes? Ab Snopes? By Godfrey, if he was Grumby, if it was Ab Snopes that shot your grandmaw, I'd be ashamed to have it known. I'd be ashamed to be caught catching him. No, sir. He ain't Grumby; he's better than that." He sat sideways on his mule with the sack over his head and his beard jerking and wagging out of it while he talked. "He's the one that's going to show us where Grumby is. They just hid them horses here because they thought this would be the last place you boys would think to look for them. And now Ab Snopes has went off with Grumby to get some more, since your grandmaw has gone out of business, as far as he is concerned. And thank Godfrey for that. It won't be a house or a cabin they will ever pass as long as Ab Snopes is with them, that he won't leave a indelible signature, even if it ain't nothing to capture but a chicken or a kitchen clock.

By Godfrey, the one thing we don't want is to catch Ab Snopes."

And we didn't catch him that night. We went back to the road and went on, and then we came in sight of the house. I rode up to Uncle Buck. "Give me the pistol," I said.

"We ain't going to need a pistol," Uncle Buck said. "He ain't even here, I tell you. You and that nigger stay back and let me do this. I'm going to find out which a way to start hunting. Get back, now."

"No," I said, "I want—"

He looked at me from under the crokersack. "You want what? You want to lay your two hands on the man that shot Rosa Millard, don't you?" He looked at me. I sat there on the mule in the slow gray cold rain, in the dying daylight. Maybe it was the cold. I didn't feel cold, but I could feel my bones jerking and shaking. "And then what you going to do with him?" Uncle Buck said. He was almost whispering now. "Hey? Hey?"

"Yes," I said. "Yes."

"Yes. That's what. Now you and Ringo stay back. I'll do this."

It was just a cabin. I reckon there were a thousand of them just like it about our hills, with the same canted plow lying under a tree and the same bedraggled chickens roosting on the plow and the same gray twilight dissolving onto the gray shingles of the roof. Then we saw a faint crack of fire and a woman's face looking at us around the crack of the door.

"Mr. Snopes ain't here, if that's what you want," she said. "He's done gone to Alabama on a visit."

"Sho, now," Uncle Buck said. "To Alabama. Did he leave any word when to expect him home?"

"No," the woman said.

"Sho, now," Uncle Buck said. "Then I reckon we better get on back home and out of the rain."

"I reckon you had," the woman said. Then the door closed.

We rode away. We rode back toward home. It was like it had been while we waited at the old compress; it hadn't got darker exactly, the twilight had just thickened.

"Well, well, well," Uncle Buck said. "They ain't in Alabama, because she told us so. And they ain't toward Memphis, because there are still Yankees there yet. So I reckon we better try down toward Grenada first. By Godfrey, I'll bet this mule against that nigger's pocketknife that we won't ride two days before we come on a mad woman hollering down the road with a handful of chicken feathers in her hand."

We didn't get Ab Snopes that day. It was February before we got him, because we had been seeing ducks and geese going north for more than a week, but we had lost count of days a long while back. At first Ringo had a pine stick, and each night he would cut a notch in it. There was a big one for Christmas and New Year's, and he had a special one for Sundays. But one night when the stick had almost forty notches in it, we stopped in the rain to make camp without any roof to get under and we had to use the stick to start a fire, because of Uncle Buck's arm. And so, when we came to where we could get another pine stick, we couldn't remember whether it had been five or six or ten days, and so Ringo didn't start another. Because he said he would fix the stick up the day we got Grumby and that it wouldn't need but two notches on it—one for the day we got him and one for the day Granny died.

We had two mules apiece, to swap onto at noon each day. We got the mules back from the hill people; we could have got a cavalry regiment if we had wanted it—of old men and women and children, too—with cotton bagging and flour sacking for uniforms and hoes and axes for arms, on the Yankee mules that Granny had loaned to them. But Uncle Buck told them that we didn't need any help; that three was enough to catch Grumby.

They were not hard to follow. One day we had about twenty notches on the stick and we came onto a house where the ashes were still smoking and a boy almost as big as Ringo and me still unconscious in the stable with even his shirt cut to pieces like they had had a wire snapper on the whip, and a woman with a little thread of blood still running out of her mouth and her voice sounding light and far away like a locust from across the pasture, telling us how many there were and which way they would likely go, saying, "Kill them. Kill them."

It was a long way, but it wasn't far. You could have put a silver dollar down on the geography page with the center of it at Jefferson and we would have never ridden out from under it. And we were closer behind them than we knew, because one night we had ridden late without coming to a house or a shed to camp in, and so we stopped and Ringo said he would scout around a little, because all we had left to eat was the bone of a ham; only it was more likely Ringo was trying to dodge helping to get in the firewood. So Uncle Buck and I were spreading down pine branches to sleep on when we heard a shot and then a sound like a brick chimney falling onto a rotten shingle roof, and then the horses, starting fast and dying away, and then I could hear Ringo yelling. He had come onto a house; he thought it was deserted, and then he said it looked too dark, too quiet. So he climbed onto a shed against the back wall, and he said he saw the crack of light and he was trying to pull the shutter open careful, but it came loose with a sound like a shot, and he was looking into a room with a candle stuck into a bottle and either three or thirteen men looking right at him; and how somebody hollered, "There they are!" and another man jerked out a pistol and one of the others grabbed his arm as it went off, and then the whole shed gave way under him, and he said how he lay there hollering and trying to get untangled from the broken planks and heard them ride away.

"So he didn't shoot at you," Uncle Buck said.

"Hit warn't none of his fault if he never," Ringo said.

"But he didn't," Uncle Buck said. But he wouldn't let us go on that night. "We won't lose any distance," he said. "They are flesh and blood, the same as we are. And we ain't scared."

So we went on at daylight, following the hoofprints now. Then we had three more notches in the stick; that night Ringo put the last notch in it that he was going to, but we didn't know it. We were sitting in front of a cotton pen where we were going to sleep, eating a shote that Ringo had found, when we heard the horse. Then the man begun to holler, "Hello! Hello!" and then we watched him ride up on a good short-coupled sorrel mare, with his neat little fine made boots, and his linen shirt without any collar, and a coat that had been good, too, once, and a broad hat pulled down so that all we could see was his eyes and nose between the hat and his black beard.

"Howdy, men," he said.

"Howdy," Uncle Buck said. He was eating a sparerib; he sat now with the rib in his left hand and his right hand lying on his lap just inside his coat; he wore the pistol on a loop of lace leather around his neck and stuck into his pants like a lady's watch. But the stranger wasn't looking at him; he just looked at each of us once and then sat there on the mare, with both his hands on the pommel in front of him.

"Mind if I light and warm?" he said.

"Light," Uncle Buck said.

He got off. But he didn't hitch the mare. He led her up and he sat down opposite us with the reins in his hand. "Give the stranger some meat, Ringo," Uncle Buck said. But he didn't take it. He didn't move. He just said that he had eaten, sitting there on the log with his little feet side by side and his elbows out a little and his two hands on his knees as small as a woman's hands and covered with a light mat of fine black hair right down to the finger nails, and not looking at any of us now. I don't know what he was looking at now.

"I have just ridden out from Memphis," he said. "How far do you call it to Alabama?"

Uncle Buck told him, not moving either, with the sparerib still raised in his left hand and the other hand lying just inside his coat. "You going to Alabama, hey?"

"Yes," the stranger said. "I'm looking for a man." And now I saw that he was looking at me from under his hat. "A man named Grumby. You people in these parts may have heard of him too."

"Yes," Uncle Buck said, "we have heard of him."

"Ah," the stranger said. He smiled; for a second his teeth looked white as rice inside his ink-colored beard. "Then what I am doing does not have to be secret." He looked at Uncle Buck now. "I live up in Tennessee. Grumby and his gang killed one of my niggers and ran my horses off. I'm going to get the horses back. If I have to take Grumby in the bargain, that will suit me too."

"Sho, now," Uncle Buck said. "So you look to find him in Alabama?"

"Yes. I happen to know that he is now headed there. I almost caught him yesterday; I did get one of his men, though the others escaped me. They passed you all sometime last night, if you were in this neighborhood then. You would have heard them, because when I last saw them, they were not wasting any time. I managed to persuade the man I caught to tell me where they are to ron-dyvoo."

"Alabama?" Ringo said. "You mean they headed back toward Alabama?"

"Correct," the stranger said. He looked at Ringo now. "Did Grumby steal your hog, too, boy?"

"Hawg," Ringo said. "Hawg?"

"Put some wood on the fire," Uncle Buck told Ringo. "Save your breath to snore with tonight."

Ringo hushed, but he didn't move; he sat there staring back at the stranger, with his eyes looking a little red in the firelight.

"So you folks are out to catch a man, too, are you?" the stranger said.

"Two is correct," Ringo said. "I reckon Ab Snopes can pass for a man."

So then it was too late; we just sat there, with the stranger facing us across the fire with the mare's reins in his little still hand, looking at the three of us from between his hat and his beard. "Ab Snopes," he said. "I don't believe I am acquainted with Ab Snopes. But I know Grumby. And you want Grumby too." He was looking at all of us now. "You want to catch Grumby. Don't you think that's dangerous?"

"Not exactly," Uncle Buck said. "You see, we done got a little Alabama Grumby evidence ourselves. That something or somebody has give Grumby a change of heart about killing women and children." He and the stranger looked at each other. "Maybe it's the wrong season for women and children. Or maybe it's public opinion, now that Grumby is what you might call a public character. Folks hereabouts is got used to having their menfolks killed and even shot from behind. But even the Yankees never got them used to the other. And evidently somebody has done reminded Grumby of this. Ain't that correct?"

They looked at each other; they didn't move. "But you are neither a woman nor a child, old man," the stranger said. He stood up, easy; his eyes glinted in the firelight as he turned and put the reins over the mare's head. "I reckon I'll get along," he said. We watched him get into the saddle and sit there again, with his little black-haired hands lying on the pommel, looking down at us—at me and Ringo now. "So you want Ab Snopes," he said. "Take a stranger's advice and stick to him."

He turned the mare. I was watching him, then I was thinking "I wonder if he knows that her off back shoe is gone," when Ringo hollered, "Look out!" and then it seemed to me that I saw the

spurred mare jump before I saw the pistol flash; and then the mare
was galloping and Uncle Buck was lying on the ground cussing and
yelling and dragging at his pistol, and then all three of us were
dragging and fighting over it, but the front sight was caught in his
suspenders, and the three of us fighting over it, and Uncle Buck
panting and cussing, and the sound of the galloping mare dying
away.

The bullet went through the flesh of the inner side of the arm
that had the rheumatism; that was why Uncle Buck cussed so bad;
he said the rheumatism was bad enough, and the bullet was bad
enough, but to have them both at once was too much for any man.
And then, when Ringo told him he ought to be thankful, that
suppose the bullet had hit his good arm and then he wouldn't even
be able to feed himself, he reached back and, still lying down, he
caught up a stick of firewood and tried to hit Ringo with it. We
cut his sleeve away and stopped the blood, and he made me cut a
strip off his shirt tail, and Ringo handed him his stick and he sat
there cussing us while we soaked the strip in hot salt water, and
he held the arm himself with his good hand, cussing a steady
streak, and made us run the strip back and forth through the hole
the bullet had made. He cussed then sure enough, looking a little
like Granny looked, like all old people look when they have been
hurt, with his beard jerking and his eyes snapping and his heels and
the stick jabbing into the ground like the stick had been with him
so long that it felt the rag and the salt too.

And at first I thought that the black man was Grumby, like I
had thought that maybe Ab Snopes was. But Uncle Buck said not.
It was the next morning; we hadn't slept much because Uncle Buck
wouldn't go to sleep; only we didn't know then that it was his arm,
because he wouldn't even let us talk about taking him back home.
And now we tried again, after we had finished breakfast, but he
wouldn't listen, already on his mule with his left arm tied across
his chest and the pistol stuck between the arm and his chest, where
he could get to it quick, saying, "Wait. Wait," and his eyes hard
and snapping with thinking. "It's something I ain't quite got yet,"
he said. "Something he was telling us last night without aiming to
have us know yet that he had told us. Something that we are going
to find out today."

"Likely a bullet that's fixing to hit you halfway betwixt both arms stid of halfway betwixt one," Ringo said.

Uncle Buck rode fast; we could watch his stick rising and falling against the mule's flank, not hard, just steady and fast, like a crippled man in a hurry that has used the stick so long he don't even know it any more. Because we didn't know that his arm was making him sick yet; he hadn't given us time to realize it. So we hurried on, riding along beside a slough, and then Ringo saw the snake. It had been warm for a week, until last night. But last night it made ice, and now we saw the moccasin where it had crawled out and was trying to get back into the water when the cold got it, so that it lay with its body on the land and its head fixed in the skim ice like it was set into a mirror, and Uncle Buck turned sideways on his mule, hollering at us: "There it is, by Godfrey! There's the sign! Didn't I tell you we would—"

We all heard it at once—the three or maybe four shots and then the sound of horses galloping, except that some of the galloping came from Uncle Buck's mule, and he had his pistol out now before he turned from the road and into the trees, with the stick jammed under his hurt arm and his beard flying back over his shoulder. But we didn't find anything. We saw the marks in the mud where the five horses had stood while the men that rode them had watched the road, and we saw the sliding tracks where the horses had begun to gallop, and I thinking quietly, "He still don't know that that shoe is gone." But that was all, and Uncle Buck sitting on his mule with the pistol raised in his hand and his beard blown back over his shoulder and the leather thong of the pistol hanging down his back like a girl's pigtail, and his mouth open and his eyes blinking at me and Ringo.

"What in the tarnation hell!" he said. "Well, let's go back to the road. Whatever it was has done gone that way too."

So we had turned. Uncle Buck had put the pistol up and his stick had begun to beat the mule again when we saw what it was, what it meant.

It was Ab Snopes. He was lying on his side, tied hand and foot, and hitched to a sapling; we could see the marks in the mud where he had tried to roll back into the underbrush until the rope stopped him. He had been watching us all the time, lying there with his face in the shape of snarling and not making a sound after he found out he could not roll out of sight. He was watching our mules' legs and feet under the bushes; he hadn't thought to look any higher yet, and so he did not know that we could see him; he must have thought that we had just spied him, because all of a sudden he began to jerk and thrash on the ground, hollering, "Help! Help! Help!"

We untied him and got him onto his feet, and he was still hollering, loud, with his face and his arms jerking, about how they had caught and robbed him, and they would have killed him if they hadn't heard us coming and run away; only his eyes were not hollering. They were watching us, going fast and quick from Ringo to me to Uncle Buck, and then at Ringo and me again, and they were not hollering, like his eyes belonged to one man and his gaped and yelling mouth belonged to another.

"So they caught you, hey?" Uncle Buck said. "A innocent and unsuspecting traveler. I reckon the name of them would never be Grumby now, would it?"

It was like we might have stopped and built a fire and thawed out that moccasin—just enough for it to find out where it was, but not enough for it to know what to do about it. Only I reckon it was a high compliment to set Ab Snopes up with a moccasin, even a little one. I reckon it was bad for him. I reckon he realized that they had thrown him back to us without mercy, and that if he tried to save himself from us at their expense, they would come back and kill him. I reckon he decided that the worst thing that could happen to him would be for us not to do anything to him at all. Because he quit jerking his arms; he even quit lying; for a minute his eyes and his mouth were telling the same thing.

"I made a mistake," he said. "I admit hit. I reckon everybody does. The question is, what are you fellows going to do about hit?"

"Yes," Uncle Buck said. "Everybody makes mistakes. Your trouble is, you make too many. Because mistakes are bad. Look at Rosa Millard. She just made one, and look at her. And you have made two."

Ab Snopes watched Uncle Buck. "What's them?"

"Being born too soon and dying too late," Uncle Buck said.

He looked at all of us, fast; he didn't move, still talking to Uncle Buck. "You ain't going to kill me. You don't dast."

"I don't even need to," Uncle Buck said. "It wasn't my grand-maw you sicked onto that snake den."

He looked at me now, but his eyes were going again, back and forth across me at Ringo and Uncle Buck; it was the two of them again now, the eyes and the voice. "Why, then I'm all right. Bayard ain't got no hard feelings against me. He knows hit was a pure accident; that we was doing hit for his sake and his paw and them niggers at home. Why, here hit's a whole year and it was me that holp and tended Miss Rosa when she never had ara living soul but them chil—" Now the voice began to tell the truth again; it was the eyes and the voice that I was walking toward. He fell back, crouching, his hands flung up.

Behind me, Uncle Buck said, "You, Ringo! Stay back."

He was walking backward now, with his hands flung up, hollering, "Three on one! Three on one!"

"Stand still," Uncle Buck said. "Ain't no three on you. I don't see nobody on you but one of them children you was just mentioning." Then we were both down in the mud; and then I couldn't see him, and I couldn't seem to find him any more, not even with the hollering; and then I was fighting three or four for a long time before Uncle Buck and Ringo held me, and then I could see him again, lying on the ground with his arms over his face. "Get up," Uncle Buck said.

"No," he said. "Three of you can jump on me and knock me down again, but you got to pick me up first to do hit. I ain't got no rights and justice here, but you can't keep me from protesting hit."

"Lift him up," Uncle Buck said. "I'll hold Bayard."

Ringo lifted him; it was like lifting up a half-filled cotton sack. "Stand up, Mr. Ab Snopes," Ringo said. But he would not stand, not even after Ringo and Uncle Buck tied him to the sapling and Ringo had taken off his and Uncle Buck's and Ab Snopes' galluses and knotted them together with the bridle reins from the mules. He just hung there in the rope, not even flinching when the lash fell, saying, "That's hit. Whup me. Lay hit on me; you got me three to one."

"Wait," Uncle Buck said. Ringo stopped. "You want another chance with one to one? You can take your choice of the three of us."

"I got my rights," he said. "I'm helpless, but I can still protest hit. Whup me."

I reckon he was right. I reckon if we had let him go clean, they would have circled back and killed him themselves before dark. Because—that was the night it began to rain and we had to burn Ringo's stick because Uncle Buck admitted now that his arm was getting bad—we all ate supper together, and it was Ab Snopes that was the most anxious about Uncle Buck, saying how it wasn't any hard feelings and that he could see himself that he had made a mistake in trusting the folks he did, and that all he wanted to do now was to go back home, because it was only the folks you had known all your life that you could trust, and when you put faith in a stranger you deserved what you got when you found that what you had been eating and sleeping with was no better than a passel of rattlesnakes. But as soon as Uncle Buck tried to find out if it actually was Grumby, he shut up and denied that he had ever even seen him.

They left us early the next morning. Uncle Buck was sick by then; we offered to ride back home with him, or to let Ringo ride back with him, and I would keep Ab Snopes with me, but Uncle Buck wouldn't have it.

"Grumby might capture him again and tie him to another sapling in the road, and you would lose time burying him," Uncle Buck said. "You boys go on. It ain't going to be long now. And catch them!" He begun to holler, with his face flushed and his eyes bright, taking the pistol from around his neck and giving it to me, "Catch them! Catch them!"

So Ringo and I went on. It rained all that day; now it began to rain all the time. We had the two mules apiece; we went fast. It rained; sometimes we had no fire at all; that was when we lost count of time, because one morning we came to a fire still burning and a hog they had not even had time to butcher; and sometimes we would ride all night, swapping mules when we had guessed that it had been two hours; and so, sometimes it would be night when we slept and sometimes it would be daylight, and we knew that they must have watched us from somewhere every day and that now that Uncle Buck was not with us, they didn't even dare to stop and try to hide.

Then one afternoon—the rain had stopped but the clouds had not broken and it was turning cold again—it was about dusk and we were galloping along an old road in the river bottom; it was dim and narrow under the trees and we were galloping when my mule shied and swerved and stopped, and I just did catch myself before I went over his head; and then we saw the thing hanging over the middle of the road from a limb. It was an old Negro man, with a rim of white hair and with his bare toes pointing down and his head on one side like he was thinking about something quiet. The note was pinned to him, but we couldn't read it until we rode on into a clearing. It was a scrap of dirty paper with big crude printed letters, like a child might have made them:

Last woning not thret. Turn back. The barer of this my promise and garntee. I have stood all I aim to stand children no children.
                                                                                              G.

And something else written beneath it in a hand neat and small and prettier than Granny's, only you knew that a man had written it; and while I looked at the dirty paper I could see him again, with his neat little feet and his little black-haired hands and his fine soiled shirt and his fine muddy coat, across the fire from us that night.

This is signed by others beside G., one of wh^{m} in particular hav^{ng} less scruples re children than he has. Nethless unders^{gnd} desires to give both you and G. one more chance. Take it, and some day become a man. Refuse it, and cease even to be a child.

Ringo and I looked at each other. There had been a house here once, but it was gone now. Beyond the clearing the road went on again into the thick trees in the gray twilight. "Maybe it will be tomorrow," Ringo said.

It was tomorrow; we slept that night in a haystack, but we were riding again by daylight, following the dim road along the river bottom. This time it was Ringo's mule that shied; the man had stepped out of the bushes that quick, with his fine muddy boots and coat and the pistol in his little black-haired hand, and only his eyes and his nose showing between his hat and his beard.

"Stay where you are," he said. "I will still be watching you."

We didn't move. We watched him step back into the bushes, then the three of them came out—the bearded man and another

man walking abreast and leading two saddled horses, and the third
man walking just in front of them with his hands behind him—a
thick-built man with a reddish stubble and pale eyes, in a faded
Confederate uniform coat and Yankee boots, bareheaded, with a
long smear of dried blood on his cheek and one side of his coat
caked with dried mud and that sleeve ripped away at the shoulder,
but we didn't realize at once that what made his shoulders look so
thick was that his arms were tied tight behind him. And then all
of a sudden we knew that at last we were looking at Grumby. We
knew it long before the bearded man said, "You want Grumby.
Here he is."

We just sat there. Because from then on, the other two men did
not even look at us again. "I'll take him now," the bearded man
said. "Get on your horse." The other man got on one of the horses.
We could see the pistol in his hand then, pointed at Grumby's back.
"Hand me your knife," the bearded man said.

Without moving the pistol, the other man passed his knife to the
bearded man. Then Grumby spoke; he had not moved until now;
he just stood there with his shoulders hunched and his little pale
eyes blinking at me and Ringo.

"Boys," he said, "boys—"

"Shut your mouth," the bearded man said, in a cold, quiet,
almost pleasant voice. "You've already talked too much. If you had
done what I wanted done that night in December, you wouldn't
be where you are now." We saw his hand with the knife; I reckon
maybe for a minute Ringo and I and Grumby, too, all thought the
same thing. But he just cut Grumby's hands loose and stepped back
quick. But when Grumby turned, he turned right into the pistol in
the bearded man's hand.

"Steady," the bearded man said. "Have you got him, Bridger?"

"Yes," the other man said. The bearded man backed to the other
horse and got on it without lowering his pistol or ceasing to watch
Grumby. Then he sat there, too, looking down at Grumby, with
his little hooked nose and his eyes alone showing between the hat
and the ink-colored beard. Grumby began to move his head from
side to side.

"Boys," he said, "boys, you ain't going to do this to me."

"We're not going to do anything to you," the bearded man said.
"I can't speak for these boys there. But since you are so delicate

about children, maybe they will be delicate with you. But we'll give
you a chance though." His other hand went inside his coat too fast
to watch; it had hardly disappeared before the other pistol flicked
out and turned once and fell at Grumby's feet; again Grumby
moved, but the pistols stopped him. The bearded man sat easy on
the horse, looking down at Grumby, talking in that cold, still,
vicious voice that wasn't even mad:

"We had a good thing in this country. We would have it yet, if
it hadn't been for you. And now we've got to pull out. Got to leave
it because you lost your nerve and killed an old woman and then
lost your nerve again and refused to cover the first mistake. Scruples," he said. "Scruples. So afraid of raising the country that there
ain't a man, woman or child, black or white, in it that ain't on the
watch for us. And all because you got scared and killed an old
woman you never saw before. Not to get anything; not for one
single Confed bank note. But because you got scared of a piece of
paper on which someone had signed Bedford Forrest's name. And
you with one exactly like it in your pocket now."

He didn't look at the other man, Bridger; he just said, "All right.
Ease off. But watch him. He's too tenderhearted to turn your back
on."

They backed the horses away, side by side, the two pistols
trained on Grumby's belly, until they reached the underbrush.
"We're going to Texas. If you should leave this place, I would
advise you to go at least that far also. But just remember that
Texas is a wide place, and use that knowledge. Ride!" he
shouted.

He whirled the mare. Bridger whirled too. As they did so,
Grumby leaped and caught the pistol from the ground and ran
forward, crouching and shouting into the bushes, cursing. He shot
three times toward the fading sound of the horses, then he whirled
back to face us. Ringo and I were on the ground, too; I don't
remember when we got down nor why, but we were down, and I
remember how I looked once at Ringo's face and then how I stood
there with Uncle Buck's pistol feeling heavy as a firedog in my
hand. Then I saw that he had quit whirling; that he was standing
there with the pistol hanging against his right leg and that he was
looking at me; and then all of a sudden he was smiling.

"Well, boys," he said, "it looks like you have got me. Durn my hide for letting Matt Bowden fool me into emptying my pistol at him."

And I could hear my voice; it sounded faint and far away, like the woman's in Alabama that day, so that I wondered if he could hear me: "You shot three times. You have got two more shots in it."

His face didn't change, or I couldn't see it change. It just lowered, looking down, but the smile was gone from it. "In this pistol?" he said. It was like he was examining a pistol for the first time, so slow and careful it was that he passed it from his right to his left hand and let it hang again, pointing down again. "Well, well, well. Sholy I ain't forgot how to count as well as how to shoot." There was a bird somewhere—a yellowhammer—I had been hearing it all the time; even the three shots hadn't frightened it. And I could hear Ringo, too, making a kind of whimpering sound when he breathed, and it was like I wasn't trying to watch Grumby so much as to keep from looking at Ringo. "Well, she's safe enough now, since it don't look like I can even shoot with my right hand."

Then it happened. I know what did happen, but even now I don't know how, in what order. Because he was big and squat, like a bear. But when we had first seen him he was a captive, and so, even now he seemed more like a stump than even an animal, even though we had watched him leap and catch up the pistol and run firing after the other two. All I know is, one second he was standing there in his muddy Confederate coat, smiling at us, with his ragged teeth showing a little in his red stubble, with the thin sunlight on the stubble and on his shoulders and cuffs, on the dark marks where the braid had been ripped away; and the next second there were two bright orange splashes, one after the other, against the middle of the gray coat and the coat itself swelling slow down on me like when Granny told us about the balloon she saw in St. Louis and we would dream about it.

I reckon I heard the sound, and I reckon I must have heard the bullets, and I reckon I felt him when he hit me, but I don't remember it. I just remember the two bright flashes and the gray coat rushing down, and then the ground hitting me. But I could smell him—the smell of man sweat, and the gray coat grinding into my face and smelling of horse sweat and wood smoke and grease—and

I could hear him, and then I could hear my arm socket, and I thought "In a minute I will hear my fingers breaking, but I have got to hold onto it" and then—I don't know whether it was under or over his arm or his leg—I saw Ringo, in the air, looking exactly like a frog, even to the eyes, with his mouth open, too, and his open pocketknife in his hand.

Then I was free. I saw Ringo straddle of Grumby's back, and Grumby getting up from his hands and knees, and I tried to raise the pistol, only my arm wouldn't move.

Then Grumby bucked Ringo off like a steer would and whirled again, looking at us, crouched, with his mouth open, too; and then my arm began to come up with the pistol, and he turned and ran. He shouldn't have tried to run from us in boots.

It took us the rest of that day and part of the night to reach the old compress. But it didn't take very long to ride home, because we had the two mules apiece to change onto now. [It would have taken less time than it did, only we found an old iron pot that we could use and so we stopped and built the fire there. There was a piece of machinery at the compress that we could have used. But we didn't stay there that long. There used to be a book at home about Borneo, that told how headhunters did it. But the book was burned up now, even if we had waited until we got home, and all I could remember was something about tree gum. So we got some pine resin, and we had a lot of salt that we wouldn't need now, and Ringo thought about making some lye ashes and we did it. And then we went on.]

It was almost dark when we rode through Jefferson, and it was raining again when we rode past the brick piles and the sooty walls that hadn't fallen down yet, and went on through what used to be the square. We hitched the mules in the cedars, and Ringo was just starting off to find a board when we saw that somebody had already put one up—Mrs. Compson, I reckon, or maybe Uncle Buck, when he got back home.

The earth had sunk too, now, after two months; it was almost level now, like at first Granny had not wanted to be dead either, but now she had begun to be reconciled. We fixed it on the headstone with a piece of wire and stood back.

"Now she can lay good and quiet," Ringo said.

"Yes," I said. And then we both began to cry. We stood there in the slow rain, crying quiet. We were tired; we had ridden a lot, and during the last week we hadn't slept much and we hadn't always had anything to eat.

"It wasn't him or Ab Snopes either that kilt her," Ringo said. "It was them mules. That first batch of mules we got for nothing."

"Yes," I said. "Let's go home. I reckon Louvinia is worried about us."

So it was good and dark when we came to the cabin. And then we saw that it was lighted like for Christmas; we could see the big fire and the lamp, clean and bright, when Louvinia opened the door long before we had got to it and ran out into the rain and began to paw at me, crying and hollering.

"What?" I said. "Father? Father's home? Father?"

"And Miss Drusilla!" Louvinia hollered, crying and praying and pawing at me, and hollering and scolding at Ringo all at once. "Home! Hit done finished! All but the surrendering. And now Marse John done home." She finally told us how father and Drusilla had come home about a week ago and Uncle Buck told father where Ringo and I were, and how father had tried to make Drusilla wait at home, but she refused, and how they were looking for us, with Uncle Buck to show the way.

So we went to bed. We couldn't even stay awake to eat the supper Louvinia cooked for us; Ringo and I went to bed in our clothes on the pallet, and went to sleep all in one motion, with Louvinia's face hanging over us and still scolding, and Joby in the chimney corner where Louvinia had made him get up out of Granny's chair. And then somebody was pulling at me, and I thought I was fighting Ab Snopes again, and then it was the rain in father's beard and clothes that I smelled. But Uncle Buck was still hollering, and father holding me, and Ringo and I held to him, and then it was Drusilla kneeling and holding me and Ringo, and we could smell the rain in her hair, too, while she was hollering at Uncle Buck to hush. Father's hand was hard; I could see his face beyond Drusilla and I was trying to say, "Father, father," while she was holding me and Ringo with the rain smell of her hair all around us, and Uncle Buck hollering and Joby looking at Uncle Buck with his mouth open and his eyes round.

"Yes, by Godfrey! Not only tracked him down and caught him

but brought back the actual proof of it to where Rosa Millard could rest quiet."

"The which?" Joby hollered. "Fotch back the which?"

"Hush! Hush!" Drusilla said. "That's all done, all finished. You, Uncle Buck!"

"The proof and the expiation!" Uncle Buck hollered. "When me and John Sartoris and Drusilla rode up to that old compress, the first thing we see was that murdering scoundrel pegged out on the door to it all except the right hand. 'And if anybody wants to see that, too,' I told John Sartoris, 'just let them ride into Jefferson and look on Rosa Millard's grave!' Ain't I told you he is John Sartoris' boy? Hey? Ain't I told you?"

Fool About a Horse

~

Yes, sir. It wasn't Pap that bought one horse from Pat Stamper and
then sold two back to him. It was Mammy. Her and Pat jest used
Pap to trade through. Because we never left home that morning
with Mammy's cream separator money to trade horses with nobody. And I reckon that if Pap had had any notion that he was
fated to swap horses with Pat Stamper, they couldn't even have
arrested him and taken him to town. We never even knowed it was
Pat Stamper that had unloaded that horse on whoever it was
Beasley Kemp got it from until we was halfway there. Because Pap
admitted he was a fool about a horse but it wasn't that kind of a
fool he meant. And once he was away from our lot and the neighbor men looking through the fence at whatever it was Pap had
traded some more of Old Man Anse Holland's bob-wire and busted
tools for this time, and Pap lying to them to jest exactly the right
amount about how old it was and how much he give for it;—once
Pap was away from there I don't reckon he was even the kind of
a fool about a horse that Mammy claimed he was when we come
up to the house that noon after we had shut the gate on the horse
we had jest traded outen Beasley Kemp, and Pap taken his shoes
off on the front gallery for dinner and Mammy standing there in
the door, shaking the cold skillet at Pap and scolding and railing
and Pap saying, "Now Vynie; now Vynie. I always was a fool about
a good horse and it ain't no use you a-scolding and jawing about
it. You had better thank the Lord that when He give me a eye for

horse-flesh He give me a little jedgment and gumption along with it."

Because it wasn't the horse. It wasn't the trade. It was a good trade, because Pap swapped Beasley a straight stock and fourteen rods of bob-wire and a old wore-out sorghum mill of Old Man Anse's for the horse, and Mammy admitted it was a good swap even for that horse, even for anything that could git up and walk from Beasley Kemp's lot to ourn by itself. Because like she said while she was shaking the skillet at Pap, even Pap couldn't git stung very bad in a horse trade because he never owned nothing that anybody would swap even a sorry horse for and even to him. And it wasn't because me and Pap had left the plows down in the bottom piece where Mammy couldn't see them from the house, and snuck the wagon out the back way with the straight stock and the wire and the sorghum mill while she thought we were still in the field. It wasn't that. It was like she knowed without having to be told what me and Pap never found out for a week yet: that Pat Stamper had owned that horse we traded outen Beasley Kemp and that now Pap had done caught the Pat Stamper sickness jest from touching it.

And I reckon she was right. Maybe to hisself Pap did call hisself the Pat Stamper of the Frenchman Bend country, or maybe even of all Beat Four. But I reckon that even when he was believing it the strongest, setting there on the top rail of the lot fence and the neighbor men coming up to lean on the fence and look at what Pap had brung home this time and Pap not bragging much and maybe not even lying much about it; I reckon that even then there was another part of his mind telling him he was safe to believe he was the Pat Stamper of Beat Four jest as long as he done it setting on that fence where it was about one chance in a million of Pat Stamper actually passing and stopping to put it to a test. Because he wouldn't no more have set out to tangle with Pat Stamper than he would have set out to swap horses with a water moccasin. Probly if he had knowed that Pat Stamper ever owned that horse we swapped outen Beasley, Pap wouldn't have traded for it at no price. But then, I reckon that a fellow who straggles by acci-dent into where yellow fever or moccasins is, don't aim to ketch fever or snakebite neither. But he sholy never aimed to tangle with Pat Stamper. When we started for town that morning with Beasley's horse and our mule in the wagon and that separator money that Mammy had been saving on for four years in Pap's pocket, we wasn't even thinking about horse trading, let alone about Pat Stamper, because we didn't know that Pat Stamper was in Jefferson and we didn't even know that he had owned the horse until we got to Varner's store. It was fate. It was like the Lord Hisself had decided to spend Mammy's separator money for a horse; it would have had to been Him because wouldn't nobody else, leastways nobody that knowed Mammy, have risked doing it. Yes, sir. Pure fate. Though I will have to admit that fate picked a good, quick, willing hand when it picked Pap. Because it wasn't that kind of a fool about a horse that Pap meant he was.

No, sir. Not that kind of a fool. I reckon that while he was setting on the porch that morning when Mammy had done said her say for the time being and went back to the kitchen, and me done fetched the gourd of fresh water from the well, and the side meat plopping and hissing on the stove and Pap waiting to eat it and then go back down to the lot and set on the fence while the neighbor men come up in two's and three's to look at Pap's new horse, I reckon maybe in his own mind Pap not only knowed as much about horse trading as Pat Stamper, but he owned head for head as many of them as Old Man Anse hisself. I reckon that while he would set there on the fence, jest moving enough to keep outen the sun, with them two empty plows standing in the furrow down in the bottom piece and Mammy watching him outen the back window and saying, "Horse trader! Setting there bragging and lying to a passel of shiftless men, and the weeds and morning glories climbing that thick in the corn and cotton that I am afraid to tote his dinner to him for fear of snakes"; I reckon Pap would look at whatever it was he had traded the mail box or the winter corn or something else that maybe Old Man Anse had done forgot he owned or leastways might not miss, and he would say to hisself: "It's not only mine, but before God it's the prettiest drove of horses a man ever seen."

II

It was pure fate. When we left for town that morning with Mammy's separator money, Pap never even aimed to use Beasley's horse at all because he knowed it probably couldn't make no

twelve-mile trip to Jefferson and get back the same day. He aimed
to go up to Old Man Anse's and borrow one of his mules to work
with ourn; it was Mammy herself that done it, taunted him about
the piece of crowbait he had bought for a yard ornament until Pap
said that by Godfrey he would show Mammy and all the rest of
them that misdoubted he knowed a horse when he seen it, and so
we went to the lot and put the new horse in the wagon with the
mule. We had been feeding it heavy as it would eat for a week now
and it looked a heap better than it did the day we got it. But even
yet it didn't look so good, though Pap decided it was the mule that
showed it up so bad; that when it was the only horse or mule in
sight, it didn't look so bad and that it was the standing beside
something else on four legs that hurt its looks. "If we jest had some
way to hitch the mule under the wagon where it wouldn't show and
jest leave the horse in sight, it would be fine," Pap said. But there
wasn't no way to do that, so we jest done the best we could. It was
a kind of doormat bay and so, with Pap standing about twenty foot
away and squinching first one eye and then the other and saying,
"Bear down on it. You got to git the hide hot to make the har
shine," I polished it down with croker sacks the best I could. Pap
thought about feeding it a good bait of salt in some corn and then
turning it to water and hide some of the ribs, only we knowed that
we wouldn't even get to Jefferson in one day, let alone come back,
besides having to stop at ever creek and load it up again. So we
done the best we could and then we started, with Mammy's separator money (it was twenty-seven dollars and sixty-five cents; it taken
her four years to save it outen her egg- and quilt-money) tied up
in a rag that she dared Pap to even open to count it before he
handed it to Uncle Ike McCaslin at the store and had the separator
in the wagon.

Yes, sir. Fate. The same fate that made Mammy taunt Pap into
starting out with Beasley's horse; the same fate that made it a hot
morning in July for us to start out on. Because when we left home
that morning we wasn't even thinking about horse trading. We was
thinking about horse, all right, because we were wondering if
maybe we wasn't fixing to come back home that night with Beasley's horse riding in the wagon and me or Pap in the traces with
the mule. Yes, sir. Pap eased that team outen the lot at sunup and
on down the road toward Frenchman's Bend as slow and careful

as arra horse and mule ever moved in this world, with me and Pap
walking up ever hill that was slanted enough to run water down
the ruts, and aiming to do that right on into Jefferson. It was the
weather, the hot day, that done it. Because here we was, about a
mile from Varner's store, and Beasley's horse kind of half walking
and half riding on the double tree, and Pap's face looking a little
more and a little more concerned ever time our new horse failed
to lift its feet high enough to make the next step, when all of a
sudden that horse popped into a sweat. It flung its head up like it
had been teched with a hot poker and stepped up into the collar,
teching the collar for the first time since the mule had taken the
weight off the breast yoke when Pap'd shaken out the whip inside
the lot; and so here we come down the last hill and up to Varner's
store and that horse of Beasley's with its head up and blowing froth
and its eyes white-rimmed like these here colored dinner plates and
Pap sawing back on the reins, and I be dog if it not only hadn't
sweated into as pretty a blood bay as you ever see, but even the ribs
didn't seem to show so much. And Pap, that had been talking
about taking a back road so as to miss Varner's store altogether,
setting there on the wagon seat exactly like he would set on the lot
fence where he knowed he would be safe from Pat Stamper, telling
Jody Varner and them other men that Beasley's horse come from
Kentucky. Jody Varner never even laughed. "Kentucky, hey?" he
says. "Sho, now. That explains why it taken it so long. Herman
Short swapped Pat Stamper a buckboard and a set of harness for
it five years ago, and Beasley Kemp give Herman eight dollars for
it last summer. How much did you give Beasley? Fifty cents?"

That's what done it. From then on, it was automatic. It wasn't
the horse, the trade. It was still a good trade, because in a sense
you might say that all Pap give Beasley for it was the straight stock,
since the bob-wire and the sorghum mill belonged to Old Man
Anse. And it wasn't the harness and the buckboard that Herman
Short give Pat Stamper: it was that eight dollars that Beasley give
Herman. That's what rankled Pap. Not that he held the eight
dollars against Herman, because Herman had done already invested a buckboard and a set of harness. And besides, the eight
dollars was still in the county, even if it was out of circulation,
belonging to Herman Short, and so it didn't actually matter
whether Herman had it or Beasley had it. It was Pat Stamper that

rankled Pap. When a man swaps horse for horse, that's one thing. But when cash money starts changing hands, that's something else; and when a stranger comes into the country and starts actual cash money jumping from hand to hand, it's like when a burglar breaks into your house and flings your clothes and truck from place to place even though he don't take nothing: it makes you mad. So it was not jest to unload Beasley's horse back onto Pat Stamper. It was to get Beasley's eight dollars back outen Pat some way. And so it was jest pure fate that had Pat Stamper camped right on the road we would take to Jefferson on the very day when me and Pap went to get Mammy's separator.

So I reckon the rest of it don't even hardly need to be told, except as a kind of sidelight on how, when a man starts out to plan to do something, he jest thinks he is planning: that what he is actually doing is giving the highball to misfortune, throwing open the switch and saying, "All right, Bad Luck; come right ahead." So here was Pat Stamper and that nigger magician of hisn camped in Hoke's pasture, right on the road we would have to pass to git to town, and here was Pap on the way to town with two live animals and twenty-seven dollars and sixty-five cents in cash, and feeling that the entire honor and pride of the science and pastime of horse trading in Yoknapatawpha County depended on him to vindicate it. So the rest of it don't even need to be told. I don't need to tell whether me and Pap walked back home or not, because anybody that knows Pat Stamper knows that he never bought a horse or a mule outright in his life; that he swapped you something for it that could at least walk out of sight. So the only point that might interest you is, what was pulling the wagon when we got back home. And what Mammy done when she said, "Where is my separator?" and Pap saying, "Now Vynie; now Vynie—" Yes, sir. When it come down to the trade, it wasn't Pat Stamper after all that Pap was swapping horses with. It was the demon rum.

Because he was desperate. After the first swap he was desperate. Before that he was jest mad, like when you dream you are right in the middle of the track and the train a-coming; it's right on you and you can't run or dodge because all of a sudden you realize you are running in sand and so after a while it don't even matter if the train catches you or not because all you can think about is being mad at the sand. That's how Pap was. For ever mile we made toward Jefferson, the madder Pap got. It wasn't at Beasley's horse, because we nursed it on toward town the same way we nursed it to Varner's store until it begun to sweat. It was them eight cash dollars that that horse represented. I don't even recollect just when and where we found out that Pat Stamper was at Jefferson that day. It might have been at Varner's store. Or it might have been that we never had to be told; that for Pap to carry out the fate that Mammy started when she taunted him about Beasley's horse, Pat Stamper would jest have to be in Jefferson. Because Pap never even taken time to find out where Pat was camped, so that when we did roll into town we had done already swapped. Yes, sir. We went up them long hills with Pap and me walking and Beasley's horse laying into the collar the best it could but with the mule doing most of the pulling and Pap walking on his side of the wagon and cussing Pat Stamper and Herman Short and Beasley Kemp and Jody Varner, and we went down the hills with Pap holding the wagon broke with a sapling pole so it wouldn't shove Beasley's horse through the collar and turn it wrong-side-outward like a sock and Pap still a-cussing Pat Stamper and Herman and Beasley and Varner, until we come to the three-mile bridge and Pap turned off the road and druv into the bushes and taken the mule outen the harness and knotted one rein so I could ride it and give me the quarter and told me to git for town and git the dime's worth of saltpeter and the nickel's worth of tar and the number ten fish hook.

So we didn't git to town until that afternoon. We went straight to Pat Stamper's camp in Hoke's pasture where I had done already passed it twice on the mule, with Beasley's horse laying into the collar sho enough now and its eyes looking nigh as wild as Pap's looked a hour later when we come outen McCaslin's back door with the separator, and foaming a little at the mouth where Pap had rubbed the rest of the saltpeter into its gums and with a couple of as pretty tarred bob-wire cuts on its chest as you could want and another one on its flank where Pap had worked the fish hook under its hide where he could tech it by drooping the rein now and then; yes, sir, turning into Hoke's pasture on two wheels and Pap sawing back on the reins and Pat Stamper's nigger running up and grabbing the bridle to keep Beasley's horse from running right into the tent where Pat slept and Pat hisself coming outen the tent with that 'ere cream-colored Stetson cocked over one eye and them eyes the color of a new plow point and jest about as warm. "That's a pretty lively looking horse you got there," Pat says.

"Hell fire, yes!" Pap says. "It durn nigh killed me and this boy both before I could git it into that ere gate yonder. That's why I got to git shut of it. I expect you to beat me, but I got to trade. So come on and beat me quick and give me something I won't be skeered to walk up to."

And I still believe that Pap was right, that it was the right system. It had been five years since Pat had seen the horse, or anyway since he had unloaded it on Herman Short, so me and Pap figured that the chance of Pat's recognizing it would be about the same as for a burglar to recognize a dollar watch that happened to snag onto his clothes in passing five years ago. And it was the right system, to rush up and say we jest had to trade instead of jest drifting up and hanging around for Pat to persuade us. And Pap wasn't trying to beat Pat bad. All he wanted was to vindicate that ere eight cash dollars. That was it: the eight cash dollars' worth of the pride of Yoknapatawpha County horse trading, and Pap the self-appointed champion and knight doing it not for profit but for honor. And I be dog if I still don't believe it worked, that Pap did fool Pat, and that it was because of what Pat aimed to swap to Pap and not because Pat recognized Beasley's horse, that he refused to trade anyway except team for team. Or I don't know. Maybe Pap was so busy fooling Pat that Pat never had to fool Pap, like a man that has jest got to do something, who no matter how hard he tries he jest half does it, while a man that don't care whether he does it or not, does it twice as good with jest half the work. So there we was: the nigger holding the two mules that Pat wanted to swap for our team, and Pat chewing his tobacco slow and gentle and steady and watching Pap with them plow point eyes, and Pap standing there with that look on his face that was desperate not because he was skeered yet but because he was having to think fast, realizing now that he had done got in deeper than he aimed to and that he would either have to shet his eyes and bust on through, or back out and quit. Because right here was where Pat Stamper showed how come he was Pat Stamper. If he had jest started in to show Pap what a bargain he would be getting in them two mules, I reckon Pap would have backed out. But Pat didn't. He fooled Pap exactly

like one first-class burglar would purely and simply refuse to tell
another first-class burglar where the safe was at.

"But I don't want to swap for a whole team," Pap said. "I
already got a good mule. It's the horse I don't want. Trade me a
mule for the horse."

"No," Pat said. "I don't want no wild horse neither. Not that
I won't trade for anything that can walk, provided I can trade my
way. But I ain't going to trade for that horse alone because I don't
want it no more than you do. What I am trading for is that mule.
And besides, this here team of mine is matched. I aim to get about
three times for the pair of them what I would get trading either of
them single."

"But you will still have a team to trade with," Pap says.

"No," Pat said. "I aim to get more from you for them than if
the team was broken. If it's a single mule you want, you better try
somebody else."

So Pap looked at the mules again. That was it. They looked all
right. They looked jest exactly all right. They didn't look too good
and they didn't look too bad. Neither of them looked quite as good
as our mule, but the two of them looked jest a leetle mite better
than Beasley's horse and one mule of anybody's. That was it. If
they had looked like a bargain, I reckon even I, a twelve-year-old
boy, would have had sense enough to tell Pap to come on and let's
git outen there. But Lord, I reckon we was doomed from the very
second when Jody Varner told about that eight dollars. I reckon
Pat Stamper knowed we was doomed the very second he looked up
and seen the nigger holding Beasley's horse outen the tent. I reckon
he knowed right then that he wouldn't have to try to trade, that
all he would need to do would be jest to say No long enough. So
that's what he done, leaning against our wagon bed with his
thumbs hooked into the top of his pants, chewing his tobacco and
watching Pap going through the motion of examining them mules
again. Because even I knowed that Pap had done already traded,
that he had done walked out into what he thought was a spring
branch and then found it was quicksand, and now he knowed he
couldn't even stop long enough to turn back. "All right," he said.
"I'll take them."

So the nigger taken Beasley's horse and the mule outen the
wagon and put our new team in, and me and Pap went on to town.

And before God, them mules still looked all right. I be dog if I didn't think that maybe Pap had walked into that Stamper quicksand and then got out again. Or maybe it was jest getting outen Stamper's reach with the harness left. Because when we got back into the road and outen sight of Stamper's camp, Pap's face begun to look like it would when he would set on the lot fence at home and tell the fellows how he was a fool about a horse but not a durn fool. It wasn't easy yet; it was jest watchful, setting there and feeling out our new team. We was right at town now and so he wouldn't have much time to feel them out, but we would have a good chance to on the road home. "By Godfrey," Pap said, "if they can walk home a-tall, I have got that ere eight dollars back, durn him."

Because that nigger of Pat Stamper's was a artist. Because I swear to Godfrey them mules looked all right. They jest looked like two ordinary not extry good mules you might see in a hundred wagons on the road. I noticed how they had a kind of jerky way of starting off, first one jerking into the collar and then jerking back and then the other jerking into the collar and then jerking back, and even after we was in the road and the wagon rolling good, one of them taken a spell of some sort and snatched hisself crossways in the traces like he aimed to go back, but then Stamper had jest told us that they was a matched team; he never had said they had worked together as a matched team, and they was a well matched team in the sense that neither one of them seemed to have any idea as to jest when the other one aimed to start moving or what direction it was going to take. But Pap got them straightened out and we went on; we was jest starting up that ere big hill into town, when they popped into a sweat jest like Beasley Kemp's horse done back yonder on the other side of Varner's store. But that was all right; it was hot enough; that was when I first taken notice that that rain was going to come up before dark; I mind how I was jest thinking how it was going to ketch us before we got home when this here sweat taken them mules. And that was all right; I didn't blame them for sweating; the trouble was, it was a different kind of sweat from the kind Beasley's horse had given us to expect. I mind how I was looking at a big hot-looking bright cloud over to the southwest when all of a sudden I realized that the wagon had done stopped going forward up the hill and was starting down it backward and then I looked in time to see both them mules this time crossways in the traces and kind of glaring at one another across the tongue and Pap trying to straighten them out and his eyes looking a right smart like the mules' eyes, and then all of a sudden they straightened out and I mind how I thought it was a good thing they happened to have their backs toward the wagon when they did, because I reckon they moved at the same time for the first time in their lives, for the first time since Pap owned them at least; and, gentlemen, here we come swurging up that hill and into town like a roach down a rathole, with the wagon on two wheels and Pap sawing back on the lines and hollering, "Hell fire, hell fire," and folks scattering, and Pap jest managed to swing them into the alley behind McCaslin's store and stopped them by locking our nigh front wheel with another wagon's and the other mules (they was hitched) holp to put the brakes on. So it was a good crowd by then, helping us to git untangled, and Pap led our team on to Uncle Ike's back door and tied them up close to the door handle and me and him went in to get the separator, with the folks still coming up and saying, "It's that team of Stamper's" and Pap kind of breathing hard and looking a right smart less easy in the face than when we had left Stamper's camp even, besides most all-fired watchful, saying, "Come on here. Let's git that durn separator of your mammy's loaded and git outen here." So we give Uncle Ike the rag with Mammy's money in it and me and Pap taken up the separator and started back out to the wagon, to where we had left it. It was still there. I mind how I could see the bed of it where Pap had drawed it up to the door, and I could see the folks from the waist up standing in the alley, and then I realized that it was about twice as many folks looking at our team as it had been when we left. I reckon Pap never noticed it because he was too busy hurrying that 'ere separator along. So I jest stepped aside a little to have a look at what the folks was looking at and then I realized that I could see the front of our wagon and the place where me and Pap had left the mules, but that I couldn't see no mules. So I don't recollect whether I dropped my side of the separator or if Pap dropped hisn or if we still carried it when we come to where we could see out the door and see the mules. They were still there. They were just laying down. Pap had snubbed them right up to the handle of Uncle Ike's back door, with the same rein run through both bits, and now they looked jest exactly like two fellows that had done hung themselves in one of these here suicide packs, with their heads snubbed up together and their tongues hanging out and their necks stretched about four foot and their legs folded back under them like shot rabbits until Pap jumped down and cut the harness. Yes, sir. A artist. He had give them to the exact inch jest enough of whatever it was, to get them into town and off the square before it played out.

And this here is what I meant when I said it was desperation. I can see Pap now, backed off into that corner behind Uncle Ike's plows and cultivators and such, with his face white and his voice shaking and his hand shaking so he couldn't hardly hand me the six bits. "Go to Doc Peabody's store," he says, "and git me a pint of whiskey and git it quick."

Yes, sir. Desperate. It wasn't even quicksand now. It was a whirlpool, and Pap with jest one jump left. He drunk that pint of whiskey in two drinks and set the empty bottle careful in the corner of Uncle Ike's warehouse, and we went back to the wagon. The mules was still up all right, and we loaded the separator in and Pap eased them away careful, with the folks all watching and telling one another it was a Pat Stamper team and Pap setting there with his face red now instead of white and them clouds were heavy and the sun was even gone now but I don't think Pap ever noticed it. And we hadn't eaten too, and I don't think Pap noticed that neither. And I be dog if it didn't seem like Pat Stamper hadn't moved too, standing there at the gate to his stock pen, with that Stetson cocked and his thumbs still hooked into the top of his pants, and Pap setting on the wagon trying to keep his hands from shaking and the team stopped now with their heads down and their legs spraddled and breathing like starting up a sawmill on a Monday morning. "I come to trade back for my team," Pap said.

"What's the matter?" Stamper says. "Don't tell me these are too lively for you, too. They don't look it."

"All right," Pap said. "All right. I jest want my team back. I'll give you four dollars to trade back. That's all I got. And I got to have them. Make your four dollars, and give me my team."

"I ain't got your team," Stamper says. "I didn't want that horse either. I told you that. So I got shet of it right away."

Pap set there for a while. It was all clouded over now, and cooler;

you could even smell the rain. "All right," Pap said. "But you still got the mule. All right. I'll take it."

"For what?" Stamper says. "You want to swap that team for your mule?" Sho. Pap wasn't trading. He was desperate, setting there like he couldn't even see, with Stamper leaning easy against the gate and looking at him for a minute. "No," he says. "I don't want them mules. Yours is the best. I wouldn't trade that way, even." He spit, easy and careful, before he looked at Pap again. "Besides, I done included your mule into another team, with another horse. You want to look at it?"

"All right," Pap said. "How much?"

"Don't you even want to see it first?" Stamper says.

"All right," Pap said. So the nigger led out the horse, a little dark brown horse; I remember how even with it clouded up to rain and no sun, how the horse shined; a horse a little bigger than the one we traded Stamper, and hog fat. Yes, sir. That's jest exactly how it was fat: not like a horse is fat but like a hog: fat right up to its ears and looking tight as a drum; it was so fat it couldn't hardly walk, putting its feet down like they didn't have no weight nor feeling in them. "It's too fat to last," Pap said. "It won't even git me home."

"That's what I think myself," Stamper said. "That's why I am willing to git shet of it."

"All right," Pap said. "But I got to try it."

"Try it?" Stamper said. Pap didn't answer. He jest got down from the wagon careful and went to the horse. It had a hackamore on and Pap taken the rein outen the nigger's hand and started to git on the horse. "Wait," Stamper says. "What you fixing to do?"

"Going to try it," Pap said. "I done traded a horse with you once today." Stamper looked at Pap again for a minute. Then he spit again and kind of stepped back.

"All right," he said. "Help him up, Jim." So the nigger holp Pap onto the horse, only the nigger never had time to jump back because as soon as Pap's weight come onto the horse's back it was like Pap had a live wire in his britches. It throwed Pap hard and Pap got up without no change on his face a-tall and went back to the horse and taken the hackamore again and the nigger holp him up again, with Stamper standing there with his hands hooked into his pants tops, watching. And the horse slammed Pap off again and

Pap got up again with his face jest the same and went back and taken the hackamore from the nigger again when Stamper stopped him. That was exactly how Pap did it, like he wanted the horse to throw him and hard, not to try to hurt hisself, but like the ability of his bones and meat to feel that 'ere hard ground was all he had left to pay for a horse with life enough in it to git us home. "Here, here," Stamper says. "Are you trying to kill yourself?"

"All right," Pap says. "How much?"

"Come on into the tent and have a drink," Stamper says.

So I waited in the wagon. It was beginning to blow a little now, and we hadn't brought no coats with us. But there was some croker sacks in the wagon that Mammy made us bring to wrap her separator in and so I was wrapping the separator up in them when the nigger led out a horse and buggy and then Pap and Stamper come outen the tent and Pap come to the wagon. He never looked at me. He jest reached in and taken the separator outen the sacks and put it into the buggy and then him and Stamper got in and druv away. They went back toward town and then they went out of sight and I seen the nigger watching me. "You fixing to git wet fo you git home," he said.

"I reckon so," I said.

"You want to eat a snack of dinner until they git back?" the nigger said.

"I ain't hungry," I said. So he went on into the tent and I waited in the wagon. Yes, sir, it was most sholy going to rain; I mind how I thought that anyway now we could use the croker sacks to try to keep dry in. Then Pap and Stamper come back and Pap never looked at me neither. He went into the tent and I could see him drinking outen a bottle and then putting the bottle back into his shirt. I reckon Stamper give him that bottle. Pap never said so, but I reckon Stamper did. So then the nigger put our mule and the new horse in the wagon and Pap come outen the tent and got in. Stamper and the nigger both holp him now.

"Don't you reckon you better let the boy drive?" Stamper says.

"I'll drive," Pap said. "By Godfrey, maybe I can't swap a horse with you, but I can still drive it."

"Sho now," Stamper said. "That horse will surprise you."

III

It did. Yes, sir. It surprised us, jest like Stamper said. It happened
jest before dark. The rain, the storm, come up before we had gone
a mile and we rode in it for two hours before we found a old barn
to shelter under, setting hunched under them croker sacks (I mind
how I thought how in a way I almost wished Mammy knew we
never had the separator because she had wanted it for so long that
maybe she would rather for Uncle Ike to own it and it safe and dry,
than for her to own it five miles from home in a wagon in the rain)
and watching our new horse that was so fat it even put its feet down
like they never had no feeling nor weight, that ever now and then,
even in the rain, would take a kind of flinching jerk like when Pap's
weight came down onto its back at Stamper's camp. But we didn't
catch on then, because I was driving now, sho enough, because Pap
was laying flat in the wagon bed with the rain popping him in the
face and him not even knowing it, and me setting on the seat and
watching our new horse change from a black horse into a bay.
Because I was jest twelve and me and Pap had always done our
horse trading along that country road that run past our lot. So I
jest druv into the first shelter I come to and shaken Pap awake. The
rain had cooled him off some, but even without that he would have
sobered quick. "What?" he says. "What is it?"

"The horse, Pap!" I hollered. "It's done changed color!"

Yes, sir. It sobered him quick. We was both outen the wagon
then and Pap's eyes popping sho enough now and a bay horse
standing there where he had went to sleep looking at a black one.
Because I was jest twelve; it happened too fast for me; I jest mind
seeing Pap tech the horse's back at a spot where ever now and then
the backband must have teched it (I tell you, that nigger was a
artist) and then the next I knowed that horse was plunging and
swurging; I remember dodging jest as it slammed into the wall and
then me and Pap heard a sound like when a automobile tire picks
up a nail: a sound like Whoosh! and then the rest of that shiny fat
black horse we had got from Pat Stamper vanished. I don't mean
that me and Pap was standing there with jest our mule left. We had
a horse too. Only it was the same one we had left home with that
morning and that we had swapped Beasley Kemp the sorghum mill

and the bob-wire and the straight stock for two weeks ago. We even got our fish hook back, with the barb still bent where Pap had bent it and the nigger had jest moved it a little. But it wasn't until we was home the next day at daylight that we found the hand pump valve behind its off fore leg.

And that's about all. Because Mammy was up and seen us pass, and so after a while we had to go to the house, because me and Pap hadn't et since twenty-four hours ago. So we went to the house, with Mammy standing in the door saying, "Where's my separator?" and Pap saying how he always had been a fool about a horse and he couldn't help it and Mammy couldn't neither and that to jest give him time, and Mammy standing there looking at him and then she begun to cry and it was the first time I ever seen her cry. She cried hard, standing there in her old wrapper, not even hiding her face, saying, "Fool about a horse! Yes, but why the horse? why the horse?"

"Now, Vynie; now, Vynie," Pap said. Then she turned and went back into the house. We didn't go in. We could hear her, but she wasn't in the kitchen, and Pap told me to go around to the kitchen and see if she was fixing breakfast and then come down to the lot and tell him, and I did but she wasn't in the kitchen. So we set on the lot fence, and then we seen her coming down the hill from the house; she was dressed and had on her shawl and sunbonnet and her gloves, and she went into the stable without looking at us and we could hear her saddling the mule and Pap told me to go and ask her if she wanted him to help her and I did and she didn't answer and I saw her face that time and so I come back and set on the fence with Pap and we saw her ride out of the barn on the mule. She was leading Beasley Kemp's horse. It was still black in places where the rain had streaked it. "If it hadn't been for that durn rain, we might could have got shet of it," Pap said.

So we went to the house then, and I cooked breakfast and me and Pap et and then Pap taken a nap. He told me to watch for her from the gallery, but me and him neither never much thought to see her soon. We never seen her until next morning. We was cooking breakfast when we heard the wagon and I looked out and it was Odum Tull's wagon and Mammy was getting outen it and I come back to the kitchen jest before Pap left for the stable. "She's got the separator," I told Pap.

"I reckon it didn't happen to be our team in Odum's wagon," Pap said.

"No, sir," I says. So we saw her go into the house with the separator.

"I reckon likely she will wait to put on her old wrapper first," Pap said. "We ought to started breakfast sooner." It did take about that long. And then we could hear it. It made a good strong sound, like it would separate milk good and fast. Then it stopped. "It's too bad she ain't got but the one gallon," Pap said. "You go and look in the kitchen." So I went, and sho enough, she was cooking breakfast. But she wouldn't let us eat it in the kitchen. She handed it out the door to us.

"I am going to be busy in here and I don't aim to have you all in the way," she said. It was all right now. Her face was quiet now; it was jest busy. So me and Pap went out to the well and et, and then we heard the separator again.

"I didn't know it would go through but one time," Pap said.

"Maybe Uncle Ike showed her how to do it," I said.

"I reckon she is capable of running it right," Pap said. "Like she wants it to run, anyhow." Then it stopped, and me and Pap started down to the barn but she called us and made us bring the dishes to the kitchen door. Then we went down to the lot and set on the fence, only, like Pap said, without no stock to look at, it wasn't no comfort in it. "I reckon she jest rode up to that durn feller's tent and said, 'Here's your team. Now you git me my separator and git it quick; I got to ketch a ride back home,' " Pap said. And then after a while we heard it again, and that afternoon we walked up to Old Man Anse's to borrow a mule to finish the lower piece with, but he never had none to spare now. So he jest cussed around a while and then we come on back and set on the fence. And sure enough, pretty soon we could hear Mammy starting it up and it running strong and steady, like it would make the milk fly. "She is separating it again," Pap said. "It looks like she is fixing to get a heap of pleasure and comfort outen it."

Lizards in Jamshyd's Courtyard

I

Along toward mid-afternoon the wagons, the saddle horses and mules would begin to arrive. From both directions they came up the valley, each in its own slow dust, with a quality profound and dramatic, like the painted barge which they hauled across the stage in Ben Hur. They came, slow, deliberate, behind the bobbing mule ears, with upon their occupants—the men, the women, the young and the old—a quality not festive, since it was too profoundly undivergent, but of holiday, of escape and of immolation like that of people going to the theater to see tragedy, to turn from the broad valley highway into the old road, the peaceful and healing scar.

So peaceful the road was, so healed of the old scars of man's old restlessness, that almost with the turning the road appeared to have run immediately into another land, another world; the weathered wagons, the plow-galled mules, the men and the women in overalls and awkward gingham, into another time, another afternoon without time or name.

For almost sixty years the road had been unmarked by wheel or hoof, so that now, where the sand darkened into the shallow water of the branch, the recent thick marks of rims and iron shoes were as startling as shouts in a church. Beyond the branch, where there was now no trace of the vanished bridge, the road began to mount. It ran straight as a plumb line, bordered by a shaggy hedgerow of spaced cedars three and four feet thick now, the boughs locked and massed now, mounting to where, out of a jungle of formal cedars, a fading dilapidation of broad formal grounds and gardens, the gaunt and austere skeleton of a huge house lifted its broken roof and topless chimneys.

It was known as the Old Frenchman's place, after its builder, who had straightened the river bed and reclaimed four thousand acres of jungle bottom land for his slaves to raise cotton on—a huge square house which the anonymous builder's nameless and un-recorded successors had been pulling down for firewood since the Civil War, set in grounds laid out by an imported English architect a hundred years ago, upon a knoll overlooking the broad acres parceled now into small shiftless farms among his shiftless and illiterate heirs at large.

They did not even remember his name. They did not know for certain if his anonymous dust lay with that of his blood and of the progenitors of saxophone players in Harlem honky-tonks, beneath the weathered and illegible headstones on a smaller knoll four hundred yards away. All that was left of him was the old mark of the river bed, and the road, and the skeleton of the house, and the legend of the gold which his slaves buried somewhere when Grant passed through the land on his Vicksburg campaign; so that for sixty years three generations of sons and grandsons, lurking into the place at night and on foot, had turned under the original surface time and again, hunting for the gold and the silver, the money and the plate.

The place was owned now by Varner, who was the principal landowner of the community; he had bought it for the taxes and kept it under the same condition.

The fresh tracks did not go on as far as the house. They went on to where, beside and along the fence to what had once been a garden, the wagons themselves stood and drew up in turn and stopped. The women kept their seats on the splint chairs in the wagon beds. The men, though, descended and went to the fence and leaned there where the earlier arrivals already stood, watching the man who was digging in the garden. He was digging alone, spading the earth steadily down the slope toward the ditch, work-ing with a certain unflagging fury. He had been digging there for a week. His name was Henry Armstid.

They had been watching him for a week, coming by wagon and on horse and mule back for ten miles, to gather, with lips full of snuff, along the fence with the decorum of a formal reception, the rapt and static interest of a crowd watching a magician at a fair. On the first day, when the first rider descended and came to the fence, Armstid turned and ran at him with the lifted shovel, cursing in a harsh, light whisper, and drove the man away. But he had quit that, and he appeared to be not even aware of them as on the successive days they gathered along the fence, talking a little among themselves in sparse syllables, watching Armstid spade the surface of the garden steadily down the slope toward the ditch, working steadily back and forth across the hillside.

Along toward sundown they would begin to watch the road, until sometime before dark the last wagon would arrive. It contained a single occupant; a weathered and patched wagon drawn by two rabbit-like mules, creaking terrifically on crazy and dishing wheels. Then the spectators would stop talking and they would turn and watch quietly while the occupant, a woman in a gray shapeless garment and a faded sunbonnet, descended and lifted down a tin pail and approached the fence beyond which Armstid still had not looked up, had not faltered in his labor.

She would set the pail into the corner of the fence and then stand there for a time, motionless, the gray garment falling in rigid folds to her stained tennis shoes, her hands rolled together into a fold of the garment. She just stood there. She did not appear to look at Armstid, to look at anything. She was his wife; the pail she brought contained cold food.

She never stayed long. He never looked up when she came and they never spoke, and after a while she would return to the crazy wagon and get in and drive away. Then the spectators would begin to drift away, mounting their wagons and creaking also supper-ward, barnward, leaving Henry alone again, spading himself into the waxing twilight with the regularity of a mechanical toy and with something monstrous in his unflagging effort, as if the toy were too light for what it had been set to do, and too tightly wound.

In the long forenoons, squatting with their slow tobacco on the porch of Varner's store two miles away, or in halted wagons along the quiet roads and lanes, or in the fields or at the cabin doors about the slow, laborious land, they talked about it.

"Still at it, is he?"

"Sho. Still at it."

"Reckon he's aiming to kill himself there in that garden."

"Well, it won't be no loss to her."

"It's a fact. Save her a trip ever' day, toting him food."

"I notice she don't never stay long out there when she comes."

"She has to get back home to get supper for them chaps of theirn and to take care of the stock."

"I reckon she won't be sorry."

"Sho. It's a fact."

"That Flem Snopes. I'll declare."

"He's a sight, sho. Yes, sir. Wouldn't no other man but him done it."

"Couldn't no other man done it. Anybody might a-fooled Henry Armstid. But couldn't nobody but Flem a-fooled Suratt."

"That's a fact, that's a fact. Sho."

II

Suratt was a sewing-machine agent. He traveled the country in a buckboard, to the rear of which was attached a sheet-iron dog kennel painted to resemble a house. It had two painted windows on each side, in each of which a painted woman's face simpered above a painted sewing machine, and into the kennel a sewing machine neatly fitted.

On successive days and two counties apart, the buckboard and the sturdy mismatched team might be seen tethered in the nearest shade, and Suratt's affable, ready face and neat, tieless blue shirt one of the squatting group on the porch of a crossroads store. Or —and still squatting—among the women surrounded by laden clotheslines and blackened wash pots at springs and wells, or decorous in a splint chair in cabin dooryards, talking and listening. He had a regular itinerary, selling perhaps three machines a year, and the rest of the time trading in land and livestock, in secondhand farm tools and musical instruments, or whatever came to his hand. He had an affable and impenetrable volubility, a gift for anecdote and gossip. He never forgot names and he knew everyone, man, mule and dog, in fifty miles. He was believed to be well fixed.

His itinerary brought him to Varner's store every six weeks. One day he arrived two weeks ahead of schedule. While across the county he had bought, for twenty dollars, of a Northerner who was

establishing a ranch to breed native goats, a contract to sell the
Northerner a hundred goats which Suratt knew to be owned near
Varner's store, in the Frenchman's Bend country. Of the four or
five men squatting along the porch of the store Suratt made his
guarded inquiries, larding them skillfully into his anecdote, and got
the information which he wanted. The next morning he drove out
to the first goat owner.

"Wish you'd got here yesterday," the man said. "I done already
sold them goats."

"The devil you have," Suratt said. "Who to?"

"Flem Snopes."

"Flem Snopes?"

Snopes was the man who ran Varner's store. Varner himself—
he was a politician, a veterinary, a Methodist lay preacher—was
hardly ever seen about the store. Snopes had been running the store
for two or three years—a squat man who might have been any age
between twenty-five and fifty, with a round full face and dull eyes,
who sat all day, between the infrequent customers, in a tilted chair
in the door, chewing and whittling and saying no word. All that
was known of him was known on hearsay, and that not his own;
it was not even known what his exact relation to Varner and the
store was, whether clerk, partner or what. He had been sitting in
his usual chair, chewing and whittling, while Suratt was getting his
information about the goats.

"He come out here last night and bought all I had," the goat
owner said.

"You mean, he come out here after dark?"

"About nine o'clock it was. I reckon he couldn't leave the store
sooner."

"Sho," Suratt said. "I reckon not." The second goat owner lived
four miles away. Suratt drove it in thirty-two minutes. "I come out
to see if you sold your goats at ten o'clock last night, or was it
half-past ten?"

"Why, yes," the man said. "It was along about midnight when
Flem got here. How did you know?"

"I knowed I had the best team," Suratt said. "That's how.
Good-by."

"What's your hurry? I got a couple of shotes I might sell."

"Sho, now," Suratt said. "They wouldn't do me no good. Soon

as they belonged to me they would get elephant-sized overnight, and bust. This here country's too rich for me."

He did not call on the other goat owner at all. He returned to Jefferson without passing Varner's store. Three miles from town, a single goat balanced with somnolent precariousness upon the roof of a barn. Beside the fence a small boy in overalls watched Suratt draw up and stop.

"What did Flem Snopes offer you for that goat, bud?" Suratt said.

"Sir?" the boy said.

Suratt drove on. Three days later Snopes gave Suratt twenty-one dollars for the contract for which Suratt had paid twenty. He put the twenty dollars away in a tobacco sack and held the other dollar in his hand. He chucked it, caught it, the squatting men along the wall watching him. Snopes had sat again, whittling.

"Well, at least I ain't skunked." Suratt said. The others guffawed, save Snopes. Suratt looked about at them, bleak, sardonic, humorous too. Two children, a boy and a girl, mounted the steps, carrying a basket. Suratt gave them the dollar. "Here, chillens," he said. "Here's something Mr. Snopes sent you."

It was three years after that when Suratt learned that Snopes had bought the Old Frenchman place from Varner. Suratt knew the place. He knew it better than anyone suspected. Perhaps once a year he drove three or four miles out of his way to pass the place, entering from the back. Why he took that precaution he could not have said; he probably would have believed it was not to be seen doing something by which he had no expectation of gaining anything. Once a year he halted his buckboard before the house and sat in the buckboard to contemplate the austere skeleton somnolent in the summer sunlight, a little sinister, thinking of the generations of men who had dug for gold there, contemplating the inscrutable desolation of cedar and brier and crapemyrtle and calycanthus gone lush and wild, sensing out of the sunny and sinister silence the ancient spent and hopeful lusts, the optimism, the effluvium of the defunct greed and despair, the spent and secret nocturnal sweat left upon the place by men as quiet now as the man who had unwittingly left behind him a monument more enduring than any obituary either carved or cast. "It's bound to be there, somewhere," Suratt told himself. "It's bound to." Then he would drive on to Varner's store two miles away or to Jefferson twelve miles away, having carried away with him something of that ancient air, that old splendor, confusing it though he did with the fleshly gratifications, the wherewith to possess them, in his peasant's mind. "It's bound to. Folks wouldn't keep on digging for it if it wasn't there somewhere. It wouldn't be right to keep on letting them. No, sir."

When he learned that Snopes had bought the place, Suratt was eating dinner in Jefferson in the restaurant which he and his brother-in-law owned. He sat on a backless and friction-smooth stool, his elbows on the friction-smooth counter, eating steak and potatoes. He became motionless, humped forward in the attitude of eating, the laden knife blade arrested halfway to his mouth, his eyes profoundly concentrant. "If Flem Snopes bought that place, he knows something about it that even Will Varner never knowed. Flem Snopes wouldn't buy a nickel mousetrap withouten he knowed beforehand it would make him back a dime."

He reached Varner's store in mid-afternoon. Snopes was sitting in the chair, chewing, whittling minutely at a piece of soft pine. There was about him, his white shirt, his blue denim trousers braced thick and smooth, a profound inertia impervious to haste like that of a cow, to the necessity for haste like an idol. "That's what makes me so mad about it," Suratt told himself. "That he can set still and know what I got to work so hard to find out. That I got to work fast to learn it and ain't got time to work fast because I don't know if I got time to make a mistake by working fast. And him just setting still." But when he mounted the steps there was upon his brown, lean face its usual expression—alert, quizzical, pleasant, impenetrable and immediate. He greeted in rotation the men who squatted along the wall.

"Well, boys," he said, "I hear Flem has done bought himself a farm. You fixing to start a goat ranch of your own, Flem? Or maybe it's just a home for the folks you trims trading." Then he said, getting his sober and appreciative laugh while Snopes chewed slowly and trimmed minutely at the stick with the profound impenetrability of an idol or a cow, "Well, if Flem knowed any way to make anything offen that old place, he'd be too durn close-mouthed to tell himself about it."

III

The three men crouched in the weeds along the ditch at the foot of the garden. The shaggy slope rose before them in the darkness to the crest where the broken roof and topless chimneys of the house stood sharp against the sky. In one of the windows a single star showed, like a feeble candle set upon the ledge. They lay in the weeds, listening to the sigh and recover of an invisible shovel halfway up the garden slope.

"Didn't I tell you?" Suratt whispered. "Didn't I? Is there e'er a man or woman in this country that don't know Flem Snopes wouldn't pay a nickel for nothing if he didn't know all the time he would make a dime back?"

"How do I know it's Flem?" the second said. His name was Vernon Tull. He was a well-to-do bachelor.

"Ain't I watched him?" Suratt said. "Ain't I laid here in these weeds two nights now and watched him come out here and dig? Ain't I waited until he left, and crawled up there and found every place where he had done filled the hole up again and smoothed the dirt back to hide it?"

"But how do I know it's Flem?" Vernon said.

"If you knowed, would you believe it was something buried there?" Suratt whispered. The third man was Henry Armstid. He lay between them, glaring up the dark slope; they could feel him trembling like a dog. Now and then he cursed in a dry whisper. He lived on a small mortgaged farm, which he and his wife worked like two men. During one season, having lost one of his mules, he and his wife did the plowing, working day about in the second trace beside the other mule. The land was either poor land or they were poor managers. It made for them less than a bare living, which the wife eked out by weaving by the firelight after dark. She wove fancy objects of colored string saved from packages and of bits of cloth given her by the women in Jefferson, where, in a faded gingham wrapper and sunbonnet and tennis shoes, she peddled the objects from door to door on the market days. They had four children, all under six years of age, the youngest an infant in arms.

They lay there in the weeds, the darkness, hearing the shovel. After a while it ceased. "He's done found it," Henry said. He surged suddenly between them. They grasped his arms.

"Stop!" Suratt whispered. "Stop! Help hold him, Vernon." They held him until he ceased and lay again between them, rigid, glaring, cursing. "He ain't found it yet." Suratt whispered. "He knows it's there somewhere; he's done found the paper maybe that tells. But he's got to hunt for it same as we will. He knows it's in that 'ere garden, but he's got to hunt for it same as us. Ain't we done watched him?" They spoke in hissing whispers, rigid, panting, glaring up the starlit slope.

"How do I know it's Flem?" Vernon said.

"Just watch, that's all," Suratt whispered. They crouched; the shadowy, deliberate motion of the digger mounted the slope. It was the sound made by a lazy man rather than by a cautious one. Suratt gripped Henry. "Watch, now!" he whispered. They breathed with hissing exhalations, in passionate and dying sighs. Then the man came into sight. For a moment he came into relief against the sky upon the crest of the knoll, as though he had paused there for an instant. "There!" Suratt whispered. "Ain't that Flem Snopes? Do you believe now?"

Vernon drew his breath quietly in like a man preparing to sleep. "It's a fact," he said. He spoke quietly, soberly. "It's Flem."

"Do you believe now?" Suratt whispered. "Do you? Do you believe now?" Between them, Henry lay cursing in a dry whisper. Beneath Vernon's and Suratt's arms his arms felt like wire cables vibrating faintly.

"All we got to do," Suratt said, "is to find where it's at tomorrow night, and then get it."

"Tomorrow night, hell!" Henry said. "Let's get up there now and find it. That's what we got to do. Before he—"

They argued with him, violent, sibilant, expostulant. They held him flat on the ground between them, cursing. "We got to find where it is the first time and dig it up," Suratt said. "We got to get Uncle Dick. Can't you see that? Can't you see we got to find it the first time? That we can't be caught looking?"

"We got to get Uncle Dick," Vernon said. "Hush, Henry. Hush, now."

They returned the next night with Uncle Dick. When Vernon and Suratt, carrying the second shovel and the pick and half carrying Uncle Dick between them, climbed up out of the ditch at the foot of the garden, they could hear Henry already digging. After concealing the buckboard in the branch bottom they had had to run to keep even within hearing of Henry, and so Uncle Dick could not yet stand alone. Yet they released him at once, whereupon he sank to the ground at their feet, from where his invisible breathing rose in reedy gasps, and as one Vernon and Suratt glared into the darkness toward the hushed, furious sound of Henry's shovel.

"We got to make him quit until Uncle Dick's ready," Suratt said. They ran toward the sound, shoulder to shoulder in the stumbling dark. Suratt spoke to Henry. Henry did not cease to dig. Suratt grasped at the shovel. Henry whirled, the shovel raised like an ax; they glared at each other, their faces strained with sleeplessness and weariness and lust. It was Suratt's fourth night without having removed his clothes; Vernon's and Henry's second.

"Touch it," Henry whispered. "Touch it."

"Wait, Henry," Suratt said. "Let Uncle Dick find where it's at."

"Get away," Henry said. "I warn you. Get outen my hole."

Uncle Dick was sitting up when Suratt and Vernon returned running and plunged down beside him and began to scrabble in the dark weeds for the second shovel. Suratt found the pick and learned the blade with his hand in one motion and flung it behind him into the darkness again, and plunged down again just as Vernon found the shovel. They struggled for it, their breathing harsh, mute, repressed. "Leave go," Suratt whispered. "Leave go." They clutched the shovel between them. Out of the darkness came the unflagging sound of Henry's digging.

"Wait," Uncle Dick said. He got stiffly to his feet—a shriveled little old man in a filthy frock coat, with a long white beard. Between sunup and sundown Suratt, seventy-two hours without having removed his clothes, drove thirty miles to fetch him from where he lived alone in a mud-daubed hut in a cane swamp. He had no other name, and he antedated all who knew him. He made and sold nostrums and charms, and they said that he ate not only frogs and snakes but bugs as well—anything that he could catch. "Wait," he said in a reedy, quavering voice. "Ther air anger in the yearth. Ye must make that 'ere un quit a-bruisin' hit, so the Lord kin show whar hit's hid at."

"That's so," Suratt said. "It won't work unless the ground is quiet. I forgot."

When they approached, Henry stood erect in his pit and threatened them with the shovel and cursed them, but Uncle Dick walked up and touched him.

"Ye kin dig and ye kin dig, young man," he said. "Fer what's rendered to the yearth, the yearth will keep withouten the will of the Lord air revealed."

Henry desisted then and lowered the shovel. Uncle Dick drove them back to the ditch. From his coat he produced a forked peach branch, from the end of which, dangling on a bit of string, swung an empty brass cartridge containing a gold-filled human tooth. He held them there for five minutes, stooping now and then to lay his hand flat on the ground. Then with the three of them at his heels —Henry rigid, silent; Suratt and Vernon speaking now and then in short, hissing whispers—he went to the fence corner and grasped the two prongs of the branch in his hands and stood there for a moment, muttering to himself.

They moved like a procession, with something at once outrageously pagan and orthodoxly funereal about them, working slowly back and forth across the garden, mounting the slope in overlapping traverses. Near the spot where they had watched the man digging last night Uncle Dick began to slow. The others clumped at his back, breathing with thick, tense breaths. "Tech my elbers," Uncle Dick said. They did so. Inside his sleeves his arms —arms thin and frail and dead as rotten wood—were jerking a little. Henry began to curse, pointless. Uncle Dick stopped; when they jarred into him they felt his whole thin body straining. Suratt made a sound with his mouth and touched the twig and found it curved into a rigid down-pointing bar, the string taut as wire. Uncle Dick staggered; his arms sprang free. The twig lay dead at his feet until Henry, digging furiously with his bare hands, flung it away. He was still cursing. He was cursing the ground, the earth.

They got the tools and began to dig, swiftly, hurling the dirt aside, while Uncle Dick, shapeless in his shapeless garment, appeared to muse upon them with detached interest. Suddenly the three of them became utterly still in their attitudes, then they leaped into the hole and struggled silently over something.

"Stop it!" Suratt whispered. "Stop it! Ain't we all three pardners alike?"

But Henry clung to the object and at last Vernon and Suratt

desisted and stood away. Henry was half stooped, clutching the object to his middle, glaring at them.

"Let him keep it," Vernon said. "Don't you know that ain't all? Come here, Uncle Dick."

Uncle Dick was motionless behind them. His head was turned toward the ditch, toward where they had hidden. "What?" Suratt whispered. They were all three motionless, rigid, stooped a little. "Do you see something? Is it somebody hiding yonder?"

"I feel four bloods lust-running," Uncle Dick said. "Hit's four sets of blood here lusting for dross."

They crouched, rigid. "Well, ain't it four of us right here?" Vernon said.

"Uncle Dick don't care nothing about money," Suratt said. "If it's somebody hiding there—"

They were running then, the tools clutched, plunging and stumbling down the slope.

"Kill him," Henry said. "Watch every bush and kill him."

"No," Suratt said, "catch him first."

They halted at the ditch bank. They could hear Henry beating along the ditch. But they found nothing.

"Maybe Uncle Dick never seen nobody," Vernon said.

"He's gone, anyway," Suratt said. "Maybe it—" He ceased. He and Vernon stared at each other; above their held breath they heard the horse. It was going at a gallop, the sound clear but faint, diminishing. Then it ceased. They stared at each other in the darkness, across their breath. "That means we got till daylight," Suratt said. "Come on."

Twice more Uncle Dick's twig sprang and bent; twice more they exhumed small bulging canvas sacks solid and unmistakable even in the dark.

"Now," Suratt said, "we got a hole apiece and till daylight to do it in. Dig, boys."

When the east began to gray they had found nothing more. At last they made Henry see reason and quit, and they filled up the holes and removed the traces of their labor. They opened the bags in the gray light. Vernon's and Suratt's contained each twenty-five silver dollars. Henry wouldn't tell what his contained. He crouched over it some distance away, his back toward them. Vernon and Suratt closed the sacks and looked at each other quietly, their blood cool now with weariness, with sleeplessness and fatigue.

"We got to buy it," Suratt said. "We got to buy it tomorrow."

"You mean today," Vernon said. Beneath a tree, in the wan light, Uncle Dick lay sleeping. He slept quiet as a child, not even snoring.

"That's right," Suratt said. "It's today now."

IV

When at noon the next day Suratt drove up to the store, there was a stranger squatting among the others on the porch. His name was Eustace Grimm, from the adjoining county—a youngish man, also in overalls, with a snuff stick in his mouth. Snopes sat in the tilted chair in the doorway, whittling.

Suratt descended and tethered his team. "Morning, gentlemen," he said.

They replied. "Be durn if you don't look like you ain't been to bed in a week, Suratt," one said. "What you up to now? Lon Quick said his boy seen your team hid out in the bottom below Armstid's two mornings ago, but I told him I didn't reckon them horses had done nothing to hide from. I wasn't so sho about you, I told him."

Suratt joined the laugh readily. "I reckon not. I reckon I'm still smart enough to not be caught by nobody around here except Flem Snopes. 'Course I take a back seat for Flem." He mounted the steps. Snopes had not looked up. Suratt looked briefly from face to face, his gaze pausing for an instant at Eustace Grimm, then going on. "To tell the truth, I am getting pretty durn tired of traipsing all over the country to make a living. Be durn if I ain't sometimes a good mind to buy me a piece of land and settle down like folks."

"You might buy that Old What-you-call-it place from Flem," Grimm said. He was watching Suratt. Suratt looked at him. When he spoke his tone was immediate, far superior to merely casual.

"That's a fact. I might do that." He looked at Grimm. "What you doing way up here, Eustace? Ain't you strayed a right smart?"

"I come up to see if I couldn't trade Flem outen—"

Snopes spoke. His voice was not cold so much as utterly devoid of any inflection. "Reckon you better get on to dinner, Eustace," he said. "Mrs. Littlejohn'll be ringing the bell soon. She don't like to be kept waiting."

Grimm looked at Snopes, his mouth still slacked for talk. He rose. Suratt looked at Snopes, too, who had not raised his head from his whittling. Suratt looked at Grimm again. Grimm had closed his mouth. He was moving toward the steps.

"If it's goats you're aiming to trade Flem for," Suratt said, "I can warn you to look out."

The others laughed, sober, appreciative. Grimm descended the steps. "That depends on how smart the fellow is that trades with Flem," he said. "I reckon Flem don't only need goats—"

"Tell her I'll be there in ten minutes," Snopes said. Again Grimm paused, looking back, his mouth slacked for speech; again he closed it.

"All right," he said. He went on. Suratt watched him. Then he looked at Snopes.

"Flem," he said, "you sholy ain't going to unload that Old Frenchman place on a poor fellow like Eustace Grimm? Boys, we hadn't ought to stand for it. I reckon Eustace has worked pretty hard for every cent he's got, and he won't be no match for Flem."

Snopes whittled with tedious deliberation, his jaw thrusting steadily.

"Of course, a smart fellow like Flem might make something offen that old place, but Eustace now— Let me tell you what I heard about one of them Grimms down there last month; it might be Eustace they tell it on." He achieved his anecdote skillfully above the guffaws. When he had finished it Snopes rose, putting his knife away. He crossed the porch, waddling thickly in his denim trousers braced neatly over his white shirt, and descended the steps. Suratt watched him.

"If it's that time, I reckon I better move too," Suratt said. "Might have to go into town this evening." He descended the steps. Snopes had gone on. "Here, Flem," Suratt said. "I'm going past Littlejohn's. I'll give you a free ride that far. Won't cost you a cent."

Again the squatting men on the porch guffawed, watching Suratt and Snopes like four or five boys twelve years old might watch and listen to two boys fourteen years old. Snopes stopped. He did not look back. He stood there, chewing with steady unhaste, until Suratt swung the buckboard up and cramped the wheel; then he got in. They drove on.

"So you done sold that old place," Suratt said. They drove at a walk. Mrs. Littlejohn's house was a quarter of a mile down the road. In the middle distance Eustace Grimm walked, his back toward them. "That 'ere Frenchman place," Suratt said.

Snopes spat over the wheel. "Dickering," he said.

"Oh," Suratt said. "Can't get Eustace to close with you?" They drove on. "What's Eustace want with that place? I thought his folks owned a right smart of land down yonder."

"Heard so," Snopes said.

They drove on. Grimm's figure was a little nearer. Suratt drew the team down to a slower walk. "Well, if a man just give what that old place is worth, I reckon most anybody could buy it." They drove on. "Still, for a man that just wanted a place to settle down, a fellow that depended on outside work for his living—"

Snopes spat over the wheel.

"Yes, sir," Suratt said. "For a fellow that just aimed to fix him up a home, say. Like me. A fellow like that might give you two hundred for it. Just the house and garden and orchard, say." The red dust coiled slow beneath the slow hoofs and wheels. Grimm had almost reached Mrs. Littlejohn's gate. "What would you take for that much of it?"

"Don't aim to sell unless I sell the whole place," Snopes said. "Ain't in no rush to sell that."

"Yes?" Suratt said. "What was you asking Eustace Grimm for the whole place?"

"Ain't asked him nothing yet. Just listened to him."

"Well, what would you ask me, say?"

"Three thousand," Snopes said.

"Three which?" Suratt said. He laughed, slapping his leg. He laughed for some time. "If you ain't a sight. Three thousand." They drove on. Grimm had reached Mrs. Littlejohn's gate. Suratt quit laughing. "Well, I hope you get it. If Eustace can't quite meet that, I might could find you a buyer at three hundred, if you get in a tight to sell."

"Ain't in no rush to sell," Snopes said. "I'll get out here." Grimm had paused at the gate. He was looking back at them from beneath his hat brim, with a gaze at once attentive and veiled.

That afternoon Suratt, Vernon and Henry made Snopes three joint notes for one thousand dollars each. Vernon was good for his.

Suratt gave a lien on his half of the restaurant which he and his brother-in-law owned in Jefferson. Henry gave a second mortgage on his farm and a chattel mortgage on his stock and fixtures, including a new stove which his wife had bought with her weaving money, and a mile of barbed-wire fence.

They reached their new property just before sundown. When they arrived a wagon, the mules still—or already—in the traces, stood on the lawn, and then Eustace Grimm came around the corner of the house and stood there, watching them. Henry ordered him off the place. He got into the wagon and they began to dig at once, though it was still light. They dug for some little time before they found that Grimm had not yet departed. He was sitting in the wagon in the road, watching them across the fence, until Henry rushed at him with his shovel. Then he drove on.

Vernon and Suratt had stopped also. Vernon watched Grimm's back as he rattled on down the road in the slow wagon. "Ain't he some kin to them Snopeses?" Vernon said. "A in-law or something?"

"What?" Suratt said. They watched the wagon disappear in the dusk. "I didn't know that."

"Come on," Vernon said. "Henry's getting ahead of us." They began to dig again. It was dark soon, but they could still hear one another.

They dug steadily for two nights, two brief summer darks broken by the daylight intervals of fitful sleep on the bare floor of their house, where even to the ground floor the sunlight reached in patchy splashes at noon. In the sad light of the third dawn Suratt stopped and straightened his back. Twenty feet away, Henry, in his pit, moved up and down with the regularity of an automaton. He was waist-deep, as though he were digging himself tirelessly into that earth whose born thrall he was; as though he had been severed at the waist, the dead torso laboring on in measured stoop and recover, not knowing that it was dead. They had completely turned under the entire surface of the garden, and standing in the dark fresh loam, his muscles flinching and jerking with fatigue, Suratt watched Henry; and then he found that Vernon was watching him quietly in turn. Suratt laid his shovel carefully down and went to where Vernon stood. They stood looking at each other while the dawn grayed upon their gaunt faces. When they spoke their voices were quiet.

"You looked close at that money of yours yet?" Suratt said.

Vernon didn't answer at once. They watched Henry as he rose and fell behind his pick. "I don't reckon I dared to," Vernon said. He laid his tool carefully on the earth also, and together he and Suratt turned and went to the house. It was still dark in the house, so they lit the lantern and took the two sacks from the hiding place in a chimney and set the lantern on the floor.

"I reckon we'd ought to thought it wouldn't no cloth sack—" Suratt said.

"Sho," Vernon said. "I reckon you can say that and leave off about the sack."

They squatted, the lantern between them, opening the sacks. "Bet you a dollar I beat you," Suratt said.

"All right," Vernon said. They laid two coins aside and examined the others, one by one. Then they looked at each other. "1901," Vernon said. "What you got?"

"1896," Suratt said. "I beat you."

"Yes," Vernon said. "You beat me." Suratt took up the wager and they hid the money again and blew the lantern out. It was lighter now, and they could see Henry quite well as he worked in his thigh-deep trench. Soon the sun; already three buzzards soared in it high against the yellow blue.

Henry did not look up at them when they reached him. "Henry," Suratt said. Henry did not pause. "When was your oldest dollar minted, Henry?" Suratt said. Henry did not falter. Suratt came nearer and touched his shoulder. "Henry," he said.

Henry whirled, raising the shovel, the blade turned edgewise, glinting a thin line of steel-colored dawn such as an ax would have.

"Git outen my hole," he said. "Git outen hit."

The Hound

To Cotton the shot was the loudest thing he had ever heard in his life. It was too loud to be heard all at once. It continued to build up about the thicket, the dim, faint road, long after the hammerlike blow of the ten-gage shotgun had shocked into his shoulder and long after the smoke of the black powder with which it was charged had dissolved, and after the maddened horse had whirled twice and then turned galloping, diminishing, the empty stirrups clashing against the empty saddle.

It made too much noise. It was outrageous, unbelievable—a gun which he had owned for twenty years. It stunned him with amazed outrage, seeming to press him down into the thicket, so that when he could make the second shot, it was too late and the hound too was gone.

Then he wanted to run. He had expected that. He had coached himself the night before. "Right after it you'll want to run," he told himself. "But you can't run. You got to finish it. You got to clean it up. It will be hard, but you got to do it. You got to set there in the bushes and shut your eyes and count slow until you can make to finish it."

He did that. He laid the gun down and sat where he had lain behind the log. His eyes were closed. He counted slowly, until he had stopped shaking and until the sound of the gun and the echo of the galloping horse had died out of his ears. He had chosen his place well. It was a quiet road, little used, marked not once in three months save by that departed horse; a short cut between the house where the owner of the horse lived and Varner's store; a quiet, fading, grass-grown trace along the edge of the river bottom, empty save for the two of them, the one squatting in the bushes, the other lying on his face in the road.

Cotton was a bachelor. He lived in a chinked log cabin floored with clay on the edge of the bottom, four miles away. It was dusk when he reached home. In the well-house at the back he drew water and washed his shoes. They were not muddier than usual, and he did not wear them save in severe weather, but he washed them carefully. Then he cleaned the shotgun and washed it too, barrel and stock; why, he could not have said, since he had never heard of finger prints, and immediately afterward he picked up the gun again and carried it into the house and put it away. He kept firewood, a handful of charred pine knots, in the chimney corner. He built a fire on the clay hearth and cooked his supper and ate and went to bed. He slept on a quilt pallet on the floor; he went to bed by barring the door and removing his overalls and lying down. It was dark after the fire burned out; he lay in the darkness. He thought about nothing at all save that he did not expect to sleep. He felt no triumph, vindication, nothing. He just lay there, thinking about nothing at all, even when he began to hear the dog. Usually at night he would hear dogs, single dogs ranging alone in the bottom, or coon- or cat-hunting packs. Having nothing else to do, his life, his heredity, and his heritage centered within a five-mile radius of Varner's store. He knew almost any dog he would hear by its voice, as he knew almost any man he would hear by his voice. He knew this dog's voice. It and the galloping horse with the flapping stirrups and the owner of the horse had been inseparable: where he saw one of them, the other two would not be far away —a lean, rangy brute that charged savagely at anyone who approached its master's house, with something of the master's certitude and overbearance; and to-day was not the first time he had tried to kill it, though only now did he know why he had not gone through with it. "I never knowed my own luck," he said to himself, lying on the pallet. "I never knowed. If I had went ahead and killed it, killed the dog. . . ."

He was still not triumphant. It was too soon yet to be proud, vindicated. It was too soon. It had to do with death. He did not believe that a man could pick up and move that irrevocable distance at a moment's notice. He had completely forgotten about the body. So he lay with his gaunt, underfed body empty with waiting, thinking of nothing at all, listening to the dog. The cries came at measured intervals, timbrous, sourceless, with the sad, peaceful, abject quality of a single hound in the darkness, when suddenly he found himself sitting bolt upright on the pallet.

"Nigger talk," he said. He had heard (he had never known a negro himself, because of the antipathy, the economic jealousy, between his kind and negroes) how negroes claimed that a dog would howl at the recent grave of its master. "Hit's nigger talk," he said all the time he was putting on his overalls and his recently cleaned shoes. He opened the door. From the dark river bottom below the hill on which the cabin sat the howling of the dog came, bell-like and mournful. From a nail just inside the door he took down a coiled plowline and descended the slope.

Against the dark wall of the jungle fireflies winked and drifted; from beyond the black wall came the booming and grunting of frogs. When he entered the timber he could not see his own hand. The footing was treacherous with slime and creepers and bramble. They possessed the perversity of inanimate things, seeming to spring out of the darkness and clutch him with spiky tentacles. From the musing impenetrability ahead the voice of the hound came steadily. He followed the sound, muddy again; the air was chill, yet he was sweating. He was quite near the sound. The hound ceased. He plunged forward, his teeth drying under his dry lip, his hands clawed and blind, toward the ceased sound, the faint phosphorescent glare of the dog's eyes. The eyes vanished. He stopped, panting, stooped, the plowline in his hand, looking for the eyes. He cursed the dog, his voice a dry whisper. He could hear silence but nothing else.

He crawled on hands and knees, telling where he was by the shape of the trees on the sky. After a time, the brambles raking and slashing at his face, he found a shallow ditch. It was rank with rotted leaves; he waded ankle-deep in the pitch darkness, in something not earth and not water, his elbow crooked before his face. He stumbled upon something; an object with a slack feel. When he touched it, something gave a choked, infantlike cry, and he started back, hearing the creature scuttle away. "Just a possum," he said. "Hit was just a possum."

He wiped his hands on his flanks in order to pick up the shoulders. His flanks were foul with slime. He wiped his hands on his shirt, across his breast, then he picked up the shoulders. He walked backward, dragging it. From time to time he would stop and wipe his hands on his shirt. He stopped beside a tree, a rotting cypress shell, topless, about ten feet tall. He had put the coiled plowline into his bosom. He knotted it about the body and climbed the stump. The top was open, rotted out. He was not a large man, not as large as the body, yet he hauled it up to him hand over hand, bumping and scraping it along the stump, until it lay across the lip like a half-filled meal sack. The knot in the rope had slipped tight. At last he took out his knife and cut the rope and tumbled the body into the hollow stump.

It didn't fall far. He shoved at it, feeling around it with his hands for the obstruction; he tied the rope about the stub of a limb and held the end of it in his hands and stood on the body and began to jump up and down upon it, whereupon it fled suddenly beneath him and left him dangling on the rope.

He tried to climb the rope, rasping off with his knuckles the rotten fiber, a faint, damp powder of decay like snuff in his nostrils. He heard the stub about which the rope was tied crack and felt it begin to give. He leaped upward from nothing, scrabbling at the rotten wood, and got one hand over the edge. The wood crumbled beneath his fingers; he climbed perpetually without an inch of gain, his mouth cracked upon his teeth, his eyes glaring at the sky.

The wood stopped crumbling. He dangled by his hands, breathing. He drew himself up and straddled the edge. He sat there for a while. Then he climbed down and leaned against the hollow trunk.

When he reached his cabin he was tired, spent. He had never been so tired. He stopped at the door. Fireflies still blew along the dark band of timber, and owls hooted and the frogs still boomed and grunted. "I ain't never been so tired," he said, leaning against the house, the wall which he had built log by log. "Like ever thing had got outen hand. Climbing that stump, and the noise that shot made. Like I had got to be somebody else without knowing it, in a place where noise was louder, climbing harder to climb, without knowing it." He went to bed. He took off the muddy shoes, the overalls, and lay down; it was late then. He could tell by a summer star that came into the square window at two o'clock and after.

Then, as if it had waited for him to get settled and comfortable, the hound began to howl again. Lying in the dark, he heard the first cry come up from the river bottom, mournful, timbrous, profound.

Five men in overalls squatted against the wall of Varner's store. Cotton made the sixth. He sat on the top step, his back against a gnawed post which supported the wooden awning of the veranda. The seventh man sat in the single splint chair; a fat, slow man in denim trousers and a collarless white shirt, smoking a cob pipe. He was past middle-age. He was sheriff of the county. The man about whom they were talking was named Houston.

"He hadn't no reason to run off," one said. "To disappear. To send his horse back home with a empty saddle. He hadn't no reason. Owning his own land, his house. Making a good crop ever year. He was as well-fixed as ere a man in the county. A bachelor too. He hadn't no reason to disappear. You can mark it. He never run. I don't know what; but Houston never run."

"I don't know," a second said. "You can't tell what a man has got in his mind. Houston might a had reason that we don't know, for making it look like something had happened to him. For clearing outen the country and leaving it to look like something had happened to him. It's been done before. Folks before him has had reason to light out for Texas with a changed name."

Cotton sat a little below their eyes, his face lowered beneath his worn, stained, shabby hat. He was whittling at a stick, a piece of pine board.

"But a fellow can't disappear without leaving no trace," a third said. "Can he, Sheriff?"

"Well, I don't know," the Sheriff said. He removed the cob pipe and spat neatly across the porch into the dust. "You can't tell what a man will do when he's pinched. Except it will be something you never thought of. Never counted on. But if you can find just what pinched him you can pretty well tell what he done."

"Houston was smart enough to do ere a thing he taken a notion to," the second said. "If he'd wanted to disappear, I reckon we'd a known about what we know now."

"And what's that?" the third said.

"Nothing," the second said.

"That's a fact," the first said. "Houston was a secret man."

"He wasn't the only secret man around here," a fourth said. To Cotton it sounded sudden, since the fourth man had said no word before. He sat against the post, his hat slanted forward so that his face was invisible, believing that he could feel their eyes. He watched the sliver peel slow and smooth from the stick, ahead of his worn knife-blade. "I got to say something," he told himself.

"He warn't no smarter than nobody else," he said. Then he wished he had not spoken. He could see their feet beneath his hat-brim. He trimmed the stick, watching the knife, the steady sliver. "It's got to trim off smooth," he told himself. "It don't dast to break." He was talking; he could hear his voice: "Swelling around like he was the biggest man in the county. Setting that ere dog on folks' stock." He believed that he could feel their eyes, watching their feet, watching the sliver trim smooth and thin and unhurried beneath the knife blade. Suddenly he thought about the gun, the loud crash, the jarring shock. "Maybe I'll have to kill them all," he said to himself—a mild man in worn overalls, with a gaunt face and lack-luster eyes like a sick man, whittling a stick with a thin hand, thinking about killing them. "Not them; just the words, the talk." But the talk was familiar, the intonation, the gestures; but so was Houston. He had known Houston all his life: that prosperous and overbearing man. "With a dog," Cotton said, watching the knife return and bite into another sliver. "A dog that et better than me. I work, and eat worse than his dog. If I had been his dog, I would not have . . . We're better off without him," he said, blurted. He could feel their eyes, sober, intent.

"He always did rile Ernest," the first said.

"He taken advantage of me," Cotton said, watching the infallible knife. "He taken advantage of ever man he could."

"He was a overbearing man," the Sheriff said.

Cotton believed that they were still watching him, hidden behind their detached voices.

"Smart, though," the third said.

"He wasn't smart enough to win that suit against Ernest over that hog."

"That's so. How much did Ernest get outen that lawing? He ain't never told, has he?"

Cotton believed that they knew how much he had got from the

suit. The hog had come into his lot one October. He penned it up; he tried by inquiry to find the owner. But none claimed it until he had wintered it on his corn. In the spring Houston claimed the hog. They went to court. Houston was awarded the hog, though he was assessed a sum for the wintering of it, and one dollar as pound-fee for a stray. "I reckon that's Ernest's business," the Sheriff said after a time.

Again Cotton heard himself talking, blurting. "It was a dollar," he said, watching his knuckles whiten about the knife handle. "One dollar." He was trying to make his mouth stop talking. "After all I taken offen him. . . ."

"Juries does queer things," the Sheriff said, "in little matters. But in big matters they're mostly right."

Cotton whittled, steady and deliberate. "At first you'll want to run," he told himself. "But you got to finish it. You got to count a hundred, if it needs, and finish it."

"I heard that dog again last night," the third said.

"You did?" the Sheriff said.

"It ain't been home since the day the horse come in with the saddle empty," the first said.

"It's out hunting, I reckon," the Sheriff said. "It'll come in when it gets hungry."

Cotton trimmed at the stick. He did not move.

"Niggers claim a hound'll howl till a dead body's found," the second said.

"I've heard that," the Sheriff said. After a time a car came up and the Sheriff got into it. The car was driven by a deputy. "We'll be late for supper," the Sheriff said. The car mounted the hill; the sound died away. It was getting toward sundown.

"He ain't much bothered," the third said.

"Why should he be?" the first said. "After all, a man can leave his house and go on a trip without telling everybody."

"Looks like he'd a unsaddled that mare, though," the second said. "And there's something the matter with that dog. It ain't been home since, and it ain't treed. I been hearing it ever night. It ain't treed. It's howling. It ain't been home since Tuesday. And that was the day Houston rid away from the store here on that mare."

Cotton was the last one to leave the store. It was after dark when he reached home. He ate some cold bread and loaded the shotgun and sat beside the open door until the hound began to howl. Then he descended the hill and entered the bottom.

The dog's voice guided him; after a while it ceased, and he saw its eyes. They were now motionless; in the red glare of the explosion he saw the beast entire in sharp relief. He saw it in the act of leaping into the ensuing welter of darkness; he heard the thud of its body. But he couldn't find it. He looked carefully, quartering back and forth, stopping to listen. But he had seen the shot strike it and hurl it backward, and he turned aside for about a hundred yards in the pitch darkness and came to a slough. He flung the shotgun into it, hearing the sluggish splash, watching the vague water break and recover, until the last ripple died. He went home and to bed.

He didn't go to sleep though, although he knew he would not hear the dog. "It's dead," he told himself, lying on his quilt pallet in the dark. "I saw the bullets knock it down. I could count the shot. The dog is dead." But still he did not sleep. He did not need sleep; he did not feel tired or stale in the mornings, though he knew it was not the dog. He knew he would not hear the dog again, and that sleep had nothing to do with the dog. So he took to spending the nights sitting up in a chair in the door, watching the fireflies and listening to the frogs and the owls.

He entered Varner's store. It was in mid-afternoon; the porch was empty, save for the clerk, whose name was Snopes. "Been looking for you for two-three days," Snopes said. "Come inside."

Cotton entered. The store smelled of cheese and leather and new earth. Snopes went behind the counter and reached from under the counter a shotgun. It was caked with mud. "This is yourn, ain't it?" Snopes said. "Vernon Tull said it was. A nigger squirl hunter found it in a slough."

Cotton came to the counter and looked at the gun. He did not touch it; he just looked at it. "It ain't mine," he said.

"Ain't nobody around here got one of them old Hadley ten-gages except you," Snopes said. "Tull says it's yourn."

"It ain't none of mine," Cotton said. "I got one like it. But mine's to home."

Snopes lifted the gun. He breeched it. "It had one empty and one load in it," he said. "Who you reckon it belongs to?"

"I don't know," Cotton said. "Mine's to home." He had come to purchase food. He bought it: crackers, cheese, a tin of sardines. It was not dark when he reached home, yet he opened the sardines and ate his supper. When he lay down he did not even remove his overalls. It was as though he waited for something, stayed dressed to move and go at once. He was still waiting for whatever it was when the window turned gray and then yellow and then blue; when, framed by the square window, he saw against the fresh morning a single soaring speck. By sunrise there were three of them, and then seven.

All that day he watched them gather, wheeling and wheeling, drawing their concentric black circles, watching the lower ones wheel down and down and disappear below the trees. He thought it was the dog. "They'll be through by noon," he said. "It wasn't a big dog."

When noon came they had not gone away; there were still more of them, while still the lower ones dropped down and disappeared below the trees. He watched them until dark came, until they went away, flapping singly and sluggishly up from beyond the trees. "I got to eat," he said. "With the work I got to do to-night." He went to the hearth and knelt and took up a pine knot, and he was kneeling, nursing a match into flame, when he heard the hound again; the cry deep, timbrous, unmistakable, and sad. He cooked his supper and ate.

With his axe in his hand he descended through his meager corn patch. The cries of the hound could have guided him, but he did not need it. He had not reached the bottom before he believed that his nose was guiding him. The dog still howled. He paid it no attention, until the beast sensed him and ceased, as it had done before; again he saw its eyes. He paid no attention to them. He went to the hollow cypress trunk and swung his axe into it, the axe sinking helve-deep into the rotten wood. While he was tugging at it something flowed silent and savage out of the darkness behind him and struck him a slashing blow. The axe had just come free; he fell with the axe in his hand, feeling the hot reek of the dog's breath on his face and hearing the click of its teeth as he struck it down with his free hand. It leaped again; he saw its eyes now. He was on his knees, the axe raised in both hands now. He swung it, hitting nothing, feeling nothing; he saw the dog's eyes, crouched.

He rushed at the eyes; they vanished. He waited a moment, but heard nothing. He returned to the tree.

At the first stroke of the axe the dog sprang at him again. He was expecting it, so he whirled and struck with the axe at the two eyes and felt the axe strike something and whirl from his hands. He heard the dog whimper, he could hear it crawling away. On his hands and knees he hunted for the axe until he found it.

He began to chop at the base of the stump, stopping between blows to listen. But he heard nothing, saw nothing. Overhead the stars were swinging slowly past; he saw the one that looked into his window at two o'clock. He began to chop steadily at the base of the stump.

The wood was rotten; the axe sank helve-deep at each stroke, as into sand or mud; suddenly Cotton knew that it was not imagination he smelled. He dropped the axe and began to tear at the rotten wood with his hands. The hound was beside him, whimpering; he did not know it was there, not even when it thrust its head into the opening, crowding against him, howling.

"Git away," he said, still without being conscious that it was the dog. He dragged at the body, feeling it slough upon its own bones, as though it were too large for itself; he turned his face away, his teeth glared, his breath furious and outraged and restrained. He could feel the dog surge against his legs, its head in the orifice, howling.

When the body came free, Cotton went over backward. He lay on his back on the wet ground, looking up at a faint patch of starry sky. "I ain't never been so tired," he said. The dog was howling, with an abject steadiness. "Shut up," Cotton said. "Hush. Hush." The dog didn't hush. "It'll be daylight soon," Cotton said to himself. "I got to get up."

He got up and kicked at the dog. It moved away, but when he stooped and took hold of the legs and began to back away, the dog was there again, moaning to itself. When he would stop to rest, the dog would howl again; again he kicked at it. Then it began to be dawn, the trees coming spectral and vast out of the miasmic darkness. He could see the dog plainly. It was gaunt, thin, with a long bloody gash across its face. "I'll have to get shut of you," he said. Watching the dog, he stooped and found a stick. It was rotten, foul with slime. He clutched it. When the hound lifted its muzzle to howl, he struck. The dog whirled; there was a long fresh scar running from shoulder to flank. It leaped at him, without a sound; he struck again. The stick took it fair between the eyes. He picked up the ankles and tried to run.

It was almost light. When he broke through the undergrowth upon the river bank the channel was invisible; a long bank of what looked like cotton batting, though he could hear the water beneath it somewhere. There was a freshness here; the edges of the mist licked into curling tongues. He stooped and lifted the body and hurled it into the bank of mist. At the instant of vanishing he saw it—a sluggish sprawl of three limbs instead of four, and he knew why it had been so hard to free from the stump. "I'll have to make another trip," he said; then he heard a pattering rush behind him. He didn't have time to turn when the hound struck him and knocked him down. It didn't pause. Lying on his back, he saw it in midair like a bird, vanish into the mist with a single short, choking cry.

He got to his feet and ran. He stumbled and caught himself and ran again. It was full light. He could see the stump and the black hole which he had chopped in it; behind him he could hear the swift, soft feet of the dog. As it sprang at him he stumbled and fell and saw it soar over him, its eyes like two cigar-coals; it whirled and leaped at him again before he could rise. He struck at its face with his bare hands and began to run. Together they reached the tree. It leaped at him again, slashing his arm as he ducked into the tree, seeking that member of the body which he did not know was missing until after he had released it into the mist, feeling the dog surging about his legs. Then the dog was gone. Then a voice said:

"We got him. You can come out, Ernest."

The countyseat was fourteen miles away. They drove to it in a battered Ford. On the back seat Cotton and the Sheriff sat, their inside wrists locked together by handcuffs. They had to drive for two miles before they reached the highroad. It was hot, ten o'clock in the morning. "You want to swap sides out of the sun?" the Sheriff said.

"I'm all right," Cotton said.

At two o'clock they had a puncture. Cotton and the Sheriff sat under a tree while the driver and the second deputy went across a field and returned with a glass jar of buttermilk and some cold food. They ate, repaired the tire, and went on.

When they were within three or four miles of town, they began to pass wagons and cars going home from market day in town, the wagon teams plodding homeward in their own inescapable dust. The Sheriff greeted them with a single gesture of his fat arm. "Home for supper, anyway," he said. "What's the matter, Ernest? Feeling sick? Here, Joe; pull up a minute."

"I'll hold my head out," Cotton said. "Never mind." The car went on. Cotton thrust his head out the V strut of the top stanchion. The Sheriff shifted his arm, giving him play. "Go on," Cotton said, "I'll be all right." The car went on. Cotton slipped a little farther down in the seat. By moving his head a little he could wedge his throat into the apex of the iron V, the uprights gripping his jaws beneath the ears. He shifted again until his head was tight in the vise, then he swung his legs over the door, trying to bring the weight of his body sharply down against his imprisoned neck. He could hear his vertebrae; he felt a kind of rage at his own toughness; he was struggling then against the jerk on the manacle, the hands on him.

Then he was lying on his back beside the road, with water on his face and in his mouth, though he could not swallow. He couldn't speak, trying to curse, cursing in no voice. Then he was in the car again, on the smooth street where children played in the big, shady yards in small bright garments, and men and women went home toward supper, to plates of food and cups of coffee in the long twilight of summer.

They had a doctor for him in his cell. When the doctor had gone he could smell supper cooking somewhere—ham and hot bread and coffee. He was lying on a cot; the last ray of copper sunlight slid through a narrow window, stippling the bars upon the wall above his head. His cell was near the common room, where the minor prisoners lived, the ones who were in jail for minor offenses or for three meals a day; the stairway from below came up into that room. It was occupied for the time by a group of negroes from the chain-gang that worked the streets, in jail for vagrancy or for selling a little whiskey or shooting craps for ten or fifteen cents. One of the negroes was at the window above the street, yelling down to someone. The others talked among themselves, their voices rich and murmurous, mellow and singsong. Cotton rose and went to the door of his cell and held to the bars, looking at the negroes.

"Hit," he said. His voice made no sound. He put his hand to his throat; he produced a dry croaking sound, at which the negroes ceased talking and looked at him, their eyeballs rolling. "It was all right," Cotton said, "until it started coming to pieces on me. I could a handled that dog." He held his throat, his voice harsh, dry, and croaking. "But it started coming to pieces on me. . . ."

"Who him?" one of the negroes said. They whispered among themselves, watching him, their eyeballs white in the dusk.

"It would a been all right," Cotton said, "but it started coming to pieces. . . ."

"Hush up, white man," one of the negroes said. "Don't you be telling us no truck like that."

"Hit would a been all right," Cotton said, his voice harsh, whispering. Then it failed him again altogether. He held to the bars with one hand, holding his throat with the other, while the negroes watched him, huddled, their eyeballs white and sober. Then with one accord they turned and rushed across the room, toward the staircase; he heard slow steps and then he smelled food, and he clung to the bars, trying to see the stairs. "Are they going to feed them niggers before they feed a white man?" he said, smelling the coffee and the ham.

Spotted Horses

I

Yes, sir. Flem Snopes has filled that whole country full of spotted horses. You can hear folks running them all day and all night, whooping and hollering, and the horses running back and forth across them little wooden bridges ever now and then kind of like thunder. Here I was this morning pretty near half way to town, with the team ambling along and me setting in the buckboard about half asleep, when all of a sudden something come swurging up outen the bushes and jumped the road clean, without touching hoof to it. It flew right over my team, big as a billboard and flying through the air like a hawk. It taken me thirty minutes to stop my team and untangle the harness and the buckboard and hitch them up again.

That Flem Snopes. I be dog if he ain't a case, now. One morning about ten years ago, the boys was just getting settled down on Varner's porch for a little talk and tobacco, when here come Flem out from behind the counter, with his coat off and his hair all parted, like he might have been clerking for Varner for ten years already. Folks all knowed him; it was a big family of them about five miles down the bottom. That year, at least. Share-cropping. They never stayed on any place over a year. Then they would move on to another place, with the chap or maybe the twins of that year's litter. It was a regular nest of them. But Flem. The rest of them stayed tenant farmers, moving ever year, but here come Flem one day, walking out from behind Jody Varner's counter like he owned it. And he wasn't there but a year or two before folks knowed that, if him and Jody was both still in that store in ten years more, it would be Jody clerking for Flem Snopes. Why, that fellow could make a nickel where it wasn't but four cents to begin with. He skun me in two trades, myself, and the fellow that can do that, I just hope he'll get rich before I do; that's all.

All right. So here Flem was, clerking at Varner's, making a nickel here and there and not telling nobody about it. No, sir. Folks never knowed when Flem got the better of somebody lessen the fellow he beat told it. He'd just set there in the store-chair, chewing his tobacco and keeping his own business to hisself, until about a week later we'd find out it was somebody else's business he was keeping to hisself—provided the fellow he trimmed was mad enough to tell it. That's Flem.

We give him ten years to own ever thing Jody Varner had. But he never waited no ten years. I reckon you-all know that gal of Uncle Billy Varner's, the youngest one; Eula. Jody's sister. Ever Sunday ever yellow-wheeled buggy and curried riding horse in that country would be hitched to Bill Varner's fence, and the young bucks setting on the porch, swarming around Eula like bees around a honey pot. One of these here kind of big, soft-looking gals that could giggle richer than plowed new-ground. Wouldn't none of them leave before the others, and so they would set there on the porch until time to go home, with some of them with nine and ten miles to ride and then get up tomorrow and go back to the field. So they would all leave together and they would ride in a clump down to the creek ford and hitch them curried horses and yellow-wheeled buggies and get out and fight one another. Then they would get in the buggies again and go on home.

Well, one day about a year ago, one of them yellow-wheeled buggies and one of them curried saddle-horses quit this country. We heard they was heading for Texas. The next day Uncle Billy and Eula and Flem come in to town in Uncle Bill's surrey, and when they come back, Flem and Eula was married. And on the next day we heard that two more of them yellow-wheeled buggies had left the country. They mought have gone to Texas, too. It's a big place.

Anyway, about a month after the wedding, Flem and Eula

went to Texas, too. They was gone pretty near a year. Then one day last month, Eula come back, with a baby. We figgured up, and we decided that it was as well-growed a three-months-old baby as we ever see. It can already pull up on a chair. I reckon Texas makes big men quick, being a big place. Anyway, if it keeps on like it started, it'll be chewing tobacco and voting time it's eight years old.

And so last Friday here come Flem himself. He was on a wagon with another fellow. The other fellow had one of these two-gallon hats and a ivory-handled pistol and a box of gingersnaps sticking out of his hind pocket, and tied to the tail-gate of the wagon was about two dozen of them Texas ponies, hitched to one another with barbed wire. They was colored like parrots and they was quiet as doves, and ere a one of them would kill you quick as a rattlesnake. Nere a one of them had two eyes the same color, and nere a one of them had ever see a bridle, I reckon; and when that Texas man got down offen the wagon and walked up to them to show how gentle they was, one of them cut his vest clean offen him, same as with a razor.

Flem had done already disappeared; he had went on to see his wife, I reckon, and to see if that ere baby had done gone on to the field to help Uncle Billy plow maybe. It was the Texas man that taken the horses on to Mrs. Littlejohn's lot. He had a little trouble at first, when they come to the gate, because they hadn't never see a fence before, and when he finally got them in and taken a pair of wire cutters and unhitched them and got them into the barn and poured some shell corn into the trough, they durn nigh tore down the barn. I reckon they thought that shell corn was bugs, maybe. So he left them in the lot and he announced that the auction would begin at sunup to-morrow.

That night we was setting on Mrs. Littlejohn's porch. You-all mind the moon was nigh full that night, and we could watch them spotted varmints swirling along the fence and back and forth across the lot same as minnows in a pond. And then now and then they would all kind of huddle up against the barn and rest themselves by biting and kicking one another. We would hear a squeal, and then a set of hoofs would go Bam! against the barn, like a pistol. It sounded just like a fellow with a pistol, in a nest of cattymounts, taking his time.

II

It wasn't ere a man knowed yet if Flem owned them things or not. They just knowed one thing: that they wasn't never going to know for sho if Flem did or not, or if maybe he didn't just get on that wagon at the edge of town, for the ride or not. Even Eck Snopes didn't know, Flem's own cousin. But wasn't nobody surprised at that. We knowed that Flem would skin Eck quick as he would ere a one of us.

They was there by sunup next morning, some of them come twelve and sixteen miles, with seed-money tied up in tobacco sacks in their overalls, standing along the fence, when the Texas man come out of Mrs. Littlejohn's after breakfast and clumb onto the gate post with that ere white pistol butt sticking outen his hind pocket. He taken a new box of gingersnaps outen his pocket and bit the end offen it like a cigar and spit out the paper, and said the auction was open. And still they was coming up in wagons and a horse- and mule-back and hitching the teams across the road and coming to the fence. Flem wasn't nowhere in sight.

But he couldn't get them started. He begun to work on Eck, because Eck holp him last night to get them into the barn and feed them that shell corn. Eck got out just in time. He come outen that barn like a chip on the crest of a busted dam of water, and clumb into the wagon just in time.

He was working on Eck when Henry Armstid come up in his wagon. Eck was saying he was skeered to bid on one of them, because he might get it, and the Texas man says, "Them ponies? Them little horses?" He clumb down offen the gate post and went toward the horses. They broke and run, and him following them, kind of chirping to them, with his hand out like he was fixing to catch a fly, until he got three or four of them cornered. Then he jumped into them, and then we couldn't see nothing for a while because of the dust. It was a big cloud of it, and them blare-eyed, spotted things swoaring outen it twenty foot to a jump, in forty directions without counting up. Then the dust settled and there they was, that Texas man and the horse. He had its head twisted clean around like a owl's head. Its legs was braced and it was trembling like a new bride and groaning like a saw mill, and him holding its head wrung clean around on its neck so it was snuffing sky. "Look it over," he says, with his heels dug too and that white pistol sticking outen his pocket and his neck swole up like a spreading adder's until you could just tell what he was saying, cussing the horse and talking to us all at once: "Look him over, the fiddle-headed son of fourteen fathers. Try him, buy him; you will get the best—" Then it was all dust again, and we couldn't see nothing but spotted hide and mane, and that ere Texas man's boot-heels like a couple of walnuts on two strings, and after a while that two-gallon hat come sailing out like a fat old hen crossing a fence.

When the dust settled again, he was just getting outen the far fence corner, brushing himself off. He come and got his hat and brushed it off and come and clumb onto the gate post again. He was breathing hard. He taken the gingersnap box outen his pocket and et one, breathing hard. The hammer-head horse was still running round and round the lot like a merry-go-round at a fair. That was when Henry Armstid come shoving up to the gate in them patched overalls and one of them dangle-armed shirts of hisn. Hadn't nobody noticed him until then. We was all watching the Texas man and the horses. Even Mrs. Littlejohn; she had done come out and built a fire under the wash-pot in her back yard, and she would stand at the fence a while and then go back into the house and come out again with a arm full of wash and stand at the fence again. Well, here come Henry shoving up, and then we see Mrs. Armstid right behind him, in that ere faded wrapper and sunbonnet and them tennis shoes. "Git on back to that wagon," Henry says.

"Henry," she says.

"Here, boys," the Texas man says; "make room for missus to git up and see. Come on, Henry," he says; "here's your chance to buy that saddle-horse missus has been wanting. What about ten dollars, Henry?"

"Henry," Mrs. Armstid says. She put her hand on Henry's arm. Henry knocked her hand down.

"Git on back to that wagon, like I told you," he says.

Mrs. Armstid never moved. She stood behind Henry, with her hands rolled into her dress, not looking at nothing. "He hain't no more despair than to buy one of them things," she says. "And us not five dollars ahead of the pore house, he hain't no more despair."

It was the truth, too. They ain't never made more than a bare living offen that place of theirs, and them with four chaps and the very clothes they wears she earns by weaving by the firelight at night while Henry's asleep.

"Shut your mouth and git on back to that wagon," Henry says. "Do you want I taken a wagon stake to you here in the big road?"

Well, that Texas man taken one look at her. Then he begun on Eck again, like Henry wasn't even there. But Eck was skeered. "I can git me a snapping turtle or a water moccasin for nothing. I ain't going to buy none."

So the Texas man said he would give Eck a horse. "To start the auction, and because you holp me last night. If you'll start the bidding on the next horse," he says, "I'll give you that fiddle-head horse."

I wish you could have seen them, standing there with their seed-money in their pockets, watching that Texas man give Eck Snopes a live horse, all fixed to call him a fool if he taken it or not. Finally Eck says he'll take it. "Only I just starts the bidding," he says. "I don't have to buy the next one lessen I ain't overtopped." The Texas man said all right, and Eck bid a dollar on the next one, with Henry Armstid standing there with his mouth already open, watching Eck and the Texas man like a mad-dog or something. "A dollar," Eck says.

The Texas man looked at Eck. His mouth was already open too, like he had started to say something and what he was going to say had up and died on him. "A dollar?" he says. "One dollar? You mean, *one* dollar, Eck?"

"Durn it," Eck says; "two dollars, then."

Well, sir, I wish you could a seen that Texas man. He taken out that gingersnap box and held it up and looked into it, careful, like it might have been a diamond ring in it, or a spider. Then he throwed it away and wiped his face with a bandanna. "Well," he says. "Well. Two dollars. Two dollars. Is your pulse all right, Eck?" he says. "Do you have ager-sweats at night, maybe?" he says. "Well," he says, "I got to take it. But are you boys going to stand there and see Eck get two horses at a dollar a head?"

That done it. I be dog if he wasn't nigh as smart as Flem Snopes. He hadn't no more than got the words outen his mouth before here was Henry Armstid, waving his hand. "Three dollars," Henry says. Mrs. Armstid tried to hold him again. He knocked her hand off, shoving up to the gate post.

"Mister," Mrs. Armstid says, "we got chaps in the house and not corn to feed the stock. We got five dollars I earned my chaps a-weaving after dark, and him snoring in the bed. And he hain't no more despair."

"Henry bids three dollars," the Texas man says. "Raise him a dollar, Eck, and the horse is yours."

"Henry," Mrs. Armstid says.

"Raise him, Eck," the Texas man says.

"Four dollars," Eck says.

"Five dollars," Henry says, shaking his fist. He shoved up right under the gate post. Mrs. Armstid was looking at the Texas man too.

"Mister," she says, "if you take that five dollars I earned my chaps a-weaving for one of them things, it'll be a curse onto you and yourn during all the time of man."

But it wasn't no stopping Henry. He had shoved up, waving his fist at the Texas man. He opened it; the money was in nickels and quarters, and one dollar bill that looked like a cow's cud. "Five dollars," he says. "And the man that raises it'll have to beat my head off, or I'll beat hisn."

"All right," the Texas man says. "Five dollars is bid. But don't you shake your hand at me."

III

It taken till nigh sundown before the last one was sold. He got them hotted up once and the bidding got up to seven dollars and a quarter, but most of them went around three or four dollars, him setting on the gate post and picking the horses out one at a time by mouth-word, and Mrs. Littlejohn pumping up and down at the tub and stopping and coming to the fence for a while and going back to the tub again. She had done got done too, and the wash was hung on the line in the back yard, and we could smell supper cooking. Finally they was all sold; he swapped the last two and the wagon for a buckboard.

We was all kind of tired, but Henry Armstid looked more like a mad-dog than ever. When he bought, Mrs. Armstid had went back to the wagon, setting in it behind them two rabbit-sized, bone-pore mules, and the wagon itself looking like it would fall all to pieces soon as the mules moved. Henry hadn't even waited to pull it outen the road; it was still in the middle of the road and her setting in it, not looking at nothing, ever since this morning.

Henry was right up against the gate. He went up to the Texas man. "I bought a horse and I paid cash," Henry says. "And yet you expect me to stand around here until they are all sold before I can get my horse. I'm going to take my horse outen that lot."

The Texas man looked at Henry. He talked like he might have been asking for a cup of coffee at the table. "Take your horse," he says.

Then Henry quit looking at the Texas man. He begun to swallow, holding onto the gate. "Ain't you going to help me?" he says.

"It ain't my horse," the Texas man says.

Henry never looked at the Texas man again, he never looked at nobody. "Who'll help me catch my horse?" he says. Never nobody said nothing. "Bring the plowline," Henry says. Mrs. Armstid got outen the wagon and brought the plowline. The Texas man got down offen the post. The woman made to pass him, carrying the rope.

"Don't you go in there, missus," the Texas man says.

Henry opened the gate. He didn't look back. "Come on here," he says.

"Don't you go in there, missus," the Texas man says.

Mrs. Armstid wasn't looking at nobody, neither, with her hands across her middle, holding the rope. "I reckon I better," she says. Her and Henry went into the lot. The horses broke and run. Henry and Mrs. Armstid followed.

"Get him into the corner," Henry says. They got Henry's horse cornered finally, and Henry taken the rope, but Mrs. Armstid let the horse get out. They hemmed it up again, but Mrs. Armstid let it get out again, and Henry turned and hit her with the rope. "Why didn't you head him back?" Henry says. He hit her again. "Why didn't you?" It was about that time I looked around and see Flem Snopes standing there.

It was the Texas man that done something. He moved fast for a big man. He caught the rope before Henry could hit the third time, and Henry whirled and made like he would jump at the Texas man. But he never jumped. The Texas man went and taken Henry's arm and led him outen the lot. Mrs. Armstid come behind them and the Texas man taken some money outen his pocket and he give it into Mrs. Armstid's hand. "Get him into the wagon and take him on home," the Texas man says, like he might have been telling them he enjoyed his supper.

Then here come Flem. "What's that for, Buck?" Flem says.

"Thinks he bought one of them ponies," the Texas man says. "Get him on away, missus."

But Henry wouldn't go. "Give him back that money," he says. "I bought that horse and I aim to have him if I have to shoot him."

And there was Flem, standing there with his hands in his pockets, chewing, like he had just happened to be passing.

"You take your money and I take my horse," Henry says. "Give it back to him," he says to Mrs. Armstid.

"You don't own no horse of mine," the Texas man says. "Get him on home, missus."

Then Henry seen Flem. "You got something to do with these horses," he says. "I bought one. Here's the money for it." He taken the bill outen Mrs. Armstid's hand. He offered it to Flem. "I bought one. Ask him. Here. Here's the money," he says, giving the bill to Flem.

When Flem taken the money, the Texas man dropped the rope he had snatched outen Henry's hand. He had done sent Eck Snopes's boy up to the store for another box of gingersnaps, and he taken the box outen his pocket and looked into it. It was empty and he dropped it on the ground. "Mr. Snopes will have your money for you to-morrow," he says to Mrs. Armstid. "You can get it from him to-morrow. He don't own no horse. You get him into the wagon and get him on home." Mrs. Armstid went back to the wagon and got in. "Where's that ere buckboard I bought?" the Texas man says. It was after sundown then. And then Mrs. Littlejohn come out on the porch and rung the supper bell.

IV

I come on in and et supper. Mrs. Littlejohn would bring in a pan of bread or something, then she would go out to the porch a minute and come back and tell us. The Texas man had hitched his team to the buckboard he had swapped them last two horses for, and him and Flem had gone, and then she told that the rest of them that never had ropes had went back to the store with I. O. Snopes to get some ropes, and wasn't nobody at the gate but Henry Armstid, and Mrs. Armstid setting in the wagon in the road, and Eck Snopes and that boy of hisn. "I don't care how many of them fool men gets killed by them things," Mrs. Littlejohn says, "but I ain't going to let Eck Snopes take that boy into that lot again." So she went down to the gate, but she come back without the boy or Eck neither.

"It ain't no need to worry about that boy," I says. "He's charmed." He was right behind Eck last night when Eck went to help feed them. The whole drove of them jumped clean over that boy's head and never touched him. It was Eck that touched him. Eck snatched him into the wagon and taken a rope and frailed the tar outen him.

So I had done et and went to my room and was undressing, long as I had a long trip to make next day; I was trying to sell a machine to Mrs. Bundren up past Whiteleaf; when Henry Armstid opened that gate and went in by hisself. They couldn't make him wait for the balance of them to get back with their ropes. Eck Snopes said he tried to make Henry wait, but Henry wouldn't do it. Eck said Henry walked right up to them and that when they broke, they run clean over Henry like a hay-mow breaking down. Eck said he snatched that boy of hisn out of the way just in time and that them things went through that gate like a creek flood and into the wagons and teams hitched side the road, busting wagon tongues and snapping harness like it was fishing-line, with Mrs. Armstid still setting in their wagon in the middle of it like something carved outen wood. Then they scattered, wild horses and tame mules with pieces of harness and single trees dangling offen them, both ways up and down the road.

"There goes ourn, paw!" Eck says his boy said. "There it goes, into Mrs. Littlejohn's house." Eck says it run right up the steps and into the house like a boarder late for supper. I reckon so. Anyway, I was in my room, in my underclothes, with one sock on and one sock in my hand, leaning out the window when the commotion busted out, when I heard something run into the melodeon in the hall; it sounded like a railroad engine. Then the door to my room come sailing in like when you throw a tin bucket top into the wind and I looked over my shoulder and see something that looked like a fourteen-foot pinwheel a-blaring its eyes at me. It had to blare them fast, because I was already done jumped out the window.

I reckon it was anxious, too. I reckon it hadn't never seen barbed wire or shell corn before, but I know it hadn't never seen under-clothes before, or maybe it was a sewing-machine agent it hadn't never seen. Anyway, it swirled and turned to run back up the hall and outen the house, when it met Eck Snopes and that boy just coming in, carrying a rope. It swirled again and run down the hall and out the back door just in time to meet Mrs. Littlejohn. She had just gathered up the clothes she had washed, and she was coming onto the back porch with a armful of washing in one hand and a scrubbing-board in the other, when the horse skidded up to her, trying to stop and swirl again. It never taken Mrs. Littlejohn no time a-tall.

"Git outen here, you son," she says. She hit it across the face with the scrubbing-board; that ere scrubbing-board split as neat as ere a axe could have done it, and when the horse swirled to run back up the hall, she hit it again with what was left of the scrub-bing-board, not on the head this time. "And stay out," she says.

Eck and that boy was half-way down the hall by this time. I reckon that horse looked like a pinwheel to Eck too. "Git to hell outen here, Ad!" Eck says. Only there wasn't time. Eck dropped flat on his face, but the boy never moved. The boy was about a yard tall maybe, in overhalls just like Eck's; that horse swoared over his head without touching a hair. I saw that, because I was just coming back up the front steps, still carrying that ere sock and still in my underclothes, when the horse come onto the porch again. It taken one look at me and swirled again and run to the end of the porch and jumped the banisters and the lot fence like a hen-hawk and lit in the lot running and went out the gate again and jumped eight or ten upside-down wagons and went on down the road. It was a full moon then. Mrs. Armstid was still setting in the wagon like she had done been carved outen wood and left there and forgot.

That horse. It ain't never missed a lick. It was going about forty miles a hour when it come to the bridge over the creek. It would have had a clear road, but it so happened that Vernon Tull was already using the bridge when it got there. He was coming back from town; he hadn't heard about the auction; him and his wife and three daughters and Mrs. Tull's aunt, all setting in chairs in the wagon bed, and all asleep, including the mules. They waked up when the horse hit the bridge one time, but Tull said the first he knew was when the mules tried to turn the wagon around in the middle of the bridge and he seen that spotted varmint run right twixt the mules and run up the wagon tongue like a squirrel. He said he just had time to hit it across the face with his whip-stock, because about that time the mules turned the wagon around on that ere one-way bridge and that horse clumb across one of the mules and jumped down onto the bridge again and went on, with Vernon standing up in the wagon and kicking at it.

Tull said the mules turned in the harness and clumb back into the wagon too, with Tull trying to beat them out again, with the reins wrapped around his wrist. After that he says all he seen was overturned chairs and womenfolks' legs and white drawers shining in the moonlight, and his mules and that spotted horse going on up the road like a ghost.

The mules jerked Tull outen the wagon and drug him a spell on the bridge before the reins broke. They thought at first that he was dead, and while they was kneeling around him, picking the bridge splinters outen him, here come Eck and that boy, still carrying the rope. They was running and breathing a little hard. "Where'd he go?" Eck says.

V

I went back and got my pants and shirt and shoes on just in time to go and help get Henry Armstid outen the trash in the lot. I be dog if he didn't look like he was dead, with his head hanging back and his teeth showing in the moonlight, and a little rim of white under his eyelids. We could still hear them horses, here and there; hadn't none of them got more than four-five miles away yet, not knowing the country, I reckon. So we could hear them and folks yelling now and then: "Whooey. Head him!"

We toted Henry into Mrs. Littlejohn's. She was in the hall; she hadn't put down the armful of clothes. She taken one look at us, and she laid down the busted scrubbing-board and taken up the lamp and opened a empty door. "Bring him in here," she says.

We toted him in and laid him on the bed. Mrs. Littlejohn set the

177 SPOTTED HORSES · 177

lamp on the dresser, still carrying the clothes. "I'll declare, you men," she says. Our shadows was way up the wall, tiptoeing too; we could hear ourselves breathing. "Better get his wife," Mrs. Littlejohn says. She went out, carrying the clothes.

"I reckon we had," Quick says. "Go get her, somebody."

"Whyn't you go?" Winterbottom says.

"Let Ernest git her," Durley says. "He lives neighbors with them."

Ernest went to fetch her. I be dog if Henry didn't look like he was dead. Mrs. Littlejohn come back, with a kettle and some towels. She went to work on Henry, and then Mrs. Armstid and Ernest come in. Mrs. Armstid come to the foot of the bed and stood there, with her hands rolled into her apron, watching what Mrs. Littlejohn was doing, I reckon.

"You men git outen the way," Mrs. Littlejohn says. "Git outside," she says. "See if you can't find something else to play with that will kill some more of you."

"Is he dead?" Winterbottom says.

"It ain't your fault if he ain't," Mrs. Littlejohn says. "Go tell Will Varner to come up here. I reckon a man ain't so different from a mule, come long come short. Except maybe a mule's got more sense."

We went to get Uncle Billy. It was a full moon. We could hear them, now and then, four mile away: "Whooey. Head him." The country was full of them, one on ever wooden bridge in the land, running across it like thunder: "Whooey. There he goes. Head him."

We hadn't got far before Henry begun to scream. I reckon Mrs. Littlejohn's water had brung him to; anyway, he wasn't dead. We went on to Uncle Billy's. The house was dark. We called to him, and after a while the window opened and Uncle Billy put his head out, peart as a peckerwood, listening. "Are they still trying to catch them durn rabbits?" he says.

He come down, with his britches on over his night-shirt and his suspenders dangling, carrying his horse-doctoring grip. "Yes, sir," he says, cocking his head like a woodpecker; "they're still a-try-ing."

We could hear Henry before we reached Mrs. Littlejohn's. He was going Ah-Ah-Ah. We stopped in the yard. Uncle Billy went on in. We could hear Henry. We stood in the yard, hearing them on the bridges, this-a-way and that: "Whooey. Whooey."

"Eck Snopes ought to caught hisn," Ernest says.

"Looks like he ought," Winterbottom said.

Henry was going Ah-Ah-Ah steady in the house; then he begun to scream. "Uncle Billy's started," Quick says. We looked into the hall. We could see the light where the door was. Then Mrs. Littlejohn come out.

"Will needs some help," she says. "You, Ernest. You'll do." Ernest went into the house.

"Hear them?" Quick said. "That one was on Four Mile bridge." We could hear them; it sounded like thunder a long way off; it didn't last long:

"Whooey."

We could hear Henry: "Ah-Ah-Ah-Ah-Ah."

"They are both started now," Winterbottom says. "Ernest too."

That was early in the night. Which was a good thing, because it taken a long night for folks to chase them things right and for Henry to lay there and holler, being as Uncle Billy never had none of this here chloryfoam to set Henry's leg with. So it was considerate in Flem to get them started early. And what do you reckon Flem's com-ment was?

That's right. Nothing. Because he wasn't there. Hadn't nobody see him since that Texas man left.

VI

That was Saturday night. I reckon Mrs. Armstid got home about daylight, to see about the chaps. I don't know where they thought her and Henry was. But lucky the oldest one was a gal, about twelve, big enough to take care of the little ones. Which she did for the next two days. Mrs. Armstid would nurse Henry all night and work in the kitchen for hern and Henry's keep, and in the afternoon she would drive home (it was about four miles) to see to the chaps. She would cook up a pot of victuals and leave it on the stove, and the gal would bar the house and keep the little ones quiet. I would hear Mrs. Littlejohn and Mrs. Armstid talking in the kitchen. "How are the chaps making out?" Mrs. Littlejohn says.

"All right," Mrs. Armstid says.

"Don't they git skeered at night?" Mrs. Littlejohn says.

"Ina May bars the door when I leave," Mrs. Armstid says. "She's got the axe in bed with her. I reckon she can make out."

I reckon they did. And I reckon Mrs. Armstid was waiting for Flem to come back to town; hadn't nobody seen him until this morning; to get her money the Texas man said Flem was keeping for her. Sho. I reckon she was.

Anyway, I heard Mrs. Armstid and Mrs. Littlejohn talking in the kitchen this morning while I was eating breakfast. Mrs. Littlejohn had just told Mrs. Armstid that Flem was in town. "You can ask him for that five dollars," Mrs. Littlejohn says.

"You reckon he'll give it to me?" Mrs. Armstid says.

Mrs. Littlejohn was washing dishes, washing them like a man, like they was made out of iron. "No," she says. "But asking him won't do no hurt. It might shame him. I don't reckon it will, but it might."

"If he wouldn't give it back, it ain't no use to ask," Mrs. Armstid says.

"Suit yourself," Mrs. Littlejohn says. "It's your money."

I could hear the dishes.

"Do you reckon he might give it back to me?" Mrs. Armstid says. "That Texas man said he would. He said I could get it from Mr. Snopes later."

"Then go and ask him for it," Mrs. Littlejohn says.

I could hear the dishes.

"He won't give it back to me," Mrs. Armstid says.

"All right," Mrs. Littlejohn says. "Don't ask him for it, then."

I could hear the dishes; Mrs. Armstid was helping. "You don't reckon he would, do you?" she says. Mrs. Littlejohn never said nothing. It sounded like she was throwing the dishes at one another. "Maybe I better go and talk to Henry about it," Mrs. Armstid says.

"I would," Mrs. Littlejohn says. I be dog if it didn't sound like she had two plates in her hands, beating them together. "Then Henry can buy another five-dollar horse with it. Maybe he'll buy one next time that will out and out kill him. If I thought that, I'd give you back the money, myself."

"I reckon I better talk to him first," Mrs. Armstid said. Then it sounded like Mrs. Littlejohn taken up all the dishes and throwed them at the cook-stove, and I come away.

That was this morning. I had been up to Bundren's and back, and I thought that things would have kind of settled down. So after breakfast, I went up to the store. And there was Flem, setting in the store-chair and whittling, like he might not have ever moved since he come to clerk for Jody Varner. I. O. was leaning in the door, in his shirt sleeves and with his hair parted too, same as Flem was before he turned the clerking job over to I. O. It's a funny thing about them Snopes: they all looks alike, yet there ain't ere a two of them that claims brothers. They're always just cousins, like Flem and Eck and Flem and I. O. Eck was there too, squatting against the wall, him and that boy, eating cheese and crackers outen a sack; they told me that Eck hadn't been home a-tall. And that Lon Quick hadn't got back to town, even. He followed his horse clean down to Samson's Bridge, with a wagon and a camp outfit. Eck finally caught one of hisn. It run into a blind lane at Freeman's and Eck and the boy taken and tied their rope across the end of the lane, about three foot high. The horse come to the end of the lane and whirled and run back without ever stopping. Eck says it never seen the rope a-tall. He says it looked just like one of these here Christmas pinwheels. "Didn't it try to run again?" I says.

"No," Eck says, eating a bite of cheese offen his knife blade. "Just kicked some."

"Kicked some?" I says.

"It broke its neck," Eck says.

Well, they was squatting there, about six of them, talking, talking at Flem; never nobody knowed yet if Flem had ere a interest in them horses or not. So finally I come right out and asked him. "Flem's done skun all of us so much," I says, "that we're proud of him. Come on, Flem," I says, "how much did you and that Texas man make offen them horses? You can tell us. Ain't nobody here but Eck that bought one of them; the others ain't got back to town yet, and Eck's your own cousin; he'll be proud to hear, too. How much did you-all make?"

They was all whittling, not looking at Flem, making like they was studying. But you could a heard a pin drop. And I. O. He had been rubbing his back up and down on the door, but he stopped now, watching Flem like a pointing dog. Flem finished cutting the sliver offen his stick. He spit across the porch, into the road. "'Twarn't none of my horses," he says.

I. O. cackled, like a hen, slapping his legs with both hands. "You boys might just as well quit trying to get ahead of Flem," he said.

Well, about that time I see Mrs. Armstid come outen Mrs. Littlejohn's gate, coming up the road. I never said nothing. I says, "Well, if a man can't take care of himself in a trade, he can't blame the man that trims him."

Flem never said nothing, trimming at the stick. He hadn't seen Mrs. Armstid. "Yes, sir," I says. "A fellow like Henry Armstid ain't got nobody but hisself to blame."

"Course he ain't," I. O. says. He ain't seen her, neither. "Henry Armstid's a born fool. Always is been. If Flem hadn't a got his money, somebody else would."

We looked at Flem. He never moved. Mrs. Armstid come on up the road.

"That's right," I says. "But, come to think of it, Henry never bought no horse." We looked at Flem; you could a heard a match drop. "That Texas man told her to get that five dollars back from Flem next day. I reckon Flem's done already taken that money to Mrs. Littlejohn's and give it to Mrs. Armstid."

We watched Flem. I. O. quit rubbing his back against the door again. After a while Flem raised his head and spit across the porch, into the dust. I. O. cackled, just like a hen. "Ain't he a beating fellow, now?" I. O. says.

Mrs. Armstid was getting closer, so I kept on talking, watching to see if Flem would look up and see her. But he never looked up. I went on talking about Tull, about how he was going to sue Flem, and Flem setting there, whittling his stick, not saying nothing else after he said they wasn't none of his horses.

Then I. O. happened to look around. He seen Mrs. Armstid. "Psssst!" he says. Flem looked up. "Here she comes!" I. O. says. "Go out the back. I'll tell her you done went in to town to-day."

But Flem never moved. He just set there, whittling, and we watched Mrs. Armstid come up onto the porch, in that ere faded sunbonnet and wrapper and them tennis shoes that made a kind of hissing noise on the porch. She come onto the porch and stopped, her hands rolled into her dress in front, not looking at nothing.

"He said Saturday," she says, "that he wouldn't sell Henry no horse. He said I could get the money from you."

Flem looked up. The knife never stopped. It went on trimming off a sliver same as if he was watching it. "He taken that money off with him when he left," Flem says.

Mrs. Armstid never looked at nothing. We never looked at her, neither, except that boy of Eck's. He had a half-et cracker in his hand, watching her, chewing.

"He said Henry hadn't bought no horse," Mrs. Armstid says. "He said for me to get the money from you today."

"I reckon he forgot about it," Flem said. "He taken that money off with him Saturday." He whittled again. I. O. kept on rubbing his back, slow. He licked his lips. After a while the woman looked up the road, where it went on up the hill, toward the graveyard. She looked up that way for a while, with that boy of Eck's watching her and I. O. rubbing his back slow against the door. Then she turned back toward the steps.

"I reckon it's time to get dinner started," she says.

"How's Henry this morning, Mrs. Armstid?" Winterbottom says.

She looked at Winterbottom; she almost stopped. "He's resting, I thank you kindly," she says.

Flem got up, outen the chair, putting his knife away. He spit across the porch. "Wait a minute, Mrs. Armstid," he says. She stopped again. She didn't look at him. Flem went on into the store, with I. O. done quit rubbing his back now, with his head craned after Flem, and Mrs. Armstid standing there with her hands rolled into her dress, not looking at nothing. A wagon come up the road and passed; it was Freeman, on the way to town. Then Flem come out again, with I. O. still watching him. Flem had one of these little striped sacks of Jody Varner's candy; I bet he still owes Jody that nickel, too. He put the sack into Mrs. Armstid's hand, like he would have put it into a hollow stump. He spit again across the porch. "A little sweetening for the chaps," he says.

"You're right kind," Mrs. Armstid says. She held the sack of candy in her hand, not looking at nothing. Eck's boy was watching the sack, the half-et cracker in his hand; he wasn't chewing now.

He watched Mrs. Armstid roll the sack into her apron. "I reckon I better get on back and help with dinner," she says. She turned and went back across the porch. Flem set down in the chair again and opened his knife. He spit across the porch again, past Mrs. Armstid where she hadn't went down the steps yet. Then she went on, in that ere sunbonnet and wrapper all the same color, back down the road toward Mrs. Littlejohn's. You couldn't see her dress move, like a natural woman walking. She looked like a old snag still standing up and moving along on a high water. We watched her turn in at Mrs. Littlejohn's and go outen sight. Flem was whittling. I. O. begun to rub his back on the door. Then he begun to cackle, just like a durn hen.

"You boys might just as well quit trying," I. O. says. "You can't git ahead of Flem. You can't touch him. Ain't he a sight, now?"

I be dog if he ain't. If I had brung a herd of wild cattymounts into town and sold them to my neighbors and kinfolks, they would have lynched me. Yes, sir.

Lion

A good part of the lives of dogs—I mean hunting dogs, bear and deer dogs—is whiskey. That is, the men who love them, who hunt hard the hard-hunting and tireless and courageous dogs, drink hard too. I know certainly that the best, the finest talk about dogs which I have heard took place over a bottle or two or three bottles maybe, in the libraries of town houses and the offices of plantation houses or, better still, in the camps themselves; before the burning logs on hearths when there were houses, or before the high blazing of nigger-fed wood before stretched and earth-pegged tarpaulins when there were not. So this story might just as well begin with whiskey too.

It was December; it was the coldest December I ever saw. We—I was just sixteen that year—had been in camp a week now and the men had run out of whiskey, and so Boon Hogganbeck and I went in to Memphis with a suitcase and a note from Major de Spain to get some more. That is, Major de Spain sent Boon in to get the whiskey, and he sent me along to get Boon back to camp with the whiskey in the suitcase and not in Boon. Boon was part Indian. They said half, but I don't think so. I think it was his grandmother who was the Chickasaw woman, niece of the chief who once owned the land which Major de Spain now owned and over which we hunted.

Boon was four inches over six feet, and he had the mind of a child and the heart of a horse and the ugliest face I ever saw. It looked as if somebody had found a walnut a little smaller than a basket ball and with a machinist's hammer had shaped the features of the face and then painted it, mostly red. Not Indian red: a fine bright ruddy color that whiskey might have had something to do with but probably mostly just happy and violent out-of-door life. The wrinkles in it—he must have been forty years old—must have come just from squinting into the sun or into the gloom of cane brakes where game had run, or have been baked into his face by camp fires while he tried to sleep on the cold November or December ground while waiting for daylight so he could get up and hunt again—as though time were just something he walked through as he did in air, to age him no more than air did. The eyes were like shoebuttons, without depth, without meanness or generosity or viciousness or gentleness or anything at all: just something to see with. He didn't have any profession or trade or even job: he just did whatever Major de Spain told him to do. Later, after Lion died, Major de Spain had him appointed marshal of Hoke's, the little town on the edge of Major de Spain's preserve. But that had not happened yet; Lion was not dead yet.

We got up at three o'clock this morning. Ad had breakfast ready and we ate, hearing the dogs under the kitchen, wakened too by the smell of the frying ham or maybe by Ad's feet on the floor overhead; we could hear Lion then, just once, short and peremptory, as the best hunter in any crowd has only to speak once to all the others except the ones that are fools, and there were no fools among Major de Spain's dogs. As he said, sometimes he had fools in the house because now and then he could not help himself. But that did not matter so much because he did not intend to hunt with them or depend on them to hunt.

Ad had the mules in the wagon, waiting too, and it was cold, the ground frozen and the stars hard and bright. I was not shivering, I was just shaking slow and steady and hard, the breakfast I had just eaten warm and comfortable inside me and my stomach still warm from it and the outside of me shaking slow and hard as if my stomach were floating loose inside me like the globe of a floating compass.

"They won't run this morning, anyway," I said. "No dog will have any nose to-day."

"Cep' Lion," Ad said. "He run a bear thu a thousand-acre ice house. Ketch him too. Other dogs don't matter because they don't keep up wid Lion nohow."

"Well, they ain't going to run this morning," Boon said, harsh and positive. "Major promised they wouldn't run till me and Quentin get back."

He was sitting on the jolting seat, his feet wrapped in towsacks and a quilt from his pallet in the kitchen wrapped around him and over his head so that he didn't look like anything at all. Ad laughed. "I like to know why Major need to wait on you. Hit's Lion he gonter use; I ain't never heard tell of you bringing no bear nor any yuther kind of meat into this camp."

"By God, he ain't going to put Lion or no other dog on nothing until I get back," Boon said. "Because he promised me. Whup up them mules; you want me to freeze to death?"

He and Ad were funny. It was Lion that made the difference, because Boon had a bad name among negroes. Yet Ad talked to him, when Lion was a factor (even though he was not mentioned), just as if Ad were another white man; and Boon let him do it. They were funny about Lion. Neither one of them owned him or had any hope of ever owning him and I don't believe it ever occurred to either of them to think, *I wish I owned that dog.* Because you didn't think of Lion as belonging to anyone, any more than you thought about a man belonging to anybody, not even to Major de Spain. You thought of the house and the woods as belonging to him and even the deer and the bear in them; even the deer and bear killed by other people were shot by them on Major de Spain's courtesy, given to them through his kindness and will. But not Lion. Lion was like the chiefs of Aztec and Polynesian tribes who were looked upon as being not men but both more and less than men. Because we were not men either while we were in camp: we were hunters, and Lion the best hunter of us all, and Major de Spain and Uncle Ike McCaslin next; and Lion did not talk as we talked, not because he could not but because he was the chief, the Sunbegotten, who knew the language which we spoke but was superior to using it himself; just as he lived under the house, under the kitchen, not because he was a dog, an animal, but for the same reason as the Aztec or the Polynesian whose godhead required that he live apart. Lion did not belong to Major de Spain at all but just happened to like him better than he did any of the rest of us, as a man might have.

Ad and Boon were funny about him. You would have almost

thought that Lion was a woman, a beautiful woman. I used to listen to them; they would wait until Major de Spain had settled down to the poker game or maybe was in bed, if we were going out early, and then Boon and Ad would each try to get Lion in to sleep on his pallet with him, Ad in the kitchen and Boon in the shed room. It would be funny. They would be so deadly serious about it, not arguing with each other but each one trying to work on Lion, persuade or tempt him; and he not caring which one he slept with, and not staying long with either one even when they persuaded him, because always Major de Spain would carry the lamp into Boon's shed or into the kitchen, as the case might be, and make them put Lion outdoors. "Damn it," he would say, "if he slept with either one of you for half the night he wouldn't even be able to trace a polecat to-morrow."

So we went on, under the iron stars, the wagon jolting in the iron ruts, the woods impenetrable and black on either hand. Once we heard two wildcats squalling and fighting off to the right and not far away. We came to the dummy line and Boon flagged the early log train and we rode into Hoke's in the warm caboose, while I slept behind the red stove and Boon and the conductor and brakeman talked about Lion and Old Ben as people talked about Sullivan and Kilrain or Dempsey and Tunney. Old Ben was a bear and we were going to run him to-morrow as we did once every year, every time in camp. He was known through the country as well as Lion was. I don't know why they called him Old Ben nor who named him except that it was a long time ago. He was known well for the shoats he had stolen and the corn cribs he had broken into and the dogs he had killed and the number of times he had been bayed and the lead which he carried (it was said that he had been shot at least two dozen times, with buckshot and even with rifles). Old Ben had lost three toes from his nigh hind foot in a steel trap, and every man in the country knew his track, even discounting the size, and so he should have been called Two-Toe. That is, that's what they had been calling two-toed bears in this country for a hundred years. Maybe it was because Old Ben was an extra bear—the head bear, Uncle Ike McCaslin called him—and everyone knew that he deserved a better name.

We were in Hoke's by sun-up, Boon and me, getting out of the warm caboose in our hunting clothes, our muddy boots, and stained khaki. Boon hadn't shaved since we came into camp, but that was all right because Hoke's was just a sawmill and a few stores, and most of the men in it wore muddy boots and khaki too. Then the accommodation came; Boon bought three packages of molasses-covered popcorn and a bottle of soda pop from the news butch and I went to sleep to the sound of his chewing. But in Memphis we did not look all right. The tall buildings and the hard pavements and the street cars made our boots and khaki look a little rougher and muddier and made Boon's whiskers look worse and his face more and more as if he should never have brought it out of the woods at all or at least out of reach of Major de Spain or somebody who knew it and could say, "Don't be afraid. He's all right; he won't hurt you"—Boon walking through the station, on the tile floor, his face moving where he was still working the popcorn out of his teeth with his tongue, his legs spraddled a little and a little stiff in the hips as if he were walking on buttered glass, and that blue stubble on his face and chin like used steel wool or like ravelings from screen wire.

We went straight and had the suitcase filled and Boon bought a bottle for himself, to take home after we broke camp, he said. But by the time we reached Hoke's again at sundown, it was all gone. He drank the first time in the washroom at the station. A man in uniform came in to tell Boon he couldn't drink there and took one look at Boon's face and didn't say anything. The next time he drank from his water glass, filling it under the edge of the counter where we were eating dinner and the waitress did tell him he could not. In the meantime he had been telling the waitress and all the other customers about Lion and Old Ben. Then he got on to the subject of the zoo some way, and his plan was to hurry back to camp, get Lion and return to the zoo where, he said, the bears were fed lady fingers and ice cream and where we would match Lion against them all, tigers and elephants included. But I got him and the suitcase aboard the train, so we were all right then, with Boon drinking right in the aisle and telling the other passengers about Lion and Old Ben; the men he buttonholed no more dared to act as if they did not want to listen than the man in the washroom had dared to tell Boon he couldn't drink there. We were back in Hoke's at sundown and I waked him and got him and the suitcase off and persuaded him to eat supper.

When we got on the caboose of the evening log train which went back into the woods, the sun was going down red and it already seemed warmer. I was the one who went to sleep again now, sitting behind the stove again while Boon and the brakeman and the conductor talked about Lion and Old Ben and the drive to-morrow; they knew what Boon was talking about. Once I waked; it was dark now and the brakeman was leaning out the window. "It's overcast," he said. "It will thaw to-night and to-morrow scent will lie to a dog's nose. Maybe Lion will get him to-morrow."

It would have to be Lion or somebody. It would not be Boon. He never could shoot. He never had killed anything bigger than a squirrel that anybody knew of, except that nigger that time. That was several years ago. They said he was a bad nigger, but I don't know. All I know is, there was some trouble and the nigger told Boon he'd better have a pistol next time he came to town and Boon borrowed a pistol from Major de Spain and sure enough that afternoon he met the nigger and the nigger outs with a dollar-and-a-half mail order pistol and he would have burned Boon up with it only it never went off. It just snapped five times and the nigger kept coming, and Boon shot four times and broke a plate-glass window and shot in the leg a nigger woman who happened to be passing before he managed to hit the nigger in the face at six feet with the last shot. He never could shoot. The first day in camp, the first drive we made, the buck ran right over him; we measured later and the buck's tracks and the five exploded shells were not fifty feet apart. We heard Boon's old pump gun go *whow whow whow whow whow* and then we heard him; they could have heard him clean up to Hoke's: "God damn, here he comes! Head him! Head him!"

The next morning we had company, people from Hoke's and from Jefferson too, who came every year for the day when Major de Spain drove Old Ben. It was gray and warmer; we ate breakfast by lamplight, with Boon frying the eggs and still talking, looking wilder and more unpredictable and more uncurried in the face than ever, and Ad sitting on his box beside the stove, pushing the heavy solid greasy cartridges into Major de Spain's carbine. And we could hear the dogs too now, in the yard where Ad had already coupled them in pairs and tied them to the fence—the snarling bursts of almost hysterical uproar; we could hear them all except Lion.

There was no sound from him, there never was; I remember how after breakfast we went out and into the damp, gray, faint light and there he stood, apart from the other dogs and not tied, just standing there and looking huge as a calf looks, or an elephant or buffalo calf, huge despite its actual size. He was part Walker, but most of him was mastiff; he was the color of a blue sorrel horse, though perhaps it was his topaz-colored eyes that made him look so dark. I remember how he stood there—big-footed, with his strong grave head and a chest almost as big as mine. Beneath the skin you could feel the long, easy, quiet, strong muscles that did not flinch with either pleasure or distaste from any touch, Major de Spain's or Boon's or Ad's or any stranger's. He stood like a horse, only different from a horse because a horse promises only speed while Lion promised—with that serene and comforting quality of a promise from a man whom you trust absolutely—an immeasurable capacity not only for courage and skill and will to pursue and kill, but for endurance, the will to endure beyond any imaginable limit to which his flesh and heart might be called. I remember him in the summer when we would go in for squirrels, how when the other dogs would be all over the bottom, chasing coon and wildcat and anything that ran and left scent, Lion would not go. He would stay in camp with us, not especially following Major de Spain or Boon or Ad in particular; just lying nearby somewhere in the attitude in which they carve lions in stone, with his big head raised and his big feet quiet before him; you would go to him and speak to him or pat him and he would turn his head slowly and look at you with those topaz eyes that were as impenetrable as Boon's, as free of meanness or generosity or gentleness or viciousness but a good deal more intelligent. Then he would blink and then you would realize that he was not looking at you at all, not seeing you at all. You didn't know what he was seeing, what he was thinking. It was like when you are sitting with your feet propped against a column on the gallery and after a while you are not even aware that you are not seeing the very column your feet are propped against.

The two mules were ready too, one for Major de Spain, who was going with Boon and Ad and the dogs; and the other for Uncle Ike McCaslin, who was going to put us on the stands. Because he and Major de Spain knew Old Ben as well as they knew each other. They knew where he denned and where he used and which direction he took when dogs jumped him. That was why we had been in camp a week and hadn't run him yet; that was the way Major de Spain did. Each year he ran Old Ben just one time, unless Old Ben happened to let himself be caught out of bounds on a visit or something and the dogs started him by accident, which did happen the second day in camp. We heard them strike something and carry it down toward the river; Lion was not with them. They went out of hearing and after a while Boon came up, cussing. But hunting was over for that day and so we went back to camp. We had not heard them again, but when we reached camp the dogs were already there, crouched back under the kitchen, huddled together as far back as they could go and Boon squatting down and peering under the kitchen at them and cussing, and Uncle Ike said it was Old Ben they had struck. Because they knew Old Ben too and the ones that didn't know him probably found out pretty quick. They were not cowards. It was just that Lion hadn't been with them to lead them in on him and bay him and hold him. Lion was with Major de Spain; they came in about an hour later with Lion on the leash and Major de Spain said it was Old Ben, that he had seen the track, still having to hold Lion on the leash because he was saving Old Ben for to-day. I remember him sitting on the mule in the gray light with his rifle across the saddle, and Boon with his old gun slung over his shoulder by a piece of cotton rope and still cussing while he and Ad struggled to hold the dogs while they untied them, and only Lion and Major de Spain calm and Major de Spain looking around at us and saying, "No deer this morning, boys. This is Old Ben's race."

He meant there must be no shooting, no noise that might turn Old Ben because he wanted everybody to have a fair chance. Uncle Ike explained that to me when he put me on my stand, after we watched Major de Spain ride away, with Lion heeled and pacing along beside the mule and Ad and Boon in front, stooped over and half running in a surging uproar of dogs as if they were running in surf.

"Stay here until you kill a bear or hear a horn, or until you haven't heard a dog in an hour," Uncle Ike said "If Lion bays him, me or Major or Boon will blow everybody in. If you don't hear anything after a while, go back to camp. If you get lost, stand right still and holler and listen. Some of the boys will hear you."

"I've got my compass," I said.

"All right. Stay right still now. He may cross the bayou right here; I have known him to do it. Don't move around. If he comes over you, give him time to get close. Then hold right on his neck." Then he rode away, into the gray gloom.

It was full daylight now; that is, it was full daylight up above the trees, because it would never be very light down here that day. I had never been in this part of the bottom before, because Major de Spain had not let us hunt here lest we disturb Old Ben before the right day. I stood there under a gum tree beside the bayou, where the black, still water ran out of the cane and across a little clearing and into the cane again. I had been on stand before where you might see a bear and I had seen bear signs. But this was different; I was just sixteen then; I kept on thinking about those dogs huddled back there under the kitchen that day and I could smell the solitude, the loneliness, something breathing out of this place which human beings had merely passed through without altering it, where no axe or plow had left a scar, which looked exactly as it had when the first Indian crept into it and looked around, arrow poised and ready. I thought about how just twenty miles away was Jefferson, the houses where people were getting ready to wake up in comfort and security, the stores and offices where during the day they would meet to buy and sell and talk, and I could hardly believe it; I thought *It's just twenty miles away. What's the matter with you?* but then the other side of me, the other thing in me would say, *Yes, and you are just a puny assortment of bones and meat that cannot get one mile from where you stand without that compass to help you and could not spend one night where you are and live without fire to keep you warm and perhaps that gun to protect yourself.*

I had forgotten that I had a gun. I had completely forgotten it. I was telling myself that black bears are not dangerous, they won't hurt a man unless they are cornered, when all of a sudden I thought, with a kind of amazed surprise, *Besides, I have a gun. Why, I have a gun!* I had clean forgotten it. I hadn't even loaded it; I broke it quickly, fumbling in my coat for shells. I was not scared any more now; I was just suffering one of those mindless and superstitious illusions which people get—I do anyway. I believed that by getting scared and failing to load my gun, I was going to fail the others and let Old Ben through. I had conferred supernatural powers on him now. I had a picture of him lurking back in the cane, watching his chance and waiting for one of us who barred his way to make a mistake, and I had made it; I believed, knew, that he would charge out of the cane and pass me before I could get loaded. I thought I should never pick up the two shells, and then I had a terrible impulse to read the size of the shot printed on the wadding to be sure, even though I knew I had only buckshot. But I didn't; I got the gun loaded and snapped it shut, already swinging toward the spot of cane where I had hypnotized myself to believe he would emerge. I think that if a bird had moved in it I should have fired.

But I never saw him. I just heard the dogs. Suddenly I knew that I had been hearing them for a second or two before I realized what it was. That must have been when they jumped him because I heard Lion, just once. His voice was not deep especially, it was just strong and full; he bayed just once somewhere in the gray light maybe a mile away, and that was all, as if he had said, "All right, Old Man. Let's go." It was the other dogs making the racket. But I never saw any of them. At the closest time they were a half mile away and they didn't pass near any stand because I heard no shots. I just stood there, crouched, holding my breath, with the safety off even though father had taught me never to take it off until I saw what I was going to shoot at; and I heard the dogs pass me and go on. Then the sound died away. I didn't move; I waited. I was thinking, maybe he will turn and come back. But I knew that he would not. He must have known where all of us were standing; he probably picked the one gap where he could have got through unseen. Because he had lived too long now, been run too many times. I stood there, still holding my gun forward, though I did slip the safety back on. I don't know how long it was; then I whirled. But it was only father. "You didn't see him?" father said.

"No, sir. But it was Old Ben, wasn't it?"

"Yes. So Uncle Ike says. He's gone across the river. He won't come back to-day. So we might as well go back to camp."

We went back to camp. Major de Spain was already there, sitting on the mule with Boon's gun in the rope sling over his shoulder now (he told how Boon had stopped just long enough to throw the gun at him and say, "Here, take the damn thing. I can't hit him with it nohow"). They had the other team in the wagon, and some of them were just loading the boat into the wagon when we came up, and Major de Spain told us how Old Ben and the dogs had crossed the river, and that Ad and Boon had swum it too, and that Uncle Ike was waiting at the river while he came back for the boat.

"He killed Kate this side of the river without even stopping," Major de Spain said. "Come on, boys. Lion wasn't five hundred yards behind him. He will bay him soon and then we will get him."

So we all went back to the river. But the boat was just a duck boat, so it wouldn't hold any more than Major de Spain and Uncle Ike. Theophilus McCaslin, Uncle Ike's grandson, said he knew about a log drift across the river about three miles down, so he and some of the others went to look for it. I wanted to go too, but father said I'd better come on back to camp so the rest of us came back to camp, with the mules and the wagon and the dead dog.

It began to rain before we got back; it rained slowly and steadily all afternoon, and we ate dinner and then Theophilus and the others came in and said they had got across the river but they couldn't hear anything and so they came back. The men played cards some but not much because every now and then somebody would go to the window and look out across the field to where the woods began, the black trees standing in the rain like a picture in ink beginning to dissolve. "He must have carried them clean out of the country," somebody said.

It was still raining at dark. But we didn't eat supper yet; we waited, and now there was somebody watching the woods all the time, and just before dark Theophilus McCaslin began to blow a horn every five minutes to guide them in. Yet when they did come, nobody saw them at all; we were all inside at the fire; we just heard the noise at the back door and then in the hall; we were still sitting down when Boon walked into the room. He was carrying something big wrapped in his hunting coat, but we didn't even look to see what it was because we were looking at Boon. He was wet and muddy and there was blood all over him, streaked by the rain. But that wasn't it. It was his face, his head. There was a bloody furrow (you could see the five claw-marks) wide as my hand starting up in his hair and running down the side of his head and right on down his arm to the wrist; there was a bloody blob hanging on the side of his head that I didn't know until the next day was his left ear,

and his right breeches' leg had been ripped off and the leg under
it looking like raw beef and the blood from it staining his boot
darker than the rain. But that wasn't it either. Because then we saw
that what he was carrying in the coat was Lion. He stood there in
the door, looking at us, and he began to cry. I never had seen a man
cry before. He stood there in the lamplight, looking big as all
outdoors and bloody as a hog, with that tough unshaven face of his
crinkled up and more like a dried walnut than ever, and the tears
streaming down it fast as rain.

"Good God, Boon!" father said. We got up then; we all kind of
surged toward him and somebody tried to touch the coat; I hadn't
even seen Major de Spain standing behind him until then.

"Get to hell away!" Boon hollered to the one who touched the
coat. "His guts are all out of him." Then he hollered, "Saddle me
a mule! Hurry!" and turned, with all of us following now, and
crossed the hall into the shed where he slept and laid Lion on his
pallet. "Damn it to hell, get me a mule!" he hollered.

"A mule?" somebody said.

"Yes!" Boon hollered. "I'm going to Hoke's and get a doctor!"

"No, you're not," Major de Spain said. "You need a doctor
yourself. One of the other boys will go."

"The hell I ain't!" Boon hollered. He looked wild, bloody and
wild as he glared round at us, then he ran out, the torn bloody
clothes flapping behind him, still hollering, "Help me catch a
mule!"

"Go and help them," father said, pushing me toward the door.
There were three of us. We were almost too late to help any; we
had to run to keep up with him. Maybe he was still crying, or
maybe he was in too much of a hurry to cry now. We kept on trying
to find out what happened but Boon couldn't even seem to hear the
questions; he was talking to himself, saddling the mule fast, cussing
and panting.

"I tried to get him back, make him stay out," he said. "I tried
to. And them others wouldn't help him, wouldn't go in." And he
did try. Ad said (Ad was there; he saw it all) that when Boon ran
in, Lion was already on the ground and that Boon caught him by
the hind leg and flung him twenty feet away, but that Lion hit the
ground already running and that he beat Boon back to Old Ben.

Then Boon got into the saddle without even touching the stir-

rups and was gone; we could hear the mule already loping. Then
we went back to the house, where Major de Spain was sitting on
the pallet with Lion's head in his lap, soaking a rag in a pan of
water and squeezing it into Lion's mouth. Lion was still wrapped
in the coat and under a blanket, to keep the air away from his
entrails. But I don't think he was suffering now. He just lay there
with his head on Major de Spain's knee and his eyes open a little
and looking yellower than ever in the lamplight; once I saw his
tongue come out and touch Major de Spain's hand. Then about
midnight (Major de Spain had sent the wagon back to the river
before he followed Boon into the house) Uncle Ike and Ad came
in with Old Ben; and Ad stood in the door too, as Boon had done,
with the tears running down his face too, and Uncle Ike told about
it, what Ad had told him: about how Lion had bayed Old Ben
against a down tree top and the other dogs would not go in, and
how Old Ben caught Lion and had him on the ground, and Boon
ran in with the hunting knife and jerked Lion back, but he would
not stay out; and how this time Boon jumped straddle of Old Ben's
back and got the knife into him, under the shoulder; Ad said that
Boon picked Old Ben clean up from behind, his arm round Old
Ben's neck and Old Ben striking backward at Boon's head and arm
while Boon worked the knife blade round until he touched the life.

Boon got back just before daylight with the doctor, and the
doctor told about that too: how Boon busted past the doctor's wife
when she opened the door and how the first thing the doctor knew
was when Boon waked him up dragging him out of the bed like a
sack of meal. He thought Boon was crazy, especially when he saw
him, the blood and all. Boon wouldn't even wait long enough to
have himself attended to; he didn't even want to wait long enough
for the doctor to put on his clothes. He wouldn't let the doctor do
anything for him now until he had fixed Lion; he just stood there
in his blood and his torn clothes and with his wild face, saying,
"Save him, Doc. By God, you had better save him!"

They couldn't give Lion chloroform; they didn't dare. They had
to put his entrails back and sew him up without it. But I still don't
think he felt it, suffered. He just lay there on Boon's pallet, with
his eyes half open and Major de Spain holding his head, until the
doctor was through. And not even Boon said, "Will he live?" We
just sat there and talked quietly until the light came and we went

out to look at Old Ben with his eyes open too and his lips snarled back and the neat slit just in front of the shoulder where Boon had finally found his life, and the mutilated hind foot and the little hard lumps under his skin which were the old bullets, the old victories. Then Ad said breakfast was ready. We ate, and I remember how that was the first time we could not hear any dogs under the kitchen, though I asked Ad and he said that they were there. It was as though Old Ben, even dead and harmless out there in the yard, was a more potent force than they were alive without Lion to lead them in, and they knew it.

The rain had stopped before midnight and about noon a thin sun came out and we moved Lion out onto the porch, in the sun. It was Boon's idea. "Damn it," he said, "he never did like to stay in the house. You know that. At least let's take him out where he can see the woods." So Boon loosened the floor boards under the pallet so that we could pick up the pallet without changing Lion's position, and we carried him out to the porch and we sat there now. The people at Hoke's had heard that we had got Old Ben and about Lion; there must have been a hundred men came in during the afternoon to look at Old Ben and then come and look at Lion, to sit and talk quietly about Lion, the races he had made and the bears he had brought to bay, and now and then Lion would open his eyes (Boon had laid him so he could look at the woods without moving) not as if he was listening to what they were saying but as if he was looking at the woods for a moment before closing his eyes again, remembering the woods again or seeing that they were still there. Maybe he was, because he waited until dark before he died. We broke camp that night; we went out in the wagon, in the dark. Boon was quite drunk by then. He was singing, loud.

This is how Lion's death affected the two people who loved him most—if you could have called Boon's feeling for him, for anything, love. And I suppose you could, since they say you always love that which causes you suffering. Or maybe Boon did not consider being clawed by a bear suffering.

Major de Spain never went back again. But we did; he made us welcome to go; it seemed to please him when we went. Father and the others who had been there that time would talk about it, about how maybe if they could just persuade him to go back once . . .

But he would not; he was almost sharp when he refused. I remember the day in the next summer when I went to his office to ask permission to go in and hunt squirrels. "Help yourself," he said. "Ad will be glad to have some company. Do you want to take anybody with you?"

"No, sir," I said. "I thought if maybe Boon . . ."

"Yes," he said. "I'll wire him to meet you there." Boon was the marshal at Hoke's now; Major de Spain called his secretary and sent Boon the wire right away. We didn't need to wait for an answer; Boon would be there; he had been doing what Major de Spain told him to for twenty years now at least. So I thanked him and then I stood there and after a minute I got up my nerve and said it:

"Maybe if you would come . . ."

But he stopped me. I don't know how he did it because he didn't say anything at once. He just seemed to turn to his desk and the papers on it without moving; and I stood there looking down at a little plumpish gray-headed man in expensive, unobtrusive clothes and an old-fashioned immaculate boiled shirt, whom I was used to seeing in muddy khaki, unshaven, sitting the mule with the carbine across the saddle, and Lion standing beside him as a thoroughbred horse stands and motionless as a statue, with his strong grave head and his fine chest; the two of them somehow queerly alike, as two people get who have been closely associated for many years in doing something which both of them love and respect. He didn't look at me again.

"No. I will be too busy. But if you have luck, you might bring me a few squirrels when you come back."

"Yes, sir," I said. "I will." So I reached Hoke's early and caught the morning log train into the woods and they put me off at our crossing. It was the same, yet different, because they were summer woods now, in full leaf, not like that iron dawn when Boon and I had flagged the train to go in to Memphis. And it was hot too. Ad was there with the wagon to meet me; we shook hands. "Mr. Boon here yet?" I said.

"Yes, suh. He got in last night. He in de woods fo daylight. Gone up to de Gum Tree."

I knew where that was. It was a single big gum just outside the woods, in an old clearing. If you crept up to it quietly just after daylight this time of year, sometimes you would catch a dozen squirrels in it, trapped there because they could not jump to another tree and dared not descend. So I told Ad to take my duffel on to the house; I would hunt up through the woods and meet Boon. I didn't say I was going by the holly knoll, but he must have known that I was, because the point where he put me down was on a direct line with the knoll and the Gum Tree. "Watch out for snakes," he said. "Dey's crawling now."

"I will," I said. He went on and I entered the woods. They were changed, different. Of course it was just the summer; next fall they would be again as I remembered them. Then I knew that that was wrong; that they would never again be as I remembered them, as any of us remembered them, and I, a boy, who had owned no Lion, knew now why Major de Spain knew that he would never return and was too wise to try to. I went on. Soon the earth began to lift under my feet and then I saw the hollies, the four pale trunks marking the four corners and inside them the wooden cross with Old Ben's dried mutilated paw nailed to it. There was no trace of grave any more; the spring flood water had seen to that. But that was all right because it was not Lion who was there; not Lion. Maybe it was nice for him now, nice for him and Old Ben both now —the long challenge and the long chase, the one with no heart to be driven and outraged, the other with no flesh to be mauled and bled. It was hot and the mosquitoes were too bad to stand still in, besides it was too late to hunt any more this morning; I would go on and pick up Boon and go back to camp. I knew these woods and presently I knew that I could not be very far from the Gum Tree.

Then I began to hear a curious sound. It sounded like a blacksmith shop—someone hammering fast on metal. It grew louder as I approached. Then I saw the clearing, the sun; the hammering, the furious hammering on metal, was quite loud now, and the trees broke and I saw the Gum Tree and then I saw Boon. It was the same Boon; he had not changed; the same Boon who had almost missed that nigger and had missed that buck; who could not shoot even when his old worn-out gun held together. He was sitting under the tree, hammering at something in his lap, and then I saw that the tree was apparently alive with frightened squirrels. I watched them rush from limb to limb, trying to escape, and rush, dart, down the trunk and then turn and dart back up again. Then I saw what Boon was hammering at. It was a section of his gun; drawing nearer, I saw the rest of it scattered in a dozen pieces about him on the ground where he sat, hunched over, hammering furiously at the part on his lap, his walnut face wild and urgent and streaming with sweat. He was living, as always, in the moment; nothing on earth—not Lion, not anything in the past—mattered to him except his helpless fury with his broken gun. He didn't stop; he didn't even look up to see who I was; he just shouted at me in a hoarse desperate voice.

Get out of here!" he said. "Don't touch them! They're mine!"

The Old People

At first there was nothing but the faint, cold, steady rain, the gray
and constant light of the late November dawn, and the voices of
the dogs converging somewhere in it. Then Sam Fathers, standing
just behind me, as he had been standing when I shot my first
running rabbit four years ago, touched me and I began to shake,
not with any cold, and then the buck was there. He did not come
into sight; he was just there, looking not like a ghost but as if all
of light were condensed in him and he were the source of it, not
only moving in it but disseminating it, already running, seen first
as you always see the deer, in that split second after he has already
seen you, already slanting away in that first soaring bound, the
antlers even in that dim light looking like a small rocking-chair
balanced on his head.

"Now," Sam said, "shoot quick and slow."

I don't remember that shot at all. I don't even remember what
I did with the gun afterward. I was running, then I was standing
over him where he lay on the wet ground still in the attitude of
running and not looking at all dead. I was shaking and jerking
again and Sam was beside me and I had his knife in my hand.

"Don't walk up to him in front," Sam said. "If he ain't dead he
will cut you all to pieces with his feet. Walk up to him from behind
and take him by the horn."

And I did that—drew the throat taut by one of the antlers and
drew Sam's knife across it, and Sam stooped and dipped his hands
in the hot blood and wiped them back and forth across my face.
Then he blew his horn and there was a moiling of dogs about us

with Jimbo and Boon Hogganbeck driving them back after they
had all had a taste of the blood. Then father and Major de Spain
sitting the horses, and Walter Ewell with his rifle which never
missed, from the barrel of which all the bluing had long since been
worn away, were looking down at us—at the old man of seventy
who had been a Negro for two generations now but whose face and
bearing were still those of the Chickasaw chief, and the white boy
of twelve with the prints of the bloody hands across his face, who
now had nothing to do but stand straight and not let the shaking
show.

"Did he do all right, Sam?" father said.

"He done all right," Sam Fathers said.

We were the white boy, not yet a man, whose grandfather had
lived in the same country and in almost the same manner as the
boy himself would grow up to live, leaving his descendants in the
land in his turn, and the old man past seventy whose grandfathers
had owned the land long before the white men ever saw it and who
had vanished from it now with all their kind, what of blood they
had left behind them running now in another race and for a while
even in bondage and now drawing toward the end of its alien
course, barren. Because Sam Fathers had no children.

His grandfather was Ikkemotubbe himself, who had named himself Doom. Sam told me about that—how Ikkemotubbe, old Issetibbeha's sister's son, had run away to New Orleans in his youth
and returned seven years later to the plantation in north Mississippi, with a French companion called the Chevalier Soeur-Blonde
de Vitry, who must have been the Ikkemotubbe of his family too
and who was already addressing Ikkemotubbe as *Du Homme,* and
the slave woman who was to be Sam's grandmother, and a gold-
laced hat and coat and a wicker basket containing a litter of puppies and a gold snuffbox of white powder. And how he was met at
the river by two or three companions of his bachelor youth, and
with the light of a smoking torch glinting on the gold-laced hat and
coat, Doom took one of the puppies from the basket and put a
pinch of the white powder from the gold box on its tongue, and at
once the puppy ceased to be a puppy. And how the next day the
eight-year-old son of Doom's cousin, Moketubbe, who was now
hereditary head of the clan (Issetibbeha was now dead) died suddenly, and that afternoon Doom, in the presence of Moketubbe and

most of the others (the People, Sam always called them), took another puppy from the basket and put a pinch of the powder on its tongue, and so Moketubbe abdicated and Doom became in fact the Man which his French friend already called him. And how Doom married the slave woman, already pregnant, to one of the slaves which he had just inherited—hence Sam Fathers' name, which in Chickasaw had been Had-Two-Fathers—and later sold them both and the child too (his own son) to my great-grandfather almost a hundred years ago.

Up to three years ago he had lived on our farm four miles from Jefferson, though all he ever did was what blacksmithing and carpentering was needed. And he lived among Negroes, in a cabin among the other cabins, he consorted with them and dressed like them and talked like them and went to a Negro church now and then. But for all that, he was still the grandson of that Indian chief and the Negroes knew it. Boon Hogganbeck's grandmother had been a Chickasaw woman too, and although the blood had run white since and Boon was a white man, it was not a chief's blood. You could see the difference at once when you saw them together, and even Boon seemed to know that the difference was there—even Boon, to whom in his tradition it had never occurred that anyone might be better born than himself. A man might be smarter, he admitted that, or richer (luckier, he called it) but not better born. He was a mastiff, absolutely faithful to father and Major de Spain, absolutely dependent upon them for his very bread, hardy, courageous enough, a slave to all the appetites and almost unrational. It was Sam Fathers who bore himself, not only toward father but toward all white men, with gravity and dignity and without servility or recourse to that impenetrable wall of ready and easy mirth which Negroes sustain between themselves and white men, bearing himself toward father not only as one man to another but as an older man to a younger one.

He taught me the woods, to hunt, when to shoot and when not to shoot, when to kill and when not to kill, and better, what to do with it afterward. Then he would talk to me, the two of us sitting under the close fierce stars on a summer hilltop while we waited for the dogs to return within hearing behind the red or gray fox they ran, or beside a fire in the November or December woods while the dogs worked out a coon's trail along the creek, or fireless in the pitch dark and the heavy dew of April mornings while we waited for daylight beneath a turkey roost. I would not question him; he did not react to questions. I would just wait and then listen and he would begin, talking about the old days and the People whom he had never known, and so could not remember himself, and in place of whom the other race into which his blood had run had supplied him with no substitute.

And as he talked about those old times and those dead and vanished men of another race from either that I knew, gradually those old times would cease to be old times and would become the present, now, not only as if they had happened yesterday but as if they were still happening and some of them had not even happened yet but would occur to-morrow, so that at last it would seem as if I myself had not come into existence yet, that none of my race nor the other race which we had brought into the land with us had come here yet; that although it had been my grandfather's and was now my father's and someday would be my land which we hunted over and now rested upon, our hold upon it actually was as trivial and without reality as that now faded and archaic script in one of the Chancery Clerk's books in the courthouse in town, and that it was I who was the guest here and Sam Fathers' voice the mouthpiece of the host.

Until three years ago there had been two of them, the other a full-blood Chickasaw, in a sense even more astonishingly lost than Sam Fathers. He called himself Jobaker, as if it were one word. Nobody knew his history at all. He was a hermit, he lived in a foul little shack at the forks of the creek four or five miles from our farm and about that far from any other habitation. He was a market hunter and fisherman and he consorted with nobody, black or white; no Negro would even cross his path and no man dared approach his hut except Sam, and perhaps once a month I would find the two of them in Sam's shop—two old men squatting on their heels on the dirt floor, talking in a mixture of negroid English and flat hill dialect and now and then a phrase of that old tongue which as time went on and I squatted there too listening, I began to learn. Then he died. That is, nobody had seen him in some time. Then one morning Sam Fathers was missing, none of the Negroes knew when nor where, until that night when some Negroes possum-hunting saw the sudden burst of flames and approached them.

It was Joe Baker's hut, but before they got anywhere near it someone shot toward them. It was Sam, but nobody ever found Joe Baker's grave.

Two days after that Sam walked to town and came to father's office. I was there when he walked in without knocking and stood there—the Indian, with the Indian face for all the nigger clothes.

"I want to go," he said. "I want to go to the big bottom to live."

"To live?" father said.

"You can fix it with Major de Spain," Sam said. "I could live in the camp and take care of it for you all. Or I could build me a little house." For a little while they both looked at each other, he and father. Then father said:

"All right. I'll fix it." And Sam went out, and that was all.

I was nine then; it seemed perfectly natural to me that nobody, not even father, would argue with Sam any more than I would. But I could not understand it.

"If Joe Baker's dead like they say," I said, "and Sam hasn't got anybody any more at all kin to him, why does he want to go into the big bottom, where he won't ever see anybody except us for a few days in the fall while we are hunting?"

Father looked at me. It was not a curious look, it was just thoughtful. I didn't notice it then. I did not remember it until later. Then he quit looking at me.

"Maybe that's what he wants," he said.

So Sam moved. He owned so little that he could carry it. He walked. He would neither let father send him in the wagon nor would he take one of the mules. He was just gone one morning, the cabin vacant in which he had lived for years yet in which there never had been very much, the shop standing idle now in which there never had been very much to do. Each November we would go into the big bottom, to the camp—Major de Spain and father and Walter Ewell and Boon and Uncle Ike McCaslin and two or three others, with Jimbo and Uncle Ash to cook, and the dogs. Sam would be there; if he was glad to see us he did not show it. If he regretted to see us depart again he did not show that. Each morning he would go out to my stand with me before the dogs were cast. It would be one of the poorer stands of course, since I was only nine and ten and eleven and I had never even seen a deer running yet.

But we would stand there, Sam a little behind me and without a gun himself, as he had stood when I shot the running rabbit when I was eight years old; we would stand there in the November dawns and after a while we would hear the dogs. Sometimes they would sweep up and past, close, belling and invisible; once we heard the five heavy reports of Boon's old pump gun with which he had never killed anything larger than a rabbit or a squirrel, and that sitting, and twice we heard from our stand the flat unreverberant clap of Walter Ewell's rifle which never missed, so that you did not even wait to hear his horn.

"I'll never get a shot," I said. "I'll never kill one."

"Yes you will," Sam said. "You wait. You'll be a hunter. You'll be a man."

And we would leave him there. He would go out to the road where the surrey would be waiting in order to take the horses and mules back; for now that he lived at the camp all the time, father and Major de Spain left the horses and the dogs there. They would go on ahead on the horses and Uncle Ash and Jimbo and I would follow in the wagon with Sam, with the guns and the bedding and the meat and the heads, the antlers, the good ones, the wagon winding on among the tremendous gums and cypresses and oaks where no axe had ever sounded, between the impenetrable brakes of cane and brier—the two changing yet constant walls just beyond which the wilderness seemed to lean, stooping a little, watching us and listening; not quite inimical because we were too small, our sojourn too brief and too harmless to excite to that, just brooding, secret, almost inattentive. Then we would emerge, we would be out of it, the line as sharp as the demarcation of a doored wall. Suddenly skeletoned cotton- and corn-fields would flow away on either hand, gaunt and motionless beneath the gray rain; there would be a house, barns, where the hand of man had clawed for an instant, holding, the wall of the wilderness behind us now, tremendous and still and seemingly impenetrable in the gray and fading light. The surrey would be waiting, father and Major de Spain and Uncle Ike dismounted beside it. Then Sam would get down from the wagon and mount one of the horses and, with the others at lead behind him, he would turn back. I would watch him for a while against that tall and secret wall, growing smaller and smaller against it. He would not look back. Then he would enter it, returning to what I believed, and thought that father believed, was his loneliness and solitude.

So the instant came; I pulled trigger and ceased to be a child forever and became a hunter and a man. It was the last day. We broke camp that afternoon and went out, father and Major de Spain and Uncle Ike and Boon on the horses and mules, Walter Ewell and old Ash and Jimbo and I in the wagon with Sam and the duffel and my hide and antlers. There could have been other trophies in the wagon too but I should not have known it, just as for all practical purposes Sam Fathers and I were still alone together as we had been that morning, the wagon winding and jolting on between those shifting yet constant walls from beyond which the wilderness watched us passing, less than inimical now and never inimical again since my buck still and forever leaped, the shaking gun-barrels coming constantly and forever steady at last, crashing, and still out of his moment of mortality the buck sprang, forever immortal, that moment of the buck, the shot, Sam Fathers and myself and the blood with which he had marked me forever, one with the wilderness which had now accepted me because Sam had said that I had done all right; the wagon winding on, when suddenly Sam checked it and we all heard that unforgettable and unmistakable sound of a deer breaking cover.

Then Boon shouted from beyond the bend of the trail and while we all sat motionless in the halted wagon, Walter and I already reaching for our guns, Boon came galloping back, flogging his mule with his hat, his face wild and amazed as he shouted down at us. Then father and the others came round the bend.

"Get the dogs!" Boon cried. "Get the dogs! If he had a nub on his head, he had fourteen points! Laying right there in that pawpaw thicket! If I'd a knowed he was there, I could a cut his throat with my pocket knife!"

"Maybe that's why he run," Walter said. "He saw you never had your gun." He was already out of the wagon, with his rifle. Then I was out too with my gun, and father and Major de Spain and Uncle Ike had come up and Boon got off his mule somehow and was scrabbling among the duffel for his gun, still shouting, "Get the dogs! Get the dogs!" And it seemed to me too that it would take them forever to decide what to do—the old men in whom the blood ran cold and slow, in whom during the intervening years between us the blood had become a different and colder substance from that which ran in me and even in Boon and Walter.

"What about it, Sam?" father said. "Could the dogs bring him back?"

"We won't need the dogs," Sam said. "If he don't hear dogs behind him he will circle back in here about sundown to bed."

"All right," Major de Spain said. "You boys take the horses. We'll go on out to the road in the wagon and wait there." So he and father and Uncle Ike got into the wagon, and Boon and Walter and Sam and I took the horses and turned back and out of the trail. We rode for about an hour, through the gray and unmarked afternoon whose light was little different from what it had been at dawn and which would become darkness without any graduation. Then Sam stopped us.

"This is far enough," he said. "He'll be coming upwind, and he don't want to smell the mules."

So we dismounted and tied them and followed Sam on foot through the markless afternoon, through the unpathed woods.

"You got time," Sam said to me once. "We'll get there before he does."

So I tried to go slower. That is, I tried to slow, decelerate, the dizzy rush of time in which the buck which I had not even seen was moving, which it seemed to me was carrying him farther and farther and more and more irretrievably away from us even though there were no dogs behind him to make him run yet. So we went on; it seemed to me that it was for another hour. Then suddenly we were on a ridge. I had never been in there before and you could not see the ridge; you just knew that the earth had risen slightly because the undergrowth had thinned a little and the ground which you could not see slanted, sloping away toward a dense brake of cane.

"This is it," Sam said. "You all follow the ridge and you will come to two crossings. You can see the tracks."

Boon and Walter went on. Soon they had disappeared, and once more Sam and I were standing motionless in a clump of switchlike bushes against the trunk of a pin oak, and again there was nothing, as in the morning. There was the soaring and somber solitude in the dim light, there was the thin whisper of the faint cold rain which had not ceased all day; then, as if it had waited for us to find our positions and become still, the wilderness breathed again. It seemed to lean inward above us, above Walter, and Boon, and Sam and me in our separate lurking-places, tremendous, attentive, impartial, and omniscient, the buck moving in it too somewhere, not running since he had not been pursued, not frightened and never fearsome but just alert too as we were alert, perhaps already circling back, perhaps quite near, conscious too of the eye of the ancient immortal Umpire. Because I was just twelve then, and that morning something had happened to me: in less than a second I had ceased forever to be the child I was yesterday. Or perhaps this made no difference, perhaps even a city-bred man, let alone a child, could not have understood it; perhaps only a country-bred one could comprehend loving the life he spills. I began to shake again.

"I'm glad it's started now," I whispered. "Then it will be gone when I raise the gun—"

"Hush," Sam said.

"Is he that near?" I whispered. We did not move to speak: only our lips shaping the expiring words. "Do you think—"

"Hush," Sam said. So I hushed. But I could not stop the shaking. I did not try, because I knew that it would go away when I needed the steadiness, since Sam Fathers had already made me a hunter. So we stood there, motionless, scarcely breathing. If there had been any sun it would be near to setting now; there was a condensing, a densifying, of what I thought was the gray and unchanging light until I realized it was my own breathing, my heart, my blood—something, and that Sam had marked me indeed with something he had had of his vanished and forgotten people. Then I stopped breathing, there was only my heart, my blood, and in the following silence the wilderness ceased to breathe too, leaning, stooping overhead with held breath, tremendous and impartial and waiting. Then the shaking stopped too, as I had known it would, and I slipped the safety off the gun.

Then it had passed. It was over. The solitude did not breathe again yet; it had merely stopped watching me and was looking somewhere else, and I knew as well as if I had seen him that the buck had come to the edge of the cane and had either seen or scented us and had faded back into it. But still the solitude was not breathing, it was merely looking somewhere else. So I did not move yet, and then, a second after I realized what I was listening for, we heard it—the flat single clap of Walter Ewell's rifle following which you did not need to wait for the horn. Then the sound of the horn itself came down the ridge and something went out of me too and I knew then that I had never really believed that I should get the shot.

"I reckon that's all," I said. "Walter got him."

I had shifted the gun forward, my thumb on the safety again and I was already moving out of the thicket when Sam said:

"Wait." And I remember how I turned upon him in the truculence of a boy's grief over the missed chance, the missed luck.

"Wait?" I said. "What for? Don't you hear that horn?"

And I remember how he was standing. He had not moved. He was not tall, he was rather squat and broad, and I had been growing fast for the past year or so and there was not much difference between us, yet he was looking over my head. He was looking across me and up the ridge toward the sound of Walter's horn and he did not see me; he just knew I was there, he did not see me. And then I saw the buck. He was coming down the ridge; it was as if he were walking out of the very sound of the horn which signified a kill. He was not running; he was walking, tremendous, unhurried, slanting and tilting his head to pass his antlers through the undergrowth, and I standing there with Sam beside me now instead of behind me as he always stood and the gun which I knew I was not going to use already slanted forward and the safety already off.

Then he saw us. And still he did not begin to flee. He just stopped for an instant, taller than any man, looking at us, then his muscles suppled, gathered. He did not even alter his course, not fleeing, not even running, just moving with that winged and effortless ease with which deer move, passing within twenty feet of us, his head high and the eye not proud and not haughty but just full and wild and unafraid, and Sam standing beside me now, his right arm lifted at full length and the hand turned palm-outward, and speaking in that tongue which I had learned from listening to him and Joe Baker, while up the ridge Walter Ewell's horn was still blowing us in to a dead buck.

"Oleh, Chief," he said. "Grandfather."

When we reached Walter he was standing with his back toward us, looking down at the deer. He didn't look up at all.

"Come here, Sam," he said quietly. When we reached him he still did not look up, standing there over a little spike buck which even last spring had still been a fawn. "He was so little I pretty near let him go," Walter said. "But just look at the track he was making. It's pretty near big as a cow's. If there were any more tracks here besides the ones he is laying in, I would swear there was another buck that I never even saw."

It was after dark when we reached the road where the surrey was waiting. It was turning cold, the rain had stopped, and the sky was beginning to blow clear. Father and Major de Spain and Uncle Ike had a fire going. "Did you get him?" father said.

"Got a good-sized swamp-rabbit with spike horns," Walter said, sliding the little buck down from his mule.

"Nobody saw the big one?" father said.

"I don't even believe Boon saw it," Walter said. "He probably jumped a stray cow back there."

Then Boon started cursing, swearing at Walter and at Sam for not getting the dogs to begin with and at the buck and all.

"Never mind," father said. "He'll be here for us next fall. Let's get started home now."

And it was after midnight when we let Walter out at his gate two miles from town and it was later still when we put Major de Spain and Uncle Ike down at Major de Spain's. It was cold, the sky was clear now; there would be a heavy frost by sunup and the ground was frozen beneath the horses' feet and beneath the wheels. I had slept a little but not much and not because of the cold. And then suddenly I was telling father, the surrey moving on toward home over the frozen ground, the horses trotting again, sensing the stable. He listened quite quietly.

"Why not?" he said. "Think of all that has happened here, on this earth. All the blood hot and fierce and strong for living, pleasuring. Grieving and suffering too of course, but still getting something out of it for all that, getting a lot out of it, because after all you don't have to continue to bear what you believe is suffering; you can always stop that. And even suffering and grieving is better than nothing; there is nothing worse than not being alive. But you can't be alive forever, and you always wear out life before you have completely exhausted the possibilities of living. And all that must

be somewhere. And the earth is shallow; there is not a great deal
of it before you come to the rock. And even that does not want to
keep things. Look at the seed, the acorns, at what happens even to
carrion when you try to bury it: it refuses too, seethes and struggles
too until it reaches light and air again, hunting the sun still. And
they—" he lifted his hand for an instant toward the sky where the
scoured and icy stars glittered "—they don't want it, need it.
Besides, what would it want, knocking about out there, when it
never had enough time about the earth as it was, when there is
plenty of room about the earth, plenty of places still unchanged
from what they were when the blood used and pleasured in them
while it was still blood?"

"But we want them," I said. "We still want them. There is plenty
of room among us for them."

"That's right," father said. "Suppose they don't have substance,
can't cast a shadow—"

"But I saw it!" I cried. "I saw it!"

"Steady," father said. For an instant his hand rested upon my
knee. "Steady. I know you did. So did I. Sam took me in there once
after I killed my first deer."

A Point of Law

Lucas pushed his chair back from the supper table and got up. He gave the sullen and watchful face of his daughter, Nat, a single grim-veiled look. "Gwine down the road," he said.

"Whar you gwine dis time er night?" his wife demanded. "Messin' around up yon in de bottom all last night; gittin' back just in time to hitch up and be in de field when de sun cotch you! You needs to be in bed if you gonter git done plantin' fo' Roth Edmonds—"

But then he was out of the house and did not need to hear her any longer, in the road now which ran pale and dim beneath the moonless sky of corn-planting time, between the fields where next month, when the whippoorwills began, he would plant his cotton, to the big gate from which the private road mounted among oaks to the crest where the bright lamps of his landlord's house gleamed.

He had nothing against George Wilkins personally. If George Wilkins had just stuck to farming, to working the land which he too share-cropped from Roth Edmonds, he, Lucas, would just as soon Nat were married to George as anybody else, sooner than most of the other buck niggers in that neighborhood. But he was not going to let George Wilkins or anybody else move into the country where he had lived for forty-five years and set up in competition with him in a business which he had established and nursed carefully and discreetly for almost twenty years, ever since he built his first still, secretly and at night since nobody needed to tell him what Roth Edmonds would do if he found out about it.

He wasn't afraid that George would cut into his established

clientele, his old regular customers, with the sort of hog swill which George Wilkins had begun to manufacture three months ago and called whisky. But George Wilkins was a fool without discretion, who sooner or later would inevitably be caught, whereupon for the next ten years every bush on Roth Edmonds' place would have a deputy sheriff squatting behind it all night long. And he, Lucas, not only wasn't going to let his daughter become the wife of a fool, he didn't intend to have a fool living on the same place he lived on.

When he reached the big house, he didn't mount the steps. Instead he stood on the ground, rapping on the edge of the veranda with his knuckles until Edmonds came to the door, peering into the darkness. "Who is it?" he said.

"Luke," Lucas said.

"Come in to the light," Edmonds said.

"I'll talk here," Lucas said.

Edmonds approached. Lucas was the older of the two; in fact, he had been on the place, living in the same house and working the same acres for twenty-five years when Carothers Edmonds' father died. Lucas was at least sixty; it was known that he had one daughter with grandchildren, and he was probably more solvent than Edmonds, since he owned nothing he had to pay taxes on and keep repaired and fenced and ditched and fertilized.

Yet now he became, not the Negro which he was, but nigger— not secret so much as impenetrable, not servile and not effacing, but standing motionless in the half-dark below the white man in an aura of timeless and impassive stupidity like a smell almost.

"George Wilkins is running a kettle in that gully behind the old west field," he said in a voice perfectly flat and uninflectioned. "If they wants the whisky too, tell um to look under his kitchen floor."

"What?" Edmonds said. He began to roar—a quick-tempered man at best: "Didn't I tell you niggers what I was going to do the first time I found a drop of white mule whisky on this place?"

"George Wilkins gonter hear you too," Lucas said. "You didn't need to told me. I been on this place forty-five years and you ain't never heard of me having no truck with no kind of whisky except that bottle of town whisky you and your paw always give me Christmas."

"I know it," Edmonds said. "You've got better sense, because you knew good and well what I would do if I ever caught you. And George Wilkins will wish by daylight . . ." Lucas stood, motionless, blinking a little, listening to the rapid clapping of the white man's angry heels and then to the prolonged and violent grinding of the telephone crank and Edmonds shouting into the instrument: "Yes! The sheriff! I don't care where he is! Find him!"

Lucas waited until he had finished. "I don't reckon you need me no more," he said.

"No," Edmonds said in the house. "Go on home to bed. I want your south creek piece all planted by tomorrow night. You doped around in it today like you hadn't been to bed in a week."

Lucas returned home. He was tired. He had been up most of last night, first following Nat to see if she was going to meet George Wilkins after he had forbidden her to, then, in his secret place in the creek bottom, finishing his final run and dismantling his still and carrying it piece by piece still farther into the bottom and concealing it, reaching home only an hour before dawn.

His house was dark save for the faint glow among the ashes in the room where he and his wife slept—the fire which he had lit on the hearth when he moved into the house forty-five years ago and which had burned ever since. The room where his daughter slept was dark. He did not need to enter it to know it was empty. He had expected it to be. George Wilkins was entitled to one more evening of female companionship, because tomorrow he was going to take up residence for a long time where he would not have it.

When he got into bed his wife said, without even waking: "Whar you been? Wawkin' de roads all night wid de ground cryin' to git planted—" Then she stopped talking without waking either, and sometime later he waked.

It was after midnight; he lay beneath the quilt on the shuck mattress, not triumphant, not vindictive. It would be happening about now. He knew how they did it—the white sheriff and revenue officers and deputies creeping up through the bushes with a drawn pistol or two, surrounding the still and sniffing like hunting dogs at every stump and disfiguration of earth until every jug and keg was found and carried back to where the car waited; maybe they would even take a sup or two to ward off the night's chill, before returning to the still to squat there until George Wilkins walked innocently in.

Maybe it will be a lesson to George Wilkins about whose daughter to fool with next time, he thought.

Then his wife was leaning over the bed, shaking him and screaming. It was just after dawn. In his shirt and drawers he ran behind her, out onto the back porch. Sitting on the ground was George Wilkins' patched and battered still; on the porch itself was an assortment of fruit jars and stoneware jugs and a keg or so and one rusted five-gallon oilcan which, to Lucas' horrified and still sleep-dulled eyes, appeared capable of holding enough liquid to fill a ten-foot horse trough. He could even see it in the glass jars—a pale, colorless fluid in which still floated the shredded corn-husks which George Wilkins' tenth-hand still had not removed.

"Whar was Nat last night?" he cried, shaking his wife by the shoulder. "Whar was Nat, old woman?"

"She lef' right behind you!" his wife cried. "She followed you! Didn't you know it?"

"I knows it now," Luke said. "Git the ax!" he said. "Bust it! We ain't got time to git it away." But they didn't have time for that either. It was the sheriff himself, followed by a deputy, who came around the corner of the house.

"Dammit, Luke," the sheriff said, "I thought you had better sense than this."

"That ain't none of mine," Lucas said. "You knows it ain't. George Wilkins—"

"Never you mind about George Wilkins," the sheriff said. "I've got him too. He's out there in the car, with that girl of yours. Go get your pants on. We're going to town."

Two hours later he was in the commissioner's office in the federal courthouse in Jefferson, inscrutable of face, blinking a little, listening to George Wilkins breathing hard beside him and to the voices of the white men:

"Confound it, Carothers," the commissioner said, "what kind of Senegambian Montague and Capulet business is this?"

"Ask them!" Edmonds said violently. "Wilkins and that girl of Luke's want to get married. Luke won't hear of it, for some reason —only I seem to be finding out now why. So last night Luke came to the house and told me Wilkins was running a still on my land because he knew damn' well what I would do because I have been telling every nigger on my place for years just what I would do the first time I caught one drop of that damn' wildcat whisky on my place—"

"And we got Mr. Roth's telephone message"—it was one of the deputies now—a plump, voluble man muddy about the lower legs and a little strained and weary in the face—"and we went out there and Mr. Roth told us where to look. But there ain't no still in the gully where he said, so we set down and thought about just where would we hide a still if we was one of Mr. Roth's niggers, and we went and looked there and sure enough after a while there it was, all took to pieces and hid careful and neat as you could want, in a brier brake in the creek bottom. Only it's getting toward daylight by that time, so we decide to come on back to George Wilkins' house and look under his kitchen floor like Mr. Roth said and then have a little talk with George.

"We get there about daybreak and what do we see but George and that gal legging it up the hill toward Luke's house with a gallon jug in each hand, only George busted the jugs on a root before we could catch them. Then Luke's wife starts to yelling in the house and we run around to the back and there is another still setting in Luke's back yard and about forty gallons of evidence stacked on his back porch like he was fixing to hold a auction sale, and Luke standing there in his drawers and shirttail hollering, 'Git the ax and bust it! Git the ax and bust it!' "

"But who do you charge?" the commissioner said. "You went out there to catch George, but all your evidence is against Luke."

"There was two stills," the deputy said. "And George and that gal both say Luke has been making and selling whisky right there in Mr. Roth's back yard for twenty years." Blinking, Lucas found Edmonds glaring at him, not in reproach and no longer in surprise, but in grim and furious outrage. Then, without even moving his eyes and with no change in his face he was no longer looking at Edmonds, but blinking quietly, listening to George Wilkins breathing hard beside him like one in profound slumber, and to the voices:

"But you can't make his own daughter testify against him."

"George can though," the deputy said. "George ain't no kin to him. Not to mention being in a fix where George has got to think of something good to say and think of it quick."

"Let the court settle all that, Tom," the sheriff said. "I was up all last night and I haven't even had my breakfast yet. I've brought you a prisoner and thirty or forty gallons of evidence and two witnesses. Let's get done with this."

"I think you've brought two prisoners," the commissioner said. He began to write on the paper before him. Lucas watched the moving hand, blinking. "I'm going to commit them both. George can testify against Luke, if he wants to. And that girl can testify against George. She's no kin to him, too."

Lucas could have paid both his and George's bonds without even altering the number of figures in his bank balance. After Edmonds had paid for the bonds, they returned to his car. George drove now, with Nat beside him in the front seat, huddled down into the corner of it. When the car stopped at the gate seventeen miles later, she sprang out, still without looking at Lucas, and ran on up the road toward his house. They drove on to the stable, where George got out too. His hat was still raked above his right ear, but his sepia face was not full of teeth as it usually was. "Go on and get your mule," Edmonds said. Then he looked at Lucas. "What are you waiting on?"

"I thought you were fixing to say something," Lucas said. "So a man's kinfolks can't tell on him in court?"

"Never you mind about that," Edmonds said. "George ain't any kin to you and he can tell plenty. And if he should start to forget, Nat ain't any kin to George and she can tell plenty. You've waited too late. If George Wilkins and Nat tried to buy a wedding license now, they would probably hang you and George both. Besides, even if Judge Gowan don't, I'm going to take both of you to the penitentiary myself as soon as you have laid by. Now you get on down to your south creek field. Don't you come out until you have finished planting it. If dark catches you, I'll send somebody down with a lantern."

He was done in the south creek piece before dark. He was back at the stable, his mule watered and rubbed down and stalled and fed and the gear hanging on its peg beside the stall door, while George was still unharnessing. Then he was walking up the hill in the beginning of twilight, toward his house, not fast; he didn't even look back when he spoke:

"George Wilkins."

"Sir," George said, behind him. Lucas neither slowed nor looked back. They went on, mounting the hill, until they reached the battered gate in the weathered fence enclosing his small dusty yard. Then Lucas stopped and looked back at George behind him, lean, foppish even in overalls, wasp-waisted, with no teeth visible now either in the face sober, not to say grave, beneath the rake of the ruined Panama hat.

"Just what was your idea?" Lucas said.

"I don't rightly know, sir," George said. "It uz mostly Nat's. We never aimed to get you in no trouble. She say maybe ifn we took and fotch dat kettle from whar you and Mister Roth told de shurf hit was and you would find hit settin' on yo' back porch, maybe when we offered to help you git shet of hit 'fo' de shurf got here, yo' mind might change about loanin' us de money to—I mean to leffin' us be married. . . ." Lucas looked at George. He didn't blink.

"Hah," he said. "There's more folks than just me in that trouble."

"Yes, sir," George said. "Hit look like it. I hope it's gonter be a lesson to me."

"I hope so too," Lucas said. "When they get done sending you to Parchman, you'll have plenty of time to study it."

"Yes, sir," George said. "Especially wid you to help me."

"Hah," Lucas said again. He continued to stare at George; he raised his voice though only a little: a single word, peremptory and cold, still staring at George: "Nat."

The girl came down the path, barefoot, in a clean, faded calico dress and a bright headrag. She had been crying.

"It wasn't me that told Mister Roth to telefoam for dem shurfs!" she said.

"My mind done changed," Lucas said. "I'm gonter let you and George Wilkins be married." She stared at him; he watched her gaze flick to George and return.

"It changed quick," she said. She watched him now. Then he knew she was not looking at him; her hand came up and touched for an instant the bright cotton handkerchief which bound her head. "Me, marry wid George and go to live in dat house whar de back porch is done already fell off of and whar I got to wawk a half er mile and back from de spring to fotch water? He ain't even got no stove!"

"My chimbley cooks good, and I can prop up de porch," George said.

"And I can get used to wawkin' a mile fer two lard buckets er water," she said.

She ceased, with no dying fall of her high, clear soprano voice, watching her father's face.

"A cookstove. And the back porch propped up. A well."

"A new back porch," she said. She might not have even spoken.

"The back porch fixed," he said. Then she was certainly not looking at him; again her hand rose, the lighter palm pale, the fingers limber and delicate, and touched the back of her headkerchief. Lucas moved. "George Wilkins," he said.

"Sir," George said.

"Come into the house," Lucas said.

The day came at last. In their Sunday clothes he and Nat and George waited at the gate until the car came down the drive. "Morning, Nat," Edmonds said. "When did you get home?"

"I got back yistiddy, Mister Roth."

"You stayed in Jackson a good while."

"Yassuh. I lef de next day after you and pappy and Gawge went to town wid de shurfs."

"You and George go on a minute," Edmonds said. They went on. Lucas stood beside the car. This was the first time Edmonds had spoken to him since that day three weeks ago, as if it had taken that long for his rage to consume itself. Or die down rather, because it still smoldered.

"I suppose you know what's going to happen to you," Edmonds said. "When that lawyer gets through with Nat, and Nat gets through with George, and George gets through with you and Judge Gowan gets through with you both. You were on this place with my father for twenty-five years, until he died. You have been on it twenty years with me. Was that still and that whisky they found in your back yard yours?"

"You knows it wasn't," Lucas said.

"All right," Edmonds said. "Was that other still they found hidden in the bottom yours?"

They looked at each other. "I ain't being tried for that one," Lucas said.

"Was that still yours, Luke?" Edmonds said. They looked at each other. The face which Edmonds saw was absolutely blank, impenetrable.

"Does you want me to answer that?" Lucas said.

"No!" Edmonds said violently. "Get in the car!"

The square and the streets leading into it were crowded with cars and wagons. Following Edmonds, they crossed the crowded sidewalk before the entrance, in a lane of faces they knew—other tenants from their own farm and from the other farms along the creek, come the seventeen miles also in battered and limping trucks and sedans, without hope of getting into the courtroom itself but only to wait on the street and see them pass—and faces they knew only by hearsay: the rich white lawyers talking to one another around cigars, the proud and powerful of the earth.

Then they were in the marble foyer, where George began to walk gingerly on the hard heels of his Sunday shoes and where Edmonds, at a touch on his arm, looked back and saw in Lucas' extended hand the thick, folded, soiled document which, opening stiffly at the old hand-smudged folds, revealed among the blunt and forthright lettering above the signature and seal, the two names in the impersonal and legible script of whatever nameless clerk: *George Wilkins* and *Nathalie Beauchamp,* and dated in October of last year.

"Do you mean," Edmonds said, "that you have had this all the time? *You have had this all the time?*" But still the face he glared at was impenetrable, almost sleepy-looking.

"You hand it to Judge Gowan," Lucas said.

It didn't take very long. They sat in a small office, on the edge of a hard bench, decorous and in silence, their backs not touching the bench's back, while the deputy marshal chewed a toothpick and read a paper. They did not stop in the courtroom. They went on through it, between the empty benches and through another door, into another office, but larger and finer and quieter, where an angry-looking man waited whom Lucas knew only from hearsay

—the United States Attorney, who had moved to Jefferson only after the administration changed eight years ago. But Edmonds was there, and behind the table sat a man whom Lucas did know, who used to come out in Old Zach Edmonds' time thirty and forty years ago and stay for weeks during the quail season, with Lucas to hold his horse for him to get down and shoot when the dogs pointed.

"Lucas Beauchamp?" the judge said. "With thirty gallons of whisky and a still sitting on his back porch in open daylight? Nonsense."

"Then there you are," the angry man said, flinging out his hands. "I didn't know anything about this either until Edmonds—" But the judge was not listening to the angry man. He was looking at Nat.

"Come here, girl," he said. Nat moved forward a step or two and stopped. Lucas could see her trembling. She looked small, thin as a lath, young; she was his youngest and last child—seventeen, born in his wife's old age and, it sometimes seemed to him, in his too. She was too young to be married and face all the troubles that married people had to get through in order to become old and find out for themselves the taste and savor of peace. Just a stove and a new back porch and a well were not enough. "You're Luke's girl?" the judge said.

"Yassuh," Nat said. "I'm name Nat. Nat Wilkins, Gawge Wilkins' wife. Dar de paper fer hit in yo' hand."

"I see it is," the judge said. "It's dated last October."

"Yes, sir, Judge," George said. "We been had it since I sold my cotton last year. We uz married den, only she won't come to live in my house unto Mister Luke—I mean to I gots a stove and de porch fixed and a well dug."

"Have you got that now?"

"Yes, sir, Judge," George said. "I'm just 'fo' gettin' hit. Soon as I gits around to de hammerin' and de diggin'."

"I see," the judge said. "Henry," he said to the marshal, "have you got that whisky where you can pour it out?"

"Yes, Judge."

"And both those stills where you can chop them up, destroy them good?"

"Yes, Judge."

"Then clear my office. Get them out of here. Get that jimber-jawed clown out of here at least."

"George Wilkins," Lucas murmured, "he's talking about you."

"Yes, sir," George said. "Hit sound like he is."

But before the next three weeks were up, he had begun to get impatient, probably because he now had so little to do. His land was all planted now, after a good season, the seeds of cotton and corn sprouting almost in the planter's wheel-print between the brief, gusty rains and the rich flood of the northing sun. One day's work a week would keep them grassed, so all he had to do now, after slopping his hogs and chopping a little cooking wood, was to lean on the fence in the morning's cool and watch them grow.

But at last in the third week he stood just inside his kitchen door and saw George Wilkins enter the lot in the dusk and go into the stable and emerge presently leading his, Lucas', fat middle-aged mare and put her in the spring wagon and drive out of the lot and on. So the next morning he went no farther than his first field and stood in the bright dew looking at his cotton until his wife began to shout at him from the house.

Nat was sitting in a chair beside the hearth where the fire had burned for forty-five years, bent forward, her long hands hanging limp between her knees, her face swollen and puffed again from crying. "Yawl and your Gawge Wilkins!" his wife said when Lucas entered. "Gawn and tell him."

"He ain't started on de well," Nat said. "He ain't even propped up de back porch. Wid all dat money you give him, he ain't even started. And I axed him and he just say he ain't got around to it yet, and I wait and I axed him again and he just say he ain't got around to it yet. Unto I told him at last that ifn he don't git started like he promised, my mind gonter change about what all I seed dat night dem shurfs come out here and so last night he say he gwine up de road a piece and do I wants to come home and stay because he mought not git back unto late and I say I can bar de door because I thought he was going to fix about starting on de well.

"And when I seed him catch pappy's mare and de wagon, I knowed dat uz whar he uz gwine. And it ain't to almost daylight when he got back and he ain't only ain't got nothin' to fix no porch and dig no well, he had done spent de money. And I told him what

I was gonter do and I was waitin' soon as Mister Roth got up and I told Mister Roth my mind done change about what I seed dat night and Mister Roth start to cussin' and say I done waited too long because I'm Gawge's wife now and de court won't listen and for me to come and tell you and Gawge both to be offen his place by sundown."

"Dar now," his wife said. "Dar's your Gawge Wilkins!" But Lucas was already moving toward the door. "Whar you gwine?" she said. "Whar we gonter move to now?"

"You wait to start worrying about where we gonter move to when Roth Edmonds starts to worrying about why we ain't gone," Lucas said.

The sun was well up now. It was going to be hot today; it was going to make cotton and corn both before the sun went down. When he reached George's house, George stood quietly out from beyond the corner of it. Lucas crossed the grassless and sun-glared yard. "Where is it?" he said.

"I hid it in de gully whar mine use to be," George said. "If dem shurfs ain't find nothing de first time, dey might think hit ain't no use to look again."

"You fool," Lucas said. "Don't you know a week ain't gonter pass from now to the next election without one of them looking in that gully just because Roth Edmonds told them there was a still in it once? When they catch you this time, you ain't gonter have no witness you done already been married to since last fall."

"Dey ain't gonter catch me," George said. "I'm gonter run dis one de way you tells me. I done had my lesson."

"You better had," Lucas said. "You take that wagon soon as dark falls and get that thing outen there. I'll show you where to put it. Hah," he said. "And I reckon this one looks about like that other one that was in that gully, too."

"No, sir," George said. "This is a good one. The worm in hit is almost new. That's how come I couldn't git him down no more on the price he axed. That porch and well money lacked two dollars of being enough, but I just made that up myself. But it ain't worryin' about gittin' caught that bothers me. What I can't keep from studyin' about is what we gonter tell Nat about that back porch and that well."

"What *we* is?" Lucas said.

"What I is then," George said. Lucas looked at him for a moment.

"George Wilkins," he said.

"Sir," George said.

"I don't give no man advice about his wife," Lucas said.

Gold Is Not Always

I

When they drew near the commissary, Lucas said: "You wait here." "No, no," the salesman said. "I'll talk to him. If I can't sell it to him, there ain't a—" Then the salesman stopped. He did not know why. He was young, not yet thirty, with the slightly soiled snap and dash of his calling, and a white man. Yet he stopped and looked at the Negro in battered overalls, whose face showed only that he was at least sixty, who was looking at him not only with dignity but with command.

"You wait here," Lucas said. So the salesman leaned against the lot fence in the bright August morning while Lucas went on up the hill and mounted the gnawed steps beside which a bright-coated young mare with a blaze and three stockings stood under a heavy comfortable saddle, and entered the commissary, with its ranked shelves of tinned food and tobacco and patent medicines, its hooks from which hung trace chains and collars and hames, and where, at a roll-top desk beside the front window, his landlord was writing in a ledger. Lucas stood quietly looking at the back of the white man's neck until the other looked around. "He's done come," Lucas said.

Edmonds swiveled his chair about, back-tilted. He was already glaring at Lucas before the chair stopped moving; he said with astonishing violence: "No!"

"Yes," Lucas said.

"No!"

"He done fotch the machine with him," Lucas said. "I seed hit work. I buried a dollar in my back yard this morning and it went right straight to whar it wuz and found it. He just wants three hundred dollars for it. We gonter find that money tonight and I can pay it back tomorrow morning"

"No!" Edmonds said. "I tell you and tell you and tell you there ain't any money buried around here. You've been here sixty years. Did you ever hear of anybody in this country with enough money to bury? Can you imagine anybody in this country burying anything worth as much as two bits that some of his kinfolks or friends or neighbors or acquaintances ain't dug up long ago?"

"You're wrong," Lucas said. "Folks finds it all the time. Ain't I told you about them two strange white men that come in here after dark one night three years ago and dug up twenty-two thousand dollars and got out again before anybody even seed um? I seed the hole whar they had done filled it up again. And the churn hit was buried in."

"Hah," Edmonds said. "Then how do you know it was twenty-two thousand dollars?" But Lucas only looked at him. It was not stubbornness. It was an infinite, an almost Jehovah-like patience, as if he, Lucas, were engaged in a contest, partially for the idiot's own benefit, with an idiot. "Your paw would a lent me three hundred dollars if he was here," he said.

"Well, I ain't," Edmonds said. "You've got damn near three thousand dollars in the bank. If I could keep you from wasting any of that on a damn machine to find buried money, I would. But then, you ain't going to use any of your money, are you? You've got more sense yourself than to risk that."

"It looks like I'm gonter have to," Lucas said. "I'm gonter ask you one more time—"

"No!" Edmonds said, again with that astonishing and explosive violence. Lucas looked at him for a time, almost contemplative. He did not sigh.

"All right," he said.

When he returned to the salesman, his son-in-law was there too —a lean-hipped, very black young man with a ready face full of white teeth and a ruined Panama hat raked above his right ear.

The salesman looked once at Lucas's face and hunched himself away from the fence. "I'll go talk to him," he said.

"No," Lucas said. "You stay away from there."

"Then what you going to do about it?" the salesman said. "Here I've come all the way from St. Louis—and how you ever persuaded them to send this machine out without any down payment in the first place, I still don't see. And I'll tell you right now, if I got to take it back and turn in an expense account for this trip and no sale, something is—"

"We ain't doing no good standing here, nohow," Lucas said. The other two followed him, back to the gate and the highroad, where the salesman's car stood. The divining machine rested on the rear seat and Lucas stood in the open door, looking at it—an oblong metal box with a handle for carrying at each end, compact and solid, efficient and businesslike and complex with its knobs and dials, and Lucas standing over it, sober and bemused. "And I seed hit work," he said. "I seed hit with my own eyes."

"Well?" the salesman said. "What you going to do? I've got to know, so I can know what to do, myself. Ain't you got three hundred dollars?" Lucas mused upon the machine. He did not look up yet.

"We gonter find that money tonight," he said. "You put in the machine and I'll show you whar to look, and we'll go halves on hit."

"Ha, ha, ha," the salesman said harshly. "Now I'll tell one."

"We bound to find hit, cap-tin," the son-in-law said. "Two white men slipped in here three years ago and dug up twenty-two thousand dollars one night and got clean away wid hit fo' daylight."

"You bet," the salesman said. "And you knew it was exactly twenty-two thousand because you found where they had throwed away the odd cents."

"Naw, sir," the son-in-law said. "Hit mought a been even more than twenty-two thousand dollars. Hit wuz a big churn."

"George Wilkins," Lucas said, still half inside the car and still without turning his head.

"Sir," the son-in-law said.

"Shut up." Now Lucas turned and looked at the salesman; again the salesman saw a face quite sober, even a little cold, quite impenetrable. "I'll swap you a mule for it."

"A mule?" the salesman said.

"When we find that money tonight, I'll buy the mule back for your three hundred dollars." The son-in-law had begun to bat his eyes rapidly. But nobody was looking at him. Lucas and the sales-man looked at one another—the shrewd, suddenly attentive face of the young white man, the absolutely impenetrable face of the Negro.

"Do you own the mule?"

"How could I swap hit to you ef 'n I didn't?"

"Let's go see it," the salesman said.

"George Wilkins," Lucas said.

"Sir," the son-in-law said. He was still batting his eyes con-stantly and rapidly.

"Go up to my barn and get my halter," Lucas said.

II

Edmonds found the mule was missing as soon as the stablemen brought the drove up from pasture that evening. She was a three-year-old, eleven-hundred-pound mare mule named Alice Ben Bolt, and he had refused three hundred dollars for her in the spring. But he didn't even curse. He merely dismounted and stood beside the lot fence while the rapid beat of his mare's feet died away in the darkling night and then returned, and the head stableman sprang down and handed him his flashlight and pistol. Then, himself on the mare and the two Negroes on saddleless mules, they went back across the pasture, fording the creek, to the gap in the fence through which the mule had been led. From there they followed the tracks of the mule and of the man who led her in the soft earth along the edge of a cotton field, to the road. And here too they could follow them, the head stableman walking and carrying the flashlight, where the man had led the unshod mule in the softer dirt which bordered the gravel. "That's Alice's foot," the head stable-man said. "I'd know hit anywhar."

Later Edmonds would realize that both the Negroes had recog-nized the man's footprints too. But at the time his very fury and concern had short-circuited his normal sensitivity to Negro behav-ior. They would not have told him who had made the tracks even if he had demanded to know, but the realization that they knew would have enabled him to leap to the correct divination and so save himself the four or five hours of mental turmoil and physical effort which he was about to enter.

They lost the tracks. He expected to find the marks where the mule had been loaded into a waiting truck, whereupon he would return home and telephone to the sheriff in Jefferson and to the Memphis police to watch the horse-and-mule markets tomorrow. There were no such marks. It took them almost an hour to find where the tracks had vanished on to the gravel, crossing it, descending through the opposite roadside weeds, to reappear in another field a hundred yards away. Supperless, raging, the mare which had been under saddle all day unfed too, he followed the two shadowy mules at the backstretched arm of the second walking Negro, cursing the darkness and the puny light which the head stableman carried, on which they were forced to depend.

Two hours later they were in the creek bottom four miles away. He was walking too now, lest he knock his brains out against a limb, stumbling and thrashing among brier and undergrowth and rotting logs and branches where the tracks led, leading the mare with one hand and fending his face with the other arm and trying to watch his feet, so that he walked into one of the mules, instinctively leaping in the right direction as it lashed out at him with one hoof, before he discovered that the Negroes had stopped. Then, cursing out loud now and moving quickly again to avoid the invisible second mule which would be somewhere to his left, he discovered that the flashlight was now off and he too saw the faint, smoky glare of the lightwood torch among the trees ahead. It was moving. "That's right," he said rapidly. "Keep the light off." He called the second Negro's name. "Give the mules to Dan and come back here and take the mare." He waited, watching the light, until the Negro's hand fumbled at his. Then he released the reins and moved around the mules, drawing his pistol and still watching the moving flame. "Hand me the flashlight," he said. He took the light from that fumbling hand too. "You and Oscar wait here."

"I better come wid you," the Negro said.

"All right," Edmonds said. "Give Oscar the mules." He didn't wait, though from time to time he could hear the Negro behind him, both of them moving as quietly and rapidly as possible. The rage was not cold now. It was hot, and there was an eagerness upon him, a kind of vindictive exultation as he plunged on, heedless of brush or log, the flashlight in his left hand and the pistol in his right, gaining rapidly on the moving torch, bursting at last out of the undergrowth and into a sort of glade, in the centre of which two men stood looking toward him, one of them carrying before him what Edmonds believed at first to be some kind of receptacle of feed, the other holding high over his head the smoking pine-knot. Then Edmonds recognized George Wilkins's ruined Panama hat, and he realized not only that the two Negroes with him had known all the time who had made the footprints, but that the object which Lucas was carrying was not any feedbox and that he himself should have known all the time what had become of his mule.

"You, Lucas!" he shouted. George flung the torch, arching, but the flashlight already held them spitted; Edmonds saw the white man now, snap-brim hat, necktie, and all, risen from beside a tree, his trousers rolled to the knees and his feet invisible in caked mud. "That's right," Edmonds said. "Go on, George. Run. I believe I can hit that hat without even touching you." He approached, the flashlight's beam contracting on to the metal box which Lucas held before him, gleaming and glinting among the knobs and dials. "So that's it," he said. "Three hundred dollars. I wish somebody would come into this country with a seed that had to be worked every day, from New Year's right on through to Christmas. As soon as you niggers are laid by, trouble starts. I ain't going to worry with Alice tonight, and if you and George want to spend the rest of it walking back and forth with that damn thing, that's your business. But I want that mule to be in her stall by sunup. Do you hear?" Edmonds had forgotten about the white man until he appeared beside Lucas.

"What mule is that?" he said. Edmonds turned the light on him for a moment.

"My mule, sir," he said.

"I've got a bill of sale for that mule," the other said. "Signed by Lucas here."

"Have you now," Edmonds said. "You can make lamplighters out of it next winter."

"Is that so?" the other said. "Look here, Mister What's-your-name—" But Edmonds had already turned the light back to Lucas, who still held the divining machine before him.

"On second thought, I ain't going to worry about that mule at all," he said. "I told you this morning what I thought about this business. But you're a grown man; if you want to fool with it, I can't stop you. But if that mule ain't in her stall by sunup tomorrow, I'm going to telephone the sheriff. Do you hear me?"

"I hears you," Lucas said.

"All right, big boy," the salesman said. "If that mule is moved from where she's at until I'm ready to move her, I'm going to telephone the sheriff. Do you hear that too?" This time Edmonds jumped, flung the light beam at the salesman, furious and restrained.

"Were you talking to me, sir?" he said.

"No," the salesman said. "I'm talking to him. And he heard me." For a while longer Edmonds held the light beam on the other. Then he dropped it, so that only their legs and feet showed, planted in the pool and its refraction as if they stood in a pool of dying water. He put the pistol back into his pocket.

"Well, you and Lucas have got till daylight to settle that. Because that mule is to be back in my barn at sunup." He turned and went back to where Dan waited, the light swinging and flickering before him; presently it had vanished.

"George Wilkins," Lucas said.

"Sir," George said.

"Find that pine-knot and light it again." George did so; once more the red glare streamed away in thick smoke, upward against the August stars of more than midnight. "Now grab a holt of this thing," Lucas said. "I got to find that money now."

But when day broke they had not found it, the torch paling away in the wan, dew-heavy light, the white man asleep on the wet earth now, drawn into a ball against the dawn's wet chill, unshaven, with his dashing city hat, his necktie, his soiled shirt and muddy trousers rolled to his knees, and his mud-caked feet whose shoes gleamed with polish yesterday. They waked him. He sat up, cursing. But he knew at once where he was, because he said: "All right now. If that mule moves one foot out of that cotton house, I'm going to get the sheriff."

"I just wants one more night," Lucas said. "That money's here."

"What about that fellow that says the mule is his?"

"I'll tend to him in the morning. You don't need to worry about that. Besides, ef 'n you try to move that mule yourself, the sheriff gonter take her away from you. You leave her whar she's at and lemme have one more night with this-here machine. Then I kin fix everything."

"All right," the other said. "But do you know what it's going to cost you? It's going to cost you just exactly twenty-five dollars more. Now I'm going to town and go to bed."

He put Lucas and George out at George's gate. They watched the car go on down the road, already going fast. George was batting his eyes rapidly. "Now whut we gonter do?" he said. Lucas roused.

"Eat your breakfast quick as you can and come on to my house. You got to go to town and get back here by noon."

"I needs to go to bed too," George said. "I'm bad off to sleep too."

"Ne'mine about that," Lucas said. "You eat your breakfast and get up to my house quick." When George reached his gate a half hour later, Lucas met him, the check already written out in his laborious, cramped, but quite legible hand. It was for fifty dollars. "Get it in silver dollars," Lucas said. "And be back here by noon."

It was just dusk when the salesman's car stopped again at Lucas's gate, where Lucas and George, carrying a long-handled shovel, waited. The salesman was freshly shaved and his face looked rested; the snap-brim hat had been brushed and his shirt was clean. But he now wore a pair of cotton khaki pants still bearing the manufacturer's stitched label and still showing the creases where they had been folded on the store's shelf. He gave Lucas a hard, jeering stare as Lucas and George approached. "I ain't going to ask if my mule's all right," he said. "Because I don't need to. Hah?"

"Hit's all right," Lucas said. He and George got into the rear seat beside the divining machine. The salesman put the car into gear, though he did not move it yet.

"Well?" he said. "Where do you want to take your walk tonight? Same place?"

"Not there," Lucas said. "I'll show you whar. We was looking in the wrong place. I misread the paper."

"You bet," the salesman said. "It's worth that extra twenty-five bucks to have found that out—" The car had begun to move. He stopped it so suddenly that Lucas and George, squatting gingerly on the front edge of the seat, lurched forward before they caught themselves. "You did what?" the salesman said.

"I misread the paper," Lucas said.

"What paper? Have you got a letter or something that tells where some money is buried?"

"That's right," Lucas said.

"Where is it?"

"Hit's put away in the house," Lucas said.

"Go and get it."

"Ne'mine," Lucas said. "I read hit right this time." For a moment longer the salesman sat, his head turned over his shoulder. Then he looked forward. He put the car in gear again.

"All right," he said. "Where's the place?"

"Drive on," Lucas said. "I'll show you."

It was not in the bottom, but on a hill overlooking the creek— a clump of ragged cedars, the ruins of old chimneys, a depression which was once a well or a cistern, the old worn-out fields stretching away and a few snaggled trees of what had been an orchard, shadowy and dim beneath the moonless sky where the fierce stars of late summer swam. "Hit's in the orchard," Lucas said. "Hit's divided, buried in two separate places. One of them's in the orchard."

"Provided the fellow that wrote you the letter ain't come back and joined it all up again," the salesman said. "What are we waiting on? Here, Jack," he said to George, "grab that thing out of there." George lifted the divining machine from the car. The salesman had a flashlight himself now, quite new, thrust into his hip pocket. He didn't put it on at once. "By God, you better find it first pop this time. We're on a hill now. There probably ain't a man in ten miles that can walk at all that won't be up here inside an hour, watching us."

"Don't tell me that," Lucas said. "Tell hit to this-here three hundred and twenty-five dollar buzz-box I done bought."

"You ain't bought this box yet, big boy," the salesman said. "You say one of the places is in the orchard. All right. Where?"

Lucas, carrying the shovel, went on into the old orchard, the others following. The salesman watched him pause, squinting at trees and sky to orient himself, then move on again, pause again. "We kin start here," he said. The salesman snapped on the light, handcupping the beam on to the metal box which George carried.

"All right, Jack," he said. "Get going."

"I better tote it," Lucas said.

"No," the salesman said. "You're too old. I don't know yet that you can even keep up with us. Get on, Jack!" So Lucas walked on

George's other side, carrying the shovel and watching the small bright dials in the flashlight's contracted beam as they went back and forth across the orchard. He was watching also, grave and completely attentive, when the needles began to spin and jerk and then quiver. Then he held the box and watched George digging into the light's concentrated pool and saw the rusted can come up at last and the bright cascade of silver dollars about the salesman's hands and heard the salesman's voice: "Well, by God! By God!" Lucas squatted also; they faced each other across the pit.

"I done found this much of hit, anyhow," he said. The salesman, one hand upon the scattered coins, made a slashing, almost instinctive blow with the other as if Lucas had reached for the coins. Squatting, he laughed harshly at Lucas across the pit.

"*You* found? This machine don't belong to you, old man."

"I bought hit," Lucas said.

"With what?"

"A mule," Lucas said. The other laughed at him, harsh and steady across the pit. "I give you a billy sale for hit."

"Which never was worth a damn. It's in my car yonder. Go and get it whenever you want to." He scrabbled the coins together, back into the can. He rose quickly out of the light, until only his legs showed in the new, still-creased cotton pants. He still wore the same low black shoes. He had not had them shined again—only washed. Lucas rose also, more slowly. "All right," the salesman said. "This ain't hardly any of it. Where's the other place?"

"Ask your finding machine," Lucas said. "Ain't it supposed to know?"

"You damn right it does," the salesman said.

"Then I reckon we can go home," Lucas said. "George Wilkins."

"Sir," George said.

"Wait," the salesman said. He and Lucas faced each other in the darkness, two shadows, faceless. "There wasn't over a hundred here. Most of it is in the other place. I'll give you ten per cent."

"Hit was my letter," Lucas said. "Hit ain't enough."

"Twenty. And that's all."

"I wants half," Lucas said. "And that mule paper, and another paper to say the finding machine belongs to me."

"Tomorrow," the salesman said.

"I wants hit now," Lucas said. The invisible face stared at his own invisible one. Both he and George seemed to feel the windless summer air moving to the trembling of the white man's body.

"How much did you say them other fellows found?"

"Twenty-two thousand dollars," Lucas said.

"Hit mought a been more," George said. "Hit wuz a big—"

"All right," the salesman said suddenly. "I'll give you a bill of sale for the machine as soon as we finish."

"I wants it now," Lucas said. They went back to the car. While Lucas held the flashlight, they watched the salesman rip open his patent brief case and jerk out of it and fling toward Lucas the bill of sale for the mule. Then they watched his jerking hand fill in the long printed form with its carbon duplicates and sign it and rip out one of the duplicates.

"You get possession tomorrow morning," he said. "It belongs to me until then. O.K.?"

"All right," Lucas said. "What about them fifty dollars we done already found? Does I get half of them?" This time the salesman just laughed, harsh and steady and without mirth. Then he was out of the car. He didn't even wait to close his brief case. They could see him half running back toward the orchard, carrying the divining machine and the flashlight both.

"Come on," he said. "Bring the spade." Lucas gathered up the two papers, the bill of sale which he had signed for the mule, and the one which the salesman had signed for the divining machine.

"George Wilkins," he said.

"Sir," George said.

"Take that mule back whar you got hit. Then go tell Roth Edmonds he can quit worrying folks about her."

III

Lucas mounted the gnawed steps beside which the bright mare stood beneath the heavy saddle, and entered the commissary, with its ranked shelves of tinned food, the hooks from which hung collars and trace chains and hames and ploughlines, its smell of molasses and cheese and leather and kerosene. Edmonds swiveled around from the roll-top desk. "Where've you been?" he said. "I sent word two days ago I wanted to see you."

"I was in bed, I reckon," Lucas said. "I been had to stay up all night for the last three nights. I can't stand hit no more like when I was a young man."

"So you've found that out at last, have you? What I wanted to see you about is that damn St. Louis fellow. Dan says he's still hanging around here. What's he doing?"

"Hunting buried money," Lucas said.

"What?" Edmonds said. "Doing what, did you say?"

"Hunting buried money," Lucas said. "Using my finding box. He rents it from me. That's why I been had to stay up all night. To go with him and make sho' I'd get the box back. But last night he never turnt up, so I reckon he's done gone back wharever it was he come from."

Edmonds sat in the swivel chair and stared at him. "Rents it from you? The same machine he sold you?"

"For twenty-five dollars a night," Lucas said. "That's what he chawged me to use hit one night. So I reckon that's the regular rent on um. Leastways, that's what I chawges." Edmonds stared at him as he leaned against the counter with only the slight shrinkage of the jaws to show that he was an old man, in his clean, faded overalls and shirt and the open vest looped across by a heavy gold watch chain, and the thirty-dollar handmade beaver hat which Edmonds's father had given him forty years ago above the face which was not sober and not grave but wore no expression whatever. It was absolutely impenetrable. "Because he was looking in the wrong place," Lucas said. "He was looking up there on that hill. That money is buried down there by the creek. Them two white men that slipped in here that night three years ago and got clean away with twenty-two thousand dollars—" At last Edmonds got himself out of the chair and on to his feet. He was trembling. He drew a deep breath, walking steadily toward the old Negro leaning against the counter, his lower lip full of snuff. "And now that we done got shut of him," Lucas said, "me and George Wilkins—" Walking steadily toward him, Edmonds expelled his breath. He had believed it would be a shout, but it was not much more than a whisper.

"Get out of here," he said. "Go home. And don't come back. Don't ever come back. When you need supplies, send your wife after them."

Pantaloon in Black

He stood in the worn, faded, clean overalls which Mannie herself had washed only a week ago, and heard the first clod strike the pine box. Soon he had one of the shovels himself, which in his hands (he was better than six feet and weighed better than two hundred pounds) resembled the toy shovel a child plays with at the shore, its half cubic foot of flung dirt no more than the light gout of sand the child's shovel would have flung.

Another member of his sawmill gang touched his arm and said, "Lemme have hit, Rider."

He didn't even falter. He released one hand in midstroke and flung it backward, striking the other across the chest, jolting him back a step, and restored the hand to the moving shovel, flinging the dirt with that effortless fury so that the mound seemed to be rising of its own volition, not built up from above but thrusting visibly upward out of the earth itself, until at last the grave, save for its rawness, resembled any other, marked off without order about the barren plot by shards of pottery and broken bottles and old brick and other objects insignificant to sight but actually of a profound meaning and fatal to touch, which no white man could have read. Then he straightened up and with one hand flung the shovel quivering upright in the mound like a javelin and turned and began to walk away, walking on even when an old woman came out of the meager clump of his kin and friends and a few old people who had known him and his dead wife both since they were born, and grasped his forearm. She was his aunt. She had raised him. He could not remember his parents at all.

"Whar you gwine?" she said.

"Ah'm goan home," he said.

"You don't wants ter go back dar by yoself. You needs to eat. You come on home and eat."

"Ah'm goan home," he repeated, walking out from under her hand, his forearm like iron, as if the weight on it were no more than that of a fly, the other members of the mill gang whose head he was giving way quietly to let him pass. But before he reached the fence one of them overtook him; he did not need to be told it was his aunt's messenger.

"Wait, Rider," the other said. "We gots a jug in de bushes—" Then the other said what he had not intended to say, what he had never conceived of saying in circumstances like these, even though everybody knew it—the dead who either will not or cannot quit the earth yet, although the flesh they once lived in has been returned to it—let the preachers tell and reiterate and affirm how they left it not only without regret but with joy, mounting toward glory: "You don't wants ter go back dar. She be wawkin yit."

He didn't pause, glancing down at the other, his eyes red at the inner corners in his high, slightly back-tilted head. "Lemme lone, Acey," he said. "Doan mess wid me now," and went on, stepping over the three-strand wire fence without even breaking his stride, and crossed the road and entered the woods. It was middle dusk when he emerged from them and crossed the last field, stepping over that fence too in one stride, into the lane. It was empty at this hour of Sunday evening—no family in wagon, no rider, no walkers churchward to speak to him and carefully refrain from looking after him when he had passed—the pale, powder-light, powder-dry dust of August from which the long week's marks of hoof and wheel had been blotted by the strolling and unhurried Sunday shoes, with somewhere beneath them, vanished but not gone, fixed and held in the annealing dust, the narrow, splay-toed prints of his wife's bare feet where on Saturday afternoons she would walk to the commissary to buy their next week's supplies while he took his bath; himself, his own prints, setting the period now as he strode on, moving almost as fast as a smaller man could have trotted, his body breasting the air her body had vacated, his eyes touching the objects—post and tree and field and house and hill—her eyes had lost.

The house was the last one in the lane, not his but rented from the local white landowner. But the rent was paid promptly in advance, and even in just six months he had refloored the porch and rebuilt and reroofed the kitchen, doing the work himself on Saturday afternoon and Sunday with his wife helping him, and bought the stove. Because he made good money: sawmilling ever since he began to get his growth at fifteen and sixteen and now, at twenty-four, head of the timber gang itself because the gang he headed moved a third again as much timber between sunup and sundown as any other, handling himself at times out of the vanity of his own strength logs which ordinarily two men would have handled with cant hooks; never without work even in the old days when he had not actually needed the money, when a lot of what he wanted, needed perhaps, didn't cost money—the women bright and dark and for all purposes nameless he didn't need to buy, and it didn't matter to him what he wore, and there was always food for him at any hour of day or night in the house of his aunt who didn't even want to take the two dollars he gave her each Saturday. So there had been only the Saturday and Sunday dice and whiskey that had to be paid for until that day six months ago when he saw Mannie, whom he had known all his life, for the first time and said to himself: "Ah'm thu wid all dat," and they married and he rented the cabin from Carothers Edmonds and built a fire on the hearth on their wedding night as the tale told how Uncle Lucas Beauchamp, Edmonds' oldest tenant, had done on his forty-five years ago and which had burned ever since. And he would rise and dress and eat his breakfast by lamplight to walk the four miles to the mill by sunup, and exactly one hour after sundown he would enter the house again, five days a week, until Saturday. Then the first hour would not have passed noon when he would mount the steps and knock, not on post or door frame but on the underside of the gallery roof itself, and enter and ring the bright cascade of silver dollars on to the scrubbed table in the kitchen where his dinner simmered on the stove and the galvanized tub of hot water and the baking-powder can of soft soap and the towel made of scalded flour sacks sewn together and his clean overalls and shirt waited, and Mannie would gather up the money and walk the half-mile to the commissary and buy their next week's supplies and bank the rest of the money in Edmonds' safe and return and they would eat once again without haste or hurry after five days—the sidemeat, the greens, the cornbread, the buttermilk from the well house, the cake which she baked every Saturday now that she had a stove to bake in.

But when he put his hand on the gate it seemed to him suddenly that there was nothing beyond it. The house had never been his anyway, but now even the new planks and sills and shingles, the hearth and stove and bed were all a part of the memory of somebody else, so that he stopped in the half-open gate and said aloud, as though he had gone to sleep in one place and then waked suddenly to find himself in another: "Whut's Ah doin hyar?" before he went on.

Then he saw the dog. He had forgotten it. He remembered neither seeing nor hearing it since it began to howl just before dawn yesterday—a big dog, a hound with a strain of mastiff from somewhere (he had told Mannie a month after they married: "Ah needs a big dawg. You's de onliest least thing whut ever kep up wid me one day, leff alone fo weeks.") coming out from beneath the gallery and approaching, not running but seeming rather to drift across the dusk until it stood lightly against his leg, its head raised until the tips of his fingers just touched it, facing the house and making no sound; whereupon, as if the animal controlled it, had lain guardian before it during his absence and only this instant relinquished, the shell of planks and shingles facing him solidified, filled, and for the moment he believed that he could not possibly enter it.

"But Ah needs to eat," he said. "Us bofe needs to eat," he said, moving on though the dog did not follow until he turned and cursed it. "Come on hyar!" he said. "Whut you skeered of? She lacked you too, same as me."

They mounted the steps and crossed the porch and entered the house—the dusk-filled single room where all those six months were now crammed and crowded into one instant of time until there was no space left for air to breathe, crammed and crowded about the hearth where the fire which was to have lasted to the end of them, in front of which in the days before he was able to buy the stove he would enter after his four-mile walk from the mill and find her, the shape of her narrow back and haunches squatting, one narrow spread hand shielding her face from the blaze over which the other hand held the skillet, had already fallen to a dry, light soilure of dead ashes when the sun rose yesterday—and himself standing there while the last of light died about the strong and indomitable beating of his heart and the deep steady arch and collapse of his chest which walking fast over the rough going of woods and fields had not increased and standing still in the quiet and fading room had not slowed down.

Then the dog left him. The light pressure went off his flank; he heard the click and hiss of its claws on the wooden floor as it surged away, and he thought at first that it was fleeing. But it stopped just outside the front door, where he could see it now and the upfling of its head as the howl began; and then he saw her too.

She was standing in the kitchen door, looking at him. He didn't move. He didn't breathe or speak until he knew his voice would be all right, his face fixed too not to alarm her.

"Mannie," he said. "Hit's awright. Ah ain't afraid."

Then he took a step toward her, slow, not even raising his hand yet, and stopped. Then he took another step. But this time as soon as he moved she began to fade. He stopped at once, not breathing again, motionless, willing his eyes to see that she had stopped too. But she had not stopped. She was fading, going. "Wait," he said, talking as sweet as he had ever heard his voice speak to a woman: "Den lemme go wid you, honey." But she was going. She was going fast now; he could actually feel between them the insuperable barrier of that very strength which could handle alone a log which would have taken any two other men to handle, of the blood and bones and flesh too strong, invincible for life, having learned, at least once with his own eyes, how tough, even in sudden and violent death, not a young man's bones and flesh perhaps but the will of that bone and flesh to remain alive, actually was.

Then she was gone. He walked through the door where she had been standing and went to the stove. He did not light the lamp. He needed no light. He had set the stove up himself and built the shelves for the dishes, from among which he took two plates by feel and from the pot, sitting cold on the cold stove, he ladled on to the plates the food which his aunt had brought yesterday and of which he had eaten yesterday, though now he did not remember when he had eaten it nor what it was, and carried the plates to the scrubbed bare table beneath the single small fading window and drew two chairs up and sat down, waiting again until he knew his voice would be what he wanted it to be.

"Come on hyar now," he said roughly. "Come on hyar and eat yo supper. Ah ain't gonter have no . . ." and ceased, looking down at his plate, breathing the strong, deep pants, his chest arching and collapsing until he stopped it presently and held himself motionless for perhaps a half minute, and raised a spoonful of the cold and glutinous pease to his mouth. The congealed and lifeless mass seemed to bounce on contact with his lips. Not even warmed from mouth-heat, pease and spoon spattered and rang upon the plate; his chair crashed backward and he was standing, feeling the muscles of his jaw beginning to drag his mouth open, tugging upward the top half of his head. But he stopped that too before it became sound, holding himself again while he rapidly scraped the food from his plate on to the other and took it up and left the kitchen, crossed the other room and the gallery and set the plate on the bottom step and went on toward the gate.

The dog was not there but it overtook him within the first half-mile. There was a moon then, their two shadows flitting broken and intermittent among the trees or slanted long and intact across the slope of pasture or old abandoned fields upon the hills, the man moving almost as fast as a horse could have covered that ground, altering his course each time a lighted window came in sight, the dog trotting at heel while their shadows shortened to the moon's curve until at last they trod them and the last far lamp had vanished and the shadows began to lengthen on the other hand, keeping to heel even when a rabbit burst from almost beneath the man's foot, then lying in the gray of dawn beside the man's prone body, beside the labored heave and collapse of the chest, the loud harsh snoring which sounded, not like groans of pain, but like someone engaged without arms in prolonged single combat.

When he reached the mill there was nobody there but the fireman, an older man just turning from the woodpile, watching quietly as he crossed the clearing, striding as if he were going to walk not only through the boiler shed but through (or over) the boiler too, the overalls which had been clean yesterday now draggled and soiled and drenched to the knees with dew, the cloth cap flung on to the side of his head, hanging peak downward over his ear as he always wore it, the whites of his eyes rimmed with red and with something urgent and strained about them.

"Whar yo bucket?" he said. But before the fireman could answer he had stepped past him and lifted the polished lard pail down from a nail in a post. "Ah just wants a biscuit," he said.

"Eat hit all," the fireman said. "Ah'll eat outen de yuthers' buckets at dinner. Den you gawn home and go to bed. You don't looks good."

"Ah ain't come hyar to look," he said, sitting on the ground, his back against the post, the open pail between his knees, cramming the food into his mouth with his hands, wolfing it—pease again, also gelid and cold, a fragment of yesterday's Sunday fried chicken, a few rough chunks of this morning's fried sidemeat, a biscuit the size of a child's cap—indiscriminate, tasteless. The rest of the crew was gathering now, the voices and sounds of movement outside the boiler shed. Presently the white foreman rode into the clearing on a horse. Rider did not look up; setting the empty pail aside, rising, looking at no one, he went to the branch and lay on his stomach and lowered his face to the water, drawing the water into himself with the same deep, strong, troubled inhalations that he had snored with, or as when he had stood in the empty house at dusk yesterday, trying to get air.

Then the trucks were rolling. The air pulsed with the rapid beating of the exhaust and the whine and clang of the saw, the trucks rolling one by one up to the skidway as he mounted them in turn, to stand balanced on the load he freed, knocking the chocks out and casting loose the shackle chains and with his cant hook squaring the sticks of cypress and gum and oak one by one to the incline and holding them until the next two men of his gang were ready to receive and guide them, until the discharge of each truck became one long rumbling roar punctuated by grunting shouts and, as the morning grew and the sweat came, chanted phrases of song tossed back and forth. He did not sing with them. He rarely ever did, and this morning might have been no different from any other—himself man-height again above the heads which carefully refrained from looking at him, stripped to the waist now, the shirt removed and the overalls knotted about his hips by the suspender straps, his upper body bare except for the handkerchief about his neck and the cap clapped and clinging somehow over his right ear, the mounting sun sweat-glinted steel-blue on the midnight-colored bunch and slip of muscles, until the whistle blew for noon and he

said to the two men at the head of the skidway: "Look out. Git out
de way," and rode the log down the incline, balanced erect in short
rapid backward-running steps above the headlong thunder.

His aunt's husband was waiting for him, an old man as tall as
he was, but lean, almost frail, carrying a tin pail in one hand and
a covered plate in the other. They too sat in the shade beside the
branch a short distance from where the others were opening their
dinner pails. The bucket contained a fruit jar of buttermilk packed
in a clean damp towsack. The covered dish was a peach pie, still
warm.

"She baked hit fer you dis mawnin," the uncle said. "She say fer
you to come home."

He didn't answer, bent forward a little, his elbows on his knees,
holding the pie in both hands, wolfing at it, the syrupy filling
smearing and trickling down his chin, blinking rapidly as he
chewed, the whites of his eyes covered a little more by the creeping
red.

"Ah went to yo house last night, but you want dar. She sont me.
She wants you ter come on home. She kept de lamp burnin' all last
night fer you."

"Ah'm awright," he said.

"You ain't awright. De Lawd guv, and He tuck away. Put yo
faith and trust in Him. And she kin help you."

"Whut faith and trust?" he said. "Whut Mannie ever done ter
Him? Whut He wanter come messin' wid me and—"

"Hush!" the old man said. "Hush!"

Then the trucks were rolling again. Then he could stop needing
to invent to himself reasons for his breathing, until after a while
he began to believe he had forgot about breathing since now he
could not hear it himself above the steady thunder of the rolling
logs; whereupon as soon as he found himself believing he had
forgotten it, he knew that he had not, so that, instead of tipping
the final log on to the skidway, he stood up and cast his cant hook
away as if it were a burnt match, and in the dying reverberation
of the last log's rumbling descent he vaulted down between the two
slanted tracks of the skid, facing the log which still lay on the truck.
He had done it before—taken a log from the truck in his hands,
balanced, and turned with it and tossed it on to the skidway, but
never with a stick of this size. So that in a complete cessation of

all sound save the pulse of the exhaust and the light free-running whine of the disengaged saw, since every eye there, even that of the white foreman, was upon him, he nudged the log to the edge of the truckframe and squatted and set his palms against the underside of it. For a time there was no movement at all. It was as if the unrational and inanimate wood had invested, mesmerized the man with some of its own primal inertia.

Then a voice said quietly: "He got hit. Hit's off de truck," and they saw the crack and gap of air, watching the infinitesimal straightening of the braced legs until the knees locked, the movement mounting infinitesimally through the belly's insuck, the arch of the chest, the neck cords, lifting the lip from the white clench of teeth in passing, drawing the whole head backward and only the bloodshot fixity of the eyes impervious to it, moving on up the arms and the straightening elbows until the balanced log was higher than his head.

"Only he ain't gonter turn wid dat un," the same voice said. "And when he try to put hit back on de truck, hit gonter kill him."

But none of them moved. Then—there was no gathering of supreme effort—the log seemed to leap suddenly backward over his head of its own volition, spinning, crashing, and thundering down the incline. He turned and stepped over the slanting track in one stride and walked through them as they gave way and went on across the clearing toward the woods even though the foreman called after him: "Rider!" and again: "You, Rider!"

At sundown he and the dog were in the river swamp four miles away—another clearing, itself not much larger than a room, a hut, a hovel partly of planks and partly of canvas, an unshaven white man standing in the door beside which a shotgun leaned, watching him as he approached, his hand extended with four silver dollars on the palm. "Ah wants a jug," he said.

"A jug?" the white man said. "You mean a pint. This is Monday. Ain't you all running this week?"

"Ah laid off," he said. "Whar's my jug?" waiting, looking at nothing apparently, blinking his bloodshot eyes rapidly in his high, slightly back-tilted head, then turning, the jug hanging from his crooked middle finger against his leg, at which moment the white man looked suddenly and sharply at his eyes as though seeing them for the first time—the eyes which had been strained and urgent this morning and which now seemed to be without vision too and in which no white showed at all—and said:

"Here. Gimme that jug. You don't need no gallon. I'm going to give you that pint, give it to you. Then you get out of here and stay out. Don't come back until—"

Then the white man reached and grasped the jug, whereupon the other swung it behind him, sweeping his other arm up and out so that it struck the white man across the chest.

"Look out, white folks," he said. "Hit's mine. Ah done paid you."

The white man cursed him. "No you ain't. Here's your money. Put that jug down, nigger."

"Hit's mine," he said, his voice quiet, gentle even, his face quiet save for the rapid blinking of the red eyes. "Ah done paid for hit." Turning his back on the man and the gun both, he recrossed the clearing to where the dog waited beside the path to come to heel again. They moved rapidly on between the close walls of impenetrable cane-stalks which gave a sort of blondness to the twilight and possessed something of that oppression, that lack of room to breathe in, which the walls of his house had had. But this time, instead of fleeing it, he stopped and raised the jug and drew the cob stopper from the fierce dusk-reek of uncured alcohol and drank, gulping the liquid solid and cold as ice water, without either taste or heat until he lowered the jug and the air got in.

"Hah," he said. "Dat's right. Try me. Try me, big boy. Ah gots something hyar now dat kin whup you."

And, once free of the bottom's unbreathing blackness, there was the moon again. His long shadow and that of the lifted jug slanted away as he drank and then held the jug poised, gulping the silver air into his throat until he could breathe again, speaking to the jug: "Come on now. You always claims you's a better man den me. Come on now. Prove hit," and drank again, swallowing the chill liquid tamed of taste or heat either while the swallowing lasted, feeling it flow solid and cold with fire past and then enveloping the strong steady panting of his lungs until they ran suddenly free as his moving body did in the silver solid wall of air he breasted, and he was all right, his striding shadow and the trotting one of the dog traveling swift as those of two clouds along the hill, the long cast of his motionless shadow and that of the lifted jug slanting across the slope as he watched the tall frail figure of his aunt's husband toiling up the hill.

"Dey tole me at de mill you wuz gone," the old man said. "Ah knowed whar to look. Come home, son. Dat ar can't help you."

"Hit done awready hope me," he said. "Ah'm awready home. Ah'm snakebit now and pizen can't hawm me."

"Den stop and see her. Leff her look at you. Dat's all she axes: just leff her look at you—" But he was already moving. "Wait," the old man cried. "Wait!"

"You can't keep up," he said, speaking into the silver air, breasting aside the silver solid air which began to flow past him almost as fast as it would have flowed past a moving horse; the faint frail voice was already lost in the night's infinitude, his shadow and that of the dog scudding the free miles, the deep strong panting of his chest running free as air now because he was all right.

Then, drinking, he discovered suddenly that no more liquid was entering his mouth; swallowing, it was no longer passing down his throat, throat and mouth filled now with a solid and unmoving column which, without any reflex of revulsion, sprang columnar and intact and still retaining the shape of his gullet, outward glinting in the moonlight, to vanish into the myriad murmur of the dewed grass. He drank again; again his throat merely filled solidly until two icy rills ran from his mouth-corners; again the intact column sprang silvering, glinting, while he panted the chill of air into his throat, the jug poised before his mouth while he spoke to it:

"Awright. Ah'm gwy try you again. Soon as you makes up yo mind to stay whar Ah puts you Ah'll leff you alone."

He drank again, filling his gullet for the third time and for the third time lowered the jug one instant ahead of the bright intact repetition, panting, indrawing the cool of air until he could breathe. He stoppered the cob carefully back into the jug and stood with the deep strong panting of his chest, blinking, the long cast of his motionless and solitary shadow slanting away across the hill and beyond, across the mazy infinitude of all the night-bound earth.

"Awright," he said. "Ah just misread de sign wrong. Hit's done done me all de help Ah needs. Ah'm awright now. Ah doan needs no mo of hit."

He could see the lamp in the window as he crossed the pasture, passing the black-and-silver yawn of the sandy ditch where he had played as a boy with empty snuff-tins and rusted harness buckles and fragments of trace-chain and now and then an actual wheel, the garden patch where he had hoed in the spring days while his aunt stood sentry over him from the kitchen window, crossing the grassless yard in whose dust he had sprawled and crept before he learned to walk, and entered the house, the room, the light itself, his head back-tilted a little, the jug hanging from his crooked finger against his knee.

"Unc Alec say you wanter see me," he said.

"Not just to see you," his aunt said. "To come home, whar we kin help you."

"Ah'm awright," he said. "Ah doan needs no help."

"No," she said. She rose from the chair and came and grasped his arm as she had grasped it yesterday beside the grave; again, as on yesterday, the forearm like iron under the hand. "No! When Alec come back and tole me how you had wawked off de mill and de sun not half down, Ah knowed why and whar. And dat can't help you."

"Hit done awready hope me. Ah'm awright now."

"Don't lie to me," she said. "You ain't never lied to me. Don't lie to me now."

Then he said it. It was his own voice, speaking quietly out of the tremendous panting of his chest which would presently begin to strain at the walls of this room too. But he would be gone in a moment.

"Nome," he said. "Hit ain't done me no good."

"And hit can't! Can't nothing help you but Him. Ax Him! Tole Him about hit! He wants to hyar you and help you!"

"Efn He God, Ah don't needs to tole Him. Efn He God, He awready know hit. Awright. Hyar Ah is. Leff Him come down hyar and do me some good."

"On yo knees!" she cried. "On yo knees and ax Him!" But it was not his knees on the floor: it was his feet, and for a space he could hear her feet too on the planks of the hall behind him and her voice crying after him from the door: "Spoot! Spoot!"—crying after him across the moon-dappled yard the name he had gone by in childhood and adolescence, before the men he worked with and the bright dark nameless women he had taken in course and forgotten until he saw Mannie that day and said, "Ah'm thu wid all dat," began to call him Rider.

It was just after midnight when he reached the mill again. The dog was gone now. This time he could not remember when nor where. At first he seemed to remember hurling the empty jug at it. But later the jug was still in his hand and it was not empty, although each time he drank now the two icy runnels streamed from his mouth-corners, sopping his shirt and overalls until he walked constantly in the fierce chill of the liquid tamed now of flavor and heat and odor too even when the swallowing stopped.

"Sides," he said, "Ah wouldn't th'ow nothin at him. Ah mout kick him efn he needed hit and was close enough. But Ah wouldn't ruint no dawg chunkin' hit."

It was still in his hand when he entered the clearing and paused among the mute soaring of the moon-blond lumber stacks, standing in the middle of the now unimpeded shadow which he was treading again now as he had trod it last night, swaying a little, blinking about him at the stacked lumber, the skidway, the piled logs waiting for to-morrow, the boiler shed all quiet and blanched in the moon: and then it was all right. He was moving again. But he was not moving, he was drinking, the liquid cold and swift and tasteless and requiring no swallowing, so that he could not tell if it were going down inside or outside; but it was all right. And now he was moving, the jug gone now and he didn't know the when or where of that either, crossing the clearing, entering the boiler shed and through it, crossing the junctureless trepan of time's back-loop to the door of the tool-room, the faint glow of the lantern beyond the plank-joints, the surge and fall of a shadow between the light and the wall, the mutter of voices, the mute click and scutter of the dice, his hand loud on the barred door, his voice loud too: "Open hit. Hit's me. Ah'm snakebit and bound to die."

Then he was inside. They were the same faces—three members of his timber gang, three or four others of the mill crew, the white night-watchman with the heavy pistol in his hip pocket and the small heap of coins and worn banknotes on the floor before him; himself standing over the kneeling and squatting circle, swaying a little, blinking, the deadened muscles of his face shaped into smiling while the white man stared at him. "Make room, gamblers," he said. "Ah'm snakebit and de pizen can't hawm me."

"You're drunk," the watchman said. "Get out of here. One of you niggers open that door and get him out of here."

"Dass awright, boss man," he said, his voice equable, almost deferential, his face still fixed in the faint rigid smiling beneath the blinking of the red eyes; "Ah ain't drunk. Ah just can't wawk straight fer dis hyar money weighin' me down."

Now he was kneeling too, the other six dollars of his last week's pay on the floor before him, blinking, still smiling at the face of the white man opposite, then still smiling, watching the dice pass from hand to hand around the circle as the watchman covered the bets, watching the soiled and palm-worn money in front of the white man gradually increase, watching the white man cast and win two doubled bets in succession, then lose one for twenty-five cents, the dice coming to him at last, the cupped snug clicking of them in his fist.

"Shoots a dollar," he said, and cast and watched the white man pick up the dice and flip them back to him. "Ah'm snake-bit," he said. "Ah kin pass wid anything," and cast, and this time one of the others flipped the dice back. "Ah lets hit lay," he said, and cast, and moved as the white man moved, catching the white man's wrist before the hand reached the dice, the two of them squatting, facing each other above the dice and the money, his left hand grasping the white man's right wrist, his face still fixed in the rigid and deadened smiling, his voice still almost deferential: "Ah kin pass even wid miss-outs. But dese hyar yuther boys—" until the hand sprang open and the second pair of dice clattered on to the floor beside the other two, and the white man wrenched it free and sprang up and back and reached the hand backward toward the pocket where the pistol was.

The razor hung between his shoulder blades from a loop of cotton string round his neck beneath his shirt. The same motion of the hand which brought the razor forward over his shoulder flipped the blade open and freed it from the cord, the blade opening on until the back edge of it lay across the knuckles of his fist, his thumb pressing the handle into his closing fingers, so that in the instant before the half-drawn pistol exploded he actually struck at the white man's throat not with the blade but with a sweeping blow of his fist, following through in the same motion so that not even the first jet of blood touched his hand or arm.

After it was over (it didn't take long; they found the prisoner on the following day, hanging from the bell rope in a negro schoolhouse about two miles from the sawmill, and the coroner had pronounced his verdict of death at the hands of a person or persons unknown and surrendered the body to its next of kin all within five minutes) the sheriff's deputy who had been officially in charge of the business was telling his wife about it. It was in the kitchen; his wife was cooking supper, and the deputy had been up and in motion ever since the jail delivery shortly after midnight and he had covered considerable ground since, and he was spent now from lack of sleep and hurried food at hurried and curious hours and, sitting in a chair beside the stove, a little hysterical too.

"Them damn niggers," he said. "I swear to Godfrey, it's a wonder we have as little trouble with them as we do. Because why? Because they ain't human. They look like a man and they walk on their hind legs like a man, and they can talk and you can understand them and you think they understand you, at least now and then. But when it comes to the normal human feelings and sentiments of human beings, they might just as well be a damn herd of wild buffaloes. Now you take this one to-day—"

"I wish you would," his wife said harshly, a stout woman, handsome once, graying now and with a neck definitely too short, who looked not harried at all but choleric. Also she had attended a club rook party that afternoon and had won the first, the fifty-cent, prize until another member had insisted on a recount of the scores and the ultimate throwing out of one entire game. "Take him out of my kitchen, anyway. You sheriffs! Sitting around that courthouse all day long talking. It's no wonder two or three men can walk in and take prisoners out from under your noses. They would take your chairs and desks and window sills too if you ever got your backsides and feet off of them that long."

"It's more of them Birdsongs than just two or three," the deputy said. "There's forty-two active votes in that connection. Me and Mayfield taken the poll-list and counted them up one day. But listen—" The wife turned from the stove, carrying a dish. The deputy snatched his feet rapidly out of the way as she passed him and went on into the dining room. The deputy raised his voice a little. "His wife dies on him. All right. But does he grieve? He's the biggest man at the funeral. Grabs a shovel before they even got the box into the grave, I heard tell, and starts throwing dirt onto her faster than a slip scraper could. But that's all right—"

His wife came back. He moved his feet again. "—maybe that's the way he felt about her. There ain't any law against that, long as he never officiated at the deceasing too. But here the next day he's the first man at the mill except the fireman, getting there before the fireman had his fire going; five minutes earlier and he could even helped the fireman wake Birdsong up so he could go home and go back to bed again or even cut Birdsong's throat then and saved everybody trouble. So he comes to work, the first man on the job, when McAndrews would have give him the day off and paid him his time too, when McAndrews and everybody else expected him to take the day off, when any white man would have took the day off no matter how he felt about his wife, when even a little child would have had sense enough to take a holiday when he could still get paid too. But not him. The first man there, jumping from one truck to another before the whistle quit blowing even, snatching up ten-foot cypress logs by himself and throwing them around like matches. And then, just when everybody has decided that that's the way to take him, that that's the way he wants to be took, he walks off the job in the middle of the afternoon without by-your-leave or thank you or good-by to McAndrews or nobody else, gets himself a whole gallon of bust-skull white-mule whiskey, comes straight back to the mill to the same crap game where Birdsong has been running crooked dice on them mill niggers for fifteen years, goes straight to the same game where he has been peacefully losing a probably steady average ninety-nine per cent of his pay ever since he got big enough to read the spots on them miss-outs, and cuts Birdsong's throat clean to the neckbone five minutes later.

"So me and Mayfield go out there. Not that we expect to do any good, as he had probably passed Jackson, Tennessee, about day-light; and besides, the simplest way to find him would be just to stay close behind them Birdsong boys. So it's just by the merest pure chance that we go by his house; I don't even remember why now; and there he is. Sitting behind the door with that razor open on one knee and his shotgun on the other? No. Asleep. A big pot of pease set clean on the stove, and him laying in the back yard asleep in the broad sun with just his head under the edge of the porch and a dog that looked like a cross between a bear and a Polled Angus steer yelling fire and murder from the back door. And he wakes up and says, 'Awright, white folks. Ah done it. Jest don't lock me up,' and Mayfield says, 'Mr. Birdsong's kinfolks ain't going to either. You'll have plenty of fresh air when they get a hold of you,' and he says, 'Ah done it. Jest don't lock me up'—advising, instructing the sheriff not to lock him up; he done it all right and it's too bad, but don't cut him off from the fresh air. So we loaded him into the car, when here come the old woman—his ma or aunt or something—panting up the road at a dog-trot, wanting to come with us, and Mayfield trying to tell her what might happen maybe to her too if them Birdsong kin catches us before we can get him locked up, only she is coming anyway and, like Mayfield says, her being in the car might be a good thing if the Birdsongs did happen to run into us, because interference with the law can't be condoned even if the Birdsong connection did carry that beat for Mayfield last summer. So we brought her along too and got him to town and into the jail all right and turned him over to Ketcham and Ketcham taken him on upstairs and the old woman coming too, telling Ketcham, 'Ah tried to raise him right. He was a good boy. He ain't never been in no trouble till now. He will suffer for what he done. But don't let the white folks git him,' and Ketcham says, 'You and him ought to thought of that before he started barbering white men without using no lather,' and locked them both up in the cell because he felt like Mayfield did, that her being there might be a good influence on the Birdsong boys if anything started if he should run for sheriff when Mayfield's term was out. So he come on back downstairs and pretty soon the chain gang come in and he thought things had settled down for a while when all of a sudden he begun to hear the yelling, not howling: yelling, though there wasn't no words in it, and he grabbed his pistol and run back upstairs and into the room where the chain gang was, where he could see through the door bars into the cell where that nigger had done tore that iron cot clean out of the floor it was bolted to and was standing in the middle of the cell, holding the cot over his head like it was a baby's cradle, yelling, and the old woman sitting hunched into the corner and the nigger says to her, 'Ah ain't going to hurt you,' and throws the cot against the wall and comes and grabs holt of that steel door and rips it out of the wall—bricks, hinges and all—and walks out into the big room, toting the door over his head as if it were a gauze wire window screen, saying, 'It's awright. Ah ain't tryin' to git away.'

"Ketcham could have shot him right there, but like he figured, if it wasn't going to be the law, then the Birdsong boys ought to have first lick at him. So Ketcham don't shoot. Instead he jumps in behind where the chain-gang niggers were kind of backed off from that steel door, hollering, 'Grab him! Throw him down!' except they hang back at first until Ketcham gets up to where he can kick the ones he can reach, batting at the others with the flat of the pistol until they rush him. And Ketcham says for a good minute he would grab them up as they come in and fling them clean across the room like they was rag dolls, still saying, 'Ah ain't tryin' to git out, Ah ain't tryin' to git out,' until at last they pulled him down, a big mass of nigger arms and heads and legs boiling around on the floor and even then Ketcham says every now and then a nigger would come flying out and go sailing through the air across the room, spraddled like a flying squirrel and his eyes sticking out in front of him like the headlights on a car, until at last they had him down and Ketcham went in and begun peeling away niggers until he could see him laying there under the pile of niggers, laughing, with tears big as glass marbles popping out of his eyes and running across his face and down past his ears and making a kind of popping sound on the floor like somebody dropping bird eggs, laughing and laughing and saying, 'Hit look lack Ah just can't quit thinking. Look lack Ah just can't quit.' And what do you think of that?"

"I think if you eat any supper in this house you'll do it in the next five minutes," his wife said from the dining room. "I'm going to clear this table then and I'm going to the picture show."

Go Down, Moses

The face was black, smooth, impenetrable; the eyes had seen too much. The Negroid hair had been treated so that it covered the skull like a cap, in a single neat-ridged sweep that had the appearance of having been lacquered, the part trimmed out with a razor, so that the head resembled a bronze head, permanent, imperishable. He wore one of those sports costumes called ensembles in the newspaper advertisements, shirt and trousers matching and cut from the same fawn-colored flannel, and they had cost too much and were draped too much, with too many pleats. He half lay on the steel cot in the steel cubicle just outside which an armed guard had stood for twenty hours now, smoking cigarettes and answering in a voice deliberately and consistently not a Southern voice the questions of the spectacled young white man sitting with a broad census taker's portfolio on the steel stool opposite.

"Samuel Worsham Beauchamp. Twenty-six. Born in the country near Jefferson, Mississippi. No family. No—"

"Wait." The census taker wrote rapidly. "That isn't the name you were sen—lived under in Chicago?"

The other snapped the ash from the cigarette. "No. It was another guy killed the cop."

"All right. Occupation—"

"Getting rich too fast."

"—none." The census taker wrote rapidly. "Parents?"

"Sure. Two. I don't remember them. My grandmother raised me."

"What's her name? Is she still living?"

"I don't know. Mollie Worsham Beauchamp. If she is, she's on Carothers Edmonds' farm. Near Jefferson, Mississippi. That all?"

The census taker closed the portfolio and rose. He was a year or two younger than the other. "If they don't know who you are here, how will they know—how do you expect to get home?"

The other snapped the ash from the cigarette, lying on the steel cot in the fine Hollywood clothes and a pair of shoes better than the census taker had ever owned. "What will that be to me?" he said.

So the census taker went away; the guard locked the steel door again. And the other lay on the steel cot smoking until they came and slit the expensive trousers and shaved the expensive coiffure and led him out of the cell.

On that same hot, bright July morning, the same hot, bright wind that shook the mulberry leaves just outside Gavin Stevens' window blew into the office too, contriving a semblance of coolness in what was merely motion. It fluttered among the county-attorney business on his desk and blew in the wild shock of his prematurely white hair above the thin, intelligent, unstable face, above the rumpled linen suit from whose lapel his Phi Beta Kappa key dangled from the watch chain—Phi Beta Kappa, Harvard; Ph.D., Heidelberg—Stevens, whose office was his hobby, although it made his living for him, and whose serious vocation was a twenty-two-year-old unfinished translation of the Old Testament back into classic Greek. Only his caller seemed impervious to it although by appearance she should have owned in that breeze no more of weight and solidity than the intact ash of a scrap of paper—a little old Negro woman with a shrunken, incredibly old face beneath a white headcloth and a black straw hat which would have fitted a child.

"Beauchamp?" Stevens said. "You live on Mr. Carothers Edmonds' place."

"I done left," she said. "I come to find my boy." Then, sitting opposite him on the hard chair and without moving, she began to chant: "Roth Edmonds done sold my Benjamin. Sold him in Egypt. Pharaoh got him—"

"Wait," Stevens said. "Wait, Aunty." Because memory, recollection, was about to click and mesh. "If you don't know where your grandson is, how do you know he's in trouble? Do you mean that Mr. Edmonds refused to help you find him?"

"It was Roth Edmonds sold him," she said. "Sold him into Egypt. I don't know whar he is. I just knows Pharaoh got him. And you the Law. I wants to find my boy."

"All right," Stevens said. "I'll try to find him. If you're not going back home, where are you going to stay in town? It may take some time, if you don't know where he went and you haven't heard from him in five years."

"I be staying with Hamp Worsham. He my brother."

"All right," Stevens said. He was not surprised. He knew Hamp Worsham, but he would not have been surprised even if he had never seen the old Negress before. They were like that. You knew them all your life, they might even have worked for you for years; they might have different names, then suddenly you learned that they were brothers or sisters, or claimed to be, and you were not surprised.

He sat in the hot motion which was not breeze and heard her toiling slowly down the outside stairs, remembering the grandson. The papers had passed across his desk before going to the district attorney five or six years ago—Butch Beauchamp, as the youth had been known during the single year he had spent in and out of the city jail, the old Negress' daughter's child, orphaned of his mother at birth and deserted by his father, whom the grandmother had taken and raised, or tried to. Because at nineteen he had quit the country and come to town, in and out of jail for gambling and fighting, and at last under serious indictment for breaking and entering a store.

Caught red-handed, whereupon he struck with a piece of iron pipe at the officer who caught him, then lay on the ground where the officer had felled him with his pistol butt, cursing through his broken mouth, his teeth fixed into something like grinning through the blood, then two nights later he had broken out of jail and was seen no more—a youth, not yet twenty-one, yet with something in him from the father who had begot and deserted him and who was now in the state penitentiary for manslaughter—some seed not only violent but bad.

"And that's who I am to find, save," Stevens thought. Because he did not for one moment doubt the old Negress' instinct. If she had also been able to divine where the boy was and what his trouble was, he would not have been surprised, and it was only later that he thought to be surprised at how quickly he did find where the boy was and what was wrong.

Edmonds' farm was seventeen miles away. But then, according to the old Negress, Edmonds had already refused to have anything to do with the business. And now Stevens comprehended what the old Negress had meant. He remembered that it was Edmonds who had sent the boy into Jefferson; he had caught the boy breaking into his commissary store and had ordered him off the place and had forbidden him ever to return. "And not the sheriff," Stevens thought. "Something broader, quicker in scope, than his would be. . . ." He rose, descended the outside stairs and crossed the empty square in the hot suspension of noon's beginning to the office of the county weekly newspaper. The editor was in—an older man, though with hair less white than Stevens', in a black string tie and an old-fashioned boiled shirt and tremendously fat.

"An old nigger woman named Mollie Beauchamp," Stevens said. "She and her husband live on the Edmonds' place. It's her grandson. You remember him—Butch Beauchamp, about five or six years ago, who spent a year in town, mostly in jail, until they finally caught him breaking into Rouncewell's store one night? Well, he's in worse trouble than that now. I don't doubt her at all. I just hope, for her sake as well as that of the great public whom I represent, that his present trouble is bad and maybe final too—"

"Wait," the editor said. He didn't even need to leave his desk. He took the press association flimsy from its spike and handed it to Stevens. "It just came in," the editor said. It was datelined from Joliet, Illinois, this morning: "Mississippi Negro, on eve of execution for murder of Chicago policeman, exposes alias by completing census questionnaire. Samuel Worsham Beauchamp. . . ."

Stevens was crossing the empty square again in the hot suspension in which noon was now several minutes nearer. He had thought he was going home to his boardinghouse for the noon meal, but he found that he was not. "Besides, I didn't lock my office door," he thought. "So it seems I didn't mean what I said I hoped." So he mounted the outside stairs again, out of the hazy and now windless sun glare, and entered his office. He stopped.

Then he said, "Good morning, Miss Worsham."

She was quite old too—thin, erect, with a neat, old-time piling of white hair beneath a faded hat of thirty years ago, in rusty black, with a frayed and faded black umbrella. She lived alone in the decaying house her father had left her, where she gave lessons in china painting and, with the help of Hamp Worsham and his wife, raised chickens and vegetables for market.

"I came about Mollie," she said. "Mollie Beauchamp. She said that you—"

He told her while she watched him, erect on the hard chair where the old Negress had sat, the rusty umbrella leaning against her knee. On her lap, beneath her folded hands, lay an immense old-fashioned beaded reticule. "He is to be executed tonight."

"Can nothing be done? Mollie's and Hamp's parents belonged to my grandfather. Mollie and I grew up together. Our birthdays are in the very same month."

"I telephoned," Stevens said. "I talked to the warden at Joliet, and to the district attorney in Chicago. He had a fair trial, a good lawyer. He had money. He was in a business called numbers, that people like him make money in." She watched him, erect, not moving. "He is a murderer, Miss Worsham. He shot that policeman in the back. A bad son of a bad father. He confessed it afterward."

"I know," she said. Then he realized that she was not looking at him, not seeing him at least. "It's terrible."

"So is murder terrible," Stevens said. "It's better this way." Then she was looking at him again.

"I wasn't thinking of him. I was thinking of Mollie. She mustn't know."

"Yes," Stevens said. "I have already talked to Mr. Wilmoth at the paper. He has agreed not to print anything. I will telephone the Memphis paper, but it's probably too late for that, even if they would. . . . If we could just persuade her to go on back home this afternoon, before the Memphis paper. . . . Out there, where the only white person she ever sees is Mr. Edmonds, and I can see him and warn him not to tell her, and even if the niggers would hear about it, they wouldn't—. And then maybe in about two or three months I could go out and tell her he is dead and buried somewhere in the

North. . . ." This time she was watching him with such an expression that he ceased talking; she sat there, erect on the hard chair, watching him until he had ceased.

"She will want to take the body back home with her," she said.

"The body?" Stevens said. The expression was neither shocked nor disapproving. It merely embodied some old, timeless, female affinity for blood and grief. Looking at her, Stevens thought: "She has walked into town in this heat. Unless Hamp brought her in in the buggy he peddles eggs and vegetables from."

"He is the only child of her oldest daughter, her own dead first child. He must come home."

"He must come home," Stevens said. "I'll attend to it at once. I'll telephone at once."

"You are kind." For the first time she stirred, moved. He watched her hands draw the reticule toward her, clasping it. "I will defray the expenses. Can you give me some idea—?"

He looked her straight in the face. He told the lie without batting an eye, quickly, easily: "Ten or twelve dollars will cover it. They will furnish a box, and there will be only the transportation."

"A box?" Again she looked at him with that expression curious and detached, as though he were a child. "He is her grandson, Mr. Stevens. When she took him to raise, she gave him my father's name. Not just a box, Mr. Stevens. I understand that can be done by paying so much a month."

"Not just a box," Stevens said. "Mr. Edmonds will want to help, I know. And I understand old Luke Beauchamp has some money in the bank. And if you will permit me—"

"That will not be necessary," she said. He watched her open the reticule; he watched her count onto the desk twenty-five dollars in frayed bills and coins ranging down to nickels and dimes and pennies. "That will take care of the immediate expenses. I will tell her—you are sure there is no hope?"

"I am sure. He will die tonight."

"I will tell her this afternoon that he is dead then."

"Would you like for me to tell her?"

"I will tell her," she said.

"Would you like for me to come out and see her then, talk to her?"

"If you will be so kind." Then she was gone, erect, her feet crisp and light, almost brisk, on the stairs, ceasing. He telephoned again, to the warden in Illinois, then to an undertaker in Joliet. Then once more he crossed the hot, empty square. He had to wait only a short while for the editor to return from dinner.

"We're bringing him home," Stevens said. "Miss Worsham and you and me and some others. It will cost—"

"Wait," the editor said. "What others?"

"I don't know yet. It will cost about two hundred. I'm not counting the telephones; I'll take care of that myself. I'll get something out of Carothers Edmonds the first time I catch him, I don't know how much, but something. And maybe fifty around the square. But the rest of it is you and me, because she insisted on leaving twenty-five with me, which is just twice what I tried to persuade her it would cost, and just exactly four times what she can afford to pay—"

"Wait," the editor said. "Wait."

"And he will come in on Number Nine the day after tomorrow and we will meet it, Miss Worsham and his grandmother, the old nigger, in my car and you and me in yours."

["Oh hell, now, Gavin! Folks will claim I have turned Republican and I'll lose what few advertisers I have got."

Stevens glared at the editor almost, with a sort of furious patience. "Are you going to let that lady meet that nigger murderer's body by herself, with nobody else there but that old nigger woman, for a lot of blackguard white men to stare at? If somebody thought to send it to your damn little sheet, dont you know it'll be in the Memphis papers tomorrow morning?" After a moment the editor looked away.

"All right," he said. "Then what?"]

"Miss Worsham and the old woman will take him back home, back where he was born. Or where the old woman raised him. Or where she tried to. And the hearse out there will be fifteen more, not counting flowers—"

"Flowers?"

"Flowers," Stevens said. "Call the whole thing two hundred and twenty-five. And it will probably be mostly you and me. All right?"

"All right," the editor said. "By Jupiter," he added, "even if I could help myself, the novelty will be almost worth it. It will be the first time in my life I ever paid money for copy I had already promised beforehand I will not print."

"Have already promised beforehand you will not print," Stevens said. And during the rest of that hot and now windless afternoon, while officials from the city hall and justices of the peace and bailiffs came fifteen and twenty miles from the ends of the county, mounted the stairs and stood in his empty office and called his name and then sat and waited and went away and returned and sat again, fuming, Stevens passed from store to store and office to office about the square—merchant and clerk, proprietor and employee, doctor and dentist and lawyer—with his set and rapid speech: "It's to bring a dead nigger home. It's for Miss Worsham. Never mind about a paper to sign: just give me a dollar. Or a half a dollar then."

And that night after supper he walked through the breathless and star-filled darkness to Miss Worsham's house on the edge of town and knocked on the paintless door. Hamp Worsham admitted him—an old man, belly-bloated from the vegetables on which he and his wife and Miss Worsham all three mostly lived, with a fringe of white hair and the face of a Roman senator and the blurred pupilless eyes of the old.

"She expecting you," he said. "She say to kindly step up to the chamber."

"Is that where Aunt Mollie is?" Stevens said.

"We all dar," Worsham said.

So Stevens crossed the lamplit hall (the entire house was still lighted by oil lamps and there was no running water in it) and preceded the Negro up the clean, paintless stairs beside the faded wallpaper, and followed the old Negro up the hall and into the clean, spare bedroom with its unmistakable faint odor of old maidens. They were all there, as Worsham had said—his wife, a tremendous woman in a bright turban leaning in the door, Miss Worsham erect again on a hard chair, the old Negress sitting in the one rocking chair beside the hearth on which even tonight a few ashes smoldered faintly.

She had a reed-stemmed clay pipe in her hand, but she was not smoking it, the ash dead and white in the stained bowl; and actually looking at her for the first time, Stevens thought: "Good Lord, she's not as big as a ten-year-old child." Then he sat too, so that the four of them—himself, Miss Worsham, the old Negress and her brother—made a circle about the brick hearth on which the ancient symbol of physical coherence smoldered.

"He'll be home the day after tomorrow, Aunt Molly," he said. The old Negress didn't even look at him; she never had looked at him.

"He dead," she said. "Pharaoh got him."

"Oh, yes, Lord," Worsham said. "Pharaoh got him."

"Done sold my Benjamin," the old Negress said. "Sold him in Egypt." She began to sway faintly back and forth in the chair.

"Oh, yes, Lord," Worsham said.

"Hush," Miss Worsham said. "Hush, Hamp."

"I telephoned to Mr. Edmonds," Stevens said. "He will have everything ready when you get there."

"Roth Edmonds sold him," the old Negress said. She swayed back and forth in the chair. "Sold my Benjamin."

"Hush," Miss Worsham said. "Hush, Mollie. Hush now."

"No," Stevens said. "No he didn't, Aunt Mollie. It wasn't Mr. Edmonds. Mr. Edmonds didn't—" ("But she certainly won't hear me," he thought. She was not even looking at him, never had looked at him.)

"Sold my Benjamin," she said. "Sold him in Egypt."

"Sold him in Egypt," Worsham said.

"Roth Edmonds sold my Benjamin."

"Sold him to Pharaoh."

"Sold him to Pharaoh and now he dead."

"I'd better go," Stevens said. He rose quickly. Miss Worsham rose too, but [the others did not even look at them—the brother and sister facing one another across the hearth and both swaying back and forth, Worsham's wife leaning against the wall, and now when Stevens looked at her he saw that her eyes were rolled upward in her skull until the pupils had vanished and only the whites showed.] He did not wait for her to precede him—he went down the hall, fast. "Soon I will be outside, then there will be air, space, breath," he thought. He could hear her behind him—the crisp, almost brisk yet unhurried feet, and beyond the feet, the voices:

"Sold my Benjamin. Sold him in Egypt."

"Sold him in Egypt. Oh, yes, Lord."

He descended the stairs, almost running. It was not far now; now he could smell it, feel it—the breathless and simple dark, and now he could manner himself to pause and wait, turning at the door, watching Miss Worsham as she approached—the high, white, erect, old-time head approaching through the old-time lamplight beyond which he could now hear the third voice, which would be that of Worsham's wife—a true, constant soprano that ran without words beneath the strophe and antistrophe of the brother and sister:

"Sold him in Egypt and now he dead."

"O, yes, Lord. Sold him in Egypt."

"Sold him in Egypt."

"And now he dead."

"Sold him to Pharaoh."

"And now he dead."

"I'm sorry," Stevens said. "I ask you to forgive me. I should have known. I shouldn't have come."

"It's all right," Miss Worsham said. "It's our grief."

And on the next bright, hot day but one the hearse and the two cars were waiting when the southbound train came in. There were more than a dozen cars waiting, but it was not until the train came that Stevens and the editor began to notice the number of Negroes and whites both. Then, with the idle white men and youths and small boys and probably half a hundred Negroes, men and women too, watching quietly, the Negro undertaker's men lifted the gray-and-silver casket from the train and carried it to the hearse and snatched the wreaths and floral symbols of mortality briskly and efficiently out and slid the casket in and replaced the flowers and clapped to the door.

Then, with Miss Worsham and the old Negress in Stevens' car with the driver he had hired and himself and the editor in the editor's car, they followed the hearse as it swung into the long hill up from the station, going fast in a whining lower gear until it reached the crest, going pretty fast still though quiet now, purring, until it slowed into the square, crossing the square, circling the Confederate monument and the courthouse while the merchants and clerks and professional men who had given Stevens the dollars and half dollars two days ago, and the ones who had not, watched quietly from doors and upstairs windows, swinging then into the street which at the edge of town would become the country road leading to the destination seventeen miles away, already picking up speed again and followed by the two cars containing the four people—the highheaded, erect lady, the old Negress, the designated paladin of justice and truth, the Ph.D. from Heidelberg—in formal component complement to the Negro murderer's catafalque, the slain wolf.

When they reached the edge of town, the hearse was going quite fast. Now they flashed past the metal sign which said in reverse, Jefferson, Corporate Limit, and the street vanished, slanting away into another long hill, becoming gravel. Stevens leaned forward and cut the switch, so that the editor's car coasted, slowing as he began to brake it, the hearse and the other car drawing rapidly away now as if in flight, the light and unrained summer dust spurting from beneath the fleeing wheels; soon they were gone. The editor turned his car clumsily, grinding the gears, sawing and filling until he was back in the road facing town again. Then he sat for a moment, his foot on the clutch.

"Do you know what she asked me this morning, back there at the station?" he said. "She said, 'Is you gonter put hit in de paper?'"

"What?" Stevens said.

"That's what I said," the editor said. "And she said it again: 'Is you gonter put hit in de paper? I wants hit all in de paper. All of hit.' And I wanted to say, 'If I should happen to know how he really died, do you want that in too?' And, by Jupiter, if I had said that and if she had known what we know even, I believe she would have said yes. But I didn't say it. I just said, 'Why, you couldn't read it, Aunty.' And she said, 'Miss Belle will show me whar to look and I kin look at hit. You put hit in de paper. All of hit.'"

"Oh," Stevens said. ("Yes," he thought. "It doesn't matter to her now. Since it had to be and she couldn't stop it, and now that it's all over and done and finished, she doesn't care how he died. She wanted him home, but she wanted him to come home right. She wanted that casket for him and those flowers and the hearse and she wanted to ride through town behind it in a car.") "Come on," he said. "Let's get back to town. I haven't seen my desk in two days."

Delta Autumn

Soon now they would enter the Delta. The sensation was familiar to him, renewed like this each last week in November for more than fifty years—the last hill at the foot of which the rich unbroken alluvial flatness began as the sea began at the base of its cliffs, dissolving away beneath the unhurried November rain as the sea itself would dissolve away. At first they had come in wagons—the guns, the bedding, the dogs, the food, the whiskey, the anticipation of hunting—the young men who could drive all night and all the following day in the cold rain and pitch camp in the rain and sleep in the wet blankets and rise at daylight the next morning to hunt. There had been bear then, and a man shot a doe or a fawn as quickly as he did a buck, and in the afternoons they shot wild turkey with pistols to test their stalking skill and marksmanship, feeding all but the breast to the dogs. But that time was gone now and now they went in cars, driving faster and faster each year because the roads were better and they had farther to drive, the territory in which game still existed drawing yearly inward as his life was drawing in, until now he was the last of those who had once made the journey in wagons without feeling it and now those who accompanied him were the sons and even the grandsons of the men who had ridden for twenty-four hours in rain and sleet behind the steaming mules, calling him Uncle Ike now, and he no longer told anyone how near seventy he actually was because he knew as well as they did that he no longer had any business making such expeditions, even by car. In fact, each time now, on that first night in camp, lying aching and sleepless in the harsh blankets, his blood only faintly warmed by the single thin whiskey-and-water which he allowed himself, he would tell himself that this would be his last. But he would stand that trip (he still shot almost as well as he had ever shot, he still killed almost as much of the game he saw as he had ever killed; he no longer knew how many deer had fallen before his gun) and the fierce long heat of the next summer would somehow renew him. Then November would come again and again in the car with two of the sons of his old companions, whom he had taught not only how to distinguish between the prints left by a buck and a doe but between the sound they made in moving, he would look ahead past the jerking arc of the windshield wiper and see the land flatten suddenly, dissolving away beneath the rain as the sea itself would dissolve, and he would say, "Well boys, there it is again."

This time though he didn't have time to speak. The driver of the car stopped it, slamming it to a skidding halt on the greasy pavement without warning, so that old McCaslin, first looking ahead at the empty road, glanced sharply past the man in the middle until he could see the face of the driver, the youngest face of them all, darkly aquiline, handsome and ruthless and saturnine and staring sombrely ahead through the steaming windshield across which the twin arms of the wiper flicked and flicked. "I didn't intend to come in here this time," he said. His name was Boyd. He was just past forty. He owned the car as well as two of the three Walker hounds in the rumble behind them, just as he owned, or at least did the driving of, anything—animal, machine or human—which he happened to be using.

"You said that back in Jefferson last week," McCaslin said. "Then you changed your mind. Have you changed it again?"

"Oh, Don's coming," the third man said. His name was Legate. He seemed to be speaking to no one. "If it was just a buck he was coming all this distance for now. But he's got a doe in here. On two legs—when she's standing up. Pretty light-colored too. The one he was after them nights last fall when he said he was coon-hunting. The one I figured maybe he was still chasing when he was gone all that month last January." He chortled, still in that voice addressed to no one, not quite completely jeering.

"What?" McCaslin said. "What's that?"

"Now, Uncle Ike," Legate said, "that's something a man your

age ain't supposed to had no interest in in twenty years." But McCaslin had not even glanced at Legate. He was still watching Boyd's face, the eyes behind the spectacles, the blurred eyes of an old man but quite sharp too; eyes which could still see a gun barrel and what ran beyond it as well as any of them could. He was remembering himself now: how last year, during the final stage by motor boat to where they would camp, one of the boxes of food had been lost overboard and how on the second day Boyd had gone back to the nearest town for supplies and had been gone overnight and when he did return, something had happened to him: he would go into the woods each dawn with his gun when the others went, but McCaslin, watching him, knew that he was not hunting.

"All right," he said. "Take Will and me on to shelter where we can wait for the truck, and you can go back."

"I'm going in," Boyd said harshly. "I'm going to get mine too. Because this will be the last of it."

"The last of deer hunting, or of doe hunting?" Legate said. This time McCaslin paid no attention to him even in speech. He still watched Boyd's savage and immobile face.

"Why?" he said.

"After Hitler gets through with it? Or Yokohama or Pelley or Smith or Jones or whatever he will call himself in this country."

"We'll stop him in this country," Legate said. "Even if he calls himself George Washington."

"How?" Boyd said. "By singing God Bless America in bars at midnight and wearing dime-store flags in our lapels?"

"So that's what's worrying you," McCaslin said. "I ain't noticed this country being short of defenders yet when it needed them. You did some of it yourself twenty years ago and did it well, if those medals you brought back home mean anything. This country is a little mite stronger and bigger than any one man or even group of men outside or inside of it either. I reckon it can cope with one Austrian paper hanger, no matter what he calls himself. My pappy and some other better men than any of them you named tried once to tear it in two with a war, and they failed."

"And what have you got left?" Boyd said. "Half the people without jobs and half the factories closed by strikes. Too much cotton and corn and hogs, and not enough for all the people to wear and eat. Too much not-butter and not even the guns. . . ."

"We got a deer camp—if we ever get to it," Legate said. "Not to mention does."

"It's a good time to mention does," McCaslin said. "Does and fawns both. The only fighting anywhere that ever had anything of God's blessing on it has been when men fought to protect does and fawns. If it's going to come to fighting, that's a good thing to mention and remember."

"Haven't you discovered in sixty years that women and children are one thing there's never any scarcity of?" Boyd said.

"Maybe that's why all I am worrying about right now is that ten miles of river we still got to run before we can make camp," McCaslin said. "Let's get on."

They went on. Soon they were going fast again—that speed at which Boyd drove, about which he had consulted neither of them just as he had given neither of them any warning when he had slammed the car to a stop. McCaslin relaxed again, watching, as he did each recurrent November while more than fifty of them passed, the land which he had seen change. At first there had been only the old towns along the river and the old towns along the edge of the hills, from each of which the planters with their gangs of slaves and then of hired labor had wrested from the impenetrable jungle of waterstanding cane and cypress, gum and holly and oak and ash, cotton patches which as the years passed became fields and then plantations, the paths made by deer and bear becoming roads and then highways, with towns in turn springing up along them and along the rivers Tallahatchie and Sunflower which joined and became the Yazoo, the River of the Dead of the Choctaws—the thick, slow, black, unsunned streams almost without current, which once each year actually ceased to flow and then moved backward, spreading, drowning the rich land and then subsiding again, leaving it still richer. Most of that was gone now. Now a man drove two hundred miles from Jefferson before he found wilderness to hunt in; now the land lay open from the cradling hills on the east to the rampart of levee on the west, standing horseman-tall with cotton for the world's looms—the rich black land, imponderable and vast, fecund up to the very cabin doorsteps of the Negroes who worked it and the domiciles of the white men who owned it, which exhausted the hunting life of a dog in one year, the working life of a mule in five and of a man in twenty—the land in which neon flashed past them from the little countless towns and constant this-year's cars sped over the broad plumb-ruled highways, yet in which the only permanent mark of man's occupation seemed to be the tremendous gins, constructed in sections of sheet iron and in a week's time though they were, since no man, millionaire though he be, would build more than a roof and walls to live in, with camping equipment to live with, because he knew that once each ten years or so his house would be flooded to the second story and all within it ruined;—the land across which there came now no scream of panther but instead the long hooting of locomotives: trains of incredible length and drawn by a single engine since there was no gradient anywhere and no elevation save those raised by forgotten aboriginal hands as refuges from the yearly water and used by their Indian successors to sepulchure their fathers' bones, and all that remained of that old time were the Indian names on the little towns and usually pertaining to water—Aluschaskuna, Tillatoba, Homachitto, Yazoo.

By early afternoon they were on water. At the last little Indian-named town at the end of the pavement they waited until the other car and the two trucks—the one containing the bedding and tents, the other carrying the horses—overtook them. Then they left the concrete and, after a mile or so, the gravel too, and in caravan they ground on through the ceaselessly dissolving afternoon with chained wheels in the lurching and splashing ruts, until presently it seemed to him that the retrograde of his recollection had gained an inverse velocity from their own slow progress and that the land had retreated not in minutes from the last spread of gravel, but in years, decades, back toward what it had been when he first knew it—the road they now followed once more the ancient pathway of bear and deer, the diminishing fields they now passed once more scooped punily and terrifically by axe and saw and mule drawn plow from the brooding and immemorial tangle instead of ruthless mile-wide parallelograms wrought by ditching and dyking machinery.

They left the cars and trucks at the landing, the horses to go overland down the river to a point opposite the camp and swim the river, themselves and the bedding and food and tents and dogs in the motor launch. Then, his old hammer double gun which was better than half as old as he between his knees, he watched even these last puny marks of man—cabin, clearing, the small and irregular fields which a year ago were jungle and in which the skeleton stalks of this year's cotton stood almost as tall and rank as the old cane had stood, as if man had had to marry his planting to the wilderness in order to conquer it—fall away and vanish until the twin banks marched with wilderness as he remembered it; the tangle of brier and cane impenetrable even to sight twenty feet away, the tall tremendous soaring of oak and gum and ash and hickory which had rung to no axe save the hunter's, had echoed to no machinery save the beat of old-time steamboats traversing it or the snarling of launches like their own of people going into it to dwell for a week or two weeks because it was still wilderness. There was still some of it left, although now it was two hundred miles from Jefferson when once it had been thirty. He had watched it, not being conquered, destroyed, so much as retreating since its purpose was now done and its time an outmoded time, retreating southward through this shaped section of earth between hills and river until what was left of it seemed now to be gathered and for the time arrested in one tremendous density of brooding and inscrutable impenetrability at the ultimate funnelling tip.

They reached the site of their last year's camp with still two hours left of light. "You go on over under that driest tree and set down," Legate told him. "Me and these other young boys will do this." He did neither. In his slicker he directed the unloading of the boat—the tents, the stove, the bedding, the food for themselves and the dogs until there should be meat in camp. He sent two of the Negroes to cut firewood; he had the cook-tent raised and the stove set up and a fire going and a meal cooking while the big tent was still being staked down. Then in the beginning of dusk he crossed in the boat to where the horses waited, backing and snorting at the water. He took the lead-ropes and with no more weight than that and his voice he drew them down into the water and held them beside the boat with only their heads above the surface as though they actually were suspended from his frail and strengthless old man's hands while the boat recrossed and each horse in turn lay prone in the shallows, panting and trembling, its eyes rolling in the dusk until the same weightless hand and the unraised voice gathered surging upward, splashing and thrashing up the bank.

Then the meal was ready. The last of light was gone now save the thin stain of it snared somewhere between the river's surface and the rain. He had the glass of thin whiskey-and-water and they ate standing in the mud beneath the stretched tarpaulin. The oldest Negro, Isham, had already made his bed—the strong, battered iron cot, the stained mattress which was not quite soft enough, the worn, washed blankets which as the years passed were less and less warm enough. Wearing only his bagging woolen underclothes, his spectacles folded away in the worn case beneath the pillow where he could reach them readily and his lean body fitted into the old worn groove of mattress and blankets, he lay on his back, his hands crossed on his breast and his eyes closed while the others went to bed and the last of the talking died into snoring. Then he opened his eyes and lay looking up at the motionless belly of canvas upon which the constant rain murmured, upon which the glow of the sheet-iron heater died slowly away and would fade still further until the youngest Negro, lying on planks before it for that purpose, would sit up and stoke it again and lie back down.

They had had a house once. That was twenty and thirty and forty years ago, when the big bottom was only thirty miles from Jefferson and old Major de Spain, who had been his father's cavalry commander in '61 and –2 and –3 and –4 and who had taken him into the woods his first time, had owned eight or ten sections of it. Old Sam Fathers was alive then, half Chickasaw Indian, grandson of a chief, and half Negro, who had taught him how and when to shoot; such a November dawn as tomorrow would be and the old man had led him straight to the great cypress and he had known the buck would pass exactly there because there was something running in Sam Fathers' veins which ran in the veins of the buck and they stood there against the tremendous trunk, the old man and the boy of twelve, and there was nothing but the dawn and then suddenly the buck was there, smoke-colored out of nothing, magnificent with speed, and Sam Fathers said, "Now. Shoot quick and shoot slow," and the gun leveled without hurry and crashed and he walked to the buck lying still intact and still in the shape of that magnificent speed and he bled it with his own knife and Sam Fathers dipped his hands in the hot blood and marked his face forever while he stood trying not to tremble, humbly and with pride too though the boy of twelve had been unable to phrase it then, "I slew you; my bearing must not shame your quitting life.

My conduct forever onward must become your death." They had
the house then. That roof, the two weeks of each fall which they
spent under it, had become his home; although since that time they
had lived during the two fall weeks in tents and not always in the
same place two years in succession, and now his companions were
the sons and even the grandsons of those with whom he had lived
in the house and the house itself no longer existed, the conviction,
the sense of home, had been merely transferred into the canvas. He
owned a house in Jefferson, where he had had a wife and children
once though no more, and it was kept for him by his dead wife's
niece and her family and he was comfortable in it, his wants and
needs looked after by blood at least related to the blood which he
had elected out of all the earth to cherish. But he spent the time
between those walls waiting for November, because even this tent
with its muddy floor and the bed which was not soft enough nor
warm enough was his home and these men, some of whom he only
saw during these two weeks, were more his kin. Because this was
his land. . . .

The shadow of the youngest Negro loomed, blotting the heater's
dying glow from the ceiling, the wood billets thumping into it until
the glow, the flame, leaped high and bright across the canvas. But
the Negro's shadow still remained, until after a moment McCaslin,
rising onto one elbow, saw that it was not the Negro, it was Boyd;
when he spoke the other turned his head and he saw in the red
firelight the sullen and ruthless profile. "Nothing," Boyd said. "Go
on back to sleep."

"Since Will Legate mentioned it," McCaslin said, "I remember
you had some trouble sleeping in here last fall too. Only you called
it coon-hunting then. Or was it Will Legate that called it that?"
Boyd didn't answer. He turned and went back to his bed. McCaslin, propped on his elbow, watched until the other's shadow sank
down the wall and vanished. "That's right," he said. "Try to get
some sleep. We must have meat in camp tomorrow. You can do
all the setting up you want to after that." Then he too lay back
down, his hands crossed again on his breast, watching the glow of
the heater. It was steady again now, the fresh wood accepted, being
assimilated; soon it would begin to fade again, taking with it the
last echo of that sudden upflare of a young man's passion and
unrest. Let him lie awake for a little while, he thought. He would

lie still some day for a long time without even dissatisfaction to disturb him. And lying awake here, in these surroundings, would soothe him if anything could, if anything could soothe a man just forty years old. The tent, the rain-murmured canvas globe, was filled with it once more now. He lay on his back, his eyes closed, his breathing quiet and peaceful as a child's, listening to it—that silence which was never silence but was myriad. He could almost see it, tremendous, primeval, looming, musing downward upon this puny evanescent clutter of human sojourn which after a single brief week would vanish and in another week would be completely healed, traceless in the unmarked solitude. Because it was his land, although he had never owned a foot of it. He had never wanted to, even after he saw its ultimate doom, began to watch it retreating year by year before the onslaught of axe and saw and log-lines and then dynamite and tractor plows, because it belonged to no man. It belonged to all; they had only to use it well, humbly and with pride. Then suddenly he knew why he had never wanted to own any of it, arrest at least that much of what people called progress. It was because there was just exactly enough of it. He seemed to see the two of them—himself and the wilderness—as coevals, his own span as a hunter, a woodsman not contemporary with his first breath but transmitted to him, assumed by him gladly, humbly, with joy and pride, from that old Major de Spain and Sam Fathers who had taught him to hunt, the two spans running out together, not into oblivion, nothingness, but into a scope free of both time and space where once more the untreed land warped and wrung to mathematical squares of rank cotton for the frantic old-world peoples to turn into shells to shoot at one another, would find ample room for both—the shades of the tall unaxed trees and the sightless brakes where the wild strong immortal animals ran forever before the tireless belling immortal hounds, falling and rising phoenix-like before the soundless guns.

Then he had slept. The lantern was lighted, the tent was full of the movement of men getting up and dressing and outside in the darkness the oldest Negro, Isham, was beating with a spoon on the bottom of a tin pan and crying, "Raise up and get yo fo clock coffy. Raise up and get yo fo clock coffy."

He heard Legate too. "Get on out of here now and let Uncle Ike sleep. If you wake him up, he'll want to go on stand. And he aint got any business in the woods this morning." So he didn't move. He heard them leave the tent; he listened to the breakfast sounds from the table beneath the tarpaulin. Then he heard them depart —the horses, the dogs, the last voice dying away; after a while he might possibly even hear the first faint clear cry of the first hound ring through the wet woods from where the buck had bedded, then he would go back to sleep again. Then the tent flap swung in and fell, something jarred against the end of the cot and a hand grasped his knee through the blanket and shook him before he could open his eyes. It was Boyd, carrying a shotgun instead of his rifle. He spoke in a harsh, rapid voice. "Sorry I had to wake you. There will be a. . . ."

"I was awake," McCaslin said. "Are you going to shoot that today?"

"You just told me last night you want meat," Boyd said. "There will be a. . . ."

"Since when did you start having trouble getting meat with your rifle?"

"All right," the other said, with that harsh, restrained, furious impatience. Then McCaslin saw in his other hand a thick oblong, an envelope. "There will be a woman here some time this morning, looking for me. Give her this and tell her I said no."

"What?" McCaslin said. "A what?" He half rose onto his elbow as the other jerked the envelope onto the blanket in front of him, already turning toward the entrance, the envelope striking solid and heavy and soundless and already sliding from the bed until McCaslin caught it, feeling through the paper the thick sheaf of banknotes. "Wait," he said. "Wait." The other stopped, looking back. They stared at one another—the old face, wan, sleep-raddled above the tumbled bed, the dark handsome younger one at once furious and cold. "Will Legate was right," McCaslin said. "This is what you called coon-hunting. And now this." He didn't lift the envelope nor indicate it in any way. "What did you promise her that you haven't the courage to face her and retract?"

"Nothing," Boyd said. "This is all of it. Tell her I said no." He was gone; the tent flap lifted on a waft of faint light and the constant murmur of the rain and fell again while McCaslin still lay half-raised on his elbow, the envelope clutched in his shaking hand. It seemed to him later that he began to hear the approaching boat almost immediately, before Boyd could have got out of sight even. It seemed to him that there had been no interval whatever: the mounting snarl of the engine, increasing, nearer and nearer and then cut short off, ceasing into the lap and plop of water under the bows as the boat slid in to the bank, the youngest Negro, the youth, raising the tent flap beyond which for an instant he saw the boat —a small skiff with a Negro man sitting in the stern beside the upslanted motor—then the woman entering, in a man's hat and a man's slicker and rubber boots, carrying the blanket-and-tarpaulin-wrapped bundle and bringing something else, something intangible, an effluvium which he knew he would recognize in a moment because he knew now that Isham had already told him, warned him, by sending the young Negro to the tent instead of coming himself—a face young and with dark eyes, queerly colorless but not ill and not that of a country woman despite the garments she wore, looking down at him where he sat upright on the cot now, clutching the envelope, the soiled underclothes bagging about him and the twisted blankets huddled about his hips.

"Is that his?" he said. "Don't lie to me!"

"Yes," she said. "He's gone."

"He's gone," he said. "You won't jump him here. He left you this. He said to tell you no." He extended the envelope. It was sealed and it bore no superscription. Nevertheless he watched her take it in one hand and manage to rip it open and tilt the neat sheaf of bound notes onto the blanket without even glancing at them and then look into the empty envelope before she crumpled and dropped it.

"Just money," she said.

"What did you expect?" he said. "You have known him long enough or at least often enough to have got that child, and you don't know him that well?"

"Not very often," she said. "Not very long. Just that week here last fall, and in January he sent for me and we went West, to New Mexico, and lived for six weeks where I could cook for him and look after his clothes. . . ."

"But no marriage," he said. "He didn't promise you that. Don't lie to me. He didn't have to."

"He didn't have to," she said. "I knew what I was doing. I knew that to begin with, before we agreed. Then we agreed again before he left New Mexico that that would be all of it. I believed him. I must have believed him. I don't see how I could have helped but believe him. I wrote him last month to make sure and the letter came back unopened and I was sure. So I didn't even know I was coming back here until last week. I was waiting there by the road yesterday when the car passed and he saw me and I was sure."

"Then what do you want?" he said. "What do you want?"

"Yes," she said. He glared at her, his white hair awry from the pillow, his eyes, lacking the spectacles to focus them, blurred, irisless and apparently pupilless.

"He met you on a street one afternoon just because a box of groceries happened to fall out of a boat. And a month later you went off and lived with him until you got a child from it. Then he took his hat and said good-bye and walked out. Haven't you got any folks at all?"

"Yes. My aunt, in Vicksburg. I came to live with her two years ago when my father died; we lived in Indianapolis until then. But my aunt had a family and she took in washing herself, so I got a job teaching school in Aluschaskuna. . . ."

"Took in what?" he said. "Took in washing?" He sprang, flinging himself backward onto one arm, awry-haired, glaring. Now he understood what it was she had brought in with her, what old Isham had already told him—the lips and skin pallid and colorless yet not ill, the tragic and foreknowing eyes. *Maybe in a thousand or two thousand years it will have blended in America and we will have forgotten it,* he thought. *But God pity these.* He cried, not loud, in a voice of amazement, pity and outrage, "You're a nigger!"

"Yes," she said.

"Then what did you expect here?"

"Nothing."

"Then why did you come here? You said you were waiting in Aluschaskuna yesterday and he saw you."

"I'm going back North," she said. "My cousin brought me up from Vicksburg the day before yesterday in his boat. He's going to take me on to Leland to get the train."

"Then go," he said. Then he cried again in that thin, not loud voice, "Get out of here; I can do nothing for you! Can't nobody do nothing for you!" She moved, turning toward the entrance.

"Wait," he said. She paused, turning. He picked up the sheaf of bank notes and laid it on the blanket at the foot of the cot and drew his hand back beneath the blanket. "Here."

"I don't need it," she said. "He gave me money last winter. Provided. That was all arranged when we agreed that would have to be all."

"Take it," he said. His voice began to rise again, but he stopped it. "Take it out of my tent." She came back and took the money. "That's right," he said. "Go back North. Marry, a man in your own race. That's the only salvation for you. Marry a black man. You are young, handsome, almost white; you could find a black man who would see in you whatever it was you saw in him, who would ask nothing from you and expect less and get even still less if it's revenge you want. And then in a year's time you will have forgotten all this; you will forget it even happened, that he ever existed. . . ." He ceased; for an instant he almost sprang again for it seemed to him that, without moving at all, she had blazed silently at him. But she had not. She had not even moved, looking quietly down at him from beneath the sodden hat.

"Old man," she said, "have you lived so long that you have forgotten all you ever knew or felt or even heard about love?" Then she was gone too; the waft of light and the hushed constant rain flowed into the tent, then the flap fell again. Lying back again, trembling, panting, the blanket huddled to his chin and his hands crossed on his breast, he heard the pop and snarl, the mounting then the descending whine of the motor until it died away and once again the tent held only silence and the sound of the rain. And the cold too: he lay shaking faintly and steadily in it, rigid save for the shaking. 'This Delta,' he thought. 'This Delta.' *This land, which man has deswamped and denuded and derivered in two generations so that white men can own plantations and commute every night to Memphis and black men can own plantations and even towns and keep their town houses in Chicago, where white men rent farms and live like niggers and niggers crop on shares and live like animals, where cotton is planted and grows man-tall in the very cracks in the sidewalks, where usury and mortgage and bankruptcy and measureless wealth, Chinese and African and Aryan and Jew, all breed and spawn together until no man has time to say which is which, or cares.* . . . 'No wonder the ruined woods I used to know don't cry for retribution,' he thought. 'The people who have destroyed it will accomplish its revenge.'

The tent flap swung rapidly in and fell. He did not move save to turn his head and open his eyes. Legate was stooping over Boyd's bed, rummaging hurriedly in it. "What is it?" McCaslin said.

"Looking for Don's skinning knife," Legate said. "We got a deer on the ground. I come in to get the horses." He rose, the knife in his hand and went toward the door.

"Who killed it?" McCaslin said. "It was Don," he said.

"Yes," Legate said, lifting the tent flap.

"Wait," McCaslin said. "What was it?" Legate paused for an instant in the entrance. He did not look back.

"Just a deer, Uncle Ike," he said impatiently. "Nothing extra." He was gone; the flap fell behind him, wafting out of the tent again the faint light, the constant and grieving rain. McCaslin lay back on the cot.

"It was a doe," he said to the empty tent.

The Bear

He was ten. But it had already begun, long before that day when at last he wrote his age in two figures and he saw for the first time the camp where his father and Major de Spain and old General Compson and the others spent two weeks each November and two weeks again each June. He had already inherited then, without ever having seen it, the tremendous bear with one trap-ruined foot which, in an area almost a hundred miles deep, had earned for itself a name, a definite designation like a living man.

He had listened to it for years: the long legend of corncribs rifled, of shotes and grown pigs and even calves carried bodily into the woods and devoured, of traps and deadfalls overthrown and dogs mangled and slain, and shotgun and even rifle charges delivered at point-blank range and with no more effect than so many peas blown through a tube by a boy—a corridor of wreckage and destruction beginning back before he was born, through which sped, not fast but rather with the ruthless and irresistible deliberation of a locomotive, the shaggy tremendous shape.

It ran in his knowledge before he ever saw it. It looked and towered in his dreams before he even saw the unaxed woods where it left its crooked print, shaggy, huge, red-eyed, not malevolent but just big—too big for the dogs which tried to bay it, for the horses which tried to ride it down, for the men and the bullets they fired into it, too big for the very country which was its constricting scope. He seemed to see it entire with a child's complete divination before he ever laid eyes on either—the doomed wilderness whose edges were being constantly and punily gnawed at by men with axes and plows who feared it because it was wilderness, men myriad and nameless even to one another in the land where the old bear had earned a name, through which ran not even a mortal animal but an anachronism, indomitable and invincible, out of an old dead time, a phantom, epitome and apotheosis of the old wild life at which the puny humans swarmed and hacked in a fury of abhorrence and fear, like pygmies about the ankles of a drowsing elephant; the old bear solitary, indomitable and alone, widowered, childless and absolved of mortality—old Priam reft of his old wife and having outlived all his sons.

Until he was ten, each November he would watch the wagon containing the dogs and the bedding and food and guns and his father and Tennie's Jim, the Negro, and Sam Fathers, the Indian, son of a slave woman and a Chickasaw chief, depart on the road to town, to Jefferson, where Major de Spain and the others would join them. To the boy, at seven and eight and nine, they were not going into the Big Bottom to hunt bear and deer, but to keep yearly rendezvous with the bear which they did not even intend to kill. Two weeks later they would return, with no trophy, no head and skin. He had not expected it. He had not even been afraid it would be in the wagon. He believed that even after he was ten and his father would let him go too, for those two November weeks, he would merely make another one, along with his father and Major de Spain and General Compson and the others, the dogs which feared to bay it and the rifles and shotguns which failed even to bleed it, in the yearly pageant of the old bear's furious immortality.

Then he heard the dogs. It was in the second week of his first time in the camp. He stood with Sam Fathers against a big oak beside the faint crossing where they had stood each dawn for nine days now, hearing the dogs. He had heard them once before, one morning last week—a murmur, sourceless, echoing through the wet woods, swelling presently into separate voices which he could recognize and call by name. He had raised and cocked the gun as Sam told him and stood motionless again while the uproar, the invisible course, swept up and past and faded; it seemed to him that he could actually see the deer, the buck, blond, smoke-colored, elongated with speed, fleeing, vanishing, the woods, the gray solitude, still ringing even when the cries of the dogs had died away.

"Now let the hammers down," Sam said.

"You knew they were not coming here too," he said.

"Yes," Sam said. "I want you to learn how to do when you didn't shoot. It's after the chance for the bear or the deer has done already come and gone that men and dogs get killed."

"Anyway," he said, "it was just a deer."

Then on the tenth morning he heard the dogs again. And he readied the too-long, too-heavy gun as Sam had taught him, before Sam even spoke. But this time it was no deer, no ringing chorus of dogs running strong on a free scent, but a moiling yapping an octave too high, with something more than indecision and even abjectness in it, not even moving very fast, taking a long time to pass completely out of hearing, leaving even then somewhere in the air that echo, thin, slightly hysterical, abject, almost grieving, with no sense of a fleeing, unseen, smoke-colored, grass-eating shape ahead of it, and Sam, who had taught him first of all to cock the gun and take position where he could see everywhere and then never move again, had himself moved up beside him; he could hear Sam breathing at his shoulder and he could see the arched curve of the old man's inhaling nostrils.

"Hah," Sam said. "Not even running. Walking."

"Old Ben!" the boy said. "But up here!" he cried. "Way up here!"

"He do it every year," Sam said. "Once. Maybe to see who in camp this time, if he can shoot or not. Whether we got the dog yet that can bay and hold him. He'll take them to the river, then he'll send them back home. We may as well go back, too; see how they look when they come back to camp."

When they reached the camp the hounds were already there, ten of them crouching back under the kitchen, the boy and Sam squatting to peer back into the obscurity where they huddled, quiet, the eyes luminous, glowing at them and vanishing, and no sound, only that effluvium of something more than dog, stronger than dog and not just animal, just beast, because still there had been nothing in front of that abject and almost painful yapping save the solitude, the wilderness, so that when the eleventh hound came in at noon and with all the others watching—even old Uncle Ash, who called himself first a cook—Sam daubed the tattered ear and the raked shoulder with turpentine and axle grease, to the boy it was still no living creature, but the wilderness which, leaning for the moment down, had patted lightly once the hound's temerity.

"Just like a man," Sam said. "Just like folks. Put off as long as she could having to be brave, knowing all the time that sooner or later she would have to be brave once to keep on living with herself, and knowing all the time beforehand what was going to happen to her when she done it."

That afternoon, himself on the one-eyed wagon mule which did not mind the smell of blood nor, as they told him, of bear, and with Sam on the other one, they rode for more than three hours through the rapid, shortening winter day. They followed no path, no trail even that he could see; almost at once they were in a country which he had never seen before. Then he knew why Sam had made him ride the mule which would not spook. The sound one stopped short and tried to whirl and bolt even as Sam got down, blowing its breath, jerking and wrenching at the rein while Sam held it, coaxing it forward with his voice, since he could not risk tying it, drawing it forward while the boy got down from the marred one.

Then, standing beside Sam in the gloom of the dying afternoon, he looked down at the rotted overturned log, gutted and scored with claw marks and, in the wet earth beside it, the print of the enormous warped two-toed foot. He knew now what he had smelled when he peered under the kitchen where the dogs huddled. He realized for the first time that the bear which had run in his listening and loomed in his dreams since before he could remember to the contrary, and which, therefore, must have existed in the listening and dreams of his father and Major de Spain and even old General Compson, too, before they began to remember in their turn, was a mortal animal, and that if they had departed for the camp each November without any actual hope of bringing its trophy back, it was not because it could not be slain, but because so far they had had no actual hope to.

"Tomorrow," he said.

"We'll try tomorrow," Sam said. "We ain't got the dog yet."

"We've got eleven. They ran him this morning."

"It won't need but one," Sam said. "He ain't here. Maybe he ain't nowhere. The only other way will be for him to run by accident over somebody that has a gun."

"That wouldn't be me," the boy said. "It will be Walter or Major or—"

"It might," Sam said. "You watch close in the morning. Because he's smart. That's how come he has lived this long. If he gets hemmed up and has to pick out somebody to run over, he will pick out you."

"How?" the boy said. "How will he know—" He ceased. "You mean he already knows me, that I ain't never been here before, ain't had time to find out yet whether I—" He ceased again, looking at Sam, the old man whose face revealed nothing until it smiled. He said humbly, not even amazed, "It was me he was watching. I don't reckon he did need to come but once."

The next morning they left the camp three hours before daylight. They rode this time because it was too far to walk, even the dogs in the wagon; again the first gray light found him in a place which he had never seen before, where Sam had placed him and told him to stay and then departed. With the gun which was too big for him, which did not even belong to him, but to Major de Spain, and which he had fired only once—at a stump on the first day, to learn the recoil and how to reload it—he stood against a gum tree beside a little bayou whose black still water crept without movement out of a cane-brake and crossed a small clearing and into cane again, where, invisible, a bird—the big woodpecker called Lord-to-God by Negroes—clattered at a dead limb.

It was a stand like any other, dissimilar only in incidentals to the one where he had stood each morning for ten days; a territory new to him, yet no less familiar than that other one which, after almost two weeks, he had come to believe he knew a little—the same solitude, the same loneliness through which human beings had merely passed without altering it, leaving no mark, no scar, which looked exactly as it must have looked when the first ancestor of Sam Fathers' Chickasaw predecessors crept into it and looked about, club or stone ax or bone arrow drawn and poised; different only because, squatting at the edge of the kitchen, he smelled the hounds huddled and cringing beneath it and saw the raked ear and shoulder of the one who, Sam said, had had to be brave once in order to live with herself, and saw yesterday in the earth beside the gutted log the print of the living foot.

He heard no dogs at all. He never did hear them. He only heard the drumming of the woodpecker stop short off and knew that the bear was looking at him. He never saw it. He did not know whether it was in front of him or behind him. He did not move, holding the useless gun, which he had not even had warning to cock and which even now he did not cock, tasting in his saliva that taint as of brass which he knew now because he had smelled it when he peered under the kitchen at the huddled dogs.

Then it was gone. As abruptly as it had ceased, the woodpecker's dry, monotonous clatter set up again, and after a while he even believed he could hear the dogs—a murmur, scarce a sound even, which he had probably been hearing for some time before he even remarked it, drifting into hearing and then out again, dying away. They came nowhere near him. If it was a bear they ran, it was another bear. It was Sam himself who came out of the cane and crossed the bayou, followed by the injured bitch of yesterday. She was almost at heel, like a bird dog, making no sound. She came and crouched against his leg, trembling, staring off into the cane.

"I didn't see him," he said. "I didn't, Sam!"

"I know it," Sam said. "He done the looking. You didn't hear him neither, did you?"

"No," the boy said. "I—"

"He's smart," Sam said. "Too smart." He looked down at the hound, trembling faintly and steadily against the boy's knee. From the raked shoulder a few drops of fresh blood oozed and clung. "Too big. We ain't got the dog yet. But maybe someday. Maybe not next time. But someday."

So I must see him, he thought. *I must look at him.* Otherwise, it seemed to him that it would go on like this forever, as it had gone on with his father and Major de Spain, who was older than his father, and even with old General Compson, who had been old enough to be a brigade commander in 1865. Otherwise, it would go on so forever, next time and next time, after and after and after. It seemed to him that he could see the two of them, himself and the bear, shadowy in the limbo from which time emerged, becoming time; the old bear absolved of mortality and himself partaking, sharing a little of it, enough of it. And he knew now what he had smelled in the huddled dogs and tasted in his saliva. He recognized fear. *So I will have to see him,* he thought, without dread or even hope. *I will have to look at him.*

It was in June of the next year. He was eleven. They were in camp again, celebrating Major de Spain's and General Compson's birthdays. Although the one had been born in September and the other in the depth of winter and in another decade, they had met for two weeks to fish and shoot squirrels and turkey and run coons and wildcats with the dogs at night. That is, he and Boon Hoggen-beck and the Negroes fished and shot squirrels and ran the coons and cats, because the proved hunters, not only Major de Spain and old General Compson, who spent those two weeks sitting in a rocking chair before a tremendous iron pot of Brunswick stew, stirring and tasting, with old Ash to quarrel with about how he was making it and Tennie's Jim to pour whisky from the demijohn into the tin dipper from which he drank it, but even the boy's father and Walter Ewell, who were still young enough, scorned such, other than shooting the wild gobblers with pistols for wagers on their marksmanship.

Or, that is, his father and the others believed he was hunting squirrels. Until the third day he thought that Sam Fathers believed that too. Each morning he would leave the camp right after break-fast. He had his own gun now, a Christmas present. He went back to the tree beside the little bayou where he had stood that morning. Using the compass which old General Compson had given him, he ranged from that point; he was teaching himself to be a better-than-fair woodsman without knowing he was doing it. On the second day he even found the gutted log where he had first seen the crooked print. It was almost completely crumbled now, healing with unbelievable speed, a passionate and almost visible relinquish-ment, back into the earth from which the tree had grown.

He ranged the summer woods now, green with gloom; if any-thing, actually dimmer than in November's gray dissolution, where, even at noon, the sun fell only in intermittent dappling upon the earth, which never completely dried out and which crawled with snakes—moccasins and water snakes and rattlers, themselves the color of the dappled gloom, so that he would not always see them until they moved, returning later and later, first day, second day, passing in the twilight of the third evening the little log pen enclosing the log stable where Sam was putting up the horses for the night.

"You ain't looked right yet," Sam said.

He stopped. For a moment he didn't answer. Then he said

peacefully, in a peaceful rushing burst as when a boy's miniature dam in a little brook gives way, "All right. But how? I went to the bayou. I even found that log again. I—"

"I reckon that was all right. Likely he's been watching you. You never saw his foot?"

"I," the boy said—"I didn't—I never thought—"

"It's the gun," Sam said. He stood beside the fence, motionless —the old man, the Indian, in the battered faded overalls and the frayed five-cent straw hat which in the Negro's race had been the badge of his enslavement and was now the regalia of his freedom. The camp—the clearing, the house, the barn and its tiny lot with which Major de Spain in his turn had scratched punily and evanescently at the wilderness—faded in the dusk, back into the immemorial darkness of the woods. *The gun,* the boy thought. *The gun.*

"Be scared," Sam said. "You can't help that. But don't be afraid. Ain't nothing in the woods going to hurt you unless you corner it, or it smells that you are afraid. A bear or a deer, too, has got to be scared of a coward the same as a brave man has got to be."

The gun, the boy thought.

"You will have to choose," Sam said.

He left the camp before daylight, long before Uncle Ash would wake in his quilts on the kitchen floor and start the fire for breakfast. He had only the compass and a stick for snakes. He could go almost a mile before he would begin to need the compass. He sat on a log, the invisible compass in his invisible hand, while the secret night sounds, fallen still at his movements, scurried again and then ceased for good, and the owls ceased and gave over to the waking of day birds, and he could see the compass. Then he went fast yet still quietly; he was becoming better and better as a woodsman, still without having yet realized it.

He jumped a doe and a fawn at sunrise, walked them out of the bed, close enough to see them—the crash of undergrowth, the white scut, the fawn scudding behind her faster than he had believed it could run. He was hunting right, upwind, as Sam had taught him; not that it mattered now. He had left the gun; of his own will and relinquishment he had accepted not a gambit, not a choice, but a condition in which not only the bear's heretofore inviolable anonymity but all the old rules and balances of hunter and hunted had been abrogated. He would not even be afraid, not even in the moment when the fear would take him completely— blood, skin, bowels, bones, memory from the long time before it became his memory—all save that thin, clear, quenchless, immortal lucidity which alone differed him from this bear and from all the other bear and deer he would ever kill in the humility and pride of his skill and endurance, to which Sam had spoken when he leaned in the twilight on the lot fence yesterday.

By noon he was far beyond the little bayou, farther into the new and alien country than he had ever been. He was traveling now not only by the compass but by the old, heavy, biscuit-thick silver watch which had belonged to his grandfather. When he stopped at last, it was for the first time since he had risen from the log at dawn when he could see the compass. It was far enough. He had left the camp nine hours ago; nine hours from now, dark would have already been an hour old. But he didn't think that. He thought, *All right. Yes. But what?* and stood for a moment, alien and small in the green and topless solitude, answering his own question before it had formed and ceased. It was the watch, the compass, the stick—the three lifeless mechanicals with which for nine hours he had fended the wilderness off; he hung the watch and compass carefully on a bush and leaned the stick beside them and relinquished completely to it.

He had not been going very fast for the last two or three hours. He went no faster now, since distance would not matter even if he could have gone fast. And he was trying to keep a bearing on the tree where he had left the compass, trying to complete a circle which would bring him back to it or at least intersect itself, since direction would not matter now either. But the tree was not there, and he did as Sam had schooled him—made the next circle in the opposite direction, so that the two patterns would bisect somewhere, but crossing no print of his own feet, finding the tree at last, but in the wrong place—no bush, no compass, no watch—and the tree not even the tree, because there was a down log beside it and he did what Sam Fathers had told him was the next thing and the last.

As he sat down on the log he saw the crooked print—the warped, tremendous, two-toed indentation which, even as he watched it, filled with water. As he looked up, the wilderness coalesced, solidified—the glade, the tree he sought, the bush, the watch and the compass glinting where a ray of sunlight touched them. Then he saw the bear. It did not emerge, appear; it was just there, immobile, solid, fixed in the hot dappling of the green and windless noon, not as big as he had dreamed it, but as big as he had expected it, bigger, dimensionless against the dappled obscurity, looking at him where he sat quietly on the log and looked back at it.

Then it moved. It made no sound. It did not hurry. It crossed the glade, walking for an instant into the full glare of the sun; when it reached the other side it stopped again and looked back at him across one shoulder while his quiet breathing inhaled and exhaled three times.

Then it was gone. It didn't walk into the woods, the undergrowth. It faded, sank back into the wilderness as he had watched a fish, a huge old bass, sink and vanish back into the dark depths of its pool without even any movement of its fins.

He thought, *It will be next fall.* But it was not next fall, nor the next nor the next. He was fourteen then. He had killed his buck, and Sam Fathers had marked his face with the hot blood, and in the next year he killed a bear. But even before that accolade he had become as competent in the woods as many grown men with the same experience; by his fourteenth year he was a better woodsman than most grown men with more. There was no territory within thirty miles of the camp that he did not know—bayou, ridge, brake, landmark tree and path. He could have led anyone to any point in it without deviation, and brought them out again. He knew game trails that even Sam Fathers did not know; in his thirteenth year he found a buck's bedding place, and unbeknown to his father he borrowed Walter Ewell's rifle and lay in wait at dawn and killed the buck when it walked back to the bed, as Sam had told him how the old Chickasaw fathers did.

But not the old bear, although by now he knew its footprint better than he did his own, and not only the crooked one. He could see any one of the three sound ones and distinguish it from any other, and not only by its size. There were other bears within those thirty miles which left tracks almost as large, but this was more than that. If Sam Fathers had been his mentor and the back-yard rabbits and squirrels at home his kindergarten, then the wilderness

the old bear ran was his college, the old male bear itself, so long
unwifed and childless as to have become its own ungendered
progenitor, was his alma mater. But he never saw it.

He could find the crooked print now almost whenever he liked,
fifteen or ten or five miles, or sometimes nearer the camp than that.
Twice while on stand during the three years he heard the dogs
strike its trail by accident; on the second time they jumped it
seemingly, the voices high, abject, almost human in hysteria, as on
that first morning two years ago. But not the bear itself. He would
remember that noon three years ago, the glade, himself and the
bear fixed during that moment in the windless and dappled blaze,
and it would seem to him that it had never happened, that he had
dreamed that too. But it had happened. They had looked at each
other, they had emerged from the wilderness old as earth, synchro-
nized to that instant by something more than the blood that moved
the flesh and bones which bore them, and touched, pledged something, affirmed something more lasting than the frail web of bones
and flesh which any accident could obliterate.

Then he saw it again. Because of the very fact that he thought
of nothing else, he had forgotten to look for it. He was still-hunting
with Walter Ewell's rifle. He saw it cross the end of a long blow-
down, a corridor where a tornado had swept, rushing through
rather than over the tangle of trunks and branches as a locomotive
would have, faster than he had ever believed it could move, almost
as fast as a deer even, because a deer would have spent most of that
time in the air, faster than he could bring the rifle sights up to it,
so that he believed the reason he never let off the shot was that he
was still behind it, had never caught up with it. And now he knew
what had been wrong during all the three years. He sat on a log,
shaking and trembling as if he had never seen the woods before nor
anything that ran them, wondering with incredulous amazement
how he could have forgotten the very thing which Sam Fathers had
told him and which the bear itself had proved the next day and had
now returned after three years to reaffirm.

And he now knew what Sam Fathers had meant about the right
dog, a dog in which size would mean less than nothing. So when
he returned alone in April—school was out then, so that the sons
of farmers could help with the land's planting, and at last his father
had granted him permission, on his promise to be back in four days

—he had the dog. It was his own, a mongrel of the sort called by Negroes a fyce, a ratter, itself not much bigger than a rat and possessing that bravery which had long since stopped being courage and had become foolhardiness.

It did not take four days. Alone again, he found the trail on the first morning. It was not a stalk; it was an ambush. He timed the meeting almost as if it were an appointment with a human being. Himself holding the fyce muffled in a feed sack and Sam Fathers with two of the hounds on a piece of plowline rope, they lay down wind of the trail at dawn of the second morning. They were so close that the bear turned without even running, as if in surprised amazement at the shrill and frantic uproar of the released fyce, turning at bay against the trunk of a tree, on its hind feet; it seemed to the boy that it would never stop rising, taller and taller, and even the two hounds seemed to take a sort of desperate and despairing courage from the fyce, following it as it went in.

Then he realized that the fyce was actually not going to stop. He flung, threw the gun away, and ran; when he overtook and grasped the frantically pinwheeling little dog, it seemed to him that he was directly under the bear.

He could smell it, strong and hot and rank. Sprawling, he looked up to where it loomed and towered over him like a cloudburst and colored like a thunderclap, quite familiar, peacefully and even lucidly familiar, until he remembered: This was the way he had used to dream about it. Then it was gone. He didn't see it go. He knelt, holding the frantic fyce with both hands, hearing the abased wailing of the hounds drawing farther and farther away, until Sam came up. He carried the gun. He laid it down quietly beside the boy and stood looking down at him.

"You've done seed him twice now with a gun in your hands," he said. "This time you couldn't have missed him."

The boy rose. He still held the fyce. Even in his arms and clear of the ground, it yapped frantically, straining and surging after the fading uproar of the two hounds like a tangle of wire springs. He was panting a little, but he was neither shaking nor trembling now.

"Neither could you!" he said. "You had the gun! Neither did you!"

"And you didn't shoot," his father said. "How close were you?"

"I don't know, sir," he said. "There was a big wood tick inside his right hind leg. I saw that. But I didn't have the gun then."

"But you didn't shoot when you had the gun," his father said. "Why?"

But he didn't answer, and his father didn't wait for him to, rising and crossing the room, across the pelt of the bear which the boy had killed two years ago and the larger one which his father had killed before he was born, to the bookcase beneath the mounted head of the boy's first buck. It was the room which his father called the office, from which all the plantation business was transacted; in it for the fourteen years of his life he had heard the best of all talking. Major de Spain would be there and sometimes old General Compson, and Walter Ewell and Boon Hoggenbeck and Sam Fathers and Tennie's Jim, too, because they, too, were hunters, knew the woods and what ran them.

He would hear it, not talking himself but listening—the wilderness, the big woods, bigger and older than any recorded document of white man fatuous enough to believe he had bought any fragment of it or Indian ruthless enough to pretend that any fragment of it had been his to convey. It was of the men, not white nor black nor red, but men, hunters with the will and hardihood to endure and the humility and skill to survive, and the dogs and the bear and deer juxtaposed and reliefed against it, ordered and compelled by and within the wilderness in the ancient and unremitting contest by the ancient and immitigable rules which voided all regrets and brooked no quarter, the voices quiet and weighty and deliberate for retrospection and recollection and exact remembering, while he squatted in the blazing firelight as Tennie's Jim squatted, who stirred only to put more wood on the fire and to pass the bottle from one glass to another. Because the bottle was always present, so that after a while it seemed to him that those fierce instants of heart and brain and courage and wiliness and speed were concentrated and distilled into that brown liquor which not women, not boys and children, but only hunters drank, drinking not of the blood they had spilled but some condensation of the wild immortal spirit, drinking it moderately, humbly even, not with the pagan's base hope of acquiring thereby the virtues of cunning and strength and speed, but in salute to them.

His father returned with the book and sat down again and opened it. "Listen," he said. He read the five stanzas aloud, his voice quiet and deliberate in the room where there was no fire now because it was already spring. Then he looked up. The boy watched him. "All right," his father said. "Listen." He read again, but only the second stanza this time, to the end of it, the last two lines, and closed the book and put it on the table beside him. " 'She cannot fade, though thou hast not thy bliss, for ever wilt thou love, and she be fair,' " he said.

"He's talking about a girl," the boy said.

"He had to talk about something," his father said. Then he said, "He was talking about truth. Truth doesn't change. Truth is one thing. It covers all things which touch the heart—honor and pride and pity and justice and courage and love. Do you see now?"

He didn't know. Somehow it was simpler than that. There was an old bear, fierce and ruthless, not merely just to stay alive, but with the fierce pride of liberty and freedom, proud enough of that liberty and freedom to see it threatened without fear or even alarm; nay, who at times even seemed deliberately to put that freedom and liberty in jeopardy in order to savor them, to remind his old strong bones and flesh to keep supple and quick to defend and preserve them. There was an old man, son of a Negro slave and an Indian king, inheritor on the one side of the long chronicle of a people who had learned humility through suffering, and pride through the endurance which survived the suffering and injustice, and on the other side, the chronicle of a people even longer in the land than the first, yet who no longer existed in the land at all save in the solitary brotherhood of an old Negro's alien blood and the wild and invincible spirit of an old bear. There was a boy who wished to learn humility and pride in order to become skillful and worthy in the woods, who suddenly found himself becoming so skillful so rapidly that he feared he would never become worthy because he had not learned humility and pride, although he had tried to, until one day and as suddenly he discovered that an old man who could not have defined either had led him, as though by the hand, to that point where an old bear and a little mongrel dog showed him that, by possessing one thing other, he would possess them both.

And a little dog, nameless and mongrel and many-fathered, grown, yet weighing less than six pounds, saying as if to itself, "I can't be dangerous, because there's nothing much smaller than I am; I can't be fierce, because they would call it just noise; I can't be humble, because I'm already too close to the ground to genuflect; I can't be proud, because I wouldn't be near enough to it for anyone to know who was casting that shadow, and I don't even know that I'm not going to heaven, because they have already decided that I don't possess an immortal soul. So all I can be is brave. But it's all right. I can be that, even if they still call it just noise."

That was all. It was simple, much simpler than somebody talking in a book about a youth and a girl he would never need to grieve over, because he could never approach any nearer her and would never have to get any farther away. He had heard about a bear, and finally got big enough to trail it, and he trailed it four years and at last met it with a gun in his hands and he didn't shoot. Because a little dog— But he could have shot long before the little dog covered the twenty yards to where the bear waited, and Sam Fathers could have shot at any time during that interminable minute while Old Ben stood on his hind feet over them. He stopped. His father was watching him gravely across the spring-rife twilight of the room; when he spoke, his words were as quiet as the twilight, too, not loud, because they did not need to be because they would last, "Courage, and honor, and pride," his father said, "and pity, and love of justice and of liberty. They all touch the heart, and what the heart holds to becomes truth, as far as we know truth. Do you see now?"

Sam, and Old Ben, and Nip, he thought. And himself too. He had been all right too. His father had said so. "Yes, sir," he said.

Race at Morning

I was in the boat when I seen him. It was jest dust-dark; I had jest fed the horses and clumb back down the bank to the boat and shoved off to cross back to camp when I seen him, about half a quarter up the river, swimming; jest his head above the water, and it no more than a dot in that light. But I could see that rocking chair he toted on it and I knowed it was him, going right back to that canebrake in the fork of the bayou where he lived all year until the day before the season opened, like the game wardens had give him a calendar, when he would clear out and disappear, nobody knowed where, until the day after the season closed. But here he was, coming back a day ahead of time, like maybe he had got mixed up and was using last year's calendar by mistake. Which was jest too bad for him, because me and Mister Ernest would be setting on the horse right over him when the sun rose tomorrow morning.

So I told Mister Ernest and we et supper and fed the dogs, and then I holp Mister Ernest in the poker game, standing behind his chair until about ten o'clock, when Roth Edmonds said, "Why don't you go to bed, boy?"

"Or if you're going to set up," Willy Legate said, "why don't you take a spelling book to set up over? . . . He knows every cuss word in the dictionary, every poker hand in the deck and every whisky label in the distillery, but he can't even write his name. . . . Can you?" he says to me.

"I don't need to write my name down," I said. "I can remember in my mind who I am."

"You're twelve years old," Walter Ewell said. "Man to man

now, how many days in your life did you ever spend in school?"

"He ain't got time to go to school," Willy Legate said. "What's the use in going to school from September to middle of November, when he'll have to quit then to come in here and do Ernest's hearing for him? And what's the use in going back to school in January, when in jest eleven months it will be November fifteenth again and he'll have to start all over telling Ernest which way the dogs went?"

"Well, stop looking into my hand, anyway," Roth Edmonds said.

"What's that? What's that?" Mister Ernest said. He wore his listening button in his ear all the time, but he never brought the battery to camp with him because the cord would bound to get snagged ever time we run through a thicket.

"Willy says for me to go to bed!" I hollered.

"Don't you never call nobody 'mister'?" Willy said.

"I call Mister Ernest 'mister'," I said.

"All right," Mister Ernest said. "Go to bed then. I don't need you."

"That ain't no lie," Willy said. "Deaf or no deaf, he can hear a fifty-dollar raise if you don't even move your lips."

So I went to bed, and after a while Mister Ernest come in and I wanted to tell him again how big them horns looked even half a quarter away in the river. Only I would 'a' had to holler, and the only time Mister Ernest agreed he couldn't hear was when we would be setting on Dan, waiting for me to point which way the dogs was going. So we jest laid down, and it wasn't no time Simon was beating the bottom of the dishpan with the spoon, hollering, "Raise up and get your four-o'clock coffee!" and I crossed the river in the dark this time, with the lantern, and fed Dan and Roth Edmondziz horse. It was going to be a fine day, cold and bright; even in the dark I could see the white frost on the leaves and bushes —jest exactly the kind of day that big old son of a gun laying up there in that brake would like to run.

Then we et, and set the stand-holder across for Uncle Ike McCaslin to put them on the stands where he thought they ought to be, because he was the oldest one in camp. He had been hunting deer in these woods for about a hundred years, I reckon, and if anybody would know where a buck would pass, it would be him.

Maybe with a big old buck like this one, that had been running the woods for what would amount to a hundred years in a deer's life, too, him and Uncle Ike would sholy manage to be at the same place at the same time this morning—provided, of course, he managed to git away from me and Mister Ernest on the jump. Because me and Mister Ernest was going to git him.

Then me and Mister Ernest and Roth Edmonds set the dogs over, with Simon holding Eagle and the other old dogs on leash because the young ones, the puppies, wasn't going nowhere until Eagle let them, nohow. Then me and Mister Ernest and Roth saddled up, and Mister Ernest got up and I handed him up his pump gun and let Dan's bridle go for him to git rid of the spell of bucking he had to git shut of ever morning until Mister Ernest hit him between the ears with the gun barrel. Then Mister Ernest loaded the gun and give me the stirrup, and I got up behind him and we taken the fire road up toward the bayou, the five big dogs dragging Simon along in front with his single-barrel britchloader slung on a piece of plow line across his back, and the puppies moiling along in ever'body's way. It was light now and it was going to be jest fine; the east already yellow for the sun and our breaths smoking in the cold still bright air until the sun would come up and warm it, and a little skim of ice in the ruts, and ever leaf and twig and switch and even the frozen clods frosted over, waiting to sparkle like a rainbow when the sun finally come up and hit them. Until all my insides felt light and strong as a balloon, full of that light cold strong air, so that it seemed to me like I couldn't even feel the horse's back I was straddle of—jest the hot strong muscles moving under the hot strong skin, setting up there without no weight at all, so that when old Eagle struck and jumped, me and Dan and Mister Ernest would go jest like a bird, not even touching the ground. It was jest fine. When that big old buck got killed today, I knowed that even if he had put it off another ten years, he couldn't 'a' picked a better one.

And sho enough, as soon as we come to the bayou we seen his foot in the mud where he had come up out of the river last night, spread in the soft mud like a cow's foot, big as a cow's, big as a mule's, with Eagle and the other dogs laying into the leash rope now until Mister Ernest told me to jump down and help Simon hold them. Because me and Mister Ernest knowed exactly where he would be—a little canebrake island in the middle of the bayou, where he could lay up until whatever doe or little deer the dogs had happened to jump could go up or down the bayou in either direction and take the dogs on away, so he could steal out and creep back down the bayou to the river and swim it, and leave the country like he always done the day the season opened.

Which is jest what we never aimed for him to do this time. So we left Roth on his horse to cut him off and turn him over Uncle Ike's standers if he tried to slip back down the bayou, and me and Simon, with the leashed dogs, walked on up the bayou until Mister Ernest on the horse said it was fur enough; then turned up into the woods about half a quarter above the brake because the wind was going to be south this morning when it riz, and turned down toward the brake, and Mister Ernest give the word to cast them, and we slipped the leash and Mister Ernest give me the stirrup again and I got up.

Old Eagle had done already took off because he knowed where that old son of a gun would be laying as good as we did, not making no racket atall yet, but jest boring on through the buck vines with the other dogs trailing along behind him, and even Dan seemed to know about that buck, too, beginning to souple up and jump a little through the vines, so that I taken my holt on Mister Ernest's belt already before the time had come for Mister Ernest to touch him. Because when we got strung out, going fast behind a deer, I wasn't on Dan's back much of the time nohow, but mostly jest strung out from my holt on Mister Ernest's belt, so that Willy Legate said that when we was going through the woods fast, it looked like Mister Ernest had a boy-size pair of empty overhalls blowing out of his hind pocket.

So it wasn't even a strike, it was a jump. Eagle must 'a' walked right up behind him or maybe even stepped on him while he was laying there still thinking it was day after tomorrow. Eagle jest throwed his head back and up and said, "There he goes," and we even heard the buck crashing through the first of the cane. Then all the other dogs was hollering behind him, and Dan give a squat to jump, but it was against the curb this time, not jest the snaffle, and Mister Ernest let him down into the bayou and swung him around the brake and up the other bank. Only he never had to say, "Which way?" because I was already pointing past his shoulder, freshening my holt on the belt jest as Mister Ernest touched Dan with that big old rusty spur on his nigh heel, because when Dan felt it he would go off jest like a stick of dynamite, straight through whatever he could bust and over or under what he couldn't.

The dogs was already almost out of hearing. Eagle must 'a' been looking right up that big son of a gun's tail until he finally decided he better git on out of there. And now they must 'a' been getting pretty close to Uncle Ike's standers, and Mister Ernest reined Dan back and held him, squatting and bouncing and trembling like a mule having his tail roached, while we listened for the shots. But never none come, and I hollered to Mister Ernest we better go on while I could still hear the dogs, and he let Dan off, but still there wasn't no shots, and now we knowed the race had done already passed the standers; and we busted out of a thicket, and sho enough there was Uncle Ike and Willy standing beside his foot in a soft patch.

"He got through us all," Uncle Ike said. "I don't know how he done it. I just had a glimpse of him. He looked big as a elephant, with a rack on his head you could cradle a yellin' calf in. He went right on down the ridge. You better get on, too; that Hog Bayou camp might not miss him."

So I freshened my holt and Mister Ernest touched Dan again. The ridge run due south; it was clear of vines and bushes so we could go fast, into the wind, too, because it had riz now, and now the sun was up too. So we would hear the dogs again any time now as the wind got up; we could make time now, but still holding Dan back to a canter, because it was either going to be quick, when he got down to the standers from that Hog Bayou camp eight miles below ourn, or a long time, in case he got by them too. And sho enough, after a while we heard the dogs; we was walking Dan now to let him blow a while, and we heard them, the sound coming faint up the wind, not running now, but trailing because the big son of a gun had decided a good piece back, probably, to put a end to this foolishness, and picked hisself up and souled out and put about a mile between hisself and the dogs—until he run up on them other standers from that camp below. I could almost see him stopped behind a bush, peeping out and saying, "What's this? What's this? Is this whole durn country full of folks this morning?" Then looking back over his shoulder at where old Eagle and the others was hollering along after him while he decided how much time he had to decide what to do next.

Except he almost shaved it too fine. We heard the shots; it sounded like a war. Old Eagle must 'a' been looking right up his tail again and he had to bust on through the best way he could. "Pow, pow, pow, pow" and then "Pow, pow, pow, pow," like it must 'a' been three or four ganged right up on him before he had time even to swerve, and me hollering, "No! No! No! No!" because he was ourn. It was our beans and oats he et and our brake he laid in; we had been watching him ever year, and it was like we had raised him, to be killed at last on our jump, in front of our dogs, by some strangers that would probably try to beat the dogs off and drag him away before we could even git a piece of the meat.

"Shut up and listen," Mister Ernest said. So I done it and we could hear the dogs; not just the others, but Eagle, too, not trailing no scent now and not baying no downed meat, neither, but running hot on sight long after the shooting was over. I jest had time to freshen my holt. Yes, sir, they was running on sight. Like Willy Legate would say, if Eagle jest had a drink of whisky he would ketch that deer; going on, done already gone when we broke out of the thicket and seen the fellers that had done the shooting, five or six of them, squatting and crawling around, looking at the ground and the bushes, like maybe if they looked hard enough, spots of blood would bloom out on the stalks and leaves like frogstools or hawberries.

"Have any luck, boys?" Mister Ernest said.

"I think I hit him," one of them said. "I know I did. We're hunting blood now."

"Well, when you have found him, blow your horn and I'll come back and tote him in to camp for you," Mister Ernest said.

So we went on, going fast now because the race was almost out of hearing again, going fast, too, like not jest the buck, but the dogs, too, had took a new leash on life from all the excitement and shooting.

We was in strange country now because we never had to run this fur before, we had always killed before now; now we had come to Hog Bayou that runs into the river a good fifteen miles below our camp. It had water in it, not to mention a mess of down trees and logs and such, and Mister Ernest checked Dan again, saying,

"Which way?" I could just barely hear them, off to the east a little, like the old son of a gun had give up the idea of Vicksburg or New Orleans, like he first seemed to have, and had decided to have a look at Alabama; so I pointed and we turned up the bayou hunting for a crossing, and maybe we could 'a' found one, except that I reckon Mister Ernest decided we never had time to wait.

We come to a place where the bayou had narrowed down to about twelve or fifteen feet, and Mister Ernest said, "Look out, I'm going to touch him" and done it.

I didn't even have time to freshen my holt when we was already in the air, and then I seen the vine—it was a loop of grapevine nigh as big as my wrist, looping down right across the middle of the bayou—and I thought he seen it, too, and was jest waiting to grab it and fling it up over our heads to go under it, and I know Dan seen it because he even ducked his head to jump under it. But Mister Ernest never seen it atall until it skun back along Dan's neck and hooked under the head of the saddle horn, us flying on through the air, the loop of the vine gitting tighter and tighter until something somewhere was going to have to give. It was the saddle girth. It broke, and Dan going on and scrabbling up the other bank bare nekkid except for the bridle, and me and Mister Ernest and the saddle, Mister Ernest still setting in the saddle holding the gun, and me still holding onto Mister Ernest's belt, hanging in the air over the bayou in the tightened loop of that vine like in the drawed-back loop of a big rubber-banded slingshot, until it snapped back and shot us back across the bayou and flang us clear, me still holding onto Mister Ernest's belt and on the bottom now, so that when we lit I would 'a' had Mister Ernest and the saddle both on top of me if I hadn't clumb fast around the saddle and up Mister Ernest's side, so that when we landed, it was the saddle first, then Mister Ernest, and me on top, until I jumped up, and Mister Ernest still laying there with jest the white rim of his eyes showing.

"Mister Ernest!" I hollered, and then clumb down to the bayou and scooped my cap full of water and clumb back and throwed it in his face, and he opened his eyes and laid there on the saddle cussing me.

"God dawg it," he said, "why didn't you stay behind where you started out?"

"You was the biggest!" I said. "You would 'a' mashed me flat!"

"What do you think you done to me?" Mister Ernest said. "Next time, if you can't stay where you start out, jump clear. Don't climb up on top of me no more. You hear?"

"Yes, sir," I said.

So he got up then, still cussing and holding his back, and clumb down to the water and dipped some in his hand onto his face and neck and dipped some more up and drunk it, and I drunk some, too, and clumb back and got the saddle and the gun, and we crossed the bayou on the down logs. If we could jest ketch Dan; not that he would have went them fifteen miles back to camp, because, if anything, he would have went on by hisself to try to help Eagle ketch that buck. But he was about fifty yards away, eating buck vines, so I brought him back, and we taken Mister Ernest's galluses and my belt and the whang leather loop off Mister Ernest's horn and tied the saddle back on Dan. It didn't look like much, but maybe it would hold.

"Provided you don't let me jump him through no more grape-vines without hollering first," Mister Ernest said.

"Yes, sir," I said. "I'll holler first next time—provided you'll holler a little quicker when you touch him next time too." But it was all right; we jest had to be a little easy getting up. "Now which-a-way?" I said. Because we couldn't hear nothing now, after wasting all this time. And this was new country, sho enough. It had been cut over and growed up in thickets we couldn't 'a' seen over even standing up on Dan.

But Mister Ernest never even answered. He jest turned Dan along the bank of the bayou where it was a little more open and we could move faster again, soon as Dan and us got used to that homemade cinch strop and got a little confidence in it. Which jest happened to be east, or so I thought then, because I never paid no particular attention to east then because the sun—I don't know where the morning had went, but it was gone, the morning and the frost, too—was up high now.

And then we heard him. No, that's wrong; what we heard was shots. And that was when we realized how fur we had come, because the only camp we knowed about in that direction was the Hollyknowe camp, and Hollyknowe was exactly twenty-eight miles from Van Dorn, where me and Mister Ernest lived—just the shots, no dogs nor nothing. If old Eagle was still behind him and

304 STORIES REVISED FOR LATER BOOKS

the buck was still alive, he was too wore out now to even say, "Here
he comes."

"Don't touch him!" I hollered. But Mister Ernest remembered
that cinch strop, too, and he jest let Dan off the snaffle. And Dan
heard them shots, too, picking his way through the thickets, hopping the vines and logs when he could and going under them when
he couldn't. And sho enough, it was jest like before—two or three
men squatting and creeping among the bushes, looking for blood
that Eagle had done already told them wasn't there. But we never
stopped this time, jest trotting on by. Then Mister Ernest swung
Dan until we was going due north.

"Wait!" I hollered. "Not this way."

But Mister Ernest jest turned his face back over his shoulder. It
looked tired, too, and there was a smear of mud on it where that
'ere grapevine had snatched him off the horse.

"Don't you know where he's heading?" he said. "He's done done
his part, give everybody a fair open shot at him, and now he's going
home, back to that brake in our bayou. He ought to make it exactly
at dark."

And that's what he was doing. We went on. It didn't matter to
hurry now. There wasn't no sound nowhere; it was that time in the
early afternoon in November when don't nothing move or cry, not
even birds, the peckerwoods and yellowhammers and jays, and it
seemed to me like I could see all three of us—me and Mister Ernest
and Dan—and Eagle, and the other dogs, and that big old buck,
moving through the quiet woods in the same direction, headed for
the same place, not running now but walking, that had all run the
fine race the best we knowed how, and all three of us now turned
like on a agreement to walk back home, not together in a bunch
because we didn't want to worry or tempt one another, because
what we had all three spent this morning doing was no play-acting
jest for fun, but was serious, and all three of us was still what we
was—that old buck that had to run, not because he was skeered,
but because running was what he done the best and was proudest
at; and Eagle and the dogs that chased him, not because they hated
or feared him, but because that was the thing they done the best
and was proudest at; and me and Mister Ernest and Dan, that run
him not because we wanted his meat, which would be too tough
to eat anyhow, or his head to hang on a wall, but because now we

could go back and work hard for eleven months making a crop, so we would have the right to come back here next November—all three of us going back home now, peaceful and separate, until next year, next time.

Then we seen him for the first time. We was out of the cut-over now; we could even 'a' cantered, except that all three of us was long past that. So we was walking, too, when we come on the dogs— the puppies and one of the old ones—played out, laying in a little wet swag, panting, jest looking up at us when we passed. Then we come to a long open glade, and we seen the three other old dogs and about a hundred yards ahead of them Eagle, all walking, not making no sound; and then suddenly, at the fur end of the glade, the buck hisself getting up from where he had been resting for the dogs to come up, getting up without no hurry, big, big as a mule, tall as a mule, and turned, and the white underside of his tail for a second or two more before the thicket taken him.

It might 'a' been a signal, a good-by, a farewell. Still walking, we passed the other three old dogs in the middle of the glade, laying down, too; and still that hundred yards ahead of them, Eagle, too, not laying down, because he was still on his feet, but his legs was spraddled and his head was down; maybe jest waiting until we was out of sight of his shame, his eyes saying plain as talk when we passed, "I'm sorry, boys, but this here is all."

Mister Ernest stopped Dan. "Jump down and look at his feet," he said.

"Nothing wrong with his feet," I said. "It's his wind has done give out."

"Jump down and look at his feet," Mister Ernest said.

So I done it, and while I was stooping over Eagle I could hear the pump gun go, "Snick-cluck. Snick-cluck. Snick-cluck" three times, except that I never thought nothing then. Maybe he was jest running the shells through to be sho it would work when we seen him again or maybe to make sho they was all buckshot. Then I got up again, and we went on, still walking; a little west of north now, because when we seen his white flag that second or two before the thicket hid it, it was on a beeline for that notch in the bayou. And it was evening, too, now. The wind had done dropped and there was a edge to the air and the sun jest touched the tops of the trees. And he was taking the easiest way, too, now, going straight as he could. When we seen his foot in the soft places he was running for a while at first after his rest. But soon he was walking, too, like he knowed, too, where Eagle and the dogs was.

And then we seen him again. It was the last time—a thicket, with the sun coming through a hole onto it like a searchlight. He crashed jest once; then he was standing there broadside to us, not twenty yards away, big as a statue and red as gold in the sun, and the sun sparking on the tips of his horns—they was twelve of them —so that he looked like he had twelve lighted candles branched around his head, standing there looking at us while Mister Ernest raised the gun and aimed at his neck, and the gun went, "Click. Snick-cluck. Click. Snick-cluck. Click. Snick-cluck" three times, and Mister Ernest still holding the gun aimed while the buck turned and give one long bound, the white underside of his tail like a blaze of fire, too, until the thicket and the shadows put it out; and Mister Ernest laid the gun slow and gentle back across the saddle in front of him, saying quiet and peaceful, and not much louder than jest breathing, "God dawg. God dawg."

Then he jogged me with his elbow and we got down, easy and careful because of that ere cinch strop, and he reached into his vest and taken out one of the cigars. It was busted where I had fell on it, I reckon, when we hit the ground. He throwed it away and taken out the other one. It was busted, too, so he bit off a hunk of it to chew and throwed the rest away. And now the sun was gone even from the tops of the trees and there wasn't nothing left but a big red glare in the west.

"Don't worry," I said. "I ain't going to tell them you forgot to load your gun. For that matter, they don't need to know we ever seed him."

"Much oblige," Mister Ernest said. There wasn't going to be no moon tonight neither, so he taken the compass off the whang leather loop in his buttonhole and handed me the gun and set the compass on a stump and stepped back and looked at it. "Jest about the way we're headed now," he said, and taken the gun from me and opened it and put one shell in the britch and taken up the compass, and I taken Dan's reins and we started, with him in front with the compass in his hand.

And after a while it was full dark; Mister Ernest would have to strike a match ever now and then to read the compass, until the stars come out good and we could pick out one to follow, because

I said, "How fur do you reckon it is?" and he said, "A little more than one box of matches." So we used a star when we could, only we couldn't see it all the time because the woods was too dense and we would git a little off until he would have to spend another match. And now it was good and late, and he stopped and said, "Get on the horse."

"I ain't tired," I said.

"Get on the horse," he said. "We don't want to spoil him."

Because he had been a good feller ever since I had knowed him, which was even before that day two years ago when maw went off with the Vicksburg roadhouse feller and the next day pap didn't come home neither, and on the third one Mister Ernest rid Dan up to the door of the cabin on the river he let us live in, so pap could work his piece of land and run his fish line, too, and said, "Put that gun down and come on here and climb up behind."

So I got in the saddle even if I couldn't reach the stirrups, and Mister Ernest taken the reins and I must 'a' went to sleep, because the next thing I knowed a buttonhole of my lumberjack was tied to the saddle horn with that ere whang cord off the compass, and it was good and late now and we wasn't fur, because Dan was already smelling water, the river. Or maybe it was the feed lot itself he smelled, because we struck the fire road not a quarter below it, and soon I could see the river, too, with the white mist laying on it soft and still as cotton. Then the lot, home; and up yonder in the dark, not no piece akchully, close enough to hear us unsaddling and shucking corn prob'ly, and sholy close enough to hear Mister Ernest blowing his horn at the dark camp for Simon to come in the boat and git us, that old buck in his brake in the bayou; home, too, resting, too, after the hard run, waking hisself now and then, dreaming of dogs behind him or maybe it was the racket we was making would wake him.

Then Mister Ernest stood on the bank blowing until Simon's lantern went bobbing down into the mist; then we clumb down to the landing and Mister Ernest blowed again now and then to guide Simon, until we seen the lantern in the mist, and then Simon and the boat; only it looked like ever time I set down and got still, I went back to sleep, because Mister Ernest was shaking me again to git out and climb the bank into the dark camp, until I felt a bed against my knees and tumbled into it.

Then it was morning, tomorrow; it was all over now until next

November, next year, and we could come back. Uncle Ike and Willy and Walter and Roth and the rest of them had come in yestiddy, soon as Eagle taken the buck out of hearing and they knowed that deer was gone, to pack up and be ready to leave this morning for Yoknapatawpha, where they lived, until it would be November again and they could come back again.

So, as soon as we et breakfast, Simon run them back up the river in the big boat to where they left their cars and pickups, and now it wasn't nobody but jest me and Mister Ernest setting on the bench against the kitchen wall in the sun; Mister Ernest smoking a cigar —a whole one this time that Dan hadn't had no chance to jump him through a grapevine and bust. He hadn't washed his face neither where that vine had throwed him into the mud. But that was all right, too; his face usually did have a smudge of mud or tractor grease or beard stubble on it, because he wasn't jest a planter; he was a farmer, he worked as hard as ara one of his hands and tenants—which is why I knowed from the very first that we would git along, that I wouldn't have no trouble with him and he wouldn't have no trouble with me, from that very first day when I woke up and maw had done gone off with that Vicksburg road-house feller without even waiting to cook breakfast, and the next morning pap was gone, too, and it was almost night the next day when I heard a horse coming up and I taken the gun that I had already throwed a shell into the britch when pap never come home last night, and stood in the door while Mister Ernest rid up and said, "Come on. Your paw ain't coming back neither."

"You mean he give me to you?" I said.

"Who cares?" he said. "Come on. I brought a lock for the door. We'll send the pickup back tomorrow for whatever you want."

So I come home with him and it was all right, it was jest fine— his wife had died about three years ago—without no women to worry us or take off in the middle of the night with a durn Vicks-burg roadhouse jake without even waiting to cook breakfast. And we would go home this afternoon, too, but not jest yet; we always stayed one more day after the others left because Uncle Ike always left what grub they hadn't et, and the rest of the homemade corn whisky he drunk and that town whisky of Roth Edmondziz he called Scotch that smelled like it come out of a old bucket of roof paint; setting in the sun for one more day before we went back

home to git ready to put in next year's crop of cotton and oats and
beans and hay; and across the river yonder, behind the wall of trees
where the big woods started, that old buck laying up today in the
sun, too—resting today, too, without nobody to bother him until
next November.

So at least one of us was glad it would be eleven months and two
weeks before he would have to run that fur that fast again. So he
was glad of the very same thing we was sorry of, and so all of a
sudden I thought about how maybe planting and working and then
harvesting oats and cotton and beans and hay wasn't jest something me and Mister Ernest done three hundred and fifty-one days
to fill in the time until we could come back hunting again, but it
was something we had to do, and do honest and good during the
three hundred and fifty-one days, to have the right to come back
into the big woods and hunt for the other fourteen; and the fourteen days that old buck run in front of dogs wasn't jest something
to fill his time until the three hundred and fifty-one when he didn't
have to, but the running and the risking in front of guns and dogs
was something he had to do for fourteen days to have the right not
to be bothered for the other three hundred and fifty-one. And so
the hunting and the farming wasn't two different things at all—
they was jest the other side of each other.

"Yes," I said. "All we got to do now is put in that next year's
crop. Then November won't be no time away."

"You ain't going to put in the crop next year," Mister Ernest
said. "You're going to school."

So at first I didn't even believe I had heard him. "What?" I said.
"Me? Go to school?"

"Yes," Mister Ernest said. "You must make something out of
yourself."

"I am," I said. "I'm doing it now. I'm going to be a hunter and
a farmer like you."

"No," Mister Ernest said. "That ain't enough any more. Time
was when all a man had to do was just farm eleven and a half
months, and hunt the other half. But not now. Now just to belong
to the farming business and the hunting business ain't enough. You
got to belong to the business of mankind."

"Mankind?" I said.

"Yes," Mister Ernest said. "So you're going to school. Because you got to know why. You can belong to the farming and hunting business and you can learn the difference between what's right and what's wrong, and do right. And that used to be enough—just to do right. But not now. You got to know why it's right and why it's wrong, and be able to tell the folks that never had no chance to learn it; teach them how to do what's right, not just because they know it's right, but because they know now why it's right because you just showed them, told them, taught them why. So you're going to school."

"It's because you been listening to that durn Will Legate and Walter Ewell!" I said.

"No," Mister Ernest said.

"Yes!" I said. "No wonder you missed that buck yestiddy, taking ideas from the very fellers that let him git away, after me and you had run Dan and the dogs durn nigh clean to death! Because you never even missed him! You never forgot to load that gun! You had done already unloaded it a purpose! I heard you!"

"All right, all right," Mister Ernest said. "Which would you rather have? His bloody head and hide on the kitchen floor yonder and half his meat in a pickup truck on the way to Yoknapatawpha County, or him with his head and hide and meat still together over yonder in that brake, waiting for next November for us to run him again?"

"And git him, too," I said. "We won't even fool with no Willy Legate and Walter Ewell next time."

"Maybe," Mister Ernest said.

"Yes," I said.

"Maybe," Mister Ernest said. "The best word in our language, the best of all. That's what mankind keeps going on: Maybe. The best days of his life ain't the ones when he said 'Yes' beforehand: they're the ones when all he knew to say was 'Maybe.' He can't say 'Yes' until afterward because he not only don't know it until then, he don't want to know 'Yes' until then. . . . Step in the kitchen and make me a toddy. Then we'll see about dinner."

"All right," I said. I got up. "You want some of Uncle Ike's corn or that town whisky of Roth Edmondziz?"

"Can't you say Mister Roth or Mister Edmonds?" Mister Ernest said.

"Yes, sir," I said. "Well, which do you want? Uncle Ike's corn or that ere stuff of Roth Edmondziz?"

Hog Pawn

Old man Otis Meadowfill was so mean as to be solvent even on his modest competence. He had just enough income without working to support himself and his gray drudge of a wife and their one child, with not one dollar over for anyone to try to borrow or sell him anything for. As a result, he could give his full time to gaining and holding unchallenged top honors for unpleasantness in our town.

The child was a quiet, modest girl whom we had still considered plain and mousy, for the simple reason that that's what the daughter of that household would have had to be, even after we had looked at her twice. This was when we learned that she had graduated valedictorian of her high school class, with the highest grades, plus a five-hundred-dollar scholarship, ever made in the school.

Only she didn't take the scholarship. It was the annual gift of one of our bankers as a memorial to his only son who had died as an army pilot in one of the first Pacific battles. When Essie Meadowfill won it, she went to the donor herself (this was the shy mouse who apparently could barely face us enough to say good morning on the street) and told him she did not need the scholarship since she had already found a job with the telephone company, but she wanted to borrow the five hundred dollars, or any part of it, to be paid back from her salary as soon as she went to work; and explained why. We (their neighbors anyway) knew that there was no bathroom in the small frame house on the edge of town. But it was only now that we learned that only in the most rudimentary sense did they bathe at all in it: how once a week, on Saturday night, winter and summer, the mother heated water on the stove and filled a zinc tub in the middle of the floor, in which single filling of water all three of them bathed in turn: first the father, then the child, and last of all the mother.

The banker's first reaction was not only outrage but rage too. He would go to old Meadowfill himself. No, better: he would send the police: a kind of public deputation of town criers of the old curmudgeon's lack of simple decency, let alone shame of it. But America, Mississippi, Jefferson, was a free country; a father and husband had the right to outrage his womenfolks provided it was done in privacy and he raised no physical hand against them. Not to mention the privacy itself which (as he told it, Essie was crying now, the first tears she had shed since childhood probably) she must have. Then the banker tried to make her take the scholarship and the loan both. But she would not; there was at least the pride of solvency which the old reprobate had bequeathed her. She just took the loan, along with the banker's promise of secrecy. Nor was it that he ever told about the weekly tub of third-hand water; it was as though the simple installation of the bath and its connecting pipes had absolved the neighbors of the check upon their tongues in little towns like Jefferson, where even bathing habits can not forever remain a secret.

So she had her bath and her job. A good one; she could indeed hold her head up now—the quiet girl whom we were still thinking of as negative and mouselike until that day suddenly last year when the recently demobilised Korean Marine sergeant was to show us all how wrong we had been—each morning along the street to the Square and the telephone exchange, and each afternoon back along the street with the shopping bags from the markets and food stores. Time was when old Meadowfill did all the shopping, haggling for left-overs in the small dingy side-street stores which catered mostly to Negroes. But now she did it, not because she was earning money now but because, once she was at work and it was obvious that her job would last as long as she wanted it, old Meadowfill retired into a wheel-chair (second-hand, of course). There was nothing wrong with him; as the town said, he was too mean for germs to inhabit and live, let alone multiply. He had consulted no doctor: he just waited until the morning following her death and went and bought the chair from the family of a paralytic old lady who had inhabited it for years, before the funeral had even left the house and pushed the chair home himself along the street and retired into it. Not completely at first; we would still see him in his yard, snarling and cursing at the small boys who made a game of raiding the sorry untended fruit trees bordering his kitchen garden, or throwing rocks (he kept a small pile of them handy) at every stray dog which crossed his land. But he never left his premises anymore; and presently he seemed to have retired permanently into the wheel-chair, sitting in it like a rocking chair in the window looking out over the vegetable patch which he no longer worked now, and the scrawny fruit trees which he had always been too stingy or perhaps simply too perverse to spray and tend enough even to harvest a salable crop.

Essie's job was not just a good one: it was getting better. Now we began to wonder why she didn't leave that house, even take her mother with her and both be free of the outrageous old man, until we learned that it was the mother herself who would not go. Whereupon we had to admit that morally the mother was right; she could have done nothing else, because of the wheel-chair. Though Uncle Gavin said there was more than that. It was not that the wife still loved him; she could not possibly have done that. It was simple fidelity: virtue itself transformed into vice by simple habit, as, according to Uncle Gavin, all human virtues become vices with habit—not only the virtues of loyalty and honor and devotion and continence, but the God-given pleasures too of wine and food and sex and the adrenalic excitement of risk which becomes gambling for money. "Besides," he said, "it's much simpler than that. They dont need to move at all. All the two of them need to do is insure his life and then poison him. Nobody would mind, not even the insurance company once their investigator came and learned the circumstances."

Anyway, they did neither: murdered him nor moved; he continued his useless and outrageous days in the wheel-chair beside the window, with the gray and defeated wife to wait on him and be vocally harried and wrangled at when he got bored with the view, and the daughter not only earning the money which fed him but even carrying the groceries home. Not to mention the bathroom. He began to use it immediately it was installed, sometimes taking two or three baths a day. Though after the wheel-chair he reverted to his old once-a-week custom, on the intervening days merely wheeling himself in, to sit fully dressed in the chair and watch the water run into and then out of the tub.

Then, about a year ago, whatever shabby gods could preserve and nourish an existence like that, even supplied him with a fillip for it. At the end of the War, Progress reached Jefferson too; the almost unused back lane on which Meadowfill's property abutted, now became an intersecting corner of an arterial highway—as soon that is as the oil company could persuade old Meadowfill to sell his orchard-late-vegetable patch which, with a strip of the next adjoining lot, comprised the site of the proposed filling station. He refused to sell it, not from simple perversity this time but because legally he could not. During the early second Roosevelt days, he had naturally been among the first to apply for relief, learning to his outraged and incredulous amazement that a finicking and bureaucratic federal government declined utterly to allow him to be a pauper and a property-owner at the same time. So he came to Uncle Gavin, choosing Uncle Gavin from among the other Jefferson lawyers for the simple reason that he, Meadowfill, knew that in five minutes he would have Uncle Gavin so mad that very likely Uncle Gavin would refuse to accept a fee for drawing the deed transferring all his propert to the (then: legally) infant child. He was wrong only in his estimate of time, since it required only two minutes for Uncle Gavin to reach a pitch of boiling enragement which carried him right in to the Chancery Clerk's vault, where in copying Meadowfill's own original deed into the new one, he discovered the conditional clause, phrase covering the outside strip of old Meadowfill's orchard which conveyed to Meadowfill himself only such warranty as the warrantor from whom Meadowfill had bought, was himself vested with. So that for a moment Uncle Gavin thought that Meadowfill's true motive might have been the delusion that the law would make good for an infant child that right which Meadowfill himself had never been able to establish. Though in the next moment he realised that a free sack or two of flour and a side of meat would be enough motive for Meadowfill. So Uncle Gavin at least was no more surprised than (he realised now) old Meadowfill himself was when the other claimant to the strip of vacant lot appeared.

His name was Snopes, though in a way he was another Meadowfill except that he actually was a bachelor. That is, he was alone when he moved in from the country and bought a scrap of what had been the grounds of one of our once-fine ante bellum colonial houses—a small back lot adjoining Meadowfill's debatable orchard-strip and hence containing that additional strip which the oil company wanted to buy, on which sat what had been the manor's carriage house until Snopes converted it into a cottage complete with kitchen; he too did his own marketing in the same dingy back-street shops which Meadowfill had used to use, doing his own cooking too; presently he was buying and selling scrubby cattle and hogs and plow-mules; presently after that he was lending small sums, secured by usurious notes, to Negroes and small farmers; presently he was buying and selling small parcels of real estate— town lots and farms; he could be found at almost any time poring over the land records in the courthouse. So when war and boom and prosperity and then the oil company reached Jefferson, nobody was really surprised (least of all Meadowfill, according to Uncle Gavin) to learn that Snopes's deed also covered that equivocal strip of old Meadowfill's vacant lot.

The oil company would not buy one without the other, and obviously they must have a clear title to the disputed strip, which meant a release from Snopes. (Naturally the company had already approached Essie Meadowfill, the recorded owner of Meadowfill's lot, first, who had answered as we anyway had foreknown: "You'll have to see papa.") Which would be a mere formality, since the company offered enough for old Meadowfill to clear his title with Snopes and hardly miss it; not to mention the fact that Snopes, who would already do pretty well out of the sale of his strip, had lived in the same town with old Meadowfill long enough by now to expect little more than a simple nuisance-value ten percent.: whose (Snopes's) financial sights would not have obfuscated at a much more modest range than that, who last year at an auction sale had bought a worn-out mule for two dollars and sold it thirty minutes later for two dollars and ten cents.

Except that old Meadowfill would not pay ten percent. for the release. Snopes was a tallish man, quite thin as became one who shopped for left-overs and cooked them himself, with a bland negative face and manner and perfectly inscrutable eyes, who said (to the oil company's purchasing agent): "All right. Five percent. then." Then he said: "All right. What will he give, then?" And bland and affable and accommodating was no description for his voice when he said next: "Well, a good citizen cant stand in the way of progress, even if it does cost him money. Tell Mr Meadowfill he can have the release for nothing."

This time old Meadowfill didn't even bother to say No. He just sat there in his wheel-chair laughing. We thought we knew why: he wasn't going to sell the lot at all now for the reason that a rival company had just bought the corner opposite; and since in the lexicon of merchandising, the immediate answer to a successful business is to build another one exactly like it as near as possible as soon as possible, sooner or later the first company would have to pay whatever old Meadowfill demanded for his lot. But a year passed; the rival station was not only finished but operating. And now we knew what we (Snopes too) should have known all the time: that old Meadowfill would never sell that lot, for the simple reason that somebody else, anybody else, would likewise benefit from the sale. So that now, in a way, even Snopes had our sympathy in his next move, which he made shortly before the thing happened to Essie Meadowfill which showed us that she was anything in the world but mousy, and though demure might still be the word for her, the other word wasn't quiet but instead determined.

One morning old Meadowfill, wheeling his chair up to the window for a long peaceful forenoon of gloating, not at the lot which he wouldn't sell but at the adjoining one which for that reason Snopes couldn't, he saw a big stray hog rooting among the worthless peaches on the ground beneath his worthless and untended trees; and even as he sat bellowing for his wife, Snopes himself crossed the lot and contrived to ease a looped rope around one of the hog's feet and half-lead half-drive it back to his own premises, old Meadowfill not actually risen from the chair, leaning in the open window bellowing curses at both of them until they disappeared.

And the next morning he was already seated in his window and so actually saw the hog come at a steady and purposeful trot up the lane from Snopes's yard and into the orchard; he was still leaning in the open window bellowing and cursing when the drab wife emerged from the house, clutching a shawl about her head, and hurried down the lane to knock for a while at Snopes's locked front door until old Meadowfill's bellowing, which had never stopped, drew her back home. By that time most of the neighborhood was there to watch what followed: the old man still bellowing indiscriminate curses and instructions from the window while his wife tried single-handed to drive the hog away from the fallen peaches and out of the unfenced lot, until almost noon, when Snopes himself appeared (from where the neighborhood already believed he had been hidden, watching), innocent, amazed and apologetic, with his looped rope and caught the hog and removed it.

Next old Meadowfill had the rifle—an aged, battered single-shot .22. That is, it looked second hand simply because it was in his possession, though this time nobody could imagine when he could have left the wheel-chair and the window (not to mention Snopes's hog) long enough to have hunted down the rifle's small-boy owner and haggled and browbeat him out of it. Because (Uncle Gavin said) you could not imagine him ever having been a boy passionate and proud for the ownership of that symbol of our brave and hardy pioneer tradition and heritage, and have kept it these long secret years as a memory (reproach too) of that pure and innocent time. But he had it, and the cartridges too—not solid bullets but loaded with tiny shot incapable of killing the hog at all and not even of hurting it at that distance, let alone driving it from the peaches. Whereupon we realised that he did not want to drive the hog away; that he too had been caught by that virulent germ of self-contest which in other people of his age becomes golf or croquet or bingo or anagrams.

He would rush his wheel-chair straight from the breakfast table, to sit immobile in ambush until the hog would appear. Then (he would have to stand up to do this) he would slowly and quietly raise the window whose grooves he kept greased for silence, and pick and deliver the shot, the hog giving its convulsive start and leap until, forgetting, it would settle down again to receive the next shot, until at last even its dull processes connected the sting with the report and after the next shot it would go home, to return no more until tomorrow morning; and finally even the peaches themselves with inimicality. For a whole week the hog did not return at all and now the neighborhood legend was that old Meadowfill had contracted with the boy who delivered the Memphis and Jackson papers (old Meadowfill did not take a paper himself, not being interested in news which cost a dollar a month) to scavenge from garbage cans and so bait his (Meadowfill's) orchard at night.

Now we more than just wondered exactly what Snopes could be up to, who might have been expected to fasten the hog up after the first time old Meadowfill shot it. Or even sold the animal, which he could still do: either fasten it up or even sell it, though probably no buyer would give the full market price per hundred for a hog which for months had been subject to daily bombardment. Until at last we believed that we had divined Snopes's intention: his hope that someday, either by error, mistake, or perhaps simply carried, swept beyond all check of morality or fear of consequences by his vice as the drunkard or gambler is by his, he (Meadowfill) would put a solid bullet in the gun. Whereupon Snopes would not merely sue him for destroying the hog: he would also invoke an old town ordinance forbidding the firing of guns inside the town limits, and beneath that compounded weight, compel Meadowfill to make his (Snopes's) lot available to the oil company by agreeing to release his own to them. Then something happened to Essie Meadowfill.

It was the Marine sergeant. We never did know where or how or when Essie managed to meet him. She had never been anywhere save occasionally to Memphis, since everyone in Jefferson sooner or later spent an afternoon in Memphis once a month. She had never missed a day from her job since she joined the company, except during her annual vacations, which as far as we knew she spent at home to take some of the burden of the wheel-chair. Yet she did it. Still carrying the parcels of her daily marketing, she was waiting at the station when the Memphis bus came in and he got down from it, whom the town had never seen before, he carrying the parcels now along the street where she was already an hour late since her passage along it could have set watches. That was when we realised that mousy had not been the word for her for years, since obviously no girl could have bloomed that much, got that round and tender and girl-looking just in that brief time since the bus arrived. And we were glad that quiet was not the word for her either. Because she was going to need the determination, whether her Marine knew it yet or not, the two of them walking into the house and up to the wheel-chair, into point-blank range of that rage compared to which the cursing of small boys and throwing rocks at dogs and even shooting live ammunition at Snopes's hog was the

mere reflexive hysteria of the moment since this intruder threatened the very system of peonage on which he lived, and saying:
"Papa, this is McKinley Smith. We're going to be married."

Perhaps she had it, walking back out to the street with him five
minutes later, and there, in full view of whoever wanted to look,
kissing him—maybe not the first time she ever kissed him but
probably the first time she ever kissed anyone without bothering
(more: caring) whether or not it was sin. Perhaps he had it too—
son of an Arkansas tenant-farmer, who probably had barely heard
of Mississippi until he met Essie Meadowfill wherever it was that
day; who, once he realised that because of the wheel-chair and the
mother, she was not going to cut away from her family and marry
him regardless, should have given up and gone back to his Arkansas.

Rather, they both had it, for the simple reason that they owned
everything else in common. They were indeed doomed and fated,
whether or not they were star-crossed too; they not only believed
and desired alike, they even acted alike. It was obvious now that
he had cast his lot in Jefferson; we had accepted him. And since
for years now the land had been filled with ex-G.I.'s going to school
whether they were fitted or not or even really wanted to or not, the
obvious thing was for him to use his G.I. privileges at our local
college, where at government expense he could see her every day
while they waited for the ultimate meanness to kill old Meadowfill.
But he not only dismissed education as immediately and finally as
Essie had, he intended to substitute the same thing in its place
which Essie did. He explained it to us: "I was a soldier for two
years. The only thing I learned was, the only place in this world
you can be safe in is a private hole, preferably with a iron lid you
can pull down on top of you. So I aim to own me a hole. Only I
aint a soldier now, so I can pick where I want it, and even make
it comfortable. I'm going to build a house."

Which he did. He bought a small lot. She chose it; it was not even
very far from where she had lived all her life. In fact, after the
house began to go up, old Meadowfill even could (he had to, unless
he went back to bed) sit in his window and watch its daily progress.
But then we already knew that she was no more going to run from
him than she was going to desert her mother. So we took this at
its true meaning: a constant warning and reminder to him that he

dared not make the mistake of dying. Perhaps from the excitement of his vendetta with Snopes's hog, we might have added, except that the contest with the hog no longer existed; not, we realised now, that Meadowfill had quit, having found a more vulnerable and tender victim to vent upon, but (this was what we realised now) the hog itself had given up. Or Snopes had, that is. The hog had made its last sortie at about the time that Essie Meadowfill startled us with the fact that she had at last found a sweetheart, and had not appeared in the orchard since. Snopes still owned it. That is, the neighborhood knew (probably by smell when the wind was right) that it was still in his back yard; he evidently had given up at last and fixed his fence or (as we believed) simply stopped leaving the gate ajar on what he considered the strategic days. Though actually we had forgot Snopes and the hog in watching the new contest, battle of attrition.

He—McKinley—built the house himself, doing all the rough and heavy work, with one professional carpenter to mark off the planks for him to saw. We watched it: the furious and impotent old man in his wheel-chair ambush behind the window, without even the hog to vent his rage on anymore, while he watched the house going up. We speculated on whether he still kept the .22 rifle loaded to his hand perhaps, perhaps just how long it would be, how much he would be able to stand, before he would lose all restraint and fire one of the shot cartridges at one of them—McKinley or even the carpenter. Presently it would have to be the carpenter, unless old Meadowfill took up jacklighting. Because one day (it was spring now) McKinley had a mule too and now we learned that he had rented a small piece of land about a mile from town and was making a cotton-crop on it. The house was about finished now, down to the millwork—doors and windows and trim—which only the professional carpenter could do, so McKinley would depart on his mule each morning at sun-rise, to be gone until night-fall. And now we knew that old Meadowfill must have raged indeed: McKinley could have got discouraged, given up and sold even the unfinished house for that modest profit at least computed at the value of his own work on it, and left Jefferson. But he couldn't have sold the unmade crop; McKinley would stay in Jefferson forever now to flout and taunt him, with only his life or his rival's death to fend him from disaster.

Then the hog came back. It simply reappeared; probably one morning old Meadowfill wheeled himself from breakfast to the window, expecting to face nothing except one more interminable day of raging and impotent outrage, when there was the hog again, rooting for the ghosts of last fall's peaches as though it had never been away: no time nor anguish nor frustration had intervened. We —I, because this was where I came in—liked to think that that's what old Meadowfill felt: the hog had never been away and so all that had happened since to outrage him had been only a dream; and even the dream to be exercised as by a thunderclap by the next shot he would make. Which was immediately; apparently we were right and he had kept the loaded rifle at his hand all the time; some of the neighbors claimed to have heard the vicious spat of it while they were still in bed.

And (the report of the shot) over the rest of the town too while some of us were still at breakfast. Though, as Uncle Gavin said, he was one of the few who actually felt the repercussion. It was about noon, he was getting ready to lock the office and go home for dinner when he heard the feet mounting the outside stairs. Then Snopes entered, the five-dollar bill already in his hand, and crossed to the desk and laid the bill on it and said, "Good morning, Lawyer. I wont keep you. I just want a little advice—about five dollars' worth." Then he told it, Uncle Gavin not even touching the bill yet, just looking from it up at Snopes who in all the time he had lived among us had never been known to pay five dollars at one time for anything he didn't know he could sell within twenty-four hours for at least twenty-five cents' profit: "It's that ere hog of mine that the old gentleman—old Mister Meadowfill—likes to shoot with them little shot."

"I heard about it," Uncle Gavin said. "All right. What do you want for your five dollars?" He told about it: Snopes standing there beyond the desk, not secret, not fawning: just bland, deferent, inscrutable. "For telling you what you already know? That, once you sue him for injuring your hog, he will invoke against you the law against livestock running loose inside the town limits? Provided you can prove an injury. Provided you can satisfy even a j.p. court why you waited this long. Tell you what you already knew last summer when he fired the first shot at it? Either fix the fence, or get rid of the hog."

"It costs a right smart to feed a hog," Snopes said.

"Then eat it," Uncle Gavin said.

"A whole hog, for just one single man?" Snopes said.

"Then sell it," Uncle Gavin said.

"That old gentleman has done shot it so much now, I doubt wouldn't nobody buy it," Snopes said.

"Then give it away," Uncle Gavin said. Then he said he stopped, because it was already too late. Snopes said, with no inflection whatever:

"Give the hog away," already turning when Uncle Gavin said:

"Here. Wait," though even then Snopes paused only long enough to look back at the bill as Uncle Gavin pushed it across the desk toward him.

"I come for legal advice," he said. "I owe a legal fee for it," and was gone, Uncle Gavin thinking fast now, not *Why did he pick on me?* because that was obvious: because of his instrumentality in Essie's deed, Uncle Gavin was the only person in Jefferson outside his family, with whom old Meadowfill had had anything resembling human contact in almost twenty years, nor even *Why did he need to notify any outsider, lawyer or not, that he intended to give that hog away?* nor even *Why did he lead me into saying the actual words first myself, technically constituting them paid-for legal advice?* but *How, by giving that hog away, is he going to compel old Meadowfill to sell that lot?*

He always said that he was not really interested in truth nor even justice: that all he wanted was just to know, to find out, whether the answer was any of his business or not; and that all means to that end were valid, provided he left neither hostile witnesses nor incriminating evidence. Only I didn't believe him; some of his methods were not only too hard, they took too long; and there are some things you wont do even to find out. But he said I was wrong; that curiosity is another one of the mistresses whose slaves decline no sacrifice. Maybe this one proved both of us right.

The trouble was, he said, he didn't know what he was looking for; he had two methods for three leads, to discover what he might not recognise in time even when he found it. He couldn't use inquiry, because the only one who knew the answer had already told him all he intended for him to know. And he couldn't use observation of the second lead, because like Snopes the hog could move too. Which left only the immobile one, the fixed quantity: old man Meadowfill.

So at daylight the next morning, he too was ambushed in his parked car where he could see old Meadowfill's house and orchard, and beyond them, Snopes's front door; and beyond that in turn, the little new house which McKinley Smith had almost finished. During the next two hours he watched McKinley depart on his mule for his cotton-patch, then Snopes himself come out of his house and walk away toward the Square and his normal day of usurious opportunism; presently it would be time for Essie Meadowfill to leave for work. Which she did, and there remained only himself in his car and old Meadowfill in his window, both (he hoped) invisible to the other. So, of the elements, only the hog was missing: assuming that it was the hog he was waiting for, which he didn't even know yet, let alone what he would do next if—when—it appeared. So that he thought that perhaps Snopes really had recognised impasse, had given up and given the hog away; and he, Uncle Gavin, had made a mare's nest.

And the next morning was the same. Which was when he should have quit too. Except that he should have quit two days ago. Because it was too late now, not that he had too much at stake because he didn't know what was at stake yet, but rather too much invested: if no more than two days of rising before dawn, to sit for two hours in a parked car without even a cup of coffee. So when he saw the hog—it was the third morning; McKinley and his mule had departed at the regular hour: so regular and normal that he had not even realised he had not seen Snopes until Essie herself came out on her way to work; he said it was one of those shocks, starts as when you find yourself waking up without even knowing until then you were asleep, so that he was already getting out of the car when he saw the hog. That is, it was the hog and it was doing exactly what he expected it to do: moving toward old Meadowfill's orchard at that rapid and purposeful trot. Only it was not quite where it should have been when he first saw it. It was going where he expected it to be going, but it was not coming exactly from where he had expected it to come. Though at the time he didn't pay much attention to that, still being in that initial surge of belated not-yet-awake alarm, just hurrying now to get across the street and the little yard and into the house and to the wheel-chair before old Meadowfill saw the hog and made the shot and so completed the pattern before he, Uncle Gavin, was close enough to read whatever it was Snopes had intended him either to read or not read, whichever it was.

But he made it. He wouldn't have stopped to knock even if there had been time, since at this hour Mrs Meadowfill would be in the kitchen washing up from breakfast. Only there was plenty of time. He reached the door and saw old Meadowfill leaning forward in the wheel-chair behind the screened window, the little rifle already half-raised in one hand. But he had not risen yet to raise the screen: he was just sitting there looking through the window at the hog, and Uncle Gavin said his face was terrible. We were all used to seeing meanness and vindictiveness and rage in it; they were normal. But this was gloating. He sat there gloating; he didn't even turn his head as Uncle Gavin crossed to the chair, he just said: "Come right in; you got a grandstand seat." And now Uncle Gavin could hear him cursing—not the hard outdoors swearing of anger or combat, but a quiet murmur of indoors foulness which, even if old Meadowfill had ever known and used, his gray hairs should have forgotten now.

Then he rose from the wheel-chair. As he did so, Uncle Gavin said he noticed the smallish lump, about the size of a brick wrapped in a piece of gunnysack, bound to the bole of one of the peach trees about forty feet from the window. But he paid no attention to it, just saying, "Stop it, Mr Meadowfill; stop it," as the old man, standing up now, set the gun beside the window and took hold of the handles on the bottom frame of the screen and jerked it upward in its greased grooves. Then the light sharp vicious spat of the shot; Uncle Gavin said he was actually looking at the screen when the wire suddenly frayed and vanished before the myriad tiny invisible pellets. And though this was impossible, he said he seemed actually to hear them hiss across old man Meadowfill's belly and chest as the old man half-leaped half-fell backward onto the chair, which rushed backward from under him, leaving him to sprawl onto the floor, where he lay for a moment with on his face an expression of incredulous and mounting outrage: not pain, just outrage, already reaching for the rifle as he began to scramble onto his knees.

"Somebody shot me!" he said in that outraged and unbelieving voice.

"Certainly," Uncle Gavin said. "That hog did. Dont try to move."

"Hog, hell!" old Meadowfill said. "It was that blank blank blank McKinley Smith!"

That was when Uncle Gavin drafted me. Though when I got there, he already had old Meadowfill back in the wheel-chair; Mrs Meadowfill must have been somewhere in the background by that time, but I suppose I didn't notice her any more than Uncle Gavin had. Old Meadowfill was no calmer yet, still raging, mad as a hornet—he wasn't hurt: just burned, blistered, the little shot barely under his skin—bellowing and cursing and still trying to get hold of the rifle which Uncle Gavin had taken away from him, but at least immobilised, by Uncle Gavin's moral force or maybe just because Uncle Gavin was standing up. He told Uncle Gavin about it—how Snopes had told Essie two days ago that he had given McKinley the hog, as a sort of house-warming present or maybe even—Snopes hoped—a wedding one someday soon. Uncle Gavin had the weapon too: a very neat home-made booby-trap; it had been a cheap single shot .22 rifle also once, sawed off barrel and stock and wrapped in the feed sack and fastened to the bole of the peach tree, a black practically invisible cord running through a series of screw eyes from the sash of the screen to the trigger, the muzzle trained at the center of the window about a foot above the sill; Mrs Meadowfill was there then so we could leave.

"If he hadn't stood up before he touched that screen, the charge would have hit him square in the face," I said.

"Do you think who set it cared about that?" Uncle Gavin said. "Whether it merely frightened and enraged him into rushing at Smith with that little rifle (it had a solid bullet in it this time, and the cartridge was the big one, the long rifle; then how old Meadowfill intended to hunt what he shot at next) and compelling Smith to kill him, or whether the shot blinded him or killed him right there in his wheel-chair and so solved the whole thing?"

"Solved it?" I said.

"It was a balance," he said. "A kind of delicate attenuated unbearable equilibrium of outrage; so delicate that the first straw's weight, no matter how trivial, would not just upset it but overturn, reverse all the qualities in it; all withheld no longer withheld, all unsold no longer unsold."

"Yes," I said. "It was pretty smart."

"It was worse," Uncle Gavin said. "It was bad. Nobody would ever have thought anyone except a Pacific veteran would have invented a booby-trap, no matter how much he denied it."

"It was still smart," I said. "Even Smith will agree."

"Yes," Uncle Gavin said. "That's why I telephoned you. You were a soldier too. I may need an interpreter to talk to him."

"I was just a major," I said. "I never had enough rank to tell anything to any sergeant, let alone a Marine one." But we didn't go [to find] Smith first; he would be in his cotton-patch now anyway. And if Snopes had been me, there wouldn't have been anybody in his house either. But there was. He opened the door himself; he wore an apron and carried a frying pan. There was even a fried egg in it. But then, thinking of that before hand wouldn't be much for who thought of that reciprocating booby-trap. And there wasn't anything in his face either.

"Gentle-men," he said. "Come in."

"No thanks," Uncle Gavin said. "It wont take that long. This is yours, I think." There was a table; Uncle Gavin laid the feed sack on it and flipped it suddenly, the mutilated rifle sliding across the table until it stopped. And still there was nothing whatever in Snopes's face or voice.

"That ere is what you lawyers call debatable, aint it?"

"Oh yes," Uncle Gavin said. "Everybody knows about finger prints now too, just like they do about space flight and booby-traps."

"Yes," Snopes said. "Are you giving it to me, or selling it to me?"

"I'm selling it to you," Uncle Gavin said. "For a deed to Essie Meadowfill for that strip of your lot the oil company wants to buy, and a release for that strip of Meadowfill's lot that your deed covers. She'll pay you what you paid for the strip, plus ten percent. of what the oil company pays her for it." And now indeed Snopes didn't move, immobile with the cold egg in the frying pan. "That's right," Uncle Gavin said. "In that case, I'd have to see if McKinley Smith wants to buy it."

He was smart, you'd have to give him that; smart enough to

know exactly how far to try. "Just ten percent.?" he said.

"You invented that figure," Uncle Gavin said. And smart enough to know when to quit trying too. He set the frying pan carefully on the floor and folded the mutilated rifle back into the feed sack.

"I reckon you'll have time to be in your office today, wont you?" he said.

And this time it was Uncle Gavin who stopped dead for a second. But he only said: "I'm going there now." And we could have met Smith at his house when he came in at sundown too. It was Uncle Gavin who wouldn't wait; it was not yet noon when we stood at the roadside fence and watched Smith and the mule come up the long black shear of turning earth like the immobilised wake of the plow's mold-board. Then he was standing across the fence from us, naked from the waist up except for his overalls and combat boots; and I remembered what Uncle Gavin had said that morning about what was withheld to be no longer withheld. He handed Smith the deed. "Here," he said.

Smith read it. "This is Essie's," he said.

"Then marry her," Uncle Gavin said. "Then you can sell that lot and buy a farm. Isn't that what you both want? Haven't you got a shirt or a jumper here with you? Get it and you can ride to town with me; Chick here will bring the mule."

"No," Smith said; he was already shoving, actually ramming the deed into his pocket as he turned back to the mule. "I'll bring him in. I'm going home first. I aint going to marry anybody without a necktie and a shave."

And one more, while we were waiting for the Baptist minister to wash his hands and put his coat on too; Mrs Meadowfill was wearing the first hat any of us had ever seen on her; it looked a good deal like the first hat anybody ever made. "But papa," Essie Smith-soon-to-be said.

"Oh," Uncle Gavin said. "You mean that wheel-chair. It belongs to me now. It was a legal fee. I'm going to give it to you for a wedding present."

II

UNCOLLECTED STORIES

Nympholepsy

Soon the sharp line of the hill-crest had cut off his shadow's head; and pushing it like a snake before him, he saw it gradually become nothing. And at last he had no shadow at all. His heavy shapeless shoes were gray in the dusty road, his overalls were gray with dust: dust was like a benediction upon him and upon the day of labor behind him. He did not recall the falling of slain wheat and his muscles had forgotten the heave and thrust of fork and grain, his hands had forgotten the feel of a wooden handle worn smooth and sweet as silk to the touch; he had forgotten a yawning loft and spinning chaff in the sunlight like an immortal dance.

Behind him a day of labor, before him cloddish eating, and dull sleep in a casual rooming house. And tomorrow labor again and his sinister circling shadow marking another day away. The hill broke briefly and sharply, soon, on its crest it was no more sharp. Here was the valley in shadow, and the opposite hill in two dimensions and gold with sun. Within the valley the town lay among lilac shadows. Among lilac shadows was the food he would eat and the sleep that waited him; perhaps a girl like defunctive music, moist with heat, in blue gingham, would cross his path fatefully; and he too would be as other young men sweating the wheat to gold, along the moony land.

Here was town anyway. Above gray walls were branches of apple once sweet with bloom and yet green, barn and house were hives from which the bees of sunlight had flown away. From here the court-house was a dream dreamed by Thucydides: you could not see that pale Ionic columns were stained with casual tobacco.

And from the blacksmith's there came the measured ring of hammer and anvil like a call to vespers.

Reft of motion, his body felt his cooling blood, felt the evening drawing away like water; his eyes saw the shadow of the church spire like a portent across the land. He watched the trickling dust from his inverted shoes. His feet were grained and grimy with dust; and cooled, took the pleasantly warm moistness of his shoes gratefully.

The sun was a red descending furnace mouth, his shadow he had thought lost crouched like a skulking dog at his feet. The sun was in the trees, dripping from leaf to leaf, the sun was like a little silver flame moving among the trees. Why, its something alive, he thought, watching a golden light among dark pines, a little flame that had somehow lost its candle and was seeking for it.

How he knew it was a woman or a girl at that distance he could not have told, but know he did; and for a time he watched the aimless movements of the figure with vacuous curiosity. The figure, pausing, took the last of the red sun in a slim golden plane that, breaking again into movement, disappeared.

For a clear moment there was an old sharp beauty behind his eyes. Then his once-clean instincts become swinish got him lurching into motion. He climbed a fence under the contemplative stare of cattle and ran awkwardly across a harvested corn field toward the woods. Old soft furrows shifted beneath his stride, causing his pounding knees to knock together and brittle corn stalks hindered his speed with wanton and static unconcern.

He gained the woods by climbing another fence and stopped for a moment while the west alchemized the leaden dust upon him, gilding the tips of his unshaven beard. Hardwood,—maple and beech trunks, were twin strips of red gold and lavender upright in earth, and stretched branches sloped the sunset to unwordable colors;—they were like the hands of misers reluctantly dripping golden coins of sunset. Pines were half iron and half bronze, sculptured into a symbol of eternal quiet, dripping gold also which the sparse grass took from tree to tree like a running fire, quenching it at last in the shadow of pines. A bird on a swinging branch regarded him briefly, sung, and flew away.

Before this green cathedral of trees he stood for a while, empty as a sheep, feeling the dying day draining from the world as a bath-tub drains, or a cracked bowl; and he could hear the day repeating slow orisons in a green nave. Then he moved forward again, slowly, as though he expected a priest to stop forth, halting him and reading his soul.

Nothing happened though. The day slowly died without a sound about him, and gravity directed him down hill along peaceful avenues of trees. Soon the violet shadow of the hill itself took him. There was no sun here, though the tips of trees were still as gold-dipped brushes and the trunks of trees upon the summit were like a barred grate beyond which the evening burned slowly away. He stopped again, knowing fear.

He recalled fragments of the day—of sucking cool water from a jug with another waiting his turn, of the wheat breaking to the reaper's blade as the thrusting horses surged to the collar, of horses dreaming of oats in a barn sweet with ammonia and the smell of sweaty harness, of blackbirds like scraps of burned paper slanting above the wheat. He thought of the run of muscles beneath a blue shirt wet with sweat, and of someone to listen or talk to. Always someone, some other member of his race, of his kind. Man can counterfeit everything except silence. And in this silence he knew fear.

For here was something that even the desire for a woman's body took no account of. Or, using that instinct for the purpose of seducing him from the avenues of safety, of security where others of his kind ate and slept, it had betrayed him. If I find her, I am safe he thought, not knowing whether it was copulation or companionship that he wanted. There was nothing here for him: hills, sloping down on either side, approaching yet forever severed by a small stream. The water ran brown under alders and willow, and without light, seemed dark and forbidding. Like the hand of the world, like a line on the palm of the world's hand—a wrinkle of no account. Yet he could drown here! he thought with terror, watching the spinning gnats above it and the trees calm and uncaring as gods, and the remote sky like a silken pall to hide his unsightly dissolution.

He had thought of trees as being so much timber but these silent ones were more than that. Timber had made houses to shelter him, timber had fed his fire for warmth, had given him heat to cook his food; timber had made him boats to go upon the waters of the earth. But not these trees. These trees gazed on him impersonally, taking a slow revenge. The sunset was a fire no fuel had ever fed, the water murmured in a dark and sinister dream. No boat would swim on this water. And above all brooded some god to whose compulsions he must answer long after the more comfortable beliefs had become out-worn as a garment used everyday.

And this god neither recognized him nor ignored him: this god seemed to be unconscious of his entity, save as a trespasser where he had no business being. Crouching, he felt the sharp warm earth against his knees and his palms; and kneeling, he awaited abrupt and dreadful annihilation.

Nothing happened, and he opened his eyes. Above the hill-crest, among tree trunks, he saw a single star. It was as though he had seen a man there. Here was a familiar thing, something too remote to care what he did. So he rose and with the star at his back, he began walking swiftly in the direction of town. Here was the stream to cross. The delay of looking for a crossing place engendered again his fear. But he suppressed it by his will, thinking of food and of a woman he hoped to find.

That sensation of an imminent displeasure and anger, of a Being whom he had offended, he held away from himself. But it still hung like poised wings about and above him. His first fear was gone, but soon he found himself running. He would have slowed to a walk if only to prove to himself the soundness of his integral integrity, but his legs would not stop running. Here, in the noncommittal dusk, was a log bridging the stream. Walk it! walk it! his good sense told him; but his thrusting legs took it at a run.

The rotten bark slipped under his feet, scaling off and falling upon the dark whispering stream. It was as though he stood upon the bank and cursed his blundering body as it slipped and fought for balance. You are going to die, he told his body, feeling that imminent Presence again about him, now that his mental concentration had been vanquished by gravity. For an arrested fragment of time he felt, through vision without intellect, the waiting dark water, the treacherous log, the tree trunks pulsing and breathing and the branches like an invocation to a dark and unseen god; then trees and the star-flown sky slowly arced across his eyes. In his fall was death, and a bleak derisive laughter. He died time and again, but his body refused to die. Then the water took him.

Then the water took him. But here was something more than water. The water ran darkly between his body and his overalls and shirt, he felt his hair lap backward wetly. But here beneath his hand a startled thigh slid like a snake, among dark bubbles he felt a swift leg; and, sinking, the point of a breast scraped his back. Amid a slow commotion of disturbed water he saw death like a woman shining and drowned and waiting, saw a flashing body tortured by water; and his lungs spewing water gulped wet air.

Churned water lapped at his mouth, trying to enter, and the light of day prisoned beneath the stream broke again upon the surface, shaped to ripples. Gleaming planes of light angled and broke the surface, moving away from him; and treading water, feeling his sodden shoes and his heavy overalls, feeling his wet hair plastered upon his face, he saw her swing herself, dripping, up the bank.

He churned the water in pursuit. It seemed that he would never reach the other side. His heavy water-soaked clothes clung to him like importunate sirens, like women; he saw the broken water of his endeavor crested with stars. Finally he was in the shadow of willows and felt wet and slippery earth under his hand. Here was a root, and here a branch. He drew himself up, hearing the trickling water from his clothing, feeling his clothing become light and then heavy.

His shoes squashed limply and his clinging nondescript garments hampered his running, heavily. He could see her body, ghostly in the moonless dusk, mounting the hill. And he ran, cursing, with water dripping from his hair, with his coarse clothing and shoes wetly complaining, cursing his fate and his luck. He believed he could do better without the shoes, so, still watching the muted flame of her running, he removed them, then he took up the pursuit again. His wet clothes were like lead, he was panting when he crested the hill. There she was, in a wheat field under the rising harvest moon, like a ship on a silver sea.

He plunged after her. His furrow broke silver in the wheat beneath the impervious moon, rippling away from him, dying again into the dull and unravished gold of standing grain. She was far ahead, the disturbance of her passage through the wheat had died away ere he reached it. He saw, beyond the spreading ripple of her passage arcing away on either side, her body break briefly against a belt of wood, like a match flame; then he saw her no more.

Still running, he crossed the wheat slumbrous along the moony land, and into the trees he went, wearily. But she was gone, and in a recurrent surge of despair he threw himself flat upon the earth. But I touched her! he thought in a fine agony of disappointment, feeling the earth through his damp clothing, feeling twigs beneath his face and arm.

The moon swam up, the moon sailed up like a fat laden ship before an azure trade wind, staring at him in rotund complacency. He writhed, thinking of her body beneath his, of the dark wood, of the sunset and the dusty road, wishing he had never left it. But I touched her! he repeated to himself, trying to build from this an incontrovertible consummation. Yes, her swift frightened thigh and the tip of her breast; but to remember that she had fled him on impulse was worse than ever. I wouldnt have hurt you, he moaned, I wouldnt have hurt you at all.

His lax muscles, emptied, felt a rumor of past labor and of labor tomorrow, compulsions of fork and grain. The moon soothed him, prying in his wet hair, experimenting with shadows; and thinking of tomorrow he rose. That troubling Presence was gone and dark and shadows only mocked him. The moonlight ran along a wire fence and he knew that here was the road.

He felt the dust stirring to his passage and he saw silver corn in fields, and dark trees like poured ink. He thought of how like running quicksilver she had looked, how like a flipped coin she had sped from him; but soon the lights of town came into view—the courthouse clock, and a luminous suggestion of streets, like a fairy land, small though it was. Soon she was forgotten and he thought only a relaxed body in a sorry bed, and waking and hunger and work.

The long monotonous road stretched under the moon before him. Now his shadow was behind him, like a following dog, and beyond it was a day of labor and sweat. Before him was sleep and casual food and more labor; and perhaps a girl like defunctive music, in this calico against the heat. Tomorrow his sinister shadow would circle him again, but tomorrow was a long way off.

The moon swam higher and higher: soon she would slide down the hill of heaven, recalling with interest the silver she had lent to tree and wheat and hill and rolling monotonous fecund land. Below him a barn took the moon for a silver edge and a silo became a dream dreamed in Greece, apple trees broke into silver like gesturing fountains. Flat planes of moonlight the town, and the lights on the courthouse were futile in the moon.

Behind him labor, before him labor; about all the old despairs of time and breath. The stars were like shattered flowers floating on dark water, sucking down the west; and with dust clinging to his yet damp feet, he slowly descended the hill.

Frankie and Johnny

I

"We'll name him Frank," said her father the prize fighter, who never won a battle nor was ever licked, confidently. "No more hustling for you, old girl. We'll get married, huh?" But, on a day, he bent his round sunny head above his mewling red child in consternation. "A girl?" he whispered in hushed amazement, "cripes, a girl! What do you know about that?" But he was a gentleman and a good sport, so he kissed the mother's hot cheek. "Buck up, old lady, dont you fret. Better luck next time, huh?"

She did not tell him there would be no next time though, but smiled wanly at him from her tumbled hair; and in the short time he knew his daughter (he was gallantly drowned trying to save a fat lady bather at Ocean Grove Park) he even became reconciled to a girl. When asked the sex of his child he was no longer sheepish about admitting it: he even took an inordinate pride in the swift sunny-headed creature. "She's me, over and over again," he told his casual acquaintances proudly; and his last connected thought as he fought the undertow with his mountainous struggling burden, was of her.

"Christ, the old bitch," he gasped, watching the spinning sky between gaping rollers; and he cursed for her size the fat soft weight killing his hard youth. But he didn't let go and swim for it, not he! Thinking of Frankie was sharper than the burning in his throat and lungs. "Poor kid, she'll have it tough now," he thought among green bubbles.

Frankie, therefore, was a girl of spirit. At least so thought Johnny, her fellow. You would have thought so too, watching the sensuous thrust of her walk and the angular sawing of her thin young arms as she'd take Johnny's arm and swing the rough synchronism of her young body along the streets of a Saturday night. Johnny's compeers thought so anyway, for when he'd take her to a dance at his Athletic club she'd put their eyes out; they followed her so thick during the music she hadn't room to dance. She knocked them cold from that first night when, lounging on the corner laughing and kidding the girls that passed, they saw her approaching. "Cheest," they said, and dared Johnny to brace her. Johnny, brave in his new suit, was nothing loath.

"Hello, kid," he said, tipping his hat gracefully and falling in beside her. Frankie gave him a level grey look. "On your way, boy," she replied, not stopping. "Aw, say—" began Johnny easily, while his pals guffawed behind them.

"Beat it, bum; or I'll slam you for a row," commanded Frankie. She didn't need to call a cop, not Frankie.

Johnny retained his sang-froid admirably. "Hit me, baby, I like it," he told her, taking her arm. Frankie did no ineffectual lady-like jerking: she took a full arm swing and her narrow palm smacked on Johnny's face. This was in front of an ex-saloon: swinging doors erupted upon tobacco-fogged lights.

"Hit me again," said Johnny, straight and red, and Frankie hit him again. A man staggered from the saloon. "Why, the—" spoke the newcomer, "knock hell out of her, you—"

Johnny's red stinging face and Frankie's white one hung like two young planets in the dingy street and he saw Frankie's nose wrinkle up. She's going to cry, thought Johnny in panic, and the man's words penetrated his singing head. He whirled upon the newcomer.

"Say, who're you talking to, fellow? What do you mean, talking that way before a lady?" He thrust his face into the man's beery one. The other, with alcoholic valor, began: "Why, you—" Johnny struck, and he went cursing into the gutter.

Johnny turned, but Frankie had fled down the street, wailing. He overtook her. "Why, baby," said Johnny. Frankie heeded him not. Cheest, what luck, and perspiring gently he led her into the mouth of a dark alleyway. He put his awkward arm about her. "Why, say, kid, it's all right, dont cry." Frankie turned to him suddenly and clung passionately to his coat. Cripes, what luck, he thought, patting her back as though she were a dog. "Say, dont cry, wont you? I never meant to scare you, sister. What you want I should do?" He looked about him, trapped. Cheest, what a fix! Suppose the gang should catch him now! Cheest, wouldn't they razz him? When in trouble, you called a cop; but Johnny, for sound reasons, evaded all intimate dealing with cops—even old Ryan who had known his father, man and boy. Cripes, what'll he do? Poor gentlemanly dull Johnny.

Then he had an inspiration. "Here, kid, brace up. You wanna go home, dont you? Tell me where you live and I'll take you, see?" Frankie raised her blurred face. How grey her eyes were, and her bright hair beneath her cheap little hat. Johnny felt how straight and firm her body was. "What's eating you, baby? Tell old Johnny your troubles: he'll fix it. Say, I never meant to scare you."

"It—it wasn't you: it was that bum back there."

"Oh, him?" He almost shouted in relief. "Say, j'ou see me slam that bimbo? Say, I knocked him off like—like—Say, I'll go back and break his neck, huh?"

"No, no," replied Frankie quickly, "it's all right. I was a fool to crybaby: I dont, mostly." She sighed. "Gee, I better be going, I guess."

"Say, I'm sorry I—I—"

"You never done nothing. You are not the first tried to pick me up. But I usually give 'em the air, right now. Gee, what do you know about us doing a fade-out right on the street, like this?"

"Why, if you aint mad at what I done and at what a fix I got you into, why, say, it means you're my girl. Say—lemme be your fellow, wont you? I'll be good to you, kid." They looked at each other and a soft wind blew over flowers and through trees and the street was no longer blind and mean and filthy. Their lips touched, and a blond morning came on hills brave in a clean dawn.

2

They walked in a park backed by dark factories; before them was the water front with water lapping at piles, and two ferry boats like a pair of golden swans caught forever in a barren cycle of courtship, to no escape.

"Listen, baby," said Johnny, "before I seen you it was like I was one of them ferry boats yonder, crossing and crossing a dark river or something by myself, a-crossing and a-crossing and never getting nowheres and not knowing it and thinking I was all the time. You know—being full of a lot of names of people and things busy with their own business, and thinking I was the berries all the time. And say, listen:

"When I seen you coming down the street it was like them two ferry boats would stop when they met instead of crossing each other, and they would turn and go off side by side together where they wasn't nobody except them. Listen, baby: before I seen you I was a young tough like what old Ryan, the cop, says I was, not doing nothing and not worth nothing and not caring for nothing except old Johnny; but when I slammed that bum back there I done it for you and not for me, and it was like a wind had blew a lot of trash and stuff out of the street.

"And when I put my arm around you and you was holding to me and crying I knowed you was meant for me and that I wasn't no longer the young tough like what old Ryan says I was; and when you kissed me it was like one morning a gang of us was beating our way back to town on a rattler and the bulls jumped us and trun us off and we walked in and I seen the day breaking acrost the water when it was kind of blue and dark at the same time, and the boats was still on the water and there was black trees acrost, and the sky was kind of yellow and gold and blue. And a wind come over the water, making funny little sucking noises. It was like when you are in a dark room or something, and all on a sudden somebody turns up the lights, and that's all. When I seen your yellow hair and your grey eyes it was like that; it was like a wind had blew clean through me and there was birds singing somewheres. And then I knowed it was all up with me."

"Oh, Johnny!" cried Frankie. They swung together, their mouths struck sharply and clung in the sweet friendly dark.

"Baby!"

3

"Say," said Frankie's mother, "who is this fellow you've took up with?" Frankie, staring across her mother's shoulder into the mir-

ror, cruelly examined the other's face. Will I look like that when
I am old? she asked herself, and something inside her replied no
passionately. The older woman's white flaccid hands fumbled in
her dyed hair, then, in rising anger pulled it savagely down. "Well,
cant you answer, or dont you think it's none of my business? What
does he do?"

"He—he—he's got a job in a garage. He's going to work up to
a racing driver." Why should she feel she must vindicate Johnny
to her mother, Johnny, who stood on his own legs and be damned
to them all?

"A job in a garage? and you, who've saw how hard life is on a
woman, and haven't no more sense than that! You, young and with
a figure men like, throwing yourself away on a damn car jumper
in dirty overalls!"

"Money aint everything."

The other stared at Frankie, speechless. At last she said: "Money
aint everything? Will you stand there and look at me and say that?
You, that have saw how I have to live? Where would you be today,
if it wasn't for what I can make? Where would the clothes to your
back be? Can your garage sweetheart buy you clothes? can he do
for you what I've done? God knows I dont want you to go the way
I've had to go, but if it's in your blood and you got to do it, I'd
rather see you on the street taking them as they come, than to see
you tied down to some damn penny pinching clerk. God, how hard
life is on us women." She turned to the mirror and began anew on
her hair, her sense of injury finding ease in voluble self pity. Frankie
watched her reflection stonily.

"When your father died without leaving a red cent behind him,
who stopped to help me? Some of them high brow dames rotten
with money, that are always fretting over social conditions? One
of them damn froze face parsons always talking about the wages
of sin and raising the poor sinner? Not so's you'd notice it! You'll
learn, like me, that men dont never help women like me for nothing; and whenever you have any dealings with 'em you got to look
out for yourself, and you got to put up a good front to get 'em and
to keep 'em. No man aint never yet helped a woman through pity.
And another thing: getting a man aint the half of it. Any woman
with sense at all can get one, its keeping him that makes the
difference between me and them poor girls you see on the streets.

And good or bad, there's one thing any woman will do: she'll try to take him away from you, whether she wants him herself or not.

"You can bet on it, there wont nobody help you any more than they did me. God knows, I wouldn't have chose this life, promising your father like I did. But he has to go and drown himself trying to pull some strange woman out of the ocean. Women always could do what ever they like with your father: he never had sense enough to either let 'em alone or to get something for his trouble. But it aint that I couldn't trust him: never a better man than him wore hair. But to have died that way, and so soon!" She faced her daughter again.

"Come here, honey."

Frankie drew near reluctantly and the other put her arms about her. Frankie's body, in spite of herself, grew taut with reluctance and the other went easily into tears. "My own daughter turns against me! After all I done and suffered for her, she turns against me! Oh God!"

Oh, dont be a fool was on the tip of Frankie's tongue, but instead she awkwardly embraced her mother. "Hush, mamma, dont take on so: I never meant nothing like that, you know I didn't. Hush, you'll ruin your make-up you put on so careful."

The other turned to the mirror again, making bird-like dabs at her face with a greasy rag. "God, I'm a sight when I cry! But, Frances, you're so—so cold; I dont know what to make of you. I swear I want you to have more of a chance than I had, and when I see you making the same mistake I did, it—it—" tears were imminent again. Frankie leaned over and embraced her mother from behind.

"There, there. I aint going to do nothing I'll regret, I promise. Come on, now, and finish dressing. You got an engagement at four, you know."

The other raised her petulant puffy face again, and put her arms around Frankie once more. This time the daughter did not draw back. "You love mamma, dont you, honey?"

"Of course I do, mamma." They kissed. "Come on, let me do your hair for you."

Her mother sighed. "All right, you're so much quicker than I am. Oh, Frankie, I wisht you was a baby again." She turned back to the dressing table with her fears and her imminent problem and her stubborn womanish incomprehensions. Frankie's fingers wrought nimbly in her mother's hair, and the phone rang.

Frankie took down the receiver, a fat voice said Who is this, and she thought at once of black cigars.

"Who do you want?"

"Well, well," jovially, "if it aint little Frances! How's the girl, anyhow? Say, you cant guess what I've got in my pocket for a cute blond kid now, can you?"

"Who do you want, please?" Frankie's tone was icy. Her mother stood at her elbow, her eyes bright with suspicion. "Who is it?" asked the other. Frankie silently tendered the instrument and crossed to a window giving on an air shaft massed with wires and filled with the dusty sound of sparrows. Her mother's voice came to her in snatches: "—yes—yes— Be down in a mo—huh? yes— sure— Be down in a moment, honey. G'bye."

She rushed back to the mirror, and dabbed at her face again. "My God, wont I ever learn better than to cry before I'm going out? What a fright I am! Where's my hat and gloves?" Frankie stood at her elbow with them. "How do I look, honey? Wisht you could go with us, such a nice drive, but still— Oh, God, oh, God, to grow old! I wont be good for much longer, hon; that's why I'm so anxious about you. Christ, what a sight I am!"

Frankie reassured her, helping to adjust her various belongings.

"I'll be back Monday," her mother spoke from the door. "There's money in the top drawer, if you need it, you know. Be a good girl." She pecked Frankie on the cheek, then suddenly clasped her close.

"There, now, run along, or you'll cry again." Frankie released herself and pushed her mother from the room. "Good-bye, have a nice time."

Her mother gone at last, Frankie raised the drawn shades and approaching the mirror she examined her reflection unsparingly, pulling the skin of her face, pinching her flesh until the bright healthy red came through.

4

Frankie lay in her bed gazing out of the window, across roof-tops, into the far dark sky. Throughout the world hundreds of girls lay like this, thinking of their lovers for a while, then of their babies. Once, Frankie used to lie thinking of Johnny, and being lonely for him at times, but now she hardly thought of him at all. Oh, she loved Johnny all right; but boys were such tactless blundering things, trying to synchronise the crude inescapable facts of life each with his own personal integrity. And you cant do this.

To tell the truth, Johnny kind of bothered her at times, going on about something that was done and that couldn't be undone. Trying to kid her, as well as himself into the belief that he could stand up like a highwayman and bid destiny halt and deliver. Gee, at times Johnny was worse than a movie.

And her mother's baffled rage had been terrible. Just as though I'd burned up a liberty bond, Frankie thought.

"And this is what you call doing something you wont regret," the other had almost screamed at her. "But what about me? What am I to do when I am too old for men to like any longer? Is this the way you repay the things I've gave you, by giving me another mouth to feed?"

Frankie tried vainly to stem the torrent of the other's anger: she would care for her mother in her turn.

"How? Can that fellow do it? Can he pay me the money I've spent on you?" But at last, even her mother's anger wore away into tears, even recriminations began to pall in her tearful trotting in and out with ice cream and toast and the few things Frankie drove herself to eat.

"What will folks think," her mother moaned, and Frankie replied tartly that people wouldn't have to think at all and therefore they wouldn't be always guessing, which was more than her mother could say. In fact, ever since the other had found out she had acted as though the whole thing were something Frankie could or should remedy. "Mother's such an awful kid, but she has been sweet to me," Frankie sighed, running her fingers lightly over her young belly, trying to imagine she could feel the baby already, staring out into the far dark sky.

She felt quite old, and very sick at the stomach; she kind of wished her mother was not such a fool. She'd kind of like to have someone she could—that she— You know how, when you've walked and walked until you're about all in and you know you car walk further if you have to, but you dont see how; and then someone comes along and gives you a lift and dont try to talk to you at all but just takes you where you are going and then lets you out? Not God: she didn't believe much in prayer. When she was five she had prayed for a doll that could open and close her eyes, and she hadn't got it.

"Oh, hell," she said, "if I just wasn't so damn sick! That's what gives me the willies so." But the nausea would pass away after a while, everything would pass away after a while. By next year all this will be forgotten, she thought—unless I've gotten into this fix again. One thing I wont ever do. I wont ever want no more toast and tea.

Frankie lay thinking of all the other girls throughout the world, lying with babies in the dark. Like the center of the world, she thought; wondering how many centers the world had: whether the world was a round thing with peoples' lives like fly-specks on it, or whether each person's life was the center of a world and you couldn't see anybody's world except yours. How funny it must look to whoever made it! Unless he, too, was the center of a world and couldn't see any other world except his. Or if he was a fly-speck on somebody else's world.

But it was more comforting to believe that she was the center of the world. That the world was centered in her belly. And I will keep it so! she told herself fiercely. I dont need Johnny nor mother to help me, neither.

"Oh, God, oh, God," her mother wailed, "what will become of us now? How can I hold up my head and meet my men friends with a daughter at home in the family way? What can I tell them?"

"Why must you tell them at all?" Frankie repeated wearily.

"And who'll look after you? Who'll give you a home? Do you think any man is going to take your brat, too?"

Frankie looked at her mother a steady moment. "Do you still think that I am waiting for some rich bird to fall for me? Do you still think that, knowing me like you ought?"

"Well, what are you going to do? Do you think marrying your fellow will help you and me? What has he got?"

Frankie turned her sick face to the wall. "I tell you again, I dont need any man to take care of me."

"Then what in the name of God," asked the other in tearful exasperation, "are you going to do? What did you do it for?"

Frankie looked at her mother again. "You old fool, I didn't do it to make Johnny marry me nor to get anything from him. I dont need Johnny nor any other man to keep me, and I never will. And if you could say the same thing you wouldn't be forever crying and pitying yourself for the things you've let life do to you."

And, having reaffirmed her personal integrity it was as though, as Johnny once said, she had been in a dark room and someone had turned up the lights. Life seemed so plain and inescapable that she wondered why she had ever let things fret her; and she thought, strangely, of the father she scarcely remembered: of the way he'd raise his round yellow head and swing her, screaming with laughter, in his hard hands. And there recurred to her a childish vision of him, triumphant though dead, among green waves.

Her mother's sobs from the other bed shuddered away into silence and dark and the measured respirations of sleep, and Frankie lay in the kindly dark, lightly stroking her young belly, staring out upon a dark world like hundreds of other girls, thinking of their lovers and their babies. She felt as impersonal as the earth itself: she was a strip of fecund seeded ground lying under the moon and wind and stars of the four seasons, lying beneath grey and sunny weather since before time was measured; and that now was sleeping away a dark winter waiting for her own spring with all the pain and passion of its inescapable ends to a beauty which shall not pass from the earth.

The Priest

His novitiate was almost completed. Tomorrow he would be confirmed, tomorrow he would achieve that complete mystical union with the Lord, which he had so passionately desired. In his studious youth he had been led to expect it daily; he had hoped to attain it through confession, through talk with those who seemed to have it; through living a purging and a self denial until the earthly fires which troubled him had burned themselves out with time. He passionately desired a surcease and an easing of the appetites and hunger of his blood and flesh, which he had been taught to believe were harmful: he expected something like sleep, a condition to which he would attain in which those voices in his blood would be stilled. Or rather, chastened. Not to trouble him more, at least: an exalted plane wherein the voices would be lost, sounding fainter and fainter, soon to be but a meaningless echo among the canyons and majestic heights of the glory of God.

But he had not gotten it. After talk with a father in his seminary he could return to his dormitory in a spiritual ecstasy, an emotional state in which his body was but the signboard bearing a flaming message to shake the world. His doubts were then allayed; he had neither doubt nor thought. The end of life was clear: to suffer, to use his blood and bone and flesh as a means for attaining eternal glory—a thing magnificent and astounding, forgetting that history and not the age made Savonarolas and Thomas a Beckets. To be of the chosen despite the hungers and gnawings of flesh, to attain a spiritual union with Infinite, to die—how could physical pleasure toward which his blood cried, be compared with this?

But, once with his fellow candidates, how soon was this forgotten! Their points of view, their callousness, were enigma to him. How could one be of the world and not of the world at the same time? And the dreadful doubt that perhaps he was missing something, that perhaps after all life was only what one could make of his short three score and ten of time, might be true. Who knows? who could know? There was Cardinal Bembo living in Italy in an age like silver, like an imperishable flower, creating a cult of love beyond the flesh, purged of all torturings of flesh. And was not this but an excuse, a palliation for this terrible fearing and doubting? was not the life of that long dead, passionate man such a one as his own: a fabric of fear and doubt and a passionate grasping after something beautiful and fine? Even something beautiful and fine meant to him a Virgin not calm with sorrow and fixed like a watchful benediction in the western sky; but a creature young and slender and helpless and (somehow) hurt, who had been taken by life and toyed with and tortured—a little ivory creature reft of her first born and raising her arms vainly upon a dying evening. In other words, a woman, with all of woman's passionate grasping for today, for the hour itself; knowing that tomorrow may never come and that today alone signifies, because today alone is hers. They have taken a child and made of her a symbol of man's old sorrows, he thought; and I too am a child reft of his childhood.

The evening was like a raised hand upon the west; night fell, and a new moon swam like a silver boat on a green sea. He sat upon his cot, staring out, while the voices of his fellows grew softer despite themselves with the magic of twilight. The world clanged without, and passed away—trolley cars and cabs and pedestrians. His companions talked of women, of love, and he said to himself: "Can these men become priests living in self denial, helping mankind?" He knew that they could, and would, which made it harder. And he recalled the words of Father Gianotti of whom he did not approve: "Throughout all of history man has instigated and engineered circumstances over which he has no control. And all he can do is to shape his sails to ride out the storm which he has himself brought about. And remember: the thing alone which does not change is laughter. Man sows, and reaps tragedy always: he puts into the earth seeds which he treasured, which are himself, and what is his harvest? Something of which he can have learned nothing and with which he cannot cope. The wise man is he who can withdraw from the world, regardless of his vocation, and laugh. Money you have, you spend it: you no longer have money. Laughter alone renews itself like the fabulous wine cup."

But mankind lives in a world of illusion, he uses his puny powers to create about him a strange and bizarre place. Even he did this, with all his religious affirmations, just as his companions did it with their eternal talk of women. And he wondered how many priests leading chaste lives relieving human suffering, were virgin, and whether or not the fact of virginity made any difference. Surely his companions could not be chaste: no one could speak of women in that familiar way and be unknown to them, and yet they would make good churchmen. It was as though a man were given certain impulses and desires without being consulted by the donor, and it remained with him to satisfy them or not. He himself could not do this, though; he could not believe that sexual impulses could disrupt a man's whole philosophy, and yet might be allayed in such a way. "What do you want?" he asked himself. He did not know: it was not so much wanting any particular thing as it was fearing that life and its meaning might be lost by him because of a phrase, empty words meaning nothing. "Surely, I should know how little words signify, in my profession."

And suppose there was something going about, some answer to the riddle of man at his hand, which he could not see. "Man wants but little here below," he thought; but to miss that little he does have!

Walking the streets, his problem became no clearer. The streets were filled with women: girls going home from work, their lithe young bodies became symbols of grace and beauty, of impulses antedating Christianity. "How many of them have lovers?" he wondered. Tomorrow I will scourge myself, I will pay penance for this in prayer and mortification, but now I shall think thoughts I have long wanted to.

Girls were everywhere: their thin garments shaped their stride along Canal street; girls going home to dinner—thinking food between their white teeth, of their physical pleasure in mastication and digestion, filled him with fire—to wash dishes; girls planning to dress and go out to dance among sultry saxophones and drums and colored lights, while they were young taking life like a cocktail from a silver salver; girls to sit at home reading books and dreaming of a lover on a white horse with silver trappings.

"Is it youth I want? Is it youth in me crying out to youth in others which troubles me? Then why does not exercise satisfy me —physical strife with other young men? Or is it Woman, the nameless feminine? Is my entire philosophy to be overthrown here? If one be born in this world to suffer such compulsions, where is my church, where that mystical union which has been promised me? And which is right: to obey these impulses and sin, or refrain and be forever tortured with the fear that I have somehow thrown away my life through abnegation?

"I will purge my soul," he told himself. Life is more than this, salvation is more than this. But ah, God, ah, God; youth is so much in the world! it is everywhere in the young bodies of girls dulled with work over typewriters or behind counters in stores, uncaged and free at last and crying for the heritage of youth, taking their soft agile bodies aboard street cars, each with her own dream, of who knows what? "Except that today is today, and is worth a thousand tomorrows and yesterdays!" he cried.

Ah, God, ah, God; he thought, if tomorrow will but come! Then surely, when I am become an ordained servant of God I will find ease; I will then know how to control these voices in my blood. Ah, God, ah, God, if tomorrow will but come!

At the corner was a cigar store with men buying tobacco, men through with work for the day and going home to comfortable dinners, to wives and children; or to bachelor rooms to prepare for engagements with mistresses or sweethearts—always women. And I, too, am a man: I feel as they do; I, too, would answer to soft compulsions.

He left Canal street, leaving the flickering electric signs to fill and empty the dusk, unseen by him and therefore lightless, just as trees are green only when looked at. Lights flared and dreamed in the wet street, the lithe bodies of girls shaped to their hurrying toward food and diversion and love, all this was behind him now; for far before him a church spire soared like a prayer arrested and articulate against the evening. His footfall said Tomorrow! Tomorrow!

"Ave Maria, deam gratiam . . . tower of ivory, rose of Lebanon. . . ."

Once Aboard the Lugger (I)

꧁~꧂

In the middle of the afternoon we made a landfall. Ever since we left the mouth of the river at dawn and felt the first lift of the sea, Pete's face had been getting yellower and yellower, until by midday and twenty four hours out of New Orleans, when we spoke to him he'd glare at us with his yellow cat's eyes, and curse Joe. Joe was his older brother. He was about thirty-five. He had some yellow diamonds big as gravel. Pete was about nineteen, in a silk shirt of gold and lavender stripes, and a stiff straw hat, and all day long he squatted in the bows, holding his hat and saying Jesus Christ to himself.

He wouldn't even drink any of the whiskey he had hooked from Joe. Joe wouldn't let us take any with us, and the Captain wouldn't have let us fetch it aboard, if he had. The Captain was a teetotaller. He had been in the outside trade before Joe hired him, where they took on cargoes of green alcohol in the West Indies and had it all flavored and aged and bottled and labeled and cased before they raised Tortugas. He said he never had been a drinking man, but if he ever had, he'd be cured now. He was a real prohibitionist: he believed that nobody should be allowed to drink. He was a New Englander, with a face like a worn doormat.

So Pete had to hook a couple of bottles from Joe, and we brought them aboard inside our pants leg and the nigger hid them in the galley, and between wheel tricks I'd go forward where Pete was squatting, holding his hat, and have a nip. Now and then the nigger's disembodied face ducked into the port, without any expression at all, like a mask in carnival, and he passed up a cup of coffee which Pete drank and like as not threw the cup at the nigger's head just as it ducked away.

"He done busted two of them," the nigger told me. "We ain't got but four left, now. I gwine give it to him in a bakingpowder can next time."

Pete hadn't eaten any breakfast, and he flung his dinner overside and turned his back while I ate mine, his face getting yellower and yellower, and when we fetched the island—a scar of sand with surf creaming along its windward flank and tufted with gnawed purple pines on a darkling twilit sea—his face and his eyes were the same color.

The Captain held inside. We passed into the island's lee. The motion ceased and we pounded along in slack water of the clearest green. To starboard the island stretched on, bastioned and sombre, without sign of any life at all. Across the Sound a low smudge of mainland lay like a violet cloud. From beyond the island we could hear the boom and hiss of surf, but inside here the water was like a mill-pond, with sunlight slanting into it in green corridors. And then Pete got really sick, leaning overside and holding his hat on.

Twilight came swiftly. The clear green of the water, losing the sun, darkened. We beat on across a pulseless surface fading slowly to the hue of violet ink. Against the sky the tall pines stood in shabby and gaunt parade. The smudge of mainland had dissolved. Low on the water where it had been, a beacon was like a cigarette coal. Pete was still being sick.

The engine slowed. "Forrard there," the Captain said at the wheel. I manned the anchor.

"Come on, Pete," I said, "Give me a hand with it. You'll feel better."

"Hell with it," Pete said. "Leave the bastard sink."

So the nigger came topside and we cleared the hawser. The engine stopped and our momentum died into a violet silence floored with whispering water.

"Let go," the Captain said. We tumbled the anchor over, the hawser rattling and hissing about our feet.

Just before dark came completely down a pale wing of rigid water and a green navigating light stood abruptly in the dusk two miles away and as abruptly faded.

"There her," the nigger said. "Gwine, too."

"What is it?"

"Rum chaser. Gwine to Mobile."

"Hope she stays there," I said. In the twilight my shirt felt warmer than I, drily so, like a garment of sand.

Pete wouldn't eat his supper, either. He sat humped in the bows, a filthy quilt about his shoulders, looking like a big disgruntled bird. He sat there while the nigger and I warped the dinghy alongside and until the Captain emerged with three spades and a flashlight. Then he refused unconditionally to get into the dinghy, and he and the Captain cursed each other at point-blank range in the darkness, in ferocious whispers.

But move he would not. So we left him there, humped in his quilt, his hat slanted in savage silhouette above the shapeless blob of the vessel lurking neither wholly hidden nor wholly revealed against the perspective of the Sound and the ghostly and sourceless echo of starlight and the new moon.

The dinghy moved in darkness, in silence save for small gurgling clucks of water as the nigger wielded the oars. At each invisible stroke I could feel the steady and fading surge of the thwart under my thighs. Milky serpentines seethed alongside, mooned with bubbled fire, in the nothingness which bore us and which slapped now and then beneath the keel with whispering, caressing shocks, as of soft and secret palms. Soon a lesser darkness smoldered laterally across the bows, the Captain humped in vague relief against it, and the nigger's rhythmic blobbing. It thickened still more. The dinghy lifted with a faint grating jar, and stopped. The new moon hung in the crests of the pines overhead.

We hauled the dinghy up. The Captain stood squinting at the skyline. The sand was white, faintly luminous in the starlight. Staring at it, it seemed to be within a hand's breadth of the face. Then as you stared it seemed to shrink dizzily away until equilibrium itself was lost, fading at last without demarcation into the spangled sky that seemed to take of the sand something of its quality of dizzy and faint incandescence and against which the pines reared their tall and ragged crests, forlorn and gallant and a little austere.

The nigger had lifted the shovels out of the dinghy and the Captain, having oriented himself, took up one of them. The nigger and I took up the other two and followed the dark blob of him across the beach and into the trees. The sand was grown over with a harsh undergrowth of some sort, tough and possessing that pointless perversity of random rusty wire. We struggled through it, the sand shifting beneath us, also with a sort of derisive perversity. The surge and hiss of surf came steadily out of the darkness upon our faces, with the cool, strong breath of the sea itself, and immediately before us the treacherous darkness burst into mad shapes and a tense, soundless uproar. For a moment it seemed that I could taste my very heart in my mouth and the nigger prodded heavily into me from behind, and in the yellow tunnel of the Captain's flashlight wildeyed and anonymous horned beasts glared at us on braced forelegs, then whirled and rushed soundlessly away with mad overreaching of gaunt flanks and tossing tails. It was like a nightmare through which, pursued by demons, you run forever on a shifting surface that gives no purchase for the feet.

My shirt felt colder than I, now, and damp, and in the dizzy darkness that followed the flash my heart consented to beat again. The nigger handed me my shovel and I found that the Captain had gone on.

"What in God's name was that?" I said.

"Wild cattle," the nigger said. "Island full of them. They'll run you in the daytime."

"Oh," I said. We slogged on and overtook the Captain halted beside a dune grown harshly over with the wirelike undergrowth. He bade us halt here while he prowled slowly about the dune, prodding at it with his shovel. The nigger and I squatted, our shovels beside us. My shirt was wet, cold to my body. The steady breathing of the sea came across the sand, among the pines.

"What are cattle doing on this island?" I whispered. "I thought it was uninhabited."

"I don't know," the nigger said. "I don't know what anything want here, walking around night and day in this sand, listening to that wind in them trees." He squatted beside me, naked to the waist, the starlight glinting faintly upon him, reflected by the sand. "Be wild, too." he said.

I killed a mosquito on the back of my hand. It left a huge, warm splash, like a raindrop. I wiped my hands on my flanks.

"Skeeter bad here," the nigger said.

I killed another on my forearm, and two bit me on the ankles at the same time, and one on the neck, and I rolled my sleeves down and buttoned my collar.

"They'll eat you up, without any shirt on," I said.

"No, sir," he said. "Skeeter dont bother me. Cant nothing off the land bother me. I got medicine."

"You have? On you?"

In the darkness somewhere the cattle moved, in dry crackling surges in the undergrowth. The nigger tugged at his middle and drew something from his waist—a cloth tobacco sack in which I could feel three small, hard objects, slung on a cord about his hips.

"Nothing from the land, eh? How about the water?"

"They aint no water charm," he said. I sat on my feet, covering my ankles, wishing I had worn socks. The nigger stowed his charm away.

"What do you go to sea for, then?"

"I dont know. Man got to die someday."

"But do you like going to sea? Cant you make as much ashore?"

The cattle moved now and then in the darkness, among the undergrowth. The breath of the sea came steadily out of the darkness, among the pines.

"Man got to die someday," the nigger said.

The Captain returned and spoke to us, and we rose and took up our shovels. He showed us where to dig, and he fell to with his own implement and we spaded the dry sand behind us, digging into the dune. As fast as we dug the sand obliterated the shovelmarks, shaling in secret, whispering sighs from above, and my shirt was soon wet and warm again, and where it clung to my shoulders the mosquitoes needled my flesh as though it were naked. We made progress however, the three rhythmic blobs of us like three figures in a ritualistic and illtimed dance against that background of ghostly incandescence and the deep breath of the sea stirring the unceasing pinetops overhead, for at last the nigger's shovel rang on metal—a single half thump, half clang which the breath of the sea took up and swept on with it among the pines and so away.

We uncovered the metal slowly, a broad, limber sheet of iron roofing, and presently the nigger and I were able to get our hands beneath the edge of it. We bent our backs and straightened our legs and heaved. The sand shifted, hissing drily. We heaved again. "Hah!" the nigger grunted beside me, and the metal sheet buckled and broke free with a single clashing report like that of a pistol fired inside a tin bucket, and it too drifted away on the breath of the sea and sand sifted down across the buckled metal and into the pit beneath it in fading whispers. Shhhhhhhhhhhhh. Shhhhhhhhhhhhhhhhhhh.

The nigger and I leaned on our shovels, panting a little and sweating a good deal, while the sea went Hush Hush through the pines. The Captain propped the corner of the metal up on his shovel and delved beneath it with his hands. I killed three more mosquitoes on my ankles and wished again that I had worn socks.

The Captain was half into the pit now, and he spoke to us again from the dry whispering of that tomb and we laid our shovels aside and helped him haul the sacks out. They were faintly damp, and sand clung to them, and we dragged them out onto the sand and the nigger and I took up one under each arm and he led the way back to the beach. The vessel was faintly visible against the starlight on the sound, a shadow among treacherous shades, motionless as an island or a rock. We stowed the sacks carefully in the dinghy and retraced our steps.

Back and forth we went, carrying those endless awkward sacks. They were difficult to hold, at best, would have been heartbreaking labor on good footing, but in shifting sand that bartered each step for the price of four, surrounded always by a soundless and vicious needling which I could not brush even temporarily off, that sense of nightmare returned ten fold—a sense of hopeless enslavement to an obscure compulsion, in which the very necessity for striving was its own derision.

We loaded the dinghy and the nigger pulled off in the darkness toward the vessel. Then I was making the trips alone, and still the sacks came out of the black gullet into which the Captain had wholly disappeared. I could hear the cattle moving about in the darkness, but they paid me no attention. With every return to the beach I tried to mark the stars, if they had moved any. But even they seemed to be fixed overhead, among the ragged crests of the pines and the constant breath of the sea in their sighing tops.

Pete returned in the dinghy with the nigger, with his hat on. He was sullen and uncommunicative, but he had stopped saying Jesus Christ. The Captain came out of his hole and looked at him, but said nothing, and with another hand the sacks moved faster, and when the nigger made his second trip out to the vessel, I had Pete for company. He worked well enough, as though his meditation on board after we left had imbued him with the necessity of getting the job done, but he spoke only once. That was when he and I got a little off the track and blundered into the cattle again.

"What the hell's that?" he said, and I knew there was a gun in his hand.

"Just some wild cattle," I said.

"Jesus Christ," Pete said, and then he paraphrased the nigger unawares: "No wonder they're wild."

Back and forth we went between the sibilant and ceaseless cavern and the beach, until at last Pete and the Captain and I stood again together on the beach waiting for the dinghy to return. Though I had not seen him moving, Orion was down beyond the high pines and the moon was gone. The dinghy came back and we went on board, and in the dark hold stinking of bilge and of fish and of what other nameless avatars through which the vessel had passed, we hauled and shifted cargo until it was stacked and battened down to the Captain's notion. He flicked the torch upon his watch.

"Three oclock," he said, the first word he had spoken since he quit cursing Pete yesterday. "We'll sleep till sunup."

Pete and I went forward and lay again on the mattress. I heard Pete go to sleep, but for a long while I was too tired to sleep, although I could hear the nigger snoring in the galley, where he had made his bed after that infatuated conviction of his race that fresh air may be slept in only at the gravest peril. My back and arms and loins ached, and whenever I closed my eyes it seemed immediately that I was struggling through sand that shifted and shifted under me with patient derision, and that I still heard the dark high breath of the sea in the pines.

Out of this sound another sound grew, mounted swiftly, and I raised my head and watched a red navigating light and that pale wing of water that seemed to have a quality of luminousness of its own, stand up and pass and fade, and I thought of Conrad's centaur, the half man, half tugboat, charging up and down river in the same higheared, myopic haste, purposeful but without destination, oblivious to all save what was immediately in its path, and to that a dire and violent menace. Then it was gone, the sound too died away, and I lay back again while my muscles jerked and twitched to the fading echo of the old striving and the Hush   Hush
         of the sea in my ears.

Once Aboard the Lugger (II)

We were still working on the pump when daylight came. The nigger fetched us coffee, which we drank without stopping. After a while I heard Pete topside. He came and peered down the companion, with his slanted straw hat and his yellow eyes. Pete was Joe's brother. Joe owned the boat. Then Pete went away. A moment later I could hear his heels thumping against the hull amidships. The exhaust pipe was still hot. It was touchy business, working around it.

All of a sudden I didn't hear Pete's heels anymore. At that moment the nigger thrust his head around the galley bulkhead.

"Boat," he whispered. The Captain and I, stooping, looked at one another, and in that silence we could hear the engine; a real engine, not a kicker like ours. It sounded like an aeroplane at half speed. The Captain whispered:

"What boat?"

"Big half-decker. Cant see but two men in her. Coming up fast." The nigger went away.

We looked at one another, listening to the boat. It came up fast. Then she shut off, and it seemed to me that I could hear the water under her stem. Then Pete spoke.

"Have we got any what?"

I could hear the voice, but not the words.

Pete spoke again. "Fish-bait? What do I want with fish-bait? This is a private yacht. Gloria Swanson and Tex Rickard are down stairs eating breakfast."

The engine went on again, then ceased, as if they were jockeying her alongside. The Captain climbed onto the engine and looked through the port.

I could hear the words this time.

"Who're you? Admiral Dewey?"

A second voice, a flat Alabama voice, said, "Shet up. Keep a-settin where you air, bud," it said.

The Captain climbed down. He leaned his bearded whisper. "Has that bastard got a gun?"

"Had one last night," I whispered. The Captain cursed in a whisper. We leaned over the engine.

"Who else you got there?" the Alabama voice said. "Shove her over closer, Ed. I dont aim to git wet no more this mawnin."

"What do you want to know for?" Pete said.

"You sit still and you'll see," the first voice said. It was a high voice, like a choir boy's. "You'll see so much you'll think you're Houdini," it said.

"Shet up," the flat voice said. The nigger thrust his head around the door. He spoke in a still whisper, like the words were shaped in silence, without breath or sound.

"They got us. What I do?"

"Go up where they can see you and get out of the way and stay there," the Captain whispered. The nigger's head went away. We could hear his bare feet hissing on the companion. Then the flat voice said, "There's a nigger" and then it sounded like someone had slammed a door, hard, in an empty house. It was like we could hear the reverberation going among the empty rooms until it ceased. Then we could hear a slow scraping against the deckhouse, and something tumbled slowly down the companion. It went slowly, like it was picking its way between falls. Then I jerked my hand away from the exhaust pipe. I was thinking, I'll have to find the soda myself, now.

Pete began cursing. His voice sounded like he was balanced on a girder or a beam.

"What the hell did you do that for?" the high voice shrieked.

"Cant stand a damn nigger," the flat voice said. "Never could. Set still, bud. Shove her over, Ed." Pete was cursing.

"Well, what did you do it for?" the high voice said. "Who do you think you are, anyway?"

"Shet up, dope. You set still, bud," the flat voice said. "He'll be a-guttin you with that pistol."

"Why cant he move, if he wants?" the high voice said. "Go on, Houdini. Move."

"Set still, bud," the flat voice said. "He wont hurt you if you behave yoself. Let him alone now, hophead. Grab a holt, there."

"Who you calling hophead?" the high voice said.

"All right, all right; I warn't, then." Pete was still cursing. He sounded like he was about to cry. I kept thinking about the soda. I was thinking, I'll ask him. When he comes down, I'll ask him. "Shet up, bud," the flat voice said. "That dont sound nice. Hurry up with that-ere rope. We aint got all day."

"Calling me a hophead," the high voice said.

"Shet up," the flat voice said. "You want I taken a wipe at yo haid with this-hyer gun bar'l? Hold her, now." The hulls jarred, scraped; a wash slapped us. Pete was still cursing. "Aint you 'shamed, cussin like that?" the flat voice said, then all of a sudden Pete's voice was cut off; his heels banged once against the hull, then something thumped against the deckhouse and we heard feet on the deck.

"Watch yourself," the Captain whispered. He went to the companion. Across the Sound I could see a low smudge of mainland, then a man was standing against it, with a shotgun.

"Hyer you air," he said. "Come out."

"All right," the Captain said. "Turn that thing away. I aint got a gun."

"You aint?" the man said. He stood aside. The Captain mounted. His upper body passed from view, his legs still climbing. "That's too bad," the man said. He grunted, like a nigger swinging an axe. The Captain lunged forward. His feet slipped off the step and his legs stuck back into the cuddy, still climbing, then they shot forward. Just before his feet disappeared his legs made a little concerted jerk and quit climbing. I found that I was still holding the pump, and I was thinking that maybe we didn't have any soda and wondering if you could cook without soda. I could hear them breaking out the forward hatch. The man looked down again.

"Come out," he said. I started up the steps and stumbled to my knees, the pump clattering on the steps.

"Leave it where it lays," the man said.

"It's the pump," I said.

"Yeuh?" I got up. He had red hair and a long red face. His eyes were china-colored. "Well, I'll be dawg, ef hyer aint another boy scout. Whut you doin way out hyer?"

"Fixing the pump," I said. "It got clogged up."

"I be dawg ef hyer aint a business now, where they got to draft chillen into it. Aint you skeered somebody'll tell yo maw on you?"

"You want me to come out?" I said.

"You better stay where you air, I reckon. G'awn and fix yo pump, so you kin git home. Wait. Turn yo backside around." I turned around. "I reckon you aint fool enough to go pullin no gun, noways, air you?"

"No," I said.

"Go ahead," he said. I felt for the pump. He squatted in the door, the shotgun across his knees. It was a sawed-off gun, like mail messengers use. I found the pump. "That's the best way," he said. "Jest ack sensible. If you haint no gun, all you risks is knockin over the haid." I fitted the pump on.

"I burned my hand pretty bad a while ago," I said.

"Yeuh? Put a little sody and butter on it."

"I cant. You killed the cook."

"Yeuh? Well, he never had no business out hyer. Place fer a nigger's behind a plow." I fitted the pump on. I could hear them in the hold and on the deck forward. The smell of the engine was beginning to make me sweat a little. I could smell where the nigger had slept last night, and another smell, as if they had broken some of the bottles. The man with the high voice was talking forward, then he came through the galley and stuck his head in the cuddy —a wop in a dirty cap and a green silk shirt without a collar. There was a diamond stud in the front of it, and he had an automatic in his hand. He looked at me.

"What about this one?" he said.

"Nothing," the other said. "Git on back there and git that stuff out." I fitted the pump.

"Call me a hophead, will you?" the wop said. "Who do you think you are, anyway?"

"Git on back there and git that stuff out," the other said. I could feel the wop looking at the back of my head.

"What do you think about it?" he said.

"Nothing," I said. I fitted the pump.

"Did you hyer me?" the man on deck said. "Git on back there and put that gun away." The wop went away. "I got durn near as much time fer a nigger as I have fer a durn dope," the man in the door said.

I looked at the pump. "I've been trying to put it on upside down," I said.

"Yeuh?" he said. A voice said something forward and topside. He rose on his haunches and looked across the deckhouse. "Bring him back hyer," he said. They came along the deck, then I saw Pete's legs. "Hyer's yo pardner needin help," the man with the shotgun said, rising. "Now you git down there and see ef you caint behave." He shoved Pete down the companion. Pete had lost his hat. His hair was mussed and there was a wild, dazed look on his face. He came down the steps like he was drunk and blundered against the wall and leaned there.

"They put you out?" I said.

He cursed, whimpering. "I never had a chance. I left my gun in my coat, and they jumped me so quick. . . . I kept telling Joe they were going to take us, some day. I kept telling—" he cursed, like he was fixing to cry. The wop came around the bulkhead, with his pistol.

"You aint done yet, air you?" the man on deck said.

"Calling me a hophead," the wop said. Then he saw Pete. "Well, well, here's Houdini. Want some more of it, Houdini?"

"Go to hell," Pete said, without looking back.

"I told you to put that gun up and stay out of here," the man on deck said.

"Hell with you," the wop said. "Who do you think you are, anyway? Want some more of it, Houdini?"

"Are you goin to git outen hyer, or am I comin down there and make you?" the man on deck said.

"Make who?" the wop said. They glared at one another.

"One mo yap outen you," the man in the door said, "and I'll tell Cap'm about you killin that nigger. I'll tell the priest—"

"I didn't!" the wop shrieked, "I didn't!" He turned toward me, waving the pistol. "You seen it!"

"We was lookin right at you," the other said. "We all seen you

364 · UNCOLLECTED STORIES

shoot him. Cant you even remember the folks you kill, you durn dope?"

The wop looked from one to the other of us. Pete was leaning against the wall, his back to the wop. The wop was slobbering a little, his whole face sort of jerking and twitching.

"I didn't," he whispered. "I didn't!" he shrieked, then he began to cry. He babbled something in Italian, tears running down his face. His face was dirty, and the tears looked like snail tracks. He crossed himself.

"'Taint no time fer prayin now," the man in the door said. "You reckon God'll pay any attention to whut you say? Git on outen hyer, you little sawed-off hophead."

"Hophead?" the wop shrieked. "Son!"

"Son!" the other said. He laid the gun down and swung his legs into the companion.

"Call me a hophead," the wop screeched, waving the pistol.

"Drop it!" the other said.

"Call me a hophead," the wop wailed. Pete was looking at him across his shoulder. The wop jerked the pistol down and Pete ducked his head away and the wop jabbed the pistol at him and shot him in the back of the head. It was a heavy Colt's and it slammed Pete into the wall. The wall slammed him again, like he'd been hit twice, and as he fell again and banged his head on the engine, the other man jumped over him, onto the wop.

The sound of the explosion kept on, slamming back and forth between the walls. It was like the air was full of it, and every time anybody moved, they jarred some more of it down, and I could smell powder and a faint scorching smell.

"Call me a hophead," the wop was screeching. The other man caught the pistol and wrenched the butt out of the wop's hand. His finger was still in the trigger guard and he arched his body to ease it, screeching sure enough, until the other tore the pistol free. Then the tall man held him by the front of his shirt and slapped him, rocking his head from side to side. They sounded like pistol shots. Then a voice topside yelled something and the man dragged the wop to the galley door and flung him through it.

"Now," he said, "git on up there. Show yo face back hyer one mo time and I'll tear it off." He came back to the companion and thrust his head out.

Pete was lying with his face against the engine. I could hear water lapping between the two hulls and I smelled scorching hair again, and I stood there waiting to be sick. The man came back.

"Hit's that-ere cutter," he said. He lifted Pete away from the engine. I quit smelling scorched hair. "Better come up outen hyer, bud," the man said. "Come on." I followed him up the steps, into the breeze. Where it blew on me I could feel myself sweating. Around the corner of the deckhouse the Captain's feet stuck, his toes flopped over. But what surprised me was that it was still early in the morning. It seemed like it ought to be noon, at least, but the sun hadn't yet reached the tops of the pines on the island. About two miles inshore I saw the cutter again, rushing along on her rigid white wings like last night, her pennon stiff as a board, and I watched her pass and thought of Conrad's centaur, the half man, half tugboat charging back and forth in the same high-eared, myopic solitude.

"Gwine to Gulfpo't," the man said. "Dance tonight, I reckon. . . . Hyer, set down and smoke a cigareet. You'll feel better." I sat down against the deckhouse, facing the island and he offered me a cigarette, but I turned my face away. "Them durn wops," he said. "You jest set hyer. We'll be done soon."

I leaned back and shut my eyes, waiting to get sick. My hand smarted, but not very much. I could hear them working back and forth between the two boats. Someone came into the engine room and went forward again, with a lot of slow, bumping sounds. Then the noise forward ceased. I could hear them in their boat now. Feet came around the deckhouse, but I didn't look up.

"Well, Houdini," the wop said, "want any more of it?"

"Git in that boat," the other man said. "Better git that pump fixed and clear outen hyer," he said. "So long."

The hulls jarred, scraped. The big engine started, the propeller swished. But I didn't look around. I sat against the deckhouse, looking at the ragged pines like illcast bronze against the cobalt sky and the blanched scar of beach and the bright green water.

The sound of the engine came back for a long time. But at last it died completely away. A sea eagle swooped balancing into one of the pines and tilted there, the sun glinting on the slow, preening motions of its wings, and I watched it, waiting to get sick.

The Captain came aft, holding onto the deckhouse. His head was bloody. Someone had doused him with a pail, and the blood had streaked down his face like thin paint. He looked at me for a while.

"Got that pump fixed?"

"I dont know. Yes. I've got it fixed."

He went down the companion, slowly. I could hear him below, then he came back with a shirt in his hand and squatted beside me and tore the shirt down the middle.

"Take a turn with this," he said. I bound up his head. Then we finished connecting the pump and started the engine and went forward. The hatch was open. It reeked horribly. I didn't look in. We got the anchor up and the Captain squared her away along the island. The breeze freshened with motion, and I leaned against the deckhouse, letting the breeze blow on me where I was sweating.

"Engineer," the Captain said. I looked back. "See about them fellers in the hold."

I went to the hatch, but I didn't look in. I sat down and swung my legs into the hatch, letting the wind blow on me.

"You, Engineer," the Captain said.

"They're all right."

"Carry them back to the galley."

"Wont they do here?"

"Carry them back to the galley."

They had smashed a lot of it. I could feel broken glass under my feet, so I shuffled my feet along the floor, pushing the glass aside. It smelled horrible.

There was a scuttle in the bulkhead. Pete went through easily. But the nigger, naked from the waist up, was pretty bloody, where they had dumped him in on the broken bottles and then trampled on him, beside the wound itself, which began to bleed again when I moved him. I wedged him into the scuttle and went around into the galley and hauled at him. I tried to slip my hand down and catch the waist of his pants, but he stuck again and something broke and my hand came free with the broken string on which his charm—a cloth tobacco sack containing three hard pellets—the charm which he had said would protect him from anything that came to him across water—hung, the soiled bag dangling at the end of it. But at last I got him through.

My hand was smarting again, and all at once we passed out of the island's lee and the boat began to roll a little, and I leaned against the grease-crusted oil stove, wondering where the soda was. I didn't see it, but I saw Pete's bottle, the one he had brought aboard with him in New Orleans. I got it and took a big drink. As soon as I swallowed I knew I was going to be sick, but I kept on swallowing. Then I stopped and thought about trying to make it topside, but I quit thinking about anything and leaned on the stove and got pretty sick. I was sick for a good while, but afterward I took another drink and then I felt a little better.

Miss Zilphia Gant

I

Jim Gant was a stock trader. He bought horses and mules in three adjoining counties, and with a hulking halfwitted boy to help him, drove them overland seventy-five miles to the Memphis markets.

They carried a camping outfit with them in a wagon, passing only one night under roof during each trip. That was toward the end of the journey, where at nightfall they would reach . . . the first mark of man's hand in almost fifteen miles of cypress-and-cane river jungle and worn gullies and second-growth pine . . . a rambling log house with stout walls and broken roof and no trace whatever of husbandry . . . plow or plowed land . . . anywhere near it. There would be usually from one to a dozen wagons standing before it and in a corral of split rails nearby the mules stamped and munched, with usually sections of harness still unremoved: about the whole place lay an air of transient and sinister dilapidation.

Here Gant would meet and mingle with other caravans similar to his, or at times more equivocal still, of rough, unshaven, overalled men, and they would eat coarse food and drink pale, virulent corn whiskey and sleep in their muddy clothes and boots on the puncheon floor before the log fire. The place was conducted by a youngish woman with cold eyes and a hard infrequent tongue. There was in the background a man, oldish, with cunning reddish pig's eyes and matted hair and beard which lent a kind of ferocity to the weak face which they concealed. He was usually befuddled with drink to a state of morose idiocy, though now and then they would hear him and the woman cursing one another in the back or beyond a closed door, the woman's voice cold and level, the man's alternating between a rumbling bass and the querulous treble of a child.

After Gant sold his stock he would return home to the settlement where his wife and baby lived. It was less than a village, twenty miles from the railroad in a remote section of a remote county. Mrs. Gant and the two-year old girl lived alone in the small house while Gant was away, which was most of the time. He would be at home perhaps a week out of each eight. Mrs. Gant would never know just what day or hour he would return. Often it would be between midnight and dawn. One morning about dawn she was awakened by someone standing in front of the house, shouting "Hello, Hello" at measured intervals. She opened the window and looked out. It was the halfwit.

"Yes?" she said. "What is it?"

"Hello," the halfwit bawled.

"Hush your yelling," Mrs. Gant said, "where's Jim?"

"Jim says to tell you he ain't coming home no more," the halfwit bawled. "Him and Mrs. Vinson taken and went off in the waggin. Jim says to tell you not to expect him back." Mrs. Vinson was the woman at the tavern, and the halfwit stood in the making light while Mrs. Gant in a white cotton nightcap leaned in the window and cursed him with the gross violence of a man. Then she banged the window shut.

"Jim owes me a dollar and six bits," the halfwit bawled. "He said you would give it to me." But the window was shut, the house silent again; no light had ever shown. Yet still the halfwit stood before it, shouting "Hello, Hello" at the blank front until the door opened and Mrs. Gant came out in her nightdress, with a shotgun and cursed him again. Then he retreated to the road and stopped again in the dawn, shouting "Hello, Hello" at the blank house until he tired himself at last and went away.

Just after sunup the next morning Mrs. Gant, with the sleeping child wrapped in a quilt, went to a neighbor's house and asked the woman to keep the child for her. She borrowed a pistol from another neighbor and departed. A passing wagon, bound for Jefferson, took her aboard and she passed slowly from sight that way, sitting erect in a shoddy brown coat, on the creaking seat.

All that day the halfwit told about the dollar and seventy-five cents which Gant had taken from him and told him Mrs. Gant would repay. By noon he had told them all singly, and hoarse, voluble and recapitulant, he would offer to stop them and tell them again as they gathered at the store over the pistol incident. An ancient mariner in faded overalls he pursued them, gesticulant, shock-haired, with a wild eye and drooling a little at the mouth, telling about the dollar and seventy-five cents.

"Jim said for me to git it from her. He said she would give hit to me."

He was still talking about it when Mrs. Gant returned ten days later. She returned the pistol with no more than thanks. She had not even cleaned it nor removed the two exploded cartridges . . . a hale, not-old woman with a broad, strong face: she had been accosted more than once during her sojourn in those equivocal purlieus of Memphis, where, with a deadly female intuition, an undeviating conviction for sin (who had never been further away from home than the county seat and who had read no magazines and seen no movies) she sought Gant and the woman with the capability of a man, the pertinacity of a Fate, the serene imperviousness of a vestal out of a violated temple, and then returned to her child, her face cold, satiate and chaste.

The night of her return she was called to the door. It was the halfwit.

"Jim says you would give me that dollar and. . . ."

She struck him, felled him with a single blow. He lay on the floor, his hands lifted a little, his mouth beginning to open in horror and outrage. Before he could shriek she stooped and struck him again, jerking him up and holding him while she beat him in the face, he bellowing hoarsely. She lifted him bodily and flung him from the porch to the ground and entered the house, where his cries had roused the child. She sat and took it onto her lap, rocking it, her heels clapping hard and rythmic at each thrust, hushing it by singing to it in a voice louder, more powerful, than its own.

Three months later she had sold the house for a good price; and she moved away, taking with her a battered trunk tied with cotton rope and the shotgun and the quilt in which the child slept. They learned later that she had bought a dressmaking shop in Jefferson, the county seat.

II

They told in the town how she and her daughter, Zilphia, lived in a single room twelve feet square for twenty-three years. It was partitioned off from the rear of the shop and it contained a bed, a table, two chairs and an oil stove. The rear window gave upon a vacant lot where farmers tethered their teams on market days and where sparrows whirled in gusty clouds about the horse and mule droppings and the refuse from the grocery store beneath. The window was barred and in it for the seven years before the county Health Officer forced Mrs. Gant to let Zilphia go to school, the farmers, hitching or unhitching, would see a wan small face watching them, or, holding to the bars, coughing: a weak hacking sound soon blown away along the air, leaving the still pale face as before with something about it of that quality of Christmas wreaths in a forgotten window.

"Who is that?" one asked.

"Gant's gal. Jim Gant. Used to live out to the Bend."

"Oh. Jim Gant. I heard about that." They looked at the face. "Well, I reckon Mrs. Gant ain't got a whole lot of use for men-folks no more." They looked at the face. "But she ain't no more than a child yet."

"I reckon Mrs. Gant ain't taking no risk."

"Hit ain't her risk. Hit's whoever's risk that would chance her."

"Hit's a fact. Sho."

That was before Mrs. Gant came upon Zilphia and the boy lying inside a worn horse-blanket in the woods one day. It was during the time when, every morning and again at one o'clock they would see the two of them going toward the school, and every noon and afternoon returning to the barred room above the vacant lot. At midmorning recess time Mrs. Gant would close the shop and when the dismissal bell rang, she would be standing at the corner of the playground, upright, erect in a shapeless dress of dull black and an oil cloth sewing apron and her bosom festooned with threaded needles; still comely in a harsh way. Zilphia would cross the playground straight to her and the two of them would sit on the stone coping above the street level, side by side and not talking while the other children ran with random shouts back and forth behind them, until the bell rang again and Zilphia returned to her books and Mrs. Gant to the shop and the seam which she had laid aside.

They told how it was a client of Mrs. Gant's that got Zilphia in school. One day in the shop she was talking to Zilphia about school; Zilphia was nine then. "All the boys and girls go. You'll like it." Her back was to the room. She did not hear the machine cease, she only saw Zilphia's eyes go suddenly blank and then fill with terror. Mrs. Gant stood over them.

"Go home," she said. Zilphia . . . she did not turn and walk away: she seemed to dissolve behind her wan, haunting face and terrified eyes. The client rose. Mrs. Gant was thrusting a wad of cloth into her arms. "Get out of here," she said.

The client fell back, her hands raised, the half-finished dress cascading to the floor. Mrs. Gant picked it up and thrust it at her again, her hands hard in a series of restrained blows. "Get out of my shop," she said. "Don't you never come here again."

Mrs. Gant went back to the room. Zilphia crouched in the corner, watching the door. Mrs. Gant drew her out by one thin arm. She began to beat Zilphia, striking her about the body with her flat hand while Zilphia's thin arm appeared to elongate like rubber hose as she silently wrenched and strained. "Bitches!" Mrs. Gant said: "bitches!" She ceased as suddenly and sat on the bed and drew Zilphia toward her. Zilphia resisted. She began to cry and vomit, her eyeballs back-rolling until only the whites showed, shrieking and retching. Mrs. Gant got her to bed and sent for the doctor.

At that time Zilphia was pole-thin, with a wan, haunted face and big, not-quite-conquered eyes, going to and from school at her mother's side, behind her small tragic mask of a face. In her third year she refused one day to go back to school. She would not tell Mrs. Gant why: that she was ashamed to never be seen on the street without her mother. Mrs. Gant would not let her stop. In the spring she was ill again, from anemia and nervousness and loneliness and actual despair.

She was sick for a long time. The doctor told Mrs. Gant that Zilphia would have to have companionship, to play with children of her own age and out-of-doors. When Zilphia was convalescent Mrs. Gant came in one day with a miniature cook stove. "Now you can have the girls in and you can cook," she said. "Won't that be nicer than visiting?" Zilphia lay on the pillow, not less white than it. Her eyes looked like holes thumbed into a piece of blotting paper. "You can have a tea party every day," Mrs. Gant said. "I'll make dresses for all the dolls."

Zilphia began to cry. She lay on the pillow, crying, her hands at her sides. Mrs. Gant took the stove away. She took it back to the store and made them return her money.

Zilphia was convalescent for a long time. She still had sudden crying fits. When she was up Mrs. Gant asked her what girls she would like to visit. Zilphia named three or four. That afternoon Mrs. Gant locked the shop. She was seen in three different parts of town, looking at houses. She stopped passers. "Who lives there?" she said. They told her. "What family have they got?" The passer looked at her. She faced him steadily: a strong, still comely woman. "Have they got any boys?"

The next day she gave Zilphia permission to visit one of them. Zilphia would go home with the girl from school on certain days and they played in the barn or, in bad weather, in the house. At a certain hour Mrs. Gant appeared at the gate in a black shawl and bonnet and she and Zilphia returned to the barred room above the lot. And each afternoon . . . behind the barn a short pasture sloped to a ditch where scrub cedars grew . . . in these cedars Mrs. Gant sat on a wooden box from the time school was out until the time for Zilphia to start home, when she would hide the box again and go around by the next street to the gate and be waiting there when Zilphia emerged from the house. She did not watch the barn or, in the winter time, the house; she just sat there . . . a woman who for twelve years had been growing into the outward semblance of a man until now at forty there was a faint shadow of moustache at the corner of her mouth . . . in the timeless patience of her country raising and her cold and implacable paranoia, in the mild weather, or with the shawl drawn close about her against the rain and cold.

In Zilphia's thirteenth year Mrs. Gant began to examine her body each month. She made Zilphia strip naked and stand cringing before her while the savage light fell through the bars and the gray winter drove above the lot. After one of these examinations . . . it was in the spring . . . she told Zilphia what her father had done and what she had done. She sat on the bed while Zilphia cringed swiftly into her clothes, telling her about it in a cold, level voice, in the language of a man while Zilphia's thin body shrank and shrank as though in upon itself, as though at the impact of the words. Then her voice ceased. She was sitting on the bed, upright, motionless, her cold mad eyes gone blank as a statue's; and standing before her, her mouth open a little, Zilphia thought of a rock or a pile from which an abruptly undammed stream has roared away.

They lived now in a kind of armistice. They slept in the same bed and ate of the same food for days in complete silence; sitting at the machine Mrs. Gant would hear Zilphia's feet pass through the room and cease beyond the stairs to the street, without even raising her head. Yet now and then she would close the shop and with the shawl about her shoulders she would repair to the less frequented streets and lanes on the edge of town and after a while she would meet Zilphia walking rapidly and aimlessly. Then together they would return home without a word between them.

One afternoon Zilphia and the boy were lying beneath the blanket. It was in a ditch in the woods on the outskirts of town, within hailing distance of the highroad. They had been doing this for about a month, lying in the mutual, dreamlike mesmeric throes of puberty, rigid, side by side, their eyes closed, not even talking. When Zilphia opened her eyes she was looking up at Mrs. Gant's inverted face and foreshortened body against the sky.

"Get up," Mrs. Gant said. Zilphia lay quietly looking up at her. "Get up, you bitch," Mrs. Gant said.

The next day Zilphia withdrew from school. In an oil cloth sewing apron she sat in a chair beside the window which gave upon the square; beside it Mrs. Gant's machine whirred and whirred. The window was not barred. Through it she watched the children with whom she had gone to school begin to fall into inevitable pairs and pass into and out of her vision, some of them as far as the minister or the church; one year she made the white gown for the girl whom she used to visit; four years later, dresses for her daughter. She sat beside the window for twelve years.

III

In the town they told about Miss Zilphia's beau, with amusement and pity and, here and there, with concern. "He'll take advantage of her," they said. "It ought not to be allowed. A person of her . . . surely they would not sell her a license, even if. . . ." She was a neat woman, with neat hair. Her skin was the color of celery and she was a little plump in a flabby sort of way. Her glasses lent a baffled, ascetic look to her face, enlarging her opaque irises. As long as she had a needle in her fingers and was unobserved, her movements were direct, assured; but on the street, in the hat and clothes which her mother made for her, they had that vague, indefinite awkwardness of the nearsighted.

"But surely you don't think that she . . . of course, her mother is crazy, but Zilphia . . . poor girl."

"It's a shame. A tramp painter. She should be protected. How her mother can be so blind I cannot. . . ."

He was a young man with black hair and eyes like wood ashes. One day Mrs. Gant found that he had been painting in the window at Zilphia's chair for two days. She moved Zilphia into the back room . . . it was now a fitting room; for two years now they had been living in a frame bungalow bleak as a calendar picture, on an obscure street . . . and when he came inside to paint the walls Mrs. Gant closed the shop and she and Zilphia went home. For eight days Zilphia had a holiday, the first in twelve years.

Robbed of her needle, of the slow mechanical manipulation, Zilphia's eyes began to pain her, and she could not sleep well. She would wake from dreams in which the painter performed monstrously with his pot and brush. In the dream his eyes were yellow instead of gray, and he was always chewing, his chin fading away into the blurred drool of the chewing; one night she waked herself by saying aloud, "He's got a beard!" Now and then she dreamed of the pot and brush alone. They would be alive, performing of themselves actions of monstrous and ritualled significance.

After eight days Mrs. Gant fell ill; idleness brought her to bed. One night they had the doctor. The next morning Mrs. Gant rose and dressed and locked Zilphia into the house and went to town. Zilphia watched from the window her mother's black-shawled figure toil slowly down the street, pausing now and then to hold itself erect by the fence. An hour later she returned, in a hired cab, and locked the door and took the key to bed with her.

For three days and nights Zilphia sat beside the bed where the gaunt, manlike woman . . . the moustaches were heavier now and grizzled faintly . . . lay rigid, the covers drawn to her chin and her eyes closed. Thus it was that Zilphia could never tell if her mother slept or not. Sometimes she could tell by the breathing, then she would search carefully and infinitesimally among the bed clothing for the keys. On the third day she found them. She dressed and left the house.

The inside of the shop was half finished, reeking of turpentine. She opened the window and took her old chair beside it. When she heard his feet at last on the stairs she found that she was sewing, without any recollection of what the garment was or when she had taken it up. With the needle in her hand she sat looking up at him, blinking a little behind the glasses until he removed them.

"I knowed, once them glasses was off," he said. "I kept looking for you and looking for you. And when she come in here and I was working I could hear her on the steps a long time, a step at a time then stop, until she was in the door yonder, holding to the door and sweating like a nigger. Even after she had done fainted she wouldn't let go and faint. She just laid there on the floor sweating and sweating and counting the money out of her purse and telling me to be out of town by sundown." He stood beside the chair, holding the glasses in his hand. She watched the dark rim of paint under his nails, smelling his odor of turpentine. "I'll get you out of it. That old woman. That terrible old woman. She'll kill you yet. I know she is crazy now. I've heard. How she's done you. I've talked to folks. When they told me where you lived at I'd walk past the house. I could feel her watching me. Like she was watching me through the window. No hiding; just standing there looking at me and waiting. One night I come into the yard. After midnight it was. The house was dark and I could feel her standing there, looking at the dark where I was and waiting. Watching me like when she fainted that day and wouldn't faint until I was out of town. She just laid there on the floor sweating, with her eyes shut, telling me to leave the job like it was and be out of town by night. But I'll get you out of it. Tonight. Now. Not ever again any more." He stood above her. The dusk was thickening; the final swirl of sparrows swept across the square and into the locust trees about the courthouse. "All the time I was watching you I kept thinking about you wearing glasses, because I used to say I wouldn't never want a woman that wore glasses. Then one day you looked at me and all of a sudden I was seeing you without the glasses. It was like the glasses was gone and I knew then that, soon as I saw you once without them, it wouldn't matter to me if you wore glasses or not. . . ."

They were married by a justice of the peace in the courthouse. Then Zilphia began to hang back.

"No," he said; "don't you see, if you go back now, if you risk her seeing you now. . . ."

"I've got to," Zilphia said.

"What has she ever done for you? What do you owe her? That terrible old woman. Don't you see, if we risk going there. . . . Come on, Zilphy. You belong to me now. You said to the judge you would do like I say, Zilphy. Now we are away, if we go back now. . . ."

"I've got to. She's my mother. I've got to."

It was full twilight when they entered the gate and went up the walk. She slowed, her hand trembled cold in his. "Don't leave me!" she said. "Don't leave me!"

"I won't ever leave you if you won't ever leave me. But we ought not to . . . Come on. It's time yet. I ain't scared for me. It's for you. Zilphy. . . ." They looked toward the house. Mrs. Gant, dressed, in the black shawl and bonnet, stood in the door with the shotgun.

"Zilphy," she said.

"Don't go," he said. "Zilphy."

"You, Zilphy," Mrs. Gant said without raising her voice.

"Zilphy," he said. "If you go in there . . . Zilphy."

Zilphia went on and mounted the steps. She moved stiffly. She seemed to have shrunk into herself, collapsing from inside, to have lost height, become awkward.

"Go in the house," Mrs. Gant said, without turning her head. Zilphia went on. "Go on," Mrs. Gant said. "Shut the door." Zilphia entered and turned, beginning to close the door. She saw four or five people halted along the fence, looking back. "Shut it," Mrs. Gant said. Zilphia shut the door carefully, fumbling a little at the knob. The house was still; in the cramped hall the shadows of the twilight loomed like a herd of motionless elephants. She could hear her heart faintly, but no other sound, no sound from beyond the door which she had closed upon her husband's face. She never saw it again.

For the next two days and nights he lay hidden without food in a vacant house across the street. Mrs. Gant locked the door, but instead of going back to bed she seated herself, fully dressed save for the oil cloth apron and the needles, in a chair at the front window, the shotgun leaning at her hand. For three days she sat there, rigid, erect, her eyes closed, sweating slowly. On the third day the painter quitted the vacant house and left town. That night Mrs. Gant died, erect and fully dressed in the chair.

IV

For the first six months she believed that he would hear about it and return for her. She set six months to the day. "He will come before then," she said. "He will have to come before then, because I am being true to him;" now that she was free she dared not even put into thinking the reasons why she should wait for him. For that reason she left the shop half finished, as he had left it, for a symbol of fidelity. "I have been faithful to you," she said.

The day came and passed. She saw it accomplish, quietly. "Now," she said, "that's finished. Thank God. Thank God." She realized how terrible the waiting and believing had been, the having to believe. Nothing was worth that. "Nothing," she said, crying quietly in the dark, feeling tranquil and sad, like a little girl at the spurious funeral of a doll; "nothing."

She had the painting completed. At first the odor of turpentine was terrible to her. It seemed to obliterate time as it had the stains of twenty-five years on the walls. Her life seemed to elongate, like rubber: from one time she seemed to see her hands prolonged into another one, fitting and pinning. Then she could think peacefully, since beyond the safe ritual of her fingers Zilphia Gant and her husband were like dolls, furious and tragic but quite dead.

The shop was doing well. Within a year she had a partner, but she lived alone in the house. She took three or four newspapers, thinking that she might some day see his name in print. After a while she was writing guarded significant letters to agony columns, mentioning incidents which only he could recognize. She began to read all the wedding notices, substituting her name for the bride's and his for that of the groom. Then she would undress and go to bed.

She would have to be careful about getting into sleep. She was much more careful about that than about getting into her clothes. But even then she sometimes slipped. Then she would lie in the dark, the mock orange bush beyond the window filling the silence with its faintest suggestion of turpentine, beginning to toss lightly from side to side like a surf getting up. She would think about Christ, whispering "Mary did it without a man. She did it;" or, rousing, furious, her hands clenched at her sides, the covers flung back and her opened thighs tossing, she would violate her ineradicable virginity again and again with something evoked out of the darkness immemorial and philoprogenitive: "I will conceive! I'll make myself conceive!"

One evening she opened the paper and began to read of a wedding in a neighboring state. She made the name substitutions as usual and had already turned the page when she realised that she was smelling turpentine. Then she realized that she had not had to make any substitution for the groom's name.

She cut the story out. The next day she went to Memphis for two days. A week later she began to receive weekly letters bearing the return address of a private detective agency. She stopped reading the papers; her subscriptions lapsed. Every night she dreamed of the painter. His back was toward her now; only by his elbows could she read the familiar action of the pot and brush. There was someone beyond him in the dream whom she could not see, hidden by that back which was less of man's than goat's.

She grew plumper, a flabby plumpness in the wrong places. Her eyes behind the shell-rimmed glasses were a muddy olive, faintly protuberant. Her partner said that she was not hygienically over-fastidious. People called her Miss Zilphia; her wedding, that three day sensation, was never mentioned. When on the weekly arrival of the Memphis letters, the postmaster rallied her on her city sweetheart, there was even in this less of insincerity than pity. After another year there was less of both than either.

By means of the letters she knew how they lived. She knew

more about each than the other did. She knew when they quarrelled and felt exultation; she knew when they were reconciled and felt raging and impotent despair. Sometimes at night she would become one of the two of them, entering their bodies in turn and crucified anew by her ubiquity, participating in ecstasies the more racking for being vicarious and transcendant of the actual flesh.

One evening she received the letter telling that the wife was pregnant. The next morning she waked a neighbor by running out of the house in her nightdress, screaming. They got the doctor and when she was well again she told that she had mistaken the rat poison for tooth powder. The postmaster told about the letters and the two looked upon her again with interest and curious pity. "Twice," they said, even though the letters continued to come; "what a shame. Poor girl."

When she recovered she looked better. She was thinner and her eyes had cleared up, and she slept peacefully at night for a while. By the letters she knew when the wife's time would be, and the day she went to the hospital. Although she had recovered completely she did not dream any more for some time, though the habit she had formed in her twelfth year of waking herself with her own weeping, returned, and almost every night she lay in the darkness and the mock orange scent, weeping quietly and hopelessly between sleep and slumber. How long must this go on? she said to herself, lying flat and still and for a time tear-flushed of even despair in the darkness and the dying rumor of turpentine; how long?

It went on for a long time. She was gone from the town for three years, then she returned. Ten years later she began to dream again. Then she was walking to and from school twice a day with her daughter's hand in hers, her manner on the street confident and assured, meeting the town with level and tranquil eye. But at night she still waked herself with her own weeping after the old habit, waking wide-eyed from a sleep in which for some time now she had been dreaming of negro men. "Something is about to happen to me," she said aloud into the quiet darkness and the scent. Then something did happen to her. One day it had happened, and after that she dreamed hardly at all any more, and then only about food.

V

At last the letter came telling of the birth of a daughter and of the mother's death. Enclosed was a newspaper clipping. The husband had been killed by a motor car while crossing the street to enter the hospital.

The next day Zilphia went away. Her partner said she would be gone a year, perhaps longer, to recover from her sickness. The letters from the city sweetheart ceased.

She was gone three years. She returned in mourning, with a plain gold band and a child. The child, a girl, had eyes like wood ashes and dark hair. Zilphia told quietly of her second marriage and her husband's death, and after a time the interest died away.

She opened the house again, but she also fixed a day nursery in the room behind the shop. The window was barred, so she need not worry about the child. "It's a nice pleasant room," she said. "Why, I grew up there, myself." The shop was doing well. The ladies never tired of fondling little Zilphia.

They still called her Miss Zilphia Gant. "Somehow you just can't conceive of her as a wife. If it were not for the child. . . ." It was no longer out of tolerance or pity now. She looked better; black became her. She was plump again in the wrong places, but to people in our town that and more is permitted a woman who has served her appointed ends.

She was forty-two. "She is as fat as a partridge," the town said. "It becomes her; it really does."

"I should be, from the way I enjoy my food," she said, pausing to chat with them on the way to and from school with little Zilphia's hand in hers and her open coat, stirring in the wind, revealing her sewing apron of black oil cloth, and the straight thin glints of needles in her black bosom and the gossamer random festooning of the thread.

Thrift

I

In messes they told of MacWyrglinchbeath how, a first-class air mechanic of a disbanded Nieuport squadron, he went three weeks' A.W.O.L. He had been given a week's leave for England while the squadron was being reequipped with British-made machines, and he was last seen in Boulogne, where the lorry set him and his mates down. That night he disappeared. Three weeks later the hitherto unchallenged presence of an unidentifiable first-class air mechanic was discovered in the personnel of a bombing squadron near Boulogne. At the ensuing investigation the bomber gunnery sergeant told how the man had appeared among the crew one morning on the beach, where the flight had landed after a raid. Replacements had come up the day before, and the sergeant said he took the man to be one of the replacements; it appeared that everyone took the man to be one of the new mechanics. He told how the man showed at once a conscientious aptitude, revealing an actual affection for the aeroplane of whose crew he made one, speaking in a slow, infrequent, Scottish voice of the amount of money it represented and of the sinfulness of sending so much money into the air in a single lump.

"He even asked to be put on flying," the sergeant testified. "He downright courted me till I did it, volunteering for all manner of off-duty jobs for me, until I put him on once or twice. I'd keep him with me, on the toggles, though."

They did not discover that anything was wrong until pay day

His name was not on the pay officer's list; the man's insistence—
his was either sublime courage or sublime effrontery—brought his
presence to the attention of the squadron commander. But when
they looked for him, he was gone.

The next day, in Boulogne, an air mechanic with a void seven-
day pass, issued three weeks ago by a now disbanded scout squadron, was arrested while trying to collect three weeks' pay, which
he said was owing to him, from the office of the acting provost
marshal himself. His name, he said, was MacWyrglinchbeath.

Thus it was discovered that MacWyrglinchbeath was a simultaneous deserter from two different military units. He repeated his
tale—for the fifth time in three days fetched from his cell by a
corporal and four men with bayoneted rifles—standing bareheaded
to attention before the table where a general now sat, and the
operations officer of the bomber squadron and the gunnery sergeant:

"A had gone doon tae thae beach tae sleep, beca' A kenned they
wud want money for-r thae beds in the town. A was ther-re when
thae boombers cam' doon. Sae A went wi' thae boombers."

"But why didn't you go home on your leave?" the general asked.

"A wou'na be spendin' sic useless money, sir-r."

The general looked at him. The general had little pig's eyes, and
his face looked as though it had been blown up with a bicycle
pump.

"Do you mean to tell me that you spent seven days' leave and
a fortnight more without leave, as the member of the personnel of
another squadron?"

"Well, sir-r," MacWyrglinchbeath said, "naught wud do they
but A sud tak' thae week's fur-rlough. I didna want it. And wi' thae
big machines A cud get flying pay."

The general looked at him. Rigid, motionless, he could see the
general's red face swell and swell.

"Get that man out of here!" the general said at last.

"'Bout face," the corporal said.

"Get me that squadron commander," the general said. "At once!
I'll cashier him! Gad's teeth, I'll put him in jail for the rest of his
life!"

"'Bout face!" the corporal said, a little louder. MacWyrglinchbeath had not moved.

"Sir-r," he said. The general, in mid-voice, looked at him, his mouth still open a little. Behind his mustache he looked like a boar in a covert. "Sir-r," MacWyrglinchbeath said, "wull A get ma pay for thae thr-r-ree weeks and thae seven hour-rs and for-rty minutes in the air-r?"

It was Ffollansbye, who was to first recommend him for a commission, who knew most about him.

"I give you," he said, "a face like a ruddy walnut, maybe sixteen, maybe fifty-six; squat, with arms not quite as long as an ape's, lugging petrol tins across the aerodrome. So long his arms were that he would have to hunch his shoulders and bow his elbows a little so the bottoms of the tins wouldn't scrape the ground. He walked with a limp—he told me about that. It was just after they came down from Stirling in '14. He had enlisted for infantry; they had not told him that there were other ways of going in.

"So he began to make inquiries. Can't you see him, listening to all the muck they told recruits then, about privates not lasting two days after reaching Dover—they told him, he said, that the enemy killed only the English and Irish and Lowlanders; the Highlands having not yet declared war—and such. Anyway, he took it all in, and then he would go to bed at night and sift it out. Finally he decided to go for the Flying Corps; decided with pencil and paper that he would last longer there and so have more money saved. You see, neither courage nor cowardice had ever functioned in him at all; I don't believe he had either. He was just like a man who, lost for a time in a forest, picks up a fagot here and there against the possibility that he might some day emerge.

"He applied for transfer, but they threw it out. He must have been rather earnest about it, for they finally explained that he must have a better reason than personal preference for desiring to transfer, and that a valid reason would be mechanical knowledge or a disability leaving him unfit for infantry service.

"So he thought that out. And the next day he waited until the barracks was empty, prodded the stove to a red heat, removed his boot and putty, and laid the sole of his foot to the stove.

"That was where the limp came from. When his transfer went through and he came out with his third-class air mechanic's rating, they thought that he had been out before.

"I can see him, stiff at attention in the squadron office, his b. o. on the table, Whiteley and the sergeant trying to pronounce his name.

" 'What's the name, sergeant?' Whiteley says.

"Sergeant looks at b.o., rubs hands on thighs. 'Mac—' he says and bogs down again. Whiteley leans to look-see himself.

" 'Mac—' bogs himself; then: 'Beath. Call him MacBeath.'

" 'A'm ca'd MacWyrglinchbeath,' newcomer says.

" 'Sir,' sergeant prompts.

" 'Sir-r,' newcomer says.

" 'Oh,' Whiteley says, 'Magillinbeath. Put it down, sergeant.' Sergeant takes up pen, writes M-a-c with flourish, then stops, handmaking concentric circles with pen above page while owner tries for a peep at b. o. in Whiteley's hands. 'Rating, three ack emma,' Whiteley says. 'Put that down, sergeant.'

" 'Very good, sir,' sergeant says. Flourishes grow richer, like sustained cavalry threat; leans yet nearer Whiteley's shoulder, beginning to sweat.

"Whiteley looks up, says, 'Eh?' sharply. 'What's matter?' he says.

" 'The nyme, sir,' sergeant says. 'I can't get—'

"Whiteley lays b. o. on table; they look at it. 'People at Wing never could write,' Whiteley says in fretted voice.

" ' 'Tain't that, sir,' sergeant says. ' 'Is people just 'aven't learned to spell. Wot's yer nyme agyne, my man?'

" 'A'm ca'd MacWyrglinchbeath,' newcomer says.

" 'Ah, the devil,' Whiteley says. 'Put him down MacBeath and give him to C. Carry on.'

"But newcomer holds ground, polite but firm. 'A'm ca'd Mac-Wyrglinchbeath,' he says without heat.

"Whiteley stares at him. Sergeant stares at him. Whiteley takes pen from sergeant, draws record sheet to him. 'Spell it.' Newcomer does so as Whiteley writes it down. 'Pronounce it again, will you?' Whiteley says. Newcomer does so. 'Magillinbeath,' Whiteley says. 'Try it, sergeant.'

"Sergeant stares at written word. Rubs ear. 'Mac—wigglin-beech,' he says. Then, in hushed tone: 'Blimey.'

"Whiteley sits back. 'Right,' he says. 'We've it correctly. Carry on.'

" 'Ye ha' it MacWyrglinchbeath, sir-r?' newcomer says. 'A'd no ha' ma pay gang wrong.'

"That was before he soloed. Before he deserted, of course. Lugging his petrol tins back and forth, a little slower than anyone else, but always at it if you could suit your time to his. And sending his money, less what he smoked—I have seen his face as he watched the men drinking beer in the canteen—back home to the neighbor who was keeping his horse and cow for him.

"He told me about that arrangement too. When he and the neighbor agreed, it was in emergency; they both believed it would be over and he would be home in three months. That was a year ago. "Twull be a sore sum A'll be owin' him for foragin' thae twa beasties,' he told me. Then he quit shaking his head. He became quite still for a while; you could almost watch his mind ticking over. 'Aweel,' he says at last, 'A doot not thae beasts wull ha' increased in value, too, wi' thae har-rd times.'

"In those days, you know, the Hun came over your aerodrome and shot at you while you ran and got into holes they had already dug for that purpose, while the Hun sat overhead and dared you to come out.

"So we could see fighting from the mess windows; we were carting off the refuse ourselves then. One day it crashed not two hundred yards away. When we got there, they were just dragging the pilot clear—all but his legs. He was lying on his back, looking up at the sky with that expression they have, until someone closed his eyes.

"But Mac—they were still calling him MacBeath—was looking at the crash. He was walking around it, clicking his tongue. 'Tzut, tzut,' he says. "Tis a sinfu' waste. Sinfu'. Tzut. Tzut. Tzut.'

"That was while he was still a three ack emma. He was a two soon, sending a little more money back to the neighbor. He was keeping books now, with a cheap notebook and a pencil, and a candle stub for nights. The first page was his bank book; the others were like a barograph of this war, tighter than a history.

"Then he was a one A.M. He began then to work over his ledger late into the night. I supposed it was because he had more money to worry him now, drawing, as he probably did, more a month than he ever had in his life, until he came to me for an N C.O.'s rating sheet. I gave it to him. A week later he had to buy a new candle. I met him.

" 'Well, Mac,' I said, 'have you decided to go for a sergeant yet?'

"He looked at me, without haste, without surprise. 'Ay, sir-r,' he says. He hadn't heard about flying pay then, you see."

Ffollansbye told about his solo:

"His new squadron were pups. I suppose as soon as he saw they were single-seaters, he realized that there would be no flying pay here. He applied for transfer to bombers. It was denied. It must have been about this time that he had the letter from his neighbor, telling that the cow had calved. I can see him now, reading the letter through to the last word, keeping all judgment and speculation and concern in abeyance until he had done, then sitting there —his pencil and paper useless in this case—weighing that delicate and unanticipated situation and its unpredictable ramifications of ownership, then deciding that circumstance would take care of it in good time.

"One day he waked up; the impulse, the need to, may have come like a germ in that letter. Not that he had ever soldiered, but now he began to show interest in the machines and in the operation of the controls, talking with the pilots, asking questions about flight, sifting and cataloguing the answers in his bunk at night. He became so—well, ubiquitous, tireless, made such an up-and-doing appearance when brass hats were about, that they made him a corporal. I suppose if I'd been there then I'd have believed that was his aim all along.

"But this time he had hitched to a star, in more than allegorical sense, it proved. It was in the middle of lunch one day when the alarm goes off. They rush out, officer and man, clutching napkins, in time to see a pup go down the aerodrome, the wings at a forty-five-degree angle, the tip practically dragging. It righted itself by putting the other wing down, and with the crash car wailing behind, it nosed up and shot perpendicularly for perhaps two hundred feet, hung for ten thousand years on the prop, flipped its tail up and vanished from view, still at that forty-five-degree angle.

" 'What—' the major says.

" 'It's mine!' a subaltern shouts. 'It's my machine!'

" 'Who—' the major says. The crash car comes wailing back, and at about a hundred m.p.h. the pup comes into view again,

388 · *UNCOLLECTED STORIES*

upside down now. The pilot wears neither goggles nor helmet; in the fleeting glimpse they have of him, his face wears an expression of wary and stubborn concern. He goes on, half rolls into a skid that swaps him end for end. He is now headed straight for the crash car; driver jumps out and flees for nearest hangar, the pup in vicious pursuit. Just as the driver, clutching head in both arms, hurls himself into the hangar, the pup shoots skyward again, hangs again on the prop, then ducks from sight, disappearance followed immediately by dull crash.

"They removed Mac from its intricate remains, intact but unconscious. When he waked he was again under arrest."

II

"And so," Ffollansbye said, "for the second time Mac had caused near apoplexy in high places. But this time he was not present. He was in detention camp, where he was calculating the amount of deficit which bade fair to be the first entry on the flying-pay page of his ledger. Meanwhile, at B.H.Q. and in London they considered his case, with its accumulated documents. At last they decided, as a matter of self-protection and to forestall him before he invented any more crimes for which K.R. & O. had no precedent, to let him have his way.

"They came and told him that he was for England and the school of aeronautics.

" 'If A gang, wull they be char-rgin' thae leetle unfor-rtunate machine against me?'

" 'No,' they said.

" 'Verra weel,' he said. 'A'm ready noo.'

"He returned to England, setting foot on his native side of the Channel for the first time in more than two years, refusing leave to go home, as usual. Perhaps it was that matter of the calf's economic legitimacy; perhaps he had figured the most minimated minimum of unavoidable outlay for the trip—knowing, too, that, whatever he discovered, he could not remain long enough to solidify against what he might find when he got there. But perhaps not. Perhaps it was just MacWyrglinchbeath."

Seven months later, a sergeant pilot, he was trundling an obsolete and unwieldy Reconnaissance Experimental back and forth

above the Somme while his officer observer spotted artillery fire
from the blunt, bathtubish nose of it. Big, broad-winged, the heavy
four-cylinder Beardmore engine thundering sedately behind and
above MacWyrglinchbeath's head, a temptation and potential victim to anything with a gun on it that could move seventy miles an
hour. But all the same, flying hours accumulated slowly in Mac-
Wyrglinchbeath's log book.

He and his officer carried on a long, intermittent conversation
as they pottered about the ancient thing between flights. The officer
was an artilleryman by instinct and a wireless enthusiast by inclination; between him and aviation was an antipathy which never
flagged. MacWyrglinchbeath's passion for accumulating flying
time was an enigma to him until, by patient probing, he learned of
the neighbor and the mounting hoard of shillings.

"So you came to the war to make money?" he said.

"Aweel," MacWyrglinchbeath said, "A wou'na be wastin' ma
time."

The officer repeated MacWyrglinchbeath's history to the mess.
A day or two later another pilot—an officer—entered the hangar
and found MacWyrglinchbeath head down in the nacelle of his
machine.

"I say, sergeant," the officer said to the seat of MacWyrglinchbeath's breeks. MacWyrglinchbeath backed slowly into complete
sight and turned over his shoulder a streaked face.

"Ay, sir-r."

"Come down a moment, will you?" MacWyrglinchbeath
climbed down, carrying a wrench and a bit of foul waste. "Robinson tells me you're a sort of financier," the officer said.

MacWyrglinchbeath laid the wrench down and wiped his hands
on the waste. "Aweel, A wou'na say just that."

"Now, sergeant, don't deny it. Mr. Robinson has told on
you. . . . Have a cigarette?"

"A'll no' mind." MacWyrglinchbeath wiped his hands on his
thighs and took the cigarette. "A smawk a pipe masel'." He accepted a light.

"I've a bit of business in your line," the officer said. "This day,
each month, you're to give me one pound, and for every day I get
back, I give you a shilling. What do you say?"

MacWyrglinchbeath smoked slowly, holding the cigarette as

though it were a dynamite cap. "And thae days when ye'll no fly?"

"Just the same. I owe you a shilling."

MacWyrglinchbeath smoked slowly for a while. "Wull ye gang wi' me as ma obsair-rver-r?"

"Who'll take up my bus? No, no: if I flew with you, I'd not need underwriting. . . . What do you say?"

MacWyrglinchbeath mused, the cigarette in his soiled hand. "'Twill tak' thinkin'," he said at last. "A'll tell ye the mor-rn."

"Right. Take the night and think it out." The officer returned to the mess.

"I've got him! I've got him hooked."

"What's your idea?" the C.O. said. "Are you spending all this ingenuity for a pound which you can only win by losing?"

"I just want to watch the old Shylock lose flesh. I should give his money back, even if I won it."

"How?" the C.O. said. The officer looked at him, blinking slowly. "They have an exchange basis between here and Gehenna?" the C.O. said.

"Look here," Robinson said, "why don't you let Mac be? You don't know those people those Highlanders. It takes fortitude just to live as they do, let alone coming away without protest to fight for a king whom they probably still consider a German peasant, and for a cause that, however it ends, he'll only lose. And the man who can spend three years in this mess and still look forward to a future with any sanity, strength to his arm, say I."

"Hear, hear!" someone cried.

"Oh, have a drink," the other said. "I shan't hurt your Scot."

The next morning MacWyrglinchbeath paid down the pound, slowly and carefully, but without reluctance. The officer accepted it as soberly.

"We'll start wi' today," MacWyrglinchbeath said.

"Righto," the officer said. "We'll start in a half hour."

Three days later, after a short conversation with Robinson, the C.O. called MacWyrglinchbeath's client aside.

"Look here. You must call that silly wager off. You're disrupting my whole squadron. Robinson says that if you're anywhere in sight, he can't even keep MacBeath in their sector long enough after the battery fires to see the bursts."

"It's not my fault, sir. I wasn't buying a watchdog. At least, I thought not. I was just pulling Mac's leg."

"Well, you look him out tomorrow and ask him to release you. We'll have Brigade about our ears at this rate."

The next morning the client talked to MacWyrglinchbeath. That afternoon Robinson talked to MacWyrglinchbeath. That evening, after dinner, the C.O. sent for him. But MacWyrglinchbeath was firm, polite and without heat, and like granite.

The C.O. drummed on the table for a while. "Very well, sergeant," he said at last. "But I order you to keep to your tour of duty. If you are reported off your patrol once more, I'll ground you. Carry on."

MacWyrglinchbeath saluted. "Verra gude, sir-r."

After that he kept to his tour. Back and forth, back and forth above the puny shell puffs, the gouts of slow smoke. From time to time he scanned the sky above and behind him, but always his eyes returned northward, where the other R. E. was a monotonous speck in the distance.

This was day after day, while Mr. Robinson, with his binocular, hung over the leading edge of the nacelle like a man in a bath who has dropped the soap overside. But every day the client returned, daily the shillings grew, until that day came when the shilling was profit, followed by another and another. Then the month was complete, and MacWyrglinchbeath paid down another pound. The profit was gone now, and his gaze was a little more soberly intent as he stared northward at brief intervals.

Mr. Robinson was leaning, down-peering, over the nacelle when the heavy engine behind him burst into thunderous crescendo and the earth pivoted one hundred and eighty degrees in a single swoop. He jerked himself up and looked behind, swinging his gun about. The sky was clear, yet they were moving at the R.E.'s sedate top speed. MacWyrglinchbeath was staring straight ahead and Robinson turned and saw, indicated by A-A bursts, the other R.E. plunging and darting like an ancient stiffkneed horse. Shrapnel unfolded and bloomed above it, and at last he made out the Fokker clinging to the R.E.'s blind spot. He swung his gun forward and cleared the mechanism with a short burst.

The two R.E.'s approached at a quartering angle, the first zigzagging just above the clinging German, all three losing altitude.

The first and last intimation the German had of the presence of the second R.E. was a burst from Robinson's gun. The German shot straight up, stalled, and burst into flames. Then MacWryglinch-beath, yawing violently to dodge the zooming German, saw Robinson fall forward over the edge of the nacelle, and at the same time a rake of tracer smoke along the fuselage beside him. He swerved; without pausing, the second German shot past and plumped full upon the tail of the first R.E., and again bullets ripped about MacWyrglinchbeath, coming from beneath now, where British infantry were firing at the German.

The three of them were not a hundred feet high when they flashed above the secondary lines and the tilted pink faces of the A-A battery. The German utterly disregarded MacWryglinch-beath. He hung upon the tail of the first R.E., which was still zigzagging in wild and sluggish yaws, and putting his nose down a little more and unfastening his belt, MacWryglinchbeath brought his machine directly above the German and a little behind him. Still the German seemed utterly unaware of his presence, and MacWyrglinchbeath put one leg over the nacelle and got from directly beneath the engine and pushed the stick forward. The German disappeared completely beneath the end of the nacelle and Robinson's dead body sprawled there; immediately afterward, MacWyrglinchbeath felt the prolonged shock. He cut the switch and climbed free of the nacelle, onto the bottom wing, where the engine wouldn't fall on him. "Sax shillin'," he said as the sudden earth swooped and tilted.

III

He climbed stiffly down from his Bristol and limped across the tarmac, toward his hut. His limp was pronounced now, a terrific crablike gait, for in the wet, chill October days his broken hips stiffened, even after fourteen months.

The flight was all in, the windows of the officers' mess glowed cheerily across the dusk; he limped on, thinking of tea, a drink, a cozy evening in his hut behind the locked door. That was against the young devils from the mess. Children they took now. The old pilots, mature men, were all dead or promoted to remote Wing offices, their places filled by infants not done with public school, without responsibility or any gift for silence. He went on and opened the door to his hut.

He stopped, the open door in his hand, then he closed it and entered the cubbyhole of a room. His batman had built the fire up in the miniature stove; the room was quite warm. He laid his helmet and goggles aside and slowly unfastened and removed his flying boots. Only then did he approach the cot and stand there, looking quietly at the object which had caught his eye when he entered. It was his walking-out tunic. It had been pressed, but that was not all. The Royal Flying Corps tabs and the chevrons had been ripped from shoulder and sleeve, and on each shoulder strap a subaltern's pip was fixed, and upon the breast, above the D.S.M. ribbon, were wings. Beside it his scarred belt lay, polished, with a new and shining shoulder strap buckled on. He was still looking soberly at them when the door burst open upon a thunderous inrush.

"Now, old glum-face!" a young voice cried. "He'll have to buy a drink now. Hey, fellows?"

They watched him from the mess windows as he crossed the aerodrome in the dusk.

"Wait, now," they told one another. "Wait till he's had time to dress."

Another voice rose: "Gad, wouldn't you like to see the old blighter's face when he opens the door?"

"Old blighter?" a flight commander sitting with a newspaper beneath the lamp said. "He's not old. I doubt if he's thirty."

"Good gad! Thirty! Gad, I'll not live to see thirty by ten years."

"Who cares? Who wants to live forever?"

"Stow it. Stow it."

"Ave, Cæsar! Morituri—"

"Stow it, stow it! Don't be a mawkish fool!"

"Gad, yes! What ghastly taste!"

"Thirty! Good gad!"

"He looks about a hundred, with that jolly walnut face of his."

"Let him. He's a decent sort. Shame it wasn't done sooner for him."

"Yes. Been a D.S.O. and an M.C. twice over by now."

"Got quite a decent clink record too. Deserted once, you know."

"Go on!"

"'Struth. And first time he was ever off the ground he nipped off alone on a pup. No instruction; ack emma then. Sort of private solo."

"I say, do you know that yarn they tell about him about hoarding his pay against peace? Sends it all home. Done it for years."

"Well, why not?" the flight commander said. "If some of you young puppies would just—" They shouted him down. "Clear off, the lot of you!" the flight commander said above the din. "Why don't you go and fetch him up here?"

They charged from the room; the noise faded in the outer dusk. The three flight commanders sat down again, talking quietly among themselves.

"I'm glad too. Trouble is, they should have done it years ago. Ffollansbye recommended him once. Dare say some ass hipped on precedent quashed it."

"Too bad Ffollansbye couldn't have lived to see it done."

"What a putrid shame."

"Yes. But you'd not know it from Mac. Ffollansbye told him when he put him up. Old Mac never said anything at all; just went on about his business. And then, when Ffollansbye had to tell him it was no go, he just sort of grunted and thanked him, and carried on as though it had never come up."

"What a ruddy shame."

"Yes. Sort of makes you glad you belong to the same squadron with a chap like that. Does his bit and be damned to you." They sat in the cozy warmth, talking quietly of MacWyrglinchbeath. Feet rushed again beyond the door; it opened and two of the deputation stood in it with their young, baffled faces.

"Well?" someone said. "Where's the victim?"

But they were beckoning the senior flight commander, in whose flight MacWyrglinchbeath was.

"Come here, skipper," they said. The senior looked at them. He did not rise.

"What's row?"

But they were merely urgent and mysterious; not until the three of them were outside did they explain. "The old fool won't take it," they said in hushed tones. "Can you believe it? Can you?"

"We'll see," the flight commander said. Beyond MacWyrglinchbeath's door the sound of voices indistinguishable and expostulant came.

The flight commander entered and thrust among them as they stood about the cot. The tunic and belt lay untouched upon it; beside it MacWyrglinchbeath sat in the lone chair.

"Clear off, now," the flight commander said, herding them toward the door. "Off with you, the whole lot." He pushed the last one out and shut the door and returned and straddled his legs before the stove.

"What's all the hurrah, Mac?"

"Weel, skipper," MacWyrglinchbeath said slowly, "thae bairns mean weel, A doot not—" He looked up. "Ye ha' disfee-gur-red ma walkin-oot tunic, and thae bairns think A sud just dress up in a' thae leather-r and brass, and gang wi' they tae thae awf-ficer-rs' mess." He mused again upon the tunic.

"Right," the flight commander said. "Shame it wasn't done a year ago. Hop into it now, and come along. Dinner's about about."

But MacWyrglinchbeath did not stir. He put his hand out slowly and musingly, and touched the gallant sweep of the embroidered wings above the silken candy stripe.

"Thae bairns mean weel, A mak' nae doot," he said.

"Silly young pups. But we're all damned glad. You should have seen the major when it came through this morning. Like a child on Christmas Eve. The lads could hardly wait until they could sneak your tunic out."

"Ay," MacWyrglinchbeath said. "They mean well, A mak' nae doot. But 'twill tak' thinkin'." He sat, slowly and gently touching the wings with a blunt hand, pitted and grained with four years of grease. The flight commander watched quietly and with what he thought was comprehension. He moved.

"Right you are. Take the night and think it out. Better show up at breakfast, though, or those devils will be after you again."

"Ay," MacWyrglinchbeath said. "'Twill tak' thinkin'."

Dark was fully come. The flight commander strode savagely back to the mess, swearing. He opened the door, and, still cursing, he entered. The others faced him quickly.

"Is he coming?"

The flight commander cursed steadily—Wing, Brigade, Staff, the war, Parliament.

"Do you think he will? Would any of you yourselves, after they'd let you rot for four ruddy years, and then gave you a second lieutenancy as though it were a Garter? The man has pride, and he's damned well right."

After his dinner MacWyrglinchbeath went to the sergeant of the officers' mess and talked with him. Then he went to the squadron commander's orderly and talked with him. Then he returned and sat on his cot—he had yet the stub of candle, for light was furnished him now; but he was well into his second pencil—and calculated. He roughly computed the cost of a new uniform and accessories, with an allowance for laundry. Then he calculated a month's average battel bill, added the amounts and subtracted the total from a subaltern's pay. he compared the result with his present monthly net, sitting above the dead yet irrevocable assertion of the figures for a long time. Then he tied the ledger up in its bit of greasy cord and went to bed.

The next morning he sought the flight commander. "Thae bairns mean well, A mak' nae doot," he said, with just a trace of apology. "And the major-r. A'm gritfu' tae ye a'. But 'twina do, skipper. Ye ken that."

"Yes," the flight commander said. "I see. Yes." Again and aloud he cursed the whole fabric of the war. "Stupid fools, with their ruddy tabs and brass. No wonder they can't win a war in four years. You're right, Mac; 'course it's no go at this late day. And I'm sorry, old fellow." He wrung MacWyrglinchbeath's limp, calloused hand hard.

"A'm gritfu'," MacWyrglinchbeath said. "A'm obleeged."

That was in October, 1918.

By two o'clock there was not a mechanic on the place. On the tarmac the squadron commander's machine stood, the engine idling; in the cockpit the major sat. He was snoring. Up and down the aerodrome the senior flight commander and a wing commander and an artillery officer raced in the squadron's car, while a fourth man in an S.E. 5 played tag with them. He appeared to be trying to set his landing gear down in the tonneau of the car; at each failure the occupants of the car howled, the artillery officer waving a bottle; each time the flight commander foiled him by maneuvering, they howled again and passed the bottle from mouth to mouth.

The mess was littered with overturned chairs and with bottles and other objects small enough to throw. Beneath the table lay two men to whom three hours of peace had been harder than that many years of fighting; above and upon and across them the unabated tumult raged. At last one climbed upon the table and stood swaying and shouting until he made himself heard:

"Look here! Where's old Mac?"

"Mac!" they howled. "Where's old Mac? Can't have a binge without old Mac!"

They rushed from the room. In his cockpit the major snored; the squadron car performed another last-minute skid as the S. E.'s propeller flicked the cap from the artillery officer's head. They rushed on to MacWyrglinchbeath's hut and crashed the door open. MacWyrglinchbeath was sitting on his cot, his ledger upon his knees and his pencil poised above it. He was taking stock.

With the hammer which he had concealed beneath the well coping four years ago he carefully drew the nails in the door and window frames and put them into his pocket and opened his house again. He put the hammer and the nails away in their box, and from another box he took his kilts and shook them out. The ancient folds were stiff, reluctant, and moths had been among them, and he clicked his tongue soberly.

Then he removed his tunic and breeks and putties, and donned the kilts. With the fagots he had stored there four years ago he kindled a meager fire on the hearth and cooked and ate his supper. Then he smoked his pipe, put the dottle carefully away, smothered the fire and went to bed.

The next morning he walked three miles down the glen to the neighbor's. The neighbor, from his tilted doorway, greeted him with sparse unsurprise:

"Weel, Wully. A thocht ye'd be comin' hame. A heer-rd thae war-r was done wi'."

"Ay," MacWyrglinchbeath said, and together they stood beside the angling fence of brush and rocks and looked at the shaggy, small horse and the two cows balanced, seemingly without effort, on the forty-five-degree slope of the barn lot.

"Ye'll be takin' away thae twa beasties," the neighbor said.

"Thae three beasties, ye mean," MacWyrglinchbeath said. They did not look at each other. They looked at the animals in the lot.

"Ye'll mind ye left but twa wi' me."

They looked at the three animals. "Ay," MacWyrglinchbeath said. Presently they turned away. They entered the cottage. The neighbor lifted a hearthstone and counted down MacWyrglinchbeath's remittances to the last ha'penny. The total agreed exactly with the ledger.

"A'm gritfu'," MacWyrglinchbeath said.

"Ye'll ha' ither spoil frae thae war-r, A doot not?" the neighbor said.

"Naw. 'Twas no that kind o' a war-r," MacWyrglinchbeath said.

"Ay," the neighbor said. "No Hieland Scots ha' ever won aught in English war-rs."

MacWyrglinchbeath returned home. The next day he walked to the market town, twelve miles away. Here he learned the current value of two-year-old cattle; he consulted a lawyer also. He was closeted with the lawyer for an hour. Then he returned home, and with pencil and paper and the inch-long butt of the candle he calculated slowly, proved his figures, and sat musing above the result. Then he snuffed the candle and went to bed.

The next morning he walked down the glen. The neighbor, in his tilted doorway, greeted him with sparse unsurprise:

"Weel, Wully. Ye ha' cam' for thae twa beasties?"

"Ay," MacWyrglinchbeath said.

Idyll in the Desert

C~~O

I

"It would take me four days to make my route. I would leave
Blizzard on a Monday and get to Painter's about sundown and
spend the night. The next night I would make Ten Sleep and then
turn and go back across the mesa. The third night I would camp,
and on Thursday night I would be home again."

"Didn't you ever get lonesome?" I said.

"Well, a fellow hauling government mail, government property.
You hear tell of these old desert rats getting cracked in the head.
But did you ever hear of a soldier getting that way? Even a West
Pointer, a fellow out of the cities, that never was out of hollering
distance of a hundred people before in his life, let him be out on
a scout by himself for six months, even. Because that West Pointer,
he's like me; he ain't riding alone. He's got Uncle Sam right there
to talk to whenever he feels like talking: Washington and the big
cities full of folks, and all that that means to a man, like what Saint
Peter and the Holy Church of Rome used to mean to them old
priests, when them Spanish Bishops would come riding across the
mesa on a mule, surrounded by the ghostly hosts of Heaven with
harder hitting guns than them old Sharpses even, because the pore
aboriginee that got shot with them heavenly bolts, they never even
saw the shooting, let alone the gun. And then I carry a rifle, and
there's always the chance of an antelope and once I killed a mountain sheep without even getting out of the buckboard."

"Was it a big one?" I said.

"Sure. I was coming around a shoulder of the canyon just about sunset. The sun was just above the rim, shining right in my face. So I saw these two sheep just under the rim. I could see their horns and tails against the sky, but I couldn't see the sheep for the sunset. I could see a set of horns, I could make out a pair of hindquarters, but because of the sun I couldn't make out if them sheep were on this side of the rim or just beyond it. And I didn't have time to get closer. I just pulled the team up and throwed up my rifle and put a bullet about two foot back of them horns and another bullet about three foot ahead of them hindquarters and jumped out of the buckboard running."

"Did you get both of them?" I said.

"No. I just got one. But he had two bullets in him; one back of the fore leg and the other right under the hind leg."

"Oh," I said.

"Yes. Them bullets was five foot apart."

"That's a good story," I said.

"It was a good sheep. But what was I talking about? I talk so little that, when I mislay a subject, I have to stop and hunt for it I was talking about being lonesome, wasn't I? There wouldn't hardly a winter pass without I would have at least one passengeı on the up or down trip, even if it wasn't anybody but one of Painter's hands, done rode his horse down to Blizzard with forty dollars in his pocket, to leave his horse at Blizzard and go down to Juarez and bust the bank with that forty dollars by Christmas day and come back and maybe set up with Painter for his range boss, provided if Painter was honest and industrious and worked hard. They'd always ride back up to Painter's with me along about New Year's."

"What about their horses?" I said.

"What horses?"

"The ones they rode down to Blizzard and left there."

"Oh. Them horses would belong to Matt Lewis by that time. Matt runs the livery stable.'ı

"Oh," I said.

"Yes. Matt says he don't know what to do. He said he kept on hoping that maybe this polo would take the country like Mah-Jong done a while back. But now he says he reckons he'll have to start him a glue factory. But what was I talking about?"

"You talk so seldom," I said. "Was it about getting lonesome?"

"Oh yes. And then I'd have these lungers. That would be a passenger a week for two weeks."

"Would they come in pairs?"

"No. It would be the same one. I'd take him up one week and leave him, and the next week I'd bring him back down to make the east bound train. I reckon the air up at Sivgut was a little too stiff for eastern lungs."

"Sivgut?" I said.

"Sure. Siv. One of them things they strain the meal through back east at Santone and Washinton. Siv."

"Oh. Siv. Yes. Sivgut. What is that?"

"It's a house we built. A good house. They kept on coming here, getting off at Blizzard, passing Phoenix where there is what you might call back east at Santone and Washinton a dude lung-ranch. They'd pass that and come on to Blizzard: a peaked-looking fellow in his Sunday clothes, with his eyes closed and his skin the color of sandpaper, and a fat wife from one of them eastern corn counties, telling how they wanted too much at Phoenix so they come on to Blizzard because they don't think a set of eastern wore-out lungs is worth what the folks in Phoenix wanted. Or maybe it would be vice versa, with the wife with a sand-colored face with a couple of red spots on it like the children had been spending a wet Sunday with some scraps of red paper and a pot of glue while she was asleep, and her still asleep but not too much asleep to put in her opinion about how much folks in Phoenix thought Ioway lungs was worth on the hoof. So we built Sivgut for them. The Blizzard Chamber of Commerce did it, with two bunks and a week's grub, because it takes me a week to get up there again and bring them back down to make the Phoenix train. It's a good camp. We named it Sivgut because of the view. On a clear day you can see clean down into Mexico. Did I tell you about the day when that last revolution broke out in Mexico? Well, one day—it was a Tuesday, about ten o'clock in the morning—I got there and the lunger was out in front, staring off to the south with his hand shading his eyes. 'It's a cloud of dust,' he says. 'Look at it.' I looked. 'That's curious,' I said. 'It can't be a rodeo or I'd heard about it. And it can't be a sandstorm,' I said, 'because it's too big and staying in one place.' I went on and got back to Blizzard on

Thursday. Then I learned about this new revolution down in Mexico. Broke out Tuesday just before sundown, they told me."

"I thought you said you saw that dust at ten o'clock," I said.

"Sure. But things happen so fast down there in Mexico that that dust started rising the night before to get out of the way of—"

"Don't tell about that," I said. "Tell about Sivgut."

"All right. I'd get up to Sivgut on Tuesday morning. At first she'd be in the door, or maybe out in front of the cabin, looking down the trail for me. But after that sometimes I would drive right up to the door and stop the team and say 'Hello' and the house still as vacant as the day it was built."

"A woman," I said.

"Yes. She stayed on, after he got well and left. She stayed on."

"She must have liked the country."

"I guess not. I don't guess any of them liked the country. Would you like a country you were just using to get well from a sickness you were ashamed for your friends to know you had?"

"I see." I said. "He got well first. Why didn't he wait until his wife got well too?"

"I guess he never had time to wait. I guess he figgered there was a right smart lot for him to do yet back yonder, being a young fellow, and like he had just got out of jail after a long time."

"That's less reason than ever for him to leave his wife sick."

"He didn't know she was sick. That she had it too."

"Didn't know?" I said.

"You take a sick fellow, a young fellow at that, without no ties to speak of, having to come and live for two years in a place where there ain't a traffic light in four hundred miles; where there ain't nothing but quiet and sunlight and them durn stars staring him in the face all night long. You couldn't expect him to pay much mind to somebody that never done nothing but cook his food and chop his firewood and haul his water in a tin bucket from a spring three quarters of a mile away to wash him in like he was a baby. So when he got well, I don't reckon he could be blamed for not noticing that she had one more burden herself, especially if that burden wasn't nothing but a few little old bugs."

"I don't know what you call ties, then," I said, "If marriage isn't a tie."

"Now you're getting at it. Marriage is a tie; only, it depends some on who you are married to. You know what my private opinion is, after having watched them for about ten years, once a week on a Tuesday, as well as carrying a letter or a telegram back and forth between them and the railroad?"

"What is your private opinion?"

"It's my private opinion, based on evidence though not hidebound; I was never a opinionated man; that they wasn't married to one another a-tall."

"What do you consider evidence?"

"Well, a letter to me from a fellow back east that did claim to be her husband might be considered as evidence. What do you think?"

"Did you kill this sheep with one shot or with two," I said.

"Sho, now," the mail rider said.

II

"This fellow got off the west bound train one morning about ten years ago. He didn't look like a lunger, maybe because he didn't have but one grip. Usually it's too late already when they come here. Usually the doctor has told them they haven't got but a month more, or maybe six months. Yet they'll get off that west bound train sometimes with everything but the cook stove. I've noticed that taking trouble just to get through the world is about the hardest habit of all to break. Owning things. I know folks right now that would hold up a train bound for heaven while they telephoned back home for the cook to run and bring them something which, not having ever had any use for it at home, they had done forgot. They could live in a house on earth with it for years without even knowing where it was, but just try to get them to start to heaven without taking it along.

"He didn't look like a lunger. He didn't look concerned enough. You take them, even while they are sitting on the baggage truck with their eyes shut while the wife is arguing with anybody in sight that her husband's lungs ain't worth as much as western folks seem to think, and they look concerned. They are right there, where it is going on. They don't care who knows that they are the most interested parties present. Like a man on horseback that's swallowed a dynamite cap and a sharp rock at the same time.

"But him. His name was Darrel, Darrel Howes. Maybe House. She called him Dorry. He just got off the train with his one grip and stood on our platform and sneered at it, the mountains, the space, at the Lord God Himself that watches a man here like a man might watch a bug, a ant.

" 'Our station ain't much,' I says. 'You'll have to give us a little time. We only been working on this country about two hundred years and we ain't got it finished yet.'

"He looked at me, a tall fellow in clothes that hadn't never seen as far west as Santone even, before he brought them. What the pitchure magazines would call a dook, maybe. 'That's all right with me,' he says. 'I don't intend to look at any of it longer than I can help.'

" 'Help yourself,' I said. 'They'll tell you in Washinton it belongs to you too.'

" 'They can have my part of it back soon then,' he says. He looked at me. 'You've got a house here. A camp.'

"I understood what he meant then, what he had come for; I hadn't never suspected it. I guess I thought he was a drummer, maybe. A perfume drummer, maybe. 'Oh,' I says. 'You mean Sivgut. Sure. You want to use it?'

"That was what he wanted, standing there in his eastern clothes like a Hollywood dook, sneering. And then I knew that he was just about scared to death. After them three or four days on the train with nobody to talk to except his own inhabitants, he had just about got himself scared to death. 'Sure,' I said. 'It's a good camp. You'll like it up there. I'm going up there today. You can go with me, if you want to look at it. I will get you back here by Thursday night.' He didn't say anything. He didn't seem to be paying any attention at all. 'You'll have a lot of time to listen to them little things before you die, my friend,' I says to myself. 'And without anybody to help you listen, neither.' I thought that that was what it was. That he was just young (there was something about him that let you know, plain as if he had told you, that he was an only child and that his ma had been a widow since before he begun to remember; anyway, you could see that he had probably spent all his life being took care of by women, women to whom he looked like quite a figger, and here when he really needed to be took care of, he was ashamed to tell them the reason of it, and scared of himself. I didn't think he knew what he wanted to do or what he would do next; I thought that all he wanted was for somebody to tell him they would do this or that next, before the time come to need to do something else even. I thought he was running from himself, trying to lose himself in some crowd or in some strange surroundings where he would get lost and couldn't keep up. I never thought different even when he asked about food. 'We'll find some at camp,' I said. 'Enough for a week.'

" 'You pass there every week do you?' he said.

" 'Sure. Every Tuesday. I get there Tuesday morning. And Thursday night this team will be champing corn in Blizzard again.'

"The team was. I was in Blizzard too, but he was up there at Sivgut. He wasn't standing in the door, watching me drive away, neither. He was down in the canyon behind the camp, chopping wood, and not making much of an out with the axe, neither. He gave me ten dollars, to buy him a week's grub. 'You can't eat no ten dollars in a week,' I said. 'Five will be all you'll want. I'll bring it to you and you can pay me then.' But that wouldn't do him. When I left there, I had his five dollars.

"I didn't buy the grub. I borrowed a buffalo robe from Matt Lewis, because the weather had changed that week and I knew it would be a cold ride for him, them two days back to town in the buckboard. He was glad to see the robe. He said the nights was getting pretty chilly, and that he would be glad to have it. So I left the mail with him and I went back to Painter's and talked Painter out of enough grub to last him until next Tuesday. And I left him there again. He gave me another five dollars. 'I'm making out a little better with the axe,' he told me. 'Don't forget my grub, this time.'

"And I didn't forget it. I carried it to him every Tuesday for two years, until he left. I'd see him every Tuesday, especially during that first winter that near about killed him, I'd find him laying on the cot, coughing blood, and I'd cook him up a pot of beans and cut him enough firewood to last until next Tuesday, and finally I took the telegram down to the railroad and sent it for him. It was to a Mrs. So-and-so in New York; I thought that maybe his ma had married again, and it didn't make sense. It just said 'I've two weeks more the less long than farewell' and there wasn't any name to it. So I signed my name to it, Lucas Crump, Mail Rider, and sent it on. I paid for it, too. She got there in five days. It took her five days to get there, and ten years to leave."

"You said two years a minute ago," I said.

"That was him. He just stayed two years. I guess that first winter maybe killed his bugs, same as boll weevils back east in Texas. Anyway, he begun to set up and to chop the wood himself, so that when I'd get there about ten o'clock she'd tell me he had done been gone since sunup. And then one day, in the spring after she come there the spring before, I saw him in Blizzard. He had walked in, forty miles, and he had gained about thirty pounds and he looked hard as a range pony. I didn't see him but for a minute, because he was in a hurry. I didn't know how much of a hurry until I saw him getting onto the east bound train when it pulled out. I thought then that he was still running from himself."

"And when you found that the woman was still up there at Sivgut, what did you think then?"

"I knew that he was running from himself then," the Mail Rider said.

III

"And the woman, you said she stayed ten years."

"Sure. She just left yesterday."

"You mean that she stayed on eight years after he left?"

"She was waiting for him to come back. He never told her he wasn't coming back. And besides, she had the bugs herself then. Maybe it was the same ones, up and moved onto a new pasture."

"And he didn't know it? Living right there in the same house with her, he didn't know she was infected?"

"How know it? You reckon a fellow that's got a dynamite cap inside him has got time to worry about whether his neighbor swallowed one too or not? And besides, she had done left a husband and two children when she got the telegram. So I reckon she felt for him to come back. I used to talk to her, that first winter when we thought he was going to die. She was a durn sight handier with that axe than he was, and sometimes there wouldn't be a thing for me to do when I got there. So we would talk. She was about ten years older than him, and she told me about her husband, that was about ten years older than her, and their children. Her husband was one of these architects and she told me about how Dorry came back from this Bow and Art school in Paris and how he went to work in her husband's office. And I guess he was a pretty stiff lick to a woman of thirty-five and maybe better, that had a husband and a house that all run themselves too well for her to meddle with, and Dorry just twenty-five and fresh from Pareesian bowleyvards and looking like a Hollywood dook to boot. So I guess it couldn't have been long before they had one another all steamed up to where they believed they couldn't live until they had told her husband and his boss that love was im-perious or im-peerious or whatever it is, and had went off to live just down the canyon from a stage settin with the extra hands all playing mouth-organs and accordions in the background.

"That would have been all right. They could have bore unreality. It was the reality they never had the courage to deny. He tried, though. She told me that she didn't know he was sick nor where he had went to until she got our telegram. She says he just sent her a note that he was gone and to not expect him back. Then she got the telegram. 'And there wasn't nothing else I could do,' she says, in a man's flannel shirt and corduroy coat. She had fell off and she didn't look thirty-five by five years. But I don't reckon he noticed that. 'There was nothing else I could do,' she says. 'Because his mother had just died the year before.' 'Sho,' I said. 'I hadn't thought of that. And since she couldn't come, you had to since he never had no grandmother nor wife nor sister nor daughter nor maid servant.' But she wasn't listening.

"She never listened to anything except to him in the bed or to the pot on the stove. 'You've learned to cook fine,' I told her. 'Cook?' she said. 'Why not?' I don't guess she knew what she was eating, if she et at all, which I never saw her do. Only now and then I would make her think that she had found herself some way to get the grub done without burning it or having it taste like throwed-away cinch-leathers. I reckon though women just ain't got time to worry much about what food tastes like. But now and then during that bad winter I'd just up and run her out of the kitchen and cook him something he needed.

"Then that next spring I saw him at the station that day, getting on the train. After that, neither of us ever mentioned him a-tall. I went up to see her next day. But we didn't mention him; I never told her I saw him get on the train. I set out the week's grub and I says, 'I may come back this way tomorrow,' not looking at her. 'I ain't got anything that goes beyond Ten Sleep. So I may come back past here tomorrow on my way to Blizzard.' 'I think I have enough to last me until next Tuesday,' she says. 'Alright,' I says. 'I'll see you then.' "

"So she stayed," I said.

"Sure. She had them herself, then. She didn't tell me for some time. Sometimes it would be two months and I would not see her. Sometimes I would hear her down in the canyon with the axe, and sometimes she would speak to me out of the house, without coming to the door, and I would set the grub on the bench and wait a while. But she would not come out, and I would go on. When I saw her again, she never looked no thirty-five by twenty years. And when she left yesterday, she didn't look it by thirty-five years."

"She gave him up and left, did she?"

"I telegraphed to her husband. That was about six months after Dorry left. The husband he got here in five days, same as she did. He was a fine fellow, kind of old. But not after making no trouble. 'I'm obliged to you,' he says first thing. 'What for?' I says. 'I'm obliged to you,' he says. 'What do you think I had better do first?'

"We talked it over. We figgered he had better wait in town until I got back. I went up there. I didn't tell her he was there. I never got that far; that was the first time I ever come out and talked like there was any such thing as tomorrow. I never got far enough to tell her he was there. I came back and told him. 'Maybe next year,' I told him. 'You try then.' She still thought Dorry was coming back. Like he would be on the next train. So the husband he went back home and I fixed the money up in an envelope and I got Manny Hughes in the postoffice to help compound a crime or whatever you do to the government, with the cancelling machine so it would look natural, and I carried it to her. 'It's registered,' I said. 'Must be a gold mine in it.' And she took it, fake number and fake postmark and all, and opened it, looking for the letter from Dorry. Dorry, she called him; did I tell you? The only thing she seemed to mistrust about it was the only thing that was authentic. 'There's no letter,' she says. 'Maybe he was in a hurry,' I says. 'He must be pretty busy to have earned all that money in six months.'

"After that, two or three times a year I would take her one of these faked letters. Once a week I would write her husband how she was getting along, and I would take the money two or three times a year, when she would about be running out, and take the letter to her, and her opening the envelope and kind of throwing the money aside to look for the letter, and then looking at me like she believed that me or Manny had opened the envelope and taken the letter out. Maybe she believed that we did.

"I couldn't get her to eat right. Finally, about a year ago, she had to go to bed too, in the same cot, the same blankets. I telegraphed her husband and he sent a special train with one of them eastern specialists that won't look at you without you got pedigree stud papers, and we told her he was the County Health officer on his yearly rounds and that his fee was one dollar and she paid him, letting him give her change for a five dollar bill, and him looking at me. 'Go on and tell her,' I said. 'You can live a year,' he said. 'A year?' she says. 'Sure,' I says. 'That'll be plenty long. You can get here from anywhere in five days.' 'That's so,' she says. 'Do you think I ought to try to write to him? I might put it in the papers,' she said. 'I wouldn't do that,' I said. 'He's busy. If he wasn't pretty busy, he couldn't make the money he's making. Could he?' 'That's so,' she said.

"So the doctor went back to New York on his special train, and he gave the husband an earfull. I had a wire from him right off; he wanted to send the specialist back, this eastern stud doctor. But he figgered by telegraph that that wouldn't do any good, so I told my substitute he could make a good job; he could make one and a half of my pay for a year. It never done no harm to let him think he was working for one of these big eastern syndicates too, as well as the government. And I took a bed roll and I camped out in the canyon below the cabin. We got a Injun woman to wait on her. The Injun woman couldn't talk enough of any language to tell her better than a rich man sent her to wait there. And there she waited, with me camped out in the canyon, telling her I was on my vacation, hunting sheep. That vacation lasted eight months. It took her a right smart while.

"Then I went back to town and telegraphed her husband. He telegraphed back to put her on the Los Angeles train on Wednesday, that he would go on to Los Angeles by airplane and meet the train, so we brought her down Wednesday. She was laying on a stretcher when the train come in and stopped and the engine uncoupled and went on down to the water tank. She was laying on the stretcher, waiting for them to lift her into the baggage car; me and the Injun woman had told her that the rich man had sent for her, when they come up."

"They?" I said.

"Dorry and his new wife. I forgot to tell that. News passes Blizzard about four times before it ever lights. News happens in Pittsburg, say. All right. It gets radioed, passing right over us to Los Angeles or Frisco. All right. They put the Los Angeles and Frisco papers into the airplane and they pass right over us, going east now to Phoenix. Then they put the papers onto the fast train and the news passes us again, going west at sixty miles an hour at two A. M. And then the papers come back east on the local, and we get a chance to read them. Matt Lewis showed me the paper, about the wedding, on Tuesday. 'You reckon this is the same Darrel House?' he says. 'Is the gal rich?' I says. 'She's from Pittsburg,' Matt says. 'Then that's the one,' I says.

"So they were all out of the cars, stretching their legs like they do. You know these pullman trains. Folks that have lived together for four days. All know one another like a family: the millionaire, the movie queen, the bride and groom with rice still in their hair like as not. He still never looked a day more than thirty, with this new wife holding to him with her face lowered, and the heads of them other passengers turning when they passed, the heads of the old folks remembering their honeymoons too, and of the bachelors too, thinking maybe a few of the finest thoughts they ever think about this world and the bride thinking a little too, maybe, shrinking against her husband and holding him and thinking enough to imagine herself walking along there nekkid and probably she wouldn't take eleven dollars or even fifteen for the privilege. They come on too, with the other passengers that would come up and pass the stretcher and glance at it and then kind of pause like a house-owner that finds a dead dog or maybe a queer-shaped piece of wood at the corner, and go on."

"Did they go on, too?"

"That's right. They come up and looked at her, with the gal kind of shrinking off against her husband and holding him, with her eyes wide, and Dorry looking down at her and going on, and she—she couldn't move anything except her eyes then—turning her eyes to follow them, because she seen the rice in their hair too by then. I guess she had maybe thought all the time until then that he would get off the train and come to her. She thought he would look like he had when she saw him last, and she thought that she would look like she had when he saw her first. And so when she saw him and saw the gal and smelt the rice, all she could do was move her eyes. Or maybe she didn't know him at all. I don't know."

"But he," I said. "What did he say?"

"Nothing. I don't reckon he recognized me. There was a lot of folks there, and I didn't happen to be up in front. I don't guess he saw me a-tall."

"I mean, when he saw her."

"He didn't know her. Because he didn't expect to see her there. You take your own brother and see him somewhere you don't expect to, where it never occurred to your wildest dream he would be, and you wouldn't know him. Let alone if he has went and aged forty years on you in ten winters. You got to be suspicious of folks to recognize them at a glance wherever you see them. And he wasn't suspicious of her. That was her trouble. But it didn't last long."

"What didn't last long?"

"Her trouble. When they took her off the train at Los Angeles she was dead. Then it was her husband's trouble. Ours, too. She stayed in the morgue two days, because when he went and looked at her, he didn't believe it was her. We had to telegraph back and forth four times before he would believe it was her. Me and Matt Lewis paid for the telegrams, too. He was busy and forgot to pay for them, I guess."

"You must still have had some of the money the husband sent you to fool her with," I said.

The Mail Rider chewed. "She was alive when he was sending that money," he said. "That was different." He spat carefully. He wiped his sleeve across his mouth.

"Have you got any Indian blood?" I said.

"Indian blood?"

"You talk so little. So seldom."

"Oh, sure. I have some Indian blood. My name used to be Sitting Bull."

"Used to be?"

"Sure. I got killed one day a while back. Didn't you read it in the paper?"

Two Dollar Wife

"Ain't she never going to be ready!" Maxwell Johns stared at himself in the mirror. He watched himself light a cigarette and snap the match backward over his shoulder. It struck the hearth and bounced, still burning, toward the rug.

"What the hell do I care if it burns the damn dump down!" he snarled, striding up and down the garish parlor of the Houston home. He stared at his reflection again—slim young body in evening clothes, smooth dark hair, smooth white face. He could hear, in the room overhead, Doris Houston and her mother shrieking at each other.

"Listen at 'em squall!" he grunted. "You'd think it was a knock-down-and-drag-out going on instead of a flounce getting into her duds. Oh, hell! Their brains are fuzzy as the cotton we grow!"

A colored maid entered the room and puttered about a moment, her vast backside billowing like a high wave under oil. She glanced at Maxwell and sniffed her way out of the room.

The screams above reached a crescendo. Then he heard rushing feet, eager and swift—a bright eager clatter, young and evanescent.

A final screech from above seemed to shoot Doris Houston into the room like a pip squeezed from an orange. She was thin as a dragonfly, honey-haired, with long coltish legs. Her small face was alternate patches of dead white and savage red.

She carried a fur coat over her arm and held onto one shoulder of her dress with the other hand. The other shoulder, with a dangling strap, had slipped far down.

Doris shrugged the gown back into place and mumbled between

her red lips. A needle glinted between her white teeth, the gossamer thread floating out as she flung the coat down and whirled her back to Maxwell. "Here, Unconscious, sew me up!" he interpreted her mumbled words.

"Good God, I just sewed you into it night before last!" Maxwell growled. "And I sewed you into it Christmas Eve, and I sewed—"

"Aw, dry up!" said Doris. "You did your share of tearing it off of me! Sew it good this time, and let it stay sewed!"

He sewed it, muttering to himself, with long, savage stitches like a boy sewing the ripped cover of a baseball. He snapped the thread, juggled the needle from one hand to the other for a moment and then thrust it carelessly into the seat cover of a chair.

Doris shrugged the strap into place with a wriggle and reached for her coat. Outside a motor horn brayed. "Here they are!" she snapped. "Come on!"

Again feet sounded on the stairs—like lumps of half-baked dough slopping off a table. Mrs. Houston thrust her frizzled hair and her diamonds into the room.

"Doris!" she shrieked. "Where are you going tonight? Maxwell, don't you dare let Doris stay out till all hours again like she did Christmas Eve! I don't care if it is New Year's! Do you hear? Doris, you come home—"

"All right! All right!" squawked Doris without looking back. "Come on, Unconscious!"

"Get in!" barked Walter Mitchell, driver of the car. "Get in back, Doris, damn it! Lucille, get your legs outa my lap! How the hell you expect me to drive?"

As the car ripped through the outer fringe of the town, a second car, also containing two couples, turned in from a side road. The drivers blatted horns at each other in salute. Side by side they swerved into the straight road that led past the Country Club. They raced, roaring, rocking—sixty—seventy—seventy-five, hub brushing hub, outer wheels on the rims of the road. Behind the steering wheels glowered two almost identical faces—barbered, young, grim.

Far ahead gleamed the white gates of the Country Club. "You better slow down!" shrieked Doris.

"Slow down, hell!" growled Mitchell, foot and accelerator both flat on the floorboards.

The other car drew ahead, horn blatting derisively, voices squalling meaningless gibberish. Mitchell swore under his breath.

Scre-e-e-e-each!

The lead car took the turn on two wheels, leaped, bucked, careened wildly and shot up the drive. Mitchell slammed his throttle shut and drifted on down the dark road. A mile from the Country Club he ground the car to a stop, switched off engine and lights and pulled a flask from his pocket.

"Let's have a drink!" he grunted, proffering the flask.

"I don't want to stop here," Doris said. "I want to go to the Club."

"Don't you want a drink?" asked Mitchell.

"No. I don't want a drink, either. I want to go to the Club."

"Don't pay any attention to her," said Maxwell. "If anybody comes along I'll show 'em the license."

A month before, just after Maxwell had been suspended from Sewanee, Mitchell had dared Doris and him to get married. Maxwell had borrowed two dollars from the Negro janitor at the Cotton Exchange, where Max "worked" in his father's office, and they had driven a hundred miles and bought a license. Then Doris changed her mind. Maxwell still carried the license in his pocket, now a little smeary from moisture and friction.

Lucille shrieked with laughter.

"Max, you behave yourself!" squawked Doris. "Take your hands away!"

"Here, give me the license," said Walter, "I'll tie it on the radiator. Then they won't even have to get out of the car to look at it."

"No you won't!" Doris cried.

"What you got to say about it?" demanded Walter. "Max was the one that paid two dollars for it—not you."

"I don't care! It's got my name on it!"

"Gimme my two dollars back and you can have it," said Maxwell.

"I haven't got two dollars. You take me back to the Club, Walter Mitchell!"

"*I'll* give you two bucks for it, Max," said Walter.

"Okay," agreed Maxwell, putting his hand to his coat. Doris flung herself at him.

"No you don't!" she cried. "I'm going to tell daddy on you!"

"What do you care?" protested Walter. "I'm going to scratch out yours and Max's names and put mine and Lucille's in. We're liable to need it!"

"I don't care! Mine will still be on it and it will be bigamy."

"You mean incest, honey," Lucille said.

"I don't care what I mean. I'm going back to the Club!"

"Are you?" Walter said. "Tell them we'll be there after while." He handed Maxwell the flask.

Doris banged the door open and jumped out.

"Hey, wait!" Walter cried. "I didn't—"

Already they could hear Doris' spike heels hitting the road hard. Walter turned the car.

"You better get out and walk behind her," he told Maxwell. "You left home with her. Get her to the Club, anyway. It ain't far —not even a mile, hardly."

"Watch where you're going!" yelped Maxwell. "Here comes a car behind us!"

Walter drew aside and flashed his spot on the other car as it passed.

"It's Hap White!" shrieked Lucille, craning her neck. "He's got that Princeton man, Jornstadt, with him—the handsome one all the girls are crazy about. He's from Minnesota and is visiting his aunt in town."

The other car ground to a halt beside Doris. The door opened. She got in.

"The little snake!" shrilled Lucille. "I bet she knew Jornstadt was in that car. I bet she made a date with Hap White to pick her up."

Walter Mitchell chuckled maliciously. " 'There goes my girl—' " he hummed.

Maxwell swore savagely under his breath.

There were already five in the other car. Doris sat on Jornstadt's lap. He could feel the warmth and the rounded softness of her legs. He held her steady drawing her back against him. Doris wriggled slightly and his arm tightened.

Jornstadt drew a deep breath freighted with the perfume of the honey-colored hair. His arm tightened still more.

A moment later Mitchell's car roared past.

Lurking between two parked cars, Walter and Maxwell watched the six from Hap White's car enter the club house. The group [passed] the girls in a bee-like clot around the tall Princeton man, whose beautifully ridged head towered over them. The blaring music seemed to be a triumphant carpet spread for him, derisive and salutant.

Walter handed his almost empty flask to Maxwell. Max tilted it up.

"I know a good place for that Princeton guy," he said, wiping his lips.

"Huh?"

"The morgue," said Max.

"Gonna dance?" asked Walter.

"Hell, no! Let's go to the cloak room. Oughta be a crap game in there."

There was. Above the kneeling ring of tense heads and shoulders, they saw the Princeton man, Jornstadt, and Hap White, a fat youth with a cherubic face and a fawning manner. They were drinking, turn about, from a thick tumbler in which a darky poured corn from a Coca-Cola bottle. Hap waved a greeting. "Hi-yi, boy," he addressed Max. "Little family trouble?"

"Nope," said Maxwell evenly. "Gimme a drink."

Max and Walter watched the crap game. Hap and Jornstadt strolled out, the music squalling briefly through the opening and closing door. Around the kneeling ring droned monotonous voices.

"E-eleven! Shoot four bits."

"You're faded! Snake eyes! Let the eight bits ride?"

"C'mon, Little Joe!"

"Ninety days in the calaboose! Let it ride!"

The bottle went around. The door began banging open and shut. The cloak room became crowded, murky with cigarette smoke. The music had stopped.

Suddenly pandemonium broke loose: the rising wail of a fire siren, the shrieks of whistles from the cotton gins scattered about the countryside, the crack of pistols and rifles and the duller boom of shotguns. On the veranda girls shrieked and giggled.

"Happy New Year!" said Walter viciously. Max glared at him, shucked off his coat and ripped his collar open.

"Lemme in that game!" he snarled.

A tall man with beautifully ridged hair had just sauntered past the open door. On his arm hung a lithe girl with honey-colored hair.

By three o'clock, Maxwell had won a hundred and forty dollars and broken the game. One by one the gamblers arose, stiffly, like people who have been asleep. The music was still droning along but the cloak room was full of flapping overcoat sleeves. Youths adjusted their ties, smoothed their already patent-leather-smooth hair.

"Is it over?" asked Maxwell.

"Damn near it!" grunted Walter.

Fat Hap White sidled in through the door. Behind him was Jornstadt, his face flushed, hesitant.

"That Princeton guy sure can put away the likker," grunted a voice behind Max. "He's still got a quart flask of prime stuff, too."

Hap White eased up beside Maxwell, speaking in a low voice.

"That license you got, Max," he hesitated.

Maxwell gave him a cold look. "What license?"

Hap dabbed at his forehead with a handkerchief. "You know, that marriage license for you and Doris. We—we want to buy it, since you won't be needing it yourself."

"I ain't selling, and it wouldn't do you any good if you did have it. It's got the names already written in it."

"We can fix that," wheedled Hap. "It's easy, Max. Johns— Jornstadt. See? They look alike on paper and there wouldn't anybody expect a county clerk to be able to write so you could read it. See?"

"Yes, I see," said Maxwell quietly, very quietly.

"It's all right with Doris," urged Hap. "Look, here's a note she sent."

Max read the unsigned scrawl in Doris' childish hand: "You leave me be, you old bigamist!" He scowled blackly.

"What say, Max?" persisted Hap.

Maxwell's lean jaw set grimly.

"No, I won't sell it; but I'll shoot Jornstadt for it—the license against his flask."

"Aw, come on, Max," protested Hap, "Jornstadt ain't no crap shooter. He's a Northerner. He don't even know how to handle the dice."

"Best two out of three, high dice," said Max. "Take it or leave it."

Hap pattered over to Jornstadt, muttered a few words. The Princeton man protested, then agreed.

"All right," said Hap. "Here's the flask. Put the license beside it on the floor."

"Where's the dice?" asked Maxwell. "Who's got some dice? Peter, gimme that set of yours."

The darky rolled the whites of his eyes. "My dice—they ain't—they—"

"Shut up and give them here!" blazed Maxwell. "We won't hurt 'em. C'mon!"

Peter fished them from his pocket.

"Here, lemme show you, Jornstadt," exclaimed Hap White.

Jornstadt handled the dice awkwardly. He fumbled them onto the floor. A five and a four showed.

"Nine!" chortled Hap. "That's a good roll!"

It was plenty good. The best Max could get was three and four —seven. The first round went to Jornstadt.

Max won the next one, however, nine against five. He clicked the dice together.

"Shall I go on shootin'?" he asked Jornstadt.

The Princeton man looked inquiringly at Hap White.

"Sure, it's all right," said Hap. "Let him shoot first."

Clickety-click! The dice tumbled from Maxwell's hand, rolled over and over and stopped.

"Whoopeee!" cheered Walter Mitchell under his breath. "Two fives! That's a winner!"

"Any use for me to shoot?" asked Jornstadt.

"Sure, take your roll," said Hap gloomily, "but you ain't got no more chance than a female in a frat house."

Jornstadt fumbled the dice awkwardly from hand to hand. He tossed them out. A five showed. The other cube spun dizzily on a corner for a spine-crawling moment and settled. Maxwell stared at the six black dots winking at him like spotty-eyed devils.

"Osky-wow-wow!" shrilled Hap White. "A natural!"

Jornstadt picked up the dice and glanced inquiringly about.

"Do I win?" he asked.

"Yes, you win," replied Maxwell evenly. He began putting on

his collar. Jornstadt handed the dice to the pop-eyed Peter. "Thank you," he said. He sauntered from the room with the gleeful Hap White, stuffing flask and license into his pocket.

The room was very still as Maxwell walked to the mirror and began adjusting his tie. One by one the youths slipped out. Maxwell was left alone. He glared into the mirror.

He heard somebody muttering to himself in the little wash room back of the partition. He recognized Peter's voice.

"Lawdy! Lawdy!" sounded the darky's querulous tones. "He jest nacherly couldn'ta made no 'leben wiff dem bones, kase dey ain't no sixes on 'em! Dem's special bones. He jest couldn't! But he did! I wish I knowed how to shoot crap like he *don't* know!"

Maxwell stared into the mirror, his lips slowly whitening. He reached to his hip pocket. The dull blue-black of an automatic pistol winked back at him from the mirror. He hesitated, returned the gun to his pocket.

"I don't want to get myself hung!" he muttered.

For long minutes he stood staring, the smoothness of his forehead wrinkled with the unaccustomed labor of intense thought. Peter still puttered around in the washroom.

Maxwell strode around the partition. He gripped the darky by the arm.

"Pete, I want you to get me something, and get it darned quick," he snarled. "Listen—"

"But, Mistuh Max, that stuff's blue lightnin'!" protested the darky. "That ain't no drinkin's for white gemmuns! All right, I's a-gwin'! I's a-gwin'!"

He was back in five minutes, with a fruit jar full of something that looked like water. Maxwell took it and shoved it into his coat pocket. A minute later Walter Mitchell came in with Jornstadt and Hap White. They had the flask.

Maxwell pulled out his fruit jar, unscrewed the cap and tilted it up.

"*This* is a man's drink," he said. "It ain't colored water like that stuff!"

Jornstadt sneered. "I never saw anything I couldn't drink," he declared. "Gimme a swig!"

"Better leave it alone," cautioned Maxwell. "I tell you it's for men."

Jornstadt flushed darkly. "Gimme that jar!"

Max handed it to him. Hap White caught a whiff and his mouth gaped open.

"That's cawn likker!" he squeaked.

"Jornstadt, don't you—"

Maxwell's elbow caught him viciously in the throat. Jornstadt, the jar already tilted, did not notice. Hap gagged, gulped and subsided, shivering slightly under Maxwell's baleful glare. Jornstadt gasped.

"Thought so," nodded Max. "Can't take it!"

"Who the hell says I can't!" snarled Jornstadt, and the jar tilted again.

The orchestra was playing "Goodnight, Sweetheart," when they left the coat room. Jornstadt's eyes were slightly glazed and he held onto Hap White's arm. Maxwell walked behind them, a thin smile on his lips. The smile was still there when he saw Jornstadt wobble to Hap White's car, his arm around Doris.

"We're headin' for Marley," he heard Hap White say. Lucille, already in the car, giggled.

"Follow them!" Maxwell snarled at Walter Mitchell. Marley was twenty-two miles away. There was a justice of the peace at Marley.

Jornstadt was sagging limply, his head on his breast. His once immaculate shirt bosom had burst open. His collar was up around his ears. Doris and Lucille supported him in the careening car. Doris was whimpering:

"I don't want to marry anybody. I want to go home. Old drunken bigamist!"

"You've got to go through with it now," said Lucille. "Both your names are on it now. If you don't it'll be forgery!"

"It says Maxwell Jornstadt!" wailed Doris. "I'll be married to both of them! It'll be bigamy!"

"Bigamy isn't as bad as forgery. We'll all be in trouble!"

"I don't wanna!"

The car slammed to a stop in front of a boxcar that had apparently got lost from its railroad. There were windows cut in it, and a door over which was a sign reading, "Justice of the Peace."

"I don't wanna be married in a boxcar!" whimpered Doris.

"It's just like a church," urged Lucille, "only there ain't no organ. A J. P. isn't a D. D., so he can't marry you in a church."

The boxcar door opened and a paunchy, oldish man carrying a flash light looked out. His nightshirt was thrust into his trousers. His braces were dangling.

"Come in! Come in!" he grumbled.

Walter Mitchell's car slid up. Maxwell got out and strolled to Hap's car.

Hap was pawing at Jornstadt; trying to rouse him.

"Let him be," grunted Maxwell. "Get the license and give it to me. I'll stand up for him."

"I don't wanna!" whimpered Doris.

They went into the boxcar. The J. P. stood with a large book in his hand. The light of an oil lamp yellowed their wan faces. The J. P. looked at Doris.

"How old are you, sister?" he asked.

Doris stared woodenly. Lucille spoke up quickly:

"She's just eighteen."

"She looks about fourteen and like she ought to be home in bed," grunted the J. P.

"She's been sitting up with a sick friend," said Lucille.

The J. P. looked at the license. Lucille gulped in her throat.

"These names—" he began. Lucille found her voice.

"Doris Houston and Maxwell Johnstadt," she said.

"Good God, don't they even know their own names!" exclaimed the J. P. "This one looks like—"

Something suddenly nuzzled into the palm of his hand. Maxwell was standing beside him, very close. The thing that nuzzled the J. P.'s hand was the hundred and forty dollars Max had won in the crap game. The J. P.'s hands closed over the roll of bills like a tomcat's claw over a mouse. He opened the big book.

"Come on," Max told Doris three minutes later. "From now on you're taking orders from me—Mrs. Johns!"

Lucille wailed. Hap White yammered. Jornstadt snored loudly in the tonneau of Hap's car.

"*Oh!*" said Doris.

The cold light of a January morning was breaking as they reached the big, garish Houston house. There was already a car standing in front of it.

"That's Doc Carberry's Chrysler!" exclaimed Maxwell. "Do you reckon somebody—"

Doris was out and running before the car stopped. "If it is it's your fault!" she wailed thinly over her shoulder: "Go away from me, you old bigamist."

Maxwell followed her into the house. He heard Dr. Carberry say:

"He'll be all right now, Mrs. Houston. I got it out; but it was a narrow escape."

Doris was screaming at her mother:

"Mamma! I'm married, Mamma! Mamma! I'm married!"

"Married!" shrieked Mrs. Houston. "My God, ain't we had enough trouble here tonight! Married! Who—"

She caught sight of Maxwell. "You!" she screeched, rushing at him, waving her pudgy hands. The diamonds on her fingers sent dazzling glints of light into his eyes. "You get out of here! Get out, I say! Get out!"

"We're mar—" began Max. "I tell you—"

Mrs. Houston rushed him into the hall, screeched a final, "Get out!" and dived back into the parlor. The billowing form of the Negro maid suddenly appeared before Max. He gave back a step.

"De front door's open," said the Negress pointedly.

"What you talking about?" demanded Max. "I tell you we're married, all right. We—"

"Ain't you kicked up enough bobbery 'round heah for one night?" demanded the Negress. "You get out now. Mebbe you telefoam t'morrow."

"Telephone!" sputtered Max. "I tell you she's my—"

"You to blame for it all!" glowered the Negress. "Leavin' the needle stickin' in de chair wheah anybody'd knowed de baby would get hold of it!"

She billowed forward. Max suddenly found himself on the front porch.

"Needle—baby—" he gurgled dazedly. "What—what—"

"You no 'count good-fo' nothin'! De baby he swallered it!"

The door closed in his face.

He started the car. It moved slowly away. "Telephone, hell," he said suddenly. "She's my—"

But he did not say it. An approaching car swung wide of him.

He did not see it. He was fumbling in his pocket. At last he drew out a crumpled cigarette. Another car swerved wildly and barely missed Maxwell's car.

The cruising driver saw only a big car moving with erratic slowness on the wrong side of the street driven by a young man in evening clothes at nine o'clock in the morning.

Afternoon of a Cow

Mr. Faulkner and I were sitting under the mulberry with the afternoon's first julep while he informed me what to write on the morrow, when Oliver appeared suddenly around the corner of the smokehouse, running and with his eyes looking quite large and white. "Mr. Bill!" he cried. "Day done sot fire to de pasture!"

"———" cried Mr. Faulkner, with that promptitude which quite often marks his actions, "——— those boys to ———!" springing up and referring to his own son, Malcolm, and to his brother's son, James, and to the cook's son, Rover or Grover. Grover his name is, though both Malcolm and James (they and Grover are of an age and have, indeed, grown up not only contemporaneously but almost inextricably) have insisted upon calling him Rover since they could speak, so that now all the household, including the child's own mother and naturally the child itself, call him Rover too, with the exception of myself, whose practice and belief it has never been to call any creature, man, woman, child or beast, out of its rightful name—just as I permit no one to call me out of mine, though I am aware that behind my back both Malcolm and James (and doubtless Rover or Grover) refer to me as Ernest be Toogood—a crass and low form of so-called wit or humor to which children, these two in particular—are only too prone. I have attempted on more than one occasion (this was years ago; I have long since ceased) to explain to them that my position in the household is in no sense menial, since I have been writing Mr. Faulkner's novels and short stories for years. But I long ago became convinced (and even reconciled) that neither of them either knew or cared about the meaning of the term.

I do not think that I anticipate myself in saying that we did not know where the three boys would now be. We would not be expected to know, beyond a general feeling or conviction that they would by now be concealed in the loft of the barn or stable—this from previous experience, though experience had never before included or comprised arson. Nor do I feel that I further violate the formal rules of order, unity and emphasis by saying that we would never for one moment have conceived them to be where later evidence indicated that they now were. But more on this subject anon: we were not thinking of the boys now; as Mr. Faulkner himself might have observed, someone should have been thinking about them ten or fifteen minutes ago; that now it was too late. No, our concern was to reach the pasture, though not with any hope of saving the hay which had been Mr. Faulkner's pride and even hope—a fine, though small, plantation of this grain or forage fenced lightly away from the pasture proper and the certain inroads of the three stocks whose pleasance the pasture was, which had been intended as an alternative or balancing factor in the winter's victualing of the three beasts. We had no hope of saving this, since the month was September following a dry summer, and we knew that this as well as the remainder of the pasture would burn with almost the instantaneous celerity of gunpowder or celluloid. That is, I had no hope of it and doubtless Oliver had no hope of it. I do not know what Mr. Faulkner's emotion was, since it appears (or so I have read and heard) a fundamental human trait to decline to recognize misfortune with regard to some object which man either desires or already possesses and holds dear, until it has run him down and then over like a Juggernaut itself. I do not know if this emotion would function in the presence of a field of hay, since I have neither owned nor desired to own one. No, it was not the hay which we were concerned about. It was the three animals, the two horses and the cow, in particular the cow, who, less gifted or equipped for speed than the horses, might be overtaken by the flames and perhaps asphyxiated, or at least so badly scorched as to be rendered temporarily unfit for her natural function; and that the two horses might bolt in terror, and to their detriment, into the further fence of barbed wire or might even turn and rush back into the actual flames, as is one of the more intelligent characteristics of this so-called servant and friend of man.

So, led by Mr. Faulkner and not even waiting to go around to the arched passage, we burst through the hedge itself and, led by Mr. Faulkner who moved at a really astonishing pace for a man of what might be called almost violently sedentary habit by nature, we ran across the yard and through Mrs. Faulkner's flower beds and then through her rose garden, although I will say that both Oliver and myself made some effort to avoid the plants; and on across the adjacent vegetable garden, where even Mr. Faulkner could accomplish no harm since at this season of the year it was innocent of edible matter; and on to the panel pasture fence over which Mr. Faulkner hurled himself with that same agility and speed and palpable disregard of limb which was actually amazing —not only because of his natural lethargic humor, which I have already indicated, but because of that shape and figure which ordinarily accompanies it (or at least does so in Mr. Faulkner's case) —and were enveloped immediately in smoke.

But it was at once evident by its odor that this came, not from the hay which must have stood intact even if not green and then vanished in holocaust doubtless during the few seconds while Oliver was crying his news, but, from the cedar grove at the pasture's foot. Nevertheless, odor or not, its pall covered the entire visible scene, although ahead of us we could see the creeping line of conflagration beyond which the three unfortunate beasts now huddled or rushed in terror of their lives. Or so we thought until, still led by Mr. Faulkner and hastening now across a stygian and desolate floor which almost at once became quite unpleasant to the soles of the feet and promised to become more so, something monstrous and wild of shape rushed out of the smoke. It was the larger horse, Stonewall—a congenitally vicious brute which no one durst approach save Mr. Faulkner and Oliver, and not even Oliver durst mount (though why either Oliver or Mr. Faulkner should want to is forever beyond me) which rushed down upon us with the evident intent of taking advantage of this opportunity to destroy its owner and attendant both, with myself included for lagniappe or perhaps for pure hatred of the entire human race. It evidently altered its mind, however, swerving and vanishing again into smoke. Mr. Faulkner and Oliver had paused and given it but a glance. "I reckin dey all right," Oliver said. "But where you reckin Beulah at?"

"On the other side of that —— fire, backing up in front of it and bellowing," replied Mr. Faulkner. He was correct, because almost at once we began to hear the poor creature's lugubrious lamenting. I have often remarked now how both Mr. Faulkner and Oliver apparently possess some curious rapport with horned and hooved beasts and even dogs, which I cheerfully admit that I do not possess myself and do not even understand. That is, I cannot understand it in Mr. Faulkner. With Oliver, of course, cattle of all kinds might be said to be his avocation, and his dallying (that is the exact word; I have watched him more than once, motionless and apparently pensive and really almost pilgrim-like, with the handle of the mower or hoe or rake for support) with lawn mower and gardening tools his sideline or hobby. But Mr. Faulkner, a member in good standing of the ancient and gentle profession of letters! But then neither can I understand why he should wish to ride a horse, and the notion has occurred to me that Mr. Faulkner acquired his rapport gradually and perhaps over a long period of time from contact of his posterior with the animal he bestrode.

We hastened on toward the sound of the doomed creature's bellowing. I thought that it came from the flames perhaps and was the final plaint of her agony—a dumb brute's indictment of heaven itself—but Oliver said not, that it came from beyond the fire. Now there occurred in it a most peculiar alteration. It was not an increase in terror, which scarcely could have been possible. I can describe it best by saying that she now sounded as if she had descended abruptly into the earth. This we found to be true. I believe however that this time order requires, and the element of suspense and surprise which the Greeks themselves have authorized will permit, that the story progress in the sequence of events as they occurred to the narrator, even though the accomplishment of the actual event recalled to the narrator the fact or circumstance with which he was already familiar and of which the reader should have been previously made acquainted. So I shall proceed.

Imagine us, then, hastening (even if the abysmal terror in the voice of the hapless beast had not been inventive enough, we had another: on the morrow, when I raised one of the shoes which I had worn on this momentous afternoon, the entire sole crumbled into a substance resembling nothing so much as that which might have been scraped from the ink-wells of childhood's school days at the beginning of the fall term) across that stygian plain, our eyes and lungs smarting with that smoke along whose further edge the border of fire crept. Again a wild and monstrous shape materialized in violent motion before us, again apparently with the avowed and frantic aim of running us down. For a horrid moment I believed it to be the horse, Stonewall, returned because after passing us for some distance (persons do this; possibly it might likewise occur in an animal, its finer native senses dulled with smoke and terror), remembering having seen myself or recognized me, and had now returned to destroy me alone. I had never liked the horse. It was an emotion even stronger than mere fear; it was that horrified disgust which I imagine one must feel toward a python and doubtless even the horse's subhuman sensibilities had felt and had come to reciprocate. I was mistaken, however. It was the other horse, the smaller one which Malcolm and James rode, apparently with enjoyment, as though in miniature of the besotted perversion of their father and uncle—an indiscriminate, round-bodied creature, as gentle as the larger one was vicious, with a drooping sad upper lip and an inarticulate and bemused (though to me still sly and untrustworthy) gaze; it, too, swerved past us and also vanished just before we reached the line of flame which was neither as large nor as fearful as it had looked, though the smoke was thicker, and seemed to be filled with the now loud terrified voice of the cow. In fact, the poor creature's voice seemed now to be everywhere: in the air above us and in the earth beneath. With Mr. Faulkner still in the lead we sprang over it, whereupon Mr. Faulkner immediately vanished. Still in the act of running, he simply vanished out of the smoke before the eyes of Oliver and myself as though he too had dropped into the earth.

This is what he had also done. With the voice of Mr. Faulkner and the loud terror of the cow coming out of the earth at our feet and the creeping line of the conflagration just behind us, I now realized what had happened and so solved Mr. Faulkner's disappearance as well as the previous alteration in the voice of the cow. I now realized that, confused by the smoke and the incandescent sensation about the soles of the feet, I had become disoriented and had failed to be aware that all the while we had been approaching a gully or ravine of whose presence I was quite aware, having looked down into it more than once while strolling in the afternoons while Mr. Faulkner would be riding the large horse, and upon whose brink or verge Oliver and I now stood and into which Mr. Faulkner and the cow had, in turn and in the reverse order, fallen.

"Are you hurt, Mr. Faulkner?" I cried. I shall not attempt to reproduce Mr. Faulkner's reply, other than to indicate that it was couched in that pure ancient classic Saxon which the best of our literature sanctions and authorizes and which, due to the exigencies of Mr. Faulkner's style and subject matter, I often employ but which I myself never use although Mr. Faulkner even in his private life is quite addicted to it and which, when he employs it, indicates what might be called a state of the most robust, even though not at all calm, wellbeing. So I knew that he was not hurt. "What shall we now do?" I inquired of Oliver.

"We better git down in dat hole too," Oliver replied. "Ain't you feel dat fire right behime us?" I had forgot about the fire in my concern over Mr. Faulkner, but upon glancing behind me I felt instinctively that Oliver was right. So we scrambled or fell down the steep sandy declivity, to the bottom of the ravine where Mr. Faulkner, still speaking, stood and where the cow was now safely ensconced though still in a state of complete hysteria, from which point or sanctuary we watched the conflagration pass over, the flames crumbling and flickering and dying away along the brink of the ravine. Then Mr. Faulkner spoke:

"Go catch Dan, and bring the big rope from the storehouse."

"Do you mean me?" said I. Mr. Faulkner did not reply, so he and I stood beside the cow who did not yet seem to realize that the danger was past or perhaps whose more occult brute intellect knew that the actual suffering and outrage and despair had yet to occur —and watched Oliver climb or scramble back up the declivity. He was gone for some time, although after a while he returned, leading the smaller and tractable horse who was adorned with a section of harness, and carrying the rope; whereupon commenced the arduous business of extricating the cow. One end of the rope was attached to her horns, she still objecting violently; the other end was attached to the horse. "What shall I do?" I inquired.

"Push," said Mr. Faulkner.

"Where shall I push?" I asked.

"I don't give a ——," said Mr. Faulkner. "Just push."

But it appeared that it could not be done. The creature resisted, perhaps to the pull of the rope or perhaps to Oliver's encouraging shouts and cries from the brink overhead or possibly to the motive power supplied by Mr. Faulkner (he was directly behind, almost beneath her, his shoulder against her buttocks or loins and swearing steadily now) and myself. She made a gallant effort, scrambled quite half way up the declivity, lost her footing and slid back. Once more we tried and failed, and then again. And then a most regrettable accident occurred. This third time the rope either slipped or parted, and Mr. Faulkner and the cow were hurled violently to the foot of the precipice with Mr. Faulkner underneath.

Later—that evening, to be exact—I recalled how, at the moment while we watched Oliver scramble out of the ravine, I seem to have received, as though by telepathy, from the poor creature (a female mind; the lone female among three men) not only her terror but the subject of it: that she knew by woman's sacred instinct that the future held for her that which is to a female far worse than any fear of bodily injury or suffering: one of those invasions of female privacy where, helpless victim of her own physical body, she seems to see herself as object of some malignant power for irony and outrage; and this none the less bitter for the fact that those who are to witness it, gentlemen though they be, will never be able to forget it but will walk the earth with the remembrance of it so long as she lives;—yes, even the more bitter for the fact that they who are to witness it are gentlemen, people of her own class. Remember how the poor spent terrified creature had for an entire afternoon been the anguished and blind victim of a circumstance which it could not comprehend, had been sported with by an element which it instinctively feared, and had now been hurled recently and violently down a precipice whose crest it doubtless now believed it would never see again.—I have been told by soldiers (I served in France, in the Y.M.C.A.) how, upon entering battle, there often sets up within them, prematurely as it were, a certain impulse or desire which brings on a result quite logical and quite natural, the fulfillment of which is incontestible and of course irrevocable.—In a word, Mr. Faulkner underneath received the full discharge of the poor creature's afternoon of anguish and despair.

It has been my fortune or misfortune to lead what is—or might be—called a quiet, even though not retired, life; and I have even preferred to acquire my experience from reading what had happened to others or what other men believe or think might have logically happened to creatures of their invention or even in inventing what Mr. Faulkner conceives might have happened to certain and sundry creatures who compose his novels and stories. Nevertheless, I would imagine that a man is never too old nor too secure to suffer what might be called experiences of initial and bizarre originality, though of course not always outrage, following which his reaction would be quite almost invariably out of character. Or rather, following which his reaction would reveal that actual character which for years he may have successfully concealed from the public, his intimates, and his wife and family; perhaps even from himself. I would take it to be one of these which Mr. Faulkner had just suffered.

Anyway, his actions during the subsequent few minutes were most peculiar for him. The cow—poor female alone among three men—struggled up almost at once and stood, hysterically still though no longer violent, trembling rather with a kind of aghast abasement not yet become despair. But for a time Mr. Faulkner, prone on the earth, did not stir at all. Then he rose. He said, "Wait," which naturally we should do until he gave further orders or instructions. Then—the poor cow and myself, and Oliver looking down from the crest beside the horse—we watched Mr. Faulkner walk quietly a few paces down the ravine and sit down, his elbows on his knees and his chin supported between his hands. It was not the sitting down which was peculiar. Mr. Faulkner did this often—steadily perhaps is a better word—if not in the house, then (in summer) well down in a large chair on the veranda just outside the library window where I would be working, his feet on the railing, reading a detective magazine; in winter in the kitchen, his stocking feet inside the oven to the stove. It was the attitude in which he now sat. As I have indicated, there was a quality almost violent about Mr. Faulkner's sedentation; it would be immobile without at all being lethargic, if I may put it so. He now sat in the attitude of M. Rodin's *Penseur* increased to his tenth geometric power say, since le penseur's principal bewilderment appears to be at what has bemused him, while Mr. Faulkner can have had no doubt. We watched him quietly—myself, and the poor cow who now stood with her head lowered and not even trembling in utter and now hopeless female shame; Oliver and the horse on the brink above. I remarked then that Oliver no longer had smoke for his background. The immediate conflagration was now over, though the cedar grove would doubtless smoulder until the equinox.

Then Mr. Faulkner rose. He returned quietly and he spoke as quietly (or even more so) to Oliver as I have ever heard him: "Drop the rope, Jack." Oliver removed his end of the rope from the horse and dropped it, and Mr. Faulkner took it up and turned and led the cow down the ravine. For a moment I watched him with an amazement of which Oliver doubtless partook; in the next moment doubtless Oliver and I would have looked at one another in that same astonishment. But we did not; we moved; doubtless we moved at the same moment. Oliver did not even bother to descend into the ravine. He just went around it while I hastened on and overtook Mr. Faulkner and the cow; indeed, the three of us were actually soldiers recovered from the amnesia of battle, the battle with the flames for the life of the cow. It has been often remarked and even insisted upon in literature (novels have been built upon it, though none of them are Mr. Faulkner's) how, when faced with catastrophe, man does everything but the simple one. But from the fund of my own experience, though it does consist almost entirely of that afternoon, it is my belief that it is in the face of danger and disaster that he does the simple thing. It is merely simply wrong.

We moved down the ravine to where it turned at right angles and entered the woods which descended to its level. With Mr. Faulkner and the cow in the lead we turned up through the woods and came presently to the black desolation of the pasture in the fence to which Oliver, waiting, had already contrived a gap or orifice through which we passed. Then with Mr. Faulkner again in the lead and with Oliver, leading the horse and the cow, and myself side by side, we retraced across that desolate plain the course of our recent desperate race to offer succor, though bearing somewhat to the left in order to approach the stable—or barnlot. We had almost reached the late hay plantation when, without warning, we found ourselves faced by three apparitions. They were not ten paces away when we saw them and I believe that neither Mr. Faulkner nor Oliver recognized them at all, though I did. In fact, I had an instantaneous and curious sense, not that I had anticipated this moment so much as that I had been waiting for it over a period which might be computed in years.

Imagine yourself, if you will, set suddenly down in a world in complete ocular or chromatic reversal. Imagine yourself faced with three small ghosts, not of white but of purest and unrelieved black. The mind, the intelligence, simply refuses to believe that they should have taken refuge from their recent crime or misdemeanor in the hay plantation before it took fire, and lived. Yet there they were. Apparently they had neither brows, lashes nor hair; and clothing epidermis and all, they were of one identical sable, and the only way in which Rover or Grover could be distinguished from the other two was by Malcolm's and James' blue eyes. They stood looking at us in complete immobility until Mr. Faulkner said, again with that chastened gentleness and quietude which, granted my theory that the soul, plunged without warning into some unforeseen and outrageous catastrophe, comes out in its true colors, has been Mr. Faulkner's true and hidden character all these years: "Go to the house."

They turned and vanished immediately, since it had been only by the eyeballs that we had distinguished them from the stygian surface of the earth at all. They may have preceded us or we may have passed them. I do not know. At least, we did not see them again, because presently we quitted the sable plain which had witnessed our Gethsemane, and presently entered the barnlot where Mr. Faulkner turned and took the halter of the horse while Oliver led the cow into its private and detached domicile, from which there came presently the sound of chewing as, freed now of anguish and shame she ruminated, maiden meditant and—I hope —once more fancy free.

Mr. Faulkner stood in the door of the stable (within which, by and by, I could hear the larger and vicious horse, Stonewall, already at his food, stamp now and then or strike the board wall with his hoof as though even in the act of eating it could not forbear making sounds of threat and derision toward the very man whose food nourished it) and removed his clothing. Then, in full sight of the house and of whoever might care or not care to see, he lathered himself with saddle soap and then stood at the watering trough while Oliver doused or flushed him down with pail after pail of water. "Never mind the clothes just now," he said to Oliver. "Get me a drink."

"Make it two," said I; I felt that the occasion justified, even though it may not have warranted, that temporary aberration into the vernacular of the fleeting moment. So presently, Mr. Faulkner now wearing a light summer horse blanket belonging to Stonewall, we sat again beneath the mulberry with the second julep of the afternoon.

"Well, Mr. Faulkner," said I after a time, "shall we continue?"

"Continue what?" said Mr. Faulkner.

"Your suggestions for tomorrow," said I. Mr. Faulkner said nothing at all. He just drank, with that static violence which was his familiar character, and so I knew that he was himself once more and that the real Mr. Faulkner which had appeared momentarily to Oliver and myself in the pasture had already retreated to that inaccessible bourne from which only the cow, Beulah, had ever evoked it, and that doubtless we would never see it again. So after a time I said, "Then, with your permission, tomorrow I shall venture into fact and employ the material which we ourselves have this afternoon created."

"Do so," Mr. Faulkner said—shortly, I thought.

"Only," I continued, "I shall insist upon my prerogative and right to tell this one in my own diction and style, and not yours."

"By ——!" said Mr. Faulkner. "You better had."

Mr. Acarius

Mr. Acarius waited until toward the end of the afternoon, though he and his doctor had been classmates and fraternity brothers and still saw each other several times a week in the homes of the same friends and in the bars and lounges and grills of the same clubs, and he knew that he would have been sent straight in, no matter when he called. He was, almost immediately, to stand in his excellent sober Madison Avenue suit above the desk behind which his friend sat buried to the elbows in the paper end of the day, a reflector cocked rakishly above one ear and the other implements of his calling serpentined about the white regalia of his priesthood.

"I want to get drunk," Mr. Acarius said.

"All right," the doctor said, scribbling busily now at the foot of what was obviously a patient's chart. "Give me ten minutes. Or why don't you go on to the club and I'll join you there."

But Mr. Acarius didn't move. He said, "Ab. Look at me," in such a tone that the doctor thrust his whole body up and away from the desk in order to look up at Mr. Acarius standing over him.

"Say that again," the doctor said. Mr. Acarius did so. "I mean in English," the doctor said.

"I was fifty years old yesterday," Mr. Acarius said. "I have just exactly what money I shall need to supply my wants and pleasures until the bomb falls. Except that when that occurs—I mean the bomb, of course—nothing will have happened to me in all my life. If there is any rubble left, it will be only the carcass of my Capehart and the frames of my Picassos. Because there will never have been anything of me to have left any smudge or stain. Until now, that has contented me. Or rather, I have been resigned to accept it. But not any more. Before I have quitted this scene, vanished from the recollection of a few headwaiters and the membership lists of a few clubs—"

"Along with the headwaiters and the clubs," the doctor said. "Predicating the bomb, of course."

"Be quiet and listen," Mr. Acarius said. "Before that shall have happened, I want to experience man, the human race."

"Find yourself a mistress," the doctor said.

"I tried that. Maybe what I want is debasement too."

"Then in God's name get married," the doctor said. "What better way than that to run the whole gamut from garret to cellar and back again, not just once, but over again every day—or so they tell me."

"Yes," Mr. Acarius said. "So they tell you. I notice how the bachelor always says *Try* marriage, as he might advise you to try hashish. It's the husband who always says *Get* married; *videlicet:* We need you."

"Then get drunk," the doctor said. "And may your shadow never grow less. And now I hope we have come at last to the nut. Just what do you want of me?"

"I want—" Mr. Acarius said. "I don't just want—"

"You don't just want to get tight, like back in school: Wake up tomorrow with nothing but a hangover, take two aspirins and a glass of tomato juice and drink all the black coffee you can hold, then at five P.M. a hair of the dog and now the whole business is over and forgotten until next time. You want to lie in a gutter in skid row without having to go down to skid row to do it. You no more intend going down to skid row than you intend having skid row coming up the elevator to the twenty-second floor of the Barkman Tower. You would join skid row in its debasement, only you prefer to do yours on good Scotch whiskey. So there's not just an esprit de sty; there's a snobbery de sty too."

"All right," said Mr. Acarius.

"All right?"

"Yes then," Mr. Acarius said.

"Then this is where we came in," the doctor said. "Just what do you want of me?"

"I'm trying to tell you," Mr. Acarius said. "I'm not just no better than the people on skid row. I'm not even as good, for the reason that I'm richer. Because I'm richer, I not only don't have anything to escape from, driving me to try to escape from it, but as another cypher in the abacus of mankind, I am not even high enough in value to alter any equation by being subtracted from it. But at least I can go along for the ride, like the flyspeck on the handle of the computer, even if it can't change the addition. At least I can experience, participate in, the physical degradation of escaping—"

"A sty in a penthouse," the doctor said.

"—the surrender, the relinquishment to and into the opium of escaping, knowing in advance the inevitable tomorrow's inevitable physical agony; to have lost nothing of anguish but instead only to have gained it; to have merely compounded yesterday's spirit's and soul's laceration with tomorrow's hangover—"

"—with a butler to pour your drink when you reach that stage and to pour you into the bed when you reach that stage, and to bring you the aspirin and the bromide after the three days or the four or whenever it will be that you will allow yourself to hold them absolved who set you in the world," the doctor said.

"I didn't think you understood," Mr. Acarius said, "even if you were right about the good Scotch where his on skid row is canned heat. The butler and the penthouse will only do to start with, to do the getting drunk in. But after that, no more. Even if Scotch is the only debasement of which my soul is capable, the anguish of my recovery from it will be at least a Scotch approximation of his who had nothing but canned heat with which to face the intolerable burden of his soul."

"What in the world are you talking about?" the doctor said. "Do you mean that you intend to drink yourself into Bellevue?"

"Not Bellevue," Mr. Acarius said. "Didn't we both agree that I am incapable of skid row? No, no: One of those private places, such as the man from skid row will never and can never see, whose at best is a grating or a vacant doorway, and at worst a police van and the—what do they call it?—bullpen. A Scotch bullpen of course, since that's all I am capable of. But it will have mankind in it, and I shall have entered mankind."

"Say that again," the doctor said. "Try that in English too."

"That's all," Mr. Acarius said. "Mankind. People. Man. I shall

be one with man, victim of his own base appetites and now struggling to extricate himself from that debasement. Maybe it's even
my fault that I'm incapable of anything but Scotch, and so our
bullpen will be a Scotch one where for a little expense we can have
peace, quiet for the lacerated and screaming nerves, sympathy,
understanding—"

"What?" the doctor said.

"—and maybe what my fellow inmates are trying to escape from
—the too many mistresses or wives or the too much money or
responsibility or whatever else it is that drives into escape the sort
of people who can afford to pay fifty dollars a day for the privilege
of escaping—will not bear mention in the same breath with that
which drives one who can afford no better, even to canned heat.
But at least we will be together in having failed to escape and in
knowing that in the last analysis there is no escape, that you can
never escape and, whether you will or not, you must reenter the
world and bear yourself in it and its lacerations and all its anguish
of breathing, to support and comfort one another in that knowledge and that attempt."

"What?" the doctor said. "What's that?"

"I beg pardon?" said Mr. Acarius.

"Do you really believe that that's what you are going to find in
this place?"

"Why not?"

"Then I beg yours," the doctor said. "Go on."

"That's all," Mr. Acarius said. "That's what I want of you. You
must know any number of these places. The best—"

"The best," the doctor said. "Of course." He reached for the
telephone. "Yes, I know it."

"Shouldn't I see it first?"

"What for? They're all alike. You'll have seen plenty of this one
before you're out again."

"I thought you said that this one would be the best," Mr.
Acarius said.

"Right," the doctor said, removing his hand from the telephone.
It did not take them long: an address in an expensive section facing
the Park, itself outwardly resembling just another expensive apartment house not too different from that one in (or on) which Mr.
Acarius himself lived, the difference only beginning inside and even

there not too great: A switchboard in a small foyer enclosed by the glass-panel walls of what were obviously offices. Apparently the doctor read Mr. Acarius's expression. "Oh, the drunks," the doctor said. "They're all upstairs. Unless they can walk, they bring them in the back way. And even when they can walk in, they don't see this very long nor but twice. Well?" Then the doctor read that one too. "All right. We'll see Hill too. After all, if you're going to surrender your amateur's virginity in debauchery, you are certainly entitled to examine at least the physiognomy of the supervisor of the rite."

Doctor Hill was no older than Mr. Acarius's own doctor; apparently there was between them the aura or memory of more than one Atlantic City and Palm Beach and Beverly Hills convention. "Look here, Ab," Doctor Hill said. "Haven't you boys come to the wrong place?"

"Does Doctor Hill think I shouldn't take up room better used or at least needed by someone else?" Mr. Acarius said.

"No, no," Doctor Hill said. "There's always room for one more in dipsomania."

"Like in adultery," Mr. Acarius's doctor said.

"We don't cure that here," Doctor Hill said.

"Do they anywhere?" Mr. Acarius's doctor said.

"Can't say," Doctor Hill said. "When do you want to start?"

"What about now?" said Mr. Acarius.

"You just get sober here, not drunk too," Doctor Hill said. "You'll have to do that much of it outside, otherwise the antitrust or the free-trade laws might get us."

"Give us four days," Mr. Acarius's doctor said. "We can certainly come in under the wire in that time."

So four days were set; Mr. Acarius let himself go into alcohol completely again for the first time since his college days. That is, he tried to, because at first it seemed to him that he was making no progress at all and in the end would let down not only his own doctor but Doctor Hill too. But by the end of the third day, reason told him he had better not try to leave his penthouse; and by the afternoon of the fourth one, when his doctor called for him, his legs themselves assured him that he could not without assistance, so that his doctor looked at him with a sort of admiration almost. "By gravy, you're even up to an ambulance. What do you say? Go in toes-up like you had come in a patrol wagon right out from under Brooklyn Bridge?"

"No," Mr. Acarius said. "Just hurry."

"What?" the doctor said. "It can't be that your mind is changing."

"No," Mr. Acarius said. "This is what I wanted."

"The brotherhood of suffering," the doctor said. "All of you together there, to support and comfort one another in the knowledge of the world's anguish, and that you must be a man and not run from it? How did it go? Peace and quiet for the lacerated and screaming nerves, sympathy, understanding—"

"All right," Mr. Acarius said. "Just hurry. I'm going to be sick."

So they did: between his own houseman and an elevator man who remembered him well and tenderly from many Christmases, down the elevator and across the foyer and into the doctor's car; then into the other small foyer again, where Mr. Acarius knew that at any moment now he was going to be sick, looking out of a sort of tilting chasm of foul bile-tasting misery at what was holding them up: some commotion or excitement at the elevator which a flashy, slightly brassy woman in an expensive fur coat, like a fading show girl, was being forcibly restrained from entering. If somebody doesn't do something pretty quick, Mr. Acarius thought, it won't matter anymore. Which apparently someone did, his own doctor perhaps, though Mr. Acarius was too miserable to tell, only that he was in the elevator at last, the door sliding to across the heavily rouged shape of the woman's scream. "Peace and quiet," his doctor said.

"All right," Mr. Acarius said again. "Just hurry."

But they made it: in the privacy of his room at last and the nurse (he did not remark when or where she came from either) even got the basin in position in time. Then he lay exhausted on his bed while the deft hands which he had anticipated divested him of his clothing and slipped his pajamas over his legs and arms, not his doctor's hands, nor—opening his eyes—even the nurse's. It was a man, with a worn almost handsome actor's face, in pajamas and dressing gown, whom Mr. Acarius knew at once, with a sort of peaceful vindication, to be another patient. He had been right, it was not even as he had merely hoped but as he had expected, lying there, empty and exhausted and even at peace at last while he watched the stranger take up his coat and trousers and move rapidly into the bathroom with them and reappear empty-handed, stooping now over Mr. Acarius's suitcase when the nurse entered with a small glass of something and a tumbler of water on a tray.

"What is it?" Mr. Acarius said.

"For your nerves," the nurse said.

"I don't want it now," Mr. Acarius said. "I want to suffer a little more yet."

"You want to what?" the nurse said.

"The man's suffering," the stranger said. "Go on, Goldie. Bring him a drink. You've got to have something to put down on his chart."

"Says you," the nurse said.

"You've got to watch Goldie," the stranger said to Mr. Acarius. "She's from Alabama."

"What time everybody's not watching you," the nurse said to the stranger. She glanced rapidly, apparently at Mr. Acarius's discarded clothing, because she said sharply, "Where's his suit?"

"I've already put it in," the stranger said, tossing Mr. Acarius's shoes and underwear and shirt into the suitcase and closing it rapidly. Then he crossed to a narrow locker in the corner and stowed the suitcase in it and closed the door, which now revealed itself to be armed with a small padlock. "You want to lock it yourself, or will you trust me?" the stranger said to the nurse.

"Hold it," the nurse said grimly. She set the tray on the table and entered the bathroom and then reappeared. "All right," she said. "Lock it." The stranger did so. The nurse approached and tested the lock and then took up the tray again. "When you want this, ring," she told Mr. Acarius. At the door she paused again, speaking this time to the stranger. "Get out of here now," she said. "Let him rest."

"Right," the stranger said. The nurse went out. The stranger watched the door for perhaps half a minute. Then he came back to the bed. "It's behind the tub," he said.

"What?" Mr. Acarius said.

"That's right," the stranger said. "You've got to watch even the good ones like Goldie. Just wait till you see the one that's coming at midnight. Boy. But we'll be all right now." He looked down at Mr. Acarius, speaking rapidly now. "My name's Miller. You're a patient of Doctor Cochrane's, aren't you?"

"Yes," Mr. Acarius said.

"That'll do it; Cochrane's got such a good reputation around here that any patient of his gets the benefit of the doubt. Judy's down stairs—Watkins's girl friend. She's already tried once to get up here. But Watkins himself hasn't a chance; Goldie's got him sewed up in his room and is watching him like a hawk. But you can do it."

"Do what?" Mr. Acarius said.

"Call down and say Judy is your guest, and to send her up," Miller said, handing Mr. Acarius the telephone. "Her name's Lester."

"What?" Mr. Acarius said. "What?"

"OK. I'll do it for you. What's your name? I didn't catch it."

"Acarius," Mr. Acarius said.

"Acarius," Miller said. He said into the telephone: "Hello. This is Mr. Acarius in twenty-seven. Send Miss Lester up, will you? Thanks." He put the receiver back and picked up Mr. Acarius's dressing gown. "Now put this on and be ready to meet her. We'll take care of the rest of it. We'll have to work fast because Goldie's going to catch on as soon as she hears the elevator."

It did go fast. Mr. Acarius in his dressing gown was barely on his feet and Miller was scarcely out of the room, when he heard the elevator stop, followed by a hard rapid clatter of female heels in the corridor. Then the next moment his room seemed to be full of people: the brassy, slightly buxom slightly faded girl whom he had left screaming in the foyer, running in and flinging herself upon him shrieking, "Darling! Darling!" with Miller and another man in pajamas and robe on her heels—an older man of at least sixty, with no actor's face this time because Shriner's conventions and nightclubs and the first-night lobbies of musical comedies were full of it—and last of all, the nurse and the elevator attendant, Mr. Acarius watching in horror the brassy girl now hissing viciously: "Hurry, you bastards, hurry!" holding the fur coat open while Miller and the other man tore savagely at the front of her dress until it fell open and revealed a half-pint bottle tucked into each lobe of her brassiere. Then the room was empty again, as suddenly and violently as it had filled, though not for long; indeed, to Mr.

Acarius it seemed almost simultaneous, superposed: The uproar
still fading up the corridor, the older patient's voice still raised in
adjuration at the nurse or whoever it was who had finally got the
two bottles, when the heels clattered again, the brassy girl entering
this time at a dead run, snatching the front of her dress and slip
into a wad at her middle and revealing a third bottle, a full pint
this time, taped high between her running legs, running to Mr.
Acarius and crying down at him: "Grab it! Grab it!" then, while
Mr. Acarius, incapable of moving, merely stared, ripping the bottle
free herself and thrusting it into the chair behind him and turning
already smoothing her skirt over her hips as the nurse entered,
saying to the nurse haughtily, in a voice of a princess or a queen:
"Have the goodness not to touch me again."

And he still crouched there, weak and trembling, while the
uproar really did die away; he was still there perhaps ten minutes
later when Miller, followed by the older man, entered. "Good
work," Miller said. "Where is it?" Mr. Acarius made a weak
gesture. Miller reached behind him and extracted a pint of whiskey.

"Did you ever see a dream . . . walking," the older man said.

"Oh yes," Miller said. "This is Watkins."

"Did you ever hear a dream . . . talking," Watkins said. "The
best place to hide it is here."

"Right." Miller said. "The geranium too."

"Go and get it," Watkins said. Miller went out. Watkins carried
the pint bottle to Mr. Acarius's bed and thrust it beneath the covers
at the foot. "And the dream that is walking and talking," Watkins
said. "This your first visit here?"

"Yes," Mr. Acarius whispered.

"You'll get used to it," Watkins said, ". . . is you," he said. Miller
returned, carrying a potted geranium under his dressing gown, and
a folded newspaper which he spread on the floor and then dumped
the plant and its nurturing earth from the pot onto the paper,
revealing another pint bottle.

"That puts us in pretty good shape," Miller said. "We may not
have to use your suit, after all."

"My suit?" Mr. Acarius whispered.

"The fire escape goes down just outside my window," Miller
said, folding the refuse of the geranium into the paper. "Last week

Watkins got hold of the key long enough to unlock the window. I've still got my shoes and shirt, but we didn't have any pants. But we're fixed now. In an emergency, one of us can climb down the fire escape and go down to the corner and get a bottle. But we won't need to now. We won't even need to risk changing the charts tonight," he said to Watkins.

"Maybe not," Watkins said, brushing the earth from the bottle, "Get a glass from the bathroom."

"Maybe we ought to put this back into the pot," Miller said, raising the folded paper.

"Put it all in the wastebasket," Watkins said. Miller dumped the paper containing the ruined geranium into Mr. Acarius's wastebasket and dropped the empty pot on top of it and went into the bathroom and returned with an empty tumbler. Watkins had already opened the bottle. He poured a drink into the tumbler and drank it. "Give him one too," he said. "He deserves it."

"No," Mr. Acarius whispered.

"Better have one," Miller said. "You don't look too good."

"No," Mr. Acarius whispered.

"You want me to send Goldie back with that bromide she tried to give you?"

"No," Mr. Acarius whispered.

"Let the man alone," Watkins said. "This is still America, even in here. He don't have to drink if he don't want to. Hide this one good too."

"Right," Miller said.

"Did you ever see a dream . . . walking," Watkins said.

And still Mr. Acarius crouched. After a while an orderly brought him a tray of supper; he sat looking at the food quietly, as though it contained poison. The nurse entered, again with the tray. This time it bore, in addition to the water, a small glass of whiskey.

"You've got to eat," she said. "Maybe this will give you an appetite."

"No," Mr. Acarius whispered.

"Come on now," the nurse said. "You must try to cooperate."

"I can't," Mr. Acarius whispered.

"OK," the nurse said. "But you must eat some of it, or I'll have to tell Doctor Hill on you."

So he tried, chewing down a little of the food anyway; presently the orderly came and removed the tray; immediately after that Miller entered rapidly and removed one of the bottles, the one Watkins had opened, from Mr. Acarius's bed. "We appreciate this," Miller said. "Sure you won't have one?"

"No," Mr. Acarius whispered. Then he could crouch again, hearing the slow accumulation of the cloistral evening. He could see the corridor beyond his door. Occasionally other men in pajamas and dressing gowns passed; they seemed to be congregating toward another lighted door up the corridor; even as he knotted the cord of his robe he could hear the unmistakable voice: "Did you ever see a dream . . . walking," then, creeping nearer, he could see inside the office or dispensary or whatever it was—a cabinet, open, the keys dangling on a ring from the lock, the nurse measuring whiskey from a brown unlabeled bottle in turn into the small glasses in the hands of the assembled devotees. "Did you ever hear a dream . . . talking," Watkins said.

"That's right," Miller said to him in a friendly voice. "Better take it while you can. It's going to be a long dry spell after Goldie goes off at midnight."

But that was not what Mr. Acarius wanted; alone with the nurse at last, he said so. "It's a little early to go to bed yet, isn't it?" the nurse said.

"I've got to sleep," Mr. Acarius said. "I've got to."

"All right," the nurse said. "Go get in bed and I'll bring it to you."

He did so, swallowed the capsule and then lay, the hidden bottle cold against his feet, though it would warm in time or perhaps in time, soon even, he would not care, though he didn't see how, how ever to sleep again; he didn't know how late it was, though that would not matter either: to call his doctor now, have the nurse call him, to come and get him, take him away into safety, sanity, falling suddenly from no peace into something without peace either, into a loud crash from somewhere up the corridor. It was late, he could feel it. The overhead light was off now, though a single shaded one burned beside the bed, and now there were feet in the corridor, running; Watkins and Miller entered. Watkins wore a woman's jade-colored raincoat, from the front of which protruded or dangled a single broken-stemmed tuberose; his head was bound in a crimson silk scarf like a nun's wimple. Miller was carrying the same brown unlabeled bottle which Mr. Acarius had seen the nurse lock back inside the cabinet two or three hours or whatever it was ago, which he was trying to thrust into Mr. Acarius's bed when there entered a nurse whom Mr. Acarius knew at once must be the new and dreaded one: an older woman in awry pince-nez, crying: "Give it back to me! Give it back to me!" She cried to Mr. Acarius: "I had the cabinet unlocked and was reaching down the bottle when one of them knocked my cap off and when I caught at it, one of them reached over my head and grabbed the bottle!"

"Then give me back that bottle of mine you stole out of my flush tank," Miller said.

"I poured it out," the nurse cried in triumph.

"But you had no right to," Miller said. "That was mine. I bought it myself, brought it in here with me. It didn't belong to the hospital at all and you had no right to put your hand on it."

"We'll let Doctor Hill decide that," the nurse said. She snatched up the brown unlabeled bottle and went out.

"You bet we will," Miller said, following.

"Did you ever hear a dream . . . talking," Watkins said. "Move your feet," he said, reaching into Mr. Acarius's bed and extracting the unopened bottle. Mr. Acarius did not move, he could not, while Watkins opened the bottle and drank from it. From up the corridor there still came the sound of Miller's moral indignation; presently Miller entered.

"She wouldn't let me use the telephone," he said. "She's sitting on it. We'll have to go upstairs and wake him up."

"She has no sense of humor," Watkins said. "Better kill this before she finds it too." They drank rapidly in turn from the bottle. "We'll have to have more liquor now. We'll have to get the keys away from her."

"How?" Miller said.

"Trip her up. Grab them."

"That's risky."

"Not unless she hits her head on something. Get her out into the corridor first, where there's plenty of room."

"Let's go upstairs and wake up Hill first," Miller said. "I'm damned if I'm going to let them get away with anything as high-handed as this."

"Right," Watkins said, emptying the bottle and dropping it into Mr. Acarius's wastebasket. Then Mr. Acarius was alone again— if he had ever been else, since there was no time to telephone anyone now, no one to telephone to: who was as isolate from help and aid here as if he had waked on an inaccessible and forgotten plateau of dinosaurs, where only beast might be rallied to protect beast from beast; he remembered in the group armed with the small ritual glasses at the dispensary one who looked like a truck driver or perhaps even a prize fighter; he might do to help, provided he was awake, though it was incredible to Mr. Acarius that anyone on the floor could still be asleep; certainly not now because at this moment there came through the ceiling overhead the sound of Doctor Hill's voice roaring with rage, Mr. Acarius lying in a kind of suffering which was almost peaceful, thinking, Yes, yes, we will save her life and then I will get out of here, I don't care how, I don't care where; still lying so while Doctor Hill's voice reached its final crescendo, followed by a curious faint sound which Mr. Acarius could define only as a suspended one: then one last thundering crash.

He was off the bed now; the nurse and an orderly running, had already shown the way: A door in the corridor which, open now, revealed a flight of concrete stairs, at the foot of which lay Watkins. He looked indeed like a corpse now. In fact, he looked more than just dead: he looked at peace, his eyes closed, one arm flung across his breast so that the lax hand seemed to clasp lightly the broken stem of the tuberose. "That's right!" Mr. Acarius cried, "tremble! You only hope he is!"

Miller had said he put the suit behind the tub; it was there, wadded. Mr. Acarius had no shirt save his pajama jacket nor shoes save his carpet slippers. Nor did he have any idea where Miller's room with its unlocked window on the fire escape was either. But he did not hesitate. I've done what I can, he thought. Let the Lord provide awhile.

Something did, anyway. He had to wait while the orderly and two patients bore Watkins into his room and cleared the corridor. Then he found Miller's room with no more effort than just selecting a door rapidly and opening it. He had had a fear of height all his life, though he was already on the dark fire escape before he even remembered it, thinking with a kind of amazement of a time, a world in which anyone had time to be afraid of anything consisting merely of vertical space. He knew in theory that fire escapes did not reach the ground and that you had to drop the remaining distance too; it was dark here and he did not know into what but again he did not hesitate, letting go into nothing, onto cinders; there was a fence too and then an alley and now he could see the sweet and empty sweep of the Park: that and nothing more between him and the sanctuary of his home. Then he was in the Park, running, stumbling, panting, gasping, when a car drew abreast of him. Slowing, and a voice said, "Hey, you!" and still trying to run even after the blue coats and the shields surrounded him: then he was fighting, swinging wildly and violently until they caught and held him while one of them sniffed his breath. "Don't strike a match near him," a voice said. "Call the wagon."

"It's all right, officer," his doctor said and, panting, helpless, even crying now, Mr. Acarius saw for the first time the other car drawn up behind the police one. "I'm his doctor. They telephoned me from the hospital that he had escaped. I'll take charge of him. Just help me get him into my car."

They did so: the firm hard hands. Then the car was moving. "It was that old man," he said crying. "That terrible, terrible old man, who should have been at home telling bedtime stories to his grand-children."

"Didn't you know there were police in that car?" the doctor said.

"No," Mr. Acarius cried. "I just knew that there were people in it."

Then he was at home, kneeling before the cellarette, dragging rapidly out not only what remained of the whiskey but all the rest of it too—the brandy, vermouth, gin, liqueurs—all of it, gathering the bottles in his arms and running into the bathroom where first one then a second and then a third crashed and splintered into the tub, the doctor leaning in the door, watching him.

"So you entered mankind, and found the place already occupied," the doctor said.

"Yes," Mr. Acarius said, crying, "You can't beat him. You cannot. You never will. Never."

Sepulture South: Gaslight

When Grandfather died, Father spoke what was probably his first reaction because what he said was involuntary because if he had taken time to think, he would not have said it: "Damn it, now we'll lose Liddy."

Liddy was the cook. She was one of the best cooks we had ever had and she had been with us ever since Grandmother died seven years ago when the cook before her had left; and now with another death in the family, she would move too, regretfully, because she liked us also. But that was the way Negroes did: left after a death in the family they worked for, as though obeying not a superstition but a rite: the rite of their freedom: not freedom from having to work, that would not occur to anyone for several years yet, not until W.P.A., but the freedom to move from one job to another, using a death in the family as the moment, the instigation, to move, since only death was important enough to exercise a right as important as freedom.

But she would not go yet; hers and Arthur's (her husband's) departure would be done with a dignity commensurate with the dignity of Grandfather's age and position in our family and our town, and the commensurate dignity of his sepulture. Not to mention the fact that Arthur himself was now serving his apogee as a member of our household, as if the seven years he had worked for us had merely been the waiting for this moment, this hour, this day: sitting (not standing now: sitting) freshly shaved and with his hair trimmed this morning, in a clean white shirt and a necktie of Father's and wearing his coat, in a chair in the back room of the jewelry store while Mr. Wedlow the jeweler inscribed on the sheet of parchment in his beautiful flowing Spencerian hand the formal notice of Grandfather's death and the hour of his funeral, which, attached to the silver salver with knots of black ribbon and sprays of imitation immortelles, Arthur would bear from door to door (not back or kitchen doors but the front ones) through our town, to ring the bell and pass the salver in to whoever answered it, not as a servant bringing a formal notification now but as a member of our family performing a formal rite, since by this time the whole town knew that Grandfather was dead. So this was a rite, Arthur himself dominating the moment, dominating the entire morning in fact, because now he was not only no servant of ours, he was not even an envoy from us but rather a messenger from Death itself, saying to our town: "Pause, mortal; remember Me."

Then Arthur would be busy for the rest of the day, too, now in the coachman's coat and beaver hat which he had inherited from the husband of Liddy's precessor who had inherited it in his turn from the husband of her precessor's precessor, meeting with the surrey the trains on which our kin and connections would begin to arrive. And now the town would commence the brief, ritual formal calls, almost wordless and those in murmurs, whispers. Because ritual said that Mother and Father must bear this first shock of bereavement in privacy, supporting and comforting one another. So the next of kin must receive the callers: Mother's sister and her husband from Memphis because Aunt Alice, Father's brother Charles's wife, would have to be comforting and support- ing Uncle Charley—as long as they could keep her upstairs, that is. And all this time the neighbor ladies would be coming to the kitchen door (not the front one now: the kitchen and back ones) without knocking, with their cooks or yardboys carrying the dishes and trays of food they had prepared to feed us and our influx of kin, and for a midnight supper for the men, Father's friends that he hunted and played poker with, who would sit up all night with Grandfather's coffin when the undertaker brought it and put him into it.

And all tomorrow too, while the wreaths and flowers arrived; and now all who wanted to could go into the parlor and look at Grandfather framed in white satin in his gray uniform with the three stars on the collar, freshly shaven too and with just a touch of rouge on his cheeks. And tomorrow too, until after our dinner, when Liddy said to Maggie and the other children: "Now you chillen go down to the pasture and play until I calls you. And you mind Maggie now." Because it was not to me. I was not only the oldest but a boy, the third generation of oldest son from Grandfather's father; when Father's turn came it would be me to say before I would have time to think: Damn it, now we'll lose Julia or Florence or whatever her name would be by that time. I must be there too, in my Sunday clothes, with a band of crape on my arm, all of us except Mother and Father and Uncle Charley (Aunt Alice was though, because people excused her because she was always a good one to run things when she got a chance: and Uncle Rodney too although he was Father's youngest brother too) in the back room which Grandfather called his office, to which the whisky decanter had been moved from the dining-room sideboard in deference to the funeral; yes, Uncle Rodney too, who had no wife—the dashing bachelor who wore silk shirts and used scented shaving lotion, who had been Grandmother's favorite and that of a lot of other women too—the traveling salesman for the St. Louis wholesale house who brought into our town on his brief visits a breath, an odor, a glare almost of the metropolitan outland which was not for us: the teeming cities of hotel bellhops and girl shows and oyster-bars, my first recollection of whom was standing at the sideboard with the whisky decanter in his hand and who had it in his hand now except that Aunt Alice's hand was on it too and we could all hear her furious whisper:

"You cannot, you shall not let them smell you like this!"

Then Uncle Rodney's: "All right, all right. Get me a handful of cloves from the kitchen." So that too, the odor of cloves inextricable from that of whisky and shaving lotion and cut flowers, was a part of Grandfather's passing for the last time from his house, we waiting still in the office while the ladies entered the parlor where the casket was, the men stopping outside on the lawn, decorous and quiet, still wearing their hats until the music started, when they would remove them and stand again, their bare heads bowed a little in the bright early afternoon sunshine. Then Mother was in the hall, in black and heavily veiled, and Father and Uncle Charley in black; and now-we crossed into the dining room where chairs had been arranged for us, the folding doors open into the parlor, so that we, the family, were at the funeral but not yet of it, as though Grandfather in his casket now had to be two: one for his blood descendants and connections, one for those who were merely his friends and fellow townsmen.

Then that song, that hymn which meant nothing to me now: no lugubrious dirge to death, no reminder that Grandfather was gone and I would never see him again. Because never again could it match what it had once meant to me—terror, not of death but of the un-dead. I was just four then; Maggie, next to me, could barely walk, the two of us in a clump of older children half concealed in the shrubbery in the corner of the yard. I at least did not know why, until it passed—the first I had ever watched—the black plumed hearse, the black closed hacks and surreys, at the slow significant pace up the street which was suddenly completely deserted, as it seemed to me that I knew suddenly the entire town would be.

"What?" I said. "A deader? What's a deader?" And they told me. I had seen dead things before—birds, toads, the puppies the one before Simon (his wife was Sarah) had drowned in a crokersack in the water-trough because he said that Father's fine setter had got mixed up with the wrong dog, and I had watched him and Sarah both beat to bloody shapeless strings the snakes which I now know were harmless. But that that this, this ignominy, should happen to people too, it seemed to me that God Himself would not permit, condone. So they in the hearse could not be dead: it must be something like sleep: a trick played on people by those same inimical forces and powers for evil which made Sarah and her husband have to beat the harmless snakes to bloody and shapeless pulp or drown the puppies—tricked into that helpless coma for some dreadful and inscrutable joke until the dirt was packed down, to strain and thrash and cry in the airless dark, to no escape forever. So that night I had something very like hysterics, clinging to Sarah's legs and panting: "I won't die! I won't! Never!"

But that was past now. I was fourteen now and that song was woman's work, as was the preacher's peroration which followed it, until the men entered—the eight pallbearers who were Father's hunting and poker and business friends, and the three honorary ones who were too old now to bear a burden: the three old men in gray too, but of privates (two of them had been in the old regiment that day when, a part of Bee, it had fallen back before

McDowell until it rallied on Jackson in front of the Henry House). So they bore Grandfather out, the ladies pressing back a little to make room for us, not looking at us, the men outside in the sunny yard not looking at the passing casket or us either, bareheaded, bowed a little or even turned slightly away as though musing, inattentive; there came one muffled startling half-hollow sound as the bearers, amateurs too, finally got the casket into the hearse, then rapidly with a kind of decorous celerity, passed back and forth between the hearse and the parlor until all the flowers were in too: then moving briskly indeed now, almost hurrying, as though already disassociated, not only from the funeral but even from death too, around the corner where the carryall waited to take them by back streets to the cemetery so they would be there waiting when we arrived: so that any Southern stranger in our town, seeing that vehicle filled with black-clad, freshly shaved men going at a rapid trot up a back street at three o'clock on Wednesday afternoon, would not need to ask what had happened.

Yes, processional: the hearse, then our surrey with Mother and Father and me, then the brothers and sisters and their wives and husbands, then the cousins in one and two and three degrees, diminishing in nearness to the hearse as their connection with Grandfather diminished, up the deserted street, across the Square as empty now as Sunday, so that my insides swelled with snobbery and pride to think that Grandfather had been this important in the town. Then along the empty street which led to the cemetery, in almost every yard of which the children stood along the fence watching with that same terror and excitement which I remembered, remembering the terror and regret with which I had once wished that we lived on Cemetery Street too so that I could watch them all pass.

And now we could already see them, gigantic and white, taller on their marble pedestals than the rose-and-honeysuckle-choked fence, looming into the very trees themselves, the magnolias and cedars and elms, gazing forever eastward with their empty marble eyes—not symbols: not angels of mercy or winged seraphim or lambs or shepherds, but effigies of the actual people themselves as they had been in life, in marble now, durable, impervious, heroic in size, towering above their dust in the implacable tradition of our strong, uncompromising, grimly ebullient Baptist-Methodist Protestantism, carved in Italian stone by expensive Italian craftsmen and shipped the long costly way by sea back to become one more among the invincible sentinels guarding the temple of our Southern mores, extending from banker and merchant and planter down to the last tenant farmer who owned neither the plow he guided nor the mule which drew it, which decreed, demanded that, no matter how Spartan the life, in death the significance of dollars and cents was abolished: that Grandmother might have split stovewood right up to the day she died, yet she must enter the earth in satin and mahogany and silver handles even though the first two were synthetic and the third was german—a ceremony not at all to death nor even to the moment of death, but to decorum: the victim of accident or even murder represented in effigy not at the instant of his passing but at the peak of his sublimation, as though in death at last he denied forever the griefs and follies of human affairs.

Grandmother too; the hearse stopped at last beside the raw yawn of the waiting pit, the preacher and the three old men in gray (with the dangling meaningless bronze medals which didn't signify valor but only reunions, since in that war all the men on both sides had been brave and so the only accolades for individual distinction were the lead ones out of the muskets of firing squads) waiting beside it, now carrying shotguns, while the pallbearers removed the flowers and then the casket from the hearse; Grandmother too in her bustle and puffed sleeves and the face which we remembered save for the empty eyes, musing at nothing while the casket sank and the preacher found a place to stop at last and the first clod made that profound quiet half-hollow sound on the invisible wood and the three old men fired their ragged volley and raised their quavering and ragged yell.

Grandmother too. I could remember that day six years ago, the family gathered, Father and Mother and Maggie and I in the surrey because Grandfather rode his horse—the cemetery, our lot. Grandmother's effigy pristine and dazzling now out of its packing case, tall on the dazzling pedestal above the grave itself, the undertaker, hat in hand, and the Negro workmen who had sweated it erect, withdrawn to one side for us, the family, to look at it and approve. And in another year, after the tedious carving in Italy and the long Atlantic ship, Grandfather too on his pedestal beside her, not as the soldier which he had been and as I wanted him, but—

in the old hard unalterable tradition of apotheosis' apogee—the lawyer, parliamentarian, the orator which he was not: in frock coat, the bare head thrown back, the carven tome carved open in one carven hand and the other extended in the immemorial gesture of declamation, this time Mother and Maggie and I in the surrey because Father was now on the horse, come for the formal private inspection and approval.

And three or four times a year I would come back, I would not know why, alone to look at them, not just at Grandfather and Grandmother but at all of them looming among the lush green of summer and the regal blaze of fall and the rain and ruin of winter before spring would bloom again, stained now, a little darkened by time and weather and endurance but still serene, impervious, remote, gazing at nothing, not like sentinels, not defending the living from the dead by means of their vast ton-measured weight and mass, but rather the dead from the living; shielding instead the vacant and dissolving bones, the harmless and defenseless dust, from the anguish and grief and inhumanity of mankind.

III

UNPUBLISHED
STORIES

Adolescence

‿✺‿

I

She was not indigenous to this section. Having been foisted upon it by the blind machinations of fate and of a still blinder county School Board, she would remain, to the end of her days, a stranger to this land of pine and rain gullied hills and fecund river bottoms. Hers should have been a background of faintly sentimental decadence, of formal ease among rites of tea and graceful pointless activities.

A smallish woman with enormous dark eyes, who found in the physically crude courtship of Joe Bunden the false romance with which she had banked the fires of her presbyterian inhibitions. The first ten months of her married life—a time of unprecedented manual labor—failed to destroy her illusions; her mental life, projected forward about her expected child, supported her. She had hoped for twins, to be called Romeo and Juliet, but she was forced to lavish her starved affections on Juliet alone. Her husband condoned this choice of name with a tolerant guffaw. Paternity rested but lightly upon him: like the male of his kind, he regarded the inevitable arrival of children as one of the unavoidable inconveniences of marriage, like the risk of wetting the feet while fishing.

In regular succession thereafter appeared Cyril, one day to be sent to the State Legislature, Jeff Davis, who was finally hung in Texas for stealing a horse; then another boy whom, her spirit broken, she was too apathetic to name at all and who, as a matter of convenience, answered to Bud, and became a professor of latin with a penchant for Catullus at a small mid-western university. The fifth and last was born four years and seven months after her marriage; but from this event she fortunately failed to recover, whereupon Joe Bunden in an unusual access of sentimental remorse named his youngest son for himself, and married again. The second Mrs Bunden was a tall angular shrew who, serving as an instrument of retribution, was known to beat him soundly on occasion with stove wood.

The first official act of the new regime was to dispense with Juliet, which became Jule; and from that day Juliet and her step-mother, between whom an instinctive antipathy had smoldered on sight, hated each other openly. It was two years later, however, before conditions became unbearable. At seven Juliet was an elfish creature, thin as a reed and brown as a berry, with narrow eyes as black and depthless as a toy animal's and a shock of sun-burned black hair. A hoyden who cuffed her duller witted brothers impartially and cursed her parents with shocking fluency. Joe Bunden, in his periodical fits of maudlin inebriation, wept at the disintegration of his family and implored her to be kinder to her step-mother. The breach between the two was impassable so at last, to attain some sort of peace, he was forced to send Juliet to his mother.

Here everything was different, so much so that her defiant protest against the existing order became only a puzzled belligerence; and, after a while, a negative sort of happiness in the absence of any emotional stress. There was work to be done here as well, in house and kitchen garden, but the two of them lived smoothly together. Her grandmother, having passed the troubling ramifications of sex, was wise; and she controlled Juliet so subtly that there was never friction between them. She possessed at last undisturbed the quiet and privacy she desired.

The household whose storm center she had been would not have known her. The change, coming at a crucial time, had purged her of her fierce sensitive pride, of her restlessness and nervous bellicosity as her former life had purged her of all animal parental affection. The mere mention of father or brothers, however, roused in her all her once uncontrolled turbulence, dormant now, but dynamic as ever.

At twelve she was unchanged. Taller and quieter, perhaps, but still brown and thin and active as a cat; hatless in faded gingham, bare feet or wearing shapeless broken shoes; shy with strangers who occasionally stopped at the house or gawky and uncomfortable in hat and stockings on their rare trips to the county seat. Her father and brothers she avoided always with a passionate animal cunning. She could climb faster and surer than a boy; and naked and flashing, she spent hours in a brown pool of the creek. Evenings she sat and dangled her legs from the edge of the porch while her grandmother from the doorway filled the quiet twilight with burning home cured tobacco.

II

A happy time, with duties to be done, and pride in her flat body, climbing and swimming and sleep. Happier still, for in her thirteenth summer she found a companion. She discovered him while swimming lazily in her pool. Looking up at a sound she saw him, in faded overalls, watching her from the bank. Once or twice before strangers, hearing the splash of her dive, had parted the underbrush upon her. As long as they watched her in silence she regarded them with a belligerent indifference, but once they tried to engage her in talk she left the water in a mounting sultry hatred and gathered up her few garments.

This time it was a boy about her own age, in a sleeveless undershirt and with the sun on his round crisp head innocent of brush, staring at her silently, and it did not even occur to her that she was undisturbed. He followed her slow movements for a while in quiet provincial curiosity and without rudeness, but at last the cool brown flashing of the water was too much for him.

"Gosh," he said, "kin I come in?"

Lazily floating she made no reply, but he waited for none. With a few uncomplex motions he divested himself of his wretched garments. His skin was like old paper, and he climbed out on a limb above the water. "Whee, watch me," he shrilled; and writhing awkwardly, dived with a prodigious splash into the pool.

"That aint divin'," she told him calmly, on his spluttering reappearance, "lemme show you." And while he floated and watched her, she climbed to the limb in turn and stood precariously erect a moment, her flat gleaming body a replica of his. She dived.

"Gosh, that's right, lemme see kin I." For an hour they took turns. At last, wearied and with humming heads, they followed the stream until the water became shallow, and lay down in the hot sand. He told her his name was Lee, "fum acrost the river;" and they lay in silent companionship, falling asleep finally, and awoke hungry. "Les git some plums," he suggested, and they returned to the pool and donned their clothes.

III

This was the happy time, so clear and untroubled that she forgot it had not been like this forever; that he and she could not remain unchanged, two animals in an eternal summer. Hunting berries when hungry, swimming in the bright hot noon, fishing in the quiet level afternoon, and scuffing the dew-heavy grass homeward in twilight. Lee, surprisingly, seemed to have no responsibilities whatever; he apparently suffered no compulsions at all, nor did he ever mention home or refer to any other life except that which the two of them led together. But this was not strange to her: her childhood had inculcated her with an early realization of the eternal feud between parent and child, and it had never occurred to her that any childhood could be different from her own.

Her grandmother had never seen Lee, and so far circumstances had fallen in with her own wishes: her grandmother should never see him. For Juliet feared the older woman would feel it her duty to interfere in some manner. So she was careful not to neglect her work in any way, or to arouse a suspicion in the other's mind. With the cunning which a child who learns young from experience gains, she realized that their companionship would remain uninterrupted only so long as it was unknown to those possessing authority over her. She did not mistrust her grandmother particularly, she did not trust any one at all; not even, though certain of herself, Lee's ability to cope with an older person's active disapproval.

August came and went, and September. Through October and early November they dived and swam; but after the first light frosts the air became perceptibly cooler, though the water was still warm. They swam now only at noon and afterward lay together, wrapped in an old horse blanket, talking and dozing and talking. Winter followed the late November rains but there was still the brown sodden woods, and they built fires and roasted corn and sweet potatoes.

Winter at last. A time of dark iron dawns and an icy floor to curl the toes of bare feet while she dressed, of fires to be built in a cold stove. Later when heat had clouded the window panes of the tight little kitchen and the dishes and churning done, she cleared a pane with the corner of her apron and staring out, saw him waiting for her, a tiny figure on the brown edge of the bottom land below the house. He had acquired an ancient single barrelled shot gun and they hunted rabbits in the skeletoned cotton and corn fields or futilely stalked ducks in the marshy back-waters. But at last winter was gone.

At last winter was gone. The wind shifted southward and the rains came: the creek was sullenly full, muddy and cold. Then the sun, and they found the first willow shoots and the first red birds like flaming arrows in the tangled brier. The fruit trees bloomed in gusts of pink and white, clustering like fragrant bees about the weathered grey hives of houses and stained hay ricks; and beneath capricious marbled skies on which slender trees drunkenly leaned the wind sucked among the pine uplands like a remote long passing of far away trains.

On the first warm day Lee waited for her impatiently. And she, clattering recklessly and ineffectively at a dark sink, could stand it no longer. "First in," he whooped when she appeared running, a damp cloth flapping behind, and they raced creekward undressing as they ran. The two plunges were simultaneous, though in her haste she had neglected to kick off her shoes. She stamped out of them to Lee's raucous merriment, gasping at the shock of the icy water.

"Why, you've got white again," she said in surprise, as he climbed the tree to dive. He was startlingly white: last summer's tan had faded from them both during the winter, and they felt almost like strangers. During the cold months, as the temperature lowered, she had donned successive layers of clothing: so that now, compared with her former bulk, she seemed extremely thin. She had also, in her fourteenth year, reached the gawky stage; and beside Lee's smooth ivory symmetry her thin arms and shoulders and little bony hips made her appear almost ugly.

The water was too cold for them so after diving once or twice they got out, shivering, and raced through the woods until their blood was warm again. Then they dressed, and Lee produced two fishing lines and a tin can containing a complexity of red worms. "It'll be warmer tomorrer," he assured her.

Not tomorrow, but in a few weeks the water was warmer, and as the days grew longer their strange whiteness of skin disappeared and soon they were as brown as ever. And another year had passed.

IV

They lay together, wrapped in the horse blanket beneath the high bright October noon, dozing and waking; almost too warm in the generated heat of their two young bodies to be perfectly comfortable. The heat, the scratchy roughness of the blanket made Juliet restless: she turned and changed the position of her limbs, and changed again. The sun beat on their faces in a slow succession of blows, too blinding to allow them to open their eyes.

"Lee," she spoke at last.

"Huh?" drowsily.

"Lee, what you goin' to do when you get to be a man?"

"Aint goin' to do nothin'. "

"Nothin'? How you goin' to get along without doin' nothin'?"

"Dunno."

She raised herself on her elbow. Lee's tousled round head was burrowed into the hot sand. She shook him. "Lee! Wake up."

His eyes were startling in his dark face, the color of wood ashes. He closed them quickly, crooking his arm above. "Aw, gosh, what you worryin' about when we grow up for? I dont want to grow up: I rather stay like this—swimmin' and huntin' and fishin'. Aint this better'n bein' a man and havin' to plow and chop cotton and corn?"

"But you cant stay like this always: you got to grow up and work some day."

"Well, les wait till we're growed up 'fore we start worryin' about it."

She lay back again and closed her eyes. Bright sun spots danced before and behind her lids, madly and redly. But she was not satisfied: her feminine insistence was not to be placated so easily. As she was vaguely troubled and sad, like the changing year, with an intimation of mortality and mutability, learning that nothing is changeless save change. They were voluptuously silent in the strong refulgence of sunlight until a sound caused Juliet to open her eyes.

Ludicrously inverted above her stood her grandmother, a shapeless hunched figure against the bland ineffable blue of the sky. The old woman and the girl stared at each other for a space, then Juliet closed her eyes again.

"Git up," said the old woman.

Juliet opened her eyes and half rose, pushing back her shock of hair with the bend of a bare arm. Lee, motionless on his back, gazed up at the figure standing over them shaking with the palsy of extreme age.

"So this is what's been goin' on behind my back, is it? This is how come you never have time to half do your work, hey? This is how come we got to have a nigger to cook and clean up?" She mumbled and chuckled, "Git up, I tell ye."

They did not move. It had all happened so quickly that their sleep-clogged brains refused to function. So they lay and stared at her while she wagged her mask of a face above them. She raised her stick and shook it.

"Git up, ye slut!" she quavered in sudden anger.

They rose and stood side by side in the implacable sunlight like two bronze carvings. The toothless mouthing face and its bleared dim eyes wavered before them.

"Stark nekked, both of ye. Your paw told me you was wild, but I never thought to find you a layin' up with some body I never see before. And this aint the first one neither, I bound you! You with your innocent ways, likin' to fish and roam the country by yerself! Do you know what you've done? Spiled yer chances for gittin' a decent, well-to-do husband, that's what you've done."

They gazed at her in speechless amazement and incomprehension.

"Ye needn't look at me in that know nothin' way: do you think to fool me after I ketched ye? Aint you a pretty pair, now?" She turned suddenly to Lee. "What's your name, boy?"

"Lee," he told her equably.

"Lee who?"

"Lee Hollowell."

"Lafe Hollowell's boy, huh?" She turned back to Juliet. "Now aint you a pretty thing, takin' up with a Hollowell? Lazy, good-for-nothin', never done a honest lick of work in his life, Lafe never; and now you aint got no better sense than to lay up with one! What you goin' to do if he gits you with child? Set down on me and let me slave for you, I reckon. If you got to have a man, you better pick one that can support you: no Hollowell never will."

Juliet sprang like a taut wire. "You—you old bitch," she screamed from the wreckage of their bright companionship. "Lee, Lee," she cried in a dull misery of despair.

The other raised her stick in a shaking hand and struck Juliet across the shoulders. "Git your clothes on and go home. Now I'll 'tend to you," as Lee sprang forward, trying to grasp the stick. It fell again, across Lee's back, and again. He leaped beyond her reach. "You git away from here," she shrilled, "git away, God damn ye! dont never let me see hide nor hair of ye, or I'll shoot you like a dog."

They stared at each other, the cautious puzzled boy and the implacable old woman terrible in her rage. Then Lee turned and donned his clothes with swift ease and was gone, whooping through the woods; leaving her, gnome-like and trembling, in the strong quiet sunlight and a slow drifting of scarlet leaves.

V

In the fierce pride of her reserve she smoldered. Outwardly, however, her demeanor was unchanged. Her life with her grandmother, she discovered, had been very pleasant; the other had controlled her to an extent, but now, having blundered once, her authority was gone forever. Meanwhile they lived together in a strained armistice, the elder impersonally querulous, and Juliet in a state resembling a corked champagne bottle.

Her grandmother was getting old, and by imperceptible degrees more and more work devolved upon Juliet. At last, in her fifteenth year, it occurred to her that she was doing nearly all the house work, as well as caring for the stock, though the older woman drove her wasted rheumatic body ineffectually at lesser tasks by the sheer dull rigidity of her will. She must have a fire now, summer and winter; and most of her time was spent sitting in the chimney corner: a toothless obscene mask and a clay pipe in a withered hand, spitting into the flames.

"Grammaw," she said, not for the first time, "let's get a cook."

"Dont need none."

"But you're gettin' old; seems like a nigger'd take a lot of work offen your hands."

"Sposin' I never done a lick, aint you strong bodied enough to tend to things? I kep' up this place twenty two year, alone."

" 'Taint any use us a-slavin' to death when we dont have to, though."

The other opened her bleared eyes and sucked her pipe to a glowing coal. "Look here, gal; dont you start a-frettin' about me 'till you hear me complain. Wait 'till you been through what I have; wait 'till you been married and kept carryin' steady for fourteen years, and seen four out of nine dead and the balance scattered to God knows where without liftin' a hand for you. You reckon when all that was over and done and Alex dead and buried, that I worried about a little work and none to bother?"

"I know you had a hard time: seems like everybody in this country has a hard time. But, grammaw; seems like we could take it easy now: you done had your trouble and I aint scarcely old enough for mine yet."

"Huh," the old woman grunted. " 'Taint nothin' but Joe Bunden talkin' in you now, rank laziness. You aint satisfied lessen you're tearin' through the woods: no time for housework any more. Great big gal like you, skeered of a little hard work! When I was your age I was cookin' and carin' for a fambly of seven, while you haint no one to do for but me. You haint got enough to do now, that's what's wrong with you." She puffed and nodded in the leaping firelight.

"But, grammaw—"

The other jerked her head up. "Listen to me, gal. I've had about all your goin's on I'm goin' to stand. I sent your paw word about that Hollowell boy, and he's comin' over to see you: like's not he'll take ye home with him."

"I dont care if he does come. I wont let him see me."

"H'mph. You will if I tell ye, like you'll go home with him if he wants ye to."

"I wont go home with him. I'd kill him before I'd let him touch me."

"Now, aint you talkin' biggity! What you need is to have a stick took to ye, and I'm a-goin' to see that Joe does it 'fore you leave here. I wont have nobody around me that wont pay me no mind, that sets out to cross me from natural cussedness."

"What have I done, grammaw, that aint what you told me?"

"What aint you done? I haint no more control over you than a sperrit; you that's eatin' my vittles every day. After I caught ye a-layin up with that triflin' Hollowell you aint paid me no more mind than if I was Joe, or that wife of his'n."

"Do you still think that Lee and me—that Lee and me—I—is that the reason you been hectorin' at me ever since?" she rushed on fiercely, "is that what you think? that me and him— Oh, God, I wisht you wasn't so old: I'd mash that old face of yours right into the fire. I'd—I'd— I hate you!"

The other stirred in the leaping shadows, the pipe dropped from her trembling hand and she bent over the hearth, vainly searching for it. "Dont talk to me that way, you slut." She fumbled for her stick, and rose. "Old or no old, I'm spry enough to lick ye to a fair-ye-well." She raised the stick, and for a space the two of them glared at each other in the intermittent quiet firelight wheeling about them.

"Just touch me with that stick, just touch me," Juliet whispered through dry lips.

"Tech you! Joe Bunden'll do that a plenty when he comes, I promise ye. And I bound ye the husband Joe's picked for you'll tech ye too; when he hears what folks say about you and that no 'count Hollowell."

"Husband?" repeated Juliet. The other croaked into laughter.

"Husband, I tell ye. But I hadn't aimed to tell ye before every thing was ready, you're so hard headed. But I guess Joe'll manage ye. I sent word to Joe that I couldn't manage you; and them folks of yourn dont want ye to home; so Joe's went and found somebody to marry ye, though God knows where he found a feller'll take ye. But that's Joe's lookout, not mine: I done what I could for ye."

"Husband?" repeated Juliet idiotically. "Do you think that you and Joe Bunden can both make me get married? Much as I hate you, I'd rather be dead than go back home; and before I'd marry anybody I'll kill you and Joe Bunden, too. You cant make me!"

The old woman raised the stick. "Shet your mouth!"

"Touch me! Touch me!" Juliet repeated in a taut whisper.

"Darin' me, be ye?" the other quavered. "Take that, then, damn ye!" The stick fell across Juliet's breast and arm and an icy wind blew through her brain. She wrested the stick from her grandmother's hand and broke it across her knee as the other recoiled in fear. She threw the pieces into the fire, and in a voice as light and dry as an eggshell she reiterated senselessly: "You made me do it, you made me do it."

The older woman's rage had evaporated. "Dont worry me, gal. Cant let me set in my own chimbley without a-naggin' and a-frettin' at me. Aint never a Bunden yet didnt set out to nag and fret me. You and your nigger! Wait 'till I'm dead: 'twont be long, thank God; then you can fill the house with folks to wait on ye." She dragged herself across the room to the monstrous lowering shadow of her bed—curtained winter and summer— "If you dont like it here, maybe your husband'll git ye a cook." She chuckled evilly, and groaned, fumbling in the dark.

Outside the sky was clear, an inverted bowl of dark water floating with stars; and her damp hair stirred upon her brow as though at the touch of a hand. Deliberately she caught and saddled their one ancient horse, and mounting from the water trough, took the road toward town, leaving the gate swinging open behind her. She turned her face once backward to the dark house, repeating: "You made me do it," then rode onward through the darkness. Soon the last spurt of dust kicked up by the horse's feet settled, and the road was empty again.

VI

Juliet passed through the next few days somehow. She and her grandmother, by an unspoken agreement, ignored the last scene; and outwardly life moved stagnantly onward, as dull and uneventful as ever. Juliet felt like one who has cast the dice and must wait an eternity for them to stop. And withal, she was vaguely apathetic as to what they might show: her reserve of volition had been expended. Her terror, her fear of what she had done, had flown in the quiet round of duties and dreaming alone in the twilight.

The house was dark, an angle of quietly leaping firelight marked the door of her grandmother's room. At first she did not see the

470 · UNPUBLISHED STORIES

old woman, then her glance found a withered hand nursing a pipe. "Juliet?" the other spoke from her corner; and Juliet entered, her scornful belligerence rising in her, and stood before the fire. The heat struck pleasantly through her skirt, against her legs. Her grandmother leaned forward until her face hung like a mask in the firelight, and spat.

"Your paw's dead," she said.

Juliet gazed at the leaping enormous shadow of the curtained bed. The measured puffs of the other's pipe beat softly against her ears like moth wings. Joe Bunden's dead, she thought, without emotion; it was as though her grandmother's words still hung suspended in the room's twilight, whispering to each other. At last she stirred.

"Paw's dead, grammaw?" she repeated.

The old woman moved again, and groaned. "The fool, the fool! All Bundens is fools born: I never see a one yet, 'ceptin' you, warn't a natural ijit. I married one, but he died 'fore he done much harm, leavin' me a run-down farm and a family of chillen. And now Joe has raised a family and left 'em improvident—lessen that woman he married has got more spunk than ever I see in her. Lafe Hollowell warn't no better, neither. Him and Joe'll make a pretty pair in hell tonight."

"What happened, grammaw," she heard herself ask, in a passionless voice.

"Happen? Joe Bunden was a fool, and Lafe Hollowell warn't no better, after him and Joe hitched up, anyway. . . . Joe and him was killed by revenuers last night, at Lafe's still. Some body rid into town late Wensday night and told Deacon Harvey, and three revenuers come down on 'em last night. Never knowed who told . . . or likely wouldn't say." The old woman nodded and smoked for a while with closed eyes. Juliet stared at the slow wheeling of shadows, quietly in a smooth blending of sadness and unutterable relief. The other's mumbling materialized about her: "That woman Joe married, soon's she heard, took and went back home. God knows what'll become of them brothers o' yourn: I aint goin' to have 'em on my hands. And Lafe's boy—what's his name? Lee?—he skun out and aint been seen since. Good riddance, I call it."

The shadows leaped up the wall, and fell; while her grandmother's words lingered in the dusk like cobwebs. She left the room, and sat down on the floor of the porch with her back against the wall and her legs stiffly before her. Joe Bunden she hated no longer, but Lee, Lee was different, his leaving was more tangible than the death of a hundred men: it was like dying herself. So she sat in the dark, watching her childhood leaving her. She remembered with painful clarity that spring in which she and Lee had first swum and fished and roamed, of those raw blustery days broken to cloud racks above the fallow rain-gullied earth; she could almost hear the cries of men plowing the muddy ground, and the tangled blackbirds slanting down wind like scraps of burned paper . . . change and death and division.

She rose at last and slowly descended the hill toward the creek, and saw a small dark figure approaching her. Lee! she thought, with a constriction of throat muscles, but it was not Lee: it was too small. The figure, seeing her, stopped, then cautiously approached. "Jule?" it said timidly.

"Who's that?" she replied sharply.

"It's me—Bud."

They stood facing each other curiously. "What are you doing here?"

"I'm goin' away."

"Goin' away? Where can you go to?"

"I dunno, somewhere. I cant stay to home no more."

"Why cant you stay to home?" Emotions she hated were stirring in her.

"Maw, she's— I hate her, I aint going to stay there no longer. I never stayed noways, 'ceptin' fer paw; and now—now paw—he's —he's—" he dropped to his knees, rocking back and forth in a recurrence of grief. Juliet drew near him in an access of pity, hating herself. He was a soiled little boy in worn overalls; she decided with difficulty that he must be about eleven years old. Beside him was a bundle knotted in a handkerchief, consisting of a chunk of cold indigestible bread and a dog-eared book of pictures which were once colored. He looked so small and lonely, kneeling in the dead leaves, and the common bond of hatred drew them together. He raised his streaked dirty face. "Oh, Jule," he said, putting his arms around her legs and burrowing his face into her sharp little hip.

She watched the fitful interruptions of moonlight torturing the bare boughs of trees. Above them the wind sucked with a far sound, and across the moon slid a silent V of geese. The earth was cold and still, waiting in dark quietude for spring and the south wind. The moon stared through a cloud rift and she could see her brother's tousled hair and the faded collar of his shirt, and her racking infrequent tears rose and slid down the curve of her cheek. At last she, too, was frankly crying because everything seemed so transient and pointless, so futile; that every effort, every impulse she had toward the attainment of happiness was thwarted by blind circumstance, that even trying to break away from the family she hated was frustrated by something from within herself. Even dying couldn't help her: death being nothing but that state those left behind are cast into.

Finally she jerked the tears from her face and pushed her brother away.

"Get up. You're a fool, you cant go anywhere like this, little as you are. Come on up to the house and see grammaw."

"No, no, Jule; I cant, I do' want ter see grammaw."

"Why not? You got to do somethin', aint you? Lessen you want to go back home," she added.

"Back to her? I wont never go back to her."

"Well, come on, then; grammaw'll know what to do."

He pulled back again. "I'm skeered o' grammaw, I'm skeered o' her."

"Well, what you goin' to do?"

"I'm goin' away, yonder way," pointing toward the county seat. She recognised his stubbornness with a sense of familiarity, knowing he could be forced no easier than she. There was one thing, however, she could do, so she cajoled him as far as the gate onto the road, and left him in the shadow of a tree. Soon she reappeared with a substantial parcel of food and a few dollars in small change —her savings of years. He took it with the awkward apathy of despair and together they moved onto the high road and stopped again, regarding each other like strangers.

"Good bye, Jule," he said at last, and would have touched her again, but she drew back; so he turned, a small ineffectual figure, up the vaguely indistinct road. She watched him until he was scarcely discernible, soon he was out of sight, and once more she turned and descended the hill.

The trees were still, bodyless and motionless as reflections now that the wind had dropped; waiting pagan and untroubled by rumors of immortality for winter and death. Far, far away across the October earth a dog howled, and the mellow long sound of a horn wavered about her, filling the air like a disturbance of still waters, then was absorbed into silence again leaving the dark world motionless about her, quiet and slightly sad and beautiful. Possum hunters, she thought, and wondered as it died away if she had heard any sound at all.

She wondered dully and vaguely how she could ever have been wrought up over things, how anything could ever make her any way but like this: quiet, and a little sorrowful. Scarcely moving herself, it seemed as though the trees swam up slowly out of the dark and moved across above her head, drawing their top-most branches through star-filled waters that parted before them and joined together when they had passed, with never a ripple or change.

Here at her feet lay the pool: shadows, then repeated motionless trees, the sky again; and she sat down and stared into the water in a sensuous smooth despair. This was the world, below her and above her head, eternal and empty and limitless. The horn sounded again all around her, in water and trees and sky; then died slowly away, draining from sky and trees and water into her body, leaving a warm salty taste in her mouth. She turned over suddenly and buried her face in her thin arms, feeling the sharp earth strike through her clothing against thighs and stomach and her hard little breasts. The last echo of the horn slid immaculately away from her down some smooth immeasurable hill of autumn quiet, like a rumor of a far despair.

Soon it, too, was gone.

Al Jackson

ᦡᦢᦣ

Dear Anderson:—

I was with a boating party across the lake over the week end, and going up the river the pilot pointed out to us the old Jackson place. They are descendants of Old Hickory, and there is only one of them left,—Al Jackson. I wish you could know him: with your interest in people he would be a gold mine to you. The man has had a very eventful life, through no fault of his own. He is himself very retiring. It is told of him no one ever saw him in wading or swimming or undressed. Something about his feet, they say, though no one knows for certain.

The pilot was telling me about his people. His mother at the age of seven held the tatting championship of her Sunday school, and as a reward they gave her the privilege of attending every religious ceremony held at her church, without having to go to the social ones, for a period of ninety-nine years. At the age of nine she could play on a melodeon her father had swapped a boat and a clock and a pet alligator for; she could sew, cook; and she increased attendance at her church three hundred percent with some sort of a secret recipe for communion wine, including among other things, grain alcohol. The pilot's father used to go to her church. In fact the whole parish finally did. They tore down two churches for wood to make fish-traps of, and one minister finally got a job on a ferry boat. The church gave her a bible with her name and favorite flower embossed in gold on it for this.

Old man Jackson won her hand when she was twelve. They say he was ravished by her prowess on the melodeon. The pilot said old man Jackson didn't have a melodeon. Old man Jackson was a character, himself. When he was eight he learned by heart one thousand verses from the new testament, bringing on an attack resembling brain fever. When they finally got a veterinary up, he said it couldn't be brain fever, though. After that he became kind of—well, call it queer: bought library paste to eat whenever he could get it, and wore a raincoat every time he took a bath. He slept in a folding bed flat on the floor and closed up on him when he retired. He invented some holes bored in for air.

It seems that Jackson finally got the idea of raising sheep in that swamp of his, his belief being that wool grew like anything else, and that if sheep stood in water all the time, like trees, the fleece would be naturally more luxuriant. By the time he had about a dozen of them drowned, he made life belts out of cane for them. And then he found that the alligators were getting them.

One of the older boys (he must have had about a dozen) discovered the alligators wouldn't bother a goat with long horns, so the old man carved imitation horns about three feet across out of roots and fastened them onto his sheep. He didn't give them all horns, lest the alligators catch onto the trick. The pilot said he figured on losing so many head a year, but in this way he kept the death rate pretty low.

Soon they found that the sheep were learning to like the water, were swimming all around in it, that in about six months they never came out of the water at all. When shearing time came, he had to borrow a motor boat to run them down with. And when they caught one and raised it out of the water, it had no legs. They had atrophied and completely disappeared.

And that was true of everyone they caught. The legs not only were gone, but that part of the sheep which was under water was covered with scales in place of wool, and the tail had broadened and flattened like a beaver's. Within another six months they couldn't even catch one with the motor boat. They had learned to dive from watching fish; and when a year had passed Jackson saw them only when they stuck their noses up for a breath of air now and then. Soon days would pass without the water being broken by one of them. Occasionally they caught one on a hook baited with corn, but it had no wool on it at all.

Old man Jackson, so the pilot says, got kind of discouraged.

Here was all his capital swimming around under water, and he was afraid they would turn Alligators before [he] could catch any of them. Finally his second boy, Claude, the wild one that was always after women, told his father that if he would give him outright half he could catch, he would get a few of them. They agreed, and so Claude would take off his clothes and go in the water. He never got many at first, though he would occasionally hem one up under a log and get him. One of them bit him pretty badly one day, and he thought to himself: "Yes, sir, I got to work fast: them things will be alligators in a year."

So he lit in, and everyday his swimming got better and he'd get a few more. Soon he could stay under water for a half an hour at a time; but out of the water his breathing wasnt so very good, and his legs were beginning to feel funny at the knee. He then took to staying in the water all day and all night and his folks would bring him food. He lost all use of his arms to the elbow and his legs to the knee; and the last time any of the family saw him his eyes had moved around to the side of his head and there was a fish's tail sticking out of the corner of his mouth.

About a year later they heard of him again. There was a single shark appeared off the coast that kept on bothering the blonde lady bathers, especially the fat ones.

"That's Claude," said old man Jackson, "he always was hell on blondes."

And so their sole source of income was gone. The family was in quite a bad way for years and years, until the Prohibition law came along and saved them.

I hope you will find this story as interesting as I have.

> Sincerely,
> William Faulkner

Dear Anderson:—

I have your letter regarding the Jacksons. I am amazed. What I had thought to be a casual story seems to be quite well known. It must be a very unusual family, and so I echo your words: How I would like to meet Al Jackson.

I have been making a few inquiries myself. It's like sluicing for gold—a speck here and a speck there. It seems that Elenor's story is scandalous. She slid down a drain pipe and eloped with a tin pedler one night. Imagine the horror felt by a family as clean as fish-herding families must be, upon learning that "Perchie," as Elenor was called, had eloped with a man who not only couldn't swim, but who had never had a drop of water upon his body in his whole life. He is so afraid of water that, having been once caught by a rainstorm while on the road, he would not leave his van to feed his horse. The storm lasted nine days, the horse died between the shafts of starvation, and the man himself was found unconscious, having eaten a pair of congress shoes he was taking as a present to old man Jackson, and having consumed the reins as far as he could reach without leaving the van. The irony of it is that he was found and saved by Claude, one of Elenor Jackson's brothers, who had paused to look into the van in the hope of finding a woman in it. (Claude was kind of bad after women, as I wrote you.)

But Al is the one I wish to meet. He is considered by every one who knows him to be the finest time of American manhood, a pure Nordic. During the war he took correspondence course after course to cure his shyness and develop will power in order to help the boys over there by making four minute Liberty loan speeches, and he is said to be the one who first thought of re-writing Goethe and Wagner and calling them Pershing and Wilson. Al Jackson likes the arts, you know.

I think you are wrong about Jackson's ancestry. This Spearhead Jackson was captured and hung from the yardarm of a British frigate in 1799. It seems he was beating up the trades with a cargo of negroes when the frigate sighted him and gave chase. As was his custom, he started throwing negroes overboard, holding the Britisher off, but a squall came up suddenly, blowing him out to sea and three days off his course. Still throwing negroes overboard he ran for the Dry Tortugas but he ran out of negroes and the Britisher overtook him and boarded him off Caracas, giving no quarter and scuttling his vessel. So Al Jackson could not have sprung from this line. Besides, Al Jackson could never have come from an ancestor who had so little regard for the human soul.

And further proof. These Jacksons quite obviously descend from Andrew Jackson. The battle of New Orleans was fought in a swamp. How could Andrew Jackson have outfought an army outnumbering him unless he had had webbed feet? The detachment which saved the day was composed of two battalions of fish-herds from Jackson's Florida swamps, half horse and half alligator they were. Also, if you will examine the statue to him in Jackson Park (and who but a Jackson could ride a horse weighing two and a half tons and hold him balanced on his hind feet?) you will see that he wears congress shoes.

Yes, I have heard the negro shooting story. But it is believed in this country to be a rank calumny. It was a man called Jack Spearman shooting Swedes for a dollar bounty in Minnesota. My version, of course, may be incorrect.

But who is this Sam Jackson? I had heard a reference to him, but upon mentioning his name to an old moonshiner who seemed to know and revere the family, he hushed up like a clam, and when I insisted, became quite angry with me. All I could get from him was the remark that it was a "dam lie."

I received most of this information from people at Herman Jackson's funeral the other day. Herman, you know, was a queer boy with a passion for education. Old man Jackson didn't believe in education. But the boy Herman was crazy to learn to read, and Al, who seems to be a cultured man, helped the boy invent a way of making pearl buttons from fish scales. Herman saved his money, and was at last admitted into the university. Of course he had to earn his way doing odd jobs. He was for a while a fish grader at the fish market, but he depended mostly on his pearl buttons. People in his boarding house objected to the smell, but on seeing the boy laboring long into the night glueing fish scales together with fish glue, they felt kind of sorry for him.

At last, at the age of eighteen he learned to read and he established a record. He read Sir Walter Scott's complete works in twelve and one half days. For two days afterward he seemed to be dazed—could not remember who he was. So a schoolmate wrote his name on a card which Herman carried in his hand, showing it to anyone who asked his name.

Then on the third day he went into convulsions, passing from convulsion to convulsion and dying after days of terrible agony. Al, they say, was quite sad over this, feeling that he was somehow to blame.

The Benevolent Order of Carp, assisted by his college fraternity, R.O.E., buried him with honors; and his funeral is said to have been one of the largest ever held in the fish-herding circles. Al Jackson was not present: he could not bear it. But he is reported to have said: "I only hope that the country which I love, the business to which I have devoted my best years, will show a like appreciation of my passing away."

If you can ever arrange for me to meet this splendid man, please do so, and I will be obligated to you.

Wm Faulkner

Don Giovanni

He had been married while quite young by a rather plain-faced girl whom he was trying to seduce, and now, at thirty-two, he was a widower. His marriage had driven him into work as drouth drives the fish down the streams into the large waters, and things had gone hard with them during the time in which he shifted from position to position and business to business be[fore] finally and inevitably gravitating into the women's clothing section of a large department store.

Here he felt that he had at last come into his own (he always got along much better with women than with men) and his restored faith in himself enabled him to rise with comfortable ease to the coveted position of wholesale buyer. He knew women's clothes and, interested in women, it was his belief that his knowledge of the things they liked gave him a grasp which no other man had on the psychology of women. But he merely speculated upon this. He remained faithful to his wife, although she was bed-ridden: an invalid.

And then when success was in his grasp and life became smooth at last for them, his wife died. He had become habituated to marriage, attached to her, and re-adjustment came but slowly. Yet in time he became accustomed to the novelty of mature liberty. He had been married so young that freedom was an unexplored field to him. He took pleasure in his snug bachelor's rooms, in his solitary routine of days: of walking home in the dusk, examining the soft bodies of girls on the streets, knowing that if he cared to take one, there was none to say No to him. His only worry was his thinning hair.

But at last, celibacy began to oppress him.

His friend and prospective host sitting with a cigar on the balcony, saw him as he turned the corner under the light and with an exclamation he sprang to his feet, kicking his chair over. Ducking quickly into the room he snapped the table lamp off and leaped upon a couch, feigning sleep.

Walking dapperly, swinging his light stick:

"How they like for a man to be bold with them. Let's see, she would have one suit of black underwear. . . . first I'll act indifferent, like I dont specially want to be with her, or as if I dont particularly care to dance tonight. Drop a remark about coming only because I had promised—that there is another woman I had rather have seen. They like a man that has other women. She'll say 'Please take me to dance' and I'll say 'Oh, I dont know if I want to dance tonight' And she'll say 'Wont you take me?' kind of leaning against me—let's see—yes, she'll take my hand, soft-talking me, well, I wont respond, wont seem to hear her. She'll keep on teasing and then I'll put my arm around her and raise her face in the dark cab and kiss her, coldly and dignified, as if I didn't care whether I did or not, and I'll say 'Do you really want to dance tonight?' and she'll say 'Oh, I dont know. I'd rather just ride around—with you' And I'll say 'No, let's dance a while'

"Well, we'll dance and I'll caress her back with my hand. She'll be watching me but I wont look at her—" he broke suddenly from his revery, finding that he had passed his friend's house. He retraced his steps, craning his neck toward the darkened windows.

"Morrison!" he sang.

No reply.

"Oh, Mor—rison!"

The dark windows were inscrutable as two fates. He knocked on the door, then stepped back to finish his aria. Beside the door was another entrance. Light streamed across a half-length lattice, like a saloon door, and beyond it a typewriter was being thumped viciously. He knocked upon the blind, tentatively.

"Hello" a voice boomed above the clacking machine. He pondered briefly then knocked again, louder.

"Come in, damn you. Do you think this is a bathroom?" the voice said, drowning the typewriter.

He opened the blind. The huge collarless man at the typewriter raised a leonine head, regarding him fretfully.

"Well?" The typewriter ceased.

"Pardon me: I'm looking for Morrison."

"Next floor," the other snapped, poising his hands. "Good night."

"But he doesn't answer. Do you know if he is in tonight?"

"I do not."

He pondered again, diffidently. "I wonder how I could find out? I'm pressed for time—"

"How in hell do I know? Go up and see, or stand out there and call him."

"Thanks, I'll go up."

"Well, go up then." The typewriter clashed pianissimo.

"May I go through this way?" he ventured mildly, politely.

"Yes, yes. Go anywhere. But for God's sake dont bother me."

He murmured thanks, sidling past the large frenzied one. The whole room trembled to the big man's heavy hands and the typewriter leaped and clattered like a mad thing. He mounted dark stairs, his friend heard him stumble, and groaned. I'll have your blood for this! he swore and the thundering oblivious typewriter beneath him. The door opened and the caller hissed Morrison! into the dark room. He swore again under his breath. The couch complained to his movement and he said:

"Wait there until I turn on the light. You'll break everything I've got, blundering around in the dark."

The guest sighed with relief. "Well, well, I had just about given you up and gone away when that man below you kindly let me come through his place."

The light came on under the other's hand.

"Oh, you were asleep, weren't you? So sorry to have disturbed you. But I want your advice."

He put his hat and stick on a table, knocking from it a vase of flowers. With amazing agility he caught the vase before it crashed, but not before the contents had liberally splashed him. He replaced the vase and quickly fell to mopping at his sleeves and coat front with a handkerchief. "Ah, the devil," he ejaculated with exasperation, "and this suit fresh from the presser, too!"

His host looked on with suppressed vindictive glee, offering him a chair. "Too bad," he commiserated insincerely. "But she wont notice it: she'll probably be interested in you."

He looked up, flattered but a little dubious of the other's tone. He smoothed his palms over his thinning hair.

"Do you think so? But, listen," he continued with swift optimism—, "I have decided where I failed before. Boldness and indifference: that is what I have always overlooked. Listen,—" with enthusiasm, "tonight I will turn the trick. But I want your advice."

The other groaned again and reclined upon the couch.

He continued: "Now, I'll act as though there was another woman had phoned me, and that I met this one only because I had promised: make her jealous to begin with, see? Now, I'll act like I dont care to dance and when she begs me to, I'll kiss her, quite indifferent, see?"

"Yes?" his friend murmured, yawning.

"So we'll go and dance, and I'll pet her a little but I wont look at her—like I was thinking of someone else. She'll be intrigued, and she'll say 'What are you thinking about so hard?' And I'll say 'Why do you want to know?' and she'll beg me to tell her, all the time dancing close to me, and I'll say 'I'd rather tell you what you are thinking of' and she'll say 'What?' right quick. And I'll say 'You are thinking about me.' Now what do you think of that? What do you reckon she'll say then?"

"Probably tell you you've got a swelled head."

The caller's face fell. "Do you think she will?"

"Dont know. You'll find out, though."

"No, I dont believe she will. I kind of thought she'd think I knew a lot about women." He mused deeply for a space. Then he burst out again: "If she does I'll say 'Perhaps so. But I am tired of this place. Let's go.' She wont want to but I'll be firm. Then I'll be bold: I'll take her right out to my place, and when she sees how bold I am she'll give in. They like bold men. What do you think of that?"

"Fine—provided she acts like she ought to. It might be a good idea to outline the plot to her, though, so she wont slip up."

"You are kidding me now. But dont you really think this scheme is sound?"

"Air tight. You have thought of everything, haven't you?"

"Certainly. That's the only way to win battles, you know. Napoleon taught us that."

"Napoleon also said something about the heaviest artillery, too," his friend remarked wickedly.

He smiled with complacence. "I am as I am," he murmured. . . .

"Especially when it hasn't been used in some time," his host continued. He looked like a hurt beast, and the other added quickly: "but are you going to try this scheme tonight, or are you just telling me of an hypothetical case?"

He regarded his watch with consternation. "Good gracious, I must run." He sprang to his feet. "Thanks for advising me. I really think I have the system for this type of woman, dont you?"

"Sure," his friend agreed. At the door he halted and rushed back to shake hands. "Wish me luck," he said over his departing shoulder. The door closed behind him and his descending feet sounded from the stairs. Then the street door; and the other stood on the balcony, watching him out of sight. The host returned to his couch and reclined again, laughing. He rose, turned out the light and lay in the dark, chuckling. Beneath him the typewriter, tireless, clattered and thundered.

Perhaps three hours later. The typewriter yet leaped and danced on the table.

"Morrison!"

The manipulator of the machine felt a vague annoyance, like knowing that someone is trying to wake you from a pleasant dream, knowing that if you resist the dream will be broken.

"Oh, Mor—risooooooon!"

He concentrated again, being conscious that the warm peaceful night without his room had been ravished of quiet. He banged louder upon his key-board to exorcise it, but there came a timid knock at his blind.

"Damn!" he said, surrendering. "Come in!" he bellowed, looking up. "My God, where did you come from? I let you in about ten minutes ago, didn't I?" He looked at his visitor's face and his tone changed. "What's the matter, friend? Sick?"

The visitor stood blinking in the light, then entered falteringly and drooped upon a chair. "Worse than that," he said despondently.

The large man wheeled heavily to face him.

"Need a doctor or anything?"

The caller buried his face in his hands. "No, no a doctor cant help me."

"Well, what is it?" the other insisted in mounting exasperation. "I'm busy. What do you want?"

The guest drew a long breath and looked up. "I've simply got to talk to someone." He lifted a stricken face to the other's heavy piercing stare. "A terrible thing happened to me tonight."

"Well, spit it out, then. But be quick."

He sighed and weakly fumbled his handkerchief, mopping his face. "Well, just as I said, I acted indifferent, said I didn't want to dance tonight. And she said, 'Aw, come on: do you think I came out just to sit on a park bench all evening?' And then I put my arm around her—"

"Around who?"

"Around her. And when I tried to kiss her she just put—"

"But where was this?"

"In a taxi. She just put her elbow under my chin and pushed me back in my corner and said 'Are we going to dance, or not? If we aint, say so, and I'll get out. I know a fellow that will take me out to dance' and—"

"In God's name, friend, what are you raving about?"

"About that girl I was out with tonight. And so we went to dance and I was petting her like I said and she said 'Lay off, brother, I aint got lumbago' And after a while she kept looking over her shoulder and then craning her head around to look over mine and getting out of step and saying, 'Pardon me' and so I said to her 'What are you thinking of?' and she said 'huh?' and I said 'I can tell you what you are thinking of' and she said 'Who, me? what was I thinking of?' still looking and bobbing her head around. Then I saw she was kind of smiling and I said 'You are thinking of me.' And she said 'Oh, was I?' "

"Good God," murmured the other, staring at him.

"Yes. And so I said, like I'd planned, 'I'm tired of this place. Let's go' She didn't want to go, but I was firm and so at last she said 'All right. You go down and get a taxi and I will fix up and come on down'

"I ought to have known there was something wrong then, but I didn't. Well, I ran on down and got a taxi. And I gave the driver ten dollars to drive us out into the country where there wasn't much passing and to stop and pretend that he had to go back down the road a ways for something, and to wait there until I honked the horn for him.

"So I waited and waited and she never came down the stairs and at last I told the driver not to go off, that I would go back and get her, and I ran back up stairs. I didn't see anything of her in the ante-room, so I went back to the dance floor." He sat for a while in lax and silent despair.

"Well?" the other prompted.

He sighed. "I swear, I think I'll give it up: never have anything to do with women any more. When I went back in again I looked around for her. And at last I saw her, dancing with another man, a big one like you. I didn't know what to think. I decided that he was a friend of hers she was dancing with until I should return, having misunderstood what I said about waiting for her on the street. But she had told me to wait for her on the street. That's what confused me.

"I stood in the door until I caught her eye finally, and signalled to her. She kind of flipped her hand at me as if she wanted me to wait until the dance was over, so I just stood there. But when the music stopped they went to a table and he called a waiter and ordered something. And she never even looked at me again!

"I began to get mad then. I walked over to them. I didn't want them and everyone else to see I was angry so I bowed to them, and she looked at me and said 'Well, well! if here aint Herbie back again. I thought you had left me and so this kind gentleman was kind enough to offer to take me home.' 'You damn right I will,' says the big one, popping his eyes at me, 'who's he?' 'Why, he's a little friend of mine,' she says. 'Well, it's time little boys like him was at home in bed.'

"He looked at me, hard, and I looked at him and said 'Come on, Miss Steinbauer, our cab is waiting.' and he said 'Herb, you aint trying to take my girl, are you?' I told him that she was with me, quite dignified, you know, and she said 'Run along, you are tired of dancing. I aint, so I am going to stay a while.'

"She was kind of smiling: I could see they were ridiculing me, and then he laughed out loud—like a horse. 'Beat it, brother' he said. 'She's gave you the air. Come back tomorrow.' Well, when I saw his fat red face full of teeth I wanted to hit him. But then I thought of creating a scene and having it in the papers with my name, so I just gave her a look and turned and walked out. Of course everybody around had seen and heared it all: there was a waiter said 'Hard luck, fellow, but they will do it' as I went out the door.

"And on top of all that, the taxi driver had gone off with my ten dollars."

The other looked at him in admiration. "God, regard your masterpiece! Balzac, despair! And here I am wasting my life, trying to make people live by means of the written word!" his face became suddenly suffused. "Get to hell out of here," he roared, "you have made me sick!"

The visitor rose and stood in limp dejection.

"But what am I to do?"

"Do? do? Go to a brothel, if you want a girl. Or if you are afraid someone will come in and take her away from you, get out on the street and pick one up: bring her here, if you want to. But in Christ's name, dont ever talk to me again. I am trying to write a novel and you have already damaged my ego beyond repair."

The large man took his arm and thrusting the door open with his foot, assisted him kindly but swiftly into the street. The blind shut behind him and he stood for a space, listening to the frantic typewriter, looking at planes of shadow, letting the night soothe him. A cat, slinking, regarded him, then flashed a swift dingy streak across the street. He followed it with his eyes in a slow misery, with envy. Love was so simple for cats—mostly noise: success didn't make much difference. He sighed, and walked away, leaving the thunderous typewriter behind him.

His decorous pace spaced away streets interesting with darkness; he walked, marvelling that he could be so despairing inwardly and yet outwardly be the same. I wonder if it does show on me? he thought. It is because I am getting old, that women are not attracted to me. Yet, that man tonight was about my age. It is something I haven't got: something I have never had.

But it was unbearable to believe this. No, its something I can do, or say, that I have not discovered yet. As he turned into the quiet street on which he lived he saw two people in a dark door-way, embracing. He hurried on.

In his room at last he slowly removed coat and vest and stood before his mirror, examining his face. His hair was getting thinner daily (cant even keep my hair, he thought bitterly) and his thirty years showed in his face. He was not fleshy, yet the skin under his chin was becoming loose, flabby. He sighed and completed his disrobing. He sat in a chair, his feet in a basin of warm water, slowly chewing a digestive tablet.

The water mounting warmly through his thin body soothed him, the pungent tablet between his slowly moving jaws gave him release from his misery. "Let's see," he pondered to his rhythmic mastication, calmly reviewing the evening, "where did I go wrong tonight? My scheme was good: Morrison himself admitted it. Let me think." His jaws ceased and his eyes brooded upon a photograph on the opposite wall. "Why is it they never act as you had calculated? You can allow for every contingency, yet they will always do something else. I have been too gentle with them: I should never give them a chance to make a fool of me. That has been my mistake every time—giving them a dinner or a show right off. The trick is to be bold with them, bring them straight here, dominate them from the start. By God, that's it."

He dried his feet swiftly, thrusting them into his bed-room slippers, and went to the telephone. "That's the trick exactly," he whispered to himself exultantly, and in his ear was Morrison's sleepy voice.

"Morrison? So sorry to disturb you, but I have got it at last." There was a muffled inarticulate sound over the wire, but he rushed on: "I learned through a mistake tonight. The trouble is, I haven't been bold enough with them: I was afraid I would be too bold and scare them off. Listen: I will bring her here at once: I will be cruel and hard, brutal, if necessary, until she begs for my love. What do you think of that?. . . . Hello! Morrison?". . . .

There was an interval filled with a remote buzzing, then a woman's voice said:

"You tell 'em, big boy; treat 'em rough."

A click: he held dead gutta percha in his hand and dead gutta percha was a round O, staring at his mouth.

Peter

Here was spring in a paved street, between walls, and here was Peter sitting on a stoop, kicking his short legs in brief serge, banging his heels rhythmically against a wooden step. Behind him an arching spacious passage way swam back between walls of an ineffable azure into which one passed as into sleep, sweeping back into light again and a shabby littered court and something green and infernal against a far wall.

"Hello," says Peter easily, above his thumping heels, above the raucous syncopation of a victrola in which has been prisoned by negroes all the tortured despair of negroes. Peter's face is round as a cup of milk with a dash of coffee in it.

"My brother is white," Peter remarks conversationally, in his sailor suit. "Are you going to draw some more?" he asks us, and an old friend stops beside us. An old friend of Peter's, that is. His flat Mongol face is as yellow as Peter's and he says: "How, Petuh? You plitty nice boy t'day? Your momma home?"

"Yes, she up stairs talkin' to man."

"Your pa home?"

"Naw," replies Peter. "I aint got no paw, I got a brother, though. He's white. Like you," he added to Spratling, whom Peter likes.

"You are pretty white yourself. Aren't you white enough?" I ask.

"I dont know. My brother he's little. When he is big like me he wont be so white, I reckon."

"Pitter," the Chinese interrupts. "Your mamma talk to man.

You go tell her she talk to man enough. You tell her? You nice boy."

"Ah, you go tell her. She dont mind. She say she can get 'em out quick as any. Sometimes she says she dont let 'em take off their hats. I guess she cant never tell when Eagle Beak's coming home."

The Chinaman, his face rife with sex, stared down that ineffable azure passage to where sunlight was like golden water between walls.

"Eagle Beak?" I repeated.

"Yes, that's right. He's the one that sleeps with mamma. He works on Dock 5. He can move more cargo than anybody on Dock 5."

"Do you like Eagle Beak?"

"Sure, he's all right. He brings me candy. The other one never done that."

"Never done that?"

"No. He never brought nothing. So mamma run him away."

The Chinaman entered the passage, we saw his dark figure gain a nimbus of sunlight and turning, disappear.

"Eagle Beak's all right. We like Eagle Beak," he added and Hercules in dark bronze passed us. "Hi, Baptis'," said Peter.

"Hi, big boy," replied the negro. "How you comin'?" he asked. The light flashed briefly, arcing downward and Peter pounced on a nickel. The man walked down the street, and a corner took him. Spring, scorned by wood and stone, took the air, filled the atmosphere itself, fretful and troubling, and Peter said: "He's all right. That's the way he always acks. You got to treat 'em like that, mamma says. And we do."

Peter with his face round and yellow as a new penny, brooded briefly. What does he see? I wondered, thinking of him as an incidental coin minted between the severed yet similar despairs of two races.

"Say," he said at last, "can you spin a top? There is a boy lives in that house can spin one end and pick it up on the string."

"Haven't you got a top?" I asked.

"Yes, the Baptis' give me one, but I aint had time to learn to spin it."

"Haven't had time?"

"Well, you see, I got so much to do. I have to sit here and tell 'em when mamma's busy talking to some body. And the others, too. I got to watch out for 'em."

"Watch out for what?"

"I dont know. Just watch out for 'em. They are nice folks here. Baptis' says we got the nicest girls in town here. But say, aint you going to draw no pictures today?"

"Yes, I am going to draw a picture of your stair case. How about coming along?"

"I might as well," Peter told Spratling. "I can see 'em just as well. But you aint going up to mamma's room, are you?"

"No, no. I'll draw the passage. But why do you ask?"

"Well, she's busy talking to that Chink that just went in. She dont like to be bothered while she's talking to some one."

"Then I wont bother her. I'll just draw a picture of the stair case."

"Well, that'll be all right, I guess."

We moved inside: it was like drowning in a sweet and azure sea. "Can I watch?" asked Peter.

"Surely you can. By the way, how would you like to be drawn?"

Peter— I dunno. Can you draw me?

Spratling— I expect so.

Peter— But say, you cant put me in a picture, can you?

A voice— Wait until that chilly breeze catch you in your B.V.D.'s.

Spratling— Certainly I can, if you want me to.

The victrola again broke into a tortured syncopation. Here were dark trees, and stars on an unknown water—all the despairs of time and breath.

A voice— Baby!

Another voice— Break dem springs, if you can.

Peter— That's Euphrosy: she got more sense than any of these gals, mamma says.

Here was a salmon colored stairway swelling upward, as satisfying as a woman's belly. Negroes brushed by us: black and tan and yellow faces wrung to an imminence of physical satisfaction. They passed us—Peter in the throes of a self-consciousness and Spratling spreading paper and choosing a crayon, and other negroes passed us, going out, slow with completion and the compulsion of imminent labor (which is worse) all having a word for Peter posing and wrung to a tortured caricature of himself.

A voice— Baby, wrap me round!
A voice— You goddam whore, I'll cut your th'oat.
A voice— And yo' heart within you melt, for the sorrows you have felt.

Steps thundered on the stairs, washed clothing flapped in a faint breeze. Negroes came, flushed and gray with sex, negroes went, languorous with repletion. The Chinaman descended. "How, Peter? You plitty boy," and went away. But Peter did not remark him.

Spratling— Lean against the wall, Peter. Stop wiggling so much! Stand as if God was looking at you.
Peter— Like this? His dark sailor suit took an impossible shape against the azure restful wall. His young body was impossible and terrible.
Spratling— Oh, hell. He cant stand that way, anyhow.

"Go ahead and draw," I advised, but he was already busy. "If you want to move, Peter," he said, "go ahead and move."
But it was a point of honor with Peter not to move. Spratling drew, squinting at him; and I knew that Peter was going to cry. The sunlight was immaculate as a virgin: hanging washed garments were planes of light and a washing line took the golden noon like a tight-rope dancer.

Voice— Baby, sun on me like a gold jail-suit. Makin' dem barrels roll. Rollin' dem barrels for you, baby.
A voice— Win th'ee hundred in a crap game last night.
A voice— Come on, big boy, git done. I cant lay here all day.
A voice— All I done, I done for you. When you sad, I'm sad; when you laugh, I laugh.
A voice— Oh, Christ, dont! I never meant it! Dont!
Peter (weeping)— My arm hurts.

Spratling— All right, move then.

Peter— I cant! You wont draw me no more.

A voice— You damn whore.

Peter— (changing his position, thinking Spratling will not notice it.) That's Joe Lee. He's always beatin' Imogene up. Joe Lee's bad.

I— Bad?

Peter— Sure. He's killed three. But he's too smart fer 'em. They cant catch him at it. Mamma always asks Imogene howcome she keeps him, but Imogene dont know. That's the way women are, mamma says.

Steps on the stairs, and here is Peter's mother, languorous as a handled magnolia petal. She is as light in color as Peter, and a woman passing says:

"Uh huh, I knowed you'd get in trouble. I told you yo' maw better not ketch you here."

"All right. Wait until Imogene beats me like she done you when she caught Joe Lee in your room last week. Then I'll talk some. Tore your hair out, she did."

"You ought to beat hell out of him, Mable," said the woman, passing on.

"Peter," said his mother.

"He's drawing me in a picture, mamma. He'll draw you too, if you will stay."

She came languorous as a decayed lily and looked at the sketch. "Huh," she said. "You come on with me," she told Peter.

Peter wept. "But he's drawing me in a picture," he told her.

"Haven't I told you about hanging around down here?"

"But he's drawing me," Peter crooking his arm about his face wept from some mature reserve of masculine vanity, seeing his life temporarily disrupted by a woman. But she took his hand and led him up the salmon stairs. At the turn she paused like a languorous damaged lily, and her dark eyes in which was all the despair of a subject race and a thinned blood become sterile except in the knowledge of the ancient sorrows of white and black, as a dog can see and hear things we cant, looked at us a moment. Then she was gone, and Peter's weeping soon died away.

While Spratling finished his sketch I watched the noon become afternoon, the sunlight change from silver to gold (if I slept and waked, I think I could know afternoon from morning by the color of the sunlight) in spite of art and vice and everything else which makes a world; hearing the broken phrases of a race answering quickly to the compulsions of the flesh and then going away, temporarily freed from the body, to sweat and labor and sing; doomed again to repair to a temporary satisfaction; fleeting, that cannot last. The world: death and despair, hunger and sleep. Hunger that tolls the body along until life becomes tired of the burden.

Spratling finished his sketch and through an ineffable azure corridor, as peaceful as sleep, we passed. Here was spring in a paved street, between walls, and here was Peter, his sorrow forgotten, in a window, saying:

"When you come next time I bet I can spin that top."

Moonlight

Approached from the rear, his uncle's house lay blank and lightless under the August moon, because his uncle and aunt had been gone two days now, on their summer vacation. He crossed the lane quartering, at once hurrying and skulking, the bottle of corn whiskey jouncing and burbling inside his shirt. On the opposite side of the lawn (he could see it above the low roofline, stippled solid and heavy and without depth on the sky) was a magnolia tree and there was a mocking bird singing in it now, on the topmost twig probably, high in the moon, as he lurked swiftly through the gate and into the shadow of the trees. Now he could not be seen as he went swiftly now across the dappled and dewdrenched lawn on his rubber soles and reached the sanctuary of the inky and vine-screened veranda. It was not some random and casual passerby so much as a neighbor whom he feared, who might be looking out a side window or even from another shadowed porch—some woman, some old woman who, representing the entire class and caste of mothers, parents, would be his mortal foe by pure instinctive reflex.

But he gained the porch without having been seen. Now there was no one to see him; now he began to believe, for the first time since he received the note, in his own luck. There was a fatality in it—the empty house, the fact that he had gained the veranda unseen. It was as though by gaining the porch unchallenged he had cast the augury, bled the bird, and this was fortune, luck: that instant when desire and circumstance coincide. It was as though they not only coincided, circumstance not only condoned desire, but were actually and suavely coercing it: he thought how, if he should miss out now, if it should not be tonight, if something occurred at this hour to betray and frustrate him, that he would be automatically absolved of all allegiance to conduct, order and even breathing.

There was a french door here, giving into the dark house, locked. From his pocket he produced the broken blade of the kitchen knife, fruit and symbol of the interminable afternoon's waiting—the periodic dissolution of his entrails into salty water while he waited for dark to come and so anneal the thralled dumb flesh with the bright sweet fires of hope. Leaning to the window, fumbling the knife blade into the crack below the latch, already trembling, he could feel the bottle inside his shirt, between shirt and flesh. When he had put it there it had been cold, chill and heavy between shirt and flesh; flesh flinched from it. But now it was hot and now he did not even feel it at all because again, just with thinking, his inside dissolved, became liquid too: the outside just the dead container like the glass of the bottle which lay against it. It (the bottle) was the emptied and rinsed eight-ounce medicine phial which he had filled from the cask of corn whiskey which his father believed to be hidden in the attic. Crouching in the hot airless attic beneath the close sun-reverberant roof, his eyes stinging and his whole being revolting, recoiling from the sharp smell of the whiskey as he sploshed it clumsily about the small mouth of the bottle, he had thought how it should have been champagne. Of course he should have had a long suave roadster and an evening suit and the Pacific Ocean beyond some eucalyptus trees (they owned a car, and his father had an evening suit, though the chance of his getting the one were about as good as of getting the other, and he had forgot about the ocean and the trees without having even known or speculated on the name of either) but certainly it should have been champagne, which he had never tasted: but then he had never tasted whiskey either but once and he didn't like it. But there was no place to get champagne; thinking of the whiskey, the homemade fiery liquor to which he was reduced, he thought in a kind of despair, in the throes of that self-doubt, that feeling that it is too good for us which we have when our heart's (or body's) desire is dropped without warning into our laps: *It's like I am going to miss out now just because I aint had time to work and get rich.*

But that was early in the afternoon. It had to be while his mother was still having her nap and before his father could be coming home from the store. Since then he had had leisure to read and re-read the note a hundred times. It was finer than anything he had ever seen on the screen:

> My dear Forgive my gardian he is old he does not realise that I am yours. See Skeet fix it for him to call me for a date tonight you meat us somewhere and I will be yours tonight even if tomorrow not goodbye but farewell forever. Destroy this. S.

He did not destroy it. He had it now, buttoned into his hip pocket, food too for the vampire feeding of the ignominy, the outrage. He wished that Mr Burchett could see it. Fumbling, working the knife blade behind the latch, he thought how, if it were not for Susan, tomorrow he would mail the note to Mr Burchett. He thought of Mr Burchett getting the note and, reading how Susan had referred to him in it not as 'uncle' but as 'guardian', he would realise his irrevocable mistake in believing that he had children to deal with. That was it: the ignominy, the outrage: not the injury. He knew that Mr and Mrs Burchett didn't think much of him, but then he didn't think much of Mr and Mrs Burchett. In fact, he did not think about them at all except when one of them got in his and Susan's way, and then he thought of them only as he thought about his own parents: as the natural and impeding adjunct to his existence and the inexplicable hazard to what he wished to do. He and Susan were in the hammock on the dark side of Mr Burchett's lawn. Susan had already said, "I haf to be in by ten-thirty" and they had heard ten strike and they were trying to gauge when thirty minutes would have passed. (He had his watch on, but that will be explained later.) But they—he, anyway—had lost time somewhere in that summer's dark scented with the sweet young smell of invisible girlflesh, somewhere between her lips and the fumbling diffidence of his half-repulsed hands, so that his first intimation was a shocking and terrific blow on his bottom, come upward from beneath the net hammock, which hurled him out of it and onto his hands and knees on the earth from where, looking wildly upward, he saw the angry man, tousleheaded, in a calflength old fashioned nightshirt and carrying a flashlight, ducking nimbly beneath the hammock rope. Mr Burchett kicked him again before he could get up, with the flat on one unlaced shoe; though, and with Susan's first shriek still ringing in his ears, he outdistanced the elder man easily within the first ten yards. That was the ignominy, the writhing. *He never had a pistol, he never even had a stick,* he thought. *He never even said nothing. He just kicked me like I was a stray dog that come up onto the gallery and wet.*

For the next ten hours of excruciating suffering he thought only of revenge. But the only revenge he could visualise was himself kicking Mr Burchett and he knew that he would have to wait at least ten years to be able to do that without he got help. And the only person he could think of whom he could ask for help was Skeet and he knew even before the thought that that was vain. He tried with mathematics to exorcise, not Mr Burchett exactly, but the outrage. Lying in bed, sleepless, writing (it seemed to him that between himself and the bed the actual shoe lay, outrageous and unavoidable, like the symbol of a curse, as though attached to his backside forever like the Ancient Mariner's albatross, however he turned) he added his and Skeet's ages—16 and 16. That made 32, and Mr Burchett was at least forty. Then he added his and Skeet's weights in pounds, and that sounded better. But there was still the unknown quantity of Skeet himself. Or rather, the known, because he asked himself, Suppose Skeet came to you and said, I want you to help me kick Doctor West or Mr Hovis: and he knew that he would have refused. Then the note came, and all this vanished. It fled: Mr Burchett, the kick, the ignominy and all, was exorcised [by] a scrap of cheap scented pink note paper scrawled over with sprawling purple ink; crouching at the dark door, working with the broken blade at the latch, he thought only, again in that despair, of how difficult seduction actually was. Because he was a virgin too. Skeet and most of the others would go down into Nigger Hollow at night sometimes and they would try to make him come, but he never had. He didn't know why: he just hadn't. And now it was probably too late. He was like the hunter who finds the game suddenly and at last and then discovers that he has never learned how to load his gun; even the other night, lying in the hammock with Susan, befogged and beclouded in his own easily repulsed ineptitude, he had not thought about it much. But now he did. *Maybe I ought to practised up on niggers first,* he thought.

The latch slipped, the dark door swung inward; the house, de-

serted and close and secret, seemed to murmur of a thousand
attitudes of love. Because his uncle and aunt were still young. His
father and mother, of course, were old. He firmly (and without
difficulty) declined to imagine or think of them in bed together. But
the uncle and aunt were different, young, besides not being especially kin to him. *If I can just get her inside,* he thought, *where
laying has done already took place, maybe just two nights ago, before
they left.*

He closed the door to where it would open at a touch, then once
more he lurked swiftly across the yard and crossed the lane and
then turned and followed it, with an air casual and no longer
skulking, to its intersection with the street and stood again in the
bitten shadow of the August oaks. The mocking bird was still
singing in the magnolia; it had never stopped; up and down the
street the verandas of the houses contained each its rocking and
murmuring blurs. He did not have to wait long. "Hi, horseface,"
Skeet said. "Where's it?"

"Where's what?"

"You know what." Skeet touched his shirt, then grasped the
bottle through the shirt and with the other hand tried to open the
shirt. He struck Skeet's hand away.

"Get away!" he said. "Go get her first."

"That aint what you said," Skeet said. "I aint going to run no
man's gash on a dry stomach." So they returned down the lane and
entered his uncle's yard again and went around to the magnolia
tree, where the mocking bird still sang and beneath which there
was a hydrant. "Gimme," Skeet said.

He passed Skeet the bottle, "Go easy on it now," he said. "I'm
going to need it." Skeet tilted the bottle. Presently he stooped,
bringing Skeet's blunt head and the tilted bottle into relief against
the sky, then he rose and snatched the bottle. "Look out!" he cried.
"Didn't I tell you I am going to need it? Go on and get her; you're
already late."

"Oke," Skeet said. He rose from the hydrant, the rust-flavored
gout of warmish stale water, and went on across the lawn toward
the street.

"Make it snappy," he called after Skeet.

"What do you reckon I am going to do?" Skeet said without
looking back. "Sit around there and jaw with old man Burchett?

I got a tail to be kicked the same as you have."

He waited again, in the thick shade of the magnolia. It should have been easy for him to do now, since he had had the entire afternoon to practise, accustom himself to waiting, in. But it was harder now, standing in the shadow, beneath the silver and sense-less and untiring bird; the bottle, again inside his shirt, felt now actually hot since his flesh, his being, now blew suddenly cool, cold —a suspension like water, of amazed and dreamy unbelief that it was actually himself who waited here for her with the cunning door behind him. Automatically he raised his arm to look at the watch on his wrist, knowing that he could not see it even if time had mattered—the watch which his mother had given him last summer when he had passed his first class scouting tests, with the Scout Emblem on the face. It had had a luminous dial then, until one day he forgot and went swimming with it on. It still kept pretty good time now and then, but now you could not see the face nor the hands anymore in the dark. *That's all I want, he thought. I just want to seduce her. I would even marry her afterward, even if I aint a marrying kind of a man.*

Then he heard her—the sweet high whinnying reasonless gig-gling which turned his bowels to water—the pale dress, the body reed-thin as she and Skeet came across the lawn toward the magno-lia. "All right, fishface," Skeet said. "Where's it?"

"You already had it."

"You said you would give me one when I brought her back."

"No I didn't. I said to wait until then to take the one I said this afternoon I would give you. But you wouldn't wait."

"No you didn't. I said this afternoon if you would give me a drink I would go and get her and you said, all right, and then tonight you said you would give me a drink when I brought her back and so here she is and so where is it?" Again Skeet grasped at the bottle inside his shirt; again he struck Skeet's hand away. "All right," Skeet said. "If you aint going to give me one, I aint going to leave." So once more he squatted, bringing Skeet's blunt swallowing profile and the tilted bottle into relief against the sky; once more he snatched the bottle away: this time with actual anger.

"Do you want to drink it all?" he cried, hissed, in a thin desper-ate voice.

"Sure," Skeet said. "Why not? She dont want none of it. And you dont like it."

"That's all right about that," he said, trembling. "It's mine, aint it? Aint it mine? What?"

"All right, all right, keep your shirt on." He looked at them. "You coming to town now?"

"No."

"Why, I told Aunt Etta I was going to the show," Susan said.

"No," he said again. "We aint coming to town. Go on, now. Go on."

For a moment longer Skeet looked at them. "Oke," he said at last. They watched him go on across the lawn.

"I guess we better go to the show," she said. "I told Aunt Etta I was, and somebody might—" He turned toward her; he was trembling now; his hands felt queer and clumsy as they touched her.

"Susan," he said; "Susan—" Now he held her, his hands numb: it was not his hands which told him that she was strained back a little, looking at him curiously.

"What's the matter with you tonight?" she said.

"Nothing," he said. He released her and tried to put the bottle into her hand. "Here," he said. "There's some water over there, in the hydrant; you can drink out of the hydrant—"

"I dont want it," she said. "I dont like it."

"Please, Susan," he said; "please." He held her, recoiled and now motionless, her body arched and tense. Then she took the bottle. For an instant he believed that she was going to drink; a fierce hot wave of triumph rushed over him. Then he heard the faint dull sound of the flask when it struck the earth and then he was embracing her—the reed-thin familiar body, the mouth, the cool comfortable unlustful kissing of adolescence, to which he succumbed as usual, floated, swimming without effort on into a cool dark water smelling of spring; for the moment betrayed, Delilah-sheared, though not for long; perhaps it was her voice, what she said:

"Now come on. Let's go to the show."

"No. Not the show." Now he felt her pause in sheer amazement. "You mean, you wont take me?"

"No," he said. He was on hands and knees now, hunting the

bottle. But there was the need for haste again and he could not find the bottle at once; besides, it did not matter. He rose; his arm about her was trembling; he had a flashing conviction that, because of its numbness and trembling, he might lose her here, at the brink.

"Oh," she said, "you're hurting me!"

"All right," he said. "Come on."

"Where are we going?"

"Just there," he said. "Just yonder." He led her on to the steps and onto the dark veranda. She was holding back and even tugging at his arm and fingers but he did not know it because there was no feeling in his arm. He just went on, stumbling a little at the steps, half dragging her up, saying, "I thought I was going to die and then I got the letter. I thought I would have to die and then the letter came" and something else deeper than that, voiceless even: *Susan! Susan! Susan! Susan!* There was a porch swing in the angle. She tried to stop there; she evidently thought that that was where he was going. When she saw it she even stopped holding back, and when they passed it she came obediently, as though passive now not with amazement but with sheer curiosity as he led her to the french door and pushed it inward. Then she stopped; she began to struggle.

"No," she said. "No. No. No. No."

"Yes. They are gone. It will be just—" He said, struggling with her, dragging her toward the door. Then she began to cry—a loud wail of shocked amazement like a struck child.

"Hush!" he cried. "Jesus, hush!" She stood backed into the wall beside the open window, wailing with the loud obliviousness of five or six. "Please, Susan!" he said. "Stop bawling! They will hear us! Stop!" He grasped her, trying to close her mouth with his hand.

"Take your nasty hands off of me!" [she] cried, struggling.

"All right, all right." He held her. He began to lead her away. He led her to the swing and drew her into it, holding her. "Hush, hush! Jesus, hush!"

"You let me alone!" she wailed. "You stop!" But she was not shrieking now, though she still wept with that terrific abandon, not struggling, fighting him now as he held her, trying to hold her quiet.

"I didn't mean anything," he said. "It was just what your note said. I thought that—"

"I didn't!" she cried. "I didn't!"

"All right, all right," he said. He held her. He held her clumsily; he realised that she was clinging to him now. He felt like wood—the carcass from which sense, sensibility, sentience, had fled along with the sweet wild fires of hope; he thought in quiet amazement: *I wouldn't have hurt her. All I wanted was just to seduce somebody.*

"You sc-scared me so bad," she said, clinging to him.

"Yes, all right. I'm sorry. I never meant to. Shhhhh, now."

"Maybe I will tomorrow night. But you scared me so."

"All right, all right." He held her. He felt nothing at all now, no despair, no regret, not even surprise. He was thinking of himself and Skeet in the country, lying on a hill somewhere under the moon with the bottle between them, not even talking.

The Big Shot

When Don Reeves was on the *Sentinel* he used to spend six nights a week playing checkers at the Police Station. The seventh night they played poker. He told me this story:

Martin is sitting in the chair. Govelli sits on the desk, his thigh hung over the edge, his hat on and his thumbs in his vest, the cigarette on his lower lip bobbing up and down while he tells Martin about Popeye running over the red light with a car full of whiskey, barely missing a pedestrian. They—the onlookers, the other pedestrians—ran the car into the curb by a sheer outraged weight of over-tried civic virtue as personified by long-suffering and vulnerable bone and flesh, and held Popeye there, the women shrieking and screaming and the pedestrian on the running board waving his puny fist in Popeye's face; and then Popeye drew a pistol —a slight man with a dead face and dead black hair and eyes and a delicate hooked little nose and no chin, crouching snarling behind the neat blue automatic. He was a little, dead-looking bird in a tight black suit like a vaudeville actor of twenty years ago, with a savage falsetto voice like a choir-boy, and he was considered quite a personage in his own social and professional circles. I understand he left more than one palpitant heart among the night-blooming sisterhood of DeSoto street when he cleared these parts. There was nothing he could do with his money save give it away, you see. That's our American tragedy: we have to give away so much of our money, and there's nobody to give it to save the poets and painters. And if we gave it to them, they would probably stop being poets and painters. And that little flat ubiquitous pistol had caused more than one masculine gland to function overtime, and at least one to stop altogether; in this case the heart also. But his principal bid for interest and admiration among them was the fact that he went each summer to Pensacola to visit his aged mother, telling her that he was a hotel clerk. Have you noticed how people whose lives are equivocal, not to say chaotic, are always moved by the homely virtues. Go to the brothel or the convict camp if you would hear the songs about sonny boy and about mother.

So the cop took them all in—the car full of liquor, the hysterical and outraged pedestrian, and Popeye and the pistol—followed by an augmenting cloud of public opinion noisy as blackbirds, and including two casual reporters.

It may have been the two reporters that tipped the scales with Martin. It couldn't have been the mere presence of liquor in the car nor the fact that Popeye was on his way to Martin's house with it when he ran past the light; the cops themselves would have seen to that, Popeye being better known to them by sight than Martin, even. It had not been ten days since Martin extricated Popeye from a similar predicament, and doubtless the cops had already got the car out of the picture as soon as they reached the station. It must have been the presence of the two reporters, those symbols of the vox pop which even this Volstead Napoleon, this little corporal of polling-booths, dared not flout and outrage beyond a certain point.

So he sits in the single chair behind the desk. I am a good mind," he says. "I am a good mind. How many times have I told you not to let that durn little rat tote a pistol? Have you and him both forgot about that business last year?"

That was when they had Popeye in jail without bond for that killing. They had him dead to rights; a cold-blooded job if there ever was one, even though Popeye had done a public service (as Martin himself said when he heard it; "If he'd just go on now and commit suicide, I'll put them both up a monument") when he did it. But anyway they had him, lying in jail there with that strange —but maybe all hop-heads are crazy—strange conviction of his invulnerability. He had a certain code like he had a certain code in his clothing, his tight black suits, limited but positive. He used to get hopped up and deliver long diatribes on the liquor traffic, using the pistol for emphasis. He wouldn't—or couldn't—drink himself, and he hated liquor worse than a Baptist deacon.

As near as anybody could discover, he never even took a child's precautions to conceal or mitigate the deed or his part in it. He wouldn't say one way or the other, wouldn't even talk about it or read the papers about himself. He just lay there on his back in the cell all day long, telling anybody—the lawyers Govelli got to save his neck, the reporters and all—that came along how, as soon as he was out, he was going to put the bee on one of the turnkeys for calling him a hop-head; telling it in the same tone he'd tell about a base ball game—if he ever went to one. All I ever heard of him doing was getting pinched by traffic cops with a car full of Govelli's liquor, and going to Pensacola to see his mother; the lawyer came down heavy on that fact at his trial. He was smart, that lawyer. The trial began as to whether or not Popeye had killed a man; it ended as to whether or not Popeye really went to Pensacola, and if he had an actual mother there. But the witness they produced may have been his mother, after all. He must have had one once—a little, cold, still, quiet man that looked like he might have had ink in his veins—something cold and defunctive, anyway. "I am a good mind," Martin says. "I am, for a fact."

Govelli sits motionless above his hooked thumbs, the cigarette wreathing slow across his face, across the neat cicatrice of his scar. It slanted down across the corner of his mouth like a white thread. "They never hung it on him," he says sullenly.

"Because why not? Because I kept them from it. Not you, not him. I did it."

"Sure," Govelli says, "you do it for nothing. Just because you are big-hearted. I'm paying for it. Paying high. And when I dont get what I pay for, I know what I can do."

They look at one another, the cigarette wreathing slow across Govelli's face. He had not moved it since he lit it there. "Are you threatening me?" Martin says.

"I dont threaten," Govelli says. "I'm telling you."

Martin drums on the desk. He is not looking at Govelli; he is not looking at anything: a thick man, not tall, sitting behind the desk with that dynamic immobility of a motionless locomotive, his fingers musing in slow taps on the desk. "Durn little rat," he says. "If he even got drunk. You can count on what a man that drinks will do. But a durn hop-head."

"Sure," Govelli says. "It's his fault you can buy snow in this town. It was him lets them sell it here."

Still Martin does not look at him, his fingers musing on the desk top. "A durn rat. And why you dont get shut of them wops and hop-heads and get some decent American boys that a man can count on. . . . Here it's not ten days since I sprung him and now he's got to wave a pistol right in the face of a crowd on the street. I'm a good mind; be durn if I aint." He drummed on the desk, looking across the room and out the window, above the tall buildings; his town. For he had built some of it, letting the contracts for a price, taking his natural cut, yet insisting on a good contract, good work—our virtues are usually by-products of our vices, you know. That's why any sort of an egoist is good to have in the civic blood system—and he ran all of it from that barren office, that cheap yellow desk and patent chair. It was his town, and those who were not glad were not anything. They were just those eternal optimists, suzerains of rented rooms and little lost jobs on stools or behind counters, waiting for that mythical flood tide of outraged humanities that never makes.

After a minute, Govelli watching him, he moved. He drew the telephone across the desk and gave a number. The telephone answered. "They've got Popeye down at the station," he said into the mouthpiece. "See to it. . . . Popeye; yes. And let me know at once." He pushed the telephone away and looked at Govelli. "I told you before it was the last time. And I mean it now. If he gets in trouble once more, you will have to get shut of him. And if they find a pistol on him, I'm going to send him to the penitentiary myself. You understand?"

"Oh, I'll tell him," Govelli said. "I've told him before he aint got any need for that rod. But this is a free country. If he wants to carry a gun, that's his business."

"You tell him I'll make it mine. You go down there and get that car and send that stuff on out to my house and then you tell him. I mean it."

"You tell them broken-down flatties to lay off of him," Govelli said. "He'd be all right if they'll just leave him be."

After Govelli departs he still sits in the chair, motionless, with that immobility of country people, before which patience is no more than a sound without any meaning. He was born and raised on a Mississippi farm. Tenant-farmers—you know: barefoot, the whole family, nine months in the year. He told me about one day his father sent him up to the big house, the house of the owner, the boss, with a message. He went to the front door in his patched overalls, his bare feet: he had never been there before; perhaps he knew no better anyway, to whom a house was just where you kept the quilt pallets and the corn meal out of the rain (he said 'outen the rain'). And perhaps the boss didn't know him by sight; he probably looked exactly like a dozen others on his land and a hundred others in the neighborhood.

Anyway the boss came to the door himself. Suddenly he—the boy—looked up and there within touching distance for the first time was the being who had come to symbolise for him the ease and pleasant ways of the earth: idleness, a horse to ride all day long, shoes all the year round. And you can imagine him when the boss spoke: "Dont you ever come to my front door again. When you come here, you go around to the kitchen door and tell one of the niggers what you want." That was it, you see. There was a negro servant come to the door behind the boss, his eyeballs white in the gloom, and Martin's people and kind, although they looked upon Republicans and Catholics, having never seen either one, probably, with something of that mystical horror which European peasants of the fifteenth century were taught to regard Democrats and Protestants, the antipathy between them and negroes was an immediate and definite affair, being at once biblical, political, and economic: the three compulsions—the harsh unflagging land broken into sparse intervals by spells of demagoguery and religio-neurotic hysteria—which shaped and coerced their gaunt lives. A mystical justification of the need to feel superior to someone somewhere, you see.

He didn't deliver the message at all. He turned and walked back down the drive, feeling the nigger's teeth too in the gloom of the hall beyond the boss' shoulder, holding his back straight until he was out of sight of the house. Then he ran. He ran down the road and into the woods and hid there all day, lying on his face in a ditch. He told me that now and then he crawled to the edge of the field and he could see his father and his two older sisters and his brother working in the field, chopping cotton, and he told me it was as though he were seeing them for the first time.

But he didn't go home until that night. I dont know what he told them, what happened; perhaps nothing did. Perhaps the message was of no importance—I cant imagine those people having anything of importance capable of being communicated by words—or it may have been sent again. And people like that react to disobedience and unreliability only when it means loss of labor or money. Unless they had needed him in the field that day, they probably had not even missed him.

He never approached the boss again. He would see him from a distance, on the horse, and then he began to watch him, the way he sat the horse, his gestures and mannerisms, the way he spoke; he told me that sometimes he would hide and talk to himself, using the boss' gestures and tone to his own shadow on the wall of the barn or the bank of a ditch: "Dont you never come to my front door no more. You go around to the back door and tell hit to the nigger. Dont you never come to my front door no more" in his meagre idiom that said 'ye' and 'hit' and 'effen' for 'you' and 'it' and 'if', set off by the aped gestures of that lazy and arrogant man who had given an unwitting death-blow to that which he signified and summed and which alone permitted him breath. He didn't tell me, but I believe that he would slip away from the field, the furrow and the deserted hoe, to lurk near the gate to the big house and wait for the boss to pass. He just told me that he didn't hate the man at all, not even that day at the door with the nigger servant grinning beyond the other's shoulder. And that the reason he hid to watch and admire him was that his folks would think he ought to hate him and he knew he couldn't.

Then he was married, a father, and proprietor of a store at the cross-roads. The process must have been to him something like the bald statement: suddenly he was grown and married and owner of a store within long sight of the big house. I dont think he remembered himself the process of getting grown and getting the store anymore than he could remember the road, the path he would traverse to reach the gate and crouch in the brush there in time. He had done it the same way. The actual passing of time, the attenuation, had condensed into a forgotten instant; his strange body—that vehicle in which we ride from one unknown station to another as in a train, unwitting when the engine changes or drops a car here and takes on one there with only a strange new whistle-blast coming back to us—had metamorphosed, inventing for him new minor desires and compulsions to be obeyed and cajoled, conquered or surrendered to or bribed with the small change left over from his unflagging dream while he lay in the weeds at the gate, waiting to see pass the man who knew neither his name nor his face nor that implacable purpose which he—the man—had got upon that female part of every child where ambition lies fecund and waiting.

So he was a merchant, one step above his father, his brothers mesmerised still to the stubborn and inescapable land. He could neither read nor write; he did a credit business in spools of thread and tins of snuff and lap-links and plow-shares, carrying them in his head through the day and reciting them without a penny's error while his wife transcribed them into the cash book on the kitchen table after supper was done.

Now the next part he was a little ashamed of and a little proud of too: his man's nature, the I, and the dream in conflict. It emerged from his telling as a picture, a tableau. The boss was an old man now, gone quietly back to his impotent vices. He still rode about the place a little, but most of the day he spent in his sock feet lying in a hammock between two trees in the yard—the man who had always been able to wear shoes all day long, all year long. Martin told me about that. "That's what I had made up my mind," he said. "Once I had believed that if I could just wear shoes all the time, you see. And then I found that I wanted more. I wanted to work right through the wanting and being able to wear shoes all the time and come out on the other side where I could own fifty pairs at once if I wanted and then not even want to wear one of them." And when he told me that he was sitting in the swivel chair behind the desk, his stocking feet propped in an open drawer.

But to get back to the picture. It is night, an oil lamp burns on an up-ended box in a narrow cuddy; it is the store-room behind the store proper, filled with unopened boxes and barrels, with coils of new rope and pieces of new harness on nails in the wall; the two of them—the old man with his white stained moustache and his eyes that dont see so good anymore and his blue-veined uncertain hands, and the young man, the peasant at his first maturity, with his cold face and the old habit of deference and emulation and perhaps affection (we must love or hate anything to ape it) and

surely a little awe, facing one another across the box, the cards
lying between them—they used wrought nails for counters—and
a tumbler and spoon at the old man's hand and the whiskey jug
on the floor in the shadow of the box. "I've got three queens," the
boss says, spreading his cards in a palsied and triumphant row.
"Beat that, by Henry!"

"Well, sir," the other says, "you had me fooled again."

"I thought so. By Henry, you young fellows that count on the
luck all the time. . . ."

The other lays his cards down. His hands are gnarled, plow-
warped; he handles the cards with a certain deliberation which at
first glance appears stiff and clumsy, so that a man would not
glance at them again: certainly not a man whose eyes are dim in
the first place and a little fuddled with drink in the second. But I
doubt if the liquor was for that purpose, if he depended on it alone.
I suspect he was as confident of himself, had taken his slow and
patient precautions just as he would have got out and practised
with an axe before undertaking to clear up a cypress bottom for
profit by the stick. "I reckon I still got it," he says.

The boss has reached for the nails. Now he leans forward. He
does it slowly, his trembling hand arrested above the nails. He leans
across the table, peering, his movement slowing all the while. It is
as though he knows what he will see. It is as though the whole
movement were without conviction, as you reach for money in a
dream, knowing you are not awake. "Move them closer," he says.
"Damn it, do you expect me to read them from here?" The other
does so—the 2, 3, 4, 5, 6. The boss looks at them. He is breathing
hard. Then he sits back and takes in his trembling hand a cold
chewed cigar from the table-edge and sucks at it, making shaking
contact between cigar and mouth, while the other watches him,
motionless, his face lowered a little, not yet reaching for the nails.
The boss curses, sucking at the cigar. "Pour me a toddy," he says.

That's how he got his start. He sold the store and with his wife
and infant daughter he came to town, to the city. And he arrived
here at just exactly the right time—the year three A. V. Otherwise
the best he could have hoped for would have been another store,
where at sixty perhaps he could have retired. But now, at only
forty-eight (there is a certain irony that oversees the doings of the
great. It's as though behind their chairs at whatever table they sit

there loom leaning and partisan shadows making each the homely and immemorial gesture for fortune and good luck and whose triumphant shout at each coup roars beneath his own exultation, tossing it high—until one day he turns suddenly himself aghast at the sardonic roar), now at forty-eight he was a millionaire, living with the daughter—she was eighteen; his wife had lain ten years now beneath a marble cenotaph that cost twenty thousand dollars among the significant names in the oldest section of the oldest cemetery: he bought the lot at a bankrupt sale—in four or five acres of Spanish bungalow in our newest subdivision, being fetched each morning by his daughter in a lemon-colored roadster doing forty and fifty miles an hour along the avenue to the touched caps of the traffic policemen, in to the barren office where he would sit in his sock feet and read in the *Sentinel* with cold and biding delusion the yearly list of debutantes at the Chickasaw Guards ball each December.

The Spanish bungalow was recent. The first year they had lived in rented rooms, the second year they moved into—the compulsion of his country rearing—the biggest house he could find nearest the downtown, the street cars and traffic, the electric signs. His wife still insisted on doing her own housework. She still wanted to go back to the country, or, lacking that, to buy one of those tiny, neat, tight bungalows surrounded by infinitesimal lawns and garden plots and aseptic chicken-runs on the highways just beyond the city limits.

But he was already beginning to affirm himself in that picture of a brick house with columns on a broad, faintly dingy lawn of magnolias; he could already tell at a glance the right names— Sandeman, Blount, Heustace—in the newspapers and the city directory. He got the house, paid three prices for it, and it killed his wife. Not the overpurchase of the house, but the watching of that man who heretofore had been superior to all occasions, putting himself with that patient casualness with which he used to hide in the brush near the gate to the big house, in the way of his neighbors, establishing a certain hedge-top armistice with the men while their wives remained cold, turning in and out of the drives in their heavy, slightly outmoded limousines without a glance across the dividing box and privet.

So she died, and he got a couple—Italians—to come in and keep house for him and the girl. Not negroes yet, mind you. He was not ready for them. He had the house, the outward shape and form, but he was not yet certain of himself, not yet ready to affirm in actual practise that conviction of superiority; he would not yet jeopardise that which had once saved him. He had not yet learned that man is circumstance.

The bungalow came five years ago, when he practically gave the house away—he had begun to learn then—and built the new one, the stucco splendor of terraces and patios and wrought iron like the ultimate sublimation of a gasoline station. Perhaps he felt that in this both himself and them—the peasant without past and the black man without future—would have at least a scratch start from very paradox.

This house was staffed by negroes, too many of them; more than he had any use for. He could not bring himself to like them, to be at ease with them: the continuous sad soft murmur of their voices from the kitchen always on the verge of laughter harked him back despite himself, who was saying "Hit aint" for "it is not" and dipping his cheap snuff in the presence of urban politicians and judges and contractors with no subjective qualms whatever, to that day when, feeling the nigger's teeth and eyeballs in the dusky hall, he tramped with stiff back down the drive from the big house and so out of his childhood forever, paced by the two voices, the one saying "You cannot run" and the other "You cannot cry."

"So I kept Tony and his wife to look after the niggers," he told me, "to give them something to do." Perhaps he believed that. Perhaps he had not even ventured to himself the monstrous shape of his ambition, his delusion. Certainly he had not to the daughter as they drove down town each morning—that was until she was sixteen; within another year one of the negroes was driving him down, since the girl was not up before ten and eleven oclock, what with dancing and riding in cars the better part of the night.

"Who were you with last night?" he would ask her, and she would tell him, with that blank, secret look, who had learned in her seventeen years more about the world, that world divorced from all reality and necessity which women rule and which had killed her mother, than he had in his forty-eight, naming off the names he wanted to hear—Sandeman and Heustace and Blount. And sometimes it was the truth, even that she had met him at a dance. She just neglected to say what dance, what place—the out-of-doors pavilion at West End Gardens, where the scions of Blount and Sandeman and Heustace would go on Saturday nights with bottles of Govelli's liquor, to pick up stenographers and shop girls. I have seen her there—a thin creature, a little overdressed despite the two months at the Washington convent. Martin took her there himself, with his list of careful addresses culled from the *Sentinel*—'Miss So-and-so, daughter of So-and-so, Sandeman Place, home for the holidays'. I like to think of the two of them on that thirty-six hour journey (it was probably, for all his power and all her little urban sophistication derived from the sycophance of clerks in shops, their first Pullman experience) while the world unrolled beyond the drawing-room window with that unforgettable thrill of first journeys, that attenuation of self, that isolation and division when we first assimilate the incontrovertible actuality of the earth's roundness while gradually but surely our spirit goes down onto four legs again to cling the closer, outfaced by its broken armistice with the horror of space.

They probably never talked to one another about what they were seeing: the new sights, mountains standing remote and profound as the ultimate unknowable into the dwarfed affirmation of the peasant with his lip full of snuff and his list of pencilled addresses and the other peasant with hair of that unmistakable shade of worn sea-grass rope: the badge and pedigree of the red-neck. And wary too, her face, her little painted face. She got quieter and quieter. Here, at home, she had a certain immediacy; she too was equal to any occasion, but in Washington it was as though the sheer accomplishing of distance, of rural ground again, had robbed her of the careful years. I like to think of them making the implacable round of the addresses in a hired car, she silent, watchful, with the beginning in her little vivid shallow face of something dark and inarticulate and profound like you see in the faces of dogs, appearing to less advantage, more hopelessly country than he who had a certain assurance through sheer limitation because he was unaware of it, since women react quicker.

He did all the talking, waiting in the quiet, vaguely cloistral reception rooms while sisters and mothers superior (he decided on a Catholic convent: he had the delusions of a Napoleon, you see; he too could on occasion rise superior to the ancient voices that

make up a man, without knowing it) entered with tranquil sibi-
lance, with their serene wimpled unearthly faces. So he left her
there: a thin awkward little figure, with her streaked cheeks and her
haunted dumb eyes. "Dont you want to be where you can get to
know the girls?" he said. "You can make friends with them here,
and then you will all come home together for the Ball in the same
car." The Chickasaw Guards ball, he meant. But I'll tell about that.

So he left her and returned home in the same clothes he had left
home in, but with a new tin of snuff. He told me about that: how
he had run out and had to make an overnight trip down into
Virginia to get another tin. He showed me the tin, chucking it in
his hand. "Cost five cents more," he said, "and cant noways com-
pare with ourn. Not no ways. Why, if I'd a sold a fellow a can of
this when I was keeping store, they'd a run me outen the country."
Sitting then he was, in his sock feet, with the *Sentinel* open at the
society page where the first rumors of the Chickasaw ball were
beginning to wake.

The yearly ball, the Chickasaw Guards, were institutions. It had
been organised and the first ball given in 1861; they—Blounts and
Sandemans and Heustaces—wore their new uniforms among the
plucked strings, their knapsacks piled in the anteroom; at midnight
the troop train left for Virginia. Four years later eighteen of them
returned, with the faded roses of that night still buttoned in their
worn tunics. For the next fifteen years it was mainly political; it
became practically a secret organization, its members scattered
about the south and interdict by the Federal government, until the
Carpet-Bagger regime slew the golden goose. Then it became social, yet still retaining its military framework as a unit of the
National Guard. Thus it was two separate organizations, with a
skeleton staff of army officers—a colonel, a major, a captain and
a subaltern—who were permitted on sufferance at its principal
annual manifestation: the December ball at which the debutantes
were presented. The actual hierarchy was social, practically hereditary, arrogating to its officers designations of a gallant, inverted
military cast with a serene disregard of military usage. In other
words, anybody that wanted to could be colonel of it, while the title
of Flag-Corporal inferred in its incumbent a sense of honor like
Launcelot's, a purity of motive like Galahad's, a pedigree like Man
o' War's. It served again in the European War, the Sandemans and

Blounts and Heustaces in the ranks, including the Flag-Corporal.

He was Doctor Blount. He was a bachelor, about forty. The office had been in his family for thirty-five years; he had held it for twelve on the day when Martin went to see him two weeks after he left his daughter in the Washington school. He didn't tell me about this himself. Not that he would have minded admitting temporary defeat, but because he knew before hand that he was going to be defeated this first time, perhaps because for the first time in his life he was having to go out and buy something instead of sitting in his office and selling it.

There was nobody he could ask, you see. He knew that his judges and commissioners and such were of no weight here, for all their linen collars. Not that he would have hesitated to use them for this purpose if he could, since, also like Napoleon, he would not have hesitated to make his illusions serve his practical ends, or vice versa if you will. And that's how a man gains practical knowlege: serving his illusions with his practical ends. By serving his practical ends with material fact he acquires only habit.

So he went to Doctor Blount, the hereditary chairman. There was also invested in him a sort of hereditary practise among old ladies like an inherited legal practise—a matter of consultations regarding diet and various polite ailments at bedsides, with perhaps coffee or a glass of wine served by a negro butler who addressed him as Mister Harrison and asked him how his mother was.

He had an office, though, and he and Martin were facing one another across the desk—the doctor with his thin face and his interrogative gaze behind pince nez on his thin nose, and his thinning hair, and the caller in a cheap unpressed suit, with something of that awkwardness, that alert and dumb foreknowledge of defeat which the daughter had carried about Washington that day.

After a moment Blount said, "Yes? You wanted to see me?"

"I reckon you dont know who I am," Martin said. It was not interrogatory, not deprecatory, promptive: it was just a statement, a fact of no interest to either of them.

"I cant say I do. Did you wish—"

"My name is Martin." Blount looked at him. "Dal Martin." Blount looked at him, his eyebrows raised a little. Then his eyes became blank while Martin watched his face.

"Ah," Blount said. "I recall the name now. You are a—contractor, isn't it? I recall seeing your name in the paper associated with the paving of Beauregard avenue. But I am not on the city commission; I am afraid. . . ." His face cleared. "Ah, I see. You have come to me with regard to the proposed new armory for the Chickasaw Guards. I see. But I—"

"It aint that," Martin said.

Blount ceased, his eyebrows arched faintly. "Then what—" Then Martin told him. I suspect he told him flat out, in a single bald sentence. And I suspect that for a minute Martin's heart surged and the leaning shadows behind him leaned nearer yet on an indrawn breath of exultation, because the doctor sat so quiet beyond the desk. "Who were your people, Mr Martin?" Blount said. Martin told him, and about the daughter, Blount listening with that cold interest, with that knowledge of that female world which Martin had not and would never have and which pierced at a single glance his illusion about the girl.

"Ah," Blount said. "I dont doubt that your daughter is in every way worthy of that high place to which she is obviously destined." He rose. "That was all you wanted with me?"

Martin did not rise. He watched Blount. "I mean, cash," he said. "I aint offering you a check."

"You have it with you?"

"Yes," Martin said.

"Good day, sir," Blount said.

Martin did not move. "I'll double it," he said.

"I said, good day, sir," Blount said.

They looked at one another. Martin did not move. Blount pressed the buzzer on the desk, Martin watching his hand. "I reckon you know I can make hit unpleasant for you," he said. Blount crossed the room and opened the door as the secretary appeared there.

"This gentleman wishes to leave," he said.

But Martin didn't give up. I imagine him sitting in his office, his sock feet in the open drawer, his lower lip bulging slowly, for he believed that all men can be led by their lusts. "Hit was the money," he said. "What use has a durn fellow like that got for money? Now, what can hit be?"

But he didn't discover that until the next year. The girl was home then, two months after he left her in Washington and a week before the ball. He met her at the station. She got off the train crying and they stood in the train shed, she crying into his overcoat and he patting her back clumsily. "Now, now," he said; "now, now. Hit dont matter. Hit dont make no difference. You can stay to home effn you'd ruther."

She looked better; grief, homesickness, pining, had refined her; pining, that innate fear of cities which the peasant loses only when he has cinctured out of a particular city an existence more bucolic, because of readier opportunities, than the one he formerly knew, his bone and flesh knew before it was his bone and flesh. At first Martin believed it was the other girls at the convent who had made her unhappy. "By God," he said, "by God, we'll show them yet. Be durn if I dont." The Mother Superior said in her letter that the girl had been quite ill, and she showed it. She looked much better. It was as though for the first time in her life she had faced something from which she could not hide behind that little mask of expensive paint and powder bearing spurious French names and applied after the manner of a Hollywood-smitten waitress in a station restaurant; behind the little urban mannerisms and all that intense and unflagging feminine preoccupation with sheltered trivialities to which, with old female cunning far longer lived and more practical than any of man's invented tenets, they cling.

But that didn't last long. Soon she was being seen again with her vivid discontented face at the brief successive night clubs with their spurious New York air—the Chinese Gardens, the Gold Slippers, the Night Boats—but withal and most dominant in her face its expression of unbelief, doubt: the peasant blood that even yet could not quite accept the reality of unlimited charge accounts at lingerie- and fur- and motor car dealers, telling her father that her escorts were Blounts and Sandemans.

He never saw them. He was too busy; he had found what it was that could move that durn fellow that had no use for money. He wouldn't have cared, anyway, just so they were not bums, the Popeyes and Monks and Reds that he used "just as I would use a mule or a plow. But no bums. I'll have you seen with no bums," he told her.

That was his only stricture. He was too busy then; it was in the next year, the late winter, he sitting in the office, his feet in the drawer, thinking about Dr Blount, when all of a sudden he had it.

THE BIG SHOT · 519

Of course the man could not be moved by personal gain, and then he had it: he would go to him and offer to donate the new armory if his daughter's name be put on the annual list for the ball.

He had no qualms then, of defeat. He went at once, on foot, not hurrying. It was as though it were all finished, like two compared letters, question and answer, dropped at the same instant into the mail box. He did not think of the other until he turned into the building. I like to think of him, a man you'd hardly notice twice, striding along the street and turning into the building and pausing in midstride for a second while into his face came a flashing illumination, a conviction while the leaning and invisible shades lifted high their triumphant hands. Then he went on again—you would not have known it—and mounted to the tenth floor and entered that office from which he had once been ordered out, and faced the man who had ejected him and made his bald offer in a single phrase: "Put my daughter's name on the list, and I will build an art gallery and name it for your grandfather that was killed in Forrest's cavalry command in '64."

And now I like to think about Dr Blount. Cant you hear him telling himself "it's for the city, the citizens; I will derive nothing from it, not one jot more than any dweller in a tenement." But the very fact that he had to argue the question with himself was an indication. Maybe it was partly because he could not tell the truth about it, yet he could not let the town believe a lie; maybe sometimes he believed it had been a dream, that he had dreamed the irrevocable words; perhaps now and then during that spring he could persuade himself so, thinking *How could I have said yes? How could I?* He had the stuff in him, you see, the old blood, the old sense of honor dead everywhere else in America except in the south and kept alive here by a few old ladies who acquiesced in '65 but never surrendered.

So one evening—it was the day upon which the matter became incontrovertible, when upon the proposed site the metal sign unveiled its fresh lettering: . . . "Blount Memorial Art Gallery. Windham and Healy, Architects . . ." he went to call upon one of them who had for fifteen years been consulting him almost every time she raised a window. They had the stuff too, you see. Not that she advised him to do what he did; she probably laughed at him, with a little sympathy and a little contempt; perhaps that was what he

couldn't stand— So that evening he came to see Martin. He had
aged ten years, Martin said, standing in the floor—he wouldn't sit
—and stating his errand baldly too: "I must ask you to let me
withdraw from our agreement."

"You mean—?" Martin said.

"Yes. Completely. On your part and my own."

"The contract is let and the ground ready to be broken," Martin
said.

Blount made a short gesture. "I know." From his inside pocket
he took a sheaf of papers. "I have here bonds in the amount of fifty
thousand dollars; they are all my own." He came and laid them on
the table at Martin's hand. "If that is not enough, perhaps you
would take my note for whatever the difference will be."

Martin did not look at the bonds. "No," he said.

Blount stood beside the table, his face lowered. "I dont think I
have made myself clear. I mean—"

"You mean, whether I agree or not, you will take her name offen
the ball list?" Blount did not answer. He stood beside the table.
"You cant do that. If you did that, I'd have to explain hit all to
the contractor, maybe to the newspapers. You hadn't thought of
that, had you?"

"Yes," Blount said. "Yes, I had thought of that."

"Then I dont know as there's ere a thing we can do about hit.
Do you?"

"No," Blount said. He had picked up something from the table,
then he put it down and turned, moving toward the door. He
looked about the room. "Nice place you have here," he said.

"Hit suits us," Martin said. Blount went on toward the door,
Martin watching him. "You done forgot your bonds," he said.
Blount turned. He came back and took up the bonds and put them
carefully into his coat again.

"I wish I could make my position clear to you," he said. "But
if I could, you would not be you and it would not be necessary. And
I would not be I, and it would not matter."

He went out then, with the negro butler—who knew who he was
—closing the door behind him, and Martin sitting in his sock feet
in the cavern of a drawing room surrounded by the soundless and
exultant chorting of his shades.

He was sitting that way in his office the next morning when

I entered. "That was news, this morning," I said.

"What was news?" he said. "I aint seen ere a paper yet."

"What? You haven't heard that Doctor Blount killed himself last night?"

"Doctor Blount? Well, I'll be durned. So he lost that money, did he?"

"What money? He cant lose any money; their estate is managed by a lawyer."

"What'd he kill himself for, then?" Martin said.

"That's what a hundred thousand people have said since eight oclock this morning."

"Well, I'll be durned," he said. "The pore, durn fool."

There was no connection in his mind, you see. With his peasant's innate and abashless distrust of all women, even his own, he could not imagine any man being concerned over the presence of one woman more or less anywhere, and as for a matter of personal honor. . . . But he had his own. Or maybe he was simply carrying out his part of the bargain. Anyway, work on the art gallery went on; by November, when the *Sentinel* published the yearly list of debutantes' names, his daughter's among them, the serene Attic shape of it stood outwardly complete against the sere foliage of the park.

And so two weeks ago he had read his daughter's name where his conviction, his delusion, had printed it ten years ago, and he now sat in the single chair behind the desk, motionless as Govelli had left him, until the telephone rang. Still without changing his position he reached his hand and drew it to him and lifted the receiver. It was Govelli.

"Yes. . . . He's out? and the car too? . . . Send it on out to my house and then you tell him what I said." He put the receiver back. "Durn them wops," he said. "I am a good mind." He looked at the telephone, motionless. "I am yet," he said. "Be durn if I aint." He opened the drawer and took out the tin of snuff, the same tin that could have been found in ten thousand overalls within a ten mile radius of the city, and uncapped it and tilted a careful and meagre measure into the cap and thence into his outdrawn lower lip and replaced the tin, his lower lip bulged faintly like ten thousand others whose owners squatted on the gnawed verandas of lost country stores about the land.

He was still sitting there when the detective, the plain-clothes man, came in with the ticket, the summons. "It was one of them rookies," the detective said. "He ought to known better. I told Hickey he ought to be fired for not knowing that yellow car, and if he hadn't been learnt to know it, him and Hickey ought to both be fired." From his shiny sloven serge coat he took a greasy bill fold and extracted the summons and laid it on the desk. "But the damn fool went on and wrote the ticket and made the pinch because she wouldn't take it. He brought her in to the station, with her telling him all the time who she was. So Hickey jumped on him with both feet. But the ticket was already made out, and with them two reporters still hanging around there that come in with Popeye, and all these damn women yelling corruption and all."

Martin looked down at the ticket, not touching it. That was the only thing she ever did that annoyed him. He hated clumsiness, you see, since notoriety always follows clumsiness, even if it's just running past the stop lights. But every now and then she would do it, and I suppose that traffic cop was the only man in town that didn't know that lemon roadster. He would tell her again and again that petty laws are the only ones that cannot be broken with impunity. Not in those words, of course. He probably preached her homilies on law observance which would not have been out of place in the Sunday School journals. But still she'd do it. Not often, but too often for him who, now that his ambition had been attained, could probably not understand how she could have the need to do anything at all save vegetate until that day in December had come and passed.

So he sat musing above the summons while the detective draped his thigh on the desk edge as Govelli had done, and removed his derby hat and took from the crown of it a half cigar and relit it. Since the south waked up about twenty-five years ago, our cities have been aping Chicago and New York. And we've done it, better than we thought. But we are blind; we dont realise that you can ape only the vices of your model, that virtue is accidental even with those who practise it. But there is still a kind of hearty clumsiness to our corruption, a kind of chaotic and exasperating innocence, and as he sat musing over the ticket he was probably thinking how much time he had to spend keeping the corruption running smooth, when they both heard the swift heels in the corridor and they looked up as the door opened and the daughter herself entered.

The detective slid from the desk and removed the cigar and lifted his hat. "Morning, Miss Wrennie," he said. The girl looked at him once, a glance swift, combative, alert, and came on to the desk and around it on the opposite side. Martin picked up the summons.

"Well," he said, "that's all. You can tell Hickey I'll see to it."

"I'll tell him," the detective said. "If it was just us, the little lady could run over all the lights, red, green, blue or purple. But you know how them reformers are when they get a chance to howl. If the women would just stay at home where they belong, they could find plenty to keep them out of mischief, I always say. But you know how they are, and then the newspapers get started."

"Yes. I'll see to it. Much obliged." The detective went out. Martin laid the summons on the desk again and sat back. "I told you before," he said, "that I wont have it. Why must you keep on doing it? You got time to stop for them."

The girl stood beside the chair. "It changed while I was in the middle of the crossing. I. . . ." He was watching her. "I was in a hurry. . . ." He could watch her mind, anticipate her words as she cast swiftly here and there behind her little painted mask, her eyes too like darting mice.

"Where were you going in all that rush?"

"I—we—It was a luncheon party at the Gayoso. We were late."

"We?"

"Yes. Jerry Sandeman."

"He is in Birmingham now. The paper says so."

"He came back last night." She spoke in the light, swift, dry voice in which a child lies. "The luncheon was for him."

He looked at her through that blindness, that stupidity which success gets upon itself. "Was it about the ball he came to see you?"

"The ball?" She looked at him across a gulf of something very like despair, harried, motionless, like a hunted animal at its last resource. "I dont want to go to it!" she cried in a thin faint voice. "I dont want to!"

"Now, now," he said. He looked at the ticket again. "Them lights. It's for your good too. Suppose you were to run over somebody. Suppose you were walking, shopping, and somebody run past it and run you down. You must remember there's good in laws as well as bad. They work two ways, if you'd stop to think."

"I will. I'll be careful. I wont again."

"See you dont, then."

She leaned down and kissed his cheek. He did not move. He watched her cross the room, tap-tapping on her brittle heels, in her bright dress, her clashing beads. The door banged behind her. He wiped his cheek with his handkerchief and examined quietly the faint scarlet smear on the linen. Then he tore the ticket in two and dropped the pieces into the spittoon.

He was still sitting there a half hour later, motionless save for the slow thrust of his lower lip, when the telephone rang again. Again it was Govelli.

"What?" Martin said. "If it's that durn hop-head again—"

"Wait," Govelli said. "It's a jam. Bad. He ran down a woman on the street. He was on the way out to your house with that stuff and she was in the street while the cop was helping her change a tire, and he caught her between the two cars. The cop that was helping her made the pinch right there." Gripping the receiver, Martin cursed steadily while the faint voice went on: ". . . hurt pretty bad . . . ambulance . . . if they get to him and he talks. . . ."

"You stay right with him," Martin said. "Dont let him open his mouth." He clapped the receiver back and went swiftly to the safe and opened it and drew out a second telephone. He did not need to give a number. "One of Govelli's boys just ran down a woman on the street. He's at the station. Get him out of town at once."

The wire hummed for a moment. Then the voice said: "It wont be easy this time. The papers are already—"

"Do you want the papers after you, or do you want me?"

Again there was silence for a moment. "All right. I'll fix it."

"And let me know. At once."

He hung up, but he did not set the telephone down. He stood before the open safe, holding the telephone in his hand, motionless save for the slow movement of his chin, for almost twenty minutes. Then it rang.

"It's fixed," the voice said. "They got him out of town before he talked."

"Good. What about the woman?"

"She's at the Charity Hospital. I'll let you know soon as I get a report."

"Good."

He put the telephone back in the safe and shut it. Then he opened it again and took out a bottle of whiskey and a tumbler. As he was pouring the drink he remembered the two cases which were to have been delivered to his house, now in Popeye's car at the Police Station. "Durn them wops," he said. He drank and returned to the desk and reached for the telephone there. As he did so it rang under his hand. It continued to ring for a long time while he waited, his hand poised above it, his lower lip thrusting slowly against his gums. Then it ceased and he lifted the receiver to his ear. It was the Charity Hospital, telling him that the girl had died without having regained consciousness, and that—

"The girl?" I said.

"The one Popeye ran over," Don said. He looked at me. "Didn't I tell you? It was his daughter."

Dull Tale

I

Seated behind his bare, neat desk, Dr Blount looked at his caller. He saw a thick, broad man, a little bald, with a gray, impassive face and muddy eyes, in a cheap suit of unpressed serge and a slovenly-tied cravat, carrying in his hand a stained hat of black felt. "You wanted to see me?" Blount said.

"You're Dr Blount," the other said.

"Yes," Blount said. He looked at the man, his face interrogative and astonished. He glanced swiftly to both sides like a man seeking a weapon or an escape. "Will you sit down?"

The caller took the single straight-backed chair beyond the desk, his hat in his hand. They looked at one another; again Blount's head made that quick, aside-jerking movement. "I reckon you dont know who I am," the caller said.

"No," Blount said. He sat rigid in his own chair, erect, watching the caller. "I cant—?"

"My name is Martin." Blount made no sign, watching the caller. "Dal Martin."

"Oh," Blount said. "I remember the name now. In the newspapers. You are the politician. But I am afraid you have wasted your time in calling on me. I do not do any more general practice. You will have to—"

"I aint sick," the caller said. He looked at Blount, thick, immobile, overflowing the narrow hard chair on which he sat. "I didn't come for that. I reckon I know more about you than you do about me."

"What did you come for?"

The caller did not cease to look at him, yet for the first time Blount let himself go easy in his chair, sitting easily, though he still watched the man with alert curiosity. "What do you want with me?"

"You are the president—" he said, presi-*dent,* like a country-man—" of this here Nonconnah soldier—"

"Oh. The Guards. Yes. I hold that office." He watched the caller; his eyes narrowed, went blank with thought. "Yes. I remember now. You were concerned some way with the paving of Beauregard Avenue. You have come to me about our new armory. I will have to disappoint you; we—"

"It aint that," Martin said.

"Not?" They looked at one another.

The caller talked in a slow, level, idiomatic voice, watching Blount steadily, his own face impassive. "I got money. I reckon you know that. It aint a secret. I got a daughter. She's a good girl. But my wife is dead and we haint no kin in Memphis, no women to look out for her. Fix it for her to know the right folks and not know the wrong folks, like a woman could. Because I want her to get ahead. I give her a better start than I had, and I want her children to have a better start still. So I got to do the best I can."

"Yes?" Blount said. He did not stiffen exactly, yet he began slowly to sit back and up in the chair, watching the gray face of the man opposite him across the desk. The caller talked, without haste, without emphasis.

"She's right popular. Going out every night, to balls at West End and them dance-houses on the edge of town. But that aint what I want for her."

"What do you want for her?"

"The Nonconnah—"

"—Guards."

"—Guards gives a ball every winter. Where the girls go, the dib —dib—"

"Debutantes," Blount said.

"Debutantes. Yes. That's what she called them, with their pictures in the paper. The ones whose folks lived in Memphis a long time, with the streets named after them. And the men too. Boys and young men. She is a good girl, even if I aint lived in Memphis all her life and aint got a street named Martin Avenue—not yet.

But she lives in a house as fine as any of them. And I can build a street named Martin Avenue."

"Ah," Blount said.

"Yes. I can do anything in this town."

"Ah," Blount said.

"I aint bragging. I'm just telling you. Other folks in Memphis will tell you."

"I dont doubt that," Blount said. "I begin to remember more about you, now. One of your monuments is out near my home."

"One of my monuments?"

"A street. It was laid three years ago and it lasted one year. Then they had to dig it up and lay it again."

"Oh," Martin said. "Wyatt Street. Them crooks. I fixed them. I burned them."

"Accept my felicitations on your public spirit. And now you want—?"

They looked at one another. Neither of them said it, the words. It was Martin who looked away. "She's a good girl," he said, in that flat, slow voice. "Good as any of them. She wouldn't shame you. Or anybody there. I'd see to that."

"You are an expert and a prophet with daughters as well as with paving contracts, are you?"

"I'd see to it. I'd give you my promise. My word."

Blount rose, quickly. He stood erect behind the desk: a slight man, not as tall as the other. "I dont doubt that you can put your daughter into a much higher place than my poor influence could," he said. "A place to which she is obviously entitled, for being her father's daughter if for nothing else. That was all you wanted with me?"

Martin had not risen. "Maybe you think I meant a check," he said. "That would have to go through the bank. I mean cash."

"You have it with you?"

"Yes."

"Good-day, sir," Blount said.

Martin did not move. "You name the figure, and I'll double it."

"Good-day, sir," Blount said.

Outside, in the corridor, the caller put on his hat slowly. He stood there for a time, motionless. He mumbled his mouth slowly, as though he were chewing something. "Hit was the money," he said at last. "What use has a durn fellow like that got for money? But it's something. You cant tell me that ere a man breathing breath. . . ."

II

Where Madison Avenue joins Main Street, where the trolleys swing crashing and groaning down the hill at the clanging of bells which warn and consummate the change of light from red to green, Memphis is almost a city. Farther up or down Main Street it is the country town magnified; the street might have been lifted bodily from the Arkansas or Mississippi hinterland: the same parking-zones carefully striped in fading and tire-scarred paint and disregarded, the same dingy windows full of brogans and glazed vermilion oxfords and underwear with fly-specked bargain-tags, the same optimistic and flamboyant fire-and-clearance sale signs painted on weathered and flapping domestic banners.

At Main and Madison though, where four tall buildings quarter their flanks and form an upended tunnel up which the diapason of traffic echoes as at the bottom of a well, there is the restless life and movement of cities; the hurrying and purposeful going to-and-fro, as though the atomic components were being snowed down within a given boundary, to rush in whatever escaping direction and vanish like snow, already replaced and unmissed. There are always people standing there. Some are beggars, with tin cups and pencils, some hawkers with toys that dance on the pavement or with nostrums; some are stenographers and clerks and youths from the schools in balloon pants and bright sweaters, waiting for trolleys; some are touts for the secret crap-and-poker games and sporting-houses; some are visitors from Arkansas and Mississippi in town for the day, or bankers and lawyers and the wives and daughters of bankers and lawyers who live in the fine houses on Peabody and Belvedere and Sandeman Park Place, waiting for husbands or for private cars. Whoever you are, if you walk past the corner three times, you will see someone whom you know and will be looked at by fifty others who will be interested in the fact of your passing; so that each afternoon when Dr Blount left his office, which was in that block, he would pause at the street door and, if it was winter time, he would draw about his throat and lower face his silk scarf and button his coat and say, "Now for the ordeal," and step out into the street as though it were a cold tub. There was a back way out of the building, but he would not take it. He would pause at the front door and then enter the ceaseless throng and walk up the street to Madison and turn toward the river, to the open parking-ground where he left his car, walking a little faster until he had reached the car and unlocked the door and got in and closed the door after him. Then he would realise that he had been sweating into his clothes. "It's because they dont know me," he would say. "They just know me as what I look like, what I hate to be; not what I am."

He would look neither to the right nor the left. The people standing at the corner—the Arkansas and Mississippi farmers in wool or gingham shirts without ties; the clerks, the mechanics, the stenographers with shining rayon legs and rouge bought at Woolworth's, would see a slight, smallish man, dapperly dressed, mistaking an eager face sick with nerves and self-doubt for that of a successful road-house owner or cotton factor or merchant; anyway, one who had money in the bank and who slept well at night in a good bed cool or warm at wish or will, in a room into which the sound of the city scarcely came. They could not know that through the fitted coat he had so long since taught himself to feel the impact of eyes that more than likely did not even remark his passing with curiosity or speculation or derision, that he now carried the impact of them on with him like specks of pepper on a piece of raw flesh, until the door of his coupe had shut behind him. In the car he felt better. He would drive back past the corner, waiting perhaps for the abrupt, savage bell and the change of lights, aware of people standing there, but not as individuals, thoughts, speculations, eyes. Then they were a part of the scene: the globular lamps curving downward and away along the diminishing asphalt like twin loops of a pearl necklace on a dark narrow bosom; the buildings, the signs, the noise: Memphis, where he had been born in the same house where his grandfather had been born before him.

He was forty. He had never married. He lived with his grandmother, an invalid of ninety, and the maiden sister of his father. He was an only child. His mother died when he was born. His father, alive, was a bluff, loud man, a practical man, an inferior and successful doctor who liked to get up at three and four oclock in

the morning and make calls among Greek and Italian immigrants
on the edge of town. When Blount was a child, his father would
sometimes tease him and lead him on and then trick him into some
exposition of self, into one of those harmless revelations, betrayals
of dignity, which are so tragic to children. He would run from the
room, followed by his father's booming shout, and run up the stairs
and into a dark closet where linen was kept, where he would
crouch. He would tremble, feel faint; he would perspire and writhe
with impotent agony, though he would not cry. He would crouch
in the dark, his eyes wide, his ears preternaturally attuned, though
he knew not what for, feeling his sweat against his clothes, feeling
his body cold under the sweat, yet still sweating. He would think
about supper, of having to go down to the table, and his stomach
would coil and knot like a fist, though he had perhaps been hungry
the moment before his father caused him to betray himself. As the
moment for the ringing of the supper bell drew near, he would live
years, suffer miseries of indecision, since the sweating would cause
his glands to overfunction; he would taste saliva and be very hungry. He would steal into the diningroom before the meal was on
the table. He would be at his place when the others came in,
motionless, his head bowed as though he waited, not a blow, but
rather to be doused without warning with a pail of water. In the
meantime his aunt had spoken to his father, and he was let be.
Sitting at his place he would watch himself with a kind of horror
eat and eat and eat. Then he knew that when he went to bed he
would fall asleep quickly and wake thirty minutes later as though
a clock had rung inside him, and be violently ill. Knowing this,
sitting in the library after supper while his father read the paper
and his aunt sewed, he would take a crying fit, inexplicable to all
of them, himself included, with the exception of his aunt, who
would believe that she knew. "He hasn't been well for a day or so,"
she would say, and she would give him medicine which he did not
need and put him to bed herself, where he would go off almost
immediately to sleep, to wake up thirty minutes later and be violently sick until nature relieved him of both supper and medicine.
When he was grown, a medical student and then a doctor himself,
he still found himself now and then, with that same horror and
despair, tricked by circumstances into corresponding self-betrayals
of his sense of fitness, though he did without the linen closet, as he

had learned to curb the ensuing desire to overeat. Nevertheless, on these occasions he still waked up thirty minutes later, nauseated, sweating, though empty and inwardly cold. Then he would believe that he was going to die and, sitting up in bed, his thin hair dishevelled, his face pale and intent, his senses taut as though the skin on his face were attuned with listening, he would time his own pulse and take his own temperature with a thermometer carried in a tube with a clip for the pocket like a fountain pen.

He had inherited his father's practice, which after fifteen years had become a matter of routine calls upon four or five old women suffering from gout and indolence, since he was comfortably well-to-do in his own right, save that his grandmother and his aunt had incomes and reversions out of the estate. He kept an office downtown however, which, though he did not know it, was the equivalent of the linen closet of his childhood; and, pausing just within the door to take that mental deep breath before stepping into the street, his "Now for the ordeal" was the counterpart of the old agony and misery of indecision that must be overcome, while he crouched in the dark closet waiting for the supper bell of his childhood.

His relations with his patients could hardly be called contacts with the contemporary scene, with any living scene. What suffering they did was from that which no doctor could alleviate or cure: it was from time and flesh. They lived in smug, solid, airless bedrooms, where they spent the hour of his visit talking of the patient's girlhood, of her parents and first children in the years immediately following the Civil War; while Blount, his face quiet though still eager, a little diffuse, talked out of the tales he had heard from his grandmother of that time, as though he had himself been there. When he was younger he was at one time, for a brief interval, conscious that he had not yet given over linen closets. "I am an old woman, myself," he told himself. "They just got the bodies mixed up and put me into the wrong one, too late." That was why, while in France, on a base hospital staff, he deliberately picked a fight with a man larger than he was and went into the affair shaking with dread but not fear and without skill or hope, and was severely beaten. But the triumph, the glow, did not even last into slumber. "It wouldn't have, if I had whipped him, even," he said to himself; the next day he was ashamed of his black eye, his missing teeth.

He asked to be, and was, transferred to another hospital, where he told of having been attacked by a patient suffering from shell-shock.

He returned home and for the next ten years he watched his practice drop away to four or five old women dying slowly and querulously in huge, ugly, wealthy houses set on streets with evocative names, of Confederate generals and battlefields: Forrest Avenue, and Chickamauga and Shiloh Place, sitting for long afternoons shut away by the close, stale walls from the uproar and the fury. "It's because I like the smell," he told himself. "I like the smell of old female flesh."

His single contact with the scene which he inhabited was his chairmanship of the Nonconnah Guards. He had held it twelve years; each December he led the ball at which the season's debutantes were presented, and though there was no smell of old female flesh here, and though he still did not know it, this office—the minor and spurious importance of choosing music and decorators and caterers and checking and approving lists of names—was another linen closet.

The Guards was organised in 1859, by fifty-one young men of the city, all bachelors. The battalion elected officers and received a National Guard charter, the major being Dr Blount's grandfather. They gave a ball that year, and in the two succeeding Decembers. In 1861 the battalion resigned its charter and joined the Confederate Army. In 1865 sixteen of them returned home. The organization was interdict by the Federal government, the sixteen members scattered about the South at the head of night-riding bands, terrorising and intimidating negroes, sometimes with reason, sometimes not. When the last of the carpetbaggers were expelled and the negro marshals and representatives who had run the state governments since the war were sent back to the cotton fields, the Guards reorganised and received its charter back and gave another ball, which it had continued to do each December. Its status was now restored; it had a skeleton staff of Regular Army officers, with an inner hierarchy of elective social officers, the ranking one being the Flag-Corporal, the office which Dr Blount held, having been elected to it in a Paris café in 1918.

III

Once his coupe had dropped down the hill from Main Street and turned through the traffic into Union Avenue, where the congestion ravelled out into swift parallel lines with no more lights and bells, he would become cool. The sweat would evaporate; he would feel a cool vacuum between his body and his clothing. His body would feel firm, as though motion isolated him, molded him anew, the man a man now, rushing in a close, closed, lonely glass cabinet along the smooth and hissing asphalt. Then he would begin to look about, to look ahead, calling the streets before he reached them: the names evocative of old lost battles, of men in—he liked to believe, to think of them—some valhalla of the undefeated, galloping with long tossing hair and brandished sabres forever on tireless horses: Beauregard, Maltby, Van Dorn; Forrest Park with a stone man gallant on a gallant stone horse; Forrest: a man without education, a soldier as Goethe was a poet, whose tactics for winning battles was to git thar fustest with the morest men, and in whose command Blount's grandfather had been killed. He passed a street, slowing, one whole side of which was already torn up and dotted with pieces of red cloth nailed limply to sticks, and in the middle distance of which Italians and negroes labored with picks and shovels. "A monument," he said. "But not more enduring than brass, thank God."

IV

The room was a bedroom, a big, square room cluttered with heavy furniture. An old woman reclined in a deep chair before the fire, wrapped in rugs. Blount sat on a straight chair beside her, leaning forward, talking. "That was the first time I ever saw him, when he was sitting there in my office, offering me money to let his daughter come to the Ball. He had the money with him. In cash. But I had never seen him before. I had heard of him, of course; especially on election years when you alls' women clubs get out reform tickets to drive the high priest of corruption out of town. But I didn't know about him. I didn't even know that he was an outlander. Maybe if I had, my civic pride— You know; if robbed we must be, let it be by our own thieves."

"Is he an outlander?" the woman said.

"He came from down in Mississippi. He owned a grocery store, maybe a filling station too, out on the edge of town at first. He lived over the store, with his wife and child; that wasn't as long ago as you'd think, considering where he lives now. His house is fine. It's bigger than the Morro Castle at the Saint Louis Fair was. It must have eight or ten acres of red tiles on the roof alone."

"How do you know all this?"

"Anybody can see his house. You cant help but see it. You can see it almost as far as you can see Sears and Roebuck's."

"I mean, about him." She was watching Blount.

"I found out. I asked. Do you think I'd let a man try to bribe me, without finding out all I could about him?"

"So you will know whether the bribe will be good or not?"

Blount stopped in midspeech. He looked at the woman. "Do you — Good Lord. I. . . . You're kidding me, as the children say nowadays. I suppose I could be bribed to betray myself; I expect that all men, modern men, can. Have their price. But not to betray people who have put trust in me."

"By electing you head of a dancing-club," the woman said.

His mouth was already shaped for talk, for rebuttal. Then he closed it. "Fiddlesticks," he said. "Why do I argue with you? You cant understand. You're just a woman. You cant understand how a man feels about valueless things, things that dont have a dollar mark on them. If this had a current price, a value in coins, I would believe you at once. Of course they wouldn't mind, the other girls, the guests. The girls wouldn't know her and the men wouldn't dance with her. She'd just have a rotten time. We know that. We aren't concerned with her."

"Who are you concerned with?"

"I dont know. That's it. I just dont know what I have to do."

"You didn't have to go and see the man again."

"How did you know—" He looked at her, his jaw slacked. His face was thin, sick, intense. He closed his jaw. "Yes. I sent for him. Wrote him a note. He came back, in the same suit. He offered to build a new armory for the Guards. We talked. He told me about himself—"

"And you accepted the armory?"

"No. You know I didn't. I would not sell the Guards to him because, once he had bought them, they would have no value; they would not be the Guards. If I could sell Forrest Park to him for instance, or sell him what Van Dorn Avenue stands for. So we talked. He was born and raised on a Mississippi plantation. Tenant-farmers; you know: barefoot, the whole family, nine months in the year. There were six children, in a one-room-and-leanto cabin, he the youngest. Sometimes nearby, but usually from a distance, he would see the owner of the land on a saddle-horse, riding over the fields among the tenants, calling them by their first names and they saying Sir to him; and from the road that passed before the big house, he (he would slip away from home, when the rest of his family were in the field) would see the owner lying in a hammock under the trees, at two and three and four oclock in the afternoon, when his own father and mother and sisters and brothers were among the shimmering cotton-rows in sweaty gingham and straw hats like things salvaged out of trash bins.

"One day his father sent him up to the big house with a message. He went to the front door. A nigger opened it, one of the few niggers in that country, neighborhood; one of a race whom his kind hated from birth, through suspicion and economic jealousy and, in this case, envy; performing, as his people did, work which niggers would not do, eating food which the niggers at the big house would have scorned. The negro barred the door with his body; while they stood so, the boss himself came up the hall and looked out at the boy in worn overalls. 'Dont you ever come to my front door again,' the boss said. 'When you come here, go to the back door. Dont you ever come to my front door again.' And there was the nigger behind the boss, in the house, grinning behind the boss' back. He —Martin—told me he could feel the nigger's white eyeballs on his back as he returned down the drive, without delivering the message, and the nigger's white teeth cracked with laughing.

"He didn't go back home. He hid in the bushes. He was hungry and thirsty, but he stayed hidden all that day, lying on his face in a ditch. When it turned afternoon he crawled to the edge of the woods, where he could see his father and his brother and his two older sisters working in the field. It was after dark when he went home. He never spoke to the boss again. He never saw him closer than on the saddle-mare, going about the fields, until he was a grown man. But he watched the boss, the way he sat the horse and wore his hat and talked; sometimes he would hide and talk to himself, using the boss' gestures, watching his shadow on the wall of the barn or the bank of the ditch: 'Dont you never come to my front door again. You go around to the back. Dont you never come to my front door again.' He swore then that some day he too would be rich, with a horse, saddled and unsaddled by niggers, to ride, and a hammock to lie in during the hot hours, with his shoes off. He had never owned shoes at all, so the comparative was to wear shoes all the time, winter and summer; the superlative, to own shoes and not even wear them.

"Then he was grown. He had a wife and a child; he owned a country store in the neighborhood. His wife could read, but he had had no chance to learn. So he memorised his credit transactions as he made them—the spools of thread, the nickles' worth of lard or axle-grease or kerosene—and recited them to her over the supper table while she wrote them down in a book. He never made a mistake, because he couldn't afford to.

"He and the boss would play poker in the store at night. They would play on an improvised table, by lamplight, using wrought nails for counters; he would have corn whiskey in a jug, a glass, spoon, a cracked mug of sugar. He never drank himself; he does not know the taste of it to this day, he told me. The boss was an old man then, with a white, tobacco-stained moustache and shaky hands and eyes that didn't see so good even by daylight. So it couldn't have been very difficult to fool him. Anyway, they would bet back and forth with the nails, the two of them. 'I've got three queens,' the boss would say, reaching for the nails. 'Beat that, by Henry.' Then the other would lay his cards down on the table; the boss would lean forward, peering, his hands arrested above the nails. 'Hit's a straight,' the other says. 'I was lucky again that time.' The boss curses; he takes up a cold cigar in his shaking hand and sucks at it. 'Pour me another toddy,' he says. 'Deal the cards.'

"He came to Memphis. He owned a grocery store at first, selling to niggers and wops on the edge of town. His wife and child lived in two rooms above the store, with a vegetable garden at the back. His wife liked it there. But when he got richer and moved into town and got still richer, she didn't like it. They lived close up, where they could see the electric signs from the upstairs window, and he was making money fast then every time there was an election, but they didn't have a vegetable garden. That was what killed her: not the money; the fact that they didn't have a garden, and that there was a negro servant in the house, which bothered her. So she died and he buried her in a private lot; the cenotaph cost twelve thousand dollars, he told me. But he could afford it, he said. He could have spent fifty thousand on it then, he said. 'Ah,' I said; 'you had some paving contracts.' 'Folks needs to walk,' he said. 'Vote, too,' I said. 'That's right,' he said. He told me he has eight hundred and ten votes that he can drop into any ballot box like so many peanut-hulls.

"Then I found out about the girl, the daughter. He told me that she knew a lot of the folks that went to the Guards' Ball; she had met them at the balls at West End and at roadhouses. She told him about it herself; almost every night she would go out to another ball, with Harrison Coates or the Sandeman boys or that Heustace one; I forget his name. She had her own car, so she would leave the house alone and meet them at the ball, she told him. And he believed it; he even called them 'balls'. 'But she's as good as they are,' he said. 'Even if they dont come to the house for her, like young fellows used to do in my day. They may not know it. But there aint nothing for them to be ashamed of. She's as good as any of them.'

"I met Harrison Coates on the street; I mean young Harrison, the one that got fired out of Sewanee last year. 'I've been hearing about these balls out at the Grotto,' I said. He looked at me. 'That's what she calls them,' I said. 'What she told her father they were. She said you and the Sandeman boys were there.'

" 'Who did?' he said.

" 'So you were there,' I said. I told him her name.

" 'Oh,' he said.

" 'So you do know her.'

" 'You know; we'd kind of take a night off and go out there. Maybe pick up a girl or two on the way out.'

" 'Without asking their names,' I said. 'Was that how you met her?'

" 'Met who?' he said. I told him again. 'Not that Martin?'

" 'The same one,' I said. 'I wont tell, though.'

" 'I was wondering where you knew her,' he said. 'Jeez; I thought—' Then he stopped.

" 'Thought what?' He just looked at me. 'What is she like?' I said.

" 'A lot of stocking and paint. Like most of them. Hack Sandeman was the one that knew her before. I dont know where. I never asked. You mean the one with that lemon-colored Duplex, dont you?'

" 'That's the one. The only car like that in town.'

" 'Sure,' he said. 'Jeez; I thought—' he stopped again.

" 'What? Thought what?'

" 'Well, she was all dressed up, in some kind of a dress with diamonds and truck. When I went up to her to meet her, there was something about her; kind of. . . .' He looked at me.

" 'Belligerent?' I said.

" 'I dont know anything about her. I never saw her before. She might be all right, for all I know. Sure; she—'

" 'I didn't mean anything by belligerent,' I said. 'I mean, like she was watching you, careful; like she was waiting to find out what you were.'

" 'Oh,' he said; 'sure. So I thought—'

" 'What?'

" 'With that car and all. We thought maybe she was somebody's sweetie. Some bird's car, maybe, and her on the loose that night and him coming in all of a sudden, looking for her and the car. From Manuel Street or Toccopola; somewhere down there.'

" 'Oh,' I said. 'You thought that?'

" 'We didn't know it was that Martin. I never paid much attention to the name, because I thought it would be faked. She would just say to meet her somewhere and we would be there, and she would come along in that yellow car and we would get in, maybe looking behind all the time; you know, watching for him.'

" 'Yes,' I said. But already Martin had told me what a good girl she was, and I know she is. I know she is just a country girl, a lot further lost than he is himself, because he at least believes he knows where he wants to go. She had no mother, you see. All she wants is silk stockings, and to drive that yellow car fast past the red lights, with the cops touching their caps to it. But that didn't suit him. He took her to Washington and put her in school. It was the first time either of them had ever been in a pullman even. She stayed three weeks, when he (he was back home again) got a letter from the Mother Superior. She had cried ever since he drove off that afternoon in a taxi-cab and left her there; when he met the train at the station she got off, still crying, newly powdered and painted above the streaked tears. She had lost fifteen pounds, he said.

"And now the Guards' Ball. Maybe he was grooming her for it all the time. And she would go, not wanting to; she would have more sense than he; and be ignored, and then it would be all over. The Ball, I mean, and his wanting her to be there willy-nilly, for her own sake, as he believes. But he cant see that. He would never see it, not even on the next day, with her and Memphis and all standing against him. He would just believe that his own flesh had betrayed him; that she was simply not the man her father was. What do you think of that?"

"Nothing," the woman said. Her eyes were closed; her head lay back on the pillow. "I've heard it before. The same story about the same fly and the same molasses."

"You think that I would? That I will?"

The woman said nothing. She might have been asleep.

V

That was in the early spring. Two months later, on a bright morning in May, when Dr Blount emerged from the elevator at his floor he saw, shapeless, patient and shabby, in silhouette against the bright windows at the end of the corridor, a man waiting at the door to his office. They entered the office; again they faced one another across the neat, bare desk.

"You have a street named for your grandpaw," Martin said. "You wont want that. Some of them have got parks named for them; ones that aint no more worthy of it, but that happen to have more money. I could do that." He wore the same tie, the same cheap and shabby suit, the same stained felt hat in his hand, speaking in the same level, flat voice of a countryman. "I'd do more than that. I'd do for you what them that deserve you and your grandpappy haven't done. The one that was killed with Forrest, I mean. My grandpappy was killed too. We never knowed what army he was in nor where he went. He just went off one day and never come back; maybe he was just tired of staying at home. But my sort dont count. There was plenty of us; always was, always will be. It's your sort, the ones that's got the names the streets and the parks would want." All the time he talked, he was looking at Blount, at the thin, sick, unpredictable face behind rimless nose glasses opposite him across the desk. "There aint no right art gallery in Memphis, and aint like to be withouten I build it. Put her name on that list, and I'll build a art gallery in Sandeman Park and name it after your grandpappy that was killed with Forrest."

VI

In the park, before the gutted pit, above the savage and random refuse of the digging, the broad sign stood upright in all weather, lettered in red on a white ground *Blount Memorial Art Gallery. Windham & Healy, Architects.* He passed it every day, but he never stopped. He would enter the park and see the sign looming suddenly above the clipped green of tended hedges on a knoll, and drive swiftly past. "It's not for me," he told himself, alone in his swift and isolated glass cabinet, moving past and on, the sign falling behind; "it's for the citizens, the city. I will derive nothing from it; not one tittle more than any dweller in a Beale or Gayoso street tenement who has carfare out here." He would drive on. What calls he made were brief. He would sit in the straight chairs, waiting for the gouty and bed-ridden women to learn of it as he used to wait in the dark closet of his childhood for the sound of the supper bell. Then he would go home, still immune, to supper with his likewise oblivious grandmother and aunt. "It's nice of the city," the aunt said. "But I must say, it's not a bit too soon." Then she would look at him, her eyes sharp, curious, with a woman's instinctive affinity for evil. "But what in the world you could have done, have said to them. . . ."

"Nothing," he said above his plate. "They did it of their own accord."

"You mean, you knew nothing about it until they began to break the ground?"

"I knew nothing," he said. After supper he would go out again, to rush alone along the dim and light-glared asphalt, turning again into the shadowy park, passing the sudden and now indecipherable loom of the sign, saying to himself, "How could I have said yes? How could I?"

Late one afternoon he stopped his car before the big house where the sick woman lived. He mounted to the same bedroom and found her in the same chair, beneath the same rug, though the cold fireplace was filled with fluted green paper. "I have wondered what has been the matter with you lately," she said. He told her, sitting forward on the hard, straight chair, talking quietly; she watching his face in the failing light. "I didn't think you were that rich," she said. "And I didn't believe that the city. . . ."

"Yes," Blount said. "He is right. Every man has his price. It's because he is right. There is something about being right that's better than being courageous or even honorable."

"So it seems," the woman said.

"The others. They have parks named for them, and this and that. Because they had the money, the cash, at the right time. It doesn't matter how they got it. Because there were not many reputable ways in those days to get money in this country; the question is, to have had it. To have had it; do you see? If Grandfather or his father had just done sixty years ago what I did, it would be all right. Do you see?"

"But they didn't," the woman said. "But that dont matter. It dont matter."

"No," Blount said. "That's done. It's all done now. But not too much done. I have enough, Grandmother and I, to cover the work that has been done, to pay the contractor his forfeit. Stop it where it is. Leave the sign too: a monument."

"Then stop it," the woman said.

"You mean, cry off?"

"Just take her name off the list. That's all you have to do. Let him build the gallery. He owes that much to the city. It's the city's money he is building it with, that's digging the hole; dont you know that?"

"No," Blount said. She had been looking at him. Now her head lay back on the pillow; again her eyes were closed as though she slept.

"You men," she said. "You poor, fool men."

"Yes," Blount said. "Us poor, fool men. But we are just men. If the city let him rob it, I am in a way responsible. But this has nothing to do with the city. At one time I had myself fooled. I believed that the city would derive from this, not I. But even a man's self cannot fool itself always. A man's self, that is. Maybe women are different. But we are just men; we cant help that. So what must I do?"

"I've told you. Strike her name off. Or let it stay on. After all, what does it matter? Suppose there were a hundred girls like that there? What would it matter?"

"Yes. She wont like it. She will be sorry. It will be terrible for him."

"For him?"

"Didn't you just say, us poor fool men?"

"Go and see him," the woman said.

"And cry off?"

"You men," the woman said. Her head lay back on the pillow; her eyes were closed. Her hands, thick, soft, swollen, ringed, lay on the chair-arms. "You poor, fool men."

VII

Martin's house was on a knoll in a new subdivision. It was in the Spanish style; a big house, with courts and balconies, looming huge in the twilight. When Blount drove up, the yellow roadster stood under the porte-cochere. He was admitted by a negro in his shirt-sleeves, who opened the door and looked out at him with a kind of insolent brusqueness. "I want to see Mr Martin," Blount said.

"He eating supper now," the negro said, holding the door. "What you want with him?"

"Get away," Blount said. He pushed the door back, and entered. "Tell Mr Martin Dr Blount wants to see him."

"Doctor who?"

"Blount." The hall was opulent, oppressive, chilly. To the right was a lighted room. "Can I go in there?" Blount said.

"What you want with Mr Martin?" the negro said.

Blount stopped and turned back. "You tell him it's Dr Blount," he said. The negro was young, saddle-colored, with a pocked face. "Go on," Blount said. The negro quit looking at Blount. He went down the hall, toward another lighted passage. Blount entered a huge, raftered drawing room that looked like a window-set in a furniture store. There were rugs that looked as though they had never been trodden on; furniture and lamps that looked like they had been sent out that morning on approval; dead, still, costly. When Martin entered, he wore the same cheap serge suit. He was in his stocking feet. They did not shake hands. They did not even seat themselves. Blount stood beside a table set with objects which also looked like they had been borrowed or stolen from a shop-window. "I must ask you to let me withdraw from our agreement," he said.

"You want to back out," Martin said.

"Yes," Blount said.

"The contract is let, and the ground broken," Martin said. "You must have seen that."

"Yes," Blount said. He put his hand into his breast. From beyond the door came a swift tap-tap-tapping of hard and brittle heels. The girl entered, already talking.

"I'm guh—" She saw Blount and stopped: a thin girl with tow-colored hair tortured about a small, savagely painted mask, the eyes at once challenging and uncertain; belligerent. Her dress was too red and too long, her mouth too red, her heels too high. She wore ear-rings and carried a cloak of white fur over her arm, though it was only August.

"This here is Dr Blount," Martin said.

She made no response, no sign at all; her glance lay for a moment upon him, quick, belligerent, veiled, and went on. "I'm gone," she said. She went on, her heels brittle and hard and swift on the hard floor. Blount heard the voice of the pock-marked negro at the front door: "Where you going tonight?" Then the front door closed. A moment later he heard the car, the yellow roadster. It whined past the windows in second gear, at high speed. From his breast pocket Blount took a sheaf of embossed papers.

"I have here bonds for fifty thousand," he said. He laid them on the table. Martin had not moved, motionless in his socks on the expensive rug. "Maybe you will take my note for the balance."

"Why dont you just scratch her name off the list?" Martin said. "Couldn't nobody prove it on you."

"I could give you a mortgage on my house," Blount said. "My grandmother holds the title to it, but I am sure—"

"No," Martin said. "You're wasting your money. Take her

name off the list. You can do that. Wont nobody be the wiser. Cant prove nothing on you. Not with your word against mine."

Blount took up from the table a carved paper-weight of jade. He examined it and put it down and stood for a time, looking down at his hand. He moved, toward the door, with a vague air, as though he had suddenly found himself moving. His face was strained, vague, though quiet. "Nice place you have here," he said.

"Hit suits us," Martin said, motionless, shabby, in his gray socks, watching him. Blount's hat still lay on the chair where he had put it. "You done forgot something," Martin said. "Your bonds." Blount returned to the table and took up the bonds. He put them carefully into his breast, his face lowered. Then he moved again.

"Well," he said, "if I could have done any good by coming, you would not be you. Or I would not be I, and it wouldn't matter anyway."

He was half way to his car when the pock-marked negro overtook him. "Here's your hat," the negro said. "You forgot it."

IX

At the corner of Main Street and Madison Avenue the next day the people, the Mississippi and Arkansas farmers, the clerks and stenographers, read the four-inch headlines *CLUBMAN SUICIDE Prominent Memphian Shoots Self in Garage. Scion of old Memphis family takes own life; leaves grandmother and unmarried aunt . . . Dr Gavin Blount . . . member of old family . . . prominent in city's social life; president of Nonconnah Guards, premier social organization . . . family well-to-do . . . can give no reason for. . . .*

It was a three-day sensation, talked of among one another by the sporting- and gambling-house touts, the stenographers and clerks, the bankers and lawyers and their wives who lived in the fine houses on Sandeman and Blount Avenue; then it was gone, displaced by a state election or something. That was in August. In November the envelope came to Martin's house number: the embossed card, the crest: the bolled cotton-stalk crossed by sabres, the lettering: *The Nonconnah Guards. December 2, 1930. 10:00 P.M.;* and in a neat clerkly hand: *Miss Laverne Martin and escort.*

As Dr Blount had said, she didn't have a good time. She returned home before midnight, in a black dress a little too smart, sophisticated, in cut, and found her father, his sock feet propped against the mantel, reading a late edition which carried the names and a blurred flash-light picture of the girls, the debutantes. She entered crying, running, her heels brittle and hard. He took her onto his lap, she still crying with a passionate abjectness; he patted her back. "There now," he said, patting her back and it jerking and shuddering under the new dress, the sophisticated and costly black lace which had been for those two hours isolated out of and by the white and pastel dresses of the girls from the old houses on Sandeman and Belvedere as though it had clothed a spectre and which would be seen perhaps twice more, glittering, savage and belligerent, at the balls at the Grottoes and the Pete's Places about the equivocal purlieus and environs of the town. "There now. The fool. The durn fool. We could have done something with this town, me and him."

A Return

ℰ⤳ℯ

I

On the day the carriage would be due, from daylight on the negro
boy would squat beside the hitched droop-eared mule, shivering
over the smoldering fire in the December rain beside the road
which came up from Mississippi, with wrapped in an oil cloth cape
a bouquet the size of a yard broom, and perhaps a hundred yards
further up the road Charles Gordon himself sitting his horse in the
rain too beneath a bare tree, watching the boy and the road. Then
the muddy carriage would come in sight and Gordon would see the
bouquet delivered and then he would ride out, bareheaded in the
rain, and bow from his saddle before the carriage window, above
the fleet soft hand, the soft eyes above the mass of red roses.

This was in 1861, the third time Lewis Randolph had come up
from Mississippi in the muddy carriage paved with hot bricks
which a footman would remove every few miles and build a fire
with the pine knots fetched along for that purpose and reheat,
accompanied on the first two occasions by her mother and father
both, to receive Gordon's bouquet on the streaming road and to
enter that evening the Nonconnah Guards Armory in Memphis on
Gordon's arm and there to dance schottische and reel and even the
new waltz while the starred and striped flag hung unwinded from
the balcony where the negro musicians with fiddles and triangles
sat. But this time, this December of 1861, only her mother accompanied her because her father was down in Mississippi organising
a company of infantry, and the flag now hanging from the musi-

cians' balcony was the new one, the starred Saint Andrew's cross, as strange and new as the unsullied gray which the young men now wore in place of the old blue.

The battalion had been organised to go to Mexico—all young men and all bachelors; a man lost his membership automatically by marriage. It was a National Guard unit, but there was also a hierarchate of hereditary and elective social officers, and the Chairman of the Committee, in west Tennessee and north Mississippi at least, ranked any major or captain, Washington, the United States and all, to the contrary notwithstanding. It was formed too late to go to Mexico however so its first deployment at strength took place, not in field equipment on a dusty Texas plain but in the blue-and-gold of full dress in the ball room of a Memphis hotel just before Christmas, with the United States flag hanging from the musicians' balcony, and repeated itself each year after that, presently in its own armory, until soon the young girls of north Mississippi and west Tennessee were being presented formally to society at those balls and an invitation (or summons) to one of them was a social cachet no less irrevocable than one from Saint James's or the Vatican.

But at the one in '61 the men wore gray instead of blue and the new flag hung where the old one had used to hang and a troop train waited in the station to depart at midnight for the East. Lewis Randolph would tell about that ball, to her single listener who in a sense had missed being present himself by only twenty-four hours. She told him about it more than once, though the first time the listener could remember was when he was about six years old —the young men (there were a hundred and four of them) in their new pristine gray beneath the new flag, the gray coats and the hooped gowns turning and swirling while the rain which had turned to snow at dusk whispered and murmured at the high windows—how at half past eleven the music stopped at a signal from Gavin Blount, who was both Chairman of the Committee and major of the battalion, and the floor was cleared—the broad floor beneath the harsh military chandeliers, the battalion drawn up in parade front beneath the flag above which the faces of the negro musicians peered, the girls in their hoops and flowers at the opposite end of the room, the guests—the chaperones, the mothers and aunts and fathers and uncles, and the young men who did not belong to the Guards—in gilded chairs along the walls. She even made the speech to the six-year-old listener, word for word as Gavin Blount had made it as he leaned easily on his propped sabre in front of the gray battalion, she (Lewis Randolph) standing in the center of the kitchen in the Mississippi house which was already beginning to fall down about their heads, in a calico dress and sunbonnet, leaning on the Yankee musket barrel which they used to poke fires with as Gavin Blount had leaned on his sabre. And as she spoke it seemed to the six-year-old listener that he could see the scene itself, that it was not his mother's voice but the voice of that young man who was already dead when the listener was born —the words full of bombast and courage and ignorance of that man who had very likely seen powder flash toward his own body and heard the bullet but who had not yet seen war:

"A lot of you have already gone. I'm not talking to them. A lot of you have made your plans to go. I'm not talking to them either. But there are some of you that could go and would go, only you believe it will be over before you could get into a fight, see a Yankee's coat tail. It's them I'm talking to." The listener could see them: the rigid gray line beneath the new flag and the white eyeballs of the negroes in the balcony, the man in the crimson sash and negligent propped sabre who would be dead in seven months, the young girls in spread skirts like a cluster of butterflies, the ranked gilded chairs beneath the high windows where the snow murmured. "You have all heard of Virginia since Bull Run. But you haven't seen it. Washington, New York. But haven't seen it." Then he drew from his coat the stamped and sealed paper and opened it and read it aloud: ... *empowered by the President of the Confederate States of America. ...*

They shouted then, the women too. They yelled. Possibly some of them had not seen the gray uniform before, but probably none of them had ever heard that sound before; the first time it fell on their ears it came from their own throats, not invented by any one individual but springing simultaneously from a race, invented (if invented) not by man but by his doom. And it outlived even the doom. The listener, the boy of six, grew to manhood and became trusted, trustworthy, and successful, with a place higher in the social and economic fabric of his chosen milieu than most others. In his forty-fifth year he made a business trip to New York, where he met the father of the man he had come to see, an old man who had been in Shields' Corps in the Valley '62. He knew it, remembered it. "Sometimes I hear it even yet," he told the southerner. "Even after fifty years. And I wake up sweating." And there was another whom the boy was to know later, a man named Mullen who had been in Forrest's cavalry command, who went West and returned on a visit and told about a youth who rode down a Kansas street in '78 yelling "Yaaaiiihhh! Yaaaiiihhh!" and firing his pistol into the saloon doors until a deputy marshal behind a garbage heap shot him off the horse with a sawed-off shotgun loaded with slugs, and how they gathered about the youth bleeding to death on the ground and Mullen said, "Son, whar was it your pappy fit?" and the youth said, "Wherever there was Yankees, same as me. Yaaaiiihhh!"

Thus the listener heard it: how at another signal from Blount the music struck up again and the girls formed single file behind Blount's partner and so passed along the battalion front, kissing the men one after another, Lewis Randolph among them, kissing a hundred and four men, a hundred and three men that is because she gave Charles Gordon a red rose from his own bouquet and even thirty years afterward the listener heard from an eye-witness that the kiss which went with it was no fleet passage of laughing lips like the touch of a flying foot on the pebble of a ford. And when the troop train departed she was in it, hoisted through a window in the blind side while on the platform itself the faces of the other girls, centered by the petal-like spread of their skirts, seemed to float like severed flowers on a dark stream, while her mother gossipped placidly and waited for her in the armory a mile away. She travelled to Nashville in a day coach full of soldiers, with Charles Gordon's cloak over her ball gown and they were married by a private (who happened to be a minister) in a battalion waiting there to entrain, on the snow-bound platform with a whole regiment for witnesses while the ice-caked telegraph wires looping overhead crackled and hummed with the outraged commands of her mother addressed to every station between Memphis and Bristol; she was married in the ball gown and the officer's cloak in the snow, with not a hair turned though she had not slept in thirty hours, in a hollow square of youthful faces none of which had heard a bullet yet all of whom believed they were going to die. Four hours later the troop train went on and fifteen hours later she was

back in Memphis, with a letter written by Gordon on the back of
a fly-specked menu from the station eating-room to the mother
who was no longer frantic but just grimly and coldly outraged.
"Married?" the mother cried. "Married?"

"Yes! And I'm going to have a baby too!"

"Nonsense! Nonsense!"

"I am! I am! I tried hard enough."

They returned home to Mississippi. It was a big square house
twenty-five miles from any town. It had a park, flower beds, a rose
garden. During that winter the two women knitted socks and
mufflers and made shirts and first aid packs for the men of the
steadily growing company and they embroidered the colors for it,
with negro girls from the quarters to pick and iron the bright
fragmentary silk. The lot, the stable, was full of strange horses and
mules, the lawns and park dotted with tents and littered with
refuse; from the high room where they worked the two women
heard all day long heavy boots in the hall and the loud voices about
the punch bowl in the diningroom while the melting frost and sleet
of the departing winter gathered in the prints of heavy heels among
the broken and ruined roses. In the evenings there would be a
bonfire and oratory, the glare of the fire red and fierce upon the
successive speakers, the motionless heads of slaves in silhouette
along the fence between the fire and the portico where the women
white and black, mistress daughter and slave, huddled in shawls
and listened to the voices orotund and sonorous and meaningless
above the gestures of flung and senseless pantomime.

At last the company departed. The talking, the boots in the hall
were gone and after a while even the rubbish and litter; the scarred
lawn healed gradually under the rains of spring, leaving only the
ruined flower beds and boxwood hedges, the house quiet again with
only the two women and the negroes in the quarters, their voices,
the measured sound of axe-strokes and the smell of woodsmoke
coming peacefully up through the long spring twilights. Now the
old monotonous unoriginal tale began. It was not new. It was just
one of the thousand repetitions through the South during that year
and the next two, not of actual suffering yet but merely that attenuation of hardship, that unceasing demand upon endurance without
hope or even despair—that excruciating repetition which is Tragedy's tragedy, as if Tragedy had a childlike faith in the efficacy of
the plot simply because it had worked once—an economic system

which had outlived its place in time, a land empty of men who rode
out of it not to engage a mortal enemy as they believed but to batter
themselves to pieces against a force with which they were une-
quipped by both heredity and inclination to cope and of which
those whom they charged and counter-charged were not cham-
pions so much as victims too; armed with convictions and beliefs
a thousand years out of date they galloped gallantly behind the
bright bunting of a day and vanished, not in battle-smoke but
beyond the irrevocable curtain-fall of an era, an age, where, flesh-
less and immolated, they might bang themselves forever against no
foe and without pain or hurt in elysian fields beneath a halted sun;
behind them proscenium and footlights died. Some of them returned to be sure, but they were shadows, dazed bewildered and
impotent, creeping back onto the darkened stage where the old tale
had had its way and surfeited: a woman or women who after the
trampling and flags and trumpets were gone looked about and
found themselves alone in remote houses about a sparsely-settled
land populated in overwhelming proportion by a race dark and,
even in normal times, unpredictable, half child and half savage, a
land, a way of living, to be held together by hands trained only for
needlework, the very holding together of which offered but one
certainty: that next year there would be even less food and security
than this year, and into which reports of far-away battles came like
momentary and soundless lightning-glares, unreal and dreamlike,
brought by word-of-mouth months after the slain had begun to rot
(these dead nameless too, whether father brother husband son or
not report would not know)—then the beginning and growing
rumor of violence and pillage nearer and nearer and the woman or
women sitting in unlighted rooms waiting for the quarters to settle
down for the night in order to bury in secret a little silver in garden
or orchard (with hands not quite so soft now) and not knowing
even then what ears might be listening from what shadow. Then
the watching and waiting, the unflagging petty struggle for existence, sustenance—ditch-bank and woods-edge combed for weeds
and acorns to support life in bodies denied even the ultimate of
starvation, denied not life but merely hope, as if the sole aim of the
debacle were clinical: merely to ascertain just how much will and
flesh could endure.

They—the two women—served it. When the house was quiet
again they began to prepare for the child which would come in the

fall. The older woman did that is, because the daughter was super-intending the planting of the year's crop, the cotton and the feed —the mother in the high room where they had made the flags, with a negro woman to help her with the ironing and the infinitesimal stitching and running of ribbons while the daughter followed the plows to the field, on a horse until the mother forced her to desist, then in a battered buckboard, the plowhands throwing down gaps in the rail fences so she could pass through and sit in the buckboard and watch the gathering of the cotton in the bright hot days of September as her father had done before her—a crop which was ginned and sent to the county seat to be sold and vanished there, disappeared, where to they did not know and had no time to try to discover for in the last week of September the child was born, a boy, they named him Randolph; there was a negro midwife but no doctor and a week later a neighbor from ten miles away rode up, a man too old for fighting: "There was a big battle up beyond Corinth. General Johnston was killed, and They are in Memphis now. You had better come to us. At least there will be a man in the house."

"Thank you," the mother said. "Mr. Randolph (he had gone into that battle without coming out of it, along with Gavin Blount, though Blount's body was later found.) will expect to find us here when he returns."

The equinoctial rains began that day. By nightfall it had turned cold and that night the daughter waked suddenly, knowing that her mother was not in the house and knowing also where the older woman would be. The child's negro nurse was asleep on a pallet in the hall but the daughter did not call, she just rose from the bed, covering the child snugly and holding to the bedpost until the waves of weakness and dizziness subsided. Then in the pair of her father's heavy shoes which she wore to the fields and with a shawl clutched about her head and shoulders and holding to the stair rail for support, she descended and entered the rain itself, the strong steady black wind full of icy rain particles which actually sup-ported her, held her erect as she leaned into it, clutching the streaming shawl but making no sound until she reached the or-chard and even then not loud but merely peremptory and urgent: "Mother! Mother!" the older woman's reply calm too, even a little irritable, from somewhere about her feet:

"Careful now. Dont you fall in too. It's my leg. I cant move."

The daughter could see a little now, as if the driving rain particles were faintly incandescent, holding in each drop something of the departed day and disseminating it—the heavy trunk which the older woman had got there single-handed from the house, how, the daughter never knew, the pit which she had dug and into which she had fallen.

"How long have you been there?" the daughter cried, already turning back toward the house, running, the older woman calling after her in that same cold sharp voice, forbidding her to call the negroes, repeating "the silver. The silver", the daughter calling toward the house, still not loud, just peremptory and urgent. Presently the nurse came with two negro men. They lifted the older woman from the pit.

"Joanna can help me into the house," she said. "You stay and see that Will and Awce bury the trunk." But the two men had to carry her, though it was not until the next morning that they found for certain the hip was broken. And though a doctor came that day the mother died three nights later from pneumonia, not telling even then how she had got the heavy trunk out there nor how long she had lain in the pit slowly filling with rain. So they buried her, and they concealed carefully the marks of digging above the buried trunk; and now in the buckboard again, the child wrapped in a blanket beside her, the daughter watched the building of a hidden pen for the hogs deep in the river bottom and the gathering and cribbing of the corn. They would have food but little else, since the cotton, the money crop, had vanished. In a row of heterogeneous and carefully labelled bottles and phials in her father's desk were the seeds hoarded in the summer from the kitchen garden; in the next spring she watched the planting of them, and in the man's shoes and now in a pair of her father's trousers, in the buckboard with the child beside her (he was to be weaned, he was to learn to walk and talk in that buckboard; he ate and slept in it across his mother's lap, feeling against his side the hard shape of the derringer in her pocket) she saw the corn planted and then gathered again. During that year she received two letters. The first one was in the shaky script of an old man (she did not even recognise it to be her father's hand at first) on soiled cheap paper in a soiled envelope, addressed to her mother from Rock Island Prison. The second she did know. It was the same bold dashing sprawl she had fetched back from Nashville on the fly-specked bill-of-fare. He had been wounded, not bad; the paragraph devoted to his stay in the Richmond hospital had an almost Lucullan tone. He had been transferred to the Department of the West, he was now having a single day with his parents, following which he would join Van Dorn's cavalry corps on an expedition (destination unstated) the conclusion of which would leave him within a day's ride of that son whom he had never seen and to whom he sent his duty. But he never reached home. One night he rode howling into Holly Springs behind Van Dorn's long floating hair and the next day his body was identified from one of his wife's letters by an old man who had shot him from his kitchen door, apparently in the act of breaking into the chicken-roost.

II

All this the listener—the man of sixty-nine, the banker trusted shrewd and successful, who had been that boy of four and five and six wearing out the last of the garments his mother had cut down to fit him out of the clothes his grandfather had left in the house (there was an old setter dog which had grown from puppyhood on a rug beside the grandfather's bed, which, blind now, followed the boy through the monotonous days of his solitary childhood in which he was not lonely simply because he had never learned what the obverse of loneliness might be, following the clothes)—remembered. But it was not from his mother that he had learned it, it was from the three negroes who remained out of the more than forty, and even at six this fact did not surprise him who had learned already without being aware of it that people dont talk about what they really suffer, they dont have to; that he who talks about suffering has not suffered yet, who talks about pride is not proud. So it seemed to him that to his mother the whole debacle, the catastrophe in which her life had collapsed about her head as the big square house was gradually doing, had been summed up forever in the figure of that young man leaning in the crimson sash on the sabre beneath the martial glare of unshaded lights on that December night in 1861, whom she would take off to the life—a thin woman (a shape too, a vessel filled with the distillation of all its thoughts and actions—the lust and folly, the courage, the cowardice, the vanity and pride and shame) middleaged before her time, in a faded calico dress and sunbonnet, leaning on the Yankee musket barrel in the barren kitchen of the ruined house, saying, "Who wants to spit into the Potomac River before Easter Sunday?"

He remembered it, sitting in his office (the private one, the cubbyhole he insisted upon keeping at the very top of the bank building, which he would retire to in the slack end of afternoon and sit smoking and watching the sun set across the River) and remembering things which had happened before remembering began and which he knew were not memory but hearsay yet heard and reheard so often and so much that he had long since given over trying to say where listening stopped and remembering started. He had a listener himself now, a man half his age who had burst unannounced into the little remote bare room ten or twelve years ago, saying, "You are her son. You are Lewis Randolph's son."—a sick intelligent face which at once gave Gordon the impression of possessing no other life, of existing nowhere else, of being as much a part of the dying and peaceful end of an old man's afternoons as the bare desk, the two chairs, the slow familiar mutations of seasonal shadows of the rounding zodiac, solstice and equinox—a sick face which seemed to be not the framework for sight nor mask for thought but merely the container of a voracious listening, employing the organ of speech only to repeat "Again. Tell it again. What did she look like? What did she do? What did she say?" And he —Gordon—could not tell him. He could not even describe her. She had been too constant; he had known nothing else, he saw her only in terms of himself and when he tried to tell it he told it only in terms of himself: of lying wrapped in the quilt, then sitting alone on the seat of the buckboard, then playing about on the earth beside it while his mother in the calico dress whose pocket sagged with the weight of the derringer which next to her breasts was one of the first objects of his remembering, the nerve-ends of his flesh as constantly aware of the hard compact shape as his infant stomach was of the breast beneath the calico, stood with her arms folded on the top rail, watching the negro plowing beyond the fence. "And he plowed fast too," he said. "While she was there." And of the derringer itself: and he did not remember this even though he was there, in the kitchen, at first asleep in the crib contrived of a wooden box beside the stove, then sitting up in it, awake yet making no sound, watching with the round eyes of infancy the scene before him—the woman in the faded calico turning at the stove, the man in blue entering, the blue crash and jangle of carbines and bayonets and sabres; he could not even know, remember, if he actually heard the derringer explode or not, all he believed he remembered was that the kitchen was empty again and suddenly he was clutched against his mother's knees, her hands hard upon him and perhaps the reek of powder in the air and perhaps not and maybe one of the negresses screaming, since all he did believe he remembered was the face beneath the faded sunbonnet and even that merely the same face which watched the negro plowing or leaned above the propped musket barrel, so that all he knew for certain was that after that day the derringer was gone, he never again felt the shape of it against his flesh when she held him: and the listener: "They came there and found her alone? What did she do? Try to remember."

"I dont know. I dont think they did anything. We didn't have anything to steal, and they didn't burn the house. I suppose they didn't do anything."

"But she. What did she do?"

"I dont know. Not even the niggers would tell me what happened. Maybe they didn't know either. 'Ask her to tell you herself, when you man enough to hear it,' they told me."

"But you were not that man," the listener said, cried, with a sort of joy, exultation. "Even if you were born of her."

"Maybe not," Gordon said.

"Yes," the listener said, quietly now, the sick intelligent face blank now even of listening: "She killed him. She buried him, hid the body. She did it alone. She didn't want help. Burying one Yankee would have been no feat for the daughter of the woman who dug a pit to hide a trunk of silver alone in the dark. Yes, she wouldn't tell even you. And you were not man enough to ask, even if you were her son."

He didn't ask and time passed and one day he entered remembering; he knew this, saw it; he was there, a year after the Surrender when his grandfather came home, from the Rock Island Prison. He came on foot, in rags. He had neither hair nor teeth, and he would not talk at all. He would not eat at the table but would take his plate of food from the kitchen and hide with it like a beast; he would not remove his clothes to go to bed and he would not sleep in the bed in his room but on the floor beneath it as the old dog had done, and the daughter and the negroes would have to clean the floor behind him of gnawed bones and filth as if he were a dog or an infant. He never spoke of the prison; they did not even know if he knew the war was over or not—thus, until the negress Joanna came to the daughter in the kitchen one morning and said, "Marster's gone."

"Gone?" the daughter said. "You mean—"

"Nome. Not dead. Just gone. Awce been hunting him since daylight. But ain't nobody seen him." They never saw him again. They dragged cisterns and old wells and even the river. They searched and asked through the country. But he was gone, leaving no trace save yesterday's bones even in the room that was his, even the clothes which had hung in the closet long since worn out by the child, even the old blind setter long since dead.

So he didn't ask about the Yankee, and to the boy of five the advent and departure of the ragged and speechless old man was the coming and going of a stranger, something actually less than human, making no mark and leaving no trace; although for some time now he had come into his heritage and been bondsman to memory, he could not even remember if he ever asked even the negress what had become of the old man who lived in the house for that short summer month. That was the last of invasions; the next would be exodus and he would lead it. For he was growing now, not fast but steadily. He would never be as tall as his father, this due not to his mother's smallness but to the paucity of food during his nursing time which caused her milk to lack the quality to make him the large bones which would have been his right. But after that time he suffered nothing from malnutrition; the two women, the white one and the black, found food for him somehow, so that he gave promise of being, even though short of stature, sound and well enough—a stocky strong boy who at twelve chopped cotton as well as the negroes and who at fifteen spelled the negro man at the plow, who was old too, a contemporary of his grandfather. Letters came and went again now and in the summer of his grandfather's disappearance they had the first one from his father's parents in Memphis. They were written invariably by the grandmother, a delicate spidery script on faded fine note paper smelling even yet of the lavender of the drawer in which they had been hidden doubtless since 1862, beginning 'Mr. Gordon says' or 'Mr. Gordon asked me to write'. Yet they were not cold, they were just baffled, still uncomprehending—they still referred to the boy as 'little Charles'—written in another age and time, venturing timidly forth: 'We would like to see him, see you both. But as Mr. Gordon and I are old and don't travel . . . since it seems to be safe to go back and forth now . . . hoping you would come and see us, come and live with us. . . .' His mother may have answered them, he did not know. He was too busy. At eight and nine he could milk, squatting on a miniature of his mother's stool in the cowshed (she would milk, she would fork hay and clean stables like a man, but she would neither cook nor sweep) and at twelve and fourteen he was fitting wagon spokes and shoeing horses, then in the evening they would sit on either side of a kitchen hearth, the boy with a smooth white-oak chip and a sharpened charred stick, the thin woman in faded calico who had not changed one iota, holding the worn speller or the table of figures and watching him across them exactly as she would watch the negro plowing across the fence. So, until the letter came for him in his sixteenth year, the grandparents in Memphis were even less to him than that other one whom at least he could follow silently up the stairs and peer through the door and watch crouched facing into the corner of the room over his plate of food like a beast—nothing, less than nothing; a semi-yearly appearance of delicate faded envelopes bearing the spidery superscription which looked not as if it had been lightly and trem-blingly traced but as though it had faded in some prolonged transi-tion into the ruined Mississippi house, had arrived there almost by accident like the almost unremarked fall of the ultimate last leaf of a dying year. Then the envelope came addressed to him. His mother handed it to him without a word. He read it in secret, then two nights later as they sat opposite each other at the kitchen hearth he said, "I'm going to Memphis," and then sat exactly as a horse which knows it cannot reach shelter faces into the final shred of quiet at the forefront of a storm. But the storm never came. His mother did not even cease to knit; it was his own voice that rose:

"I've got a right to. He's my grandfather. I want—"

"Did I say you didn't have?"

"I'm going to get rich. I'm going to be rich as any carpet-bagger. So I can—" He was about to say *So I can do more for you,* only he realized that she would never permit anyone to do more for her than she could do for herself, not even him. "Don't think I'm going up there just because they are rich and haven't got any folks!"

"Why shouldn't you, if you want to? He's your grandfather, just as you said. And rich. Why shouldn't you ride around in a broad-cloth coat on a blooded horse all day long if you want to? When do you want to go?" Now was his time to say *All right. I won't go. If you have made out for both of us here this long, I can make out for both of us from now on.* But he didn't say it. Because she did believe he was going up there for the fine horse and the broadcloth, and it was too late now; it was to be years yet before, sitting in his small bare afternoon cubbyhole, the smoke of the good cigar peaceful and windless about his head, he would say to himself with humorous admiration, "By God! I believe she even faked that letter herself." So he said nothing, and after a moment she quit looking at him and spoke to the negress over her shoulder, and he realized that she had never even ceased knitting: "Get the trunk down from the attic, Joanna. And tell Awce to have the wagon hitched up at daylight."

She didn't go to the railroad station with him. She didn't even kiss him goodbye; she just stood in the kitchen door in that late fall dawn—the thin woman in the faded calico, not so much middle-aged as of no age and almost of no sex, who years ago had put off over night and forever youth and womanhood too like the virgin's confirmation dress, who advanced impervious through time like the prow of a vessel through water, no more permanently marked by the succeeding seas. The railroad was twenty-five miles away. He had one suit, four home spun shirts, a pair of sheets and two towels made of flour sacking, a black gum tooth brush and a lump of home made soap in a tin can, ten silver dollars and the letter bearing his grandparents' address sewn into his waistband. He had never seen a railroad until he climbed with the cowhide trunk into the box car. He had been in it sixteen hours without even water when the car stopped for the last time. But even then he did not get out at once. He took from his waist band the page which bore his grandfather's address and folded it carefully and began to tear

it across and across again and again until there was no more
purchase for his fingers, watching the fragments flutter down onto
the cinders. *I'll write her* he thought. *I'll write to her first thing and
tell her.* Then he thought *No. Damn if I will. If she wants to believe
that about me, let her believe it.*

His first job was in a cotton compress, loading and unloading the
bales from freight cars and steamboats. He worked side by side
with negroes, the crew boss was a negro. Once a month he wrote
the letter home telling nothing save that he was well. *If she wants
to believe I am riding around in a frock-tailed coat on that horse,
let her,* he thought. Then one day his name was called, he looked
up and saw an old man in a good suit and linen, leaning on a stick,
trembling, saying in a shaking voice: "Charles. Charles."

"My name is Randolph," he said.

"Yes, yes; of course," the grandfather said. "Why didn't you—
we wouldn't have known if your mother hadn't—the only letter we
have had from her in a year—"

"Mother? But she couldn't have known—You mean she knew
I wasn't living with you?"

"Yes. Just that you were in Memphis, working. And we
wouldn't have known—wouldn't have—"

She knew, he thought, in a surge of pride and vindication: *She
knew all the time I wasn't going to. She knew all the time.* He tried
to explain it; that was the next Sunday—a tall solid quiet dim brick
house among magnolias, a plump small woman in black, with soft
tiny trembling ineffectual hands and baffled blue eyes, the heavy
shuttered parlor, the portrait, the dashing gallant face beneath the
draped old flag and the sabre, above the mantle; he tried to explain
it.

"You don't need to work, labor among negroes," the grandfather said. "School. The University, a position waiting for you in the
office." He looked at the calm obdurate face. "Is it because I have
a Yankee for a partner? He lost his son too. That was why he came
South: trying to find him. Our sons at least died at home."

"No sir. It ain't that. It's because I want—she would want—"
only he realized that it would not bear saying, would never bear
saying to any stranger, not even to his father's father. So he said,
"I aim to be rich. And I reckon the only money that's worth a
hundred cents on the dollar is the money you earn yourself. And

in the South cotton is money. And I reckon the only way to learn cotton is to be where you can touch it, pick it up. Try to," he added with that sardonic humor beyond his years. "Pick up one end of it at least."

"But you will come here to live? You can do that."

"Could I pay board?" Then he said, "No sir. I got to do this my own way. The way I—she would. . . . I'll come every Sunday."

He went on Sundays and Wednesday evenings too, so that twice a week now he went to church. He had been to church but once before, to a negro church with Joanna, to a Sunday afternoon baptising. He slipped away. That is, he did not announce to his mother where he was going. He did not believe that she would object very much, forbid him. It was just that, though they accepted God as a force in the world which they held nothing either for or against, like weather, and with which, like weather, they had long since reached a working basis of live and let live, they did not go to church—this principally doubtless because there was no white church nearby and because his mother had not yet learned to condense a week's work into six days, as men had learned to do it. But he went now; he did it with his eyes open; even at sixteen and seventeen he told himself with that stolid and sardonic humor, *I reckon when she hears about this she will call it fudging too.* So he wrote her about it himself, receiving after a while an acknowledgement of the letter but no reference to church; in fact he received few letters of any sort from her—scrawls on scraps of paper in a savage masculine hand ending always with a formal acknowledgement (in the third person) to his grandparents; when at the end of the first twelve months he wrote to her that he had saved two hundred dollars and was coming to fetch her to Memphis to live, he received no reply at all. He went home, also in a box car, even though he now had two hundred dollars this time in an ancient money belt he had bought in a pawn shop. The wagon met him— the same mules, the same old negro man in the same patched garments; it might have been standing there ever since that day a year ago when he had got out of it; he found his mother in the cow-shed with a manure fork. She would not return to Memphis with him and for a while she even refused the two hundred dollars. "Take it," he said. "I don't need it. I don't even want it. I've got a better job now. I'm going to be rich," he said, cried, bragging:

the boastful loud dream (he was seventeen): "Soon I can begin to fix up the house. You can have a carriage too," ceasing, finding the cold steady gaze on him, not on his face; his mouth. "Don't you worry," he said. "It ain't just money I love, want. I reckon you know that by now."

And I reckon she does he thought, because she took the money, thrust it uncounted into the pocket of the faded dress; from the wagon he looked back once and saw her standing with the two pails in the door to the cowshed. His new job was runner for a cotton broker. He sent money home each month now, expecting and receiving no acknowledgement. In fact, she stopped writing to him at all now, even though he did not always return home at the end of each twelve months, the months accumulating into years and marked only by the home cured hams which she sent up at Thanksgiving and Christmas and which he ate with his grandparents. "I don't like writing letters," she wrote him. "And you are all right now and you ought to know I'm all right. I always have been." *Always had been and always will be* he thought. *Only I am just finding out how little she seems to have thought of me once.* So he waited this time until he had saved twelve hundred dollars. He went home, he reached the rotting house at dusk and watched her emerge from the cowshed with the two pails full now, as though, like the instance of the wagon, no time had elapsed since he had seen her last three years ago. And now she would not even let him do anything to the house. "Awce will prop it up before it actually falls down," she told him. But she accepted the twelve hundred dollars, without comment as usual, but this time without protest: and now time began to go fast with him, as it does for the young who have a single idea. He was now a clerk in the brokerage house, in six years a partner; he had an actual bank account now, a sum too large to be carried about in a money belt, and he was married; at times he would pause in a kind of amazement, not winded but as a strong horse pauses momentarily just to breathe, and think *I am thirty. I am forty* and he would not be able to remember just when, in what summer, he had seen her last, fetched her grandchildren down for her to look at, the occasions interchangeable and identical—the same two milk pails either full or empty, the same thin erect woman showing no age, the very graying of whose hair but reaffirmed her imperviousness to time, the same faded sunbonnet and dress, only the printed figure in the calico different, as if the change from one dress to another constituted the only alteration; then one day *I am fifty and she is sixty-nine* and in his hearse-like limousine and president now of that bank where he had made his first deposit and now a millionaire in his own right, who had become his grandfather's heir twenty years ago and declined the bequest, turning the estate into an endowed refuge for childless old women, he drove down into Mississippi beside the railroad where the old box car had run and then over the road once interminable beneath the laborious wagon and so up to the house which Awce (long since dead too, his place taken by a fourteen year old boy who was a man himself now, who plowed fast too when the white woman stood at the fence to watch him) had propped up. But she would not come to Memphis. "I'm all right, I tell you," she said. "Didn't I get along all right with Joanna for years? I reckon me and Lissy (Joanna's and Awce's daughter, Melissande her name, though probably none save the son remembered it) can do the same."

"But you don't have to do the milking," he said. She didn't answer this at all. "And I reckon you won't promise to write oftener either, will you?" She would not, so he stopped at a crossroad store a few miles away, the proprietor of which agreed to ride out to the house once a week and send him a report, which the proprietor did, the letter arriving five months later saying that his mother was ill and he returned and for the first time in his life he saw her in bed, the face still cold and indomitable and withal a little outraged at the failure of her flesh.

"I'm not sick," she said. "I could get up this minute if I wanted to."

"I know it," he said. "You're going to get up. You are coming to Memphis. I'm not asking you to this time. I'm telling you. Never mind your things. I'll come back to-morrow and move them. I'll even bring the cow back with me in the car." Perhaps it was because she was on her back and helpless and knew it. Because after a moment she said,

"I want Lissy to go too. Hand me the box on the mantel there." It was a cardboard shoebox; It had sat there for thirty years, he remembered it, and it contained every penny he had ever sent her or brought her, in the original bills, even in the original folds.

And now, as Gordon told his listener, he realized that she had never been in a car before. Not a moving car that is, though she had sat for a moment in the first one he had brought there; she had set the two milk pails down and got into it in the faded sunbonnet and dress and sat for a second and grunted grimly once and got out, although the negro chauffeur had given the negress Lissy a ride out to the main road and back. But she got into it without demurring, refusing to let him carry her, walking out to the car and standing beside it while the excited and wellnigh hysterical negress fetched out the few hurriedly wrapped bundles and bags. Then he helped her in and closed the door and he thought that the click of the door would be the end, just as the captive's freedom ends with the click of the handcuffs, but he was wrong. He told that too: It was night now, the car ran now on a paved road and already the glare of the city lay ahead and he sitting beside the small, still, shawl-wrapped figure clutching a basket on its knees, thinking with that amazement how never in his life before had he seen her lying down or even sitting down for this long, when she leaned suddenly forward and said in a faint sharp voice: "Stop. Stop." and even his negro obeyed her as Awce and Awce's successor did, the car slowing, the brakes squealing, and she leaning forward over the basket, peering out. "I want to stop here," she said and he looked out too and saw what she seemed to be looking at—a neat toylike bungalow among neat shrubs in a small trim lot.

"It's a nice place isn't it," he agreed. "Drive on Lucius."

"No," she said. "I ain't going any further. I want to stop here."

"In that house? that belongs to somebody. We can't stop there."

"Then buy it and turn them out, if you are rich as you tell me." And he told that too: How they sat there in the halted car filled with the loud consternation of the negress Lissy who saw the prospect of Memphis steadily vanishing out of her life. But the mother was adamant. She would not even go into Memphis to wait. "Take me back to Holly Springs," she said. "I'll stay with Mrs. Gillman. You can buy it tomorrow and come and get me."

"Will you promise not to go back home?"

"I ain't going to promise anything. You just buy that house. Because I ain't coming any further." So he took her back to Holly Springs, to the old friend with whom she had gone to school in girlhood, knowing she would not stay there and she did not; he made a last trip down to Mississippi and fetched her and the negress out of the old house once more and into the new one, where the cow and her chickens were already installed, and left her there. She would never come into town though now he could drive out each Sunday evening to see her, in the faded gingham and the sunbonnets, standing in the summer twilights in a swirling cloud of chickens, the hem of the apron clutched up in one hand and the other arm performing the immemorial gesture of the sower of seed. Then one afternoon he was sitting in the small bare cubby hole which he called his office when the door burst open and he looked up into the sick face of the man who was shouting at him:

"She is your mother! Lewis Randolph is your mother!" crying, "My name is Gavin Blount too. I'm his great-nephew," crying, "Didn't you know? He and Charles Gordon were both in love with her. They both proposed to her that same day: they cut a deck of cards to see who would propose first and Gavin Blount won. But she gave Charles Gordon the rose."

III

Each afternoon from that office window Gordon could look down into Battery Park and see Blount sitting on a bench facing the River. He was always alone and he sat there, in an overcoat in winter or in the linens of summer, among the old spiked cannon and the bronze plaques, for an hour sometimes, even in the rain.

He had known Blount for a long time now, yet even after twelve years he still regarded the other with tolerance and some affection and a little contempt. Because to him—the sane co-ordinated man with his healthy stocky mind—the life which Blount led was no life for a man. It was not even a woman's life. A doctor, Blount had inherited from his father a practice which, by twenty years of unflagging effort, he had reduced to the absolute minimum; what cases now entered his office came between the covers of medical journals, what patients passed his door consisted of himself.

He was sick. Not physically, but born sick. He lived with two maiden aunts in a solid well-preserved heavy house built without grace of brick in a street which was, fifty years ago, one of the select residential districts of the city but which now was a clutter of garages and plumbing shops and decayed rooming-houses backed by a section of negro tenements, and he came to town each morning just as Gordon did though not to any office (there would be days when he would not even visit that office whose door still bore his father's name) but to spend the day in the Nonconnah Guards Club, then to the River, the Battery, in the afternoon, to sit among the spiked old cannon and the bragging bas-reliefs, and at least once each week to sit for ten minutes or an hour in that high room whose proprietor and occupant had already come to think of him as existing nowhere else. "You ought to get married," Gordon once told him. "That's all that's wrong with you. How old are you?"

"Forty-one," Blount said. "Admitting for the moment that there is anything wrong with me: Do you know why I have never married? It's because I was born too late. All the ladies are dead since 1865. There's nothing left now but women. Besides, if I married I'd have to give up the chairmanship of the Guards." And that, the Nonconnah Guards, was, according to Gordon, both his sickness and his sanitarium. He had been chairman of the Committee for seventeen years now, ever since he had inherited it from a man named Sandeman who had inherited it in his turn from a man named Heustace who had inherited it on the field of Shiloh from the first Gavin Blount. That was the sickness—a man still young yet who had firmly removed himself out of the living world in order to exist in a past and irrevocable time, whose one contact with the world of living people was the weighing and discarding of submitted names of anonymous young girls hoping to attend a dance, according to a scale of values postulated by the uncaring dead; a man in whom the machinery for living lay as pristine and unworn and motionless as on the day he received it like that of an unlaunched hull rotting slowly and quietly in the ways, who spent his time sitting solitary among a few mute rusting guns and verdigrised bronze plates in the intervals of sitting across a table from a man twice his age and saying, "Tell me again about that. When she leaned on the musket barrel and told you. Tell it again. Maybe there were parts of it you forgot before."

So he told it again: how the girls fell in line and kissed the members of the battalion one by one, and how the niggers were fiddling again now only his mother said you couldn't hear it, and how he said to her once (he was fifteen then and it seemed to him that he had listened to it a right considerable of times), "How do you know you couldn't hear it?" and his mother estopped for that moment, standing there on the musket barrel and glaring at him, her mouth still open for talking beneath the sunbonnet which she wore indoors and out, which, so he told Blount, he believed she put on each morning even before her shoes and petticoat. "I bet when you came to Charley Gordon they couldn't even see the niggers' elbows working," he told her.

"What you mean is, they didn't need to listen," Blount said. "What you mean is you could hear 'Look away, look away' without having to listen then. There are folks that can still hear it, even after seventy years," he added. "That cant hear anything else."

"But you cant live now and then both," Gordon said.

"You can die trying."

"You mean, you will die trying."

"All right. What if I do? Who will be harmed by it?"

That was the first time Gordon told the other he should marry, saying it again on the afternoon when Blount had burst in with his astonishing request and in a condition even more hysteric than when he had burst in twelve years ago crying You are her son, you are Lewis Randolph's son—the wild sick intelligent face—the doctor who, as he said, preferred an anecdote to an appendectomy, who spent his days weighing the names of candidates for an annual ball like the head of a new and still precarious revolutionary government choosing his cabinet and ministers. "So I am to drag her, a woman almost ninety years old, in by main force from where she is contented and comfortable, to go to a dance with a lot of prancing jellybeans."

"But don't you see? She attended the first one. I mean the real first one, the first one that meant anything, when the Guards were really born, when they sang Dixie under that flag most of them had never seen before and she kissed a hundred and four men and gave Charles Gordon the rose. Can't you see?"

"But why mother? There must be one woman still alive here in Memphis who was there that night."

"No," Blount said. "She's the last one. And even if there were others alive she would still be the last one. It was not one of the others that left on that troop train that night with a Confederate officer's cloak over a hooped ball gown and the flower still in her hair, to be married bareheaded in the snow in a square of troops

Correction

Page 569

like a court martial and spend four hours with the husband she was never to see again. And now to have her attend the la—this one, to enter the ball room on my arm like she did seventy years ago on Charles Gordon's."

"You started to say the last one. Is this the last one you are going to hold, or is it the last one you expect to attend yourself? I thought only death or marriage could relieve you of your chairmanship."

"I'm not getting any younger."

"For marriage or for dying?" Blount did not answer. Apparently he was not listening either, the intelligent tragic face downlooking, sick, and bemused. Suddenly he looked up, full at the other, and Gordon knew that he was sicker than he or anyone else suspected.

"You say for me to marry," he said. "I can't marry. She wouldn't have me."

"Who wouldn't have you?"

"Lewis Randolph."

So he departed, and Gordon sat bemused too. But there was nothing sick about him—this stocky solid man, gray successful and sane, sitting in his sober good broadcloth and his enormous immaculate old-fashioned cuffs, the expensive cigar burning in the clipped hand soft and smooth now but which still had not forgot the shape of a plow handle, rousing, waking suddenly, saying aloud: "Well, by damn. By damn if I don't do it."

So two days later his secretary telephoned Blount's home; within an hour Blount was in the office. "Well, I persuaded her," Gordon said. "She's coming in. But not to the ball. I expect that will be too much for her. We'll just call it dinner at my house, with a few guests. I'll have Henry Heustace and his wife. She's only about twenty years older than they are. We'll see about the ball later." Only Blount was not listening to this either.

"Persuaded her," he said. "Lewis Randolph at the Nonconnah Guards ball. Charley Gordon, and now Gavin Blount. How did you do it?"

"How do you think? What's the one sure way to persuade any woman, maiden wife or widow, to go anywhere? I told her there was an eligible bachelor who wanted to marry her."

And so, three weeks later still, sitting among his guests above the fine linen and crystals and silver and cut flowers of his heavy diningroom he thought *maybe Gavin Blount never saw her before*

at all but by God this is the first time I ever saw her at a table with
actual linen on it and more than one dish and knife and fork and
drinking vessel—the thin erect figure with perfectly white hair, in
a shawl and an absolutely unrelieved black silk dress which still
showed the creases and still smelled of the thin pungent bark in
which it had been folded away, reaching Memphis at last who had
been on the road for a few months under twenty years, arriving
once more in a dissolving December dusk and entering the house
which she had never seen before, the cold sharp unfaded eyes
glancing once at the bouquet of red roses which the servant and
not the donor presented, who (the donor) peered up the hall from
within the room which Gordon called office after the old fashion,
and cried: "That can't be her. It can't be. Yes it is. It can't be
anyone else," saying, "No. Not in to table. I want to sit across from
her. So I can look at her, watch her," and the son said,

"Watch her what? Get tangled up in a lot of new-fangled knives
and spoons?" and the other:

"Tangled up? Lewis Randolph? Do you think the woman that
carried that derringer around in her apron pocket for three years
until the time came to use it could be outcountenanced or confounded by all the Post-postulations in existence?"

And she was not. The son watched Heustace precede the butler
and draw her chair and saw her pause just an instant and look at
the array of silver with a quick comprehensive country woman's
glance, and that was all. So he knew then that he need not have
worried about her at all, telling himself with the old humor that
it was a good thing for him she did not know he had worried.
Because, as Blount might have put it and as his, Gordon's, son
actually did, she had already stolen the show, not only on the part
of Heustace, the only guest present approximating her own generation, but of the other couple of Gordon's own time and of the
young woman who was his son's guest and the young man who was
his daughter's, not to mention the face which hung opposite her
above a bowl of flowers like a stricken and fading moon about to
sink beyond a hedge: so that he stopped watching his mother and
began to watch Blount; he saw his mother raise a spoon full of soup
and he thought *She ain't going to like it and she is going to say so*
out loud and then he began to watch Blount thinking *He's the one*
that needs worrying about, thinking *Yes. A damn sight sicker than*

anybody knows. So he was taken by surprise too, not, he realized later, that he actually had expected the evening to pass without incident but that it had begun so quickly, before they had even got settled at table; he was watching Blount, aware that Heustace was talking to his mother about the war days in Memphis, the Yankees in the city, which Heustace remembered; he heard Heustace say, "Conditions in the country were different, of course. There was not even a moral check on them there," when he saw Blount move a little, thrust his chair back, the sick moonlike face leaned forward above his untasted soup as he began to speak with a curious rapid intensity; and then suddenly Gordon knew what was coming as if he had read Blount's mind, he saw the other faces leaning forward into the abrupt silence as though Blount's intensity had communicated somehow even to them.

"The trouble is," Blount said, "We never could keep our Yankees in the right proportion. We were like a cook with too much raw material. If we could just have kept the proportion down to ten or twelve to one of us, we could have made a good war out of it. But when they wouldn't play fair, when the overflow of them took to prowling about the country where only women and children were left, a single woman and a child maybe, and a hand full of scared niggers—" The mother was staring at Blount. She had just bitten a piece of bread, the bread still lifted and she chewing as people without teeth chew, and now she had ceased chewing and was watching Blount exactly as she used to watch the nigger plowing beyond the fence. "Half of them prowling around the back doors of houses away back in the country while all the men were away fighting the other half million of them, gone in good faith, believing that the women and children would be safe even from Yankees—" Now she chewed again, twice; Gordon saw the two rapid motions of her jaw before she ceased again and glanced both ways along the table, at the other faces leaning forward with an identical expression of intense amazement, the glance rapid and cold, the cold eyes pausing no longer on the son's face than on any other. Then she put her hands on the table and began to thrust her chair back.

"Now mother," Gordon said; "now mother." But she was not rising: it was as though she had merely pushed her chair back to give herself room to talk in, thrusting it sharply back and leaning forward, her hands, one of which still held the bitten bread, on the edge of the table, staring at the man who sat opposite her in exactly the same attitude, and now her voice, though not rapid, was as cold and efficient as her gaze had been: and the son, waiting for his body to obey him and move also, thought *How hope to stop it, when she has had to wait seventy years for some one to tell it to.*

"It was just five of them that I ever saw," she said. "Joanna said there were more out in front, still on their horses. But I never saw them. It was just five that came round to the kitchen door, walking. They came to the kitchen door and walked in. Walked right into my kitchen without even knocking. Joanna had just come down the hall yelling that the whole front yard was full of Yankees and I was just turning from the stove where I was heating milk for him—" she did not move, she did not even indicate Gordon with a movement of her head or eyes. "I had just said 'Hush that yelling and take that child up off the floor' when those five tramps came right into my kitchen without even taking off their hats—" And still Gordon could not begin to move. He sat too, ringed by the amazed faces from among which the faces of his mother and Blount leaned toward each other above the bowl of flowers, the one cold, articulated beneath the white hair, the other resembling something expensive and fragile and on the point of falling from a mantel or shelf onto a stone floor, the voice coming from it in a passionate and dying whisper:

"Yes. Yes. Go on. And then what?"

"The pan of boiling milk was sitting on the stove like this. I took it up, just like this—" Then she moved; she and Blount both rose at the same instant as though they were two puppets worked by a single wire. They faced each other for a second, an instant, motionless like two dolls in a Christmas window above the bright glitter of the table, against the background of amazed and incredulous faces. Then she took up her bowl of soup and flung it at Blount's head, then, facing him, her butter knife clutched in her hand and pointed at Blount as though it were a small pistol, she repeated the phrase with which she had ordered the soldiers out of the house —a phrase such as steamboat mates used and which Gordon believed she did not even know she knew until that moment seventy years ago when she needed it.

Later, after the tumult of cheering and yelling had ceased, he was able to reconstruct it somewhat—the two of them, both small, rigid, back-leaning, facing each other, the one with the gleaming little knife clutched and steady at Blount's middle, the other, his face and shirtfront splashed with soup, his head erect and the sick face exalted like that of a soldier having a decoration pinned on him, about them both the roar, the tumult of cheering voices. When Gordon finally overtook her she was sitting in a chair in the parlor, trembling though still bolt upright. "Call Lucius," she said. "I want to go home."

"Why it was fine," he said. "Can't you hear them still? You never heard more noise than that even on that other night when you came up to the ball."

"I'm going home," she said. She rose. "Call Lucius. I want to go out the back door." So he took her back into that room he called his office until the car came.

"Is it those words you forgot and used?" he said. "That's nothing nowadays. You find them in all the books. Some of them, that is."

"No," she said. "I just want to go home." So he put her into the car then, and returned to the office. Blount was there, sitting quietly in a chair, clutching a damp stained napkin.

"I'll get you a fresh shirt," Gordon said.

"No," Blount said. "Never mind."

"You're not going to the ball that way, are you?" The other didn't answer. A decanter sat on the table. Gordon unstoppered it and poured a neat drink and pushed the glass toward Blount. But the other did not move to take it.

"I know why you stopped feeling the derringer now," he said. "It wasn't that the need for it had passed away. Because they might have come back, another lot of them. Maybe they did. You wouldn't have known it. It was because she found out she wasn't worthy to be protected by a bullet, a clean bullet that Charles Gordon would have said was all right, when she found out she could be surprised and tricked into using language she didn't even know she knew, Charles Gordon didn't know she knew, that Yankees and niggers had heard her use." Now he looked at Gordon. "I want your pistol." Gordon looked at him. "Come, Ran. I can go home and get one. You know that." For an instant longer Gordon looked at him. Then he said, quietly, immediately:

"All right. Here you are." He took the pistol from the desk and gave it to Blount. And yet, after the other had gone, Gordon's mind misgave him a little—this man whose business was judging character, anticipating the progression of human actions, who had done it for so long that at times they appeared to be snap judgments but were not, and in which he had complete faith, not only because they had been almost invariably right. Never-the-less, this time he had misgivings, though presently he admitted to himself that they were not due to his affection for Blount so much as to his pride in his judgment. However, right or wrong, it was done now, so he sat smoking quietly until he heard the car return and presently the negro, Lucius, entered. "I'm expecting a message," Gordon said. "I don't think it will come until in the morning, though it may come to-night. But when it does, bring it up to me."

"Yes sir," the negro said. "Even if you are asleep?"

"Yes," Gordon said. "Whether I'm asleep or not. As soon as it comes."

It did not arrive until morning however. That is, he did not get it until it appeared on the tray with his early cup of coffee, though when he saw that it was a package and not just an envelope he did not even listen for an answer to his question as to why he had not been wakened last night to receive it but instead he merely extracted the note and returned the newspaper-wrapped object to the negro. "Put this back in the desk," he said.

So it was relief he felt, an emotion such as any woman might feel, not the vindication of a man's, a banker's, judgment (*I'm getting old* he thought) as a penance, for the strengthening of his soul, he did not even read the note until he had drunk his coffee. It was written in pencil on the back of a soiled handbill announcement of a chain store grocery: *You seem to have been right again, if being told you are right can be any satisfaction to you anymore. I said once that she and her kind can take it and we can't and so that's what's wrong with us and you said Maybe and I was wrong, which both you and I expected. But you were wrong too because I can take it because why shouldn't I? because Gavin Blount beat him at last. It might have been Charles Gordon she gave the rose to but by God it was Gavin Blount she threw the soup plate at.*

A Dangerous Man

Women know things that we dont know, haven't yet learned, may never learn, I suppose. Perhaps it is that a man has everything, what he believes is right and what he believes is wrong and what he believes ought to happen and must happen and what he believes ought not to happen and cant happen, all neatly ticketed and catalogued and fitted into a pattern.

We called Mr Bowman a dangerous man, because he reacted in a proper and thoroughly masculine way, co-ordinating to a certain simple masculine creed with a kind of violent promptitude, without misgiving or remorse. One morning Zack Stowers came into the express office, a naked pistol in his hand. A drummer had insulted his wife; he had overtaken the man just as he sprang into the station bus and drove away from the hotel.

"Hey?" Mr Bowman said—he is a little deaf—leaning into the grille, cupping his ear. Stowers repeated, waving the pistol. The drummer had a friend with him; he himself might need support.

"Sure," Mr Bowman said immediately. He took from the cash drawer the pistol that belonged to the company and dropped it into his hip pocket and paused at the rear door to call back to his wife: "Going down to the depot a minute." He came around the partition without stopping for his coat and followed Stowers to the street. Stowers' buggy was there. They got in and drove to the station at a slashing gallop while people along the street turned to look after them.

There were two of them. "There they are," Stowers said. "See that tall one in the green hat, and the short one carrying two grips?"

"You mean that narrow-sterned man with his coat on his arm?" Mr Bowman said, leaning a little forward as they galloped across the broad plaza before the station. They spoke in tense, calm, impersonal voices, like two men raising a long pole or a ladder.

"No, no," Stowers said, reins, whip and pistol indiscriminate in his hands; "that tall fellow in the green hat just turning to look this way."

"Oh, yes," Mr Bowman said, "I got him. Now he's looked at us, you want to shoot him now?"

"No, no. You just keep them covered. I want to talk to him first."

"Better shoot him now," Mr Bowman said. "He's done looked around."

"No, no; you wait like I say."

"All right," Mr Bowman said. "But it wont be in the back now, since he's looking at us."

They descended, not waiting to hitch the team. The fat drummer had turned too now, and still holding the two bags he watched them approach with a kind of grave horror. His hat was on the back of his head, and with his round eyes and his round mouth he looked like the photograph of a small fat boy in a sailor hat. He cast over his shoulder one glance: he and his companion were now as completely isolated as though they were the last two men.

"Which one you want?" Mr Bowman said, producing his pistol, contemplating the two drummers like a not particularly hungry dog would two quarters of dressed beef.

"Wait, now, durn you," Stowers said. "Just watch them."

"Hey?" Mr Bowman said, cupping his ear with the hand that held the pistol. Stowers laid his pistol down and began to take off his coat.

"What's this, friend?" the tall drummer said.

"You going to fight him fist-and-skull, are you?" Mr Bowman said.

"Here, friend," the tall drummer said. He looked over his shoulder. "Here, folks, I demand—"

"Let me fight him," Mr Bowman said. "You hold the pistol on them so they wont run."

"No," Stowers said, flinging his coat down. "It's my business."

"I'll fight them both," Mr Bowman said. "Fight them both at once."

"No," Stowers said through his teeth, glaring at the tall drummer.

"Here, folks," the tall drummer said, glancing quickly about, but not daring to look too long away from Stowers; "I demand—"

Stowers struck him, leaping bodily from the ground to do so, then they were swinging at one another. Mr Bowman moved aside and approached the fat drummer, who still held the two bags.

"It's a mistake, mister," the fat drummer said. "I swear to God. I swear to God he aint done nothing to his wife. He dont even know her. And if he did, there aint a man living has more respect for a woman than him."

"You want to fight too?" Mr Bowman said.

"I swear so help me God, mister."

"Come on. I'll lay the gun on the ground between us. Come on."

The train came in, roared down and past, jarring. The tall drummer looked over his shoulder, swung again at Stowers, then turned and leaped away. Stowers sprang after him, then whirled and ran back and caught up his pistol, and then two bystanders caught and held him, struggling and cursing.

"Now, now;" they said, "now, now."

When the train pulled out Mr Bowman and Stowers returned to the buggy, Stowers dabbing at his mouth and spitting. "Durn it," he said, "I kind of got carried away for a minute. I was so mad. . . . He kept on saying he wasn't the one I was hunting."

"No matter," Mr Bowman said. "He put up a pretty good fight. Mine wouldn't even do that."

He is the express agent—a thick-built man who shows no age at all. Ruddy faced, his nose hooks a little and his hot hazel eyes hook a little, and he has a thatch of sparse, fine, vigorous reddish hair, and what would be, with a man more careful or aware of his appearance, a bald spot. He walks on the balls of his feet, with a light, mincing step like a prize-fighter gone a little stiff in the joints, and his clothes are always a little too short or too tight and too gaily colored in an innocent, slovenly way.

He looks like he might be thirty-eight, yet he has a nephew grown, married and a father; a boy whom Mr and Mrs Bowman said was Mr Bowman's nephew. Yet my aunt says he is an adopted child, taken by them from an orphanage. He grew up in the tight, small house where they live, and went to school and worked in the express office on Saturday when he got big enough, and got to be a man and went away and married; and now they own two dogs, fox terriers, fat, insolent, illtempered beasts with red choleric eyes, that ride with them in the car on Sundays and follow Mr Bowman around all during the week, at the office and on the street, and snarl and snap viciously at our hands when we offer to pet them. They snarl and snap at Mr Bowman too, but at Mrs Bowman they do not snarl. They do not exactly avoid her, but they regard her with a certain respect, insolent but alert, remaining in the office only when Mr Bowman is there.

Minnie Maude, who lives at Mrs Wiggins' boarding house across the street, told me that one day they had a terrible fight because Mr Bowman wanted to wash the dogs in the kitchen one cold day. She said that Mrs Bowman's cook told Mrs Wiggins' cook that after that Mrs Bowman would not even let him keep the dogs in the kitchen at night and that Mr Bowman would slip back after they went to bed and let the dogs in and that he gave the cook a dollar a week extra to turn them out in the morning when she came, and clean up after them.

Mr Bowman is the agent, but Mrs Bowman is the office itself, the Company, as far as we are concerned. She is there all day long in a clean, full-length apron, with black alpaca gauntlets on her arms—a flat-faced woman with a full eye and a broad smile full of gold teeth and a wealth of virulent copper curls which you know cannot be authentic. Full-breasted, broad of hip, duck-legged; tireless, pleasant in a brusque, ready way, she looks like a handsome and prosperous washerwoman. And never more so than on Sunday, when she dresses in flowered silk and a broad-brimmed red hat and they and the dogs drive into the country and return with the car full of dogwood or red-gum and sumach, with which she decorates their dark and transiently frequented little house.

"You break off too much," Mr Bowman says. She does not reply, her back turned to him and her arms lifted, her dress drawn across her firm arms and shoulders, her broad thighs. Then they go back to the kitchen, the dogs at Mr Bowman's heels and with two wary eyes on Mrs Bowman, where he takes from the cupboard a gallon jug of white whiskey, and they drink it neat from thickish tumblers, drink for drink. "It'll be withered in two days, anyway," he says. "If everybody took as much as you do, there wont be any left in fifty years."

"What of it?" she says. "Do you expect to be here then? I dont."

The next morning, Mrs Bowman already in the car and honking the horn impatiently for him, he waters the branches clumsily, sploshing water about; that evening when they return from the office he repeats it. "You're going to drown them dead," she says.

"They aint nothing but trash, anyhow," he says.

"Then throw them out. I dont want my house all splashed up with water."

The next morning they are late and in a hurry and he does not stop to water them; that evening they are late getting home. The next day it is too late, anyway. But he waters them just the same. When they return that evening the cook has thrown them out. She has to go with Mr Bowman into the back yard and show him where she put them, so that he can see they are withered and dead.

"It's a sight, the way they go on," the cook told. "Fighting about them dogs, and if it aint the dogs, it's Mr Joe's room again. Her wanting to change it so they can both have a bedroom, and him cussing and hollering scandalous whenever she mentions it. And them setting in my kitchen, drinking outen that jug and cussing one another like two men. But she stands right up to him. Makes him take them dogs out to the garage to wash them even on the coldest days."

The express office was a sinecure. At first he had the office in a small hamlet. One night he was checking up, in the office alone, when at a sound he turned and looked into the muzzle of a pistol.

"Put them up," the robber said. Even in the act of raising his hands he looked quickly about; as his right hand rose it brought with it the heavy metal cash-box and in the same motion he flung it at the robber's face and then leaped straight into the exploding pistol. Lying together on the floor, heaving and striking silently at one another, he took the pistol away from the robber and killed him with it: a man with a criminal record and a five thousand dollar reward. He bought a house with the five thousand dollars; the company gave him the easy office he now holds.

When he first came to our town he also operated an eating-place at the station, which his wife ran until one day there was some trouble with a locomotive engineer, whereupon he sold out and his wife came to help him in the office. Not that he distrusted her: it was merely his few firm and simple convictions of human conduct. He neither trusted or loved her the less nor hated the engineer the more, though for a year after that the engineer would go across to the fireman's side and crouch behind the boiler-head when he went through the station.

Soon his wife was running the office and he was doing only the outside work, hauling and such, the two dogs beside him on the truck, meeting the early train and the late one, without an overcoat in the bitterest weather. An active, though not talkative, man; full-blooded: so much so as to be impervious to cold; so much so that the very heat of his desire for children perhaps consumed and sterilised the seed in that deep provision of nature's for frustrating them who would try to force nature beyond her own provisions, since he would doubtless have tried to make his son a more Bow-man-ish Bowman than himself, or killed him trying.

So he is hardly ever in the office at all, as the absence of the dogs attested. Yet we never saw him, even with his abundant time, loafing and talking with the idle men about the square, until lately.

Women know things we dont know. Minnie Maude is twenty-two: she chews the gum behind the wicket of the Rex theatre across the street from the express office. "You wait," she says. "He's a little late today, but you wait and you'll see." So we wait, and after a while the car drives up and he gets out. His name is Wall. He sells insurance or something: a dapper little man with a handsome face in a bleakly effeminate way, like the face of a comely woman sea-captain—that sort of cold eyes. We watch him enter the express office.

"Good Lord," I say; "the man's—"

"Do you see them dogs anywhere?" Minnie Maude says. I look at her. "He's out delivering the express from number twenty-four. Dont you reckon he knows that?"

"Good Lord," I say again.

Minnie Maude's finger is slender against the softly squashed strawberry of her painted mouth; the smooth, minute corrugations of her musing gum show between her small teeth. She says in a musing tone; her eyes have a musing, faraway look, older

than time or sin: "Them big women that have to fight the way
they look all the time, they always take them little feisty men." I
thought of that too, remembering how Wall had once shown me
a thumbed notebook—his stud-book, he called it—containing
probably a hundred feminine names and telephone numbers scattered about north Mississippi and into Memphis. And why he
should dare that man for that woman who should be old enough
to be his mother or at least his aunt. But that's one of the things
that women know and we never will, not even Wall, for all his
notebook full of names.

But you have to admire his courage, his conviction of invulnerability, and when Minnie Maude, still seeing unbelief in my eyes,
says, "They spent week-end before last in Mottson, registered as
man and wife," I say:

"Hush. Do you want to cause a killing?"

She looks at me. "Who killing?"

"If you volunteer that information to everyone who stops
here as you did to me, dont you know Mr Bowman will hear
it? If they've got away with it this long, and even that I cant
see how—"

She is watching me, her eyes no longer faraway; in them is that
curious, weary tolerance with which they look at children sometimes. "Dont kid yourself, honey," she says.

"What do you mean?" I say. But I suppose she doesn't know.
I suppose, knowing so much that is immediate and significant, they
dont have to know. And so I went away.

He wears colored shirts; every afternoon he drinks coffee in the
café with the men of the town dropping in and out again; outside
the door the two dogs crouch, alert, choleric, lunging and snapping
at the small boys who pause to chivvy them. When he emerges they
fall in at his heels and halt again while he enters the drug store and
buys a magazine, then with the magazine rolled under his arm, his
hands in his pockets and his coat open upon his gaudy shirt and
tie, he goes home.

Once I stopped him on the street, contriving to do it casually.
It was raining that day, but his only concession was to button the
top button of his coat, from beneath which a corner of the magazine peeped.

"Fine day for reading," I said.

"Hey?" he said, cupping his ear, his slightly apoplectic eyes glaring pleasantly at me.

"Your magazine," I said, touching it with my finger. "Do you ever read Balzac?"

"What's that? Movie magazine? I dont think I ever saw it."

"He's a man," I said. "A writer."

"What does he write?"

"He wrote a good story about a banker named Nucingen."

"I dont pay no attention to their names," he said. He drew out the magazine and made to open it. It was *The Ladies' Home Journal.*

"I doubt if there's one in there this month," I said. "You'll get it wet, anyway."

So he buttoned it into his coat again and went on, the dogs at his heels. I followed to the corner and saw him pass the express office on the opposite side of the street, his gait not hurried nor slackened, his head slanted into the rain. After a while I saw him cross the street and enter his tight little yard and hold the gate open for the dogs to precede him.

"He wash them dogs everyday," the cook told. "Got a pair of these here long-sleeve gloves to catch them with. Then he sets the tub right in the middle of the kitchen floor and takes off the gloves and them dogs cutting his hands up like a razor and him cussing them scandalous. But he wash them right there, biting and all, and she dont say nothing about it. Then he gets out that magazine and sets there in my kitchen, in my way and me trying to git supper, reading about how to raise chillen right and asking me can I cook this or that where it's got the picture with it to show. Me, that's been cooking for better white folks than him for forty years. If he dont like the way I cook, he better git another one."

Evangeline

I

I had not seen Don in seven years and had not heard from him in six and a half when I got the wire collect: HAVE GHOST FOR YOU CAN YOU COME AND GET IT NOW LEAVING MY-SELF THIS WEEK. And I thought at once, 'What in the world do I want with a ghost?' and I reread the wire and the name of the place where it was sent—a Mississippi village so small that the name of the town was address sufficient for a person transient enough to leave at the end of the week—and I thought, 'What in the world is he doing there?'

I found that out the next day. Don is an architect by vocation and an amateur painter by avocation. He was spending his two weeks' vacation squatting behind an easel about the countryside, sketching colonial porticoes and houses and negro cabins and heads—hill niggers, different from those of the lowlands, the cities.

While we were at supper at the hotel that evening he told me about the ghost. The house was about six miles from the village, vacant these forty years. "It seems that this bird—his name was Sutpen—"

"—Colonel Sutpen," I said.

"That's not fair," Don said.

"I know it," I said. "Pray continue."

"—seems that he found the land or swapped the Indians a stereopticon for it or won it at blackjack or something. Anyway—this must have been about '40 or '50—he imported him a foreign architect and built him a house and laid out a park and gardens (you can still see the old paths and beds, bordered with brick) which would be a fitten setting for his lone jewel—"

"—a daughter named—"

"Wait," Don said. "Here, now; I—"

"—named Azalea," I said.

"Now we're even," Don said.

"I meant Syringa," I said.

"Now I'm one up," Don said. "Her name was Judith."

"That's what I meant, Judith."

"All right. You tell, then."

"Carry on," I said. "I'll behave."

II

It seems that he had a son and a daughter both, as well as a wife —a florid, portly man, a little swaggering, who liked to ride fast to church of a Sunday. He rode fast there the last time he went, lying in a homemade coffin in his Confederate uniform, with his sabre and his embroidered gauntlets. That was in '70. He had lived for five years since the war in the decaying house, alone with his daughter who was a widow without having been a wife, as they say. All the livestock was gone then except a team of spavined work-horses and a pair of two year old mules that had never been in double harness until they put them into the light wagon to carry the colonel to town to the Episcopal chapel that day. Anyway, the mules ran away and turned the wagon over and tumbled the colonel, sabre and plumes and all, into the ditch; from which Judith had him fetched back to the house, and read the service for the dead herself and buried him in the cedar grove where her mother and her husband already lay.

Judith's nature had solidified a right smart by that time, the niggers told Don. "You know how women, girls, must have lived in those days. Sheltered. Not idle, maybe, with all the niggers to look after and such. But not breeding any highpressure real estate agents or lady captains of commerce. But she and her mother took care of the place while the men were away at the war, and after her mother died in '63 Judith stayed on alone. Maybe waiting for her husband to come back kept her bucked up. She knew he was

coming back, you see. The niggers told me that never worried her
at all. That she kept his room ready for him, same as she kept her
father's and brother's rooms ready, changing the sheets every week
until all the sheets save one set for each bed were gone to make lint
and she couldn't change them anymore.

"And then the war was over and she had a letter from him—
his name was Charles Bon, from New Orleans—written after the
surrender. She wasn't surprised, elated, anything. 'I knew it would
be all right,' she told the old nigger, the old one, the greatgrand-
mother, the one whose name was Sutpen too. 'They will be home
soon now.' 'They?' the nigger said. 'You mean, him and Marse
Henry too? That they'll both come back to the same roof after what
has happened?' And Judith said, 'Oh. That. They were just children then. And Charles Bon is my husband now. Have you forgotten that?' And the nigger said, 'I aint forgot it. And Henry Sutpen
aint forgot it neither.' And (they were cleaning up the room then)
Judith says, 'They have got over that now. Dont you think the war
could do that much?' And the nigger said, 'It all depends on what
it is the war got to get over with.'

"What what was for the war to get over with?"

"That's it," Don said. "They didn't seem to know. Or to care,
maybe it was. Maybe it was just so long ago. Or maybe it's because
niggers are wiser than white folks and dont bother about *why* you
do, but only about *what* you do, and not so much about that. This
was what they told me. Not her, the old one, the one whose name
was Sutpen too; I never did talk to her. I would just see her, sitting
in a chair beside the cabin door, looking like she might have been
nine years old when God was born. She's pretty near whiter than
she is black; a regular empress, maybe because she is white. The
others, the rest of them, of her descendants, get darker each generation, like stairsteps kind of. They live in a cabin about a half mile
from the house—two rooms and an open hall full of children and
grandchildren and greatgrandchildren, all women. Not a man over
eleven years old in the house. She sits there all day long where she
can see the big house, smoking a pipe, her bare feet wrapped
around a chair rung like an ape does, while the others work. And
just let one stop, let up for a minute. You can hear her a mile, and
her looking no bigger than one of these half lifesize dolls-of-all-
nations in the church bazaar. Not moving except to take the pipe

out of her mouth: 'You, Sibey!' or 'You, Abum!' or 'You, Rose!'
That's all she has to say.

"But the others talked; the grandmother, the old one's daughter,
of what she had seen as a child or heard her mother tell. She told
me how the old woman used to talk a lot, telling the stories over
and over, until about forty years ago. Then she quit talking, telling
the stories, and the daughter said that sometimes the old woman
would get mad and say such and such a thing never happened at
all and tell them to hush their mouths and get out of the house.
But she said that before that she had heard the stories so much that
now she never could remember whether she had seen something
or just heard it told. I went there several times, and they told me
about the old days before the war, about the fiddles and the lighted
hall and the fine horses and carriages in the drive, the young men
coming thirty and forty and fifty miles, courting Judith. And one
coming further than that: Charles Bon. He and Judith's brother
were the same age. They had met one another at school—"

"University of Virginia," I said. "Bayard attenuated 1000 miles.
Out of the wilderness proud honor periodical regurgitant."

"Wrong," Don said. "It was the University of Mississippi. They
were of the tenth graduating class since its founding—almost charter members, you might say."

"I didn't know there were ten in Mississippi that went to school
then."

"—you might say. It was not far from Henry's home, and (he
kept a pair of saddle horses and a groom and a dog, descendant of
a pair of shepherds which Colonel Sutpen had brought back from
Germany: the first police dogs Mississippi, America, maybe, had
ever seen) once a month perhaps he would make the overnight ride
and spend Sunday at home. One weekend he brought Charles Bon
home with him. Charles had probably heard of Judith. Maybe
Henry had a picture of her, or maybe Henry had bragged a little.
And maybe Charles got himself invited to go home with Henry
without Henry being aware that this had happened. As Charles'
character divulged (or became less obscure as circumstances cir-
cumstanced, you might say) it began to appear as if Charles might
be that sort of a guy. And Henry that sort of a guy too, you might
say.

"Now, get it. The two young men riding up to the colonial

portico, and Judith leaning against the column in a white dress—"

"—with a red rose in her dark hair—"

"All right. Have a rose. But she was blonde. And them looking at one another, her and Charles. She had been around some, of course. But to other houses like the one she lived in, lives no different from the one she knew: patriarchial and generous enough, but provincial after all. And here was Charles, young—" We said, "and handsome" in the same breath. ("Dead heat," Don said) "and from New Orleans, prototype of what today would be a Balkan archduke at the outside. Especially after that visit. The niggers told how after that, every Tuesday A.M. Charles' nigger would arrive after his allnight ride, with a bouquet of flowers and a letter, and sleep for a while in the barn and then ride back again."

"Did Judith use the same column all the time, or would she change, say, twice a week?"

"Column?"

"To lean against. Looking up the road."

"Oh," Don said. "Not while they were away at the war, her father and brother and Charles. I asked the nigger what they—those two women—did while they were living there alone. 'Never done nothin. Jes hid de silver in de back gyarden, and et whut dey could git.' Isn't that fine? So simple. War is so much simpler than people think. Just bury the silver, and eat what you can git."

"Oh, the war," I said. "I think this should count as just one: Did Charles save Henry's life or did Henry save Charles' life?"

"Now I am two up," Don said. "They never saw each other during the war, until at the end of it. Here's the dope. Here are Henry and Charles, close as a married couple almost, rooming together at the university, spending their holidays and vacations under Henry's roof, where Charles was treated like a son by the old folks, and was the acknowledged railhorse of Judith's swains; even acknowledged so by Judith after a while. Overcame her maiden modesty, maybe. Or put down her maiden dissimulation, more like—"

"Ay. More like."

"Ay. Anyway, the attendance of saddle horses and fast buggies fell off, and in the second summer (Charles was an orphan, with a guardian in New Orleans—I never did find out just how Charles came to be in school way up in North Mississippi) when Charles decided that perhaps he had better let his guardian see him in the flesh maybe, and went home, he took with him Judith's picture in a metal case that closed like a book and locked with a key, and left behind him a ring.

"And Henry went with him, to spend the summer as Charles' guest in turn. They were to be gone all summer, but Henry was back in three weeks. They—the niggers—didn't know what had happened. They just knew that Henry was back in three weeks instead of three months, and that he tried to make Judith send Charles back his ring."

"And so Judith pined and died, and there's your unrequited ghost."

"She did no such thing. She refused to send back the ring and she dared Henry to tell what was wrong with Charles, and Henry wouldn't tell. Then the old folks tried to get Henry to tell what it was, but he wouldn't do it. So it must have been pretty bad, to Henry at least. But the engagement wasn't announced yet; maybe the old folks decided to see Charles and see if some explanation was coming forth between him and Henry, since whatever it was, Henry wasn't going to tell it. It appears that Henry was that sort of a guy, too.

"Then fall came, and Henry went back to the university. Charles was there, too. Judith wrote to him and had letters back, but maybe they were waiting for Henry to fetch him at another weekend, like they used to do. They waited a good while; Henry's boy told how they didn't room together now and didn't speak when they met on the campus. And at home Judith wouldn't speak to him, either. Henry must have been having a fine time. Getting the full worth out of whatever it was he wouldn't tell.

"Judith might have cried some then at times, being as that was before her nature changed, as the niggers put it. And so maybe the old folks worked on Henry some, and Henry still not telling. And so at Thanksgiving they told Henry that Charles was coming to spend Christmas. They had it, then, Henry and his father, behind closed doors. But they said you could hear them through the door: 'Then I wont be here myself,' Henry says. 'You will be here, sir,' the colonel says. 'And you will give both Charles and your sister a satisfactory explanation of your conduct': something like that, I imagine.

"Henry and Charles explained it this way. There is a ball on Christmas eve, and Colonel Sutpen announces the engagement, which everybody knew about, anyway. And the next morning about daylight a nigger wakes the colonel and he comes charging down with his nightshirt stuffed into his britches and his galluses dangling and jumps on the mule bareback (the mule being the first animal the nigger came to in the lot) and gets down to the back pasture just as Henry and Charles are aiming at one another with pistols. And the colonel hasn't any more than got there when here comes Judith, in her nightdress too and a shawl, and bareback on a pony too. And what she didn't tell Henry. Not crying, even though it wasn't until after the war that she gave up crying for good, her nature changing and all. 'Say what he has done,' she tells Henry. 'Accuse him to his face.' But still Henry wont tell. Then Charles says that maybe he had better clear off, but the colonel wont have it. And so thirty minutes later Henry rides off, without any breakfast and without even telling his mother goodbye, and they never saw him again for three years. The police dog howled a right smart at first; it wouldn't let anybody touch it or feed it. It got into the house and got into Henry's room and for two days it wouldn't let anybody enter the room.

"He was gone for three years. In the second year after that Christmas Charles graduated and went home. After Henry cleared out Charles' visits were put in abeyance, you might say, by mutual consent. A kind of probation. He and Judith saw one another now and then, and she still wore the ring, and when he graduated and went home, the wedding was set for that day one year. But when that day one year came, they were getting ready to fight Bull Run. Henry came home that spring, in uniform. He and Judith greeted one another: 'Good morning, Henry.' 'Good morning, Judith.' But that was about all. Charles Bon's name was not mentioned between them; maybe the ring on Judith's hand was mention enough. And then about three days after his arrival, a nigger rode out from the village, with a letter from Charles Bon, who had stopped tactfully you might say, at the hotel here, this hotel here.

"I dont know what it was. Maybe Henry's old man convinced him, or maybe it was Judith. Or maybe it was just the two young knights going off to battle; I think I told you Henry was that sort of a guy. Anyway, Henry rides into the village. They didn't shake hands, but after a while Henry and Charles come back together. And that afternoon Judith and Charles were married. And that evening Charles and Henry rode away together, to Tennessee and the army facing Sherman. They were gone four years.

"They had expected to be in Washington by July fourth of that first year and home again in time to lay-by the corn and cotton. But they were not in Washington by July fourth, and so in the late summer the colonel threw down his newspaper and went out on his horse and herded up the first three hundred men he met, trash, gentles and all, and told them they were a regiment and wrote himself a colonel's commission and took them to Tennessee too. Then the two women were left in the house alone, to 'bury the silver and eat what they could git.' Not leaning on any columns, looking up the road, and not crying, either. That was when Judith's nature began to change. But it didn't change good until one night three years later.

"But it seemed that the old lady couldn't git enough. Maybe she wasn't a good forager. Anyway, she died, and the colonel couldn't get home in time and so Judith buried her and then the colonel got home at last and tried to persuade Judith to go into the village to live but Judith said she would stay at home and the colonel went back to where the war was, not having to go far, either. And Judith stayed in the house, looking after the niggers and what crops they had, keeping the rooms fresh and ready for the three men, changing the bedlinen each week as long as there was linen to change with. Not standing on the porch, looking up the road. Gittin something to eat had got so simple by then that it took all your time. And besides, she wasn't worried. She had Charles' monthly letters to sleep on, and besides she knew he would come through all right, anyway. All she had to do was to be ready and wait. And she was used to waiting by then.

"She wasn't worried. You have to expect, to worry. She didn't even expect when, almost as soon as she heard of the surrender and got Charles' letter saying that the war was over and he was safe, one of the niggers come running into the house one morning saying, 'Missy. Missy.' And she standing in the hall when Henry came onto the porch and in the door. She stood there, in the white dress (and you can still have the rose, if you like); she stood there; maybe her hand was lifted a little, like when someone threatens you with a stick, even in fun. 'Yes?' she says. 'Yes?'

" 'I have brought Charles home,' Henry says. She looks at him; the light is on her face but not on his. Maybe it is her eyes talking, because Henry says, not even gesturing with his head: 'Out there. In the wagon.'

" 'Oh,' she says, quite quiet, looking at him, not moving too. 'Was—was the journey hard on him?'

" 'It was not hard on him.'

" 'Oh,' she says. 'Yes. Yes. Of course. There must have been a last . . . last shot, so it could end. Yes. I had forgot.' Then she moves, quiet, deliberate. 'I am grateful to you. I thank you.' She calls then, to the niggers murmuring about the front door, peering into the hall. She calls them by name, composed, quiet: 'Bring Mr Charles into the house.'

"They carried him up to the room which she had kept ready for four years, and laid him on the fresh bed, in his boots and all, who had been killed by the last shot of the war. Judith walked up the stairs after them, her face quiet, composed, cold. She went into the room and sent the niggers out and she locked the door. The next morning, when she came out again, her face looked exactly as it had when she went into the room. And the next morning Henry was gone. He had ridden away in the night, and no man that knew his face ever saw him again."

"And which one is the ghost?" I said.

Don looked at me. "You are not keeping count anymore. Are you?"

"No," I said. "I'm not keeping count anymore."

"I dont know which one is the ghost. The colonel came home and died in '70 and Judith buried him beside her mother and her husband, and the nigger woman, the grandmother (not the old one, the one named Sutpen) who was a biggish girl then, she told how, fifteen years after that day, something else happened in that big decaying house. She told of Judith living there alone, busy around the house in an old dress like trash would wear, raising chickens, working with them before day and after dark. She told it as she remembered it, of waking on her pallet in the cabin one dawn to find her mother, dressed, crouched over the fire, blowing it alive. The mother told her to get up and dress, and she told me how they went up to the house in the dawn. She said she already knew it, before they got to the house and found another negro woman and two negro men of another family living three miles away already in the hall, their eyeballs rolling in the dusk, and how all that day the house seemed to be whispering: 'Shhhhhh. Miss Judith. Miss Judith. Shhhhhh.'

"She told me how she crouched between errands in the hall, listening to the negroes moving about upstairs, and about the grave. It was already dug, the moist, fresh earth upturned in slowly drying shards as the sun mounted. And she told me about the slow, scuffing feet coming down the stairs (she was hidden then, in a closet beneath the staircase); hearing the slow feet move across overhead, and pass out the door and cease. But she didn't come out, even then. It was late afternoon when she came out and found herself locked in the empty house. And while she was trying to get out she heard the sound from upstairs and she began to scream and to run. She said she didn't know what she was trying to do. She said she just ran, back and forth in the dim hall, until she tripped over something near the staircase and fell, screaming, and while she lay on her back beneath the stairwell, screaming, she saw in the air above her a face, a head upside down. Then she said the next thing she remembered was when she waked in the cabin and it was night, and her mother standing over her. 'You dreamed it,' the mother said. 'What is in that house belongs to that house. You dreamed it, you hear, nigger?'"

"So the niggers in the neighborhood have got them a live ghost," I said. "They claim that Judith is not dead, eh?"

"You forget about the grave," Don said. "It's there to be seen with the other three."

"That's right," I said. "Besides those niggers that saw Judith dead."

"Ah," Don said. "Nobody but the old woman saw Judith dead. She laid out the body herself. Wouldn't let anybody in until the body was in the coffin and it fastened shut. But there's more than that. More than niggers." He looked at me. "White folks too. That is a good house, even yet. Sound inside. It could have been had for the taxes anytime these forty years. But there is something else." He looked at me. "There's a dog there."

"What about that?"

"It's a police dog. The same kind of dog that Colonel Sutpen brought back from Europe and that Henry had at the university with him—"

"—and has been waiting at the house forty years for Henry to come home. That puts us even. So if you'll just buy me a ticket home, I'll let you off about the wire."

"I dont mean the same dog. Henry's dog howled around the house for a while after he rode off that night, and died, and its son was an old dog when they had Judith's funeral. It nearly broke up the funeral. They had to drive it away from the grave with sticks, where it wanted to dig. It was the last of the breed, and it stayed around the house, howling. It would let no one approach the house. Folks would see it hunting in the woods, gaunt as a wolf, and now and then at night it would take a howling spell. But it was old then; after a while it could not get very far from the house, and I expect there were lots of folks waiting for it to die so they could get up there and give that house a prowl. Then one day a white man found the dog dead in a ditch it had got into hunting food and was too weak to get out again, and he thought, 'Now is my chance.' He had almost got to the porch when a police dog came around the house. Perhaps he watched it for a moment in a kind of horrid and outraged astonishment before he decided it wasn't a ghost and climbed a tree. He stayed there three hours, yelling, until the old nigger woman came and drove it away and told the man to get off the place and stay off."

"That's fine," I said. "I like the touch about the dog's ghost. I'll bet that Sutpen ghost has got a horse, too. And did they mention the ghost of a demijohn, maybe?"

"That dog wasn't a ghost. Ask that man if it was. Because it died too. And then there was another police dog there. They would watch each dog in turn get old and die, and then on the day they would find it dead, another police dog would come charging full-fleshed and in midstride around the corner of the house like somebody with a wand or something had struck the foundation stone. I saw the present one. It isn't a ghost."

"A dog," I said. "A haunted house that bears police dogs like plums on a bush." We looked at one another. "And the old nigger woman could drive it away. And her name is Sutpen too. Who do you suppose is living in that house?"

"Who do you suppose?"

"Not Judith. They buried her."

"They buried something."

"But why should she want to make folks think she is dead if she isn't dead?"

"That's what I sent for you for. That's for you to find out."

"How find out?"

"Just go and see. Just walk up to the house and go in and holler: 'Hello. Who's at home?' That's the way they do in the country."

"Oh, is it?"

"Sure. That's the way. It's easy."

"Oh, is it."

"Sure," Don said. "Dogs like you, and you dont believe in haunts. You said so yourself."

And so I did what Don said. I went there and I entered that house. And I was right and Don was right. That dog was a flesh-and-blood dog and that ghost was a flesh-and-blood ghost. It had lived in that house for forty years, with the old negro woman supplying it with food, and no man the wiser.

III

While I stood in the darkness in a thick jungle of overgrown crepe myrtle beneath a shuttered window of the house, I thought, 'I have only to get into the house. Then she will hear me and will call out. She will say "Is that you?" and call the old negress by her name. And so I will find out what the old negress' name is too.' That's what I was thinking, standing there beside the dark house in the darkness, listening to the diminishing rush of the dog fading toward the branch in the pasture.

So I stood there in the junglish overgrowth of the old garden, beside the looming and scaling wall of the house, thinking of the trivial matter of the old woman's name. Beyond the garden, beyond the pasture, I could see a light in the cabin, where in the afternoon I had found the old woman smoking in a wirebound chair beside the door. "So your name is Sutpen too," I said.

She removed the pipe. "And what might your name be?"

I told her. She watched me, smoking. She was incredibly old: a small woman with a myriadwrinkled face in color like pale coffee and as still and cold as granite. The features were not negroid, the

face in its cast was too cold, too implacable, and I thought suddenly, 'It's Indian blood. Part Indian and part Sutpen, spirit and
flesh. No wonder Judith found her sufficient since forty years.' Still
as granite, and as cold. She wore a clean calico dress and an apron.
Her hand was bound in a clean white cloth. Her feet were bare. I
told her my business, profession, she nursing the pipe and watching
me with eyes that had no whites at all; from a short distance away
she appeared to have no eyes at all. Her whole face was perfectly
blank, like a mask in which the eyesockets had been savagely
thumbed and the eyes themselves forgotten. "A which?" she said.

"A writer. A man that writes pieces for the newspapers and
such."

She grunted. "I know um." She grunted again around the pipe
stem, not ceasing to puff at it, speaking in smoke, shaping her
words in smoke for the eye to hear. "I know um. You aint the first
newspaper writer we done had dealings with."

"I'm not? When—"

She puffed, not looking at me. "Not much dealings, though. Not
after Marse Henry went to town and horsewhupped him outen he
own office, out into the street, wropping the whup around him like
a dog." She smoked, the pipe held in a hand not much larger than
the hand of a doll. "And so because you writes for the newspapers,
you think you got lief to come meddling round Cunnel Sutpen's
house?"

"It's not Colonel Sutpen's house now. It belongs to the state. To
anybody."

"How come it does?"

"Because the taxes haven't been paid on it in forty years. Do you
know what taxes are?"

She smoked. She was not looking at me. But it was hard to tell
what she was looking at. Then I found what she was looking at.
She extended her arm, the pipe stem pointing toward the house, the
pasture. "Look yonder," she said. "Going up across the pahster."
It was the dog. It looked as big as a calf: big, savage, lonely without
itself being aware that it was lonely, like the house itself. "That
dont belong to no state. You try it and see."

"Oh, that dog. I can pass that dog."

"How pass it?"

"I can pass it."

She smoked again. "You go on about your business, young white gentleman. You let what dont concern you alone."

"I can pass that dog. But if you'd tell me, I wouldn't have to."

"You get by that dog. Then we'll see about telling."

"Is that a dare?"

"You pass that dog."

"All right," I said. "I'll do that." I turned and went back to the road. I could feel her watching me. I didn't look back. I went on up the road. Then she called me, strongvoiced; as Don said, her voice would carry a good mile, and not full raised either. I turned. She still sat in the chair, small as a big doll, jerking her arm, the smoking pipe, at me. "You git out of here and stay out!" she shouted. "You go on away."

That's what I was thinking of while I stood there beside the house, hearing the dog. Passing it was easy: just a matter of finding where the branch ran, and a hunk of raw beef folded about a half can full of pepper. So I stood there, about to commit breaking and entering, thinking of the trivial matter of an old negress' name. I was a little wrought up; I was not too old for that. Not so old but what the threshold of adventure could pretty well deprive me of natural judgment, since it had not once occurred to me that one who had lived hidden in a house for forty years, going out only at night for fresh air, her presence known only to one other human being and a dog, would not need to call out, on hearing a noise in the house: "Is that you?"

So when I was in the dark hall at last, standing at the foot of the stairs where forty years ago the negro girl, lying screaming on her back, had seen the face upside down in the air above her, still hearing no sound, no voice yet saying, 'Is that you?' I was about ready to be tied myself. I was that young. I stood there for some time, until I found that my eyeballs were aching, thinking, 'What shall I do now? The ghost must be asleep. So I wont disturb her.'

Then I heard the sound. It was at the back of the house some-where, and on the ground floor. I had a seething feeling, of vindica-tion. I thought of myself talking to Don, telling him "I told you so! I told you all the time." Perhaps I had mesmerised myself and still had a hangover, because I imagine that judgment had already recognised the sound for that of a stiff key in a stiff lock; that someone was entering the house from the rear, in a logical flesh-

and-blood way with a logical key. And I suppose that judgment knew who it was, remembering how the uproar of the creekward dog must have reached the cabin too. Anyway, I stood there in the pitch dark and heard her enter the hall from the back, moving without haste yet surely, as a blind fish might move surely about and among the blind rocks in a blind pool in a cave. Then she spoke, quietly, not loud, yet without lowering her voice: "So you passed the dog."

"Yes," I whispered. She came on, invisible.

"I told you," she said. "I told you not to meddle with what aint none of your concern. What have they done to you and yo'n?"

"Shhhhh," I whispered. "If she hasn't heard me yet maybe I can get out. Maybe she wont know—"

"He aint going to hear you. Wouldn't mind, if he did."

"He?" I said.

"Git out?" she said. She came on. "You done got this far. I told you not to, but you was bound. Gittin out is too late now."

"He?" I said. "He?" She passed me, without touching me. I heard her begin to mount the stairs. I turned toward the sound, as though I could see her. "What do you want me to do?"

She didn't pause. "Do? You done done too much now. I told you. But young head mulehard. You come with me."

"No; I'll—"

"You come with me. You done had your chance and you wouldn't take it. You come on."

We mounted the stairs. She moved on ahead, surely, invisible. I held to the railing, feeling ahead, my eyeballs aching: suddenly I brushed into her where she stood motionless. "Here's the top," she said. "Aint nothing up here to run into." I followed her again, the soft sound of her bare feet. I touched a wall and heard a door click and felt the door yawn inward upon a rush of stale, fetid air warm as an oven: a smell of old flesh, a closed room. And I smelled something else. But I didn't know what it was at the time, not until she closed the door again and struck a match to a candle fixed upright in a china plate. And I watched the candle come to life and I wondered quietly in that suspension of judgment how it could burn, live, at all in this dead room, this tomblike air. Then I looked at the room, the bed, and I went and stood above the bed, surrounded by that odor of stale and unwashed flesh and of death which at first I had not recognised. The woman brought the candle to the bed and set it on the table. On the table lay another object —a flat metal case. 'Why, that's the picture,' I thought. 'The picture of Judith which Charles Bon carried to the war with him and brought back.' Then I looked at the man in the bed—the gaunt, pallid, skull-like head surrounded by long, unkempt hair of the same ivory color, and a beard reaching almost to his waist, lying in a foul, yellowish nightshirt on foul, yellowish sheets. His mouth was open, and he breathed through it, peaceful, slow, faint, scarce stirring his beard. He lay with closed eyelids so thin that they looked like patches of dampened tissue paper pasted over the balls. I looked at the woman. She had approached. Behind us our shadows loomed crouching high up the scaling, fishcolored wall. "My God," I said. "Who is it?"

She spoke without stirring, without any visible movement of her mouth, in that voice not loud and not lowered either. "It's Henry Sutpen," she said.

IV

We were downstairs again, in the dark kitchen. We stood, facing one another. "And he's going to die," I said. "How long has he been like this?"

"About a week. He used to walk at night with the dog. But about a week ago one night I waked up and heard the dog howling and I dressed and come up here and found him laying in the garden with the dog standing over him, howling. And I brought him in and put him in that bed and he aint moved since."

"You put him to bed? You mean, you brought him into the house and up the stairs by yourself?"

"I put Judith into her coffin by myself. And he dont weigh nothing now. I going to put him in his coffin by myself too."

"God knows that will be soon," I said. "Why dont you get a doctor?"

She grunted; her voice sounded no higher than my waist. "He's the fourth one to die in this house without no doctor. I done for the other three. I reckon I can do for him too."

Then she told me, there in the dark kitchen, with Henry Sutpen upstairs in that foul room, dying quietly unknown to any man, including himself. "I got to get it off my mind. I done toted it a long time now, and now I going to lay it down." She told again of Henry and Charles Bon like two brothers until that second summer when Henry went home with Charles in turn. And how Henry, who was to be gone three months, was back home in three weeks, because he had found It out.

"Found what out?" I said.

It was dark in the kitchen. The single window was a pale square of summer darkness above the shagmassed garden. Something moved beneath the window outside the kitchen, something big-soft-footed; then the dog barked once. It barked again, fulltongued now; I thought quietly, 'Now I haven't got any more meat and pepper. Now I am in the house and I cant get out.' The old woman moved; her torso came into silhouette in the window. "Hush," she said. The dog hushed for a moment, then as the woman turned away from the window it bayed again, a wild, deep, savage, reverberant sound. I went to the window.

"Hush," I said, not loud. "Hush, boy. Still, now." It ceased; the faint, soft-big sound of its feet faded and died. I turned. Again the woman was invisible. "What happened in New Orleans?" I said.

She didn't answer at once. She was utterly still; I could not even hear her breathe. Then her voice came out of the unbreathing stillness. "Charles Bon already had a wife."

"Oh," I said. "Already had a wife. I see. And so—"

She talked, not more rapidly, exactly. I dont know how to express it. It was like a train running along a track, not fast, but you got off the track, telling me how Henry had given Charles Bon his chance. Chance for what, to do what, never did quite emerge. It couldn't have been to get a divorce; she told me and Henry's subsequent actions showed that he could not have known there was an actual marriage between them until much later, perhaps during or maybe at the very end, of the war. It seemed that there was something about the New Orleans business that, to Henry anyway, was more disgraceful than the question of divorce could have been. But what it was, she wouldn't tell me. "You dont need to know that," she said. "It dont make no difference now. Judith is dead and Charles Bon is dead and I reckon she's done dead down yonder in New Orleans too, for all them lace dresses and them curly fans and niggers to wait on her, but I reckon things is different down there.

I reckon Henry done told Charles Bon that at the time. And now Henry wont be living fore long, and so it dont matter."

"Do you think Henry will die tonight?"

Her voice came out of the darkness, hardly waisthigh. "If the Lord wills it. So he gave Charles Bon his chance. And Charles Bon never took it."

"Why didn't Henry tell Judith and his father what it was?" I said. "If it was reason enough for Henry, it would be reason enough for them."

"Would Henry tell his blooden kin something, withouten there wouldn't anything else do but telling them, that I wont tell you, a stranger? Aint I just telling you how Henry tried other ways first? and how Charles Bon lied to him?"

"Lied to him?"

"Charles Bon lied to Henry Sutpen. Henry told Charles Bon that them wasn't Sutpen ways, and Charles Bon lied to Henry. You reckon if Charles Bon hadn't lied to Henry, that Henry would have let Charles Bon marry his sister? Charles Bon lied to Henry before that Christmas morning. And then he lied to Henry again after that Christmas morning; else Henry wouldn't have never let Charles Bon marry Judith."

"How lied?"

"Aint I just told you how Henry found out in New Orleans? Likely Charles Bon took Henry to see her, showing Henry how they did in New Orleans, and Henry told Charles Bon, 'Them ways aint Sutpen ways.' "

But still I couldn't understand it. If Henry didn't know they were married, it seemed to make him out pretty much of a prude. But maybe nowadays we can no longer understand people of that time. Perhaps that's why to us their written and told doings have a quality fustian though courageous, gallant, yet a little absurd. But that wasn't it either. There was something more than just the relationship between Charles and the woman; something she hadn't told me and had told me she was not going to tell and which I knew she would not tell out of some sense of honor or of pride; and I thought quietly, 'And now I'll never know that. And without it, the whole tale will be pointless, and so I am wasting my time.'

But anyway, one thing was coming a little clearer, and so when she told how Henry and Charles had gone away to the war in seeming amity and Judith with her hour old wedding ring had taken care of the place and buried her mother and kept the house ready for her husband's return, and how they heard that the war was over and that Charles Bon was safe and how two days later Henry brought Charles' body home in the wagon, dead, killed by the last shot of the war, I said, "The last shot fired by who?"

She didn't answer at once. She was quite still. It seemed to me that I could see her, motionless, her face lowered a little—that immobile, myriad face, cold, implacable, contained. "I wonder how Henry found out that they were married," I said.

She didn't answer that either. Then she talked again, her voice level, cold, about when Henry brought Charles home and they carried him up to the room which Judith had kept ready for him, and how she sent them all away and locked the door upon herself and her dead husband and the picture. And how she—the negress; she spent the night on a chair in the front hall—heard once in the night a pounding noise from the room above and how when Judith came out the next morning her face looked just like it had when she locked the door upon herself. "Then she called me and I went in and we put him in the coffin and I took the picture from the table and I said, 'Do you want to put this in, Missy?' and she said, 'I wont put that in,' and I saw how she had took the poker and beat that lock shut to where it wouldn't never open again.

"We buried him that day. And the next day I took the letter to town to put it on the train—"

"Who was the letter to?"

"I didn't know. I cant read. All I knew, it was to New Orleans because I knowed what New Orleans looked like wrote out because I used to mail the letters she wrote to Charles Bon before the war, before they was married."

"To New Orleans," I said. "How did Judith find where the woman lived?" Then I said: "Was there— There was money in that letter."

"Not then. We never had no money then. We never had no money to send until later, after Cunnel had done come home and died and we buried him too, and Judith bought them chickens and we raised them and sold them and the eggs. Then she could put money in the letters."

"And the woman took the money? She took it?"

She grunted. "Took it." She talked again; her voice was cold and steady as oil flowing. "And then one day Judith said, 'We will fix up Mr Charles' room.' 'Fix it up with what?' I said. 'We'll do the best we can,' she said. So we fixed up the room, and that day week the wagon went to town to meet the train and it come back with her in it from New Orleans. It was full of trunks, and she had that fan and that mosquito-bar umbrella over her head and a nigger woman, and she never liked it about the wagon. 'I aint used to riding in wagons,' she said. And Judith waiting on the porch in a old dress, and her getting down with all them trunks and that nigger woman and that boy—"

"Boy?"

"Hers and Charles Bon's boy. He was about nine years old. And soon as I saw her I knew, and soon as Judith saw her she knew too."

"Knew what?" I said. "What was the matter with this woman, anyway?"

"You'll hear what I going to tell you. What I aint going to tell you aint going to hear." She talked, invisible, quiet, cold. "She didn't stay long. She never liked it here. Wasn't nothing to do and nobody to see. She wouldn't get up till dinner. Then she would come down and set on the porch in one of them dresses outen the trunks, and fan herself and yawn, and Judith out in the back since daylight, in a old dress no better than mine, working.

"She never stayed long. Just until she had wore all the dresses outen the trunks one time, I reckon. She would tell Judith how she ought to have the house fixed up and have more niggers so she wouldn't have to fool with the chickens herself, and then she would play on the piano. But it never suited her neither because it wasn't tuned right. The first day she went out to see where Charles Bon was buried, with that fan and that umbrella that wouldn't stop no rain, and she come back crying into a lace handkerchief and laid down with that nigger woman rubbing her head with medicine. But at suppertime she come down with another dress on and said she never seed how Judith stood it here and played the piano and cried again, telling Judith about Charles Bon like Judith hadn't never seed him."

"You mean, she didn't know that Judith and Charles had been married too?"

She didn't answer at all. I could feel her looking at me with a kind of cold contempt. She went on: "She cried about Charles Bon a right smart at first. She would dress up in the afternoon and go promenading across to the burying ground, with that umbrella and the fan, and the boy and that nigger woman following with smelling bottles and a pillow for her to set on by the grave, and now and then she would cry about Charles Bon in the house, kind of flinging herself on Judith and Judith setting there in her old dress, straight-backed as Cunnel, with her face looking like it did when she come outen Charles Bon's room that morning, until she would stop crying and put some powder on her face and play on the piano and tell Judith how they done in New Orleans to enjoy themselves and how Judith ought to sell this old place and go down there to live.

"Then she went away, setting in the wagon in one of them mosquito-bar dresses too, with that umbrella, crying into the hankcher a while and then waving it at Judith standing there on the porch in that old dress, until the wagon went out of sight. Then Judith looked at me and she said, 'Raby, I'm tired. I'm awful tired.' "

"And I'm tired too. I done toted it a long time now. But we had to look after them chickens so we could put the money in the letter every month—"

"And she still took the money? even after she came and saw, she still took it? And after Judith saw, she still sent it?"

She answered immediately, abrupt, levelvoiced: "Who are you, questioning what a Sutpen does?"

"I'm sorry. When did Henry come home?"

"Right after she left, I carried two letters to the train one day. One of them had Henry Sutpen on it. I knowed how that looked wrote out, too."

"Oh. Judith knew where Henry was. And she wrote him after she saw the woman. Why did she wait until then?"

"Aint I told you Judith knew soon as she saw that woman, same as I knew soon as I saw?"

"But you never did tell me what. What is there about this woman? Dont you see, if you dont tell me that, the story wont make sense."

"It done made enough sense to put three folks in their graves. How much more sense you want it to make?"

"Yes," I said. "And so Henry came home."

"Not right then. One day, about a year after she was here, Judith gave me another letter with Henry Sutpen on it. It was all fixed up, ready to go on the train. 'You'll know when to send it,' Judith said. And I told her I would know the time when it come. And then the time come and Judith said, 'I reckon you can send that letter now' and I said 'I done already sent it three days ago.'

"And four nights later Henry rode up and we went to Judith in the bed and she said, 'Henry. Henry, I'm tired. I'm so tired, Henry.' And we never needed no doctor then and no preacher, and I aint going to need no doctor now and no preacher neither."

"And Henry has been here forty years, hidden in the house. My God."

"That's forty years longer than any of the rest of them stayed. He was a young man then, and when them dogs would begin to get old he would leave at night and be gone two days and come back the next night with another dog just like um. But he aint young now and last time I went myself to get the new dog. But he aint going to need no more dog. And I aint young neither, and I going soon too. Because I tired as Judith, too."

It was quiet in the kitchen, still, blackdark. Outside the summer midnight was filled with insects; somewhere a mockingbird sang. "Why did you do all this for Henry Sutpen? Didn't you have your own life to live, your own family to raise?"

She spoke, her voice not waisthigh, level, quiet. "Henry Sutpen is my brother."

V

We stood in the dark kitchen. "And so he wont live until morning. And nobody here but you."

"I been enough for three of them before him."

"Maybe I'd better stay too. Just in case. . . ."

Her voice came level, immediate: "In case what?" I didn't answer. I could not hear her breathe at all. "I been plenty enough for three of them. I dont need no help. You done found out now. You go on away from here and write your paper piece."

"I may not write it at all."

"I bound you wouldn't, if Henry Sutpen was in his right mind and strength. If I was to go up there now and say, 'Henry Sutpen, here a man going to write in the papers about you and your paw and your sister,' what you reckon he'd do?"

"I dont know. What would he do?"

"Nummine that. You done heard now. You go away from here. You let Henry Sutpen die quiet. That's all you can do for him."

"Maybe that's what he would do: just say, 'Let me die quiet.' "

"That's what I doing, anyway. You go away from here."

So that's what I did. She called the dog to the kitchen window and I could hear her talking to it quietly as I let myself out the front door and went on down the drive. I expected the dog to come charging around the house after me and tree me too, but it didn't. Perhaps that was what decided me. Or perhaps it was just that human way of justifying meddling with the humanities. Anyway, I stopped where the rusted and now hingeless iron gate gave upon the road and I stood there for a while, in the myriad, peaceful, summer country midnight. The lamp in the cabin was black now, and the house too was invisible beyond the cedartunnelled drive, the massed cedars which hid it shaggy on the sky. And there was no sound save the bugs, the insects silversounding in the grass, and the senseless mockingbird. And so I turned and went back up the drive to the house.

I still expected the dog to come charging around the corner, barking. 'And then she will know I didn't play fair,' I thought. 'She will know I lied to her like Charles Bon lied to Henry Sutpen.' But the dog didn't come. It didn't appear until I had been sitting on the top step for some time, my back against a column. Then it was there: it appeared without a sound, standing on the earth below the steps, looming, shadowy, watching me. I made no sound, no move. After a while it went away, as silent as it came. The shadow of it made one slow dissolving movement and disappeared.

It was quite still. There was a faint constant sighing high in the cedars, and I could hear the insects and the mockingbird. Soon there were two of them, answering one another, brief, quiring, risinginflectioned. Soon the sighing cedars, the insects and the birds became one peaceful sound bowled inside the skull in monotonous miniature, as if all the earth were contracted and reduced to the dimensions of a baseball, into and out of which shapes, fading, emerged fading and faded emerging:

"And you were killed by the last shot fired in the war?"

"I was so killed. Yes."

"Who fired the last shot fired in the war?"

"Was it the last shot you fired in the war, Henry?"

"I fired a last shot in the war; yes."

"You depended on the war, and the war betrayed you too; was that it?"

"Was that it, Henry?"

"What was wrong with that woman, Henry? There was something the matter that was worse to you than the marriage. Was it the child? But Raby said the child was nine after Colonel Sutpen died in '70. So it must have been born after Charles and Judith married. Was that how Charles Bon lied to you?"

"What was it that Judith knew and Raby knew as soon as they saw her?"

"Yes."

"Yes what?"

"Yes."

"Oh. And you have lived hidden here for forty years."

"I have lived here forty years."

"Were you at peace?"

"I was tired."

"That's the same thing, isn't it? For you and Raby too."

"Same thing. Same as me. I tired too."

"Why did you do all this for Henry Sutpen?"

"He was my brother."

VI

The whole thing went off like a box of matches. I came out of sleep with the deep and savage thunder of the dog roaring over my head and I stumbled past it and down the steps running before I was good awake, awake at all, perhaps. I remember the thin, mellow, farcarrying negro voices from the cabin beyond the pasture, and then I turned still half asleep and saw the façade of the house limned in fire, and the erstblind sockets of the windows, so that the entire front of the house seemed to loom stooping above me in a wild and furious exultation. The dog, howling, was hurling itself against the locked front door, then it sprang from the porch and ran around toward the back.

I followed, running; I was shouting too. The kitchen was already gone, and the whole rear of the house was on fire, and the roof too; the light, longdried shingles taking wing and swirling upward like scraps of burning paper, burning out zenithward like inverted shooting stars. I ran back toward the front of the house, still yelling. The dog passed me, fulltongued, frantic; as I watched the running figures of negro women coming up across the redglared pasture I could hear the dog hurling itself again and again against the front door.

The negroes came up, the three generations of them, their eyeballs white, their open mouths pinkly cavernous. "They're in there, I tell you!" I was yelling. "She set fire to it and they are both in there. She told me Henry Sutpen would not be alive by morning, but I didn't—" In the roaring I could scarce hear myself, and I could not hear the negroes at all for a time. I could only see their open mouths, their fixed, whitecircled eyeballs. Then the roaring reached that point where the ear loses it and it rushes soundless up and away, and I could hear the negroes. They were making a long, concerted, wild, measured wailing, in harmonic pitch from the treble of the children to the soprano of the oldest woman, the daughter of the woman in the burning house; they might have rehearsed it for years, waiting for this irrevocable moment out of all time. Then we saw the woman in the house.

We were standing beneath the wall, watching the clapboards peel and melt away, obliterating window after window, and we saw the old negress come to the window upstairs. She came through fire and she leaned for a moment in the window, her hands on the burning ledge, looking no bigger than a doll, as impervious as an effigy of bronze, serene, dynamic, musing in the foreground of Holocaust. Then the whole house seemed to collapse, to fold in upon itself, melting; the dog passed us again, not howling now. It came opposite us and then turned and sprang into the roaring dissolution of the house without a sound, without a cry.

I think I said that the sound had now passed beyond the outraged and surfeited ear. We stood there and watched the house dissolve and liquefy and rush upward in silent and furious scarlet, licking and leaping among the wild and blazing branches of the cedars, so that, blazing, melting too, against the soft, mildstarred sky of summer they too wildly tossed and swirled.

VII

Just before dawn it began to rain. It came up fast, without thunder or lightning, and it rained hard all forenoon, lancing into the ruin so that above the gaunt, unfallen chimneys and the charred wood a thick canopy of steam unwinded floated. But after a while the steam dispersed and we could walk among the beams and plank ends. We moved gingerly, however, the negroes in nondescript outer garments against the rain, quiet too, not chanting now, save the oldest woman, the grandmother, who was singing a hymn monotonously as she moved here and there, pausing now and then to pick up something. It was she who found the picture in the metal case, the picture of Judith which Charles Bon had owned. "I'll take that," I said.

She looked at me. She was a shade darker than the mother. But there was still the Indian, faintly; still the Sutpen, in her face. "I dont reckon mammy would like that. She particular about Sutpen property."

"I talked to her last night. She told me about it, about everything. It'll be all right." She watched me, my face. "I'll buy it from you, then."

"It aint none of mine to sell."

"Just let me look at it, then. I'll give it back. I talked to her last night. It'll be all right."

She gave it to me then. The case was melted a little; the lock which Judith had hammered shut for all time melted now into a thin streak along the seam, to be lifted away with a knifeblade, almost. But it took an axe to open it.

The picture was intact. I looked at the face and I thought quietly, stupidly (I was a little idiotic myself, with sleeplessness and wet and no breakfast)—I thought quietly, 'Why, I thought she was blonde. They told me Judith was blonde. . . .' Then I came awake, alive. I looked quietly at the face: the smooth, oval, unblemished face, the mouth rich, full, a little loose, the hot, slumbrous, secretive eyes, the inklike hair with its faint but unmistakable wiriness—all the ineradicable and tragic stamp of negro blood. The inscription was in French: *A mon mari. Toujours. 12 Aout, 1860.* And I looked again quietly at the doomed and passionate face with its thick, surfeitive quality of magnolia petals—the face which had unawares destroyed three lives—and I knew now why Charles Bon's guardian had sent him all the way to North Mississippi to attend school, and what to a Henry Sutpen born, created by long time, with what he was and what he believed and thought, would be worse than the marriage and which compounded the bigamy to where the pistol was not only justified, but inescapable.

"That's all there is in it," the negro woman said. Her hand came out from beneath the worn, mudstained khaki army overcoat which she wore across her shoulders. She took the picture. She glanced once at it before closing it: a glance blank or dull, I could not tell which. I could not tell if she had ever seen the photograph or the face before, or if she was not even aware that she had never seen either of them before. "I reckon you better let me have it."

A Portrait of Elmer

Elmer drinks beer upon the terrace of the Dome, with Angelo beside him. Beside him too, close against his leg, is a portfolio. It is quite new and quite flat. Sitting so among the artists he gazes across the boulevard Montparnasse and seems to gaze through the opposite gray building violetroofed and potted smugly with tile against the darkling sky, and across Paris itself and France and across the cold restless monotony of the Atlantic itself, so that for the twilit and nostalgic moment he looks about in lonely retrospect upon that Texas scene into which his mother's unselfish trying ambition had haled at implacable long last his resigned and static father and himself, young then still and blond awkward, alone remaining of all the children, thinking of Circumstance as a tireless detachment like the Postoffice Department, getting people here and there, using them or not at all obscurely, returning them with delayed impersonal efficiency or not at all.

He remarks on this. Angelo awaits his pleasure with unfailing attentive courtesy as always, with that spirit of laissez-faire which rules their relationship, claims the same privilege himself and replies in Italian. To Elmer it sounds as though Angelo is making love to him, and while autumn and twilight mount Montparnasse gravely Elmer sits in a warm bath of words that mean nothing whatever to him, caressing his warming beer and watching girls in a standardised exciting uniformity of dress and accompanied by men with and without beards, and he reaches down his hand quietly and lightly and touches the portfolio briefly, wondering which among the men are the painters and which again the good painters, thinking *Hodge, the artist. Hodge, the artist.* Autumn and twilight mount Montparnasse gravely.

Angelo, with his extreme vest V-ing the soiled kaleidoscopic bulge of his cravat, with a thin purplish drink before him, continues to form his periods with a fine high obliviousness of the fact that Elmer has learned no Italian whatever. Meaningless, his words seem to possess an aesthetic significance, passionate and impersonal, so that at last Elmer stops thinking *Hodge, the artist* and looks at Angelo again with the old helpless dismay, thinking How to interrupt with his American crudeness the other's inexhaustible flow of courteous protective friendship? For Angelo, with an affable tact which Elmer believed no American could ever attain, had established a relationship between them which had got far beyond and above any gross question of money; he had established himself in Elmer's life with the silken affability of a prince in a city of barbarians. And now what is he to do, Elmer wonders. He cannot have Angelo hanging around him much longer. Here, in Paris, he will soon be meeting people; soon he will join an atelier, (again his hand touches lightly and briefly the briefcase against his leg) when he has had a little more time to get acclimated, and has learned a little more French, thinking quickly *Yes. Yes. That's it. When I have learned a little more French, so that I can choose the best one to show it to, since it must be the best. Yes yes. That is it.* Besides, he might run into Myrtle on the street any day. And to have her learn that he and Angelo were inseparable and that he must depend on Angelo for the very food he eats. Now that they are well away from Venice and the dungeon of the Palazzo Ducale, he no longer regrets his incarceration, for it is of such things—life in the raw— that artists are made. But he does regret having been in the same jail with Angelo, and at times he finds himself regretting with an ingratitude which he knows Angelo would never be capable of, that Angelo had got out at all. Then he thinks suddenly, hopefully, again with secret shame, Maybe that would be the best thing, after all. Myrtle will know how to get rid of Angelo; certainly Mrs Monson will.

Angelo's voice completes a smooth period. But now Elmer is not even wondering what Angelo is talking about; again he gazes across the clotting of flimsy tables and the serried ranks of heads and shoulders drinking in two sexes and five languages, at the seemingly endless passing throng, watching the young girls white and soft and canny and stupid, with troubling bodies which he must believe were virginal, wondering why certain girls chose you and others do not. At one time he believed that you can seduce them; now he is not so sure. He believes now that they just elect you when they happen to be in the right mood and you happen to be handy. But surely you are expected to learn from experience (meaning a proved unhappiness you did get as compared with a possible one that missed you) if not how to get what you want, at least the reason why you did not get it. But who wants experience, when he can get any kind of substitute? To hell with experience, Elmer thinks, since all reality is unbearable. I want what I think I want when I think I want it, as all men do. Not a formula for stoicism, an antidote for thwarted desire. Autumn and twilight mount Montparnasse gravely.

Angelo, oblivious, verbose, and without selfconsciousness, continues to speak, nursing his thin dark drink in one hand. His hair is oiled sleekly backward; his face is shaven and blue as a pirate's. On either side of his brief snubbed nose his brown eyes are spaced and melting and sad as a highly bred dog's. His suit, after six weeks, is reasonably fresh and new, as are his cloth topped shoes, and he still has his stick. It is one of those slender jointed bamboo sticks which remain palpably and assertively new up to the moment of loss or death, but the suit, save for the fact that he has not yet slept in it, is exactly like the one which Elmer prevailed on him to throw away in Venice. It is a mosaic of tan-and-gray checks which seems to be in a state of constant mild explosion all over Angelo, robbing him of any shape whatever, and there are enough amber buttons on it to render him bullet proof save at point blank range.

He continues to form his periods with a fine high obliviousness, nursing his purplish drink in his hand. He has not cleaned his finger nails since they quitted Venice.

2

He met Myrtle in Houston, Texas, where he already had a bastard son. That other had been a sweet brief cloudy fire, but to him

Myrtle, arrogant with youth and wealth, was like a star: unattainable for all her curved pink richness. He did not wish to know that after a while those soft distracting hips would become thicker, heavy, almost awkward; that straight nose was a little too short; the blue ineffable eyes a trifle too candid; the brow low, pure and broad a trifle too low and broad beneath the burnished molasses-colored hair.

He met her at a dance, a semi public occasion in honor of departing soldiers in 1917; from his position against the wall, which he had not altered all evening, he watched her pass in a glitter of new boots and spurs and untarnished proud shoulder bars not yet worn thin with salutes; with his lame back and his rented tailcoat he dreamed. He was a war veteran already, yet he was lame and penniless, while Myrtle's father was known even in Texas for the oil wells which he owned. He met her before the evening was over; she looked full at him with those wide heavencolored eyes innocent of any thought at all; she said, "Are you from Houston?" and "Really." with her soft mouth open a little to indicate interest, then a banded cuff swept her away. He met Mrs Monson also and got along quite well with her—a brusque woman with cold eyes who seemed to look at him and at the dancers and at the world too even beyond Texas with a brief sardonic perspicuity.

He met her once; then in 1921, five years after Elmer had returned from his futile and abortive attempt at the war, Mr Monson blundered into three or four more oil wells and Mrs Monson and Myrtle went to Europe to put Myrtle in school, to finish her, since two years in Virginia and a year in the Texas State University had not been enough to do this.

So she sailed away, leaving Elmer to remember her lemoncolored dress, her wet red mouth open a little to indicate interest, her wide ineffable eyes beneath the pure molasses of her hair when he was at last presented; for suddenly, with a kind of horror, he had heard someone saying with his mouth, "Will you marry me?" watching still with that shocked horror her eyes widen into his, since he did not wish to believe that no woman is ever offended by a request for her body. "I mean it," he said; then the barred sleeve took her. I do mean it, he cried silently to himself, watching her lemoncolored shortlegged body disseminating its aura of imminent fat retreating among the glittering boots and belts, to the music become already martial which he could not follow because of his back. *I still mean it, he cries soundlessly, clutching his beer among the piled saucers of Montparnasse, having already seen in the Herald that Mrs Monson and Myrtle are now living in Paris, not wondering where Mr Monson is since these years, not thinking to know that Mr Monson is still in America, engaged with yet more oil wells and with a certain Gloria who sings and dances in a New Orleans nightclub in a single darkish silk garment that, drawn tightly between her kind thighs and across her unsubtle behind, lends to her heavy white legs an unbelievably harmless look, like drawn beef; Perhaps, he thinks with a surge of almost unbearable triumph and exultation, They have seen me too in the papers, maybe even in the French one: Le millionair americain Odge, qui arrive d'etre peintre, parce-qu'il croit que seulment en France faut-il L'ame d'artiste rever et travailler tranquil; en Amerique tout gagne seulment*

3

When he was five years old, in Johnson City, Tennessee, the house they were temporarily living in had burned. "Before you had time to move us again," his father said to his mother with sardonic humor. And Elmer, who had always hated being seen naked, whose modesty was somehow affronted even in the presence of his brothers, had been snatched bodily out of sleep and rushed naked through acrid roaring and into a mad crimson world where the paradoxical temperature was near zero, where he stood alternately jerking his bare feet from the iron icy ground while one side of him curled bitterly, his ears filled with roaring and meaningless shouting, his nostrils with the smell of heat and strange people, clutching one of his mother's thin legs. Even now he remembers his mother's face above him, against a rushing plume of sparks like a wild veil; remembers how he thought then, Is this my mother, this stark bitter face? Where [is] that loving querulous creature whom he knew? and his father, leanshanked, hopping on one leg while he tried to put on his trousers; he remembers how even his father's hairy leg beneath the nightshirt seemed to have taken fire. His two brothers stood side by side nearby, bawling, while tears from tight eyesockets streaked their dirty faces and blistered away and that yelping scarlet filled their gaping mouths; only Jo was not crying,

Jo, with whom he slept, with whom he didn't mind being naked. She alone stood fiercely erect, watching the fire in dark scrawny defiance, ridiculing her wailing brothers by that very sharp and arrogant ugliness of hers.

But as he remembers she was not ugly that night: the wild crimson had given her a bitter beauty like that of a Salamander. And he would have gone to her, but his mother held him tight against her leg, binding him to her with a fold of her night gown, covering his nakedness. So he burrowed against the thin leg and watched quietly the shouting volunteers within the house hurling out the meagre objects which they had dragged for so many years over the face of the North American continent: the low chair in which his mother rocked fiercely while he knelt with his head in her lap; the metal box inscribed Bread in chipped curling gold leaf and in which he had kept for as long as he could remember a dried and now wellnigh anonymous bird's wing, a basket carved from a peachstone, a dogeared picture of Joan of Arc to which he had added with tedious and tonguesucking care an indigo moustache and imperial (the English made her a martyr, the French a saint, but it remained for Hodge, the artist, to make her a man), and a collection of cigar stubs in various stages of intactness, out of an upstairs window onto the brick walk.

She was not ugly that night. And always after that, after she had disappeared between two of their long since uncounted movings and there was none of the children left save himself, the baby—after he saw her one more time and then never again, when he remembered her it was to see her again starkly poised as a young thin ugly tree, sniffing the very sound of that chaos and mad dream into her flared nostrils as mobile as those of a haughty mare.

It was in Jonesboro, Arkansas, that Jo left them. The two boys had before this refused the gambit of their father's bland inactivity and their mother's fretful energy. The second one, a dull lout with a pimpled face, deserted them in Paris, Tennessee, for a job in a liverystable owned by a man with a cruel heavy face and an alcoholcured nose and a twenty-two ounce watch chain; and in Memphis the eldest, a slight quiet youth with his mother's face but without her unconquerable frustration, departed for Saint Louis. Jo left them in Jonesboro, and presently Elmer and his mother and father moved again.

But before they moved, there came anonymously through the mail ("It's from Jo," his mother said. "I know it," Elmer said) a box of paints: cheap watercolors and an impossible brush bristling smartly from a celluloid tube in which the wood stem would never remain fixed. The colors themselves were not only impossible too, they were of a durability apparently impervious to any element, except the blue. It compensated for the others, seeming to possess a dynamic energy which the mere presence of water liberated as the presence of spring in the earth liberates the hidden seed. Sultry, prodigious, it was as virulent as smallpox, staining everything it touched with the passionate ubiquity of an unbottled plague.

He learned to curb it in time, however, and with his already ungainly body sprawled on the floor, on wrapping paper when he could get it or on newspapers when not he painted blue people and houses and locomotives. After they had moved twice more however the blue was exhausted; its empty wooden dish stared up at him from among the other glazed discs, all of which had by now assumed a similar dun color, like a dead mackerel's eye in fixed bluish reproach.

But soon school was out, and Elmer, fourteen and in the fourth grade, had failed again to make the rise. Unlike his brothers and sister, he liked going to school. Not for wisdom, not even for information: just going to school. He was always dull in his books and he inevitably developed a fine sexless passion for the teacher. But this year he was ravished away from that constancy by a boy, a young beast as beautiful to him as a god, and as cruel. Throughout the whole session he worshipped the boy from a distance: a blind and timeless adoration which the boy himself wrote finis to by coming suddenly upon Elmer on the playground one day and tripping him violently to earth, for no reason that either of them could have named. Whereupon Elmer rose without rancor, bathed his abraded elbow, and emotionally free again, fled that freedom as though it were a curse, transferring his sheeplike devotion once more to the teacher.

The teacher had a thick gray face like heavy dough; she moved in that unmistakable odor of middle-aged virgin female flesh. She lived in a small frame house which smelled as she smelled, with behind it a small garden in which no flowers ever did well, not even hardy Octoberdusty zinnias. Elmer would wait for her after school on the afternoons when she remained with pupils who had failed in the day's tasks, to walk home with her. For she saved all her wrapping paper for him to paint on. And soon the two of them, the dowdy irongray spinster and the hulking blond boy with almost the body of a man, were a matter for comment and speculation in the town. Elmer did not know this. Perhaps she did not either, yet one day she suddenly ceased walking home through the main streets, but instead took the nearest way home, with Elmer lumbering along beside her. She did this for two afternoons. Then she told him not to wait for her anymore. He was astonished: that was all. He went home and painted, sprawled on his stomach on the floor. Within the week he ran out of wrapping paper. The next morning he went by the teacher's house, as he had used to do. The door was closed. He went and knocked, but got no answer. He waited before it until he heard the school bell ringing four or five blocks away; he had to run. He did not see the teacher emerge from the house when he was out of sight and hurry also toward the still ringing bell along a parallel street, with her thick doughlike face and her blurred eyes behind her nose glasses. Then it became spring. That day, as the pupils filed from the room at noon, she stopped him and told him to come to her house after supper and she would give him some more paper. He had long since forgot how at one time his blond slow openwork inner life had been marked and fixed in simple pleasure between walking home with her by afternoon and coming by her house in the mornings to walk with her to school until she stopped him; forgetting, he had forgiven her, doglike: always with that ability to forgive and then forget as easily; looking, he did not see her eyes, he could not see her heart. "Yessum," he said. "I will."

It was dark when he reached her door and knocked; high above the reddening bitten maples stars flickered; somewhere in that high darkness was a lonely sound of geese going north. She opened the door almost before his knock had died away. "Come in," she said, leading the way toward a lighted room, where he stood clutching his cap, his overgrown body shifting from leg to leg; on the wall behind him his shadow, hulking, loomed. She took the cap from him and put it on a table on which was a fringed paper doily and a tray bearing a teapot and some broken food. "I eat my supper here," she said. "Sit down, Elmer."

"Yessum," he said. She still wore the white shirtwaist and the dark skirt in which he always saw her, in which he perhaps thought of her in slumber even. He sat gingerly on the edge of a chair.

"Spring outside tonight," she said. "Did you smell it?" He watched her push the tray aside and pick up a crust which had lain hidden in the shallow shadow of the tray.

"Yessum," he said. "I heard some geese going over." He began to perspire a little; the room was warm, close, odorous.

"Yes, spring will soon be here," she said. Still he did not see her eyes, since she now seemed to watch the hand which held the crust. Within the savage arena of light from the shaded lamp it contracted and expanded like a disembodied lung; presently Elmer began to watch crumbs appear between the fingers of it. "And another year will be gone. Will you be glad?"

"Ma'am?" he said. He was quite warm, uncomfortable; he thought of the clear high shrill darkness outside the house. She rose suddenly; she almost flung the now shapeless wad of dough onto the tray.

"But you want your paper, dont you?" she said.

"Yessum," Elmer said. *Now I will be outside soon* he said. He rose too and they looked at one another; he saw her eyes then; the walls seemed to be rushing slowly down upon him, crowding the hot odorous air upon him. He was sweating now. He drew his hand across his forehead. But he could not move yet. She took a step toward him; he saw her eyes now.

"Elmer," she said. She took another step toward him. She was grinning now, as if her thick face had been wrung and fixed in that painful and tragic grimace, and Elmer, still unable to move, seemed to drag his eyes heavily up the black shapeless skirt, up the white shirtwaist pinned at the throat with a barpin of imitation lapis-lazuli, meeting her eyes at last. He grinned too and they stood facing one another, cropping the room with teeth. Then she put her hand on him. Then he fled. Outside the house he still ran, with the noise in his ears still of the crashing table. He ran, filling his body with air in deep gulps, feeling his sweat evaporating.

O and thy little girlwhite all: musical with motion Montparnasse and Raspail: subtle ceaseless fugues of thighs under the waxing moon of death:

Elmer, fifteen, with a handleless teacup, descends steps, traverses sparse lawn, a gate; crosses a street, traverses lawn not sparse, ascends steps between flowering shrubs, knocks at screen door, politely but without diffidence.

Velma her name, at home alone, pinksoftcurved, plump sixteen. Elmer enters with his teacup and traverses dim quietness among gleams on nearmahogany, conscious of tingling remoteness and pinksoftcurves and soft intimation of sheathed hips in progression, and so on to the pantry. Helps to reach down sugar jar from where it sits in a pan of water against ants, but sees only in white cascade of sugar little white teeth over which full soft mouth and red never quite completely closed and her plump body bulging her soiled expensive clothing richly the aromatic cubbyhole in the halfdark. Touched sugar hands in the halfdark hishing cling by eluding, elude but not gone; bulging rabbitlike things under soiled silk taut softly, hishing ceaseless cascade of tilted sugar now on the floor hishing: a game.

It whispers its blanched cascade down the glazed precipice of the overflowed cup, and she flees squealing, Elmer in lumbering pursuit, tasting something warm and thick and salt in his throat. Reaches kitchen door: she has disappeared; but staring in vacuous astonishment toward the barnyard he sees a vanishing flash of skirts and runs after across the lot and into the high odorous cavern of the barn.

She is not in sight. Elmer stands baffled, bloodcooling, in the center of the trodden dungimpregnated earth; stands in baffled incertitude, bloodcooling in helpless and slowmounting despair for irretrievable loss of that which he had never gained, thinking *So she never meant it. I reckon she is laughing at me. I reckon I better try to scrape up that spilled sugar before Mrs Merridew gets home.* He turns toward the door, moving. As he does so a faint sound from overhead stops him. He feels a surge of triumph and fright that stops his heart for the moment. Then he can move toward the vertical ladder which leads to the loft.

Acrid scent of sweated leather, of ammonia and beasts and dry dust richly pungent; of quiet and solitude, of triumph fear change. Mounts the crude ladder, tasting again thick warm salt, hearing his heart heavy and fast, feels his bodyweight swing from shoulder to shoulder upward, then sees yellow slants of cavernous sunlight latticed and spinning with golden motes. Mounts final rung and finds her, breathless and a little frightened, in the hay.

In the throes of puberty, that dark soft trouble like a heard forgotten music or a scent or thing remembered though never smelt nor seen, that blending of dread and longing, he began consciously to draw people: not any longer lines at full liberty to assume any significance they chose, but men and women; trying to draw them and make them conform to a vague shape now somewhere back in his mind, trying to imbue them with what he believed he meant by splendor and speed. Later still, the shape in his mind became unvague concrete and alive: a girl with impregnable virginity to time or circumstance; darkhaired small and proud, casting him bones fiercely as though he were a dog, coppers as though he were a beggar leprous beside a dusty gate.

4

He left his mother and father in Houston when he went to the war. But when he returned, someone else had the house, as usual. He went to the agent. A bright busy bald youngish man, the agent stared at Elmer's yellow hospital stick in a fretful hiatus, visibly revolving the word Hodge in his mind. Presently he rang a bell and a brisk pretty Jewess smelling of toilet water not soap, came and found the letter [they] had left for him. The agent offered Elmer a cigarette, explaining how the war kept him too busy to smoke cigars. Our War, he called it. He talked briefly about Europe, asking Elmer a few questions such as a clothes dealer might ask of a returned African missionary, answering them himself and telling Elmer a few facts in return: that war was bad and that he was partowner of some land near Fort Worth where the British government had established a training field for aviators. But at last Elmer read the letter and went to see his people.

His father had liked Houston. But his mother would want to move though, and sitting in the daycoach among the smells of peanuts and wet babies, nursing his yellow stick from whose crook the varnish was long since handworn, he remembered and thought of that Joblike man with pity tempered by secret and disloyal relief that he himself would no more be haled over the face of the earth at what undirected compulsion drove his mother. From the vantage point of absence, of what might almost be called weaning, he wondered when she would give up: this too (compensating for the recent secret disloyalty) tempered by an abrupt fierce wave of tenderness for her bitter indomitable optimism. For he would return to Houston to live, now that his parents did not need him and hence there was none to expect him any longer to do anything. He would live in Houston and paint pictures.

He saw his father first, sitting on the small front porch; already he had known exactly what the house would look like. His father was unchanged, static, affable, resigned; age did not show on him at all, as it never had, on his cunning cherubic face, his vigorous untidy thatch. Yet Elmer discerned something else, something his father had acquired during his absence: a kind of smug unemphatic cheeriness. And then (sitting also on the porch where his father had not risen, also in a yellow varnished chair such as may be bought almost anywhere for a dollar or two) without any feeling at all, he listened to his father's cheery voice telling him that his mother, that passionate indomitable woman, was dead. While his father recited details with almost gustatory eulogism he looked about at the frame house, painted brown, set in a small dusty grassless treeless yard, recalling that long series of houses exactly like it, stretching behind him like an endless street into that time when he would wake in the dark beside Jo, with her hand sharp and fierce in his hair and her voice in the dark fierce too: "Elly, when you want to do anything, you do it, do you hear? Dont let nobody stop you." and on into the cloudy time when he had existed but could not remember it. He sat in his yellow varnished chair, nursing his yellow varnished stick, while his father talked on and on and dusk came for two hundred unhindered miles and filled the house where his mother's fretful presence seemed to linger yet like an odor, as though it had not even time for sleep, let alone for death.

He would not stay for supper, and his father told him how to find the cemetery with what Elmer believed was actual relief. "I'll get along all right," Elmer said.

"Yes," his father agreed heartily, "you'll get along all right. Folks are always glad to help soldiers. This aint no place for a young man, nohow. If I was young now, like you are—" The intimation of a world fecund, waiting to be conquered with a full

rich patience, died away, and Elmer rose, thinking if his mother
had been present now, who refused always to believe that any flesh
and blood of hers could get along at all beyond the radius of her
fretful kindness. Oh, I'll get along, he repeated, now to that thin
spirit of her which yet lingered about the house which had at last
conquered her, and he could almost hear her rejoin quickly, with
a kind of triumph: That's what your sister thought, forgetting that
they had never heard from Jo and that for all they knew she might
be Gloria Swanson or J.P.Morgan's wife.

He didn't tell his father about Myrtle. His father would have said
nothing at all, and that brisk spirit of his mother's energy would
have said that Myrtle wasn't a bit too good for him. Perhaps she
knows, he thought quietly, leaning on his stick beside the grave
which even too seemed to partake of her wiry restless imperma-
nence, as clothes assume the characteristics of the wearer. At the
head was a small compact palpably marble headstone surmounted
by a plump stone dove, natural size. And above it, above the
untreed hill, stretched an immeasurable twilight in which huge
stars hung with the impersonality of the mad and through which
Adam and Eve, dead untimed out of Genesis, might still be seeking
that heaven of which they had heard.

Elmer closed his eyes, savoring sorrow, bereavement, the sentimental loneliness of conscious time. But not for long: already he
was seeing against his eyelids Myrtle's longwaisted body in the
lemoncolored dress, her wet red halfopen mouth, her eyes widen-
ing ineffably beneath the burnished molasses of her hair, thinking
Money money money. *Anyway, I can paint now* he thought, striking his stick into the soft quiet earth *A name. Fame perhaps. Hodge,
the painter*

5

Angelo is one of those young men, one of that great submerged
mass, that vigorous yet heretofore suppressed and dominated class
which we are told has been sickened by war. But Angelo has not
been sickened by war. He had been able to perform in wartime
actions which in peacetime the police, government, all those who
by the accident of birth or station were able to override him, would
have made impossible. Naturally war is bad, but so is traffic, and

the fact that wine must be paid for and the fact that if all the women a man can imagine himself in bed with were to consent, there would not be time in the alotted three score and ten. As for getting hurt, no Austrian nor Turk nor even a carabiniere is going to shoot him with a gun, and over a matter of territory he has never seen and does not wish to see. Over a woman, now— He watches the seemingly endless stream of women and young girls in hushed childish delight, expressing pleasure and approbation by sucking his breath sharply between his pursed lips. Across the narrow table his companion and patron sits: the incomprehensible American with his predilection for a liquid which to Angelo is something like that which is pumped from the bowels of ships, whom he has watched for two months now living moving breathing in some static childlike furious brooding world beyond all fact and flesh; for a moment, unseen, Angelo looks at him with a speculation which is almost contempt. But soon he is immersed again in his own constant sound of approbation and pleasure while autumn, mounting Montparnasse, permeates the traffic of Montparnasse and Raspail, teasing the breasts and thighs of young girls moving musical in the lavender glittering dusk between old walls beneath a sky like a patient etherised and dying after an operation.

Elmer has a bastard son in Houston. It happened quickly. He was eighteen, big blond awkward, with curling hair. They would go to the movies, say twice a week, since (her name is Ethel) she was popular, with several men friends of whom she would talk to him. So he accepted his secondary part before it was offered him, as if that was the position he desired, holding her hands in the warm purring twilight while she told him how the present actor on the screen was like or unlike men she knew. "You are not like other men," she told him. "With you, it's different: I dont need to be always...." in the sleazy black satin which she liked staring at him with something fixed and speculative and completely dissimulant about her eyes. "Because you are so much younger than I am, you see; almost two years. Like a brother. Do you see what I mean?"

"Yes," Elmer said, statically awash in the secret intimacy of their clasped faintly sweating hands. He liked it. He liked sitting in the discreet darkness, watching the inevitable exigencies of human conduct as established and decreed by expatriate Brooklyn button- and pants-manufacturers, transposing her into each cellu-loid kiss and embrace, yet not aware that she was doing the same thing even though he could feel her hand lax and bloom barometri-cally in his own. He liked kissing her too, in what he believed to be snatched intervals between mounting the veranda and opening the door and again when noises upstairs had ceased and the ta-blelamp would begin to make her nervous.

Then they went to four movies in succession, and then on the fifth evening they did not go out at all. Her family was going out and she did not like to leave the house completely untenanted. He was for starting the kissing then, but she made him take a chair across the table while she took one opposite and told him what type of man she would some day marry; of how she would marry only because her parents expected it of her and that she would never give herself to a man save as a matter of duty to the husband which they would choose for her, who would doubtless be old and wealthy: that therefore she would never lose love because she would never have had it. That Elmer was the sort of man she, having no brothers, had always wanted to know because she could tell him things she couldn't even bring herself to discuss with her mother.

And so for the following weeks Elmer existed in a cloying jungle of young female flesh damply eager and apparently unappeasable (ballooning earnestly at him, Elmer with that visual detachment of man suffering temporary or permanent annihilation thought of an inferiorly inflated toy balloon with a finger thrust into it) though at first nothing happened. But later too much happened. "Too much," she told him from the extent of her arms, her hands locked behind his head, watching his face with dark dissimulant intent-ness.

"Let's get married then," Elmer said, out of his mesmerism of enveloping surreptitious breasts and thighs.

"Yes," she said. Her voice was detached, untroubled, a little resigned; Elmer thought *She's not even looking at me* "I'm going to marry Grover." This was the first he had heard of Grover.

I'm not running away, Elmer told himself, sitting in the inkblack boxcar while the springless trucks clucked and banged beneath him; It's because I just didn't think I could feel this bad. The car was going north, because there was more north to go in than south.

And there was also in his mind something beyond even the surprise and the hurt and which he refused to even think was relief; what he told himself was, Maybe in the north where things are different, I can get started painting. Maybe in painting I can forget I didn't think that I could feel this bad. And again maybe he had but belatedly reached that point at which his sister and brothers had one by one broken the spell of progression which their mother had wound about them like the string around a top.

Oklahoma knew him; he worked in Missouri wheatfields; he begged bread for two days in Kansas City. At Christmas he was in Chicago, spending day after day erect and sound asleep before pictures in galleries where there was no entrance fee; night after night sitting in railroad stations until the officials waked them all and the ones who had no tickets would walk the bitter galeridden streets to another station and so repeat. Now and then he ate.

In January he was in a Michigan lumbercamp. For all his big body, he worked in the roaring steamopaque cookshack which smelled always soporific of food and damp wool, scrubbing the bellies of aluminum pots which in the monotonous drowse of the long mornings reminded him of the empty wood dish of blue in the paint box of his childhood.

At night there was plenty of rough paper. He used charcoal until he found a box of blue washing powder. With that and with coffee-dregs and with a bottle of red ink belonging to the cook, he began to work in color. Soon the teamsters, axmen and sawyers discovered that he could put faces on paper. One by one he drew them, by commission, each describing the kind of clothing, dresssuit, racecourse check, or mackinaw, in which he wished to be portrayed, sitting patiently until the work was finished, then holding with his mates gravely profane aesthetic debate.

When February broke, he had grown two inches and filled out; his body was now the racehorse body of nineteen; sitting about the steaming bunkhouse the men discussed him with the impersonality of surgeons or horseracers. Soon now the rigid muscles of snow would laxen, though reluctant yet. Gluts of snow would slip heavily soundless from the boughs of spruce and hemlock and the boughs would spring darkly free against the slipping snow; from the high blue soon now the cries of geese would drift like falling leaves, wild, fantastical, and sad. In the talk of sex nightly growing more and more frequent about the bunkhouse stove, Elmer's body in relation to women was discussed; one night, through some vague desire to establish himself and formally end his apprenticeship to manhood, he told them about Ethel in Houston. They listened, spitting gravely on the hissing orange stove. When he had finished they looked at one another with weary tolerance. Then one said kindly: "Dont you worry, bub. It's harder to get one than you think."

Then it was March. The log drive was in the river, and over the last meal in the bunkhouse they looked quietly about at one another, who perhaps would never see the other faces again, while between stove and table Elmer and the cook moved. The cook was Elmer's immediate superior and czar of the camp. He reminded Elmer of someone; he coddled him and harried him and cursed him with savage kindness: Elmer came at last to dread him with a kind of static hypnosis, letting the cook direct his actions, not joyously but with resignation. He was wiry and hightempered; when men came in late to meals he flew into an almost homicidal rage. They treated him with bluff caution, shouting him down by sheer volume while he cursed them, but not offering to touch him. But he kept the kitchen clean and fed them well and mended their clothes for them; when a man was injured he tended the invalid in a frenzy of skillful gentleness, cursing him and his forbears and posterity for generations.

When the meal was over, he asked Elmer what he intended to do now. Elmer had not thought of that; suddenly he seemed to see his destiny thrust back into his arms like a strange baby in a railroad waitingroom. The cook kicked the stove door to savagely. 'Let's go to that goddam war. What do you say?"

He certainly reminded Elmer of someone, especially when he came to see Elmer the night before Elmer's battalion entrained for Halifax. He sat on Elmer's bunk and cursed the war, the Canadian government, the C.E.F. corps brigade battalion and platoon, himself and Elmer past present and to come, for they had made him a corporal and a cook. "So I aint going," he said. "I guess I wont never get over. So you'll just have to do the best you can by yourself. You can do it. By God, dont you take nothing off of them, these Canucks or them Limey bastards neither. You're good as any of them, even if you dont have no stripes on your sleeve or no goddam brass acorns on your shoulders. You're good as any of them and a dam sight better than most, and dont you forget it. Here. Take this. And dont lose it." It was a tobacco tin. It contained needles of all sizes, thread, a pair of short scissors, a pack of adhesive tape and a dozen of those objects which the English wittily call French letters and the French call wittily English letters. He departed, still cursing. Elmer never saw him again.

Soldiering on land had been a mere matter of marching here and there in company and keeping his capbadge and tunic buttons and rifle clean and remembering whom to salute. But aboard ship, where space was restricted, they were learning about combat. It was with hand grenades and Elmer was afraid of them. He had become reconciled to the rifle, which a man aimed and pulled trigger with immediate results, but not this object, to which a man did something infinitesimal and then held it in his hand, counting three in the waiting silence before throwing it. He told himself that when he had to, he would pull the pin and throw it at once, until the stocky sergeant-major with eyes like glass marbles and a ribbon on his breast told them how the Hun had a habit of catching the bomb and tossing it back like a baseball.

"Nah," the sergeant-major said, roving his dead eyes about their grave faces, "count three, like this." He did something infinitesimal to the bomb while they watched him in quiet horrified fascination. Then he pushed the pin back and tossed the bomb lightly in his hand. "Like that, see?"

Then someone nudged Elmer. He quit swallowing his hot salt and took the bomb and examined it in a quiet horror of curiosity. It was oval, its smug surface broken like a pineapple, dull and solid: a comfortable feel, a compact solidity almost sensuous to the palm. The sergeant-major's voice said sharply from distance: "Come on. Like I showed you."

"Yes, sir," Elmer's voice said while he watched his hands, those familiar hands which he could no longer control, toying with the bomb, nursing it. Then his apish hands did something infinitesimal and became immobile in bland satisfaction and Elmer stared in an utterly blank and utterly timeless interval at the object in his palm.

"Throw it, you bloody bastard!" the man beside him shouted before he died. Elmer stared at his hand, waiting; then the hand decided to obey him and swung backward. But the hand struck a stanchion before it reached the top of the arc and he saw the face of the man next to him like a suspended mask at his shoulder, utterly expressionless, and the dull oval object in the air between them growing to monstrous size like an obscene coconut. Then his body told him to turn his back and lie down.

How green it looks, he thought sickly. Later, while he lay for months on his face while his back healed and young women and old looked upon his naked body with a surprising lack of interest, he remembered the amazing greenness of the Mersey shores. That was about all he had to think of. These people didn't even know where Texas was, taking it to be a town in British Columbia apparently as they talked to him kindly in their clipped jerky way. On a neighboring cot and usually delirious was a youth of his own age, an aviator with a broken back and both feet burned off. It's as hard to kill folks as it is to get them, Elmer thought, thinking *So this is war:* white rows of beds in a white tunnel of a room, grayclad nurses kind but uninterested, then a wheel chair among other wheelchairs and now and then lady lieutenants in blue cloaks with brass insigne; thinking *But how green it looked* since it was quiet now, since the aviator was gone. Whether he died or not Elmer neither knew nor cared.

It seemed greener than ever when he saw it again from shipdeck as they dropped down with the tide. And with England at last behind, in retrospect it seemed greener still, with an immaculate peace which no war could ever disturb. While they felt through the Zone and into the gray Atlantic again he slept and waked, touching at times his head where endless pillows had worn his hair away, wondering if it would grow out again.

It was March again. For eleven months he had not thought of painting. Before they reached midocean it was April; one day off Newfoundland they learned by wireless that America had entered the war. His back did not hurt so much as it itched.

He spent some of his backpay in New York. He not only visited public and semipublic galleries, but through the kindness of a preserved fat woman he spent afternoons in private galleries and homes. His sponsor, a canteen worker, had once been soft pink and curved, but now she was long since the wife of a dollarayear man in Washington, with an income of fifty thousand. She had met

Elmer in the station canteen and was quite kind to him, commiserating the mothy remnant of his once curling hair. Then he went south. With his limp and his yellow stick he remained in New Orleans in an aimless hiatus. Nowhere he had to go, nowhere he wanted to go, he existed not lived in a voluptuous inertia mocking all briskness and haste: grave vitiating twilights soft and oppressive as smoke upon the city, hanging above the hushed eternal river and the docks where he walked smelling rich earth in overquick fecundity—sugar and fruit, resin and dusk and heat, like the sigh of a dark and passionate woman no longer young.

He was halted one day on Canal Street by a clotting of people. A hoarse man stood on a chair in the center of the throng, a fattish sweating prosperous man making a Liberty Loan speech, pleading on the streets for money like a beggar. And suddenly, across the clotting heads, he saw a slight taut figure as fiercely erect as ever, watching the orator and the audience with a fierce disgust. "Jo!" Elmer cried. *"Jo!"*

money we earn, work and sweat for, so that our children
not have to face what we are now   able to earn this money? By
the protection which this country, this American nation showing the
old dying civilizations   freedom   she calls on you what
will you say

The crowd stirred in a slow hysteria and Elmer lunged his maimed body, trying to thrust through toward where he still saw the fierce poise of her small hat. "For Christ's sake," someone said: a youth in the new campaign hat and the still creased khaki of recent enlistment; "whatcher in such a rush about?"

boys over there   finish it before others must die   duty
of civilization to stamp forever

"Maybe he wants he should enlist," another, a plump Jewish man clutching a new thousand dollar bill in his hand, shrieked. "This var— In Lithuania I have seen yet O God," he shrieked in Elmer's face.

"Pardon me. Pardon me." Elmer chanted, trying to thrust through, trying to keep in sight the unmistakable poise of that head.

"Well, he's going in the wrong direction," the soldier said, barring the way. "Recruiting office is over yonder, buddy." Across his shoulder Elmer caught another glimpse of the hat, lost it again.

price we must pay for having become the greatest nation
Word of God in the Book itself

The crowd surged again, elbowing the filaments of fire which lived along his spine. "This var!" the Jew shrieked at him again. "Them boys getting killed already O God. It vill make business: In Lithuania I have seen—"

"Look out," a third voice said quickly; "he's lame; dont you see his stick?"

"Yes, sure," the soldier said. "They all get on crutches when assembly blows."

"Pardon me. Pardon me." Elmer chanted amid the laughter. The black hat was not in sight now. He was sweating too, striving to get through, his spine alive now with fiery ants. The orator remarked the commotion. He saw the soldier and Elmer's sick straining face; he paused, mopping his neck.

"What's that?" he said. "Wants to enlist? Come here, brother. Make room, people; let him come up here." Elmer tried to hold back as the hands touched began to push and draw him forward as the crowd opened.

"I just want to pass," he said. But the hands thrust him on. He looked over his shoulder, thinking, I am afraid I am going to puke, thinking, I'll go. I'll go. Only for God's sake dont touch my back again. The black hat was gone. He began to struggle; at last his back had passed the stage where he could feel at all. "Let me go, goddam you!" he said whitely. "I have already been—"

But already the orator, leaning down, caught his hand; other hands lifted and pushed him up onto the platform while once more the sweating man turned to the crowd and spoke. "Folks, look at this young man here. Some of us, most of us, are young and well and strong: we can go. But look at this young man here, a cripple, yet he wants to defy the beast of intolerance and blood. See him: his stick, limping. Shall it be said of us who are sound in body and limb, that we have less of courage and less of love of country than this boy? And those of us who are unfit or old; those of us who cannot go—"

"No, no," Elmer said, jerking at the hand which the other held. "I just want to pass: I have already been—"

"—men, women, let everyone of us do what this boy, lame in the very splendor of young manhood, would do. If we cannot go ourselves, let everyone of us say, I have sent one man to the front; that though we ourselves are old and unfit, let everyone of us say, I have sent one soldier to preserve this American heritage which our fathers created for us out of their own suffering and preserved to us with their own blood; That I have done what I could that this heritage may be handed down unblemished to my children, to my children's children yet unborn—" The hoarse inspired voice went on, sweeping speaker and hearers upward into an immolation of words, a holocaust without heat, a conflagration with neither light nor sound and which would leave no ashes.

Elmer sought for another glimpse of that small hat, that fierce disdainful face, but in vain. It was gone, and the crowd, swept up once more in the speaker's eloquence, as suddenly forgot him. But she was gone, as utterly as a flame blown out. He wondered in sick despair if she had seen, not recognising him and not understanding. The crowd let him through now.

dont let the German Beast think that we, you and I, refused, failed, dared not, while our boys our sons are fighting the good fight bleeding and suffering and dying to wipe forever from the world

He shifted his stick to the palm which had become callous to it. He saw the Jew again, still trying to give away his thousand dollar bill; heard diminishing behind him the voice hoarse and endless, passionate, fatuous, and sincere. His back began to hurt again.

6

Musical with motion Montparnasse and Raspail: evening dissolves swooning: a thin odor of heliotrope become visible: with lights spangling yellow green and red. Angelo gains Elmer's attention at last and with his thumb indicates at a table nearby heavy eyes in sober passive allure, and a golden smile above a new shoddy fur neckpiece. He continues to nudge Elmer, making his rich pursed mouthsound: the grave one stares at Elmer in stoic invitation, the other one crops her goldrimmed teeth at him before he looks quickly away. Yet still Angelo grimaces at him and nods rapidly, but Elmer is obdurate, and Angelo sits back in his chair with an indescribable genuflexion of weary disgust.

"Six weeks ago," he says in Italian, "they fetched you into the political dungeon of Venice, where I already was, and took from you your belt and shoelaces. You did not know why. Two days later I removed myself, went to your consul, who in turn removed you. Again you did not know how or why. And now since twenty-three days we are in Paris. In Paris, mind you. And now what do we do? We sit in caffees, we eat, we sit in caffees; we go and sleep. This we have done save for the seven days of one week which we spent in the forest of Meudon while you made a picture of three trees and an inferior piece of an inferior river—this too apparently for what reason you do not know, since you have done nothing with it, since for thirteen days now you have shown it to no one but have carried it in that affair beside your leg, from one caffee to another, sitting over it as though it were an egg and you a hen. Do you perhaps hope to hatch others from it, eh? or perhaps you are waiting until age will make of it an old master? And this in Paris. In Paris, mind. We might as well be in heaven. In America even, where there is nothing save money and work."

Musical with motion and lights and sound, with taxies flatulent palevaporous in the glittering dusk. Elmer looks again: the two women have risen and they now move away between the close tables with never a backward glance; again Angelo makes his sound of exasperation explosive but resigned. But musical with girlmotion Montparnasse and Raspail and soon Angelo, his friend and patron forgotten in the proffered flesh, expresses his pleasure and approbation between his pursed lips, leaving his patron to gaze lonely and musing through the gray opposite building and upon that Texas hill where he stood beside his mother's grave and thought of Myrtle Monson and money and of Hodge, the painter.

Someone died and left the elder Hodge two thousand dollars. He bought a house with it, almost in revenge, it might be said. It was in a small town innocent of trees where, Hodge said in humorous paraphrase, there were more cows and less milk and more rivers and less water and you could see further and see less than anywhere under the sun. Mrs Hodge, pausing in her endless bitter activity, gazed at her husband sedentary, effacing, as inevitable and inescapable as disease, in amazement, frankly shocked at last. "I thought you was looking for a house that suited you," Hodge said.

She looked about at those identical rooms, at the woodwork (doorframes and windows painted a thir rew white which only brought into higher relief the prints of hands long moved away to print other identical houses about the earth), at walls papered with a serviceable tan which showed the minimum of stains and drank light like a sponge. "You did it just for meanness," she said bitterly, going immediately about the business of unpacking, for the last time.

"Why, aint you always wanted a home of your own to raise your children in?" Hodge said. Mrs Hodge suspended a folded quilt and looked about at the room which the two older boys would probably never see, which Jo would have fled on sight; and now Elmer, the baby, gone to a foreign war.

It could not have been nature nor time nor space, who was impervious to flood and fire and time and distance, indomitable in the face of lease contracts which required them to rent for a whole year to get the house at all. It must have been the fact of possession, rooting, that broke her spirit as a caged bird's breaks. Whatever it was, she tried to make morningglories grow upon the sawfretted porch, then she gave up. Hodge buried her on the treeless intimation of a hill, where unhampered winds could remind her of distance when she inevitably sickened to move again, though dead, and where time and space could mock at her inability to quicken and rise and stir; and he wrote Elmer, who was lying then on his face in a plaster cast in a British hospital while his spine hurt and the flesh inside the cast became warmly fluid like a film of spittle and he could smell it too, that his mother was dead and that he (Hodge) was as usual. He added that he had bought a house, forgetting to say where. Later, and with a kind of macabre thoughtfulness, he forwarded the returned letter to Elmer three months after Elmer had visited home for that brief afternoon and returned to Houston.

After his wife's death Hodge, cooking (he was a good cook, better than his wife had ever been) and doing his own sloven housework, would sit after supper on the porch, whittling a plug of tobacco against tomorrow's pipe, and sigh. Immediately that sigh would smack of something akin to relief, and he would reprimand himself in quick respect for the dead. And then he would not be so sure what that sigh signified. He contemplated the diminishing future, those years in which he would never again have to go anywhere unless he pleased, and he knew a mild discomfort. Had he too got from that tireless optimist an instinct for motion, a

gadfly of physical progression? Had she, dying, robbed him of any
gift for ease? As he never went to church he was intensely religious,
and he contemplated with troubled static alarm that day when he
too should pass beyond the veil and there find his wife waiting for
him, all packed up and ready to move.

And then, when that had worn off and he had decided since he
could not help that, to let Heaven's will be done since not only was
that best but he couldn't do anything about it anyway, three men
in boots came and, to his alarmed and pained astonishment, dug
an oilwell in his chickenyard so near that he could stand in the
kitchen door and spit into it. So he had to move again, or be washed
bodily out of the county. But this time he merely moved the house
itself, turning it around so he could sit on the veranda and watch
the moiling activity in his erstwhile henyard with static astonishment and, if truth be told, consternation. He had given Elmer's
Houston address to one of the booted men, asking him if he would
mind looking Elmer up next time he was in Houston and telling
him about it. So all he had to do then was to sit on his front porch
and wait and muse upon the unpredictableness of circumstance.
For instance, it had permitted him to run out of matches tonight,
so instead of shredding his whole plug for smoking, he reserved
enough to chew until someone came tomorrow who had matches;
and sitting on the veranda of the first thing larger than a foldingbed
which he had ever owned, with his most recent tribulation skeletoned and ladderlatticed high against the defunctive sky, he
chewed his tobacco and spat outward into the immaculate dusk.
He had not chewed in years and so he was a trifle awkward at first.
But soon he was able to arc tobacco juice in a thin brown hissing,
across the veranda and onto a parallelogram of troubled earth
where someone had once tried to make something grow.

The New Orleans doctor sent Elmer to New York. There he
spent two years while they fixed his spine, and another year recov-
ering from it, lying again on his face with behind his mind's eye
the image of a retreating shortlegged body in a lemoncolored dress,
but not retreating fast now, since already, though lying on his face
beneath weights, he was moving faster. Before departing however
he made a brief visit to Texas. His father had not changed, not
aged: Elmer found him resigned and smugly philosophical as ever

beneath this new blow which Fate had dealt him. The only change in the establishment was the presence of a cook, a lean yellow woman no longer young, who regarded Elmer's presence with a mixture of assurance and alarm; inadvertently he entered his father's bedroom and saw that the bed, still unmade at noon, had obviously been occupied by two people. But he had no intention of interfering, nor any wish to; already he had turned his face eastward; already thinking and hope and desire had traversed the cold restless gray Atlantic, thinking *Now I have the money. And now fame. And then Myrtle*

And so he has been in Paris three weeks. He has not yet joined a class; neither has he visited the Louvre since he does not know where the Louvre is, though he and Angelo have crossed the Place de la Concorde several times in cabs. Angelo, with his instinct for glitter and noise, promptly discovered the Exposition; he took his patron there. But Elmer does not consider these to be painting. Yet he lingered, went through it all, though telling himself with quick loyalty, It wont be Myrtle who would come here; it will be Mrs Monson who will bring her, make her come. He has no doubt but that they are in Paris. He has been in Europe long enough to know that the place to look for an American in Europe is Paris; that when they are anywhere else, it is merely for the weekend.

When he reached Paris, he knew two words of French: he had learned them from the book which he bought at the shop where he bought his paints. (It was in New York. "I want the best paints you have," he told the young woman, who wore an artist's smock. "This set has twenty tubes and four brushes, and this one has thirty tubes and six brushes. We have one with sixty tubes, if you would like that," she said. "I want the best," Elmer said. "You mean you want the one with the most tubes and brushes?" she said. "I want the best," Elmer said. So they stood looking at one another at this impasse and then the proprietor himself came, also in an artist's smock. He reached down the set with the sixty tubes—which, incidentally, the French at Ventimiglia made Elmer pay a merchant's import duty on. "Of course he vants the best," the proprietor said. "Cant you look at him and tell that? Listen, I vill tell you. This is the vun you vant; I vill tell you. How many pictures can you paint vith ten tubes? Eh?" "I dont know," Elmer said. "I just want the best." "Sure you do," the proprietor said; "the vun that vill paint the most pictures. Come; you tell me how many pictures you can paint vith ten tubes; I tell you how many you can paint vith sixty." "I'll take it," Elmer said.)

The two words were *rive gauche.* He told them to the taxi driver at the Gare de Lyons, who said, "That is true, monsieur," watching Elmer with brisk attentiveness, until Angelo spoke to him in a bastard language of which Elmer heard *millionair americain* without then recognising it. "Ah," the driver said. He hurled Elmer's baggage and then Angelo into the cab, where Elmer already was, and drove them to the Hotel Leutetia. So this is Paris, Elmer thought, to the mad and indistinguishable careening of houses and streets, to canopied cafes and placarded comfort stalls and other vehicles pedalled or driven by other madmen, while Elmer sat a little forward, gripping the seat, with on his face an expression of static concern. The concern was still there when the cab halted before the hotel. It had increased appreciably when he entered the hotel and looked about; now he was downright qualmed. This is not right, he thought. But already it was too late; Angelo had made once his pursed sound of pleasure and approbation, speaking to a man in the dress uniform of a field marshal in his bastard tongue, who in turn bellowed sternly, "*Encore un millionair americain.*" It was too late; already five men in uniform and not were forcing him firmly but gently to sign his name to an affidavit as to his existence, and he thinking *What I wanted was a garret* thinking with a kind of humorous despair *It seems that what I really want is poverty*

He escaped soon though, to Angelo's surprise, astonishment, and then shrugged fatalistic resignation. He took to prowling about the neighborhood, with in his hand the book from which he had learned *rive gauche,* looking up at garret windows beneath leads and then at the book again with helpless dismay which he knew would soon become despair and then resignation to the gold braid, the funereal frock coats, the piled carpets and the discreet lights among which fate and Angelo had cast him, as though his irrevocable horoscope and been set and closed behind him with the clash of that barred door in the Palazzo Ducale in Venice. He had not even opened the box of paints. Already he had paid a merchant's duty on them; he could well have continued to be the merchant which the French had made him and sold them. Then one day he strayed into the Rue Servandoni. He was merely passing through it, hopeful still with fading hope, when he looked through open doors, into a court. Even in the fatal moment he was telling himself *It's just another hotel. The only difference will be that living here will be a little more tediously exigent and pettily annoying* But again it was too late; already he had seen her. She stood, hands on hips in a clean harsh dress, scolding at an obese man engaged statically with a mop—a thin woman of forty or better, wiry, with a harried indefatigable face; for an instant he was his own father eight thousand miles away in Texas, not even knowing that he was thinking *I might have known she would not stay dead* not even thinking with omniscient perspicuity *I wont even need the book*

He didn't need the book. She wrote on a piece of paper the rate for the rooms; she could have made it anything she wished. He told himself that, housed again, static, dismayed, and relieved, while she nagged at him about his soiled clothes, examining and mending them, prowling furiously among his things and cleaning his room furiously (Angelo lived on the floor above him) while she jabbed French words and phrases into his mouth and made him repeat them. *Maybe I can get away some night,* he told himself. *Maybe I can escape after she is asleep and find an attic on the other side of town;* knowing that he would not, knowing that already he had given up, surrendered to her; that, like being tried for a crime, no man ever escapes the same fate twice.

And so soon (the next day he went to the American Express Co. and left his new address) his mind was saying only Paris. Paris. The Louvre, Cluny, the Salon, besides the city itself: the same skyline and cobbles, the same kindlooking marbles thighed as though for breeding—all that merry sophisticated coldblooded dying city to which Cezanne was dragged now and then like a reluctant cow, where Manet and Monet fought points of color and line; where Matisse and Picasso still painted: tomorrow he would join a class. That night he opened the box of paints for the first time. Yet, looking at them, he paused again. The tubes lay in serried immaculate rows, blunt, solid, torpedolike, latent. *There is so much in them,* he thought. *There is everything in them. They can do anything;* thinking of Hals and Rembrandt; all the tall deathless giants of old time, so that he turned his head suddenly, as though they were in the room, filling it, making it seem smaller than a hencoop, watching him, so that he closed the box again with quiet and aghast dismay. Not yet, he told himself. I am not worthy yet. But I can serve. I will serve. I want to serve, suffer too, if necessary.

The next day he bought watercolors and paper (for the first time since reaching Europe he showed no timorousness nor helplessness in dealing with foreign shopkeepers) and he and Angelo went to Meudon. He did not know where he was going; he merely saw a blue hill and pointed it out to the taxi driver. They spent seven days there while he painted his landscape. He destroyed three of them before he was satisfied, telling himself while his muscles cramped and his eyes blurred with weariness, I want it to be hard. I want it to be cruel, taking something out of me each time. I want never to be completely satisfied with any of them, so that I shall always paint again. So when he returned to the Rue Servandoni, with the finished picture in the new portfolio, on that first night when he looked at the tall waiting spectres, he was humble still but no longer aghast.

So now I have something to show him, he thinks, nursing his now lukewarm beer, while beside him Angelo's pursed sound has become continuous. Now, when I have found who is the best master in Paris, when I go to him and say Teach me to paint, I shall not go emptyhanded; thinking *And then fame. And then Myrtle* while twilight mounts Montparnasse gravely beneath the year turning reluctant as a young bride to the old lean body of death. It is then that he feels the first lazy, implacable waking of his entrails.

7

Angelo's pursed sound has become continuous: an open and bland urbanity, until he sees that his patron has risen, the portfolio under his arm. "We eat-a, eh?" he says, who in three weeks has learned both of French and English, while Elmer has not yet learned how to ask where the Louvre and the Salon are. Then he indicates Elmer's beer. "No feeneesh?"

"I've got to go," Elmer says; there is upon his face that rapt, inturned expression of a dyspeptic, as though he is listening to his insides, which is exactly what Elmer is doing; already he moves away. At once a waiter appears; Elmer still with that rapt, not exactly concerned expression but without any lost motion, gives the waiter a banknote and goes on; it is Angelo who stays the waiter and gets change and leaves a European tip which the waiter snatches up with contempt and says something to Angelo in French; for reply and since his patron is going on, walking a little faster than ordinary, Angelo merely takes time to reverse his sound of approbation by breathing outward through his pursed lips instead of inward.

And now musical with motion Michel also, though it is in the Place de l'Observatoire that Angelo overtakes his patron, where even then he still has to trot to keep up. Angelo looks about, his single eyebrow lifted. "No eat-a now?" he says.

"No," Elmer says. "The hotel."

"Otel?" Angelo says. "Eat-a first, eh?"

"No!" Elmer says. His tone is fretted, though not yet harried and not yet desperate. "Hotel. I've got to retire."

"Rittire?" Angelo says.

"Cabinet," Elmer says.

"Ah," Angelo says; "cabinet." He glances up at his patron's concerned, at once very alert and yet inwardlooking face; he grasps Elmer by the elbow and begins to run. They run for several steps before Elmer can jerk free; his face is now downright alarmed.

"Goddamn it, let go!" He cries.

"True," Angelo says in Italian. "In your situation, running is not what a man wants. I forgot. Slow and easy does it, though not too slow. Coraggio," he says, "we come to her soon." And presently the pay station is in sight. "Voila!" Angelo says. Again he takes his patron's arm, though not running; again Elmer frees his arm, drawing away; again Angelo indicates the station, his single eyebrow high on his skull, his eyes melting, concerned, inquiring; again he reverses his sound of approbation, indicating the station with his thumb.

"No!" Elmer says. His voice is desperate now, his expression desperate yet determined. "Hotel!" In the Garden, where Elmer walks with long harried strides and Angelo trots beside him, twilight is gray and unsibilant among the trees; in the long dissolving arras people are already moving toward the gates. They pass swiftly the carven figures in the autumntinged dusk, pass the bronze ones in solemn nowformless gleams secretive and brooding;

both trotting now, they pass Verlaine in stone, and Chopin, that sick feminine man like snow rotting under a dead moon; already the moon of death stands overhead, pleasant and affable and bloodless as a procuress. Elmer enters the Rue Vaugirard, trotting with that harried care, as though he carries dynamite; it is Angelo who restrains him until there is a gap in the traffic.

Then he is in the Rue Servandoni. He is running now, down the cobbled slope. He is no longer thinking *What will people think of me* It is as though he now carries life, volition, all, cradled dark and sightless in his pelvic girdle, with just enough of his intelligence remaining to tell him when he reaches the door. And there, just emerging, hatless, is his landlady.

"Ah, Monsieur Odge," she says. "I just this moment search for you. You have visitors; the female millionaires American Monson wait you in your chamber."

"Yes," Elmer says, swerving to run past her, not even aware that he is speaking to her in English. "In a minute I will—" Then he pauses; he glares at her with his harried desperate face. "Mohsong?" he says. "Mohsong?" then: "Monson! *Monson!*" Clutching the portfolio he jerks his wild glare upward toward his window, then back to the landlady, who looks at him in astonishment. "Keep them there!" he shouts at her with savage ferocity. "Do you hear? Keep them there! Dont let them get away. In a minute I will—" But already he has turned, running toward the opposite side of the court. Still galloping, the portfolio under his arm, he rushes up the dark stairs while somewhere in his desperate mind thinking goes quietly *There will be somebody already in it. I know there will* thinking with desperate despair that he is to lose Myrtle twice because of his body: once because of his back which would not let him dance, and now because of his bowels which will give her to think that he is running away. But the cabinet is empty; his very sigh of relief is the echo of his downwardsighing trousers about his legs, thinking Thank God. Thank God. Myrtle. *Myrtle.* Then this too flees; he seems to see his life supine before the secret implacable eyeless life of his own entrails like an immolation, saying like Samuel of old: Here I am. Here I am. Then they release him. He wakes again and reaches his hand toward the niche where scraps of newspaper are kept and he becomes utterly immobile while time seems to rush past him with a sound almost like that of a shell.

He whirls; he looks at the empty niche, surrounded by the derisive whistling of that dark wind as though it were the wind which had blown the niche empty. He does not laugh; his bowels too have emptied themselves for haste. He claps his hand to his breast pocket; he becomes immobile again with his arm crossing his breast as though in salute; then with a dreadful urgency he searches through all his pockets, producing two broken bits of crayon, a dollar watch, a few coins, his room key, the tobacco tin (worn silver smooth now) containing the needles and thread and such which the cook had given him ten years ago in Canada. That is all. And so his hands cease. Imbued for the moment with a furious life and need of their own, they die; and he sits for a moment looking quietly at the portfolio on the floor beside him; again, as when he watched them fondle the handgrenade on board the transport in 1916, he watches them take up the portfolio and open it and take out the picture. But only for the moment, because again haste descends upon him and he no longer watches his hands at all, thinking Myrtle. Myrtle. *Myrtle.*

And now the hour, the moment, has come. Within the Garden, beyond the dusk and the slow gateward throng, the hidden bugle begins. Out of the secret dusk the grave brazen notes come, over-taking the people, passing the caped policemen at the gates, and about the city dying where beneath the waxing and bloodless moon evening has found itself. Yet still within the formal twilight of the trees the bugle sounds, measured, arrogant, and sad.

With Caution and Dispatch

The general, flanked by his A.D.C. and the aerodrome colonel and adjutant and a few wives and several who were not wives, stood in the windy sun and read aloud the paper whose contents they had already known since yesterday:

"... squadron on this date of blank March 1918, will depart and proceed, forthwith and under arms and with caution and dispatch, to destination known henceforth as zero."

Then he folded the paper away and looked at them—the three flight-commanders at attention, behind them the Squadron—the young men gathered from the flung corners of the Empire (and including Sartoris, the Mississippian, who had not been a Briton since a hundred and forty-two years)—and behind them in turn, the line of waiting aeroplanes dull and ungleaming in the intermittent sun across which the general's voice still came, telling again the old stale tale: Waterloo and the playing fields of Eton and here a spot which is forever England. Then the voice was in actual retrograde in a long limbo filled with horses—Fontenoy and Agincourt and Crécy and the Black Prince—and Sartoris whispering to his neighbor from the side of his rigid mouth: "What nigger is that? He's talking about Jack Johnson."

But at last the general was done with that too. He faced them —an old man, a kindly man doubtless, certainly in no way as martial and splendid as the Horse Guards Captain A.D.C. all blood and steel in his red hatband and tabs and brassard and the wisps and loops of lapidary-like burnished chain at his shoulders and armpits where that old chain mail of Crécy and Agincourt had been blown off him in the long intervening years by a hard and constant wind, leaving only that wispy residuum. "Goodbye and goodluck, and give them hell," the general said. He took the flight-commanders' salute. The three flight-commanders turned. Britt, the senior, with his M.C. and his Mons Star and his D.F.C. and his Gallipoli ribbon (so that he was gaudier above the left pocket than even the Guards captain), roved his hard eyes from face to face along the Squadron and spoke as he could speak: in that voice cold and precise as a surgeon's knife, which never failed to reach any ear it was intended for and no further, certainly not back to the general:

"For gad's sake try to keep formation until we reach the Channel. At least try to look like something to the taxpayers while we are over England. If you should straggle and land behind their lines, what do you do?"

"Burn the crate," someone said.

"If you have time; it doesn't really matter. But if you crash anywhere behind our lines, in France or England either, what had you better do, by gad?" This time a dozen voices answered.

"Get the clock."

"Right," Britt said. "Let's get along."

The band was playing now, though it was soon drowned by engines. They took off in turn and climbed to a thousand feet and formed echelon of flights, Britt leading with B flight, of which Sartoris was number three. Britt paraded them back across the aerodrome in a shallow dive. They passed, quite low, to the fluttering of feminine handkerchiefs; Sartoris could see the steady rising and falling of the drummer's arm and the shifting glints of brass among the horns as if the sound they made were about to become visible and then audible. But it did not; the engines drummed again and they climbed on away toward the east and south.

It was a drowsy, hazy day of early spring. At five thousand feet greening England slid slowly beneath them, neat and quilted, the aeroplanes shifting slightly and constantly, rising and falling within their own close integration, within their own loud drone. In no time at all, it seemed to Sartoris, the flat unglinting gleam of the Channel lay before them and the cloudbank beyond it which was France; there was an aerodrome just beneath them. Then Britt was signalling. He was going to loop in formation: salute and farewell to home; naturally it would have occurred to someone to play horse for a while since there was nothing urgent in France—only a Hun break-through over the collapsed Fifth Army and General Haig with our backs to the wall and believing in the justice and sanctity of our cause. They were looping; they were over the top of the loop, upside down. There was a Camel right side up and heading directly toward Sartoris and about ten feet away; it would be one out of A flight whose position was just behind him. He had lost altitude; he had fallen out of the loop without knowing it. But he hadn't; Britt's Camel was just off his right wing, where it should have been.

He ruddered outward and pushed forward on the stick. He would stall now for sure, and he did; he was spinning, he had missed the other Camel somehow and he felt its slipstream as he passed through it. He closed the throttle and stopped the spin and slapped the throttle open again, climbing, frightened and raging. The squadron was below him now, the gap still carefully intact where he should have been between Britt and Atkinson at number five. Then Britt was pulling away, climbing too. "All right," Sartoris said. "If that's what you want." Only if Britt could have been the one which almost rammed him. He did not know who it had been; he had not had time to read the letter or number. *I was too close,* he thought, *to see anything as big as a letter or a number. I would have to look at it head-on from five inches, find the one with a twisted pin in one of the boss bolt-heads or something.* He dived at Britt, who turned sharply away. He turned too, to get onto Britt's tail. But he never got Britt into his Aldis because Britt was gone, he was too good for him; Sartoris did not even need to look back to know that Britt was now on his tail. They looped twice in one anothers' slipstream as if they were bolted together. *He was probably right on the back of my goggle-strap for a whole belt,* Sartoris thought.

The altimeter had never quite caught up with him but it said about seven thousand feet when he stalled deliberately at the top of the third loop and just before he spun he saw Britt pass him, already rolling into an Immelman turn. He spun for what he thought was about a thousand feet and dived out; with the engine full out he dived on and then zoomed terrifically, still climbing on after the Camel began to shudder and labor. Two thousand feet below him, the squadron was completing another sedate circle; either Sibleigh or Tate, the other flight commanders, had moved up into Britt's place. Five hundred feet below him Britt was circling too, looking up and jabbing violently downward with his arm. "Certainly," Sartoris said. He put his nose straight down. When he passed Britt, he was doing a hundred and sixty; when he dived across Tate's or Sibleigh's nose or whoever it was leading now, he was at terminal velocity; the engine was making a terrific racket; if the Camel just held together, he would have enough speed to zoom back two thousand feet and maybe even loop the squadron a time or two. Then his pressure gauge blew out. He came out of the dive, already working the hand-pump, but nothing happened; he switched the valve to the gravity tank but still nothing happened, the propeller merely continued to flop over in the wind of its own creation. He was less than two thousand feet now and he remembered the aerodrome which had been somewhere beneath them when Britt decided to loop and he found it, less than two miles away. But it was upwind, so in a silence containing now only the whistling of wires, he turned his back upon it. Then he heard Britt coming up behind him; he made the dud engine signal as Britt passed. Now he had found a field—an oblong of sprouting grain bounded on both sides by hedgerows, at one end a copse, at the other a low stone wall, lying right for the wind. Britt passed him again, shaking his fist. "I didn't do it," Sartoris said. "Come look at the gauge and the valve if you dont believe me." He made the last turn, upwind; he would come in over the wall. The field was all right; anyone who had had as much as forty hours on Camels could land one in it, but not even Sibleigh, who was the best Camel pilot he had ever seen, could have flown it out again. He was coming in just right, overshooting just exactly enough. He fishtailed a little, still overshooting just exactly enough to have the extra height and speed if he should need it; he cut the switch and used another feather's weight of rudder, raising the nose a hair's breadth, already beginning to get his tail down as the wall passed under him, getting the tail down a little more toward the mazy green. He was making a beautiful landing. He was making the best landing he had ever made; he was making the best dead-stick Camel landing he had ever seen. He had made it, the stick back to his stomach; he was on the ground. He was already reaching for the catch of his safety-belt when the Camel rolled into the moist depression which he had not even seen and stood slowly up on its nose. While he stood beside it, stanching the blood from his nose where one of the gun-butts had struck him, Britt roared past again, shaking his fist, and went streaking off hopping hedges toward where the aerodrome lay.

It was not as far as he had thought; he had not finished his cigarette when a motorcycle and sidecar burst through the hedge-row and came up. It contained a private and a corporal. "Shouldn't be smoking, sir," the corporal said. "Against regulations to smoke near a crash."

"This is not a crash," Sartoris said. "All I did was bust the prop."

"It's a crash, sir," the corporal said.

"Well, I'm going to get away from it," Sartoris said. "I take you both to witness: the clock was still on it when you took over."

"It's all right, sir," the corporal said. Sartoris got into the side-car. On the road they passed the lorry and crew going to dismantle the Camel and fetch it in. The private took him to the orderly office. There was a captain with a black eye-patch and a casual's blue armband, and a major wearing an observer's single wing.

"Hurt?" the major said.

"Just my nose bled a little," Sartoris said.

"What happened?"

"Pressure blew, sir."

"Did you switch to gravity?"

"Yes, sir," Sartoris said. "Your corporal's probably found the valve still over."

"Doubtless," the major said. *You could have come up there and looked at it too,* Sartoris thought. *I'd have liked to see you making that landing.* "Your people have gone on. I dont know anything for you to do but report to Pool. Do you?"

"No, sir," Sartoris said.

"Ring up Pool, Harry," the major said. The adjutant talked into the phone for a while. Then the major talked into it. Sartoris waited. He was beginning to itch a little inside his sidcot in the warm room. "They want to talk to you," the major said. Sartoris took the phone. It was a colonel's voice, maybe even a general's, though he decided at once that it knew too much what it was talking about to be a general's:

"Well? What happened?"

"Pressure blew, sir."

"I suppose you dived it right off the aeroplane," the voice said.

"Yes, sir," Sartoris said, looking out the window and scratching himself where the knitted vest beneath his shirt was really beginning to itch.

"What?" the voice said.

"Sir?"

"I asked you if you dived deliberately until you lost your pres—"

"Oh. No, sir. I thought you asked if I had switched to gravity."

"Of course you switched to gravity!" the voice said. "I never yet knew a pilot with a dud engine who ever failed to do everything, including standing on the wing and cranking his own propeller. Report to your aerodrome tonight. Then in the morning you will go to Brooklands. They will have another Camel for you. Take it and proceed—" *with caution and dispatch,* Sartoris thought. But the voice did not say that. It said, "—without blowing any more pressure gauges until you overtake your squadron. Do you think you can find it?"

"I can ask along," Sartoris said.

"You can what?" But that was all right; the connection was broken by then, and if Sartoris knew military telephone systems, that particular number could not possibly come up again for at least thirty minutes, by which time he should be well on his way back to London.

This was by way of the daily leave-train up from Dover—a casual among the other casuals though not yet maimed. But when he reached London, he decided not to report at the aerodrome. A casual, officially in France and corporeally in England, he therefore did not exist at all; he decided to preserve that anonymity. Even if nothing unpleasant occurred to him at the aerodrome, he knew and respected the infinite capacity and fertility, not so much of the complex military hierarchate itself, as of some idle staff-wallah waking suddenly from a doze. Certainly he would have been forced to present himself to the Transport Officer for the zone of South England and the Channel. And he could imagine that—himself who since noon yesterday had not existed in England at all, despite the fact that he still occupied space, projected suddenly among the orderly hum of clerks and N.C.O.'s and subalterns and at last captains who not only had never heard of him, they would not want to; would merely be exasperated at this interruption of the busy peaceful forms to be countersigned; would merely be enraged by his patient and passive need.

So he left his flying gear at the Royal Automobile Club and, alien and unattached and almost obfuscate, he stood at the curb-edge of that London, that England in that spring of 1918—the women, the soldiers, the women, the Waacs, the V.A.D.'s, the women in the uniforms of bus- and tram-conductors and in the no-uniform of the old trade, the old dishonored one which always flourishes in war-time since the quick-wived know that death will probably cuckold them anyhow—the posters: ENGLAND EXPECTS; the placards: BEAT THE BOCHE WITH BOVRIL; the bulletins: LINES HOLDING BEFORE AMIENS, OLD SOMME BATTLE-FIELDS—and moved among them, the foreigner come out of curiosity to chance his life in the old-men's wars, not even aware that he was watching the laboring heart of a nation in one of its blackest hours.

When he reached Brooklands the next morning, it was raining. The Camel was ready, though the guns were not mounted. Also, they tried with logic and reason to dissuade him. "It'll be filthy over the Channel. You're a casual; why dont you wash yourself out, go back to town until tomorrow?"

But he would not. "I'm already a day late, besides washing out that aeroplane yesterday. Britt was cross-eyed then. He'll be fit to be tied if I'm not there by lunchtime." They had maps all ready for him, with his course plotted to the Squadron (it was just south of Amiens) and intermediate aerodromes where he could refuel. He had no requisition for the Camel either, but he had known that here he would be dealing with people who were anything in the world except professional soldiers—either actual flying people or people who, despite the last three and a half years, were still by inclination and thought and behavior civilians and so were interested only in getting on with the war. So they let him sign the receipt for the aeroplane and started him up. Just as he opened the throttle he thought he heard someone shouting, but he was already moving then so he went on and took off. When he could look back at the field again, he saw that they were waving at him, and when he made another circle, they had unrolled a groundstrip with the symbol to land. But if anything was wrong with the aeroplane, they would not have needed to run out a groundstrip to get him back down, and if it was something like a wheel missing so that he would have to crash to land, he might as well do that in France as here. Besides, there was nothing wrong with the Camel; he rocked it and horsed it about a little; it was a good Camel, only it was a little too light in the tail for him (They always were, as the factory or anybody else rigged them; he liked an aeroplane that, once the slightest pressure was removed from the stick, went upstairs like an express elevator. But that could be remedied at the Squadron.) and it handled like a feather; he came down onto the race track and ran his wheels the whole length of the back-stretch and, with the help of the crosswind which obtained at that point, made the three-quarters turn, skidding only a little and this only because of the mud, before he had to take off again to keep from hitting the outside rail.

He climbed to a thousand feet and got onto his course. The nimbus was there; he stayed just under it, passing from one rain-patch to the next. It never became severe, though it never let up either, so that, once the compass settled down and he had fiddled with the fine adjustment until he got the engine to running right he got his head well down into the office below the windscreen, out of the rain. But presently the rain really began to come down. He could see off to his left the flat gleam where the Thames estuary began to open; he was off-course, too far east, so he corrected for it and flew on, whereupon suddenly and without warning he flew full tilt into wet invisibility. He put his nose down; the movement originated not in his brain but in his hand. The aeroplane had disappeared; there was only the edge of the windscreen, the instrument panel, the rim of the cockpit. The compass was jerking back and forth. When he tried to steady it, it began to oscillate violently for ninety degrees or more, and although the throttle was full out, the air speed was dropping. For a second all pressure went completely off the stick and a terrific vibration set up; the brute was about to spin and he had less than a thousand feet.

He burst out beneath the cloud, into fleeing patches of scud and driving rain. When he breathed again and his heart was once more back where it belonged, he was flying due east at a hundred and forty miles an hour, less than five hundred feet above the scudding and streaming earth. When he got the spinning compass stopped at last and was back on course, there was neither glint nor gleam of water in front of him. Instead, he saw the fixed and steadfast rim of England annealed into a solid wall of eastward-slanting rain. There was a town beneath him; it could have been either Dover or Folkestone. There was a lighthouse on a headland; it could have been anywhere between the Lizard and the Downs for all he knew. There would be coast defense aerodromes along here, but if he landed at one of them he would once more relinquish without recourse and succumb without hope to the rigid brazen oakleaves and the iron scarlet tabs the instant his wheels touched the ground. And he was all right now; he could see for almost a mile and all he needed to do was to stay out of the clouds and as long as rain continued to fall out of them, they would remain at least five hundred feet up, propped by the myriad spears of rain itself.

So he didn't even look for an aerodrome. With the twelve on his compass-spool rigidly bisected by the lubber's line, he sped over the escarpment, the granite bastion of the land, and at a hundred and twenty miles an hour he let down to about fifty feet above the water and got his head back down beneath the windscreen out of the rain. The Channel was twenty-six miles at its narrowest point; even if he happened to be exactly there, which was not probable, he would have at least ten minutes before he would need to worry about the opposite cliff or however else France began. So he went on, his head well down in the office, one eye on his watch and the other watching the water between his left shoulder and the cockpit rim to hold his altitude and his course by the direction in which the chop was moving, when—it had not been six minutes; he was only halfway across—the air, the rain, roared with a tremendous bellowing. It was not in front of him, it was everywhere: above, beneath, inside of him; he was breathing it, he was flying in it as he had been breathing and flying in the air. He looked up. Directly in front of him and apparently about twenty-five feet away, was a tremendous Brazilian flag. It was painted on the side of a ship which looked as long as a city block and rose taller than any cliff. *I've already crashed,* he thought. He did three things as one: he slapped the throttle full on and snatched the stick back and shut his eyes; the Camel went up the side of the ship like a hawk, a gull up a cliff-face. *Why dont I crash?* he thought. He opened his eyes. The Camel was hanging on its propeller, no longer moving. Opposite it, the mast of the ship ended in a canvas-hooded crowsnest out of which two faces, rigid with soundless yelling, glared at him; later he remembered how even at that moment he thought, *They aint Spick faces; they are English faces.* But there was no movement; actually the two of them, the aeroplane and the crowsnest, hung as solitary and peaceful in the rainfilled nothingness as two last year's birdnests. *I've got my prop and wheels up over it,* Sartoris thought. *Now if I can just get my tail over.* Only, if he tried to use his rudder, he would stall and spin. *But I have already stalled,* he thought. So he crossed the controls, he rammed one wing down and stamped the opposite rudder against the firewall. Then he was over; the crowsnest fled upward and away. The wing of the bridge shot past; there was a yelling and soundless English face on it too. There was a lifeboat in davits; he passed either above it or between it and the ship, he did not know which, though he had struck nothing yet. Then he knew that he had passed beneath a funnel-stay. He was travelling sideways down the after well-deck; there was a ventilator riding now in the angle between his wings and the aeroplane's body though still he had felt no shock, and two seamen were running madly toward a door in the break of the poop. He cut the switch. *If I dont crash quick I'm going to run out of ship and be in the ocean,* he thought. The second man hurled himself through the door, leaving it open behind him. Sartoris realised that the Camel apparently intended to follow him. Anyway, he had two gun-butts to have to try to dodge this time. And suppose they had given him a night-flying Camel with wing-flares on it. Or just suppose it had had bombs.

When the racket of banging metal and tearing cloth and snapping sticks ceased, Sartoris, his nose bleeding again, was sitting on the deck beside a jagged hole (that ventilator had vanished completely; he had never seen it) from which a waft of hot oil came, and the quiet panting of engines. Then a harsh, embittered Liverpool-trawler voice said:

"Now yer for it. Dont you know you can be clinked for duration for landing in neutral territory?"

2

He was standing beside the Liverpool boatswain, leaning his flowing blood away from himself and groping for the knee-pocket of his sidcot where he had wadded the handkerchief yesterday, while another strong and enraged voice roared through a megaphone from the bridge: "Get it off the ship! Heave it overboard! Jump!" A second calmer voice said reasonably:

"It will float."

"Let it! Get it off this ship! Break out axes and chop it up and heave it overboard!"

"Here," Sartoris said, "I've got to get the clock."

"And get that man below!" the megaphone roared. "Knock him in the head if you have to!" Now there was a second man at his other elbow. Then he was moving rapidly toward the door in the poop which the Camel had tried to enter.

"Wait," he said. "I've got to get that clock——" Then he was passing through the door. Already he could hear behind him the sound of axes; looking back, he saw two men running toward the rail with the Camel's entire tail-group.

He was being rushed through a long corridor lit at the far end by a single wan bulb. The deck felt not only cold but greasy; that was when he discovered that he was carrying his right flying-boot, still buckled, in his hand and that both the woolen sock and the silk one he had worn beneath it were gone. The men stopped, halting him; the boatswain opened a door. Beyond it was a room lit by another wan and dingy bulb; he remembered enough of the cattleboat in which he had come to Europe a year ago to enlist to recognise it as the third mate's or the third engineer's room. "Here," he said. "Look here——" A hand came into his back. Almost impersonal, it shot him inward. He tripped over the sill and caught balance and turned as the door slammed in his face. He heard the bolt shoot home as he grasped the knob. "Dammit, I'm a Flying Corps officer," he said. "You cant——" Only he must be a little hysterical still, shouting against a locked door that they couldn't do something they had already done. But they would have to back him up that he had tried to get the clock.

He bathed his nose gingerly at the washstand. There was no mirror, but he could feel it; if he crashed another one, he would need a periscope merely to walk around with. Then he took off the other flying-boot and changed the woolen sock to his left foot, so that he now had a sock on each foot, and put on the boots and went and lay or the bunk, listening to the faint shudder and pulse of the engines and watching the faint swinging of the garments from the bulkhead hooks, among which no sleeve bore any stripe, no button any insigne.

Now Britt would be fit to be tied. He would have to go back to Brooklands and get another Camel. That meant he couldn't possibly hope to reach the Squadron until tomorrow. The watch inside his right wrist still ticked, but the guard and crystal and all three of the hands were gone, vanished into that bizarre limbo of crashes where shoes and socks and luck tokens and goggles and sometimes even ties and braces disappeared; he didn't know what time it was. But it had been four minutes past twelve a second before he looked ıp and saw the painted flag in front of him, and even if he should reach Brooklands in time to leave this afternoon, they probably wouldn't let him have another Camel without an official order. That meant he would not only have to spend the rest of the afternoon signing bumf as to what had become of the present one, he would have to explain how he had got hold of it to begin with without following authorised procedure. If he reached shore tonight, reached England again at all even. He had not recognised the flag he had almost flown through, except there was too much yellow and green in it to belong out of South America, yet the men who had hauled him out of the crash and flung him in here without even pausing to see if he were hurt or not, had been English. There was apparently skulduggery of some sort here; the ship might be going anywhere—Scandinavia or Russia even. There was a porthole just over the bunk, the glass painted heavily with black paint behind a heavy metal grating. If he only had a screwdriver or an icepick or something long enough to reach and break the glass, he would probably see land. It would be France (not that it would do him any good; even if the ship would stop and put him ashore in France, the best he could hope for would be to reach the Squadron sometime after dark, walking); the ship was going east and he had crashed on the right side of it, the Camel boring its willful and invincible head to start a right-hand spin and he was still on the right side of it. He even knew how the land would look, rising at long last out of the heaving desolation of the ocean as he had seen it after fifteen days in the cattleboat—a tall and sudden loom of mist-swathed perpendicularity out of a lateral and unstable waste above the green and crashing seas at dawn which a relieving look-out, passing him at the midships rail, had told him was Bishop's Rock. . . .

Ten hours later he waked blinking into the fierce eye of an electric torch. The dim ceiling bulb was out; the garments now hung motionless among their shifting shadows as the torch moved. This time the two men wheeled up to flank him with such wooden and interlocked precision that he needed neither the white gaiters nor the rifles to tell him they were marines. "Nah then, Kitchener," a voice beyond the torch said, and he recognised that too—the composite voice of the Chief Warrant Officer within three or four years of honorable retirement, whose only superior in uniform or out of it was that one of equal age and rank in the battle fleet flagship. "Who's in charge of this party?" Sartoris said. "I'm an officer. If I'm under arrest, it must be—"

"Hup," the voice beyond the torch said. They tramped back up the dim corridor empty now of any shudder and murmur of motion. They wheeled. The torch went off behind him and they wheeled again. Then he was in a hard black wind, rainless now and much colder, beneath a low driving scud. Then he began to see a little; it was the deck where he had crashed. Three shadows waited.

"Right, Bos'un?" a new voice said, an officer's voice this time.

"Right, sir," the voice of the torch said. Then Sartoris could see the shape and angle of the officer's cap.

"Look here," he said.

"Right, then," the new voice said. They crossed the deck. There was a rope ladder beyond the rail; it might have descended the black and eyeless iron flank into the North Sea itself. But something containing human life surged toward him and sank away and surged up beneath him again; hands touched him, a voice said, "Let go," and he was in the longboat. He was in something, sitting on a thwart between his two marines, among the shadowy unison of oars, aware of the strong running of the black sea, the black depths of the strong sea, a thin plank's thickness away. Then there was another ladder, another black iron flank, after the first one so shallow seemingly that he might have stood up in the boat and caught the gunwale. But it was taller than that. Then he was on another lightless and cluttered deck. There was a shape which he did not know yet was a torpedo tube, a canted muzzle which he did know was an archie gun, and four raked funnels out of all proportion to the hull they rose from, which, as he walked on it, surged into violent motion. It heeled; it seemed to squat and then rush with a roar of water into full speed as aeroplanes themselves did not do.

He saw that speed once. He was following the officer. They were climbing; abruptly the hard black wind leaned at him; there was a motionless shape bulky in garments, with a binocular, then across the canvas bridge screen he saw the narrow and driving bows between two boiling and tremendous wings of white water. Then the wind was gone. He sidled past a dim light in which the spokes of a mahogany wheel shifted slightly. A door closed behind him and beyond a table on which a chart was spread beneath a down-ward-hooded light, he presently distinguished a man in a leather jacket looking at him. The man said nothing at all. He just sat behind the table, looking at Sartoris, then, without moving whatever, he stopped. "This way," the officer said. Then they were dodging along a cramped passage humming with that speed and narrow as a bright-lit tomb.

"What was that for?" Sartoris said.

"Nothing," the officer said. "He just wanted to look at you." The wardroom was oblong, steel-painted. It contained a long table and little else. When they entered, the boatswain said, "hup!" and the two marines came to attention and once more fell in on either side of him with that metronome-like precision. Now there were six midshipmen coming to attention in their simple and unrelieved blue, resembling any six boys out of any high school team back home in America; resembling six elected out of a nation's junior entirety by some standard of incredible excellence. "Dammit," the officer said, "I told you to beggar off." They went out, dissolved, vanished. The officer unbuttoned his peacoat and muffler. His face was perhaps thirty, blunt and quite cold. One whole side of it was covered by a puckered, sheet-lightning scar. Then Sartoris saw beneath the peacoat, unrelieved by any other ribbon and so near the same color as the tunic as to be almost indistinguishable, the ribbon of the Victoria Cross. "What do you call yourself?" the officer said.

"Second Lieutenant, Flying Corps," Sartoris said. "See?" He opened his sidcot until his wings were exposed. The other glanced at them for a moment absolutely without interest.

"That's not hard to come by," he said.

"Not hard?" Sartoris said. "It took me eight months. I never heard of anybody doing it much quicker."

"Why were you on that ship?"

"I crashed on it."

"I know. Why?"

"I didn't see it. I had my head down inside out of the rain. When he blew the whistle at me, I just had time to pull straight up. I stalled. Did they expect me to go into the water?"

"Cant say," the other said. "Where were you going?"

"Trying to catch up with my squadron," Sartoris said. "Where would I be going out there where that ship was?"

"Cant say," the other said. "Have you had anything to eat?"

"Not since breakfast."

"Have the steward get him what there is," the officer said.

"Hup," the boatswain said.

The new room was even smaller than the one in the other ship; the marine standing just inside the door, his rifle at order arms and his head within four inches of the ceiling, seemed to fill it, dwarf it to the proportions of a child's doll-house. For just a moment it resembled the other. There was the built-in bunk, but with clean blankets, and the washstand. But there was not even a black-painted port; the walls were unbroken, and he had re-entered not only the sound of the speed but of the water too. It seemed to him that he could have laid his hand against the wall and felt the steel shell trembling to the long and constant roar of flying water just outside of it.

The steward entered, with a mug of strong hot bitter tea and some cold meat and bread. He ate and then he wanted a cigarette, but they had been in the same knee-pocket where he had wadded the bloody handkerchief yesterday; they were gone too. So he lay on the clean bunk beneath the single bright bulb, within two feet of the lock of the sentry's rifle, listening to the seethe and roar of water just beyond the steel wall, until after a while it seemed to him that the intact fragility of the shell depended upon its speed alone for intactness as aeroplanes did and that if it ever slowed, it would be crushed inward by the very weight of water in which it would come to rest. He didn't know where he was going. He had thought he did yesterday, and he had been wrong. But he had never heard of a destroyer up the Thames as far as London. And he had slept at least ten hours yesterday before the flashlight waked him. So he must have been well up the North Sea by then, and he tried to remember some East Coast ports but he could not. Besides, they were probably somewhere up about the Firth of Forth anyway; maybe that's where they were going. Which meant that he probably wouldn't get back to Brooklands to get another Camel until the day after tomorrow; when he reached the Squadron now, Britt would probably have him shot. *V.C.,* he thought, feeling the roaring drive of the hull. But you had to be British-born to get that, or Britt's M.C. either, which in his opinion was next. *But I'm going to get something,* he thought. He was. He was going to get it on the coming fifth of July. But he would have only to have been born at all to get what he was going to get. *Maybe I can shoot dice with somebody for a spare iron cross,* he thought.

This time he was being shaken awake. It was a first lieutenant with the Provost Marshal's brassard. The vessel was still now; there was no seethe and roar of water, and when he crossed the deck between two armed land military police, there was no longboat, no black ocean. Instead, the vessel lay alongside a stone quay and there was a harbor beneath the beginning of dawn, and a dark encircling city. But it was not London. "It's not London," he said.

"Hardly," the lieutenant said. So he was somewhere in the Firth of Forth, as he had anticipated. Maybe Edinburgh, since it seemed to be a city—if Edinburgh came down to the water. Then he might reach London tonight. Then he could spend tomorrow explaining about the old Camel and getting a new one. He might reach the Squadron the day after tomorrow. There was a sentry at the end of the pier. A warrant officer-of-the-guard had to be turned out before they could pass—why, Sartoris didn't know, since the lieutenant and his two men must have passed him once already, and all any of them could possibly want would be for them to pass and get on. But even in just two days he had forgotten the land, forgotten the old stale smell of base-colonel's hat. But maybe in two days he would be in France; Britt and Tate and Sibleigh all said that when you got really close to the war, you were free of it.

Then they were in a car among the dark and empty streets; presently they turned into a courtyard where other cars and motorcycle couriers came and went before a big house with lights in it. It may not have been just what he had expected of an Edinburgh courtyard, but it was no railway station, not even a Scottish one, and he had been to Turnberry and Ayr. Then he found that he had expected that too; he was inside, in a tremendous orderly room full of couriers and messengers and corporal clerks and telephonists, busy, peaceful, and reeking with the olden invincible stink; he might have been trying to find someone to give him another aeroplane for all the attention which was paid him. "Listen," he said. "I'm—" It seemed like a week; it was incredible that the Squadron had left for France only two days ago. "—two days behind my squadron now. Maybe you'd better telephone—" he named the colonel at the aerodrome from which the Squadron had departed.

"They will attend to that," the lieutenant said.

"Who will?" Sartoris said.

"They will," the lieutenant said. "If they want him."

In comparison to the other two, his new room looked like a flying field. He lay on that iron cot too, taking his helmet off—he had pushed his goggles back over his head just before he cut the Camel's switch; they were all right—since he would be here some time, waiting until they should send for him; he wished now that he hadn't slept so much since noon yesterday. After a while they brought him breakfast. It was a good enough breakfast, but it stank too of the old curse of the Sam Browne belt married to the typewriter, and since he was in Scotland now, he could have done with a native breakfast; they could even keep the food. Well, he would probably even get that drink in about two days when he got to France. So he lay on the cot while the handless watch inside his right wrist ticked and ticked. Now I've *been here two hours,* he thought. *Now I've been here four hours,* he thought. Then he had been there six hours, because a corporal finally came to the door and gave him a cigarette and told him it was twelve minutes to eleven oclock. So he quit waiting, because they would never send for him. He would never get to France. He had tried once, and he was in Scotland. Next time he would be somewhere in the Baltic countries or Scandinavia, the third time it would be Russia or Iceland. He would become a legend in all the allied armed forces; he saw himself an old man, wild-faced and with a long white beard, scrabbling up the cliff somewhere between Brest and Ostend fifty or sixty years from now, piping the number of a disbanded and forgotten squadron, crying, "Where's the war? Where is it? Where is it?" . . . The sentry and the same lieutenant were at the door. Sartoris rose from the cot.

"Are they ready for me?" he said.

"Yes," the lieutenant said. Sartoris came toward the door. "Dont you want your hat?" the lieutenant said.

"Wont I be coming back here?" Sartoris said.

"I dont know. Do you want to?" So Sartoris went back and got his helmet. Then the three of them were in a long corridor. Then Sartoris and the lieutenant were mounting stairs. There was another corridor where the couriers came and went. Then the lieutenant was gone, and another man was standing against the light, looking at him. It was Britt.

"What are you doing in Scotland?" Sartoris said.

"Gad's teeth," Britt said. "Put on your bloody hat and come along out of here."

3

"I'm in France," Sartoris said. They were in the courtyard where the motorcycles of the couriers rushed and popped; there was a flight-commanderish looking car and a motorcycle sidecar with an Ak Emma driver waiting.

"You're in France," Britt said. "The name of this place is Boulogne. How old are you?"

"I'll be twenty-one next month," Sartoris said. "If I can stay out of jail that long."

"You really ought to write your memoirs. If you wait until you are thirty, so much will have happened to you that you cant remember it. You pick out the one ship in all European waters probably that really doesn't want anyone to look at it, and you land an aeroplane on it—"

"They were not Spicks," Sartoris said. "That was a Spick flag of some sort, but they were English. They hauled me out of that Camel without even stopping to see if I was hurt or not and threw me—"

"And just who commissioned you to go scouring up and down the Channel examining ships?"

"But there was something funny—'

"Certainly there was," Britt said. "That's why they locked you up so quickly and called for someone to come get you. Very likely they thought you were a hun spy—or worse still, from the Hague. But anyway, that ship is not your business; it's theirs—the war-wallahs in London or wherever. You are not even supposed to have seen any ship at all; I promised that in your name. There's a lot goes on in this war, and the others too I suppose, that subalterns and captains too are not supposed to see."

"All right," Sartoris said. "Then what did I do?"

"Then you were taken off it by a destroyer. Not just any ordinary boat; one of his Majesty's ships of war—just because it wasn't a first class battleship doesn't signify—is detached from submarine patrol three hundred miles away and sent under forced draught at night to intercept you and take you aboard like you had been the first sea lord himself, and bring you back. Dont you think that's worth going into the book?"

"It's not worth being arrested for." Now Britt was looking at him. He looked up and met Britt's cold eyes.

"That's not what you were arrested for." They looked at one another. "You were posted out to a squadron three days ago. You haven't got there yet."

After a moment Sartoris said, "So they thought I was afraid. You thought I was too."

"What would you have thought? You are posted to France for the first time. You depart but you dont even get to the Channel. You pull out of formation for no reason—"

"There was somebody out of A flight right in front of me in that loop! I was close enough on him to see a bent pin in his hub!"

"—for no reason and climb up to eight thousand feet and dive the pressure right off and then with a half-mile aerodrome not a mile away, you stand on your nose in a bit of grain that even Sibleigh couldn't have flown a Camel out of. And then you disappear. You are ordered to report at a certain place. You dont report there. You aren't heard of again until the next day, when you suddenly appear at Brooklands, where they have been ordered to have an aeroplane ready for you. They let you have it, though you have no authority to get it yet; you take off just before the message arrives to hold you. They signal you to land but you ignore it. Then you and the aeroplane disappear. You have departed ostensibly for your squadron in France; you should reach it in an hour and a half at the outside. But you dont. You vanish, until sometime that afternoon the master of that ship wirelesses frantically that you have apparently crashed deliberately on what you doubtless thought was a neutral vessel—which automatically means internment for duration, as you certainly knew."

"I never saw it," Sartoris said. "I just had time to pull up and stall. It was either the ship or the water. I—"

"It's all right now," Britt said. "I know better now, because no man is going to try deliberately to land a Camel on a sixty-foot steel deck in the middle of the Channel. All that's forgotten now. You never saw any ship; no one need know where you were; you just crashed, and this morning you reached Boulogne and I met you."

"What do you want me to do now?"

"The tender is for you. It will take you to Candas. Atkinson will meet you there, to show you the way back to the Squadron. You and he are to get two new Camels. The one you have will be yours. So right side up this time, what?"

"Dont bother," Sartoris said. He got into the sidecar. He could have seen something of France, at least of the back areas of war. *So they thought I was afraid,* he thought. Atkinson was waiting at the aircraft park.

"Where have you—" he said.

"Never mind about that too," Sartoris said. The Camels were ready too. Atkinson blinked at him.

"They are keeping lunch for us," he said. "Come along."

"I dont want any. You go on and eat." *So they thought I was afraid,* he thought. Atkinson blinked at him.

"Then I shant either," he said. "We can get something in the mess." The mechanics started them up and they took off. It seemed as though he hadn't even seen an aeroplane in a month. But he hadn't forgotten it. He would never forget how to fly—even if he was afraid. He took off in a fierce climbing turn. This one was even lighter in the tail than the one at Brooklands and it pulled even better; he was upstairs before Atkinson was off the ground almost. He came around and overtook Atkinson and rammed his wing in between Atkinson's wing and tailgroup, whereupon Atkinson's head jerked around, shaped with alarmed yelling. Atkinson waved him frantically off and slipped away at last, whereupon Sartoris pulled up and climbed and came at Atkinson from behind now, seeing Atkinson's alarmed face jerking back toward him first over one shoulder then over the other; he dogfought Atkinson for a while, chivvied him that is, since all Atkinson would do was to wave him off with that frantic rage, diving at him, zooming away, diving, going all out until he had pulled ahead enough to turn and come at Atkinson headon, until this time when he came up and set his wing into the notch between Atkinson's wing and tailgroup, Atkinson did nothing save shake his fist at him. But his head kept on jerking around to watch Sartoris' wingtip until presently Sartoris saw that Atkinson was flying gradually off to the right and soon they would be headed toward where Paris ought to be. Besides, he was having trouble holding his Camel back; it didn't want to stay there; when he throttled back slow enough, vibration got so bad he couldn't even read his compass.

So he pulled away and smoothed out his engine, whereupon at once he began to draw ahead of Atkinson. But he knew about where the aerodrome was, and Atkinson watched him draw away without showing any concern. So he must be going in the right direction. He could find some aerodrome anyway; the wrong one wouldn't matter since a frightened person is really not responsible. And sure enough, there was something which must be the church at Amiens standing up out of the plain; he saw the multiple spring-branch beginnings of the Somme and then the incredibly straight road which went to Roye. Then he saw the aerodrome; it was an aerodrome all right because there was the railroad right beside it. He looked back. Atkinson was coming sedately along three or four miles back, so it must even be the right aerodrome, and when he saw the train moving along at full speed beside the aerodrome a good deal faster than a man could walk, he knew it was. There really should be a telephone line along the track, though the train would probably be enough since he would either have to land cross-wind or come in over the train since he would run out of petrol if he sat upstairs and waited for it to finish passing, as a Camel only flew three hours by using the gravity tank when the other went dry. Only he was afraid; he couldn't seem either to keep on remembering that or forgetting that or something; he would be afraid of trains too maybe; certainly he was afraid of France and so he couldn't be expected to land on it: he would naturally be expected to land on the tarmac in front of the mess door. So he came along full-out and cross-wind about ten feet above the moving train as though he were going to land on it and then banked into the wind until he was going straight toward the mess and when he believed he had just enough speed to roll him up in front of the mess he shut off and let the Camel settle. He had a little too much speed, if anything, but then he intended to make one of those side-slipping Sibleigh landings where when you started it you had to go on and make it because it was too late then to change your mind, so he slipped until he was exactly right for his roll and straightened out, getting his tail down, getting it down a little more; only in the split second before hand, he knew he hadn't got it down enough. He bounced. The mess looked closer than the ship had looked, though not as large. But he would have to get over it. He slapped at the throttle. But instead of the throttle, his hand struck the mixing-valve. The engine popped and died. The Camel bounced again and went over on its back.

He was farther from the mess than it had seemed; the people watching him in front of it no longer seemed to be standing on his lower wing. It was quite a big field; he seemed to walk for a good while, leaning the flow of his bleeding nose away from himself (he still had no handkerchief) until he reached them. An orderly almost met him at the door with the damp towel. Britt watched him. "Feel all right now?" Britt said.

"It was just my nose," Sartoris said. "You would think it would have got used to crashing by this time."

"It's young yet," Britt said. "Give it time.—Look here," he said. "We aren't together somehow. I dont believe you quite have the right point of view about this. It cost the government the equivalent of three enemy aircraft to train you and get you out here. And now you have washed out three of ours before you have seen the front lines. Dont you see? you will have to shoot down six huns before you can even start counting." The orderly came up with something else. It was a pair of goggles. Then Sartoris discovered that this time only the rims of his own sat on his forehead. Britt took the goggles from the orderly and handed them to him.

"What's this for?" he said.

"They're goggles," Britt said. "You fly with them. You are going to Candas to get a Camel. And look. Get back and crash this one before tea if you can." Sartoris took the goggles.

"Wont dinner do?" he said. "This one may burn. It would be prettier after dark."

"No; tea," Britt said. "General Ludendorff should be here by then with your iron cross. He's only over beyond Amiens now."

Snow

❧

"Father," the child said, "what was Europe like before all the people in it began to hate and fear Germans?"

The man didn't answer. He sat behind the opened newspaper so that all visible of him were his hands in their braided khaki sleeves and his legs in pale cuffless gabardine and his feet in strapped military shoes. On the Sunday of Pearl Harbor he was an architect, successful, a husband and father, in his late thirties. On the next day he dug up the old records of the military school of his youth and now he was a subaltern of engineers, at home with three days' leave between his refresher-course and active duty, where, he did not yet know.

He didn't answer the child. The paper didn't even rattle while he looked at what was not even a column head on that inside page but just a caption: *Nazi Governor of Czodnia Slain by Companion*, and below the caption, the two blurred telephoto pictures: the cold, satiated, handsome Prussian face which he had never seen and would not see now and did not want to, and the woman's face which he had seen once and did not want ever to see again either —a face a little older than when he had seen it fifteen years ago and no longer a peasant's face now, anything but a peasant's now that the mountains and the quiet valley which had bred it had been blotted forever from it by the four or five years' triumphal pageantry of power and destruction and human suffering and blood, and below the two faces, the three lines of type enclosed in a neat box like an obituary: *It is reported from Belgrade that the German Governor of Czodnia, General von Ploeckner, was stabbed to death last week by the Frenchwoman who had been his companion for several years.*

"Except she wasn't French," the man said. "She was Swiss."

"What, Father?" the child said. "What did you say?"

When we came around the mountain's shoulder, we could see the sun again. Beyond the curving rampart of dirty snow the plows had thrown up, the whole valley lay full of sun beneath us—a tranquil and silent golden wash as still as a millpond, holding in suspension the violet-shadowed snow of the valley floor and touching in the last slow fading moment of day's withdrawal the steeple of the church and the taller chimneys and the flanks of the mountains themselves as they boomed, rushed upward in soundless rigidity of rock, to the rose and saffron and lilac of the high snows which would never melt although in the valley it was spring and in Paris the chestnuts would be already in bloom.

Then we saw the funeral. Don had stopped at the dirty tumbled parapet and was looking down into the valley through the glass, the half-Zeiss, which he had bought for fifty lire in the Milan pawnshop. It had only one lens but as Don said it cost only two dollars and forty-something cents and a Zeiss without any lenses at all would be worth that; a Zeiss autograph on two tomato cans would be worth that. But in its day it must have been the best glass Zeiss ever made because now, during the time you could bear to look through it at all, without the other eye to brace against you could feel your eyeball being pulled out of your skull like a steel marble to a magnet. But we soon learned to turn the glass over every few seconds and divide the strain, as Don was doing now as he stood spraddled against the dirty parapet like a ship's officer behind his bridge dodger. He was from California. He was about the shape of a grain elevator and almost as big. "I love snow," he said, turning the glass. "At home we never have it except in Hollywood. When we leave Switzerland tomorrow I'm going to fill the other side of the glass with it to remember you by."

"A little snow might help that glass anyway," I said.

"Or a piece of beefsteak," he said.

Then I noticed that he hadn't turned the glass in five or six and then eight and then ten seconds; I could feel my eyeball too being drawn to that unendurable moment just before the burst and spring of the blind annealing water. Then he lowered the glass and turned his head and his streaming eye, bending over a little as if his nose were bleeding while the water ran down his face. "That's a man they're carrying," he said.

"A man who're carrying?" I said. Then I had the glass and then I could actually feel it: not just the one eyeball drawing out of my skull but dragging the other one behind it, around behind my nose to fill the vacated socket, and I turned the glass and then again. But I had already seen them too, crawling black and tiny across the valley floor, toward the village, their crawling shadows long across the snow before them—a dot, then two sets of dots joined together by what they carried, then one dot and then two more in single file, and the one directly behind the men who bore the body wore skirts too.

"The one in front's a priest," Don said. "Give me the glass." Then we had it in turn, but each time there was nothing behind them but the jumble of rock at the mountain's base from which they had emerged: no house nor hut from which a body could have been borne but only the jumbled base and then the soundless roar of cliff to which even ice could not cling, up and up to where the shadow of the ledge which turned its hip was as trivial as a thread. Then I also saw that the snow-furrow the crawling dots were making lay not only behind them but in front of them too. I handed the glass toward Don and mopped my face off with my handkerchief. "They went to get him and are coming back," Don said. "He fell."

"Maybe it's a path. A road."

Don took the glass and slipped the strap over his head. The pawnshop man never could find any case for it. Maybe he had already sold it to somebody else for fifty lire. "He fell," Don said. "You no like?"

"I said all right," I said. "Come on. Dont you see the sun?" Because it was gone. It had left the valley while we stood there; only the high snow held it now, lying rosy and substanceless as cloud against the sky already changing from green to violet. We went on; the road looped and switch-backed away beneath us, into dusk. There were lights in the village now, flickering and trembling as lights do across water or maybe from beneath water, and then suddenly there was no more snow. We had left it, emerged from it, whereupon it was instantaneously colder, as if there had been something of warmth in the snow's radiance but now there was nothing but the twilight and the cold. And then between two blinks the village itself had tilted onto one edge and I thought again how no square foot of this country was really level; even the villages in the valleys only looked level from above. So maybe all the earth looked flat while you were falling toward it or maybe you couldn't bear to look or maybe you couldn't help but look. "You like snow still?" I said. "Maybe we fill spyglass for now, before we run out of it."

"Maybe I no like for now," Don said. He was in front; he always went down hill faster. So he was in the valley first, the mountains ceasing as the snow had ceased and becoming the valley and almost at once the valley was the village, the road a cobbled street, mounting again, and he was there first too. "They're in the church now," he said. "Some of them are. One or two of them must be. At least one of them is." Then I saw it too: the little harsh square stone-steepled box that looked like it might have dated back to the Lombard kings, the candle-light falling out through the open door, and the people—men and women and even a child or two—gathered quietly before the door as I once saw a group waiting outside the blank wall of a little Alabama jail where a hanging was to take place. Our hobnails clashed and rang on the cobbles like the hooves of drayhorses on a hill as without even breaking stride Don slanted off toward it.

"Wait," I said. "He fell. So what? Come on. I'm hungry. Let's go eat."

"Maybe he didn't fall," Don said. "Maybe a friend pushed him. Maybe he jumped off on a bet. We came to Europe to observe customs. You never saw a funeral just like this, even in Alabama."

"All right," I said. "Suppose he—" But we were too close now; you could never tell, at least in the parts of Europe we had seen, just what language anyone spoke or just how many different ones he didn't quite speak. So we went on toward what still looked like an empty church because all the people that we could see were on the outside of it, the heads turning and watching us quietly as we came up.

"Messieurs," Don said. "Mesdames."

"Messieurs," one of them said after an instant—a little man, fiftyish and snuffy: a mail carrier if I ever saw one, just as there had been a mail carrier with his leather pouch outside the Alabama jail that day. The other faces still turned and still watched us and then watched us no more when we stopped among them where we could see into the church too—a stone cubicle not much bigger than a sentry-box in which the soft cold candle-light, washing upward and already fading about the plaster agony of the shadowy lifesize crucifix, seemed to compound again the icy chill which our leaving the snow had seemed to establish, and the candles and the coffin and the woman kneeling beside it in a hat and a fur coat that were not bought in any Swiss city either, and the priest busy at something at the back with an air exactly like that of a busy and abstracted housewife, and the other man, a peasant with the mark of the mountains on him even if he hadn't got it driving cattle back and forth to pasture at dawn and dusk, standing in a pew near the aisle halfway back. Then even as we looked into the church the priest crossed behind the coffin and paused beneath the crucifix, his robes hushed and sibilant as if the cold faint washing of the candle-light had become audible, and genuflected, curtsied almost as little girls are taught to do, and was gone, somewhere out the back or the side, and the other man came out of the pew and came up the aisle toward us. And I saw no movement, I merely felt it, but when the man reached the door and came out there were only three of us there—myself and Don and the little postman—as the man stooped and picked up an ice axe with five or six pitons strung on it and passed us without looking at us at all and was gone too. And the reason the postman was still there was because Don was holding him by the arm and I remembered how someone had told us before we left Paris that you could say anything you wanted to any European but dont put your hand on him and without doubt this one would be a servant of the State too and it would be the same as violating a gendarme or a station agent. I could not see the others at all, I could just feel them watching from the darkness while Don held the postman like a little boy caught stealing apples in front of the open door beyond which the woman in the fur coat and the Paris hat still knelt with her forehead against the coffin as if she had gone to sleep. Don's French was all right. It never always said what he thought it was, but nobody ever failed to understand him.

"That dead," he said. "He fell? He stroked himself to the foot of the mountain?"

"Yes, monsieur," the postman said.

"And the woman who grieves. The milady from Paris. His wife?"

"Yes, monsieur." The postman jerked at the arm Don held.

"I see," Don said. "A stranger. A client for the climbing. A rich French. Or perhaps an English milord who buys his wife's clothes in Paris."

Now the postman was struggling. "No! No French! No English! Of this village! Assez, monsieur! Assez donc, alors—"

But Don held him. "Not the guide who came out of the church and picked up the ice axe and the little bijoux. The other one. Who remains. The husband who is dead in the box."

But now it was too fast for me. The postman was free now and for a while even Don stood there like a silo with a hose of water or maybe of light gravel being played on it, until the postman ceased and flung up one arm and was gone too and only Don stood there blinking down at me, the half-Zeiss looking like a child's toy on his chest.

"Of this village," he said. "Her husband. And a Paris hat and I'll bet you that coat cost thirty or forty thousand francs."

"I heard that too," I said. "What was he saying when he really pulled the plug?"

"That they were both guides, the one that came out and got the ice axe, and the one in the coffin. And all three of them are of this village, the Paris hat and that fur coat too. And she and the one in the coffin are married and one day last fall all four of them climbed—"

"All four of who?" I said.

"Yes," Don said. "So would I. —climbed the mountain and you dont often hear of professional guides falling but this one managed it somehow and it was too late to get him then until the snow went away again in the spring and so the snow went away again and yesterday his wife came back and this afternoon they fetched him in so his wife can depart again but as there is no train until tomorrow morning suppose we avail ourselves of her to satisfy our curiosity or better still mind our own business and so goodnight messieurs."

"Came back from where?" I said. "Going back to where?"

"Yes," Don said. "So do I. Let's go find the inn."

It could be in but one direction since there was but one street and we were already in it. And presently we saw it, our hobnails clashing in the chill air of full night now, the chill mountain air which was like ice water. But spring was in it: that vivid newness of spring which caused the lamps in the scattered windows rising tier by invisible tier against the slopes to flicker and tremble still even as distance had made them do. The door was two steps down from the street. Don opened it and we entered the low bright warm clean room with its stove and wooden tables and benches and the woman who knitted as always in the little cage at the end of the bar and the mountain men at the bar whose faces turned as one face when we entered.

"Gruss Gott, messieurs," Don said.

"You just say that in Austria," I said.

But (again after an infinitesimal moment) a voice said, "Gruss Gott."

"No you dont," Don said. We slipped our rucksacks and sat at one of the tables. Then the woman said, knitting rapidly, her blondined and marcelled head bent over her knitting, not even looking up when she spoke:

"Messieurs?"

"Deux bieres, Madame," Don said.

"Brune ou blonde, Messieurs?"

"Blonde, Madame. And we would sleep too."

"Bon, Messieurs."

And the beer came too, blond as gold in the glass mugs manufactured like as not in Pittsburgh or Akron or Indianapolis, almost before we were done asking for it, as if, knowing we would be there sooner or later, they had had it ready for us. The waiter even wore a dinner jacket over his apron, maybe the first dinner jacket by geography outside the Peace Palace at Lausanne. He had a few rotten teeth in the face of a handsome consumptive stable-swipe and within the next ten seconds we discovered that he not only spoke better English than we did but, when he forgot to try too hard, better American too.

"Cet mort-la," Don said. "Cet homme du voisonage qui tomba—"

"So you're the ones that tried to put the lug on Papa Grignon," the waiter said.

"On who?" Don said.

"The mayor. Back there at the church."

"I thought he was the postman," I said.

The waiter didn't even glance at me. "You missed the sword and the manure-cart," he said. "You're thinking of Hollywood. This is Switzerland." He never glanced at the rucksacks either. He didn't need to. He could have spoken a paragraph or a page and said no more.

"Yes," Don said. "Walking. We like it. The man that fell."

"All right," the waiter said. "So what?"

"A guide," Don said. "With a wife in a Paris hat and a forty-thousand-franc fur coat. Who was there on the mountain with them when he fell. I may have heard of guides falling, but I never heard of one taking his wife along on a professional job, on a climb with a paying client. Because the mayor said there were four of them, and one of them was another guide—"

"All right," the waiter said. "Brix and his wife and Emil Hiller and the client. It was the day Brix and his wife had set to get married on, after the season was over last fall, after Brix had made all the jack he could while the climbing lasted and there wouldn't be anything ahead but just the winter to be married in. Only the night before the wedding Brix gets a blue from the client that the client's already in Zurich and to meet him tomorrow morning. So Brix puts the wedding off and him and Hiller meet the train and the client gets off with the eight or ten thousand francs' worth of climbing junk Brix and Hiller have helped him buy during the last five years and that afternoon they climb to the Bernardines' and the next day—"

"The bride," Don said.

"They took her with them. They held the wedding that morning, like Brix had planned. He had put it off when he got the blue until him and Hiller could climb the client to wherever he wanted to go and then bring him back and put him back on the train again but the first thing the client heard about when he got off the train was the wedding so he took charge of the wedding and—"

"Wait," Don said. "Wait."

"He had the jack," the waiter said. He hadn't moved anymore. He wasn't even wiping off the table that didn't need it as we might have expected. He just stood there. "The Big Shot. Brix and Hiller had been dragging him over the easy climbs around here for the last four or five years, between the times when he would be merging something else for another two million kroner or francs or lire. Not that he couldn't have done better. He was a little older than you but not much. He didn't want to. He climbed for a holiday, to get his picture in his hometown paper maybe. And you dont climb for a holiday. You chisel yourself the holiday and spend it and maybe the dough that should have gone on your wife's teeth too, climbing. And there was the jack, the extra jack, and Brix was probably close enough to marriage by then to have realised he wasn't going to ever see much more of what he could call spare money. So the Big Shot took charge and they held the wedding and the Big Shot himself gave away the bride and signed the register—"

"Didn't she have any people?" Don said.

"The married daughter of her mother's half-sister," the waiter said. "She lived with them but maybe everybody's half-first cousin dont marry somebody that has for his boss a man that not only has the jack but is easy with it too as long as he runs the way it is being spent. And so the Big Shot signed the register first and the priest blessed the climb too, up to the Bernardines' where the Big Shot will give the wedding supper and back home tomorrow for the Big Shot to catch his train to Milan and merge something else, because a little child could make that climb alone almost if the weather just held off. So they climbed to the Bernardines' that afternoon and the Big Shot gave the wedding supper and the next morning they are on the *glacis* where Brix hadn't intended to be except that something had gone wrong, the weather probably, they usually say it's the weather, and maybe they should have stayed holed-up at the Bernardines' but there was the Big Shot's train and everybody dont want to dedicate his life to hauling lugs up and down mountains and dont ever intend to want to, and maybe Brix should have left his wife at the Bernardines' but everybody dont want to get married either and dont ever intend to want to. Anyway the Big Shot is where Brix shouldn't have taken him, doing whatever it was that Brix and Hiller should have known he would do, and he goes off the ledge and takes Mrs Brix with him and the two of them take Brix and so there they are: Hiller anchored on the ledge with his end of the rope, and Mrs Brix and then the Big Shot and then Brix at the other end of it, dangling down the ice-face. But at least the Big Shot drops his axe in time to miss Brix with it which is lucky because it's an overhang that Brix cant reach with his axe and nobody ever pulled up three people swinging clear, at least not around here, and naturally Brix aint going to ask the guy who is paying for the trip to cut the rope just so Hiller can pull up a guide's wife that was a deadhead and never had any business there anyway. So Brix cuts between himself and the Big Shot and then Hiller pulls up two all right and the next afternoon Mrs Brix and the Big Shot left on the train and after a while the snow—"

"Wait," Don said. "The bride? the widow?"

"They waited twenty-four hours. The Big Shot laid over a full day. Hiller took them back to the Bernardines' that afternoon to come down by the road in the morning, and Hiller and one of the brothers went down the *glacis* that night to make a try for Brix. But there was too much snow so Hiller came on down to the village and got some help (the Big Shot was guaranteeing that too. He was offering a good piece of jack for finding Brix now) and when daylight came Hiller and the other boys tried to go in from the bottom. But there was too much snow and would be until it went in the spring so finally even Hiller admitted they would have to wait and so the Big Shot and Mrs Brix took the train. And after a while the snow—"

"But her people," Don said. "You said she had some people. That—"

"—daughter of her mother's half-sister and her husband. Or maybe the priest knew. He was at the station that afternoon when she and the Big Shot left. Maybe the half-first cousin and her husband were leaving it to the priest. Or maybe it was the jack again. Or maybe she just couldn't hear the priest. She didn't look much like she could hear or see either that afternoon when she got on the train."

"Nothing?" Don said. "Not anything?"

"Well, she could walk," the waiter said. "What do you want to eat? the ragout, or do you want some ham and eggs?"

"But she came back," Don said. "At least she came back."

"Sure. On the train last night. The snow began to go last month and last week Hiller wired the Big Shot he thought it was O.K. now so she got off the midnight train last night and checked her bag and sat in the station until Hiller showed up at daylight and they went out and found Brix and brought him in and if she gets cold down there at the church tonight she can always go back to the station and sit there until the train goes back tomorrow. What do you want to eat?"

"But her people," Don said. "That. . . ."

"What do you want to eat?" the waiter said.

"Maybe they're married now," Don said.

"What do you want to eat?" the waiter said.

"Maybe she loves him now," Don said.

"All right. What do you want to eat?"

"You speak United States well," Don said.

"I lived there. Chicago. Sixteen years. What do you want to eat?"

"Maybe he was good to her," Don said. "Even if he was an Italian, a foreigner—"

"He was a German," the waiter said. "We dont like Germans in this country. What do you want to eat?"

"The ragout," Don said.

So we ate the food that was good anywhere in Europe or anywhere else that French was spoken; we mounted the clean stairs to the little clean room beneath the steep pitch of the eaves and lay between the clean chill sheets which even of themselves smelled of snow. Then the sun came from beyond the opposite mountains now, slanting long in the valley and then shortening, not driving the shadow of the mountains before it but obliterating the shadow as the rising tide consumes a beach, until when we left the inn the valley was full of sun. And I thought again how even when this country was level it was level by separate steps because when we looked back from the station, the village was once more beneath us; we looked down into the true valley from what we had merely taken for the valley, standing again in snow, between the crumpled ramparts of snow which the plows had hurled up into a gutter funnelling not only the shining rails but the living light and sun too into the black orifice of the tunnel until soon the tunnel too would overflow and the mountain it pierced dissolve in fierce light.

We entered the buvette. "Gruss Gott, messieurs," Don said. Again a voice answered "Gruss Gott" and we drank the beer blond as the morning itself in the glass mugs, which back home in America to drink before noon and that only on a hot day was as unheard of as bringing a dishpan of peas with you to shell during church, yet which all through the Tyrol we had drunk for breakfast too. Then the train came and Don said, "Gruss Gott, messieurs," and again somebody answered and we went out into the bright unbearable snow-glare and walked along the train to our third-class carriage and turned and looked back and except for the snow and the sun it might have been last night again: the quiet mountain peasant faces though not so many as last night and all men now and they might have been there anyway as people in American little towns meet through trains, and the guide named Hiller who had come out of the church last night standing before the steps of a first-class carriage beside the woman with the Paris hat and the fur coat and the face which was a peasant's face too for a while yet because it would take more than just six months to efface the mountains and the valley and the village and the spring festivals on the green if there was a green and if people in Switzerland held spring festivals, and the cows driven back and forth to the high pastures and milked for the cheese and the milk chocolate or whatever it was Swiss girls did.

Then we heard the little wan frantic horns too and she took something from her purse and gave it to the man and got into the train and we got in too, the train moving, already picking up speed as it passed the man and he turned and flipped the twinkling coin, into the plow-seethed snow-bank moving faster still as it crashed into the blackness of the tunnel which after the snow was like a blow across the eyes and then crashed from blackness into fierce light like another blow, going faster and faster, lurching and swinging on the curves and crashing again from dazzle to blackness and blackness to dazzle while steadily on either hand the peaks in their pastel gradations from that unbearable radiance swung with the tremendous deliberation of ruminant celestial mastodons under the mounting morning and into the blaze of noon and through and past it and on into one last fading swoop that even we could tell was now downgrade, and it was there: the whole long slope of the *Côte d'Or,* the shelving roof-pitch of a continent slanting away into the drowsing haze where Paris was, and the last white peak slid slowly past the window and was gone.

"I'm glad of it," I said.

"Yes," Don said. "I dont want anymore snow forever. I dont want to see any snow for a long time."

"It was just the same," the man said. "The people in Europe have hated and feared Germans for so long that nobody remembers how it was."

NOTES AND
BIBLIOGRAPHY

Notes

꩜

ABBREVIATIONS:

DCPA   Dorothy Commins Private Archive.

ESPL   *Essays, Speeches & Public Letters by William Faulkner,* ed. James B. Meriwether, New York, Random House, 1965.

NOS   *William Faulkner: New Orleans Sketches,* ed. Carvel Collins, New York, Random House, 1968.

FCVA   William Faulkner Collections, University of Virginia Library.

JFSA   Jill Faulkner Summers Private Archive.

NYPL   New York Public Library, Astor, Lenox, and Tilden Foundations.

ROUM   Rowan Oak papers, University of Mississippi Library.

Ambuscade

This story appeared in *The Saturday Evening Post,* CCVII (29 Sept. 1934), 12–13, 80, 81, as the first in a promised series. Printed in brackets on page 9 is one passage from the typescript which did not appear in the *Post* and which Faulkner did not restore when he rewrote the story to become the first chapter of his novel *The Unvanquished* (1938). There were thirteen other passages from the typescript which did not appear in the *Post,* but all were very brief and not important to the story's form or content. In the novel, Faulkner enlarged the first half of the story substantially, deepening it, enriching the prose style, and elaborating the Sartoris and Strother family relationships as he laid the groundwork for the material to follow. He filled in the portrait of John Sartoris and heightened the reader's awareness of the war, both the fighting in the field and the preparations at home to protect the livestock and the silver from the imminent arrival of Yankee troops. Faulkner also reinforced the sense of the chapter's structure by using numerals to divide it into five parts.

Repository: ROUM, ms. fragments and 23-pp. ts.

Retreat

This story appeared in *The Saturday Evening Post,* CCVII (13 Oct. 1934), 16–17, 82, 84, 85, 87, 89. There were nearly two dozen minor changes made between the typescript and the magazine version. Thirteen of them were indentions for new paragraphs, and a space was inserted in the text just before the departure for Memphis. The Yankees became just "they" rather than "They," and "one another" was changed to "each other." Ringo's "Great God, Bayard," and a Yankee's "goddamn" were both deleted, but two new phrases were introduced into the story about the rose cuttings from Mrs. Compson which Granny took on the trip. The last two lines of the story were deleted. When Faulkner revised the story to become the second chapter of *The Unvanquished,* he amplified the comic material about Granny's stratagems to protect the chest of silver and wrote half a dozen important pages on Uncle Buck and Uncle Buddy McCaslin which prefigured his treatment of them in *Go Down, Moses.* He also described in some detail their part in the raising of John Sartoris's regiment. He added to Bayard and Ringo's search for the stolen mules, to their meeting with Sartoris, and to the subsequent attack on the Yankees. Faulkner emphasized the division in the story, just before the departure for Memphis, by numbering the first and second parts. Where the *Post* version had used the expletive "son," Faulkner changed it to "son of a bitch." He also restored the two last lines of the story, which are printed here in brackets.

Repository: ROUM, 10-pp. ms. and 32-pp. ts.

Raid

This story was published in *The Saturday Evening Post,* CCVII (3 Nov. 1934), 18–19, 72, 73, 75, 77, 78. The deletions from the typescript were minimal. The expletive "Great God" was cut at both occurrences. When Drusilla spoke of the life a Southern woman could expect before the war, she said "you settled down forever more while your husband got children on your body for you. . . ." Both the husband and "on your body" disappeared in the printed version, as did "on your body" once more in the same context fourteen lines later—presumably too physical a phrase for a family magazine. The initial letters of pronouns referring to the hated Yankees were reduced from upper to lower case in eleven places, and twenty-six indentions produced new paragraphs. There were five minor changes in phrasing. When Faulkner revised the story to become the third chapter of *The Unvanquished,* he extended Granny's foray by two days and expanded the material about the war's destruction of the railroad, supplying a seven-page passage in which a joust between Federal and Confederate locomotives would stand as contrast to the grim realities of warfare which Bayard and Ringo would experience later. He also introduced numbers to divide the chapter into three parts.

Repository: ROUM, 11-pp. ms. and 35-pp. ts.

Skirmish at Sartoris

On 4 October 1934 Faulkner sent a story called "Drusilla" to *The Saturday Evening Post.* On 26 November he wrote his agent, Morton Goldman, that he would get around to rewriting it as soon as he finished typing his new novel, *Pylon.* [1] But the *Post* did not buy the story, and Goldman sold it to *Scribner's Magazine,* where it appeared without alteration in Volume XCVII (April 1935), 193–200, under the new title "Skirmish at Sartoris." When Faulkner revised it as Chapter VI of *The Unvanquished,* he deleted material which had provided background for *Scribner's* readers. He cut one sentence establishing Granny's death and deleted a sixteen-line recapitulation of major events in "Raid" together with Drusilla's appeal to be allowed to ride with John Sartoris's troop. He also shortened the time elapsed since "Raid" from two years to eighteen months and altered the divisions of the story. After the flashback he made a new section with the number 2 and then changed what had been part II, beginning with the arrival of Mrs. Habersham, to part 3

Repository: ROUM, 10-pp. ms. and 32-pp ts.

The Unvanquished

This story appeared in *The Saturday Evening Post,* CCIX (14 Nov. 1936), 12–13, 121, 122, 124, 126, 128, 130. In the late spring of 1937, when Faulkner revised it, he used tearsheets from the *Post,* pasting one column on each page and typing in other parts. The proportions of tearsheets to typescript were about equal, and there were no significant differences in the text between the magazine form and the book form apart from the insertion of three numerals to divide Chapter IV. The material was retitled "Riposte in Tertio," and the original title was used to give the new book its name.

Repository: ROUM, 13-pp. ms.

---

[1] In an undated letter to Goldman, Faulkner said he had finished the novel "yesterday." The last page of the ms of *Pylon* bears the date "25 November 1934."

Vendée

When this story first went to *The Saturday Evening Post* in September of 1934, editor Graeme Lorimer liked it but requested that Faulkner "bring about the boys' revenge on Grumby more swiftly and keep Grumby in character throughout." Faulkner did so and made a number of other clarifying changes in the first half of the story. He carefully rewrote passages from typescript pages 8–13 and 18–19, totaling more than a thousand words in all. He described Uncle Buck, Ringo, and Bayard as they tracked Ab Snopes toward Grenada at the same time that they pursued Grumby and his men. This material also included the first meeting with Grumby and the treatment of the wound he inflicted on Uncle Buck. Yance's name was changed to Joby, and more than two dozen new paragraphs were created by indention. The end of the magazine version told the reader only that Grumby was pegged out on the door of the old compress, whereas deleted material from the typescript plainly said that he looked like a flayed coon, and one passage, here included in brackets, describes obliquely what seems to have been the process by which the boys flayed Grumby and partially cured his hide before they pegged it to the compress door. After a long interval the story finally appeared in Volume CCIX (5 Dec. 1936), 16–17, 86, 87, 90, 92, 93, 94. In revising the story to become Chapter V of *The Unvanquished*, Faulkner supplied additional material about the pursuit of Grumby, the kill, and the placing of his severed hand on Rosa Millard's grave. Faulkner also supplied numbers to divide the chapter into four parts.

Repository: ROUM, 12-pp. ms. and 32-pp. ts.

Fool About a Horse

It may have been in the late winter or early spring of 1935 that Faulkner wrote a ten-page manuscript which he entitled "Fool About a Horse." A nameless narrator relayed the story told in the disused law office of "Grandfather" while a servant named Roskus operated the fan against the summer heat and served the drinks. The only Roskus in Faulkner's work is Roskus Gibson, who works for the Compsons and figures in *The Sound and the Fury*. This suggests that this story, like several others, began with one of the Compson children, in this case Quentin MacLachan Compson III, who related the tale told by the sewing-machine agent V. K. Suratt to Grandfather, presumably Jason Lycurgus Compson, Jr., and Doc Peabody. It was the story of the losing encounter of Pap, his father Lum Suratt, with Pat Stamper, to the considerable disadvantage not only of Pap but also the boy's

Mammy, Vynie Suratt. Later, in an undated letter Faulkner probably wrote in March of 1935 to Morton Goldman, he said he did not know whom to try a new story ("Lion") on, "since I made such a bust about the Post with FOOL ABOUT A HORSE. . . ." Whatever the bust was, Faulkner did not give up on the story, and in the summer of 1935 he asked Goldman to send it to *Scribner's Magazine* with the assurance that he would rewrite it if necessary. *Scribner's* bought the story, and it appeared there in Volume C (Aug. 1936), 80–86. A surviving thirty-three-page typescript is different enough from the *Scribner's* version to suggest that Faulkner did a very thorough job of revision. In the magazine there was no narrator interposed between the reader and the witness of the trading contest who described it in the first person. This witness was no longer identified as Suratt, and the passages describing Suratt were deleted. Faulkner thus eliminated not only the conjectural Quentin Compson but also Grandfather and Doc Peabody and the setting in Grandfather's office. The other changes were many without being major. One thing Faulkner did was to smooth out the narrator's dialect. Whereas he pronounced the impersonal pronoun "hit" in the typescript, in the magazine it usually became "it," and "misdoubted" became "thought." Some changes worked in the opposite direction, however, as "might" became "mought" and "fire" became "fahr." But most of the paragraphs of the typescript underwent changes of some kind as Faulkner sharpened the story, working meticulously to convey the narrator's speech precisely as he wanted it. In the winter of 1938–39, at work on what would become his novel *The Hamlet,* Faulkner revised the story, incorporating it into part 2 of Chapter Two in Book One, "Flem." Now the nameless narrator, who had been Suratt in the typescript, became V. K. Ratliff. And Lum Suratt, who had become just Pap, had been replaced as the story's protagonist by Ab Snopes. Vynie Suratt, later just Mammy, had become "Miz Snopes." Faulkner made at least as many revisions between the magazine version and the book version as he had earlier made between the typescript version and the magazine version. Most of the changes came in the first half of the story, where he compressed a number of pages. There were obvious changes: Varner's store became Whiteleaf; McCaslin's store became Cain's store, and Uncle Ike McCaslin was replaced by Cain. Faulkner also eliminated the Roman numerals II and III which had separated the parts of the magazine story. Although he had not altered the main facts of the trading match between Ab Snopes and Pat Stamper and its consequences, he had, in effect, had Ratliff retell the whole story, with many changes in diction, sentence structure, and sequence to sharpen his tale yet again.

Repository: FCVA.

Lizards in Jamshyd's Courtyard

The evolution of this story shows how painstakingly Faulkner worked on his fiction and how many stages might separate the inception and the final version of a story. Perhaps as early as the late 1920's Faulkner began a manuscript entitled "Omar's Eighteenth Quatrain." (It was actually the seventeenth in Edward FitzGerald's first edition of his translation of *The Rubáiyát of Omar Khayyám*, eighteenth in the third, fourth, and fifth editions.) One six-page fragment, a two-page fragment, and three separate pages testify to Faulkner's determination to get the story right. With no internal divisions, the six-page fragment in Faulkner's tiny script follows Suratt from Mrs. Littlejohn's boarding house to Henry Armstid's farm. Joined by a third man named Vernon, they drive in Suratt's buckboard with its sewing-machine housing out to the Old Frenchman's place, where Faulkner paused for a philosophical disquisition on the now anonymous early settler who gave the tract its name. The three men squat hidden in the bushes listening to the shoveling, which Suratt assures them is the sound of Flem Snopes searching for buried treasure. Soon afterward, when the sound ceases, Suratt dispels some of Vernon's doubts by accosting a lone departing rider in the dark night, who turns out to be Flem on his way back to Frenchman's Bend. With Vernon still skeptical and Henry a fanatical believer, Suratt returns the next night to Henry's farm with Uncle Dick, the dowser. The two eat hurriedly and set out once again for the Old Frenchman's place. Joined by Vernon, the three men complete the journey and then take pick and shovels from Suratt's buckboard to begin digging wherever Uncle Dick might find a lode. There the fragment breaks off. The other single pages are slight variants of the episodes at Henry's house, of Uncle Dick's appearance, and of the skulking in the bushes at the Old Frenchman's place. On one of the pages Flem had installed one Elmer Vance as caretaker at the place. This was followed by Suratt's dickering with Flem over a sale price. On the two connected pages (the second of them actually comprising only eight lines), Vernon discovers that the oldest coin in the sack he had found had been minted in 1901; Suratt's, in 1894. Here Faulkner brought the story swiftly, almost abruptly, to an end, as Henry keeps digging madly in his hole, visited once a day by his gaunt wife bringing him food. To the lounging onlookers he digs with "the regularity of a mechanical toy . . . with something monstrous in his unflagging motions. . . ." The only complete manuscript, eight unnumbered pages entitled "Lizards in Jamshyd's Courtyard," shows, on seven of the pages, one or more paste-ons cut from a previous manuscript. Part I introduces Suratt and follows him through the goat-buying deal (which took place three years before) to his learning of Flem's purchase of the Old Frenchman's place. Part II shows him there, spying on Flem, then bringing Vernon Tull and Henry Armstid with him. When Uncle

Dick, the dowser, finds buried coins, they determine to buy the place from Flem. Part III relates the purchase, for $3,000, the unsuccessful search for more coins, and Ratliff's realization that they have been duped. Part IV describes the crowd watching Armstid dig and then the men on the porch of Varner's store commenting on Flem and his triumph. A number of typescript fragments of varying lengths show Faulkner trying different arrangements and development of his material. The only complete typescript, one of thirty pages (which could antedate the eight manuscript pages), begins with a description of the Old Frenchman's place and Suratt and then goes on to the goat-buying deal. This section ends with Suratt learning of Flem's new purchase. Only a space rather than Roman numerals separates the parts of this version. Next Faulkner shows Suratt and his two partners spying on Flem. Another section is devoted to Uncle Dick. In the next section, Suratt dickers with Flem. In the next, the three men buy the place. The sixth section shows them digging. Then Suratt realizes they have been tricked, while Armstid continues his furious efforts. The seventh and last part shows the spectators observing Armstid and ends with the comments of the men at Varner's Store. The last six lines of dialogue are almost identical with those in the eight-page manuscript version. On his sending schedule Faulkner noted that he sent the story to *The Saturday Evening Post* on 16 May 1930, but then he canceled that date and substituted "5-27-30." Faulkner's correspondence with the *Post*[1] reveals that he sent in two versions of the story, that the editors liked the first one rather than the second, and that they had indicated acceptance by 5 August 1930 and confirmed this on 18 August, although Faulkner recorded on his sending schedule an acceptance date of 7 August. Because of the radical difference in the *Post* version—putting the mad Armstid and his observers first rather than last—it seems likely that the typescript the editors accepted was substantially different from the one discussed above. The story appeared in *The Saturday Evening Post,* CCIV (27 Feb. 1932), 12–13, 52, 57. It was probably the winter of 1938–39 when Faulkner began to use elements of the story in *The Hamlet.* The most obvious change was in Suratt's name: he was now V. K. Ratliff. And Odum Bookwright had replaced Vernon Tull as one-third owner of the Old Frenchman's place. There were other changes deriving from Faulkner's integration of the materials of the short story into his novel. For one, Flem Snopes did not buy the Old Frenchman's place; Will Varner deeded it to Mr. and Mrs. Flem Snopes as a part of his daughter Eula's dowry. Faulkner expanded the goat-buying story which is section II of the magazine story to become part 2 of Chapter Three in Book One of the novel, and he ended it with Flem sitting proprietorially in front of the Old Frenchman's place. Then, in part 1 of Chapter Two of Book Four, he launched into the much expanded tale. In rewriting sections III and IV

[1]James B. Meriwether, "Faulkner's Correspondence with *The Saturday Evening Post,*" pp. 466–67.

oᶠ the magazine story he made a number of specific changes. For example, the purchase price in dollars of the Old Frenchman's place was not specified, but the presumptive date of the coins to be found, 1861, was specified, presumably to make more immediately apparent the meaning of the clue that tells Ratliff for certain that they have been duped into buying a salted mine. Finally, Faulkner took section I' of the magazine story, rearranged and expanded it, and used it in part 2 of the chapter to end the novel.

Repositories: JFSA, mss. fragments; ROUM, 8-pp. ms., tss. fragments, and 30-pp. ts.

The Hound

Faulkner sent this story to *The Saturday Evening Post* on 17 November 1930. They refused it, as *Scribner's* and *The American Mercury* did subsequently. On 8 May 1931 it was accepted by *Harper's*, where it appeared in Volume CLXIII (Aug. 1931), 266–74. In 1934 it was reprinted in *Doctor Martino and Other Stories*, now out of print. In the late winter of 1938–39, Faulkner interpolated it into *The Hamlet*. The most striking change was Ernest Cotton's new name and identity: he was no longer a bachelor; he was now Mink Snopes, with a wife and two children. In part 1 of Chapter One, in Book Three, "The Long Summer," Faulkner set up the conflict between him and Jack Houston. Rather than penning up Houston's hog and winning a court judgment against Houston of one dollar as a pound fee, as Cotton had done in the story, Mink allowed his scrub yearling bull to stray into Houston's pasture, where Houston wintered it and then won a court judgment against Snopes of three dollars for pasturage. There were other changes, such as the elimination of the men's colloquy on the porch of Varner's store about Houston's disappearance, and the addition of the unsuccessful intrusion of Lump Snopes into Mink's attempts to dispose of the body, Lump being determined to find the fifty dollars he was convinced Houston had been carrying. Though many of the passages were identical with those in the story, Faulkner had expanded it considerably and deepened the portraiture of both Snopes and Houston. He would recount the story again in both *The Town* (1957) and *The Mansion* (1959) as he completed the Snopes trilogy. By the time he was writing *The Mansion*, he was telling the story for the fourth time, and discrepancies in these accounts in the trilogy presented a problem for Faulkner's editor, Albert Erskine. Faulkner was perfectly amenable to the idea of changes which would reconcile this last version with the others, but he was not seriously concerned about them. He wrote Erskine· 'When I first wrote the story of Houston's murder, Mink was a bachelor named Something Cotton. Apparently changing his name and his condition (possibly his motivation too, though I have forgot the original story, called THE HOUND) hasn't outraged too many academical gumshoes, so I doubt if this will either."

Spotted Horses

This story provides another example of the indefatigable persistence with which Faulkner worked at his short stories. At some time between the late fall of 1926 and early 1927, he was at work on the beginnings of two novels.[1] One of them, *Flags in the Dust,* he would go on to complete, and it would be published as *Sartoris* (1929). The other, *Father Abraham,* he put aside, but it would eventually be completed as *The Hamlet.* Faulkner had stopped work on *Father Abraham* after writing 14,000 words which introduced Flem Snopes as a successful banker in Jefferson and then, in an extended flashback which made up most of the twenty-five legal-size pages of the manuscript, introduced the Varners and other residents of Frenchman's Bend and went on to recount Flem's return from Texas, followed by the auction of the spotted horses and the immediate aftermath. At some point Faulkner wrote the story of the horse auction in a version told solely through dialogue, without quotation marks and with many phonetic spellings, a typescript whose pages were numbered 204–23, as though they had been extracted from a collection of some sort. He called this version "As I Lay Dying." In another recasting, he used the title "Abraham's Children." It was probably early November of 1928 when Faulkner took to Alfred Dashiell, an editor at *Scribner's Magazine,* a twenty-one-page typescript also entitled "As I Lay Dying." In this one, a man driving for his uncle on a political junket (as Faulkner said he himself had done) told the story of the auction. Dashiell refused it. On 25 August 1930 Faulkner sent *Scribner's* a 15,000-word version of the story under the title "The Peasants." It was the most effective version yet, but now it was too long for *Scribner's.* In early January of 1931, however, the editor Kyle Crichton wrote Faulkner that if he could cut it to 8,000 words and still retain its flavor, *Scribner's* would take it. Encouraged by Dashiell as well, Faulkner revised the story and renamed it "Aria Con Amore" but sent it on 2 February 1931 to *The Saturday Evening Post.* When the *Post* refused it, Faulkner sent the sixteen-page version to *Scribner's.* Now the story was told by yet another narrator, V. K. Suratt, who spoke directly to the reader as to another resident of Frenchman's Bend. On 20 February, Dashiell wrote Faulkner that they would take it but asked if he could change the title. Faulkner suggested simply "Horses" and apparently set to work on a revision which expanded the sixteen-page version to 8,000 words. It finally appeared as "Spotted Horses" in Volume LXXXIX (June 1931), 585–97. An eight-page fragment entitled "The Peasants" begins with the first sighting of the ponies by the men on the porch of Varner's store and

[1]See James B. Meriwether, "Sartoris and Snopes: An Early Notice," *The Library Chronicle of The University of Texas,* VII (Summer 1962), 36–39.

breaks off as Henry Armstid is about to compel his wife to help him catch the pony he has bought from the Texan—not yet named Buck Hipps. Told in the third person, the fragment is divided by Roman numerals into six parts. It is difficult to determine if this was the manuscript which preceded the 15,000-word typescript which Faulkner sent to *Scribner's* on 25 August 1930 or if it was another treatment of the story which he attempted later. In September of 1939 Faulkner retold the story once more as part I of Chapter One of "The Peasants," Book Four of *The Hamlet*. Using an omniscient narrator instead of Ratliff, he recast the story, expanding it to thirty-seven pages and bringing it closer to *Father Abraham* than to "Spotted Horses." This retelling in general resembled the narrative line of the eight-page manuscript fragment called "The Peasants," though the treatment was fuller and more detailed, with minor variations in the order of incidents and dialogue. Now the Texan had a name, Buck Hipps. Jody Varner appeared on the scene, as did others from Frenchman's Bend. In two changes, Admiral Dewey Snopes was replaced by Wallstreet Panic Snopes and I. O Snopes's place was taken by Lump Snopes. Ratliff was still very much in evidence, urging the others not to buy the horses and still carrying some of the narrative burden in his dialogue. But now, released by the switch to an omniscient narrator from the constant constraint of Ratliff's dialect, Faulkner was free to use his poetic prose to the fullest advantage. The comic, satiric, and poignant elements of the tale all benefited from these changes and from its expansion.

Repositories: NYPL, 25-pp. ms. fragment *(Father Abraham)*. FCVA, 51-pp. carbon ts. fragment and 54-pp. carbon ts. *(Father Abraham);* 3-pp. ts. fragment ("Abraham's Children"). ROUM, 18-pp. ts. ("As I Lay Dying"). JFSA, 8-pp. ms. fragment and 58-pp. ts. ("The Peasants"); 16-pp. ts. ("Aria Con Amore") and 21-pp. ts. ("As I Lay Dying").

Lion

It was probably the late winter or early spring of 1935 when Faulkner wrote this story. He doubtless tried to sell it to at least one of the large-circulation weekly magazines, but it was *Harper's* which purchased it and printed it in Volume CLXXII (Dec. 1935), 67–77. In September of 1941 Faulkner used much of the material of the story in section 3 of "The Bear," which was really a novella and which would be the fifth and longest part of the novel *Go Down, Moses* (1942). Whereas the magazine version had been narrated by sixteen-year-old Quentin Compson, now Faulkner employed an omniscient narrator, and Quentin's role was assumed by young Ike McCaslin. This permitted Faulkner to obtain the maximum dramatic effect from the climactic conflict between Old Ben and Lion and Boon by narrating it as it happened, rather than having it told as Quentin and the others heard it after the fact from old Ike McCaslin and Ad, the cook, who was now renamed Ash. Faulkner also interpolated into the story the collapse of Sam Fathers after Old Ben's death and then Sam's own passing. In *Go Down, Moses,* Ike would not then or later have produced offspring, as he obviously had done in order to have the grandson in the story named after Ike's father. Boon was still violent, but he had not killed a Negro, as the reader had been told in the magazine version. Faulkner also expanded the liquor-buying expedition to Memphis, deriving more humor from Boon's behavior than he had done in the earlier treatment of the material. He also enlarged and deepened the last portion of the *Harper's* story, so much so that he chose to use it not in section 3, but in section 5 to conclude "The Bear," gaining both power and resonance from Ike's meditation and irony through Boon's frenzy and the implied juxtaposition of past and present.

The Old People

Faulkner apparently sent this story to *The Saturday Evening Post* as soon as he finished it. When the *Post* refused it, he sent it to his agent, Harold Ober, who received the nineteen-page typescript on 3 October 1939. During the next five months it was refused by *The American Magazine, Collier's, Country Gentleman, Redbook, Cosmopolitan,* and *This Week.* When Faulkner asked Ober to offer it to one of the quality monthlies, he sent it to *Harper*'s, which bought the story on 28 June 1940 and published it in Volume CLXXI (Sept. 1940), 418–25. A typescript which survives is a seventeen-page rough draft with manuscript additions, cancellations, and numerous typographical errors. Presumably the nineteen-page typescript (and certainly the typescript, perhaps the same one, which was used as setting copy by *Harper's*) was a heavily revised and expanded version of the earlier one. In the most significant single revision, the narrator's father was no longer identified as Mr. Compson. This element in the seventeen-page typescript shows that the story was then conceived as being narrated by Quentin Compson, a function he had performed in "Fool About a Horse," "A Justice," and "Lion," though it was only in the latter two that Quentin was still present in the printed version. Every page of the magazine version of the story shows variants from the typescript, and in many paragraphs there are as many deletions as additions. All of the changes, however, seem to be those of a writer who is sharpening his rendering of detail, searching for more precise depiction, and extracting all possible resonance from his tale. New individual paragraphs describe Doom's tactics on his return to the tribe, the pursuit of the great buck by the boy and Sam Fathers, Sam's physical appearance just before the buck manifests himself to them, and finally, a passage near the end of the story in which the boy's father, accepting his son's account of the reappearance of the mighty totem animal, links him to all the life lived on earth before them, conjoining him with all the blood shed, and meditating on how "suffering and grieving is better than nothing." One of Faulkner's smaller alterations was to change Sam's salute to the buck from "Ole" (perhaps too reminiscent of bullfights) to "Oleh." Editorial or authorial tidying up included the deletion of the numbers 2 and 3 which separated sections of the story and indention to create half a dozen new paragraphs. When Faulkner revised the story in the summer of 1941 to make it the fourth segment of *Go Down, Moses,* he enlarged it by approximately a thousand words and restored the numbers, deleted in the magazine version, dividing it into three parts. But there were many more notable changes necessitated by the integration of the material into the saga of the relationships of black and white families which formed the basis of *Go Down, Moses.* The heavily revised story was now told in the third person, and the magazine version's narrator, earlier Quentin Compson, became young Ike McCaslin. General Compson took the place that had been occupied by Ike McCaslin as an old man in the *Harper's* version. Ike's cousin, McCaslin Edmonds, took the place of "father," earlier Mr. Compson. The servant, Jimbo, became Tennie's Jim. Now there was a closer bond between Ike and Sam Fathers than there had been between Sam and Quentin. And here Sam was the son, not the grandson, of Ikkemotubbe, the Chickasaw chief who had sold the child and his mother into slavery, into servitude under the McCaslins rather than the Compsons. In keeping with the thematic concerns of the novel of which it was now a part, the story dealt at greater length with Sam's mixed blood, with betrayal, and with the links between past and present as well as with what Ike learned as a boy from Sam in the Big Woods foreshadowing what Ike would do when he grew to be a man

Repository: FCVA.

A Point of Law

It was probably late in 1939 when Faulkner completed this story. Harold Ober received a twenty-two-page typescript of it on 4 January 1940 and sent it to *The Saturday Evening Post.* The *Post* refused it, but on 31 January it was bought by *Collier's*, where it appeared in Volume CV (22 June 1940), 20–21, 30, 31. The typescript apparently does not survive, but another, of twenty-one pages, bearing Faulkner's name and address, shows something of the story's evolution. Although elements of the narrative are the same as in the magazine version, there are changes in every paragraph of the latter. Faulkner clarified references by using names rather than pronouns. He cut whole paragraphs but also added new ones, accounting for the additional page in the typescript Ober received. Some of this new material elaborated on the interplay between Lucas and Roth Edmonds and Lucas and George Wilkins. The twenty-one-page typescript is also divided into three parts by numbers which were omitted from the *Collier's* version. In the spring of 1941 Faulkner was at work on *Go Down, Moses*. Chapter One of "The Fire and the Hearth," the second of the book's seven segments, reached Robert K. Haas at Random House on 5 June. It began with nine pages revealing the threat that George Wilkins's still posed to Lucas Beauchamp and setting forth something of the Beauchamp-McCaslin-Edmonds background which would be elaborated in the segments to come. Faulkner also laid the groundwork for another theme when Lucas discovered what he thought was buried treasure while hiding his still before informing on George Wilkins to Carothers Edmonds. In part 2 of this first chapter, Faulkner followed Lucas to Carothers Edmonds's home, but then, before Lucas stated his business, Faulkner interpolated fourteen new pages narrating the crucial relationship, years before, between Lucas, Edmonds's father, Zack Edmonds, and Molly Beauchamp, both Lucas's wife and Edmonds's foster mother. In sections 3 and 4, which completed "The Fire and the Hearth," Faulkner finished the comic story of the moonshining case, its final disposition, and its aftermath. Some lines and even passages were identical with those in the *Collier's* version, but Faulkner had expanded this treatment of the material. He had also made the Negro dialect less heavy, and in preparing for the more serious, and even tragic, aspects of the novel which were yet to come, he had restored one passage, only slightly altered, from the twenty-one-page typescript which did not appear in *Collier's*. As Carothers Edmonds looked at Lucas he thought, *"I am not only looking at a face older than mine and which has seen and winnowed more, but at a man most of whose blood was pure ten thousand years when my own anonymous beginnings became mixed enough to produce me."*

Repository: FCVA.

Gold Is Not Always

On 19 February 1940 Harold Ober received from Faulkner a twenty one-page typescript of this story. It was declined by *Collier's, Redbook, Country Gentleman, Harper's,* and *The Saturday Evening Post* before *The American Mercury* bought it on 16 September. It appeared there in Volume CLXVI (Nov. 1940), 563–70. Although the twenty-one-page typescript apparently does not survive, there is a nineteen-page typescript which is close to the printed version. There are changes in every paragraph, but they are minor, with only two added passages differentiating the version in *The American Mercury* from that in this typescript. One of these amplifies the tracking of Edmonds's missing mule and the other further describes the growing frenzy of the divining-machine salesman. In the summer of 1941 Faulkner used this story in writing Chapter Two of "The Fire and the Hearth." Although he wrote two pages of new material, and though the dialect was again much less pronounced than it had been, the material was much closer to the magazine version than was the portion of the story that had derived from "A Point of Law."

————

Repository: FCVA.

Pantaloon in Black

Harold Ober received a twenty-four-page typescript of this story from Faulkner on 18 March 1940. He tried unsuccessfully to place it with *Collier's*, *The American Magazine, Redbook,* and *The Saturday Evening Post* before selling it to *Harper's* on 9 August. It was published in Volume CLXXXI (Oct. 1940), 503–13. A carbon copy of the typescript reveals that apart from three sentences and two phrases deleted from the dialogue between the deputy sheriff and his wife, the changes in the published version were minor and consisted chiefly of creating twenty-one new paragraphs. When Faulkner used the story as the third segment of *Go Down, Moses,* he may have had the carbon typescript in front of him. He added a few phrases in addition to one of the sentences that had been cut from the typescript to produce the magazine version. He also changed Mayfield to Maydew and canceled almost every one of the new paragraphs that had been introduced into the magazine version.

————

Repository: FCVA.

Go Down, Moses

Faulkner wrote this story in July of 1940. Pressed for money, he told Harold Ober on 24 July that he had sent it directly to *The Saturday Evening Post.* It was refused there, but on 17 September *Collier's* bought it, and the story appeared there in Volume CVII (25 Jan. 1941), 19–20, 45, 46. In an early fourteen-page typescript Faulkner had at first called the murderer Henry Sutpen Coldfield, and he had told the census-taker that his grandmother's name was Rosa Sutpen. On the next page Faulkner changed his name to Carothers Edmonds Beauchamp and then to Samuel Worsham Beauchamp, his grandmother becoming Mollie Beauchamp and her brother becoming Hamp Worsham rather than Hamp Benbow. Faulkner grafted these two pages onto a version of the story which had begun in Gavin Stevens's office rather than the murderer's cell. A seventeen-page typescript, a carbon copy, probably of the one that went to the *Post,* retained these changes. The *Collier's*

version varied only slightly from this one. Two passages from the
typescript not in the magazine version and not restored by Faulkner
for inclusion in *Go Down, Moses* are printed in brackets. Three new
spaces were added in the magazine version to separate segments of the
story. By late August of 1941 Faulkner had sent to Robert K. Haas at
Random House the version that he wanted to use as the seventh and
concluding portion of *Go Down, Moses.* Now he used numbers to divide the scene in the cell from the rest of the story. The other changes,
like this one, were minor, and they were fewer than those he made in
any of the other stories which became a part of *Go Down, Moses.*

Repository: FCVA.

Delta Autumn

Harold Ober received an eighteen-page typescript of this story on 16
December 1940. *The Saturday Evening Post, Collier's, Harper's, The
Atlantic Monthly, The American Mercury,* and *The American Magazine*
all declined it before *Story* bought it on 2 December 1941 and published it in Volume XX (May-June 1942), 46–55. A rough typescript of
eighteen pages shows that Faulkner had made many revisions before
typing the version that went to Ober. They were stylistic changes
which occurred in nearly every paragraph. In one substantive change,
Faulkner deleted the name Coughlin from Don Boyd's listing of types
of potential American dictators and added the names of Yokohama,
Smith, and Jones. On a Sunday in December of 1941, probably the 7th,
Faulkner wrote his Random House editor, Saxe Commins, "DELTA
AUTUMN needs to be rewritten to get matter into it pertinent to the
story this mss. tells." The manuscript was, of course, *Go Down, Moses,*
and the rewriting by which it would become the sixth section of the
novel involved several crucial changes: Don Boyd became Carothers
"Roth" Edmonds, great-great-great-grandson of old Lucius Quintus
Carothers McCaslin (the grandfather of Ike McCaslin); and Edmonds's
mulatto mistress became the great-great-great-granddaughter of old
Lucius Quintus Carothers McCaslin. Thus Roth repeated the old
man's miscegenation and incest. Ike was ten years older than he had
been in the magazine story, and, in keeping with other parts of *Go
Down, Moses,* he had had a wife, the reader was told, but not children,
as in the story. New passages picked up threads such as his unhappy
marriage and the contrast between past and present, as seen in the
land, the hunt, and the men themselves. New dialogue between Ike
and Roth's mistress emphasized the McCaslin family history, including
the old wrongs now in part repeated. Contrary to Faulkner's practice
in some other stories, he broke up long paragraphs from the magazine

version into shorter paragraphs, but he restored one visual element that had been dropped in the magazine: from an earlier typescript: the hunt took place in a "△-shaped section of earth between hills and River. . . ." And the list of potential dictator types was changed again, as Faulkner deleted Pelley and Yokohama and added "Roosevelt or Willkie. . . ."

Repository: FCVA.

The Bear

In July of 1941 Faulkner began work on a story, really a novella, which would become the fifth and longest segment of *Go Down, Moses.* By 9 September the first two parts of it had reached Random House in New York. In the interval before section 3 followed them on 9 November, Faulkner had taken time to fashion some of this material into a story, bearing the same title as the novella, which he hoped would alleviate his perennial financial problems. He used most of the first section of the novella and the initial pages of the second section up to the point at which the fyce had attempted to attack Old Ben. Faulkner added material to end the story: material which would later form a part of section 4 of the novella, where Ike's cousin and father surrogate, McCaslin Edmonds, would quote Keats's "Ode on a Grecian Urn" to help the boy understand courage and forbearance and something of truth as well. Simplifying for the magazine's audience, Faulkner now called Ike simply "the boy," and McCaslin became simply his father. Harold Ober received the story on 27 October and sent it to *The Saturday Evening Post.* On 5 November he wrote Faulkner that the editors wanted him to clarify the ending, to make clear that the truth referred to was the actions of the boy, the old man, the bear, and the dog, because these things had come from the heart, and the boy's father had said that truth was all things that touched the human heart. Faulkner replied that the story was "a rewritten chapter of a book under way." It was a hurriedly written first draft, he said, and he proceeded to rewrite, closely following the editors' suggestion. On 14 November, Ober was able to write Faulkner that the *Post* had accepted the story as revised. It was printed in Volume CCXIV (9 May 1942), 30–31, 74, 76, 77.

Race at Morning

After Faulkner completed this story he took it to Harold Ober on 21 September 1954. It was intended for *The Saturday Evening Post,* which bought it two days later and published it in Volume CCXXVII (5 March

1955), 26–27, 103, 104, 106. In early 1955 Random House decided to publish a collection of Faulkner's hunting stories. He would provide new intercalated material to link them together. With the addition of a little more than a dozen new lines within the story, it became the fourth and last in the book entitled *Big Woods* (1955).

Repository: DCPA, 20-pp ts.

Hog Pawn

It may have been October of 1954 when Faulkner wrote this story. It resembled some of the stories collected in *Knight's Gambit* (1949), in which Charles "Chick" Mallison narrated episodes of his Uncle Gavin Stevens's detective work in Yoknapatawpha County. A twenty-five-page rough draft in typescript survives. On 13 March 1955 a typescript was received at the Harold Ober office, where the story was retyped in twenty-eight pages and sent to *Life*. On 29 January, *Life* refused it, as did *Collier's* two weeks later. It remained in Harold Ober's files until Faulkner asked Ober to send it to him for revisions which would make it a part of *The Mansion* (1959), completing the Snopes trilogy. "Hog Pawn" was returned to him on 13 March 1958, but it was late that year or early in the next when he reached the point in Chapter Fourteen of "Flem," the novel's third and final book, at which he could integrate the story into the novel. Faulkner rewrote and expanded, making numerous changes. As in some of the other stories in *Knight's Gambit*, Charles Mallison was in the forefront with his Uncle Gavin without being the narrator. (He had not been identified by name in the story, but his relationship to Stevens coupled with his tone made it clear that he was.) However, the third-person narration presented many of the events as they impinged upon his consciousness and sensibilities. Now he participated in more of the action, keeping the early morning vigil in the car with his uncle and then rushing into the Meadowfill house just before the shot rang out. There were numerous minor changes: Essie Meadowfill worked for a bank rather than the telephone company, and her suitor was demoted from being an ex-Marine Corps sergeant to a corporal. But the major thematic elaboration was to work this story of Snopes villainy (he now had a first name: Res, short for Orestes) into the Snopes saga and the fight waged against Snopesism by men such as Gavin Stevens and V. K. Ratliff. Faulkner also brought Jason Compson back into his fiction and used the motif of land deals and returned war veterans to link this material with other parts of the novel.

Repository: FCVA

Nympholepsy

On 10 March 1922 Faulkner published a prose sketch entitled "The Hill" in *The Mississippian,* the student newspaper of the University of Mississippi, where he had published a poem entitled "L'Apres-Midi d'un Faune" two and a half years earlier. "Nympholepsy," which James B. Meriwether dates from "early in 1925, within the first month or two of his arrival in New Orleans,"[1] not only combines elements of the two earlier works but also foreshadows the courthouse of Yoknapatawpha County and some of its less fortunate inhabitants.

Repository: NYPL, 8-pp. ts.

Frankie and Johnny

On 4 January 1925 Faulkner left Oxford for New Orleans, planning to work his passage across to Europe and support himself with his writing until he made his reputation abroad as Frost and Eliot had done. His stay lengthened into six months, however, while he wrote in the congenial atmosphere of New Orleans and published his work in the New Orleans *Times-Picayune* and a new magazine based there called *The Double Dealer.* His first appearance was in the latter. It was a 3,000-word piece in the January-February number entitled "New Orleans" and it comprised eleven sketches.[2] The third of them, entitled "Frankie and Johnny," was a first-person account in 450 words by a young gangster of his meeting with the yellow-haired, grey-eyed girl who briefly becomes his sweetheart. It was apparently condensed from part 2 of the unpublished story (which was actually untitled by Faulkner), with the first paragraph omitted and slight changes in the remainder. Later Faulkner would rework and expand material from "Frankie and Johnny" for "The Kid Learns," which appeared on May 31 in the *Times-Picayune.*[3] There the liaison resulted in Johnny's death, and though his girl friend was renamed Mary and called "Little Sister Death" at the end, she was still unmistakably the grey-eyed girl of the original story. In the last paragraph of this story, the pregnant Frankie, "a strip of fecund seeded ground," will remind some readers of Dewey Dell Bundren in *As I Lay Dying,* "a wet seed wild in the hot blind earth."

[1]This sketch was first published by James B. Meriwether with an introduction and editorial corrections in "Nympholepsy," *The Mississippi Quarterly,* XXVI (Summer 1973), 403–9.
[2]*NOS,* pp. 3–14.
[3]*NOS,* pp. 86–91.

Repository: FCVA, 23-pp. ts. This story was first published by James B. Meriwether with an introduction and editorial corrections in "Frankie and Johnny," *The Mississippi Quarterly,* XXXI (Summer 1978), 453–64.

The Priest

During his New Orleans stay Faulkner worked on what he hoped would be a series of short stories and prose sketches for the Sunday magazine section of the New Orleans *Times-Picayune* to be entitled "The Mirror of Chartres Street." Although only the first of the pieces he published there bore the title "Mirrors of Chartres Street," Faulkner used his projected general title for the series on typescripts of stories which actually appeared simply under their own titles. "The Priest" bore the number five, and according to James B. Meriwether, it was intended to follow "Jealousy," which appeared on 1 March 1925 as the fourth in the series of stories. Meriwether suggests that " 'The Priest' was rejected for fear of offending some readers of the paper" and notes that Faulkner made use of some of its elements as well as its title in a 222-word segment of "New Orleans" in *The Double Dealer.* [1]

Repository: NYPL, 8-pp. carbon ts., unnumbered.

Once Aboard the Lugger (I) and (II)

On many occasions Faulkner told of working as a bootlegger during his 1925 stay in New Orleans. He knew an Italian family, he said, whose sons brought in Cuban alcohol for their mother to transform into gin, Scotch, and bourbon for sale in the family café. Faulkner's brother Jack thought that his bootlegging experience was not extensive, that he might have made a trip or two out into the gulf primarily as a passenger. Whatever the extent of his involvement, it gave him material for fiction, from characters such as Pete Ginotta, in *Mosquitoes,* to those in these two stories. When he came to write his semi-autobiographical "Mississippi"[2] nearly thirty years later, he would recount the material in a cohesive summary of the two stories without the violence of the latter one (violence of a sort that recalls the relationship of Popeye and Tommy in *Sanctuary*). Faulkner once told Frederick L. Gwynn that he had destroyed two novels. These two stories may constitute all he was able to salvage from one of those novels. Less than a dozen manuscript pages and four dozen typed pages

[1]The sketch was first published by James B. Meriwether with an introduction and editorial corrections in "The Priest," *The Mississippi Quarterly,* XXIX (Summer 1976), 445–50.
[2]*ESPL,* pp. 30–31.

survive. However, the same material that constitutes the second of these stories, whose typed pages are numbered 1–14, had also been typed out in another version whose numbering ran from 11–27. Then Faulkner had crossed out these typed numbers and renumbered them by hand from 252–268, where they seemed to serve as the end of the book. (One manuscript page also bears the subtitle "The Prohibition Industry in Southern Waters.") The first of the stories was apparently submitted unsuccessfully to *Scribner's Magazine* in November of 1928 and finally published in *Contempo* I (1 Feb. 1932), 1, 4. In mid-December of 1928 Faulkner again sent a story entitled "Once Aboard the Lugger" to *Scribner's* and it too was refused. It seems likely that it was the second, unpublished, story. The young engineer-narrator may remind some readers of the young steward, David West, of *Mosquitoes.* It seems likely that "Once Aboard the Lugger" may date from about the same time. Faulkner seems to have taken his title, for purposes of ironic contrast, from an English school song:

> We're good at games like rugger
> And snooker and lacrosse,
> And once aboard the lugger
> We are never at a loss.

Repository: ROUM

Miss Zilphia Gant

By mid-December of 1928, when Faulkner submitted this story to *Scribner's Magazine,* it had already been there once before. It was refused both times and later rejected by *The American Mercury* as well. In March of 1930 it was purchased by *The Southwest Review,* though it would prove to be too long for that magazine, which sold it in turn to the Book Club of Texas. It appeared under that imprint, in a special edition of 300 copies, with an introduction by Henry Nash Smith on 27 June 1932.

Repository: FCVA, 9-pp. ms., 18-pp. ts., 23-pp. ts. University of Texas Humanities Research Center, 23-pp. carbon ts.

Thrift

This story appeared in *The Saturday Evening Post,* CCIII (6 Sept. 1930), 16–17, 76, 82. It was Faulkner's third story to appear in a national magazine ("A Rose for Emily" was published in April in *Forum* and "Honor" in *The American Mercury* in July of the same year), and it was selected for inclusion in the annual Doubleday *O. Henry Memorial Award Prize Stories.* As a predominantly comic treatment of aerial warfare in the Great

War, it offers a contrast (as does "With Caution and Dispatch") to the tragicomic "Turnabout" and the tragic "Ad Astra" and "All the Dead Pilots."[1]

———————

Repository: FCVA, ms. and ts. fragments.

Idyll in the Desert

Submitted without success to a total of seven magazines in 1930 and 1931, this story was published in a limited edition of 400 copies by Random House on 10 December 1931. Faulkner would again use the situation of a woman who left her husband and two children to flee to the west with a lover in *The Wild Palms.*

———————

Repository: FCVA, 4-pp. ms. and 19-pp. ts.

Two Dollar Wife

At some point after his return from Europe in December of 1925, possibly in early 1927 when he was working on *Sartoris* (1929) or even, perhaps, a year or two later, Faulkner wrote three pages of a story he called "The Devil Beats His Wife."[2] He did not complete this tale of the domestic problems of a young woman named Doris and her husband, Hubert, and the successful efforts of Della, their maid, to solve them. However, something of Della's qualities got into the character of Dilsey when Faulkner was working on *The Sound and the Fury* in 1928. Other elements of the story underwent various transmutations. In late 1933 or early 1934 Faulkner's agent, Morton Goldman, asked Faulkner about a story called "Christmas Tree." Faulkner replied, "The CHRISTMAS TREE story which you mention was a continuation of that one by the same title which you now have, the same characters who got married at the dance, with the dice and the forged license, etc. I wrote it first years ago, and I have mislaid it. I rewrote it from memory, the first part, in the short story which you now have, and I had forgot the characters' names: hence the difference." Pressed for money, Faulkner told Goldman that if an editor showed an interest, he was willing to send a synopsis of the rest of the story or rewrite it from memory. At one time or another he wrote at least four versions —manuscript and typescript, complete and incomplete—under this title. In what may have been a one-page synopsis written when Faulkner worked for Metro-Goldwyn-Mayer in 1932, his characters were Howard

———————

[1]*Collected Stories of William Faulkner,* pp. 475–510, 407–30, and 511–31.
[2]See James B. Meriwether, "Two Unknown Faulkner Short Stories," *Recherches anglaises et américaines* (Strasbourg), IV (1971), 23–30.

Maxwell, Mrs. Houston, and her daughter, Doris. In another version of fifteen manuscript pages, Faulkner followed the story of Howard and Doris through their marriage to a happy ending. Even so, "Christmas Tree" never sold, and Faulkner was feeling the same financial pressure acutely in the spring and summer of 1935. It was probably then that he rewrote his story of the bizarre courtship of Doris Houston and Howard Maxwell, now renamed Maxwell Johns. *College Life* was advertising a $500 short-story contest, and this may have led to the story's submission there. It was accepted and published in Volume XVIII (Jan. 1936), 8–10, 85, 86, 88, 90, but it won no prize in the contest.

Repositories: FCVA, 1-p. ts. ROUM, ms. fragment and 15-pp. ms. ("Christmas Tree").

Afternoon of a Cow

Experimenting with a number of verse forms and styles following his return home at the end of World War I, Faulkner wrote a forty-line poem of frustrated love in the summer of 1919 and borrowed its title from a work by Stéphane Mallarmé, "L'Apres-Midi d'un Faune." It appeared in *The New Republic* on 16 August 1919 and in the University of Mississippi student newspaper, *The Missisippian,* in revised form on 29 October. On 28 January of the next year he published there a poem inviting comparison with one by François Villon. Faulkner's was called "Une Ballade des Femmes Perdues." Such poetry unsurprisingly provoked various responses. One, appearing in *The Mississippian* on 12 May 1920, took the form of a poem entitled "Une Ballade d'une Vache Perdue," in which the authors (probably Drane Lester and Louis M. Jiggitts), using the pen name of Lordgreyson, described the heifer Betsy, lost and wandering far from home. It was an amusing tour de force, which Faulkner may have had in mind seventeen years later, "one afternoon," he recalled, "when I felt rotten with a terrible hangover." He was then working unhappily for Twentieth Century-Fox. After dinner on 25 June 1937, Faulkner read to his guests a story entitled "Afternoon of a Cow," which, he told them, had been written by a talented boy named Ernest V. Trueblood. The only one who seemed to appreciate Faulkner's *jeu d'esprit* was his house guest and French translator, Maurice Coindreau. The next day Faulkner gave him a carbon copy of his typescript as a souvenir. In February of 1939, working on part 2, Chapter One, of "The Long Summer," Book Three of *The Hamlet,* Faulkner apparently thought back to this story and appropriated elements of it for the mock chivalric romantic treatment of Ike Snopes's love for Jack Houston's cow. He completed the story in part 3, which ended the chapter. Not long afterward, when German authorities forbade the printing of American books in occupied France, "the reading of novels by Faulkner and Hemingway," said Jean Paul Sartre, "became for some a symbol of resistance." So it was not inappropriate that Francophile

Faulkner should have approved the first publication of "Afternoon of a Cow" in Maurice Coindreau's translation in Algiers in *Fontaine,* 27–28 (June-July 1943), 66–81. In early 1947 editor Reed Whittemore asked for the story for a special number of the quarterly *Furioso.* "Sell the piece if you can," Faulkner wrote his agent, Harold Ober. "Maybe it is funny, as I thought myself. I suppose I tried it on the wrong people." So "Afternoon of a Cow" finally appeared in English, under the name of Ernest V. Trueblood, in *Furioso,* 2 (Summer 1947), 5, 8, 9, 10, 13, 16, 17, a decade after it was written and nearly three decades after "L'Apres-Midi d'un Faune" and "Une Ballade d'une Vache Perdue."

Repository: DCPA, 17-pp. carbon ts.

Mr. Acarius

Faulkner delivered a nineteen-page typescript of this story to Harold Ober on 19 February 1953, shortly after he completed it. It was then called "Weekend Revisited." Ober had it retyped and wrote Faulkner that he was sending it to *The New Yorker* to Lillian Ross, who had discussed the story with Faulkner and expected to recommend it. On 5 March, however, William Shawn wrote Ober that they could not use it. On 7 April, *Collier's* made the same decision, as *Esquire* would too. Faulkner remained confident about the story. When he wrote Ober on 11 November 1954 he asked if there was any news about it, and added, "I think [it] is not only funny but true. . . ." But he would not live to see it published. It finally appeared in his favorite market for short fiction, *The Saturday Evening Post,* CCXXXVIII (9 Oct. 1965), 26–27, 29, 31.

Repositories: JFSA, ts. DCPA, carbon ts.

Sepulture South: Gaslight

Faulkner's friend Anthony West had sent him a photograph Walker Evans had made of a shaded cemetery. In the foreground were a half-dozen life-sized marble effigies. Not long after Faulkner arrived in New York about mid-September of 1954, West met him one day in the offices of *Harper's Bazaar.* Faulkner told him that it was a fine photograph. Hoping for a piece for the *Bazaar,* West asked Faulkner if he wanted to write anything about it. Though he was noncommital, he set to work on it not long afterward. Fragments remain of one version called "Sepulchure South: in Gaslight" and another entitled "Sepulchre South: Gaslight."[1]

[1] See James B. Meriwether, "Two Unknown Faulkner Short Stories," *Recherches anglaises et américaines* (Strasbourg), IV (1971), 23–30.

Faulkner finished the piece before the end of the month and sent it to West. It appeared as "Sepulture South: Gaslight," in *Harper's Bazaar,* LXXXVIII (Dec. 1954), 84–85, 140–41.

———————

Repository: DCPA, ms. and ts. fragments.

Adolescence

Very early in his career Faulkner had composed poems which followed conventional pastoral and ballad models. Then, on 17 March 1922, he published an essay extolling American materials and language as sources of dramatic art.[1] A sketch published a week earlier had employed an itinerant laborer as its sole human figure.[2] Faulkner later said that he wrote "Adolescence" in the early 1920's. Though it contains imagery suggesting particular Faulkner poems, it moves in the same direction as the essay and the sketch while foreshadowing future fiction. Joe Bunden's wife anticipates Addie Bundren of *As I Lay Dying* in her marriage to a man beneath her, in her childbearing, and in her death. Her daughter, Juliet, has the slim boyish figure of a number of Faulkner women to come, such as Pat Robyn in *Mosquitoes.* Juliet's relationship with Lee Hollowell, with the developing erotic overtones reinforced by nude swimming and bundling in a rustic setting, suggests elements in the relationships between Donald Mahon and Emmy in *Soldiers' Pay* and Harry Wilbourne and Charlotte Rittenmeyer in *The Wild Palms.*

———————

Repository: FCVA, 26-pp. ts.

Al Jackson

In the late winter of 1925 Faulkner cemented his friendship with Sherwood Anderson. The two enjoyed not only telling stories to each other, they also exchanged letters which were conscious exercises in the tradition of the tall tale. When Anderson read the first letter, he suggested that Faulkner rewrite it.[3] When he did, Anderson wrote a reply elaborating on the story and introducing a fishherd named Flu Balsam who had become involved with Faulkner's character, Al Jackson, and a Texas horse trader.[4]

[1]"Books and Things: American Drama: Inhibitions," *EPP,* pp. 93–98.
[2]"The Hill," *William Faulkner: Early Prose and Poetry,* ed. Carvel Collins, Boston, Little Brown, 1962, pp. 90–92.
[3]*ESPL,* pp. 7–8.
[4]*Letters of Sherwood Anderson,* ed. Howard Mumford Jones, with Walter Rideout, Boston, Little, Brown and Company, 1953, pp. 162–64

Faulkner replied with the second letter.[1] He would introduce some of the material into his novel *Mosquitoes.*

———

Repository: The Newberry Library, two 3-pp. tss.

Don Giovanni

This story was apparently intended, like a number of others Faulkner wrote in New Orleans in the first half of 1925, for the New Orleans *Times-Picayune.* On the first page he typed his name and the address "624 Orleans Alley/ New Orleans." Though the story was never published, Faulkner characteristically salvaged parts of it for use in perhaps three novels. The protagonist, Herbie, would become Mr. Talliaferro in Faulkner's second novel, *Mosquitoes;* Morrison would become Dawson Fairchild; the unnamed writer would become the sculptor Gordon; and Miss Steinbauer would become Jenny. Morrison and the writer, inhabiting the same building, suggest Faulkner's friends Sherwood Anderson and William Spratling, the latter Faulkner's New Orleans host. Herbie's thinning hair and faulty digestion are reminiscent of T. S. Eliot's J. Alfred Prufrock, who would be alluded to even more directly in *Mosquitoes.* In Miss Steinbauer's repulse of Herbie, she employs the tactics Eula Varner would use on the schoolteacher, Labove, in *The Hamlet.* The description of the telephone in the last lines of the story would be repeated in *Pylon.* In Faulkner's typescript he began with a paragraph which he repeated verbatim—the fifth paragraph of the story as it is printed here—but neglected to delete it at the first occurrence. It has been deleted here.

———

Repository: NYPL, 12 unnumbered ts. pp.

Peter

In March of 1925, after Faulkner moved into a spare room in William Spratling's apartment at 624 Orleans Alley, he would sometimes accompany Spratling on sketching expeditions which took him into different parts of New Orleans. A young architect teaching at Tulane University, the versatile Spratling kept busy with his own drawing and painting as well as detail drawing for local architects. Two of Faulkner's sketches printed in the New Orleans *Times-Picayune*—"Out of Nazareth" and "Episode" —related encounters on such expeditions. In the former, Faulkner described Spratling as one "whose hand has been shaped to the brush as mine

———

[1] See also Walter B. Rideout and James B. Meriwether, "On the Collaboration of Faulkner and Anderson," *American Literature,* XXXV (March 1963), 85–87.

has (alas!) not. . . ."[1] Although the seven unnumbered typescript pages of this story do not bear Faulkner's name, they are certainly his work. It is difficult to date them in the sequence of New Orleans sketches that he wrote during the first half of 1925. Like "The Priest," this one certainly contained elements that would have offended readers of the *Times-Picayune*. And Faulkner must certainly have realized that some of the language if not the subject matter of "Peter" would have been taboo for a newspaper in 1925. The story in this form was probably a rough draft and perhaps in part experimental, with its shift at mid-point from dialogue in quotation marks to drama-form dialogue and then back again—the kind of thing he would do in *Mosquitoes* (1927), his second novel, which he based on this period of his life in New Orleans. The imagery he used to describe Peter's mother also looked forward to future work: the portrait of Charles Bon's wife in "Evangeline" and *Absalom, Absalom!* (1936).

Repository: NYPL.

Moonlight

According to William Faulkner, the first version of this story was written around 1919 or 1920 or 1921 and was "about the first short story I ever wrote."[2] The sixteen-page typescript of this version which survives is incomplete. In it, Robert Binford and his friend George drink drugstore Coca-Colas on a hot Saturday night as they size up two "flusies" whom they agree to try to "make" later after George has kept a date with his girl, Cecily. With Robert's help, she has slipped out to meet George, who tries to entice her into an empty house. She resists, but when she finally yields to George's entreaties, he changes his mind. As they walk back downtown, she promises to meet him at the house the next night. There is a resemblance between elements in this story and parts of Faulkner's first novel, *Soldiers' Pay* (1926), in which Cecily Saunders takes George Farr first as her lover and then as her husband. On 3 November 1928 Alfred Dashiell rejected a story called "Moonlight" which he said he had seen before at *Scribner's Magazine.*[3] Faulkner referred to the story again in an undated letter to his agent, Morton Goldman, which may have been written in the early spring of 1935. This version of "Moonlight" comes from a fourteen-page typescript much closer to the mature style of Faulkner than the sixteen-page version which may represent its earliest form after the manuscript.

Repository: FCVA.

[1] *NOS,* pp. 46–54, 104–7.
[2] James B. Meriwether, *The Literary Career of William Faulkner,* p. 87.
[3] See James B. Meriwether, "Faulkner's Correspondence with *Scribner's Magazine,*" *Proof* 3 (1973), 253–82.

The Big Shot

Like "Mistral," "Snow," and "Evangeline," this story employs a first-person narrator and a confidant named Don who shares the narrative function. Don was probably based on William Spratling, the New Orleans friend with whom Faulkner traveled in 1925 to Europe, the scene of the first two stories mentioned above. "The Big Shot" was submitted unsuccessfully to *The American Mercury* at some time prior to 23 January 1930 and subsequently to four other magazines. The style suggests that it was written after the stories Faulkner wrote in New Orleans but before more mature writing of the later 1920's such as *Sartoris*. Elements in this story would appear in several later works. The most familiar character is Popeye, whose appearance and background here are much as they would be in *Sanctuary*. Some of the characteristics of Wrennie Martin suggest a first study of Temple Drake, of the same novel. Dal Martin is remarkable in his foreshadowing of elements in characters as disparate as Thomas Sutpen, Wash Jones, and Flem Snopes. The slight he receives at the hands of the plantation owner whose tenant his father is anticipates Sutpen's similar traumatic experience, which similarly motivates Sutpen in his determination to acquire possessions which will permit him to rise in the world. Martin's relationship to the plantation owner, particularly as the latter lies in a hammock and drinks toddies mixed by Martin, suggests several scenes between Wash Jones and Thomas Sutpen in *Absalom, Absalom!* Martin's rise, as he becomes a merchant and achieves affluence yet retains his countryman's ways, resembles the rise of Flem Snopes in the Snopes trilogy, and the cenotaph he raises over his wife's grave may even foreshadow that of Eula Varner Snopes. Dr. Gavin Blount's link with the dead past would eventually contribute to the characterization of Gail Hightower in *Light in August*.[1]

Repository: FCVA, 37-pp. ts.

Dull Tale

This reworking of "The Big Shot" was sent to *The Saturday Evening Post* on 14 November 1930 but met with no more success than the earlier story. Typed on the same machine, it shows many other similarities: the resemblance of Martin and Flem Snopes, Blount and Hightower, and, in his "eager face sick with nerves and self-doubt," a similarity between Blount and the Horace Benbow of *Sartoris* and *Sanctuary*. As a child, hiding in

[1]For further commentary, see Béatrice Lang, "An Unpublished Faulkner Story: 'The Big Shot,'" *The Mississippi Quarterly,* XXVI (Summer 1973), 312–24.

a dark closet and later retching, Blount also suggests Joe Christmas in *Light in August.* The theme of women's affinity for evil would also recur in *Light in August* and *Sanctuary.* Perhaps the most interesting aspect of this story for the student of Faulkner's work is the opportunity it affords, when compared with "The Big Shot," to observe him doing what he did so often and so indefatigably: changing his narrative point of view—here even his ending—in his unremitting search for the most effective way to tell a story.

Repositories: JFSA, 33-pp. ts. ROUM, fragments of mss. and ts.

A Return

On 7 November 1930 Faulkner sent a story entitled "Rose of Lebanon" to *The Saturday Evening Post,* which rejected it. He tried twice more in the next year to sell it, without success. But these efforts were not without worthwhile results, for it appears that something of the obsession with the past of Gavin Blount, M.D., went into the creation of Gail Hightower, D.D., in *Light in August.* Similarly, the death of Charley Gordon in a Holly Springs chicken roost foreshadowed that of Hightower's grandfather. Subsequently Faulkner reworked the material, retelling it in "A Return." Faulkner's agent, Harold Ober, received the story from Faulkner on 13 October 1938. He apparently tried unsuccessfully to sell it, and a letter from Ober to Faulkner on 2 November 1938 applauds Faulkner's decision to rewrite the story. Whether or not he actually did so, the story was never published. In the thirty-one-page typescript of "Rose of Lebanon," Faulkner began in present time, with Dr. Gavin Blount telling one of his patients the story of Lewis Randolph. In the fifty-three typescript pages of "A Return," he not only changed the chronology but identified the Major commanding Charles Gordon's unit as an earlier Gavin Blount and also made him Gordon's unsuccessful rival for Lewis Randolph's hand. He also greatly intensified Dr. Gavin Blount's feeling for that lady. (In this story, contrary to Faulkner's usual practice, he used the apostrophe in *can't* and *don't* more often than he omitted it, possibly in an attempt to conform to magazine style. The inconsistencies have been preserved here.)

Repositories: FCVA, ms. fragment ("Rose of Lebanon"). ROUM, 10-pp. ms. and 31-pp. ts. ("Rose of Lebanon"), and 53-pp. ts. ("A Return").

A Dangerous Man

This story was sent on 6 February 1930 to *The American Mercury,* which rejected it. There had been several earlier treatments of the material, complete and incomplete, in both manuscript and typescript. The story had apparently originated with Estelle Faulkner. Called "A Letter" and then "A Letter to Grandmamma," it had been at least partially typed with Estelle's name on the title page. It was about a woman with a difficult past: a hard father and a cruel husband who was perhaps a murderer. The couple lived on money sent by his mother, and when he left his wife he concealed the fact for fear his mother would stop the money. The wife was befriended by a railroad agent, but here the manuscript and typescript fragments of that version broke off. This version, with its shift of emphasis to Mr. Bowman, may have involved some of Faulkner's memories of his father, who ran a livery stable and transfer company in Faulkner's youth and who had himself been a freight agent in Faulkner's infancy. Like Mr. Bowman, Murry Falkner was also known for his violent temper and his readiness to use his fists and, if necessary, the pistol he carried.

Repositories: JFSA, ms. and ts. fragments. ROUM, 13-pp. ts. and fragments of mss. and tss.

Evangeline

Faulkner had mentioned his New Orleans friend William Spratling in the New Orleans sketches "Out of Nazareth," "Episode," and "Peter." He had also used him as a model for one of the characters in "Don Giovanni." After the two men traveled together from Genoa to Paris in 1925, Faulkner had used Spratling as the basis for the character Don in "Mistral," which was refused by magazines in June and July of 1930 and finally published by Faulkner in *These 13* in 1931. "Snow," which Faulkner sent to his agent, Harold Ober, in 1942 (but which may have been a revision of an earlier version), likewise employed Don and an "I" narrator to tell the story. Using the two again in "Evangeline," Faulkner sent it on 17 July 1931 to *The Saturday Evening Post,* which refused it, and then on 26 July to *The Woman's Home Companion,* which also refused it. In the early months of 1934 he returned to the material, substituting two characters named Chisholm and Burke for the "I" narrator and Don, and ultimately replacing Chisholm and Burke with Quentin Compson and Shreve McCannon to tell the Sutpen story in what would become *Absalom, Absalom!* The title of the story would reappear as the name of the wife and one of the daughters of Calvin Burden when *Light in August* was published in October of 1932.

Repositories: ROUM and JFSA, 15-pp. ms. and 40-pp. ts.

A Portrait of Elmer

By August of 1925 Faulkner was spending most of his working hours in Paris on a novel entitled *Elmer*. On 10 September he wrote his mother, "The novel is going elegantly well—about 27,500 words now." Three days later, however, he wrote that he had put the novel away and was about to start another one. But *Elmer* was still on his mind, for when he wrote his mother again on 21 September he told her that he had put it away temporarily and that it was half done. He seemed well satisfied with it. "Elmer is quite a boy," he wrote. "He is tall and almost handsome and he wants to paint pictures. He gets everything a man could want—money, a European title, marries the girl he wants—and she gives away his paint box. So Elmer never gets to paint at all." He resumed work on the manuscript, but when it had reached 31,000 words, probably in October or November, he put it aside for good. Faintly autobiographical, written in an experimental style including passages heavy with Freudian imagery, the story had begun to founder when Faulkner introduced decadent British aristocrats into his plot. Many years later he told James B. Meriwether that it was "funny, but not funny enough."[1] Not all of this work was lost, however, for elements of the novel were used in *Mosquitoes*, *The Wild Palms*, and *The Hamlet*. Nor did he abandon his efforts to salvage the original conception. Fragments entitled "Growing Pains" and "Elmer and Myrtle" may represent early efforts to start the novel, but they may also represent false starts at short-story treatments of the material. Another fragment, "Portrait of Elmer Hodge," was certainly an attempt at a short-story version. "A Portrait of Elmer" dates from the middle 1930's. On 30 October 1935 Faulkner's agent, Morton Goldman, offered a fifty-seven-page typescript of the story to Bennett Cerf of Random House. On 7 November, Cerf wrote Faulkner that he was sorry they had not received it in time to make a limited edition for Christmas and that they might possibly do it the following fall. But Cerf had some reservations about undeveloped themes and about the ending especially. He told Faulkner he thought that at the story's present length "you are squandering some of the finest material you ever had for a longer book as well as some of the best writing of yours I have ever seen." Nothing came of the plan to publish the story as a limited edition in the fall of 1936, by which time Faulkner had become a Random House author.

Repository: ROUM; the 123-pp. typescript of *Elmer* is in FCVA.

[1]For detailed treatments, see Thomas L. McHaney, "The Elmer Papers: Faulkner's Comic Portraits of the Artist," *The Mississippi Quarterly*, XXVI (Summer 1973), 281–311, and Cleanth Brooks, *William Faulkner: Toward Yoknapatawpha and Beyond* (1978), pp. 115–20.

With Caution and Dispatch

Faulkner made extensive use of his brief R.A.F. experience, most notably in short stories such as "All the Dead Pilots" and his novel *A Fable*. He said that this story had its inception about the time of "Turn About," which was published in *The Saturday Evening Post* for 5 March 1932. "With Caution and Dispatch" was still unsold in 1939, however, when Faulkner rewrote at least part of it on the back of pages of the typescript setting copy of *The Hamlet*. An incomplete forty-seven-page typescript of the story which may date from that time supplies a bridge in the activities of young John Sartoris between his early R.F.C. service and his fatal mission as related in "All the Dead Pilots" and *Sartoris*. This forty-seven-page version has elements in common with a hundred-page unproduced film script entitled *A Ghost Story* which Faulkner wrote for Howard Hawks, particularly in its treatment of Sartoris's wartime love affairs, carried out for the most part in competition with brother officers who outrank him. Faulkner revised the forty-seven-page version chiefly by means of judicious cutting (though he did add a little over a page of new material), eliminating a detailed description of Sartoris's efforts to evade Flight Commander Britt, an account of their visit to a country home in Kent, and then Sartoris's unauthorized excursion to London for a farewell to a girl named Kit, as well as the immediate aftermath. The forty-seven-page fragment breaks off as Sartoris's Camel is about to crash on the ship's deck in the Channel. The typescript of the revised version, printed here, is divided into two segments, each numbered sequentially beginning with the number 1. Part 1 of the story consists of seventeen typed pages. Parts 2 and 3 of the story comprise a twenty-one-page typed segment of the story, the first page of which bears the story's title together with Faulkner's name and address, as though he had concluded that the whole of "With Caution and Dispatch" was too long for magazines such as the *Post* and *Collier's* unless divided into two installments. Faulkner's agent, Harold Ober, offered the story for sale but had to inform Faulkner on 23 April 1940 that it had been rejected as "too dated."

Repositories: FCVA, 47-pp. ts. Estate of Howard Hawks, 100-pp. ts. JFSA, 38-pp. ts.

Snow

Faulkner's trip to Europe in 1925 with William Spratling provided him with useful material for later work. In "Mistral," which may have been written not long after his return home, a first-person narrator and his friend, Don, tried to solve an Alpine murder case. No magazine bought it, and so Faulkner included it in his short-story volume *These 13* (1931). At some time during that year Faulkner used the two principals of "Mistral" in another mystery story, "Evangeline." These factors suggest that Faulkner may well have thought of the present story of love and death in the Alps as early as the time of "Mistral," perhaps even written it, tried unsuccessfully to sell it, and later revised it, principally by an updated introduction, although there is at present no concrete evidence to support this conjecture. (The portraits of the Prussian general and his fiancée will remind some readers of Caddy Compson and her German general as Faulkner sketched them in October of 1945 in the Appendix, "The Compsons," which he wrote for Malcolm Cowley's *The Portable Faulkner* [1946].) Harold Ober's records reveal that he received a twenty-one-page version of "Snow" on 17 February 1942. Ober wrote back that it was a beautiful story but that he was afraid that it was suited only for a literary magazine. The next day, when he wrote Faulkner that *Harper's* had rejected "Knight's Gambit," he said that both that story and "Snow" would have a much better chance of selling if Faulkner could simplify them. On 21 February, Faulkner replied that he could probably simplify "Snow" although it did not seem too obscure to him. Ober submitted it as it was, and on 15 April, when he wrote Faulkner to say that *The American Mercury* had declined it, he quoted a paragraph of detailed criticism from editor Edward Weeks. Busy with other work, Faulkner did not revise it. On 6 May, Ober informed him that one editor had called the story an example of Faulkner's writing at its "elliptical worst" and another had declared it "confused." It was 22 July when Ober received another version of "Snow" consisting of eighteen typed pages. "It is rewritten," Faulkner told Ober, "simplified, still an implied story as before, but I have tried to fill the gaps, etc. and make it explicit as well." The most noticeable change was from third-person narration to first, so that the form of this story now followed that of "Mistral" and "Evangeline." The deletions included peripheral descriptions of Don's appearance and his efforts to speak French as well as a sketch of the train that he and the narrator boarded. The anti-Nazi sentiments were still clear but more effective because less heavy-handed. The revision was to no avail. Ober could not sell it, and the story appears here for the first time.[1]

Repositories: FCVA, 21-pp. ts. and 18-pp. carbon ts. JFSA, 18-pp. ts.

[1]For further commentary, see Frank Cantrell, "An Unpublished Faulkner Short Story: 'Snow,'" *The Mississippi Quarterly*, XXVI (Summer 1973), 325–30.

Bibliography

For biographical, bibliographical, and textual material in the notes to these stories I have drawn principally upon these sources:

Joseph Blotner, *Faulkner: A Biography,* New York, Random House, 1974.
————, *Selected Letters of William Faulkner,* New York, Random House, 1977.
James B. Meriwether, *The Literary Career of William Faulkner: A Bibliographical Study,* Princeton, N.J., Princeton University Library, 1961; revised edition: Columbia, S.C., University of South Carolina Press, 1971.
————, "The Short Fiction of William Faulkner: A Bibliography," *Proof: The Yearbook of American Bibliographical and Textual Studies,* I (1971), 293–329.

Each of these works is fully indexed, and the interested reader will find them convenient to use for further study of Faulkner's short stories.

The Literary Career of William Faulkner reproduces a schedule of Faulkner's submission of stories to magazines and his agent, Ben Wasson, in 1930 and 1931. A useful essay in conjunction with this material is Max Putzel's "Faulkner's Sending Schedule," *The Papers of the Bibliographical Society of America,* 71 (First Quarter, 1977), 98–105.

The following works are cited in the Notes. Faulkner works referred to by abbreviations and unannotated Faulkner works are not listed here.

Brooks, Cleanth, *William Faulkner: Toward Yoknapatawpha and Beyond,* New Haven and London, Yale University Press, 1978.
Cantrell, Frank, "An Unpublished Faulkner Short Story: 'Snow,'" *The Mississippi Quarterly,* XXVI (Summer 1973), 325–30.
Faulkner, William. *Mayday,* South Bend, Ind., The University of Notre Dame Press, 1976, Afterword by Carvel Collins.

Jones, Howard Mumford, ed., with Walter B. Rideout, *Letters of Sherwood Anderson*, Boston, Little, Brown and Company, 1953.

Lang, Béatrice, "An Unpublished Faulkner Short Story: 'The Big Shot,'" *The Mississippi Quarterly*, XXVI (Summer 1973), 313–24.

McHaney, Thomas L., "The Elmer Papers: Faulkner's Comic Portraits of the Artist," *The Mississippi Quarterly*, XXVI (Summer 1973), 281–311.

Meriwether, James B., "Faulkner's Correspondence with *The Saturday Evening Post*," *The Mississippi Quarterly*, XXX (Summer 1977), 461–75.

——————, "Faulkner's Correspondence with *Scribner's Magazine*," *Proof* 3 (1973), 253–82.

——————, "Frankie and Johnny," *The Mississippi Quarterly*, XXXI (Summer 1978), 453–64.

——————, "Nympholepsy," *The Mississippi Quarterly*, XXVI (Summer 1973), 403–9.

——————, "The Priest," *The Mississippi Quarterly*, XXIX (Summer 1976), 45–50.

——————, "Sartoris and Snopes: An Early Notice," *The Library Chronicle of The University of Texas*, VII (Summer 1962), 36–39.

——————, "Two Unknown Faulkner Short Stories," *Recherches anglaises et américaines* (Strasbourg), IV (1971), 23–30.

Polk, Noel, " 'Hong Li' and *Royal Street:* The New Orleans Sketches in Manuscript," *The Mississippi Quarterly*, XXVI (Summer 1973), 344–45.

Rideout, Walter B., and James B. Meriwether, "On the Collaboration of Faulkner and Anderson," *American Literature*, XXXV (March 1963), 85–87.

The following works deal with William Faulkner's short stories and his techniques of revision, especially in the cases of stories in this volume which were later revised to become parts of books.

Brooks, Cleanth, "A Note on Faulkner's Early Attempts at the Short Story," *Studies in Short Fiction*, 10 (Fall 1973), 381–88.

Burggraf, David Leroy, "The Genesis and Unity of Faulkner's *Big Woods*," Ph.D. dissertation, Ohio University, 1976.

Carothers, James B., "William Faulkner's Short Stories," Ph.D. dissertation, University of Virginia, 1970.

Cox, Leland Holcombe, Jr., "Sinbad in New Orleans: Early Short Fiction by William Faulkner: An Annotated Edition," Ph.D. dissertation, 1978.

Creighton, Joanne V., *William Faulkner's Craft of Revision: The Snopes Trilogy, "The Unvanquished" and "Go Down, Moses,"* Detroit: Wayne State University Press, 1977.

——————, "Revision and Craftsmanship in the Hunting Trilogy of *Go Down, Moses*," *Texas Studies in Language and Literature*, XV (Fall 1973), 577–92.

Early, James, *The Making of "Go Down, Moses,"* Dallas, Southern Methodist University Press, 1972.

Gregory, Eileen, "Faulkner's Typescripts of *The Town,*" in *A Faulkner Miscellany,* Jackson, University Press of Mississippi, 1974, pp. 113–38.

——————, "A Study of the Early Versions of Faulkner's *The Town* and *The Mansion,*" Ph.D. dissertation, University of South Carolina, 1975.

Grimwood, James Michael, "Pastoral and Parody: The Making of Faulkner's Anthology Novels," Ph.D. dissertation, Princeton University, 1977.

Harter, Carol Ann Clancey, "The Diaphoric Structure and Unity of William Faulkner's *Go Down, Moses,*" Ph.D. dissertation, State University of New York at Binghamton, 1970.

——————, "The Winter of Ike McCaslin: Revisions and Irony in Faulkner's 'Delta Autumn,'" *Journal of Modern Literature,* 1 (1970), 209–25.

Hochberg, Mark R., "The Unity of *Go Down, Moses,*" *Tennessee Studies in Literature,* 21 (1976), 58–65.

Holmes, Edward M., *Faulkner's Twice-Told Tales: His Re-Use of His Material,* The Hague, Mouton, 1966.

Kibler, James E., Jr., "A Study of the Text of William Faulkner's *The Hamlet,*" Ph.D. dissertation, University of South Carolina, 1970.

Klotz, Marvin, "Procrustean Revision in Faulkner's *Go Down, Moses,*" *American Literature,* 37 (March 1965), 1–16.

Lisca, Peter, "*The Hamlet:* Genesis and Revisions," *Faulkner Studies,* 3 (Spring 1954), 5–13.

Meriwether, James B., "The Place of *The Unvanquished* in William Faulkner's Yoknapatawpha Series," Ph.D. dissertation, Princeton University, 1958.

Millgate, Jane, "Short Stories into Novels: A Textual and Critical Study of Some Aspects of Faulkner's Literary Method," M.A. thesis, University of Leeds, 1962.

Momberger, Philip, "A Critical Study of Faulkner's Early Sketches and *Collected Stories,*" Ph.D. dissertation. Johns Hopkins University, 1972.

Ploegstra, Henry A., "William Faulkner's *Go Down, Moses:* Its Sources, Revisions, and Structure," Ph.D. dissertation, University of Chicago, 1966.

Roth, Russell, "The Brennan Papers: Faulkner in Manuscript," *Perspective,* 2 (Summer 1949), 219–24.

Serruya, Barbara B., "The Evolution of an Artist: A Genetic Study of William Faulkner's *The Hamlet,*" Ph.D. dissertation, University of California at Los Angeles, 1974.

Simpson, Hassell Algernon, "The Short Stories of William Faulkner," Ph.D. dissertation, Florida State University, 1962.

Tick, Stanley, "The Unity of *Go Down, Moses,*" *Twentieth Century Literature,* 8 (July 1962), 67–73.

Watkins, Floyd C., and Thomas Daniel Young, "Revisions of Style in Faulkner's *The Hamlet,*" *Modern Fiction Studies,* 5 (Winter 1959), 327–336.

Wills, Arthur, "A Study of Faulkner's Revisions," *Exercise Exchange,* 10 (March 1963), 14–16.

Winn, James A., "Faulkner's Revisions: A Stylist at Work," *American Literature,* 41 (May 1969), 231–50.

ABOUT THE EDITOR

JOSEPH BLOTNER grew up in Scotch Plains, New Jersey, but lived and taught in the South for fifteen years. Educated at Drew, Northwestern, and the University of Pennsylvania, he interrupted his schooling to fly with the 8th Air Force in England during World War II. He then taught at the Universities of Idaho, Virginia, and North Carolina (Chapel Hill). At Virginia he was a member, and later chairman, of the Balch Committee, under whose auspices William Faulkner became Writer-in-Residence there. His writings on Faulkner include *Faulkner: A Biography, Selected Letters of William Faulkner, Faulkner in the University* (with Frederick L. Gwynn) and *William Faulkner's Library: A Catalogue.* His other books are *The Political Novel, The Fiction of J. D. Salinger* (with Frederick L. Gwynn), and *The Modern American Political Novel: 1900–1960.*

Twice a Guggenheim Fellow and twice Fulbright Lecturer in American Literature at the University of Copenhagen, Professor Blotner has lectured extensively in the United States and Europe on American Literature and particularly the work of Faulkner. During 1977 he served as the first William Faulkner Lecturer at the University of Mississippi. He and his wife, Yvonne, live in Ann Arbor, where he is Professor of English at the University of Michigan.